Inclusive Education for the 21st Cε

Thoroughly revised throughout, this bestselling book returns in a new edition to take an even more comprehensive look at the question: How can teachers and schools create genuinely inclusive classrooms that meet the needs of every student? *Inclusive Education for the 21st Century* provides a rigorous overview of the foundational principles of inclusive education and the barriers to access and participation.

It explores evidence-based strategies to support diverse learners, including specific changes in curriculum, pedagogy and assessment practices, and the use of data. It addresses the needs of all students, as well as those with complex learning profiles, including mental health issues. This second edition is rich with new content, including 11 new chapters which address learning from international experience, multi-tiered systems of support, leading inclusive education reform, and the importance of language and supporting friendships. A new section has been added to provide explicit support for implementing systemic inclusive education reform from the policy level right through to classroom practice. A new series of podcasts, featuring interviews with expert chapter authors, offers an engaging complement to the chapter topics and content.

With many schools still operating under 20th-century models that disadvantage students, this book presents the deep knowledge, tools, and strategies to better equip pre- and in-service teachers and leaders to make inclusive education a reality in all schools.

Linda J. Graham is Professor and Director of The Centre for Inclusive Education (C4IE) at Queensland University of Technology (QUT). She leads several externally funded research projects specialising in the inclusion and exclusion of students who experience difficulties in school and with learning.

Inclusive Education for the 21st Century

Theory, Policy, and Practice

Second Edition

Edited by Linda J. Graham

Routledge
Taylor & Francis Group

LONDON AND NEW YORK

Designed cover image: Cover image: © Squirt Creative

First published 2024
by Routledge
4 Park Square, Milton Park, Abingdon, Oxon OX14 4RN

and by Routledge
605 Third Avenue, New York, NY 10158

Routledge is an imprint of the Taylor & Francis Group, an informa business

British Library Cataloguing-in-Publication Data
A catalogue record for this book is available from the British Library

Library of Congress Cataloging-in-Publication Data
Names: Graham, Linda J. (Linda Jayne), editor.
Title: Inclusive education for the 21st century : theory, policy and
    practice / Linda J. Graham.
Description: Second edition. | New York, NY : Routledge, [2023] |
    Includes bibliographical references and index.
Identifiers: LCCN 2023025798 (print) | LCCN 2023025799 (ebook) |
    ISBN 9781032396866 (hardback) | ISBN 9781032396859 (paperback) |
    ISBN 9781003350897 (ebook)
Subjects: LCSH: Inclusive education. | Children with disabilities—Education.
Classification: LCC LC1200 .I545 2023 (print) | LCC LC1200 (ebook) |
    DDC 371.9/046—dc23/eng/20230718
LC record available at https://lccn.loc.gov/2023025798
LC ebook record available at https://lccn.loc.gov/2023025799

ISBN: 978-1-032-39686-6 (hbk)
ISBN: 978-1-032-39685-9 (pbk)
ISBN: 978-1-003-35089-7 (ebk)

DOI: 10.4324/9781003350897

Typeset in Goudy
by Apex CoVantage, LLC

This second edition is dedicated to the same children and young people as the first. Those millions of students with disability whose right to an inclusive education has been denied due to a lack of clarity and explicit guidance as to what inclusion is and what educators can do to achieve it.

It is also dedicated to my late friend, the indomitable parent advocate, and neurodiversity rights pit bull, Louise Kuchel. Don't worry Lou. We've got this.

Contents

Foreword

The aim of this book is to provide educators with the theoretical and practical knowledge necessary to uphold students' human right to an inclusive education. Familiar readers will already know that, even though inclusive education is about all students, students with a disability are deliberately foregrounded in this book. This is because all other students benefit from the frameworks, conditions, and practices afforded by inclusion, and the human right to inclusive education is extended to *all* through those with disability. But this can only happen if we implement genuine systemic inclusive education reform; that is, if we make inclusive practices happen all of the time, in every classroom.

I have more faith now than ever before that it is only a matter of time before we achieve this. There has been an immense response to this book from education providers, educators, parents, and allied health practitioners who—together—have made the first edition an international best-seller. Its popularity virtually guaranteed the invitation to publish another one. I thank you all for that, because the more people who know what genuine inclusion is, and why and how we can enact it, the more chance we have of making it happen.

While there are many champions for inclusive education and of this book, I want to acknowledge some early standouts. Ballarat Catholic Education Diocese came straight out of the blocks, hosting a principal's forum and providing a copy of the book to each delegate in early 2020. Inclusive educator Loren Swancutt also broke early, hosting an online book club through her School Inclusion Network for Educators Facebook Community Group. Former Assistant Regional Director Trudy Graham in Central Queensland and inclusive educator India Lennerth in South Australia have also led book clubs, and I know that the late great parent advocate and founder of Square Peg Round Whole, Louise Kuchel, sent copies of the book to Education Ministers to educate them as to what real inclusion is (and what it is not).

There is still much to do, and we know from the *Royal Commission into Violence, Abuse, Neglect and Exploitation of People with Disability*, which commenced just prior to this book being published for the first time, that there are deep societal issues that affect how people with disability are treated. Over the last three and a bit years, we have all borne witness to harrowing stories of violence, abuse, neglect, and exploitation. Witnesses have provided testimony of multiple actors in multiple sectors across multiple states and in schools of all types—mainstream, special and alternative—engaging in harmful or inappropriate practices. The prevalence of the failure to include has caused some to question whether all students can or should be included in mainstream schools, but this is missing the point, emphasised (again) in the second chapter of this book. The mainstream _is_ the problem. Or more precisely, the parallel system of mainstream plus other streams to house those who can't or won't fit the mainstream. It astonishes me that something so simple appears impossible to grasp. Of course, inclusion won't work if this is how it is actioned!

At its heart, inclusion involves a fundamental reconceptualisation of schooling. It means abandoning the mainstream and all the practices geared around the 'average' student, redrawing the margins to encompass everyone, and implementing quality accessible practices that work for as many students as possible, and then making sure to quickly identify who those practices still aren't working for and providing them with relevant reasonable adjustments and targeted evidence-based support. This was being said long before the inclusion was defined in General Comment No. 4 on Article 24 of the Convention on the Rights of Persons with Disabilities; it isn't new and nor is it impossible. And with the growing tribe of passionate advocates reading and sharing this book, nor do I believe its achievement is far away.

Linda J. Graham
Director, *Centre for Inclusive Education*
Queensland University of Technology

Contributors

Editor

Professor Linda J. Graham is Director of the Centre for Inclusive Education (C4IE) and a Professor in the Faculty of Creative Industries, Education and Social Justice at Queensland University of Technology (QUT). Linda is currently Lead Chief Investigator on several externally funded research projects, including the Accessible Assessment Linkage study funded by the Australian Research Council (ARC). She has published more than 100 books, chapters, and journal articles, as well as numerous pieces published in *The Conversation*. Linda identifies as hearing impaired and is one member of a wonderfully neurodiverse family.

Authors

Associate Professor Jennifer Alford is an Associate Professor in the Griffith Institute of Education Research, Griffith University, Queensland, Australia. She has been a teacher educator for 22 years in English as an additional language, literacy, and intercultural studies. She is a current Australian Research Council fellow investigating critical literacy with migrant and refugee-background youth.

Professor Peter Blatchford is Emeritus Professor in Psychology and Education at the IOE, UCL Faculty of Education and Society. He has directed research programs on Teaching Assistants in schools (DISS), school class size differences (CSPAR), collaborative group work (SPRinG), grouping practices in schools, school breaktimes, and education of children with SEND.

Dr Francis Bobongie-Harris is a Zendath Kes and South Sea Islander from Yuwi Country. She is a senior lecturer and researcher with the C4IE at QUT. She is an early childhood educator with experience working in New Zealand and Australia.

Associate Professor Terri Bourke is an Associate Professor at QUT. She has held a number of leadership positions including Course Coordinator, Academic Program Director, and presently Academic Lead Researcher. She teaches into a number of curriculum and discipline units specifically in geography. Her research interests include professional standards, professionalism, accreditation processes, assessment in geographical education, and teaching about, to and for diversity.

Dr Emma C. Burns is an ARC DECRA Fellow and Senior Lecturer of Educational Psychology in the School of Education at Macquarie University, Australia. Her research focuses on the socio-motivational factors and processes that impact adolescents' adaptive engagement, achievement, and development, especially in STEM. Her research uses advanced quantitative research methodology.

Professor Marilyn Campbell is a professor at QUT. She is a registered teacher and psychologist and member of the C4IE. Her main clinical and research interests are anxiety disorders in young people and the effects of bullying, especially cyberbullying in schools.

Professor Suzanne Carrington is a professor in the C4IE at QUT. She has 30 years of experience working in universities including teaching, research, international development, and various leadership roles. Suzanne's areas of expertise are in inclusive education, ethical/transformative leadership for inclusive schools, disability, and teacher preparation for inclusive schools.

Ms Melissa Close works as an Outreach and Engagement Officer with the C4IE at QUT. She has over a decade of experience as an educator in international and domestic settings. She holds a Master of Education (Leadership and Management) and is currently pursuing a Master of Philosophy at QUT focused on the systemic implementation of social and emotional learning in educational settings in Australia and the United States.

Ms Juliet Davis is a Research Fellow in the Griffith Criminology Institute, Griffith University, Australia. She writes on justice responses to non-recent abuse, historical injustice, and policy wrongs, with a particular focus on money justice. Her current research centres on redress for institutional abuse of children in Australia and internationally.

Dr Kate de Bruin is a former high school teacher and Senior Lecturer in inclusive education at Monash University, Australia. Her research is based on a human rights approach to education and draws on the Multi-Tiered Systems of Support (MTSS) framework to examine funding models, as well as system, school, and classroom level practices that are supported by evidence, with specific attention to the inclusion students with a disability.

Dr Elizabeth Dickson is a Senior Lecturer in the Law School at QUT. Her PhD (2007) considered the effectiveness of discrimination law in delivering equality of educational opportunity to people with disabilities. Elizabeth researches, teaches, and consults in the areas of discrimination law and education law.

Ms Gaenor Dixon is Director, Therapies and Nursing in the Department of Education, Queensland, Australia. As a dual qualified speech language pathologist and teacher, Gaenor has worked in education policy and schools in two Australian states for more than 25 years.

Ms Libby English is an occupational therapist who is experienced in supporting schools. Her interests include communication, therapeutic relationships and how allied health professionals and schools can work together using MTSS.

Dr Katarzyna Fleming is a senior lecturer and researcher in Sheffield Institute of Education at Sheffield Hallam University, United Kingdom (UK). Her research interests encompass parent-practitioner partnerships, co-production, co-creation in Higher Education, inclusive education, Community of Philosophical Inquiry, and critical pedagogies. Katarzyna is also a founder of Co-productive Partnerships Network. Twitter @kfleming100 @co_productive https://katarzynafleming.com/

Dr Jeanine Gallagher is an experienced educator, having been a teacher and school leader in primary and secondary schools. She continues to support schools at a strategic policy level. Her research interests include the teacher work, collaborative inclusive practices, and the use of data to inform learning, teaching, and assessment for students with disability.

Dr Amy Gaumer Erickson is an associate research professor at the University of Kansas, United States of America (USA). She is a co-author of *The Skills That Matter: Teaching intrapersonal and interpersonal competencies in any classroom* and *Teaching Self-Regulation: Seventy-five instructional activities to foster independent, proactive students.* Her practice-based research guides educators to embed intrapersonal and interpersonal instruction within content-area coursework. She can be reached through the *College and Career Competency Framework* website: http://www.cccframework.org/.

Associate Professor Jenna Gillett-Swan is an Associate Professor and researcher at QUT. Her work aims to understand and address inequity and threats to wellbeing in student educational experiences through participatory rights-based approaches to educational transformation and school improvement. She works with students, teachers, and leaders across primary, secondary, and tertiary education contexts. Jenna is co-leader of the *Health and Wellbeing* Research Program in the *C4IE* and co-convenor of the EERA *Research on Child Rights and Education* network.

Dr Callula Killingly is a Postdoctoral Fellow with the C4IE at QUT. Callula's background is in cognitive psychology. Her research interests include reading development and intervention, and learning and memory processes.

Dr Carly Lassig is a Senior Lecturer with the C4IE at QUT. She has 20 years of experience working in education, as a classroom teacher, university educator and researcher, and consultant. Carly's areas of expertise are in inclusive education, inclusive pedagogies such as differentiation and Universal Design for Learning (UDL), the experiences and views of parents of students with disability, gifted education and talent development, and creativity.

Mrs Lara Maia-Pike is the Coordinator with the C4IE and an Associate Fellow of the Higher Education Academy. Lara is a PhD candidate at QUT, investigating the post-school transition planning experiences of students with disability in secondary schools.

Ms Cátia Malaquias is an Australian lawyer, board director and human rights and inclusion advocate. She has participated in United Nations processes on the rights of people with disability including the development of General Comment No. 4 (Right to Education). In 2021, Catia was recognised by Australasian Lawyer as one of Australia's Most Influential Lawyers. In 2018 she won a Human Rights Award from the Australian Human Rights Commission. Catia is currently undertaking PhD studies at Curtin University (Perth, Western Australia).

Dr Glenys Mann is a Senior Lecturer with the C4IE at QUT. She has 30 years of experience working in inclusive education as a school consultant, university educator, researcher, and advocate. Glenys' areas of expertise are in inclusive education, disability, the experiences, and views of parents of students with disability, parent-teacher partnerships, and teacher preparation for inclusive schools.

Dr Sofia Mavropoulou is Senior Lecturer in the School of Early Childhood and Inclusive Education and Program Leader for the Inclusion & Exclusion Program with the C4IE at QUT. She has 27 years of experience as a teacher educator, researcher, and consultant. Sofia's research interests are in autism, tiered educational supports, social understanding and inclusion, and the experiences of parents of autistic children.

Dr Kevin F. McGrath is an independent researcher and former primary school teacher, based in Sydney, Australia, and affiliated with the Integrated Behavioral Health Research Institute, California, USA. His research focuses on the importance of student-teacher relationships and on teacher gender as a facet of workforce diversity.

Dr Marijne Medhurst is a Research Fellow in the Centre for School and System Improvement (CSSI) at the Australian Council for Educational Research (ACER), Australia. Marijne's expertise is in inclusive education, classroom assessment, and school improvement. Marijne has previously worked as a research assistant at ACU and QUT on various projects.

Dr Pattie Noonan is an associate research professor at the University of Kansas, USA, where she centers her work on providing and evaluating professional development related to improving education for all students. She is a co-author of *The Skills That Matter: Teaching intrapersonal and interpersonal competencies in any classroom* and *Teaching Self-Regulation: Seventy-five instructional activities to foster independent, proactive students,* along with curricula, student assessments and process tools. She can be reached through the *College and Career Competency Framework* website: http://www. cccframework.org/.

Dr Daniel Quin is an Educational and Developmental Psychologist. His work focuses on building relationships between students, families, and teachers in school settings. Daniel completed his doctoral thesis on the role of teacher support in students' engagement in school. His published academic papers are on student teacher relationships and school suspension.

Professor Beth Saggers is a Professor with the C4IE at QUT. She has more than 30 years of experience working across a range of education contexts and universities including teaching, and research. Beth's areas of expertise are in autism, challenging and complex needs, research translation to practice, social-emotional wellbeing, student voice, and stakeholder perspectives.

Associate Professor Ilektra Spandagou is Associate Professor at the Sydney School of Education and Social Work, the University of Sydney, Australia. Ilektra has more than 20 years of experience of researching and teaching internationally in the areas of inclusive education policy and practice, comparative education, disability, and curriculum differentiation.

Professor Jacqueline Specht is a Professor and Director of the Canadian Research Centre on Inclusive Education in the Faculty of Education, Western University. Her research expertise is in the areas of inclusive education, teacher development, and psychosocial aspects of individuals with disabilities.

Mrs Loren Swancutt is an experienced teacher and school leader from North Queensland, Australia. She has been seconded to system advisory roles, supporting principals and school teams to advance inclusive education practices. Loren is a doctoral candidate at QUT and is National Convenor of the School Inclusion Network for Educators (SINE).

Ms Haley Tancredi is a PhD candidate at QUT and is investigating the impact of teachers' use of accessible pedagogies on the classroom experiences and engagement of students with language and/or attentional difficulties. She is a speech pathologist, a senior research assistant with QUT's C4IE, and is a chief investigator on the Central Queensland Region Inclusion Action Research Project.

Professor Penny Van Bergen is a professor of educational psychology and current Head of School in the School of Education, University of Wollongong, New South Wales. Her research focuses on social factors contributing to child and adolescent development (e.g., memory and learning, emotional competence, wellbeing), including broader relationship quality and specific interactional techniques.

Professor Elizabeth Walton (D.Ed) is Professor of Education at the School of Education University of Nottingham, UK, and Visiting Professor at the School of Education, University of the Witwatersrand, South Africa. Her research interests in inclusive education are teacher education, language, and knowledge in the field.

Associate Professor Rob Webster is a Reader in Education at the University of Portsmouth, UK. He has worked with Peter Blatchford on a series of ground-breaking research projects relating to special educational needs, inclusion, and the role and impact of teacher aides/teaching assistants.

Glossary

Ability grouping Targeting pedagogy towards small groups of students based on their skills or achievement.

Ableist To make judgements and decisions that affect others based on able-bodied experience and critical without reflection.

Access The opportunity to engage in experiences and activities, pedagogical practices, the curriculum, and assessment activities unimpeded by barriers.

Accommodations/Adaptations The term used in some countries to describe reasonable adjustments. In Australia, the preferred term is adjustments.

Adjustments A process or action that takes place to remove or minimise barriers to accessing the curriculum, teachers' pedagogical practices or assessment, for a student with disability.

Alteration Where curriculum is changed and other material is added—for example, providing orientation and mobility lessons for students with vision impairment or teaching a student who is non-speaking how to use a communication device.

Augmentation Where curriculum is changed and other material is added—for example, providing orientation and mobility lessons for students with vision impairment or teaching a student who is non-verbal how to use a communication device.

Backward mapping The identification of desired results, or achievement standards, and using these to determine what acceptable evidence of success looks like contextually. Teachers then use this information to map out learning experiences and instruction that supports and scaffolds students toward successful achievement.

Barriers A concept describing the result of the interaction between a person with an impairment and social, political, and environmental impediments affecting their access and participation. Barriers can result in a student with disability not being able to participate on the same basis as a student who does not have a disability.

Categorical resource allocation method The use of disability categories to determine eligibility for individually targeted special education funding.

Complex learning profiles Students with complex learning profiles include students described as having a combination of impairments affecting behaviour, cognition, communication, emotional regulation, mobility, and/or sensory processing. Students in this group can also include students who have experienced Childhood

Complex Trauma arising from abuse, neglect, and exclusion from education. Significant barriers may exist for students with complex learning profiles. Teachers work in collaboration with the student, the student's family, and other professionals to make adjustments and regularly review their impact. Students with complex learning profiles often require substantial and/or extensive adjustments to the learning environment, the curriculum, pedagogical practices, and assessment processes to enable them to participate in meaningful, age-appropriate learning experiences alongside their same-age peers in inclusive classrooms.

Differentiation   Proactively planning varied approaches to what and how students learn in order to be inclusive of student diversity. Differentiation can take place in content, process, product, affect, and the environment.

Direct discrimination   Occurs when a school decides to treat a student with a disability differently to other students on the basis of their disability.

Equality   The equal and exact division of resources.

Equity   The division of resources based on a commitment to impartiality, fairness, and social justice. Equality is not the same thing as equity.

Exclusion   The process of directly or indirectly denying or preventing students with disability access to education.

Extensive adjustments   The fourth level of adjustments according to the NCCD, which are *always ongoing* to overcome barriers experienced by students. These could include highly individualised adjustments to all curriculum materials and assessments, alternative modes of communication, highly specialised assistive technology, intensive and individualised ongoing intervention, or personal care assistance.

Inclusive education   A fundamental human right and process of systemic reform in education that aims to eliminate barriers, enabling all students to participate in learning experiences and the learning environment with their same-aged peers. Inclusive education differs from exclusion, segregation, and integration.

Indirect discrimination   Occurs when a school unintentionally puts in place a policy or practice which they believe to be fair, but which has a detrimental impact on a student with a disability.

Integration   A process of placing students with disability in existing educational institutions, where the student is expected to adapt and change in order to participate in learning experiences and the learning environment. Integration is not compatible with inclusion.

Mainstream   Educational structures that are built for most (but not all) students. Mainstream is not a synonym for or compatible with inclusive education.

Medical model of disability   A perspective on disability that regards people with disability as 'objects' and their characteristics as 'deficits' to be remedied or cured.

Modifications   Where a student may access learning *in a different way* to their peers, for example, where they are assessed against different outcomes to their peers.

Multi-Tiered Systems of Support (MTSS)   A system-wide approach that addresses the academic, behavioural, and social-emotional needs of all students. The multi-tiered system provides increasingly intensive levels of support, with Tier 1 offering classroom-level, universal instruction; Tier 2 providing targeted support to small groups; and Tier 3 offering intensive, individualised support.

National Disability Insurance Scheme (NDIS)   A Federally funded scheme for people with permanent and significant disability under the age of 65 in Australia. The aim is to increase participation in activities of the person's choosing, through support and services. The NDIS does not replicate education-funded support but can fund self-care at school, specialised transport to school and equipment (e.g., wheelchairs and communication devices).

Nationally Consistent Collection of Data on School Students with Disability (NCCD)   An annual data collection process where teachers indicate the type and level of adjustment that is provided for students with disability. Additional funding is provided to schools when student receive supplementary, substantial, or extensive adjustments.

On the same basis   When the opportunities and choices that are available to the student with disability are comparable to those available to a student who does not have a disability.

Quality Differentiated Teaching Practice (QDTP)   The first level of adjustments according to the NCCD, incorporating the provision of *occasional* support within the context of the types of practices that are routinely used by teachers within the resources of the classroom. It represents the baseline level of high-quality, intentional teaching that is provided to all students.

Readiness   A student's current knowledge, understanding and skills, and the knowledge and skills yet to be learned and understood. Readiness is about what students already bring to a new learning experience.

Reasonable adjustments   Adjustments to lessons, subjects, courses, and extra-curricular activities that enable students with disability to participate in education and balances the interests of all parties (including the student and the school community).

Restraint   See restrictive practice.

Restrictive practice   Includes any practice used to respond to the behaviour of a student that: 1) contains or secludes the student in a room or area from which exit is prevented or impeded; 2) uses chemical, mechanical, or physical restraint on the student; or 3) restricts access of the student.

Segregation   Education provided in a separate environment. Segregated settings mean that students with disability are not educated with their same-age peers. This is not inclusive education.

Social and emotional learning (SEL)   The process of acquiring skills that help students to manage their emotions, build positive relationships, and make responsible decisions. SEL involves developing self-awareness, social awareness, self-management, relationship skills, and responsible decision-making abilities.

Social model of disability   Perspective on disability that sees disability as being imposed by society's failure to accommodate persons with impairments. It positions disability as a societal failure, rather than an attribute or condition located within an individual.

Special provisions   The term used in Queensland, Australia, to describe the provision of reasonable adjustments to conditions of assessment, particularly in the secondary school years.

Substantial adjustments   The third level of support according to the NCCD, which includes supports that are offered *more frequently at most times* to overcome significant barriers experienced regularly by students. These might include alternative formats for many tasks, regular support by specialists, or regular assistance with personal care, social interaction, communication, or behaviour.

Supplementary adjustments   The second level of adjustments according to the NCCD, supports that are needed at *specific and intermittent times* to overcome barriers students sometimes experience. For example, there may be a need for modifications to the built environment to be used, intermittent support provided by specialists (e.g., occasional speech pathology advice), or assistive technology used for some tasks, or intermittent targeted support for students' learning, such as structured task analysis, or students' behavioural or social interactions.

Universal approaches/design principles   Approaches that facilitate accessibility, participation and inclusion with fewer individual adjustments needed, through planning and designing curriculum, pedagogy, assessment, and environments that are accessible for all.

Universal Design for Learning (UDL)   An educational approach that understands and values diversity and applies this understanding to facilitate accessible and equitable learning. It is characterised by multiple means of engagement, representation, and expression.

Part I

Foundations Of and
For Inclusion

Chapter 1

Inclusive education

Three (and a bit) years on

Linda J. Graham

In December 2019, Queensland University of Technology (QUT) hosted an Inclusive Education Forum to launch both the first edition of *Inclusive Education for the 21st Century*, and QUT's new *Centre for Inclusive Education*. At the time there were whispers that a novel coronavirus had been detected in a wet market in Wuhan, China but none of us knew what was to erupt soon thereafter. Most of us were far more concerned about the raging bushfires that were decimating enormous areas of New South Wales, Victoria, and South Australia, and which had for the first time reached Northern New South Wales and Southeast Queensland. Watching scorched koalas beg water from passing cyclists, and kangaroos hop through the ocean shallows to escape the encroaching inferno on land, was heartbreaking as was the cost to their and our habitats. Once the fires abated and our absent prime minister returned from holidaying in Hawaii, my colleagues and I started 2020 full of hope that this year would be better. Authors of the first edition chapters began the year by updating their teacher education units and submitting abstracts for international conferences; conferences we would never attend, in places we never went due to the first pandemic in over 100 years. By March, things were looking decidedly dodgy and, although some of us were still travelling interstate, it had to be for important reasons and senior executive approval was needed. In fact, I flew out of Adelaide, South Australia[1] on the last flight to leave, as lockdowns began. The units and activities that my colleagues had so carefully planned were upended and we became heartily sick of an overused verb: *pivot*.

Then transpired a strange time in our lives. My family and I were glued to the television every morning, watching what was happening overseas. Australians, especially academics who get the opportunity to travel to far off places, often grumble about the distance between us and the rest of the world, but I remember feeling very reassured by our living on an island continent, even if the heat is unbearable three months of every year. As chaos unfolded, first in Italy and then in the United States, we sat anxiously awaiting outbreaks that had the potential to take a loved one. We shared memes about toilet paper and gave lectures and held birthday parties over Zoom. We cursed the internet and the government that had ratcheted back fibre to the node, all the while

1 Such a great place, I highly recommend it, especially the nearby Barossa, Eden, and Clare valleys.

DOI: 10.4324/9781003350897-2

watching case numbers unfurl on the screen and measuring our own mortality: "Yeah, okay, I'm under 50 chronologically, but physically . . .?" Somewhat surprisingly, given all this counting and stressing and sharing of memes, people got on with their lives and, as in many other incredibly disruptive times in history, people came together and put their shoulders to the wheel, only this time virtually.

At the forefront of the pandemic were of course, doctors and nurses; some of whom lost their own lives. But so too at the frontline were educators, for they were deemed "essential workers" (Beames et al., 2021). So, while the rest of us huddled in front of screens, teachers and principals went to work, first teaching online, and then returning to abandoned classrooms. The emergent evidence was that young children were at much less risk from COVID-19 with adolescents slightly more so. The evidence for those with compromised immune systems, like many of those with disability, was not so rosy. Many of those students stayed home with parents who struggled to keep their day job, while also teaching their child/ren. This burden fell more on primary carers, yet they did not complain, for they knew of countless others who had no work at all because they were in jobs that could not be conducted from home.

The fact that we have an ageing teacher workforce and that the essential workers who had to return to schools—so that parents could work and (economic) life could go on—were not as impervious to COVID-19 as the children they were being called to mind/teach was raised loudly by professional associations and academics. To my mind, and I think many of those essential workers, the global response was "It is what it is". The education workforce responded by returning to the classroom, doing their best to avoid infection by cleaning surfaces and encouraging the application of liberal doses of hand sanitiser. Only later did we discover through the work of QUT's Distinguished Professor Lidia Morawska that the coronavirus is airborne, although she and other scientists had been warning of this almost from the beginning of the pandemic (Davey, 2020).

Inclusion suffered during this period as teachers struggled to juggle both face-to-face and online teaching for those who still could not (or would not) attend school with face-to-face taking precedence. To date, I am still hearing about the impact of lockdowns on student attendance with the effect most severe for students with mental health problems, such as anxiety and depression, some of whom found lockdown to be a blessed reprieve. So too for students on the autism spectrum and those with so-called 'behavioural difficulties' who have always found school a hostile environment. Somewhat depressingly, I heard of students being suspended for not engaging with online learning, although I wasn't all that surprised given that we know from our research on the overrepresentation of Indigenous students in the use of exclusionary discipline that some students are still suspended for truancy (as counterproductive as that is), and that Indigenous kids are overrepresented among them (Graham et al., 2023). Callula Killingly and I have since been examining Queensland suspension and exclusion statistics in relation to attendance, and worryingly we discovered that risk ratios for students in priority equity groups went *up* in 2020, while overall suspensions went down. What this means is that school still isn't working for quite a lot of kids and we simply cannot continue to blame the students—or their disability, gender, culture, sexuality, language, and/or social background—in lieu of reforming school education such that it adequately caters for *everyone*.

As in the aftermath of the 2019–20 bushfires, there are green shoots arising among the embers, even though we still aren't sure that the pandemic is over or whether we are simply now in a new normal. We all need to hear a good news story though and Chapter 8 delivers that in spades. See, even as the world as we knew it was ending, education system and school leaders joined classroom teachers in putting their shoulders to the inclusive education reform wheel. Mid-2021, QUT's Centre for Inclusive Education (C4IE) worked with the leadership of Central Queensland (CQ) Region to build knowledge of inclusive education across the region with the aim of equipping system and school leaders to lead the systemic inclusive education reform needed to ensure that school education *can* adequately cater for everyone. That December, myself, Haley Tancredi, and Associate Professor Terri Bourke travelled to Rockhampton[2] to learn what CQ system and school leaders needed to know about inclusion and how we might help them achieve their inclusive education vision for CQ. At the very same time, the Premier of Australia's most populous state of New South Wales decided that it was time that we all learnt to 'live with the virus', a decision that just so happened to coincide with the long-awaited opening of the Queensland/New South Wales border. This decision, as inevitable and economically necessary as it might have been, sparked outbreaks in Queensland which had, until that time, been relatively protected from coronavirus, compared to our southern states. Absolute chaos ensued as too few teachers were fully vaccinated and hence the formal start to the school year was delayed by two weeks (O'Flaherty, 2022), commencing on February 7th instead of January 21st. Then, just weeks later, a 'rain bomb' parked itself above Southeast Queensland. The ensuing floods affected 39 of Queensland's 77 local government areas, damaging many schools that had only just re-opened, sending many students back home with no electricity and no internet.

This was the backdrop to two of the studies informing new chapters in this book: Chapter 8: Leading Inclusive Education Reform, which I have already mentioned, and Chapter 11: Accessible Pedagogies. To be honest, it is a miracle that any research got conducted in the last few years given the natural disasters we have experienced, although how natural are they really when global warming and climate change are human made? In 2022, I watched exhausted teachers, principals, and support staff step up one more time to participate in research on top of their already packed day jobs with the aim of improving their own knowledge and practice such that it might make a difference in the effectiveness of their school and in the lives of their students. Due to the hard work and good will of our many participants, we have collected oodles of data which we are now analysing to try and make inclusion as easy as possible to achieve for those teachers and principals, so that *all* their students can thrive.

Chapter 11 of this second edition of *Inclusive Education for the 21st Century* provides a small window into the Accessible Assessment Linkage Project, which was funded by

---

2 Known affectionately as "Rocky", Rockhampton is the beef capital of Australia and now one of my favourite places!

the Australian Research Council in 2018, commenced in 2019, paused for the year of 2020, recommenced in the crucible of 2021, and is now in its final year. The project used eye-tracking technology and video-recorded classroom observations, teacher surveys and interviews, student focus groups and interviews, and a range of standardised measures to assess students' language, engagement, executive function and attention, and reading comprehension. That we were able to conduct such rigorous classroom-based research at all given the maelstrom of the past few years is incredible and even more so are the positive results for which we have many willing students and dedicated educators, partners, and team members to thank. We are looking forward to sharing the outcomes of more research from that project in a sibling book to this one titled, *Accessible Assessment and Pedagogies: Improving student outcomes through inclusive practice*. It will be published by Routledge in 2024, lest there be some other major curveball coming our way, and fingers crossed there won't be!

In the meantime, let's get back to this second edition of *Inclusive Education for the 21st Century*. As much as I would love to say that there has been a revolution since the first edition of this book and that we have now entered inclusion nirvana, we are still not there, yet. Although I have seen excellent examples of quality teaching in the many classroom observations that I and my colleagues have conducted in the last two years, I very rarely see evidence of *accessible* quality teaching or quality *inclusive practice*. This is a critical point that I've made before (Graham et al., 2022) but which I don't think is made often enough. Quality teaching is not enough on its own, it must be accessible because students cannot benefit from instruction they cannot access. Yet, as Haley and I explain in Chapter 11, the accessibility of classroom teaching is not an explicit focus in existing measures of quality teaching. This is partly due to the development of those measures by researchers in general education and a tendency for research to focus on what works for most and then doing something extra for the students missed by those approaches (Graham et al., 2022), rather than beginning from the standpoint of what we need to do to include *all*.

This problem is exacerbated by the *Disability Discrimination Act 1992* (DDA; Cth), together with its subordinate legislation, the *Disability Standards for Education 2005* (DSE; Cth). Elizabeth Dickson, a discrimination law expert, examines both in Chapter 5 of this second edition. A signature problem with our current national legislative framework is that it requires the provision of reasonable adjustments to avoid discrimination but does not impose a positive duty to prevent barriers through the proactive application of universal design. This leaves students vulnerable not only to experiencing barriers but also to never receiving adjustments, particularly those students with a less obvious disability. This is a major problem and one that must be addressed through urgent reform to bring our legislative framework into line with modern evidence-based inclusive practice by which the aim is to widen the scope of universal quality first teaching to encapsulate and successfully serve as many students as possible. As discussed in Chapter 9, another new chapter explaining Multi-Tiered Systems of Support (MTSS), the benefit of high quality, evidence based, accessible instruction like that outlined in Chapter 11 is that it reduces the number of students who need something more, either in the form of reasonable adjustments or through targeted interventions. Not only does this cost less because learning needs are met sooner and through universal provision (which costs less per student), but it also prevents the frustration and stigma that result from students trying and failing due to the existence of common barriers that their teachers have not anticipated and removed because they do not experience those barriers themselves. This is the outcome of ableism, one of five fundamental concepts of inclusive education outlined in Chapter 4.

So, how much of a problem is this, *really*? I think it's a huge one because I seem to find anti-examples nearly everywhere I go. You know when you buy a new car and suddenly that make, model, and colour appears everywhere, when it didn't before? It's not that heaps of people have suddenly gone out and bought the same car in the same week as you; it's because you are now intimately familiar with that car and so you can distinguish it from all the other cars. It's the same with inclusive practice. Once you know what it is, you can pick it from a mile away. And it is also plain as day when it's not there. But, if you *don't* experience barriers or know what inclusive practice is, you won't find anything missing. And that's the problem we face. How do we convince educators who don't experience barriers to change their practice, especially when some, as discussed in Chapter 8, are of the view that human rights and anti-discrimination legislation aren't 'compelling'? And how do we help educators to examine their own and others' practice with the objective of making it more accessible and therefore more inclusive, when inclusion often isn't top among their many competing priorities? Don't get me wrong, we have come a long way over the years and schools are doing many positive things. However, the default is not inclusive, and the mainstream is still the de facto mode. I reprise my definition of mainstream in Chapter 2 because I am still having to explain this point all the time, even to people who research in this area. And I do so because the reports from multiple reviews, inquiries and, most recently, the three Public Hearings of the *Royal Commission into Violence, Abuse, Neglect and Exploitation of People with Disability* (DRC; 2019, 2021, 2022) attest to our collective failure to discern the difference between integration into the mainstream and genuine inclusive education. Why is this allowed to go on? Is it that children and people with disability don't really matter in the hierarchy of value that we have constructed through some sort of telepathic consensus? What sits underneath that? Let's lift the rug and have a little peek at ourselves . . .

During the pandemic, we learned about 'essential workers' and then, when the budget ballooned to frightening proportions and businesses were dying, we heard that *all* workers are essential, especially those that are *spenders*. But we saw something else too. Something disturbing. In the first phases of the vaccine rollout, we witnessed the national failure to prioritise people with disability (Knaus, 2021), many of whom are immunocompromised and some living in share homes, with the outcome that people with disability had not been fully vaccinated by the time governments decided we *all* needed to live with the virus. Perhaps that is because some people are more likely *to* live, e.g., those who are young, healthy, and able-bodied, and therefore able to work?

It was a similar situation for Indigenous Australians living in regional and remote areas who also were not fully vaccinated in time and, of course, it all began in aged care; the management of which has been various forms of debacle since the kerosene baths of the early 2000s. Now that the statistics are no longer rolling across our screens and we are no longer hearing a daily count of deaths from COVID-19,[3] it is hard to know the true impact of the bungled vaccine rollout and the collective decision to let rip. But it makes reading Chapter 3 even more salient for we can see shades of those latent eugenicist beliefs about human value that once led to the industrialised extermination of people deemed 'useless eaters' due to their perceived inability to contribute to economic activity and collective prosperity in what has happened here and now.

So yes—as I said in the first edition of this book—we have been talking about inclusion for a long time and we still aren't there, although I do feel that we are also somehow closer now that we have been in years past, as there are many good things happening in government departments which are currently crafting inclusive education policy frameworks,[4] and education providers investing in the professional learning of their staff. However, as inclusive education is the human right that enables all other rights,[5] it is too important to leave to good will and happenstance. And that is exactly what is being risked without Australian government leadership in the form of a national inclusive education strategy with measurable targets and accountability for systems and sectors should those targets not be achieved.

In the first edition of this book, I noted that progress had been made in New Brunswick, Canada (New Brunswick Department of Education and Early Childhood Development, 2013). This second edition features an international comparison of the enablers of and barriers to systemic inclusive education reform in three regions of the world: Canada (focusing largely on New Brunswick), Italy, and Portugal (Chapter 7). The Inclusion & Exclusion Research Program team from C4IE—led by Professor Suzanne Carrington—have examined what each of these jurisdictions did, with the aim of providing Education Ministers and system leaders with recommendations based on evidence of what has, and has not, worked elsewhere.

I also mentioned in the previous edition that the segregation of students with disability continues to increase in some countries, Australia being one of them and England being another. I'm disappointed by what has been happening in England for the last decade or so (it feels like a very long time, so the years are perhaps best left uncounted). We used to look towards the UK as an early visionary in the field of inclusive education but no longer. That is not due to any faults in the work of the early luminaries—like Mike Oliver, Tom Shakespeare, and Len Barton—but, rather, due to another virus that appears to have taken hold in England; that of neo-traditionalism. Inclusive education, together with the practices required to achieve it, is decried by neo-traditionalists who still like children to be seen and not heard, especially unruly children who do things for inexplicable reasons and who 'won't' (i.e., *can't*) fit into neatly designated boxes or be taught by any old teacher, no matter how poor they are at teaching (to learn more, read

---

3 Note: this does not mean infections and deaths are no longer happening. We just aren't hearing about them.
4 Hello Northern Territory! I have such high hopes for you.
5 I chortled when I read recently that this statement was described as "self-aggrandising" in a blog criticising QUT's submission to the Senate Inquiry into The Issue of Increasing Disruption in Australian Classrooms. To learn more, refer to the very first sentence of Chapter 3.

Graham, 2018). The immense waters separating our nations are no match for the viral load carried by Edu-Twitter,[6] nor do they help when outfits like the Centre for Independent Studies ferry over neo-traditionalist luminaries like Katherine Birbalsingh, the Head Teacher of Michaela Community School, where she has had undoubted success at raising achievement but has done so using an authoritarian process through which I cannot imagine Australian culture surviving.

This is not flippancy and nor am I equating misbehaviour with Australian culture. Let me explain . . .

I was born the child of British (Scottish and Northern Irish) expats living in Zimbabwe and emigrated to Australia when I was two years old. That happened partly due to political unrest in Zimbabwe and partly due to my father being called up for national service. My white colonial parents read the writing on the wall and hot-footed it out of Africa in 1974. I think we ended up in Australia purely because my father got a job with an Australian firm. They didn't know anything about the place. But nor had they known anything about Africa either. We moved to Sydney and braved it for three years, but my mother found 1970s Australia somewhat uncouth and depressingly isolated, so we left bound for London in 1977. On the six-week journey through Asia, my father received a better job offer and instead of becoming English, my brother, sister, and I became Irish instead, much to the horror of my Protestant grandparents, especially the Northern Irish ones who kept telling me when we travelled up from Dublin, "You're not *Irish*, you're BRITISH!!"[7] Not surprisingly, I was a very confused child and my favourite books are emblazoned with my full address, including the country code (see Figure 1.1). It also didn't endear me to the local urchins when I earnestly corrected their description of me as Australian by referring to myself as an international citizen.

Anyway, we emigrated back to Australia in 1983, because the bottom dropped out of the Irish economy and my brother had been expelled from two private schools and was getting up to serious mischief with the local hoodlums. My mother was also seriously lonely. Dublin, at that time, wasn't exactly welcoming of Protestants. That's why my brother, sister, and I were in private schools. All public schools in the Republic of Ireland back then were Catholic. Needless to say, all the neighbourhood kids were too.

---

6 Although, Twitter's effectiveness has significantly diminished since being taken over by Elon Musk. Kind of happy about that really.
7 Meanwhile, I arrived in Dublin with an accent and my friends all considered me Australian. I don't know whether my accent was Australian at that time, but I've been confused ever since.

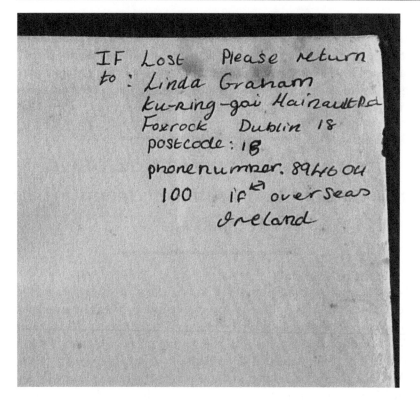

Figure 1.1 Just in case you didn't believe me!

Even though we were outsiders in Dublin, I did not want to leave, and I did not like Australia at all when we arrived. By this stage I had a lovely Irish accent but all that did was make me the object of ridicule and every Irish joke known to humankind. It took until 2005 for me to call myself Australian and it was the result of my first solo trip overseas to a non-English speaking country where Qantas lost my bags and I had to try to navigate a different language. The warm flood of recognition and love for Australia that I felt when hearing a chorus of Aussie accents on joining the queue to board the LA to Brisbane flight home was enough to convince me that, yes, I am Australian, and I bloody love this country! One of the things that I love most about it is its irreverence, its directness, and its attitude. In other words, I love the Australian culture. And that is what I fear will be lost if Australian schools slavishly adopt the discipline practices espoused by English neo-traditionalists. That doesn't mean I endorse misbehaviour or anything else I'm bound to be misquoted as saying. It means that our governments, our schools, and our educators need to be extremely careful to ensure that practices and systems are developed and adapted so that they are appropriate for our unique context and that they respect Australian egalitarian values.

This is especially important given that most citizens in this country are immigrants, just like me. The only ones who aren't are the traditional owners of these lands: the First Nations peoples of the land that is now called Australia. And we should never again import and impose people, processes, and practices from other countries with the glib assurance that because they worked in some place far away, they will work equally as well here, without adaptation and/or that the goal of that practice is respectful of our culture and is neither assimilatory, nor imperialistic. So, while chapters in this book *do* draw on international experiences and propose recommendations, each is underpinned by this caveat: we must be ever conscious of the unique characteristics of our student populations, which can be vastly different depending on their location in this immense land, as well as their language and cultural background. This, incidentally, is why I had a foundational layer of culturally appropriate pedagogy drawn into the MTSS model that we recommended in the final report of the *Inquiry into Suspension, Exclusion and Expulsion processes in South Australian government schools* (Graham et al., 2020) and why I did *not* recommend Positive Behaviour Intervention Supports (PBIS) as a standalone response to student behaviour. South Australia opted instead for PBIS, which disappointed me no end because PBIS will not alone address the myriad drivers beneath the exclusion data we analysed for the South Australia Inquiry. Nor will PBIS address overrepresentation of priority equity groups (Graham et al., 2023), especially in relation to disability, because that is being driven by the lack of accessibility in curriculum, pedagogy and assessment, and the failure to provide *relevant* reasonable adjustments.

Even though MTSS proved to be a bridge too far for South Australia, I still had high hopes that the other recommendations they accepted would put downward pressure on segregation rates. For example, I recommended that their system of Flexible Learning Options (FLO) be abolished (Graham et al., 2020). The Marshall Liberal National Party (LNP) government, which had instigated the Inquiry, accepted the recommendation to abolish FLO because the evidence showed that students were not attending, which meant that they weren't getting suspended and, while some stakeholders took that on face value as evidence of success, the reality is that many students 'in' FLO, were not *really* in FLO, and were instead being lost to the system. However, the Marshall LNP government lost the 2022 election and the new government, led by Premier Peter Malinauskas of the South Australian Labor Party (ALP), has since rescinded the previous government's decision to abolish FLO, electing to 'redesign' it instead. Of course, if I thought that was a good idea, I would have recommended it.

Another LNP government to recently bite the dust was that led by (now former) Premier Dominic Perrottet in New South Wales. Interestingly, these two former LNP state governments have been the only ones in the country to take seriously the rising use of exclusionary discipline and to endeavour to do something about it. I have been fascinated by the apparent dissonance whereby state Labor governments—for example, in Western Australia and Queensland—have been largely impervious to parent and community concerns about escalating suspension and exclusion rates, whereas Liberal National state governments have been the ones to investigate and respond. I find this baffling given that Labor is the party of equity and social justice. The political stonewalling over the last five years from both Western Australia and Queensland state governments compared to the reform efforts of LNP governments in South Australia and New South Wales, together with the backtracking by new ALP governments in those two reforming states, has convinced me that state Labor governments are hopelessly conflicted, given their deep ties to the union movement and, because—even though union membership is at an all-time low in Australia—teachers' associations are among the strongest remaining unions. And, although many teacher colleagues have told me that they are only a member of the union for the indemnity insurance, those unions wreak inordinate power on the basis of that membership. This is an issue that needs to be investigated and addressed because the unions are a significant barrier to systemic inclusive education reform. This poses us with an interesting conundrum because state Labor governments are not going to address this problem themselves and, while the LNP governments of New South Wales and South Australia did try to implement good reforms, the LNP is also vulnerable to conservative ideology. Certainly, at the federal level, the LNP has been more interested in waging culture wars than implementing evidence-based reform, and this has been as true in education as it has in other portfolios. Federal Labor, is I think inclusive education's last real hope, for Federal Labor under the Rudd government ratified the CRPD and endorsed UNDRIP, whereas the previous Howard LNP government refused.

My point is this: education in this country is intensely political, but the impact of that politicisation on progress is never openly acknowledged. Further, the education policy decisions that are made (or not made) by governments are never the explicit focus of inquiries or reviews. The problem is always framed from the perspective of deficiencies in students, parents, teachers, and/or academics and never the failure of governments to follow the advice they received or to pay attention to the evidence they were presented. Nor is the focus ever directed towards the problems underlying the problem at hand. For example, at the time of writing this chapter, there is a Senate Inquiry being conducted into "the issue of increasing disruption in Australian classrooms". Let's just examine this bold statement for a second . . . The Senate Inquiry is premised entirely on the case that there is "increasing disruption", but is there? What evidence is there to support this claim? Turns out the claim is based on the difference in results from two surveys from the OECD's *Program of International Student Assessment* (PISA): the first occurred in 2009 (Organisation for Economic Co-operation and Development [OECD], 2010), and the second in 2018 (OECD, 2019). In 2018, Australia was ranked 69th out of 76 OECD nations and this statistic was gobbled up by the media and wielded by bloggers with nary a sideways glance at the (flawed) analysis underpinning it.

A team of us in the Centre for Inclusive Education is now investigating these data for ourselves but even a cursory glance should have been enough to signal to the Senate that these rankings were not a rigorous enough premise on which to base an Inquiry. Stay with me while I explain why!

The PISA disciplinary climate data is based on five survey items:

(1) Students don't listen to what the teacher says
(2) There is noise and disorder
(3) The teacher has to wait a long time for students to quiet down
(4) Students cannot work well
(5) Students don't start working for a long time after the lesson begins

Students in the year 2000 were required to rate these items on a 4-point scale: 'never', 'some lessons', 'most lessons', or 'every lesson' for their home language lessons (e.g., in Australia this would be English). However, in 2009, the wording on the scale changed to: 'never or hardly ever', 'in some lessons', 'in most lessons', and 'in all lessons'. While the 2009 report glosses over these differences with the statement, "[s]imilar questions were asked in PISA 2000, so responses can be compared across time" (p. 96), the reporting changed as well. I get stuck into that issue later in this section but for now, let me say that as someone in inclusive education, I'm highly dubious of the requirement for students to rate a double negative, e.g., "Students don't listen to what the teacher says . . . never or hardly ever?" Just reading the reports is doing our collective heads in, so I can only imagine how hard it was for students to complete the items, especially for those with a different first language to that of the survey or for those who had a disability impacting language and information processing. We will look at this into the future because it will be interesting to examine the results by language diversity within the samples and, while Confucian cultures have already been raised as a potential factor contributing to the most recent rankings (Lee, 2021), mono vs. multilingualism is worth looking at also, as is the relative inclusiveness of systems, schools, and classrooms. But I digress. Let's keep looking at PISA.

In 2009, 38 participating countries were ranked on students' responses to items (1) and (3), and two response options were collapsed: 'never or hardly ever' and 'in some lessons'. Countries were ranked in descending order based on the percentage of students' responses to these two items and differences between PISA 2000 and PISA 2009 were calculated. Although ranked 28th for responses to the first item and 25th for the second in 2009, Australia was deemed to have an average disciplinary climate that had not significantly changed between the two timepoints. So far, so good, right? Well, in 2018, the OECD changed things up again, this time collapsing all items into a disciplinary climate index that encompasses all five items rated on the aforementioned 4-point scale. Index scores were used to rank countries but, this time, 79 countries participated; 77 of which were ranked in descending order. Australia came in at 69th (quelle horreur!) and it is on this basis that the Senate has instigated an Inquiry into *increasing* disruption in Australian classrooms. But is that appropriate? Let's see.

First, Australia has not fallen from 28th or 25th in the ranking to 69th, for the number of participating countries has changed over time and so therefore have the rankings. To be clear, the number of countries participating in PISA has grown from 43 in the first assessment in 2000 to 65 in 2009 and to 79 countries in 2018. And, because comparisons can only be made between countries that participated in each assessment, the number of countries in the rankings has changed from 38 in 2009 to 77 in 2018. Sure, we'd like to be closer to the top of that ranking than to the bottom but, here's my second caveat: the types of countries participating in PISA 2009 and PISA 2018 substantively changed due to the entrance of Asian countries, like Singapore, and an amalgamate of four provinces in China: B-S-J-Z (China). Unlike Australia, these jurisdictions/systems are grounded in Confucian culture, which has a profound effect on teacher-student relationships, classroom interactions, and climate (Lee, 2021). Third, buried in the statistical data is the fact that there was a significant difference between timepoints in the responses of Australian students for *only two* of the five items: Item (3) "The teacher has to wait a long time for students to quiet down", and Item (4) "Students cannot work well". Item (5) also declined (-1.8%) but not significantly, while Items (1) and (2) improved (both +0.8%), but again not significantly.[8] And, here is my fourth caveat: in the 2018 PISA report, countries are ranked *only* on the percentage of students who responded, 'never or hardly ever', while 'in some lessons' is dropped from the analysis. The case for increasing disruption in Australian classrooms therefore rests entirely on a 3.7% decrease in the number of students saying their teacher never or hardly ever has to wait a long time for students to quiet down (is your head hurting yet?), and a 2.8% decrease in the number saying students never or hardly ever cannot work well. Given that there was no difference in students' responses between PISA 2000 and 2009, that suggests that there has been NO change in more than 20 years for three of the five items. Those figures don't scream crisis to me . . . My final caveat—for now—is that there are *no tests of significance between countries*, so we do not know whether there is a statistically significant difference in Australian students' responses to the OECD average or how much of a difference there is to the countries clustered at the top of the ranking.

To claim that there is increasing disruption in Australian classrooms based on a fall in rankings is therefore hugely problematic. Similar points have been made numerous times over the years in relation to the rankings for student achievement in reading, mathematics, and science, but at least in those cases, countries with statistically indistinguishable performances are grouped together and given the same rank. Not so in the rankings for disciplinary climate where countries with statistically identical disciplinary index scores are ranked above and below each other. For example, Australia and Belgium received Index scores of 0.20 and 0.21, respectively, yet Australia is ranked 69th and Belgium 70th. There's a snowball's chance in hell that a 0.01 difference is significant, so why is it being used to inform a ranking? That's not what I'd call responsible data analysis or reporting. And nor is it responsible to base a taxpayer funded inquiry on them.

My view is this: if our politicians are going to look at rankings then let's look at them *all*. Let's consider, for example, that Australia is sitting at the top of ranked countries in terms of the hours that teachers spend in face-to-face teaching. I say this because Australian teachers spend more hours teaching than the OECD average (838.28 hours/year vs. 800.45 hours, respectively) and considerably more than their counterparts in Korea (516.98), which—incidentally—is ranked first in classroom disciplinary climate. *Coincidence?* I think not. Further, there are some other details in the PISA data that do not seem to have made it into the Senate Inquiry Terms of Reference. For example, for the index of disciplinary climate, the difference between advantaged students and disadvantaged students in Australia (0.34) is double that of Korea (0.17). Interesting, isn't it? Let's consider for a moment why that is.

---

8 Note: an increase is positive, while a decrease is negative.

Australian schools are among the most segregated in the world, and this too is the result of government decision-making. Our poorest students are grouped together in the most disadvantaged schools, which—far from receiving the greatest support from government—actually receive the least. We have known since the Coleman et al. (1966) study on equitable educational opportunity in the United States that concentrating advantage through selection, streaming and segregation not only confers further advantage to already advantaged students, but that it has an even greater deleterious effect on the disadvantaged who are denied the benefits of being educated with socially, behaviourally, and academically advanced peers. In other words, inclusion through mixed-ability schools and classes is more beneficial to student learning than segregation, yet we select, stream, and segregate as though this evidence doesn't exist. Sadly, Australia's response to the Coleman study and the decades of research that have followed—including that which has found similar results by reanalysing the Coleman study data using multilevel modelling (Borman & Dowling, 2010), and that which has investigated the benefits of mixed-attainment teaching (Taylor et al., 2017) and inclusion (for more read Chapter 6)—has been the education policy equivalent of "Hold my beer!", especially since the Howard LNP government fuelled federal funding of non-government schools between 1996 and 2007.

Despite attempts to address inequity in Australian schooling by the Rudd and Gillard Labor governments from 2007 to 2013, the Morrison LNP government baked in this inequity even further by in 2019 legislating an 80:20 split, whereby the federal government contributes 80% of the Schooling Resource Standard (SRS) for non-government schools (Catholic and Independent), but only 20% of the SRS for government (public) schools (Cobbold, 2021). Conversely, state governments are required to contribute 80% of the SRS for public schools, and 20% of the SRS for non-government, however, as no state government funds the full 80% for government schools, these schools remain *under*funded, even though they enrol the neediest students (Cobbold, 2021). The effects of concentrating disadvantage into underfunded public schools, which are already stratified by postcode, is never raised by conservative commentators and neo-traditionalists stoking talk of a crisis in student behaviour. My point is this: education is inherently political, and many decisions are made not on the evidence, but on the level of pressure that is brought to bear by stakeholders and lobby groups. Not all of these are equally powerful, which is why Edu-Twitter bloggers and teacher unions have a much greater say in education policy and practice than students, despite students outnumbering teaching staff nationally by some 3.7 million. It is also why we have governments that continue to build and expand special schools in the name of 'parent choice'. It actually isn't ever a matter of parent choice because firstly there are enrolment criteria that, for example in Queensland, require the student to not just have a disability but to have an intellectual disability, and also because many parents want their child to be in an inclusive school alongside their peers and siblings but are forced to 'choose' a segregated setting because their local school is a mainstream school, not an inclusive one.

In Chapter 2, I explain the difference between the two with illustrations from observed practice. I then define genuine inclusive education, as well as three common but incompatible models of provision (exclusion, segregation, integration) that often exist alongside each other, but which are often confused with inclusion. Next, I explain the long history behind inclusive education with the addition of some very recent history which, in resonating with the past, further underscores the urgency of systemic inclusive education reform. Lastly, I point to the emergence of yet more green shoots. While there have been some unedifying moments in the last three and a bit years, we are getting there and like I said in the foreword, I'm inspired by the good will and passion of so many educators, parents, allied health professionals, policy officers and disability advocates who are making things happen. This book aims to help us all by putting forward an achievable vision, helping all stakeholders understand why this is the right work, and providing evidence-based frameworks and practices to equip educators with the knowledge necessary to achieve it. Together, we can do this, and I welcome you to the good fight with open arms. The kids are worth it. Every single one of them.

References

Beames, J. R., Christensen, H., & Werner-Seidler, A. (2021). School teachers: The forgotten frontline workers of COVID-19. *Australasian Psychiatry, 29*(4), 420–422. https://journals.sage pub.com/doi/pdf/10.1177/10398562211006145

Borman, G. D., & Dowling, M. (2010). Schools and inequality: A multilevel analysis of Coleman's equality of educational opportunity data. *Teachers College Record, 112*(5), 1201–1246. https://doi.org/10.1177/016146811011200507

Cobbold, T. (2021). The unwinding of Gonksi-Part 3: Morrison abandons needs-based funding. Working Paper. *Analysis and Policy Observatory.* https://apo.org.au/node/311814

Coleman, J. S., Campbell, E. Q., Hobson, C. J., McPartland, J., Mood, A. M., Weinfeld, F. D., & York, R. L. (1966). *Equality of educational opportunity.* Government Printing Office.

Davey, M. (2020, May 6). Coronavirus and airborne transmission: Scientists warn Australia to be on guard. *The Guardian.* https://www.theguardian.com/world/2020/may/06/coronavirus-and-airborne-transmission-scientists-warn-australia-to-be-on-guard

Disability Discrimination Act 1992 (Cth).

Disability Standards for Education 2005 (Cth).

Graham, L. J. (2018). Student compliance will not mean 'all teachers can teach': A critical analysis of the rationale for 'no excuses' discipline. *International Journal of Inclusive Education, 22*(11), 1242–1256. https://doi.org/10.1080/13603116.2017.1420254

Graham, L. J., Killingly, C., Laurens, K. R., & Sweller, N. (2023). Overrepresentation of Indigenous students in school suspension, exclusion, and enrolment cancellation in Queensland: is there a case for systemic inclusive school reform? *The Australian Educational Researcher, 50,* 167–201. https://doi.org/10.1007/s13384-021-00504-1

Graham, L. J., McCarthy, T., Killingly, C., Tancredi, H., & Poed, S. (2020). *Inquiry into suspension, exclusion and expulsion processes in South Australian Government schools.* The Centre for Inclusive Education. https://www.education.sa.gov.au/documents_sorting/docs/support-and-inclusion/engagement-and-wellbeing/student-absences/report-of-an-independent-inquiry-into-suspensions-exclusions-and-expulsions-in-south-australian-government-schools.pdf

Graham, L. J., Tancredi, H., & Gillett-Swan, J. (2022). What makes an excellent teacher? Insights from junior high school students with a history of disruptive behavior. *Frontiers in Education, 7,* 1–12. https://doi.org/10.3389/feduc.2022.883443

Knaus, C. (2021, April 22). Australians with disability forgotten in coronavirus vaccine roll-out, advocates say. *The Guardian*. https://www.theguardian.com/australia-news/2021/apr/22/australians-with-a-disability-forgotten-in-coronavirus-vaccine-rollout-advocates-say

Lee, J. (2021). Teacher–student relationships and academic achievement in Confucian educational countries/systems from PISA 2012 perspectives. *Educational Psychology, 41*(6), 764–785. https://doi.org/10.1080/01443410.2021.1919864

New Brunswick Department of Education and Early Childhood Development. (2013). *Policy 322, Inclusive Education*. https://www2.gnb.ca/content/dam/gnb/Departments/ed/pdf/K12/policies-politiques/e/322A.pdf

O'Flaherty, A. (2022, March 23). Rising COVID cases numbers leave Queensland schools struggling with staff shortages. *ABC News*. https://www.abc.net.au/news/2022-03-23/queensland-schools-face-staff-shortages-covid-19-cases-increase/100933334

Organisation for Economic Co-operation and Development. (2010). *PISA 2009 Results: What makes a school successful? Resources, policies and practices (Volume IV)*. OECD iLibrary. http://dx.doi.org/10.1787/9789264091559-en

Organisation for Economic Co-operation and Development. (2019). *PISA 2018 Results (Volume III): What school life means for students' lives*. OECD iLibrary. https://doi.org/10.1787/acd78851-en

Royal Commission into Violence, Abuse, Neglect and Exploitation of People with Disability. (2019). *Public Hearing 2: Inclusive education in Queensland—preliminary inquiry*. https://disability.royalcommission.gov.au/public-hearings/public-hearing-2

Royal Commission into Violence, Abuse, Neglect and Exploitation of People with Disability. (2021). *Public Hearing 7: Barriers experienced by students with disability in accessing and obtaining a safe, quality and inclusive school education and consequent life course impacts*. https://disability.royalcommission.gov.au/public-hearings/public-hearing-7

Royal Commission into Violence, Abuse, Neglect and Exploitation of People with Disability. (2022). *Public Hearing 24: The experience of children and young people with disability in different education settings*. https://disability.royalcommission.gov.au/rounds/public-hearing-24-experience-children-and-young-people-disability-different-education-settings

Taylor, B., Francis, B., Archer, L., Hodgen, J., Pepper, D., Tereshchenko, A., & Travers, M. C. (2017). Factors deterring schools from mixed attainment teaching practice. *Pedagogy, Culture & Society, 25*(3), 327–345. https://doi.org/10.1080/14681366.2016.1256908

Chapter 2

What is inclusion... and what is it not?

Linda J. Graham

Academics in the field of inclusive education were for a long time reluctant to define inclusion, although those of us writing and researching in inclusive education all knew what it was. Inclusion has often been described as a journey and not a destination, or as a process and not a place (Runswick-Cole, 2011) and this language was as much an attempt to correct prior failed attempts at 'mainstreaming' and 'integration' (Danforth & Jones, 2015), as it was to capture and protect inclusion's inherent flexibility and on-going nature. An attempt to prevent 'inclusion' from being reduced to a checklist. This is because inclusive education is more than a set of practices. It is also a philosophy: a way of thinking about people, about diversity, about learning and about teaching. Not surprisingly, this way of thinking can be hard to define. However, in the absence of a clear definition, distortions flourish and are difficult to correct. I provide three examples to illustrate such distortions in practice later in this chapter.

The Committee responsible for the *Convention on the Rights of Persons with Disabilities* (CRPD; United Nations, 2006) recognised this problem in 2016. For a decade, inclusive education had been a human right through Article 24 of the CRPD which articulates 'The Right to Education' and, even though ratifying countries like Australia were legally bound by the CRPD, there had been slow progress in implementing inclusive education. The CRPD Committee published *General Comment No. 4* (GC4; United Nations, 2016) on Article 24 to make clear the legal obligations of States parties, as well as the steps necessary to achieve immediate progressive realisation. As discussed in Chapter 3, GC4 is the most comprehensive and authoritative instrument explaining the human right to inclusive education. It outlines in detail what is required to implement inclusive education with authenticity and fidelity. Critically, GC4 not only defines inclusion, but it defines forms of provision that are antithetical to inclusion (exclusion, segregation) or which are commonly rebadged as inclusion (integration).

Inclusion is defined in GC4 (United Nations, 2016, para 11) as:

> a process of systemic reform embodying changes and modifications in content, teaching methods, approaches, structures and strategies in education to overcome barriers

DOI: 10.4324/9781003350897-3

with a vision serving to provide all students of the relevant age range with an equitable and participatory learning experience and environment that best corresponds to their requirements and preferences.

The key words here are systemic reform, changes and modifications, overcome barriers, relevant age range, equitable, participatory, experience and environment, and requirements and preferences. In the absence of deep knowledge of inclusive education, however, these words may come to be misinterpreted in both policy and practice.

Systemic reform	Means transforming the education system—it means no more 'mainstream plus special'. It demands reform to the ways in which disability support funding is allocated (de Bruin et al., 2020). It means teaching *all* teachers to be teachers of students with disability, not just some teachers. It means making both the learning experiences and the environments in which children are expected to learn accessible to *all* and not just some.
Overcome barriers	Is a direct reference to the social model of disability in which disability is conceptualised as an outcome of the interaction between a person with an impairment and the social, political, environmental barriers that impede their access and participation.
Equitable	Means fair. It does not mean the same. It refers to the principle of giving more to those who have less to equalise opportunity and redress disadvantage (Chapter 4). Both terms are encapsulated in the concept of 'reasonable adjustments' (see Chapter 5).
Preferences and participatory	These words refer to consultation, voice, and participation in decision-making, as well as all aspects of schooling (see Chapter 13).
Requirements	Is a rights-based term and replaces the word 'needs', which is special education language that positions people with disability as dependant, implying burden. It is language that is inconsistent with inclusive education (see Chapter 4).[1] Students with disability have *rights*, they do not have 'needs'.

(Continued)

1 The UK really needs to wake up to this and stop using the awful phrase "Special Educational Needs and Disability" and the equally awful but ubiquitous acronym "SEND". Perhaps start by watching the CoorDown's #NotSpecialNeeds World Down Syndrome Day campaign: https://www.youtube.com/watch?v=kNMJaXuFuWQ

(Continued)

Changes and modifications and relevant age range	Means teaching to diversity, rather than the middle, using proactive universal design principles to plan accessible learning experiences and making reasonable adjustments to ensure access to grade-level curriculum and assessment, working alongside same-age peers (see Chapters 11 and 12). It means no more teaching to the middle with add-ons. And no more scribbling in scrapbooks for children like Daniel (Figure 2.1) and no more 'SEP kids' working on a number line while their 'mainstream' peers are doing geometric shapes (Figure 2.2). It means consistent and effective provision of *accessible* quality first teaching to all students, such that none are left behind by barriers that do not need to be there or by the failure to provide adjustments.

The examples of classroom practice discussed later in this chapter are clearly at odds with this definition of inclusion. Neither 'Daniel' nor the 'SEP kids' were provided with relevant grade-level curriculum, and nor was their experience participatory. The environments into which those children were placed were not conducive to learning and judging from students' lack of engagement with learning, nor were these environments consistent with their requirements and preferences. Rather, these classroom examples are more appropriately described by the other definitions provided in para 11 of GC4: integration, segregation, and exclusion.

Integration is:	A process of placing persons with disabilities in existing mainstream educational institutions, as long as the former can adjust to the standardised requirements of such institutions.
Segregation is:	When the education of students with disabilities is provided in separate environments designed or used to respond to a particular or various impairments, in isolation from students without disabilities.
Exclusion is:	When students are directly or indirectly prevented from or denied access to education in any form. (United Nations, 2016, para 11).

Most of what currently happens in Australian schools is integration, not inclusion. Schools are still largely organised as they have always been, except for minor changes to accommodate students who are required to 'adjust' to remain in that setting. If they can't, some are then subjected to partial enrolment, restricted hours of attendance, (in)formal suspension, segregation into 'Responsible Thinking Rooms', referral to flexible learning options, or enrolment in distance education. These trajectories end at different points through home schooling, early school leaving, and enrolment cancellation or exclusion. Given that integration is the model most confused with inclusion, it is worth illustrating. Integration is when:

- units of work are planned for a year level by a Head of Department to then be adjusted by Special Education or Learning Support teachers for individual students with a 'verified' disability (and only those students).
- a student on the autism spectrum is 'included' in a busy and visually overwhelming mainstream classroom with a pair of noise-cancelling headphones and an aide to deal with the inevitable meltdowns.
- 'included' students are pounded by developmentally inappropriate vocabulary, rapid-fire verbal instruction, and abstract concepts because "that's just how I teach" (for more see Chapter 11).

Integration is business as usual with add-ons (if students are lucky).

The long-overdue definitions of exclusion, segregation, integration, and inclusion that have been written into GG4 are a potential gamechanger for the implementation of inclusive education globally. But, to fully understand these definitions and to change educational practice accordingly, we need to know why these distinctions had to made.

The History of Inclusive Education

Perhaps one of the reasons that inclusion is described as a journey is that this word also describes its history: the story of how and why inclusive education came to be. It is important for anyone involved with inclusion to understand this history because it highlights the differences between inclusive education and everything that came before it. This, in turn, enables educators to know when educational provision is truly inclusive or whether that provision belongs more properly to a former evolutionary stage. The four definitions articulated earlier effectively describe these stages. Without their place in history, there would be no need to define them and there would be nothing from which to distinguish inclusive education. If these stages had been consigned to history, there would not be the need to define them at all. But the evidence is that they still exist. And we need to stamp them out.

The history of inclusive education varies across the world. Some countries are just discovering the concept for the first time. Others like the United States, the United Kingdom, and Australia, have been engaging with its foundational concepts since the 1970s (Chapter 4). Each is at a different point in the evolution process, and some are sadly going backwards. Whilst outstanding examples of inclusive schools can be found in many education systems around the world, none—aside perhaps from those discussed in our new Chapter 7—can claim to have implemented inclusive education systemically. The various stages of implementation internationally have further muddied the waters because some countries are still in the process of implementing mass education. Inclusive education has struggled for political traction in some developing countries due to the sheer scale of the reforms needed to modernise their education systems and because it is sometimes perceived as a white colonialist idea imposed by rich countries from the Global North (Walton, 2018). For this reason, there are no clear historical periods to which we can confidently point as complete. Rather, there shades of each in all systems, even in rich countries with mature education systems, like

Australia, where home schooling and part-time enrolments are increasing, especially of students on the autism spectrum (Poed et al., 2017).

That said, there are some broad historical features that are important to understand. Until the late 1800s, children with disability did not attend school. Most were institutionalised or kept at home. This is what GC4 refers to as *exclusion* and it still occurs in many developing countries around the world. In Australia, this began to change in the 1860s with the opening of special schools by the Royal Institute for Deaf and Blind Children. For the next 60 years, education for children with disability was considered a private concern until government special schools began opening in the early 1900s (Graham & Jahnukainen, 2011). From the 1940s, governments took over from charities, establishing an increasing number of special schools and classes. At this point, however, children who previously would always have attended their local school began being directed to new settings for students described as 'maladjusted', 'feebleminded', and 'educationally subnormal' (McRae, 1996). In other words, where special education once helped children previously excluded from schooling to receive some form of education, it began leading to a different form of exclusion: *segregation*. And it was rampant. Questions started being asked at very high levels about who was being segregated and for what reasons. For example, in 1968 the President of the Council for Exceptional Children in the United States, Lloyd Dunn, raised concerns about the overrepresentation of children from culturally and linguistically diverse backgrounds in segregated special educational settings. Change some of the language and he could easily be talking about the segregated settings currently proliferating in systems that are meant to be progressing inclusive education: special 'behaviour' schools, support classes, flexible learning options, and alternative education settings.

> The number of special day classes for the retarded has been increasing by the leaps and bounds. The most recent 1967–68 statistics compiled by the United States Office of Education now indicate that there are approximately 32,000 teachers of the retarded employed by local school systems—over one-third of all special educators in the nation. In my best judgement, about 60 to 80% of the pupils taught by these teachers are children from low-status backgrounds—including Afro-Americans, American Indians, Mexicans and Puerto-Rico Americans; those from non-standard English-speaking, broken, disorganised and inadequate homes and children from other non-middleclass environments. This expensive proliferation of self-contained special schools and classes raises serious educational and civil rights issues which must be squarely faced. It is my thesis that we must stop labelling these deprived children as mentally retarded. Furthermore, we must stop segregating them by placing them into our allegedly special programs.
>
> (Dunn, 1968, pp. 5–6)

The fact that this impassioned argument was being made by the president of the premier body for special education in the United States over 50 years ago shows just how long and circuitous the journey to inclusion has been. Similar arguments were being made at the time in the United Kingdom, where research was also highlighting the overrepresentation of poor children, especially those with black or brown skin (Graham, 2012). The difference between the two nations was in the ethnicity of those segregated but, while their ethnicity may have differed, their backgrounds did not. In each case, segregated students were poor white children from the working classes, the descendants of the African slave trade, and immigrants from other language and cultural backgrounds. The Australian experience has mirrored developments in the United Kingdom and United States, but always with some delay. For example, research has only relatively recently documented the overrepresentation of Indigenous students in segregated special educational settings (Graham, 2012; Sweller et al., 2012), and still nothing has been done about it. This is despite a global movement that began some 60 years ago, a decade and a half before Lloyd Dunn made his final address as President.

What Happened 60 Years Ago?

Several factors combined to create impetus for broad political, social, and educational change, including but not limited to the birth of an international human-rights legal framework that led to the CRPD, which we discuss in Chapter 3. Among this combination of factors was the result of the *Brown v Board of Education* (*Brown*; 1954) class action at the height of the civil rights movement in the United States in which it was declared that "separate educational facilities are inherently unequal" (Smith & Kozleski, 2005, p. 272). While *Brown* was concerned with racial segregation and the inferior educational opportunities offered to African Americans, it influenced the outcome of another right to education class action, *PARC v The Commonwealth of Pennsylvania* (*PARC*; 1971), in which it was argued that the segregation of children with intellectual disability violated the principles of *Brown* (Smith & Kozleski, 2005). The successful *PARC* class action led to the passage of the *Education for All Handicapped Children Act* in 1975, now known as the *Individuals with Disabilities Education Act* (IDEA). This United States federal law enshrined two important doctrines: (i) that *all* children were entitled to a free and appropriate public education, to be provided (ii) in the least restrictive environment. While interpretations of the words 'appropriate' and 'least restrictive' have proved problematic over time, IDEA was a major step forward for American students with disability and their families.

The United States is a fundamentally different place to Australia or the United Kingdom, and this is one of the reasons that the history of inclusive education looks different across the Pacific and Atlantic oceans. The United States has different political and judicial systems, and many of the reforms that have eventually travelled across the world have come about due to legal actions by Americans with disability and/or their parents. Australia and the United Kingdom are more alike due to a shared history and their adoption of the Westminster system of government. Here changes occur through political pressure and changes to government legislation and policy, but also because Australia tends to 'policy borrow' from the United Kingdom and United States (Graham & Jahnukainen, 2011). A pattern of the United States leading and the United Kingdom and Australia following is evident in Table 2.1 below; however, it would be a mistake to think that the United States has always led well. For example, the United States is a signatory to the CRPD, but it has not ratified it and is therefore not legally bound by it, although in some ways its own bill of rights provides for greater protections for students than are provided in many countries that have ratified the CRPD, including this one.

Table 2.1 Key Historical Events in the Journey Towards Inclusive Education

Year	Title	Origin
1948	Universal Declaration of Human Rights	United Nations
1954	*Brown v Board of Education*	United States
1959	Declaration on the Rights of the Child	United Nations
1965	Convention on Racial Discrimination	United Nations
1971	Universal Declaration on the Rights of Persons with Mental Retardation	United Nations
1971	*PARC v The Commonwealth of Pennsylvania*	United States
1973	The Karmel Report *Schools in Australia: Report of the Interim Committee for the Australian Schools Commission*	Australia
1975	Education for All Handicapped Children Act	United States
1975	Declaration on the Rights of Disabled Persons	United Nations
1978	The Warnock Report *Special Educational Needs: Report into the Committee of Enquiry into the Education of Handicapped Children and Young People*	United Kingdom
1981	International Year of Disabled Persons	International
1989	Convention on the Rights of the Child	United Nations
1990	Individuals with Disabilities Education Act	United States
1990	World Declaration on Education for All and Framework for Action to Meet Basic Learning Needs (UNESCO)	Jomtien, Thailand
1992	Disability Discrimination Act	Australia
1994	Salamanca Statement & Framework for Action on Special Needs Education (UNESCO)	Salamanca, Spain
2005	Disability Standards for Education	Australia
2006	Convention on the Rights of Persons with Disabilities	United Nations
2012	Goal 4: Quality Education, #Envision2030: Sustainable Development Goals	United Nations
2016	General Comment No. 4 on Article 24: Right to Inclusive Education	United Nations
2018	Queensland Department of Education Inclusive Education Policy Statement	Queensland, Australia

Within three years, IDEA was followed by what is known as 'The Warnock Report', which was the result of a parliamentary inquiry led by Baroness Warnock in the United Kingdom (see Table 2.1). The report recommended—among other things—that initial teacher education programs include at least one mandatory unit to prepare *all* classroom teachers to teach students with disability. The Warnock Report was hugely influential both in the UK and Australia, but it was the International Year of Disabled Persons in 1981 that had the most effect in Australia (Forlin, 2006), contributing:

to a national policy consensus that every child should be able to attend their neighbourhood school where possible and in the best interests of the child. Enrolment statistics indicate the number of students enrolled in government special schools across
Australia dropped by 37% from 23,350 in 1982 to 14,768 in 1992.

(Graham & Jahnukainen, 2011, p. 266)

This was an important achievement but, returning to the definitions that have been
at the heart of this chapter, transferring students from segregated to mainstream settings
does not equal inclusion. And we have been caught in this liminal space ever since.
Despite the development of national anti-discrimination legislation in the form of the
Disability Discrimination Act 1992 (Cth) and the *Disability Standards for Education 2005*
(DSE; Cth) (see Chapter 5), the necessary changes to shift from integrating students
with disability into a mainstream that was designed with only some students in mind
to the type of systemic reform and flexibility in practice articulated in GC4 have not
happened, at the systemic level. At this point, it is worth reprising my point about the
mainstream because I am still having to explain this point all the time, even to people
who research in this area.

The Mainstream

If we are ever to realise inclusive education, there are some things that we must get
straight. Language is one of them. Too often, the terms inclusive and mainstream are
used interchangeably, when they are—in fact—mutually incompatible. Let us turn to
recent events in Australia for a helpful example. In 2017, right-wing Senator Pauline
Hanson decided to juggle a metaphorical can of petrol while holding a lighted match
by suggesting to the media that students with disability, and especially those on the
autism spectrum, should be removed from mainstream schools (Norman & Borrello,
2017). The Senator claimed to represent the voice of teachers and argued that these
students would be better served in special classes and that their presence in 'the mainstream' negatively affects classroom teachers and other children. People with disability,
advocates, parents of children with a disability, and inclusive education experts lined up
to condemn her comments. Many cited the empirical evidence showing superior outcomes of inclusive education for students both with and without disability (Graham, &
de Bruin, 2017); evidence that Kate de Bruin re-examines in Chapter 6 of this second
edition. What none of us did, because we knew the nuance would be lost in the throes
of ill-informed public debate, was say:

"Well, no, if inclusion is interpreted to mean placing students with a disability into
unreconstructed 'mainstream' schools—schools that we know were designed with
the 'average' student in mind—then of course it doesn't work. But 'it', in this case,
isn't inclusion. 'It' is integration and we abandoned that in the 1990s because we
learned all the way back then that 'it' doesn't work".

Conflating the concept of inclusive education with the concept of a mainstream creates many problems going forward. Most frustrating is the associated claim that 'inclusion does not work' and the inside thought of many inclusive education experts is again:

"Well yeah, students with a disability and especially those on the autism spectrum should *not* be included in 'the mainstream'. That's because it [the mainstream] was built for some, not *all* and its very existence depends on the co-existence of a parallel special education system into which students who do not fit a system that was never designed for them can be directed. The truth is that 'the mainstream' is *not* inclusive and it is of no surprise whatsoever that students with a disability (and many others) do not thrive there."

Everyone involved with inclusive education simply *must* use precise terminology going forward. For much of the last 25 years, inclusive education stakeholders have been grappling with the problem of how to make inclusion happen, when so few key stakeholders understand what it really is. There are at least two aspects to this problem, which has made it difficult to solve. Aspect 1 is an artefact of what former US Defence Secretary Donald Rumsfeld once referred to as "unknown unknowns" (Launer, 2010, p. 628), which is an extension of Bradley's (1997) concept of unconscious incompetence. In other words, it is easy to believe a school is inclusive when a common definition of inclusive education is lacking and impossible to make that school inclusive if a flawed definition is applied, as this will result in the belief that inclusion has already been achieved. Aspect 2 is the gradual appropriation of both the concept and language of inclusion by special education (Walton, 2015). This appropriation started in the early 2000s as a response to policies that promoted inclusive education, threatening the careers and professional status of all those wedded to the paradigm it sought to replace. This appropriation has fuelled Aspect 1 by muddying the waters and confusing educators, who have applied exclusionary practices in the genuine belief that they were being inclusive. Cátia Malaquias, founder of the advocacy organisation Starting with Julius, and co-founder of All Means All, Australian Alliance for Inclusive Education, calls this 'fauxclusion'. It is an apt term for the rebadging that has so far thwarted the genuine development of inclusive education.

Fauxclusion

When conducting observations for a six-year longitudinal study investigating factors contributing to the development of disruptive behaviour, I asked the deputy principal of one participating school why there were so many adults in one classroom and why there seemed to be two classes in the one small room. The deputy looked at me like

Figure 2.1 An 'inclusive class' in School 5 (Year 4, 2018). Artist: Olivia Tomes.

I was from another planet and then informed me—with an edge in her voice—that their school was an 'inclusive school' and that the class I had just been observing was an 'inclusive class'. Her tone suggested that I had asked an insulting question and she began to walk away, believing it had been answered. But, of course, I was now very interested to know more (e.g., if this is an inclusive class, then what do the *other* classes look like?) and persisted with a request for clarification. Looking slightly annoyed, the deputy explained that they had closed their Special Education Program (SEP) because of the Department's new inclusion policy. This class was now an 'inclusive class' because it now included 'the SEP kids' who were being taught by 'the SEP teacher'. The other half of the class was comprised by the 'mainstream kids' who were being taught by 'the mainstream teacher'. The teachers were 'co-teaching' this new 'inclusive' class. Readers of the first edition of this book will be familiar with these stories but stay with me because, wait . . . there's more!

As Figure 2.1 illustrates, this 'inclusive class' had three adults and two classes being taught in the one room. On the left are 'the mainstream kids' with the 'mainstream teacher' who is teaching them 'mainstream curriculum': Grade 4 geometry using coloured shapes. On the right are 'the SEP kids' with 'the SEP teacher' who has drawn a number line on a portable whiteboard. These students are also in Grade 4, although most have been placed on Prep/Grade 1 Individual Curriculum Plans (ICPs).

The SEP teacher asks, "Is 18 closer to 10 or 20?" Most students in the group yell out, "20", but some answer "10." The teacher says, "the right answer is 20!" But does not explain why 10 is wrong or why 20 is closer.

(Field notes, Grade 4, 2018)

The purpose of the lesson is to work out the missing numbers on a timeline. The problem is that the work is pitched far below the groups' capability and students are clearly bored, some fidgeting and others deliberately calling out the wrong answer. I can tell because of the amusement it generates in the group. Nor is what the 'SEP kids' are learning aligned with grade-level curriculum.[2] Sitting in the middle of the classroom and forming a human barrier between the two groups is the teacher aide who remains largely motionless during the entire two-hour observational cycle, except to occasionally tell students in the 'mainstream group' to stop fidgeting and do their work. She has her back to the 'SEP group'. The noise is tremendous, but the students are not responsible; rather, it is a consequence of two teachers struggling to be heard over each other as they both attempt to individually instruct their own classes sandwiched next to each other in the same room.

This is not inclusion. Nor is the example of another 'inclusive class' we observed in School 3. As illustrated in Figure 2.2, this class featured two empty desks at the front of the room and a table with two chairs in the corridor. When we began observing we assumed that a couple of students were absent on that day, hence the empty desks. However, about half an hour into the morning session, a teacher aide arrives with a student whom we will call 'Daniel'. Daniel and the aide sit at the two desks at the front of the classroom. The class teacher does not even look their way.

The aide hands Daniel a large scrap book that has some single words written on the pages in coloured pencil. The words are quite large and look like the handiwork of a much younger child. Daniel begins doodling in the scrapbook while the aide stares listlessly into the distance. The classroom teacher continues with the other students, calling out instructions from his chair at the front of the room, which he rarely leaves. They are doing some form of literacy activity that involves a poem the teacher had obtained from a Russian website because it had blanked out words. The plan for the lesson was for the students to complete the poem by inserting what they thought the missing words should be. Daniel's scrapbook doodling is unrelated, and the aide provides him with no instruction. After about 20 minutes, he and the aide move to the desk and chairs in the outside corridor. The teacher ignores their departure, just as he ignored their entrance. Daniel begins using an iPad and the aide sits next to him staring into space and offering no support.

We followed and assessed Daniel, along with the more than 240 children in the longitudinal study, since they all began school in Prep. In Grade 1, Daniel received weekly speech therapy from an external agency but did not test low enough on standardised language assessment to be 'verified' in the Speech Language Impairment category for

---

2 For more on how to achieve this, read Chapter 12.

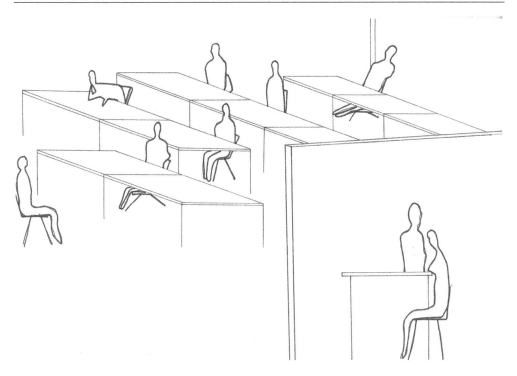

Figure 2.2 An 'inclusive class' in School 3 (Year 4, 2018). Artist: Olivia Tomes.

individual funding through Queensland's Education Adjustment Program. Eventually, in Grade 3, he was verified under the Intellectual Impairment category and placed on a Prep ICP. For us, this is a huge concern as our data suggests that he is capable of far more. For example, while his word-level reading scores were below average in Grade 1, with targeted intervention this could have been addressed and potentially lifted to average. Instead, his word-level reading scores declined so much over the next two years that they fell in the 'very poor' category. When we asked his Grade 3 teacher what her chief concern about Daniel would be, she responded: "There's no real chief concern because I know that [Daniel] will never be with his peers academically. He's in Grade 3 and he's on a prep ICP. We've put him on the prep ICP so that he can experience success." It is an indictment of our collective understanding of inclusive education that this child's ghostly presence in 'the mainstream' is being taken as evidence of inclusion.

When two groups are sandwiched into one classroom with a separate teacher for each group, as depicted in Figure 2.2, this goes beyond integration. This is new territory, a half-way house between integration and segregation for the only attempt to integrate is through the physical co-location of the two groups. The curriculum and teaching are separate, and there is no peer interaction. Even when this 'inclusive class' goes to science and the same science lesson is delivered across groups, the 'SEP kids' are positioned at a separate desk and taught by the 'SEP teacher'. Not surprisingly, the two groups do not mix in the playground, which, as Kate de Bruin outlines in Chapter 6, denies children the social benefits of genuine inclusion. While this 'inclusive class' might not exactly fit the description of segregation above, it is further to that end of the segregation-inclusion continuum than it is integration (see Figure 2.3). The other example of an 'inclusive class' is also closer to segregation than integration. In this example, Daniel is a satellite orbiting the physical approximation of a class. He is not included in any way, and he is not being taught anything. This failure flows upstream. Daniel's local high school created a 'Prep/Grade 1' class in Grade 7 to accommodate vast increases in the number of students coming from local primary schools on P/1 Individual Curriculum Plans. Not only is this not inclusion but it makes real inclusion much harder to achieve. And it leads to social and economic exclusion; the insidious form of exclusion that still occurs in rich, developed nations like Australia.

Both of these stories emerged from classroom observations conducted in primary schools serving disadvantaged communities. Is it different in high schools? What about high schools in *average* socioeconomic communities? Is inclusion better in those schools?

Since the first edition of this book was published, I have been leading the Accessible Assessment Project, funded by the Australian Research Council (ARC) Linkage Projects Scheme. The project is being conducted in partnership with three secondary schools, the Queensland Curriculum and Assessment Authority, the Queensland Secondary Principals Association, and Speech Pathology Australia. Chapter 10 describes one of the pedagogical interventions implemented in the second year of the project, the aim of which was to improve the accessibility of everyday classroom teaching. I am immensely grateful to our partners for supporting this research and to Associate Professor Jill Willis for convincing them to back us because without them this research may never have happened. Why? Well, we submitted an expression of interest to another

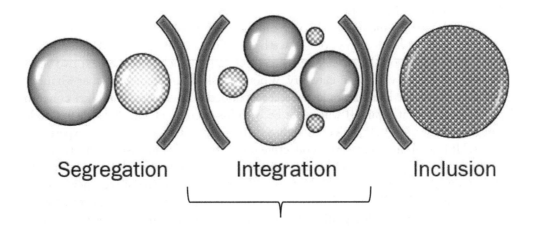

Segregation   Integration   Inclusion

Social and economic exclusion

Figure 2.3 Features and outcomes of the real 'continuum of provision.

potential partner but, while the EOI was successful, the project never eventuated because no one within the organisation could fathom what we wanted to do or why we wanted to do it. Every decision-maker that we spoke to thought that students with language disorders were those from English as an Additional Language or Dialect (EALD) backgrounds,[3] and none could understand why we would want to use eye-tracking to measure the accessibility of English assessment task sheets. Thankfully, three visionary leaders (two principals and one English Head of Department) *did* get it and came to the rescue.

Much excellent work is happening in these schools but as is often the case, inclusive practice was not highest in a very long list of competing priorities. This is not because educators don't care or because they can't be bothered. It is because there is a hierarchy of knowledge in school education (as there is in university teacher education), and inclusive education—just like the students it is about—is very much on the periphery and not generally part of the main action, which is where it needs to be. The result is integration: teaching to the middle with add-ons, although frankly we didn't see many add-ons in these high school classrooms. I suspect some are being provided in 'Learning and Enrichment Teams' in 'Diverse Learning Hubs'. Even though we identified 63 students with disability in the classes that we were observing, we also found limited evidence of quality accessible teaching (see Chapter 11) and almost never saw adjustments being made for those students. This is despite around a third of those 63 students being counted in and receiving funding through the *Nationally Consistent Collection of Data on School Students with a Disability*, colloquially known as NCCD (de Bruin et al., 2020). We also know that most of those 63 students were not being consulted on adjustments or about how their learning could be supported because we asked them, and they had no idea what we were talking about. Very few of their parents or carers had been consulted either, despite some of those parents being strong advocates for their children and expressing concern about their child's learning progress. It is with some frustration that I note our prediction of this eventuality in our chapter on the NCCD in the first edition of this book, when we warned, "there is still insufficient accountability [in NCCD] to ensure that students are in fact being consulted in the design and implementation of adjustments, or even that the adjustments claimed were ever delivered" (de Bruin et al., 2020, p. 146).

Readers of this book will know that education providers are obligated to consult students in the identification, design, and implementation of reasonable adjustments as per the DSE, but it very rarely happens with the result being that adjustments either don't happen or they are not relevant and are therefore ineffective. Put it this way, how useful is extra time in an exam when you have no idea what the task is or what the questions mean? Incidentally, the DSE were reviewed for the third time in 2020 and such failures were once again noted in the review report, just as they were in 2010 and in 2015, but these failures have still not been addressed through root-and-branch revision of legislation to impose a positive duty on education providers to deliver relevant reasonable adjustments and supports.

---

3 Not our focus. Read Chapter 9 for an excellent distinction between these groups

An updated list of relevant government reviews and inquiries over the past two decades is provided in Table 2.2. Since publication of the first edition of this book there have been several additions to this list at both state and federal level which have each in their own way highlighted the inequities in various education systems across Australia. For example, the final report of the Productivity Commission's (2022) *Review of the National School Reform Agreement* properly recognises students with disability in its consideration of priority equity groups and this is a major step forward given these students can account for 40% or more of students in some regions of the country.

This list now also includes the much-awaited *Royal Commission into Violence, Abuse, Neglect and Exploitation of People with Disability* (DRC), which commenced in late 2019,

Table 2.2 Relevant Government Reviews and Inquiries from 2000 to 2023

Year	Review/Inquiry	Level of Government
2002	Australian Government Senate Inquiry into the Education of Students with Disabilities (Commonwealth of Australia, 2002)	National
2006	New South Wales Auditor-General's Report Performance Audit: Educating Primary School Students with Disabilities (Audit Office of New South Wales, 2006)	NSW
2010	New South Wales Parliamentary Inquiry into the Provision of Education for Students with Disability or Special Needs (General Purpose Standing Committee No. 2, 2010).	NSW
2012	Review of the Disability Standards for Education (Australian Government Department of Education, Employment and Workplace Relations, 2012)	National
	Review of the Experiences of Students with Disabilities in Victorian schools (Victorian Equal Opportunity and Human Rights Commission, 2012)	VIC
2015	Review of the Disability Standards for Education (Urbis, 2015)	National
	ACT Report of the Expert Panel on Students with Complex Needs and Challenging Behaviour (Shaddock et al., 2015)	ACT
	Report of the Select Committee on Access to the South Australian Education System for Students with a Disability (Parliament of South Australia, 2017)	SA
2016	Access to Real Learning: Current levels of access and attainment for students with disability in the school system, and the impact on students and families associated with inadequate levels of support (Commonwealth of Australia, 2016)	National
	Victorian Review of the Program for Students with Disabilities (Victoria Department of Education and Training, 2016)	VIC
	New South Wales Audit Office Supporting students with disability in New South Wales public schools (Audit Office of New South Wales, 2016)	NSW

Year	Review/Inquiry	Level of Government
2017	Review of Education for Students with Disability in Queensland state schools (Deloitte Access Economics, 2017)	QLD
	New South Wales Parliamentary Inquiry into Students with a Disability or Special Needs in New South Wales schools (Portfolio Committee No. 3, 2017)	NSW
2019	Strengthening school and system capacity to implement effective interventions to support student behaviour and wellbeing in NSW public schools: An evidence review (Pearce et al., 2019)	NSW
2020	Inquiry into Suspension, Exclusion and Expulsion Processes in South Australian government schools (Graham et al., 2020)	SA
2021	Final Report of the 2020 Review of the Disability Standards for Education 2005 (Australian Government Department of Education, 2020).	National
2022	Review of the National School Reform Agreement (Australian Government Productivity Commission, 2022)	National
2023	Senate Inquiry into The Issue of Increasing Disruption in Australian Classrooms	National
2019–2023	Royal Commission into Violence, Abuse, Neglect and Exploitation of People with Disability	National

after years of lobbying by disability activists, families, and advocates. And while the final report of the DRC is being written at the same time as this second edition, and we are yet to learn of its recommendations, all three DRC Hearings on education (Hearing 2, 7, and 24; Royal Commission into Violence, Abuse, Neglect and Exploitation of People with Disability, 2019, 2021, 2022) laid bare, once again, the cracks into which students in key priority equity groups, including those with disability, fall. Note that the list in Table 2.2 is not exhaustive and there may be reviews or inquiries that I missed, however, the key point of this list is that these failures have been noted over and over again, since the beginning of this 21st century. The responsibility to address them ultimately lies with governments, for we know what needs to be done but the decision to do what is *right*—rather than what is politically popular or expedient—hasn't yet been made. Not to the extent that it needs to be to embark on the immediate progressive implementation of systemic inclusive education reform that is necessary to eradicate 'inclusive classrooms' like those described at the beginning of this chapter; reform that we are required to undertake not only to meet our human-rights obligations but to make sure that kids like Daniel stop being passed over by schools teaching to the middle with (but often without) add-ons.

Lobby groups on opposing sides—mainstream and special—argue that our current policy and practice inertia is because inclusion is 'too hard'. But the truth is old practices die hard. The lack of a clear definition of inclusion, together with unwillingness to let go of the status and power inferred by 'specialist' knowledge, has induced a stalemate, the victims of which are students with disability, their parents, and the dedicated teachers and principals who 'go it alone' and put the rights of their students first. Those teachers and principals need opportunities to acquire deep knowledge through quality teacher education and professional development that is evidence-based. They need the backing of a critical mass. They need colleagues who pull their own weight, and they need unions that defend them by ensuring *all* their members shoulder the load equally. They need employers that will support them as they make changes because people are frightened by change, and some complain loudly. They need networks from which they can source advice and quality resources that can show them how it can be done. They need educated parents who understand that *every* child has a right to an inclusive education and that their child's right does not trump the rights of students with disability to be included, even if that child has challenging behaviour (Gillett-Swan & Lundy, 2022). These are what might be called the 'conditions of possibility' (Foucault, 1972) for inclusion and some of these conditions are now emerging in Australia. Why now? Because the recipients of a substandard level of education that leads to social and economic exclusion have had enough, and they are beginning to contact the media when education providers breach legislation that entitles them to reasonable adjustments. Because governments can only conduct reviews and inquiries that all report the same thing for so long. Because Australia is legally bound by the CRPD and the Committee has made it very clear through GC4, whether our government/s agree with it or not, what inclusive education is and what must be done to achieve it. And because we all need to join the 21st century. *We are, after all, now almost a quarter of the way through it.*

I noted in the first edition of this book that here are green shoots emerging and, while I have been recounting a bit of doom and gloom in this chapter, I am buoyed by their growth. Educators are beginning to support each other through collaborative networks on social media, providing advice and resources, as well as affirmation and solidarity. The School Inclusion Network for Educators (SINE) on Facebook is one such network and it now has over 6500 members nationally. Successive Australian governments have invested in the NCCD, which allocates disability loadings based on the adjustments that teachers make to enable students with a disability to access and participate in education (de Bruin et al., 2020), as per the DSE, although both really need to be reviewed and their processes significantly tightened. And as I noted in my opening acknowledgements, there are now many dioceses, regions, and schools providing this book to educators and school leaders to support their learning. Educators are investing in their own knowledge by reading this book, using it as a discussion piece for book clubs, and buying it for their principals. Parents are doing the same. This is a critical linchpin for success because teachers and school leaders cannot make inclusion a reality without deep knowledge of inclusive education, its guiding philosophy, fundamental concepts, frameworks, and practices. It has oft been said that inclusion is everyone's business, and this second edition has been written to help everyone involved develop the deep knowledge necessary to make inclusion a reality in every system, every sector, every region, every school, and every classroom.

Keep up the good fight, #Inclusionistas!

References

Audit Office of New South Wales. (2006). *Educating primary school students with disabilities.* Department of Education. https://www.audit.nsw.gov.au/sites/default/files/pdf-downloads/2006_Sep_Report_Educating_Primary_School_Students_with_Disabilities.pdf

Audit Office of New South Wales. (2016). *Supporting students with disability in NSW public schools.* Department of Education. https://www.audit.nsw.gov.au/sites/default/files/pdf-down loads/2016_May_Report_Supporting_students_with_disability_in_NSW_public_schools.pdf

Australian Government Department of Education, Employment and Workplace Relations. (2012). *Report on the review of Disability Standards for Education 2005.* https://www.education.gov.au/swd/resources/2010-report-review-disability-standards-education-2005

Australian Government Department of Education. (2020). *Review of the Disability Standards for Education 2005.* https://www.education.gov.au/disability-standards-education-2005/2020-review-disability-standards-education-2005

Australian Government Productivity Commission. (2022). *Review of the National School Reform Agreement, Study Report.* https://www.pc.gov.au/inquiries/completed/school-agreement/report/school-agreement.pdf

Bradley, F. (1997). From unconscious incompetence to unconscious competence. *Adults Learning (England), 9*(2), 20–21.

Brown v Board of Education [1954] 347 U.S. 483.

Commonwealth of Australia. (2016). *Access to real learning: Current levels of access and attainment for students with disability in the school system, and the impact on students and families associated with inadequate levels of support.* https://www.aph.gov.au/Parliamentary_Business/Committees/Senate/Education_and_Employment/students_with_disability/Report

Commonwealth of Australia. (2002). *Inquiry into the education of students with disabilities.* Commonwealth of Australia. https://www.aph.gov.au/binaries/senate/committee/eet_ctte/comple ted_inquiries/2002-04/ed_students_withdisabilities/report/report.pdf

Danforth, S., & Jones, P. (2015). From special education to integration to genuine inclusion. In P. Jones, & S. Danforth (Eds.), *Foundations of inclusive education research* (pp. 1–21). Emerald Publishing.

de Bruin, K., Graham, L. J., & Gallagher, J. (2020). What is the NCCD and what does it mean for my practice? In L. J. Graham (Ed.), *Inclusive education for the 21st century: Theory, policy and practice* (pp. 122–158). Routledge.

Deloitte Access Economics. (2017). *Review of education for students with disability in Queensland state schools.* Deloitte Access Economics. http://education.qld.gov.au/schools/disability/docs/disability-review-report.pdf

Disability Discrimination Act 1992 (Cth).

Disability Standards for Education 2005 (Cth).

Dunn, L. M. (1968). Special education for the mildly retarded—Is much of it justifiable? *Exceptional Children, 35*(1), 5–22. https://doi.org/10.1177/001440296803500101

Education for All Handicapped Children Act (1975).

Forlin, C. (2006). Inclusive education in Australia ten years after Salamanca. *European Journal of Psychology of Education, 21*(3), 265.

Foucault, M. (1972). *Archaeology of knowledge* (A. M. Sheridan, Trans.). Pantheon Books.

General Purpose Standing Committee No. 2. (2010). *The provision of education to students with a disability or special needs.* The Committee. https://www.parliament.nsw.gov.au/lcdocs/inquir ies/1837/100716%20The%20provision%20of%20education%20to%20students%20with.pdf

Gillett-Swan, J. K., & Lundy, L. (2022). Children, classrooms and challenging behaviour: do the rights of the many outweigh the rights of the few? *Oxford Review of Education*, 48(1), 95–111. https://doi.org/10.1080/03054985.2021.1924653

Graham, L. J. (2012). Disproportionate over-representation of Indigenous students in New South Wales government special schools. *Cambridge Journal of Education*, 42(2), 163–176. https://doi.org/10.1080/0305764X.2012.676625

Graham, L. J., & de Bruin, K. (2017, June 22). Pauline Hanson is wrong—we need to include children with disability in regular classrooms. *The Conversation*. https://theconversation.com/pauline-hanson-is-wrong-we-need-to-include-children-with-disability-in-regular-classrooms-79897

Graham, L. J., & Jahnukainen, M. (2011). Wherefore art thou, inclusion? Analysing the development of inclusive education in New South Wales, Finland, and Alberta. *Journal of Education Policy*, 26(2), 263–288. https://doi.org/10.1080/02680939.2010.493230

Graham, L. J., McCarthy, T., Killingly, C., Tancredi, H., & Poed, S. (2020). *Inquiry into suspension, exclusion and expulsion processes in South Australian Government schools*. The Centre for Inclusive Education. https://www.education.sa.gov.au/documents_sorting/docs/support-and-inclusion/engagement-and-wellbeing/student-absences/report-of-an-independent-inquiry-into-suspensions-exclusions-and-expulsions-in-south-australian-government-schools.pdf

Individuals with Disabilities Education Act.

Launer, J. (2010). Unconscious incompetence. *Postgraduate Medical Journal*, 86(1020), 628–628. https://doi.org/10.1136/pgmj.2010.108423

McRae, D. (1996) *The integration/inclusion feasibility study*. NSW Department of School Education.

Norman, J., & Borrello, E. (2017, June 29). Pauline Hanson under fire for 'bigoted' call to remove children with disabilities from mainstream classrooms. *ABC News*. https://www.abc.net.au/news/2017-06-21/pauline-hanson-under-fire-repulsive-bigoted-comments-autism/8640328

PARC v The Commonwealth of Pennsylvania [1971] 334 F. Supp. 1257.

Parliament of Australia. (n.d.). *The issue of increasing disruption in Australian school classrooms*. https://www.aph.gov.au/Parliamentary_Business/Committees/Senate/Education_and_Employment/DASC#:~:text=On%2028%20November%202022%20the,date%20to%2016%20November%202023.

Parliament of South Australia. (2017). *Report of the Select Committee on access to the South Australian education*. http://www.a4.org.au/sites/default/files/Report%20of%20the%20Select%20Committee%20on%20Access%20to%20the%20South%20Australian%20Education%20System%20for%20Students%20with%20a%20Disability.pdf

Pearce, N., Cross, D., Epstein, M., Johnston, R., & Legge, E. (2019) *Strengthening school and system capacity to implement effective interventions to support student behaviour and wellbeing in NSW public schools: An evidence review*. Telethon Kids Institute. https://education.nsw.gov.au/content/dam/main-education/student-wellbeing/attendance-behaviour-and-engagement/media/documents/telethon-kids-institute-final-report.pdf

Poed, S., Cologon, K., & Jackson, R. (2017). *Gatekeeping and restrictive practices with students with disability: Results of an Australian survey*. Paper presented to the 2017 Inclusive Education Summit, University of South Australia, Adelaide. http://allmeansall.org.au/wp-content/uploads/2017/10/TIES-4.0-20172.pdf

Portfolio Committee No. 3. (2017). *Education of students with a disability or special needs in New South Wales*. The Committee. https://www.parliament.nsw.gov.au/lcdocs/inquiries/|2416/170921%20-%20Final%20report.pdf

Royal Commission into Violence, Abuse, Neglect and Exploitation of People with Disability. (2019). *Public Hearing 2: Inclusive education in Queensland—preliminary inquiry.* https://disability.royalcommission.gov.au/public-hearings/public-hearing-2

Royal Commission into Violence, Abuse, Neglect and Exploitation of People with Disability. (2021). *Public Hearing 7: Barriers experienced by students with disability in accessing and obtaining a safe, quality and inclusive school education and consequent life course impacts.* https://disability.royalcommission.gov.au/public-hearings/public-hearing-7

Royal Commission into Violence, Abuse, Neglect and Exploitation of People with Disability. (2022). *Public Hearing 24: The experience of children and young people with disability in different education settings.* https://disability.royalcommission.gov.au/rounds/public-hearing-24-experience-children-and-young-people-disability-different-education-settings

Royal Commission into Violence, Abuse, Neglect and Exploitation of People with Disability. (n.d.). https://disability.royalcommission.gov.au/

Runswick-Cole, K. (2011). Time to end the bias towards inclusive education? *British Journal of Special Education, 38*(3), 112–119. https://doi.org/10.1111/j.1467-8578.2011.00514.x

Shaddock, A., Packer, S., & Roy, A. (2015). *Schools for all children and young people: Report of the expert panel on students with complex needs and challenging behaviour.* https://www.education.act.gov.au/__data/assets/pdf_file/0003/856254/Attach-4-Expert-Panel-Report-Web.pdf

Smith, A., & Kozleski, E. (2005). Witnessing Brown: Pursuit of an equity agenda in American education. *Remedial and Special Education, 26*(5), 270–280. https://doi.org/10.1177/07419325050260050201

Sweller, N., Graham, L. J., & Van Bergen, P. (2012). The minority report: Disproportionate representation in Australia's largest education system. *Exceptional Children, 79*(1), 107–125. https://doi.org/10.1177/001440291207900106

United Nations. (2006). *Convention on the Rights of Persons with Disabilities (CRPD).* https://www.un.org/disabilities/documents/convention/convoptprot-e.pdf.

United Nations. (2016). *General Comment No. 4, Article 24: Right to Inclusive Education (CRPD/C/GC/4).* https://digitallibrary.un.org/record/1313836?ln=en

Urbis. (2015). *2015 Review of the Disability Standards for Education 2005.* https://www.education.gov.au/swd/resources/final-report-2015-review-disability-standards-education-2005

Victoria Department of Education and Training. (2016). *Review of the program for students with disabilities.* https://www.education.vic.gov.au/Documents/about/department/PSD-Review-Report.pdf

Victorian Equal Opportunity and Human Rights Commission. (2012). *Held back: The experiences of students with disabilities in Victorian schools.* https://www.humanrights.vic.gov.au/static/a6db183a9b13ac2dd426637e362d55eb/Resource-Held_back_report-2012.pdf

Walton, E. (2015). *The language of inclusive education: Exploring speaking, listening, reading and writing.* Routledge.

Walton, E. (2018). Decolonising (Through) inclusive education? *Educational Research for Social Change, 7,* 31–45. https://doi.org/10.17159/2221-4070/2018/v7i0a3

Chapter 3

Inclusive education as a human right

*Cátia Malaquias, Juliet Davis, Jenna Gillett-Swan, &
Linda J. Graham*

Education is both a right and a means to the realisation of other rights. It is generative in that education enables the development of the capabilities necessary for full and meaningful participation in modern society (Galliott & Graham, 2014). The United Nations therefore requires that education be available, accessible, acceptable, and adaptable, with the "best interests of the child a primary consideration" (United Nations, 1989, Article 3). Education must also be afforded to *all*, without discrimination of any kind, "on the basis of equality of opportunity" (United Nations, 2016, para 13). This means that all humans, regardless of their presumed ability, have a right to education. This has not always been the case historically, and many individuals around the world are still denied the basic right to education. This happens often and not just in developing countries where, for example, there is still a struggle to ensure equality of educational opportunity for girls (Hodal, 2017). In any country—whether it is developing or already developed—students with disability are the group at greatest risk of discrimination and exclusion (Srivastava et al., 2015).

In wealthy, developed countries the problem is more insidious and often disguised through the "benevolent humanitarianism" (Tomlinson, 1982, p. 6) of special education, which is translated through a discourse that displaces education with 'care' and rights with 'needs'. As discussed in Chapter 4, such words position people with disability as dependent on the abled, implying burden and a hierarchy of humanity. They fuel the misperception, rooted within our shared history, that some people are educable, and others are not, that 'education' is only for those who can profit from it and that this type of education is the business of regular 'mainstream' schools. That same misperception underpins the all-too-common belief that there are 'special' places and 'special' people who are more suited to the care of 'special' children because they use 'special' practices (see Chapter 6). But this is segregation, not education, and what passes for education in these settings is often not very 'special' at all. Rather, in the words of the late, great Stella Young: "The word 'special', as it is applied to disability, too often means 'a bit shit'" (Young, 2013). Sensory rooms, life skills, and Individual Curriculum Plans that do not extend children's knowledge and experience by exposing them to rich grade-level content are not 'special' and do not qualify as quality education.

In countries that have ratified the *Convention on the Rights of the Child* (CRC; United Nations, 1989) and the *Convention on the Rights of Persons with Disabilities* (CRPD;

DOI: 10.4324/9781003350897-4

United Nations, 2006a), there is formal recognition that *all* children have a right to a quality education, and that children with disability—specifically—have the right to an *inclusive* education. Educators' knowledge and understanding of children's rights, however, are critical for these rights to be realised. To understand why education is a human right, it is necessary to understand the origins of human rights generally and why understanding, respecting, and enacting rights is so important. It is not just because society has an obligation to do so. Knowing why we have rights enables us to recognise rights breaches when they occur and provides us with the knowledge and ability to rectify them. Rights breaches in education still frequently occur, even in more privileged contexts. Media coverage of abuse and restrictive practices (such as having isolation boxes or 'sanctuary' cages in the classroom) has provided a stark reminder of the more sinister side of some current educational practices occurring in localised contexts. For children with disability, it appears that many of these practices are becoming normalised and justified as suitable responses to assure the safety and protection of both the child and other children in the class. As more examples of restrictive practices perpetrated against children with disability emerge, the line between the atrocities perpetrated against people with disability in the past and current practices starts to fade.

Human Rights and the Treatment of People with Disability

Historically, people with disability have not been treated well. In the early part of the 20th century, people with physical, intellectual, and psychological disabilities were the first minority group to be targeted by the German Nazi regime, which drew upon and exploited the public attitudes, pseudoscientific beliefs, and economic tensions of the era. During World War I, a reallocation of resources from German asylums led to higher mortality rates among residents due to hunger and disease (Mostert, 2002). Widespread acceptance of this shift in resources highlighted an implicit public view that people with disability contributed less to society and were therefore less valuable than their able fellow citizens (Mostert, 2002). In 1920, Karl Binding and Alfred Hoche published their influential work, *Permission for the Destruction of Life Unworthy of Life*, in which they asserted that the right to life was not intrinsic; rather, it was earned by an individual's economic contribution to their community (Hudson, 2011). According to Binding and Hoche, people with disability were "useless eaters" whose lives should be sacrificed to safeguard the state's resources (Mostert, 2002).

This brutal form of economic rationalism was supplemented by the pseudoscientific ideas of Social Darwinism and eugenics. Social Darwinism distorted Charles Darwin's biological theory of evolution to assert that biological and social characteristics were heritable. It was believed that these characteristics had the power to influence the population's overall 'quality', if allowed to be passed down the generations. Eugenics promoted a program of human breeding in which desirable attributes could be enhanced through a higher birth rate and unwanted social and biological traits could be eradicated through selective 'breeding' and/or reproductive sterilisation (Barta, 2001; Gallagher, 2008). In Australia, these ideas manifested in the murder, abduction, and forced assimilation of First Nations peoples (Barta, 2001), with the intention of "breeding out the colour" to achieve "racial purity" and a white Australia (McGregor, 2002, p. 286). Although the idea of "an Australia without Aborigines was both imagined and canvassed" (Barta, 2001, p. 37) in the early 1800s, Germany was the first to issue a compulsory sterilisation law in furtherance of 'social hygiene'. The Law for the Prevention of Hereditarily Diseased Offspring, enacted by the Nazi regime in 1933 as one of its first official acts, ordered the compulsory sterilisation of specific categories of the 'hereditarily ill' (Mostert, 2002). These specific categories included people with "mental retardation", "grave bodily malformation", schizophrenia, Huntington's chorea, blindness, epilepsy, hereditary deafness, and hereditary alcoholism (Mostert, 2002, p. 159). The regime established 220 Health Courts in which a jurist and two doctors determined who would be sterilised (Mostert, 2002). Botched and experimental sterilisation procedures caused the deaths of thousands of young people (Evans, 2004). The Nazi eugenics program was further promoted by the 1935 Nuremberg Laws, including the Marriage Health Law, which prevented the marriage of any person with an intellectual disability or a contagious or hereditary disease (Mostert, 2002). Propaganda films and literature promoted the "mercy killing" of those "lives unworthy of life" (Benedict et al., 2009, p. 514).

On 18 August 1939, a directive was issued by the State Ministry of the Interior compelling all doctors and midwives to register any infant with a "congenital deformity" or "mental retardation" up to the age of three (Mostert, 2002, p. 161). Soon after, this age limit was raised to 16 years (Benedict et al., 2009). Medical practitioners were paid a small fee for each referral and were fined heavily for any failure to report. Later, teachers were also required to report any of their students who fell within the directive (Mostert, 2002). The records of these children were sent to the Reich Health Ministry, where they were marked for life or death by three 'medical experts' (Evans, 2004). Children selected for extermination were sent to special killing wards in 28 health facilities across Germany. There, they were poisoned, starved, intentionally exposed to the cold, or given a lethal injection by medical staff. The children's bodies were then cremated, although some were first autopsied in the interest of Nazi 'science'. Ashes were then sent to their families with a death certificate bearing a false cause of death (Benedict et al., 2009).

The children's killing program established the bureaucratic processes and willing workforce necessary for the next stage in the Nazi regime's extermination campaign: the involuntary 'euthanasia' of adults with disability. This program, named Aktion T4 as per the address of its headquarters at Tiergartenstrasse 4 in Berlin, required the registration of asylum patients with epilepsy, senile dementia, schizophrenia, and "feeble-mindedness", those who were criminally insane or had been institutionalised for more than five years, foreigners and "racial aliens" (Mostert, 2002, p. 163). The large number of potential victims identified through this process prompted the Nazis to find a more 'efficient' killing method: carbon-monoxide poisoning in specially constructed gas chambers, with the flow of gas administered by physicians (Gallagher, 2008). Operations commenced in 1940, and asylum inmates were transported by bus to six killing centres spread across Germany (Mostert, 2002). After the victims were killed, their gold teeth and dental bridges were extracted prior to a mass cremation (Mostert, 2002).

While the authorities tried to keep their activities secret by providing the families of those killed with urns of anonymous ashes and fictitious causes of death, public suspicion was soon aroused. Concerned families caused a general outcry, which was taken up by German Roman Catholic Bishop Clemens von Galen in a powerful sermon on 3 August 1941 (Benedict et al., 2009). Faced with open accusations of homicide and fearing public backlash, the regime shut down the killing centres. Although the official Aktion T4 program ceased, the killings did not. The mass killing of people with disabilities once more became the responsibility of physicians and nurses in medical institutions. This period of "wild euthanasia" saw a reversion to "low-tech" methods of killing people in their care, including starvation, lethal injection, and exposure (Evans, 2004, p. 68; Mostert, 2002). These decentralised killings continued unabated for both adults and children until several months *after* the fall of the Nazi regime in April 1945 (Benedict et al., 2009). Post-war prosecutors estimated that over 80,000 adults with disability were murdered as part of the official Aktion T4 program (Mostert, 2002), and the later "decentralised" killings are estimated to account for a further 150,000 to 200,000 victims (Foth, 2014, p. 220). These death tolls demonstrate the scale of violence experienced by people with disability as a victim group during the Holocaust.

Emergence of International Human-Rights Laws and Institutions

In the waning days of World War II, representatives of the chief Allied powers met to discuss preparations for a new international organisation, later known as the United Nations (Mazower, 2004). The horrors of the two World Wars and the scale of the Nazi atrocities provided political momentum for the development of an international bill of rights (Duranti, 2012; Waltz, 2002). Proclaimed just three years after the 1945 signing of the *United Nations Charter*, the *Universal Declaration of Human Rights* (UDHR) set out the human-rights agenda of the new world order (United Nations, 1948). Article 1 of the UDHR articulates one of the most foundational human-rights principles, that of *equality*, in its statement that "all human beings are born free and equal". Article 3 confirms the intrinsic right of every person to "life, liberty, and security". In drafting this article, the Human Rights Commission drew upon the Nazi regime's mass killing of children and adults with disabilities (Morsink, 1999).

But the dehumanisation of people with disability did not begin or end with World War II and its immediate aftermath. Mass institutionalisation was still the norm well into the second half of the 20th century. The 'medical model' of disability—which treats people with disability as 'objects' and their characteristics as 'defects' to be remedied or cured—resulted in many people with disability being perceived as subhuman and in-educable. In the 1960s, the eyes of the American public were finally opened to the horror of the institutionalisation of people with disability by the mass media and broadcast television. Burton Blatt's 1966 photographic essay entitled *Christmas in Purgatory* was a visual exposé of several state institutions in the eastern United States and contains the following account of the grim conditions that he encountered:

> The infant dormitories depressed us the most . . . Very young children, one and two years of age, were lying in cribs, without interaction with any adult, without playthings, without any apparent stimulation . . . The 'Special Education' we observed in the dormitories for young children was certainly not education. But it was special. It was among the most especially frightening and depressing encounters with human beings we have ever experienced.
>
> (Blatt, 1966, p. 34)

In 1968, television reporter Bill Baldini investigated the conditions at Pennhurst State School, an institution for children with intellectual disability in Pennsylvania. Reporting the details of what he had seen there affected him so much that he could not present the final five-minute segment. The deinstitutionalisation movement followed due to public outrage, with the closure of mass institutions and the reintegration of children and adults with disability back into the community. The 1970s and 1980s brought increasing recognition of human and civil rights for people with disability and acknowledgement of their demand for access, equality, and full participation within the community, although initial progress was slow and hampered by poor planning and preparation. The birth of the inclusive education movement in the 1990s was supported by the gradual recognition of children as rights-holders and the increasing advocacy and protection surrounding the need for adults to recognise children as humans in their own right.

The Importance of Education for Rights Realisation

Following the formation of the United Nations in 1945, and the development and ratification[1] of the UDHR in 1948, there was need for further development and formalisation of a rights treaty specifically for children. While the UDHR applies to children, the United Nations recognised the unique status of childhood as requiring "the need to extend particular care to the child" (United Nations, 1989: preamble). The United Nations' development of an international treaty specifically for children built upon the earlier *Declaration of the Rights of the Child* (1959) adopted by the United Nations in 1959. Consisting of ten principles, it then formed the basis of what is currently known as the *United Nations Convention on the Rights of the Child* (UNCRC; United Nations, 1989). The current Convention's development began in 1979 following a first draft

---

1 The ratification of an international convention generally refers to a commitment beyond its signature— it means that a signatory country undertakes to change its own domestic laws to realise the purposes of the convention.

proposed by Poland (Lee, 2010), which coincided with the International Year of the Child. Adopted by the United Nations in 1989 and consisting of 54 Articles, the UN-CRC mandates clear obligations for States parties to assure the rights in the Convention for all children, including the right to non-discrimination and the right to education (United Nations, 1989). With the exception of the United States, all United Nations member states have ratified the Convention (United Nations, n.d.-a), emphasising the international importance of the rights of the child.

Each child's 'education rights' can be understood in three interconnected ways: (i) rights *to* education, (ii) rights *in* education, and (iii) rights *through* education. The child's right *to* education is provided through Articles 28 and 29 of the UNCRC (United Nations, 1989) and incorporates provision and organisational aspects, such as the guarantees associated with free and compulsory education, and equality of opportunity, as well as the aims of education (Article 29). The aims of education (Article 29) also stipulate that education should foster the development of individuals to their fullest potential. A child's rights *in* education are provided through the right to protection from discrimination (Article 2) and the right to protection from violence (Article 19), as well as the right to freedoms associated with participation, communication, and association (Articles 12–15). Finally, a child's rights *through* education involve rights education as a means to foster and further "the development of respect for human rights and fundamental freedoms" (Article 29(b)). Being educated about rights is considered the most effective means of combating possible rights breaches because a person cannot defend their rights or the rights of others if they know nothing (or little) about them.

Recognition of the Rights of People with Disability

The decade from 1983 to 1992 was proclaimed "the United Nations Decade of Disabled Persons" by the United Nations General Assembly (United Nations, n.d.-b). With the adoption of the UNCRC in 1989—which ensured the right of all children to receive education without discrimination on any grounds—the notion of 'equal access' to education for students with disability also developed traction. The 1990 World Declaration on "Education for All" was the first instrument to make express reference to people with disability (United Nations Educational, Scientific and Cultural Organisation [UNESCO], 1990). Four years later, the World Conference on Special Needs Education specifically called for the education of students with disability in regular schools. It produced the Salamanca Statement (1994), which was supported by 90 countries, including Australia. Article 2 of the Statement concluded: "Regular schools with [an] inclusive orientation are the most effective means of combatting discriminatory attitudes, creating welcoming communities, building an inclusive society and achieving education for all" (UNESCO, 1994, p. ix).

This was the first time that an international instrument had unequivocally championed *inclusive* education for students with disability and emphasised the relationship between inclusive education and an inclusive society. The movement towards the education of students with disability in regular schools, rather than segregated 'special' schools, was gathering momentum. With increased international attention to children's rights came greater focus on the relative rights of people with disability and recognition by the international community that, despite some progress, existing human-rights mandates had been insufficient to protect and promote the rights of people with disability. In 2001, the United Nations General Assembly accepted a proposal for the development of an *International Convention on the Protection and Promotion of the Rights and Dignity of Persons with Disabilities*. Eventually known as the *Convention on the Rights of Persons with Disabilities* (CRPD), it was developed with very significant participation of people with disability and disabled people's organisations from all over the world (Kayess, 2019).

This landmark human-rights treaty was formally adopted in 2006, came into force in 2008, and has since been ratified by 186 nations (United Nations, 2023). While the CRPD is a major achievement for the approximately 1.3 billion people with disability around the globe (World Health Organisation, 2022), the darker period preceding it is still in living memory for many today. This history still influences social attitudes and contemporary policy, including in education (de Bruin, 2022), leading to unconscious bias and low expectations of people with disability who are perceived to fail purely through some fault of their own, and not due to barriers to their access and participation that society has failed to anticipate and address through universal design and reasonable adjustments. A recent example of such failure in practice is the Queensland government's purchase of trains that breach the *Disability Discrimination Act 1992* (Cth) by not providing access for people with disability (Roe, 2018). The issue of access is just as important and even more complicated in education, as access extends beyond the 'where' of physical access to encompass the 'what' and the 'how' of curriculum and pedagogy. Access across these domains remains a live issue in education, despite the CRPD expressly requiring States parties to ensure accessibility (Article 3(f); Article 9) and to provide "reasonable accommodation" for students with disability (Article 2, Definitions; Article 24.2(c)).

The right of persons with disability to education is outlined in Article 24 of the CRPD, which explicitly proclaims their right to *inclusive* education, prohibits their exclusion from the general education system on the basis of disability, and requires reasonable accommodation of individual requirements to be provided. While this recognition and protection of *inclusive* education is ground-breaking, in reality the concept of inclusive education has generally been poorly implemented; it is often misunderstood, sometimes deliberately misused and even actively resisted, including by "professional groups involved in special education, such as teachers, psychologists and testing centres" (Council of Europe Commissioner for Human Rights, 2017, pp. 10–11). This is despite its recognition as a fundamental obligation of each State party that has ratified the CRPD, and a correlative human right of people with disability (Cukalevski & Malaquias, 2019). It was in recognition of these and other issues—following a decade of jurisprudence by the United Nations Committee on the Rights of Persons with Disabilities (CRPD Committee) affirming the obligations of States parties to take necessary measures to ensure the realisation of this right and further identifying its contours—that the decision was made to develop and adopt a General Comment on Article 24 (Cisternas Reyes, 2019). A General Comment (sometimes called a General Recommendation) is a guidance instrument that explains the meaning and scope of a particular provision of a United Nations human-rights treaty and may include recommendations to States parties on how best to comply with their obligations under that provision (Byrnes, 2020).

The Right to Inclusive Education

The adoption of the CRPD in 2006 provided unambiguous support for inclusive education through Article 24: Right to Education, which states as its first principle in Article 24.1: "States parties recognize the right of persons with disabilities to education. With a view to realizing this right without discrimination and on the basis of equal opportunity, States parties shall ensure an *inclusive education* [emphasis added] system at all levels" (United Nations, 2006a).

Article 24.2 further requires States parties to ensure that:

(a) Persons with disabilities are not excluded from the general education system on the basis of disability and that children with disabilities are *not excluded* from free and compulsory primary education, or from secondary education, on the basis of disability,
(b) Persons with disabilities can access an *inclusive, quality and free* primary education and secondary education *on an equal basis with others in the communities in which they live*,
(c) *Reasonable accommodation* of the individual's requirements is provided,
(d) Persons with disabilities receive the support required, *within the general education system*, to facilitate their effective education,
(e) Effective individualised support measures are provided in environments that maximize academic and social development, *consistent with the goal of full inclusion* (United Nations, 2006a, emphasis added).

Although the CRPD was the first legally binding international human-rights instrument to contain a reference to the concept of inclusive education and to commit States parties to the progressive realisation of its achievement, it did not define inclusive education or identify the scope of the concept. This lack of interpretive guidance permitted perceived 'wiggle room' in Article 24 to be exploited (Graham et al., 2023) and undoubtedly hampered compliance with its requirements.

Following almost a decade's worth of country reports and Concluding Observations urging States parties to implement Article 24 of the CRPD, the CRPD Committee held a Day of General Discussion on Article 24 (15 April 2015, Palais des Nations, Geneva), commencing the process of developing a General Comment on Article 24. Just over a year later—following a comprehensive international consultation process with States parties, Disabled Person's Organisations, and civil society—General Comment No. 4 on Article 24: Right to Education was adopted by the CRPD Committee on 26 August

2016. At 24 pages, *General Comment No. 4* (GC4; United Nations, 2016) is the most comprehensive and authoritative international instrument explaining the human right to inclusive education and its substantive elements and identifying its core features. Importantly, GC4 reflects the applicable jurisprudence on the right to education for people with disability under the CRPD and is instructive of the principles that the CRPD Committee will apply in reviewing compliance by individual countries with their legal obligations under Article 24.

Article 24 and GC4 together make clear that quality inclusive education is the means by which students with disability realise their universal human right to education, with *inclusion* and *quality* being the two main pillars of this right (Cisternas Reyes, 2019). Further, the terms that GC4 defines, and the concepts and processes it outlines to implement inclusive education, should now be used as guidance to all engaged in education, including researchers, educators, parents, advocates, and policymakers. It is not for anyone to contest the right of students with disability to be educated with their same-age peers in inclusive classrooms and to be provided with reasonable adjustments. This is their fundamental human right, formally recognised and explained by the United Nations treaty body responsible for monitoring implementation of the CRPD and agreed to by all States parties ratifying the CRPD, including Australia. Australia was one of the first signatories to the CRPD and ratified it in July 2008 (Australian Law Reform Commission, n.d.). On 30 July 2009, Australia ratified the Optional Protocol to the CRPD (United Nations, 2006b) which provides the CRPD Committee with additional powers and functions in relation to inquiries and complaints from individuals or groups about violations of the CRPD. The CRPD Committee recently upheld, for the first time ever, a complaint against Australia under the Optional Protocol, in relation to the failure to provide audio descriptions on free-to-air television (United Nations, 2022). In 2018, the CRPD Committee also determined its first ever complaint in relation to education, holding that an executive action by Spain that required a student with disability to learn in a segregated 'education centre' was in violation of the student's human right to inclusive education. In doing so, the CRPD Committee affirmed the student's right to learn in a regular classroom with accommodations and supports consistent with Article 24 and GC4 (United Nations, 2018b).

Content of CRPD General Comment No. 4

One of the most significant aspects of GC4 is in the definitions that it provides. For a long time, scholars in inclusive education have resisted defining inclusion, with some referring to it somewhat ambiguously as a 'process' and not a 'place' (Booth, 1996). The origin for the focus on process is the failed attempt at 'mainstreaming'—otherwise known as integration—during the 1970s. In the years following deinstitutionalisation, the main objective was to transfer students with disability from institutions to segregated special schools and then to mainstream schools. Within a decade, however, it became clear that more radical change was needed lest the move result purely in a change of scenery, leaving physical, attitudinal, curricular, and pedagogical barriers in place. This is the history that precipitated the inclusive education movement's later emphasis on process, in addition to placement. The historical background is understood by academics within inclusive education but not by many other stakeholders, which has made it easy for special education to appropriate the language of inclusion to claim that the segregation of students with disability into special schools and classes is, in fact, 'inclusive'. Some go as far as to reject the notion of place entirely:

> This misconception that inclusion refers to a place and not a process is very pervasive. The current Australian view is restricted to the concept of an inclusive school as a place where everyone belongs, is accepted, and where special education needs students are supported and cared for by their peers and other members of the school community. This is a Utopian view, where there are no references to the processes and learning environments needed to achieve authentic educational outcomes for *all* students.
>
> (Forbes, 2007, p. 67)

Assisting this appropriation has been a confluence of factors, first of which has been the reluctance of some inclusive education scholars to define inclusion (Loreman et al., 2014). In the early 2000s, this lack of definition was accompanied by a deliberate broadening of the concept of inclusion to distance inclusive education from special education (Loreman et al., 2014). During the same period, inclusive education also became closely associated with the "Education for All" movement led by UNESCO, which is principally focused on access to education for children in developing countries (Miles & Singal, 2010). Although access, participation, and equality of opportunity for all children are undeniably relevant to the goal of inclusion, together these factors inadvertently led to an elasticity in the concept that Naraian (2013) argues has diluted inclusive education's original "insurrection-ary edge" (p. 361). The fact remains that the entire movement began with the desegregation of students with disability and has evolved due to the need to reconceptualise schooling so that it is accessible to all, beginning with those who experience the greatest barriers to equality of access: students with disability. Importantly, the original concept of inclusive education is also informed by other fundamental disability-rights concepts, including the social model of disability and inclusive language, which were forged through the lived experience and work of disability activists. At its core, therefore, inclusive education is and has always been about disability. This is a strength and not a weakness, for the empirical research evidence shows that the practices that benefit students with disability benefit *all* students (see Chapters 6 and 11).

The CRPD Committee appears to be cognisant of both this background and the confusion that exists in understanding and practice (Cisternas Reyes, 2019). In defining inclusive education through the application of human-rights principles, GC4 has broken a stalemate that until now has led some educators to believe that the enrolment of a student with disability and/or the provision of an individualised program regardless of setting is *inclusive*. In providing four key definitions (see Table 3.1), GC4 distinguishes these forms of provision as "segregation" and "integration", removing any doubt as to what is meant by the term "inclusion".

GC4 further clarifies these definitions, noting that the obligation of States parties to ensure progressive realisation of Article 24 "is not compatible with sustaining two systems of education: mainstream and special/segregated education systems" (para 39), thus making it clear that fulfilment of the goal of inclusive education entails the existence of a single education system with no parallelism (Cisternas Reyes, 2019). GC4 also recognises that "the right to non-discrimination includes the right not to be segregated and to be provided with reasonable accommodation" (para 13). This is affirmed in General Comment No. 6 on equality and non-discrimination, which states that the segregation on the basis of disability is a form of discrimination and segregated education settings are discriminatory (United Nations, 2018a).

Another important principle recognised in GC4 relates to inclusive education as a right of the child, as distinct from a choice of the parent. This is consistent with international human-rights jurisprudence in relation to children as rights-holders more broadly (Levesque, 1994). Further, the notion of 'parental choice' must also be seen in the context of education systems that have long avoided the systemic reform necessary to achieve genuine inclusion by providing what is commonly called 'a continuum of placement options'. Arguably, real choice must be free and informed. In a system where 'gatekeeping' practices are recognised as being widespread, and parents are compelled and even coerced into 'choosing' segregated placement (Jenkin et al., 2018; Poed et al., 2017), segregation is at best a false choice.[2] In recognition of these

Table 3.1 Key Definitions in General Comment No. 4

Exclusion	when students are directly or indirectly prevented from or denied access to education in any form.
Segregation	when the education of students with disabilities *is* provided in separate environments designed or used to respond to a particular or various impairments, in isolation from students without disabilities.
Integration	a process of placing persons with disabilities in *existing* mainstream educational institutions, as long as the former can adjust to the standardized requirements of such institutions.
Inclusion	involves a process of systemic reform embodying changes and modifications in content, teaching methods, approaches, structures, and strategies in education to *overcome* barriers with a vision serving to provide all students of the relevant age range with an equitable and participatory learning experience and environment that best corresponds to their requirements and preferences. Placing students with disability in regular classes without appropriate structural changes to, for example, organization, curriculum and teaching and learning strategies does *not* constitute inclusion.

Adapted from United Nations (2016, para 11).

2 See also the testimony of disability representative organisations during public hearings of the Royal Commission into Violence, Abuse, Neglect and Exploitation (2022).

issues, GC4 frames inclusive education as "the right of the individual learner, and not, in the case of children, the right of a parent or caregiver. Parental responsibilities in this regard are 'subordinate to the rights of the child" (para 10). It is worth noting that while there is some limited recognition in international law of parents' rights to choose alternative schools to ensure that their children's education corresponds to their own religious or moral convictions, there is no equivalent parental right in relation to schools that segregate students on the basis of disability, and such a right would violate applicable international human-rights law standards of equality and non-discrimination (Kayess, 2019). The issue was considered in detail in a comprehensive legal opinion, provided by an eminent human-rights law expert to the *Royal Commission into Violence, Abuse, Neglect and Exploitation* (Disability Royal Commission) in Australia, that concluded that there is no international right or obligation to support parental choice for segregation (Byrnes, 2020). The opinion specifically considered Article 13 of the *International Covenant on Economic, Social and Cultural Rights* (ICESCR; United Nations, 1966), stating:

> The liberty of parents in relation to the education of their children guaranteed by Article 13.3 of the ICESCR is not to be interpreted as guaranteeing them a right to choose special schools whether in the public system or in a private school, Article 13.3 on its terms may not extend to such a choice in any case. However, even if it did, the Article 13.3 guarantee must also be read in light of the non-discrimination guarantee in Article 2.2 of the ICESCR.

The legal opinion, which appears to have been sought by the Royal Commission to evaluate the legal basis for the Australian government's broader "contentions that the CRPD permits the indefinite or long-term maintenance of segregated special schools" (Byrnes, 2020, p. 4) in reliance on Article 13 of ICESCR and the notion of 'parent choice', further confirmed that the interpretation of Article 24 outlined in GC4 is the one "that would be reached by the proper application of the accepted rules of treaty interpretation" (Byrnes, 2020, p. 1) and that GC4 provides "a sound legally based working definition of the concept" of inclusive education (p. 24).

The Australian government's contentions in defence of segregated education are not only flawed as a matter of international law, as the legal opinion systematically explains, they effectively contradict Australia's own position during the drafting of the CRPD. At that time Australia had led the way in arguing in favour of a clear statement in the treaty that students with disability are to be educated "within the general education system and the communities in which they live" (United Nations, 2006a, p. 61) and did not support embedding exceptions and the notion of 'choice' in it. Australia then went on to ratify the CRPD in 2008 without lodging any interpretive declarations or reservations to limit its obligations under Article 24 (although it lodged declarations in respect of CRPD requirements relating to legal capacity, involuntary treatment, and migration) thereby accepting its full legal effect. This is in contrast with the United Kingdom, Mauritius, and Suriname, as the only States parties to seek to limit their obligations under Article 24 on ratification of the CRPD. In the case of the United Kingdom, it specifically sought to do this to preserve its dual-tracked system of "mainstream and special schools" (United Nations, 2023, IV.15). It seems clear that the status of segregation and the obligation of States parties under Article 24 to progressively phase out segregated settings was well understood by States parties, and notably by Australia, at the time of the negotiation and ratification of the CRPD.

It is worth noting that the Australian government's attempts to contest and limit its obligations under the CRPD appear to be a post-ratification development evident during the period of conservative Liberal/National coalition governments from 2013 to early 2022, which some commentators have perceived as one of decline in Australia's international human-rights standing, marred by volatile relationships between the government and national and international human-rights institutions and hostile rhetoric towards them (Barlow et al., 2015; Davidson, 2019), as well as attempts to weaken the Australian Human Rights Commission though funding cuts and political interference in the appointments of Commissioners (Maguire, 2022). While human rights are always vulnerable to politicisation, following the election of the Labor federal government in May 2022, Australia's new Attorney General signalled a commitment "to restore a human-rights based approach to public life in Australia" and has already sought to distance the current government's approach from its predecessor, describing it as a "shameful period . . . [during which] . . . 'human rights' was not a phrase that regularly passed the lips of coalition ministers" (Dreyfus, 2022, n.p.).

It remains to be seen whether the new Labor government will uphold this promise to embrace a human-rights approach or will instead continue the regressive stance of its predecessor to appease State governments and groups invested in the maintenance of the 'dual system' status quo and the segregation of students on the basis of disability. Either way, the long-term maintenance of segregated settings is not accepted by the CRPD Committee or other relevant United Nations independent bodies and experts engaged with human rights in education (Malaquias, 2022) or indeed the Australian disability community (Disabled Persons Organisations Australia, 2020), which has already shown its preparedness to use international legal mechanisms to compel Australia's compliance with the human-rights principles it formally endorsed in ratifying the CRPD.

Note that under international law, the delivery of education to students with disability in segregated 'special' settings, as a form of disability discrimination, is not equivalent to the delivery of education in schools established for the purpose of the transmission and promotion of religious, ethnic, cultural, or linguistic identity. The latter are directed to the preservation of cultural diversity and reflect specific rights of cultural minorities recognised under a range of international human-rights instruments such as the *Declaration on the Rights of Persons belonging to National or Ethnic, Religious and Linguistic Minorities* (United Nations, 1989) and, more recently, Article 14 of the *United Nations Declaration on the Rights of Indigenous Peoples* (UNDRIP; United Nations, 2007) which is discussed below. In the context of education, these rights effectively guarantee the liberty of religious, ethnic, cultural, or linguistic minorities to establish their own private schools subject to applicable standards and limitations. The distinction is also relevant in understanding the role of bilingual sign language Deaf education schools as schools for the promotion and transmission of sign language and Deaf culture, provided such schools meet appropriate standards (Graham et al., 2023), including ensuring access to the regular curriculum and delivering "teaching [to] children who are deaf and other children who wish to be taught through the national sign language" (International Disability Alliance, 2020, Annex p. 9). In this regard, the CRPD recognises that Deaf people have a unique "dual category status, being [seen as] both persons with disabilities and cultural-linguistic minorities" (Murray et al., 2018, p. 39; CRPD, Articles 24.3(b) and 30.4; GC4, para 35(b)(c)).

Although this issue was not explicitly addressed by GC4, it was considered in detail in the *International Disability Alliance's Global Report on Inclusive Education* (2020) which seeks to put forward the perspective of international peak representative organisations of people with disability in the context of the achievement of Sustainable Development Goal 4 on inclusive education. The report affirms that "inclusive education is incompatible with a system of segregated education" (International Disability Alliance, 2020, p. 5), while also recognising the role of inclusive bilingual sign language schools as part of an inclusive education system (Graham et al., 2023). However, this recognition does not exempt the requirement for other educational environments to be inclusive of Deaf and Deaf-blind students (GC4, para 58 and 71).

GC4 also calls on education systems to apply Universal Design for Learning (UDL), which involves developing flexible ways for students to learn (see Chapter 11). In addition, the General Comment clarifies that any support measures provided must be compliant with the goal of inclusion. Accordingly, they must be designed to strengthen opportunities for students with disability to participate alongside their peers, rather than marginalise them (para 33). Finally, as Table 3.2 shows, GC4 identifies nine core features of inclusive education necessary to ensure progressive realisation of inclusive education (para 12).

Through its jurisprudence reflected in GC4, the CRPD Committee has taken a strong stance on the importance of the right to inclusive education and provided specific recommendations to States parties bound by international law to implement their obligations under the CRPD. As the relevant United Nations treaty monitoring body, the CRPD Committee can use a range of mechanisms to ensure compliance with these obligations by education systems around Australia and internationally, including a formal periodic reporting process with specific recommendations to the relevant State party, in the form of 'concluding observations'. In addition, the CRPD's Optional Protocol provides a further mechanism through the CRPD Committee's jurisdiction to receive and examine individual complaints and petitions and undertake inquiries where there is evidence of grave individual and systematic violations of the CRPD. It is ultimately through such processes that international human-rights law principles are recognised, developed, and internalised by individual States parties into domestic legal and policy frameworks.

When the first edition of this book was published, these international law processes, together with the guidance provided by GC4 in 2016, were having a material effect, particularly in the Australian state of Queensland which was the first in Australia to incorporate the four key definitions (inclusion, integration, segregation, and exclusion) and nine core features of inclusive education in its 2018 Inclusive Education Policy Statement (Queensland Department of Education, 2018). The statement was developed in response to Recommendation 4.2 of the Disability Review (Deloitte Access

Table 3.2 Core Features of Inclusive Education Outlined in General Comment No. 4

1	Whole systems approach	All resources are invested toward advancing inclusive education, and toward introducing and embedding the necessary changes in institutional culture, policies, and practices.
2	Whole education environment	Committed leadership of educational institutions is essential to introduce and embed the culture, policies, and practices to achieve inclusive education at all levels.
3	Whole person approach	Recognition is given to the capacity of every person to learn, and high expectations are established for all learners . . . inclusive education offers flexible curricula, teaching and learning methods adapted to different strengths, requirements, and learning styles . . . it commits to ending segregation within educational settings by ensuring inclusive classroom teaching in accessible learning environments with appropriate supports. The education system must provide a personalised educational response, rather than expecting the student to fit the system.
4	Supported teachers	All teachers and other staff [in learning environments] receive education and training giving them the core values and competencies to accommodate inclusive learning environments.
5	Respect for and value of diversity	All students must feel valued, respected, included, and listened to. Effective measures to prevent abuse and bullying are in place.
6	Learning-friendly environment	A positive school community and accessible environment where everyone feels safe, supported, stimulated and able to express themselves.
7	Effective transitions	Learners with disabilities receive the support to ensure the effective transition from learning at school to vocational and tertiary education, and finally to work.
8	Recognition of partnerships	Involvement of parents/caregivers and the community must be viewed as assets with resources and strengths to contribute.
9	Monitoring	Inclusive education must be monitored and evaluated on a regular basis to ensure that segregation or integration is not happening either formally or informally.

Adapted from United Nations (2016, para 12).

Economics, 2017) by Disability and Inclusion branch staff in consultation with stakeholder groups, including Queensland Collective for Inclusive Education, All Means All—Australian Alliance for Inclusive Education, and leading academics in inclusive education. The resultant policy statement was the first in Australia to use the definitions from international human-rights law to guide state education reforms. It was released in March 2018, and later received international recognition through an award from The Zero Project, an initiative of the Essl Foundation aimed at recognising and supporting implementation of the CRPD.

However, and despite the significant efforts of committed system and school leaders and educators, implementation of genuine inclusive education in Queensland has been stymied by actions that contradict the words enshrined in policy. The most obvious example of this contradiction in action is an increase in the segregation of students with disability through the construction of new special schools and the expansion of existing special schools (Carrington et al., 2022). While the Queensland government did keep its options open by stating in its 2018 Inclusive Education Policy that "the department will continue to offer parents the choice of enrolling their child, who meets set criteria in highly individualised programs, including through special schools and academies" (np.), there was genuine intent at the time of policy development to engage in the progressive realisation of systemic inclusive education reform that is outlined in GC4. As demonstrated in Chapter 8, there is still genuine intent and real passion among system leaders and educators in Queensland, however, evidence from overseas indicates that genuine systemic inclusive education reform cannot easily be achieved while also maintaining parallel systems of education (Carrington et al., 2022; see also Chapter 7). Genuine inclusive education reform, whether it be in Queensland or anywhere else in the world, requires the ultimate decision-makers—state, and federal Ministers of Education—to both share and demonstrate the passion and commitment of our educators. That passion and commitment needs to be matched by respect for international human-rights law, something that settler-colonies like Australia have a poor track record in doing. For an example, we need look no further than our slow response to the UNDRIP.

United Nations Declaration on the Rights of Indigenous Peoples

The fundamental human right to education has been expressed in a number of international instruments, some of which apply the right in respect of specific groups or contexts. Article 14 of the UNDRIP expresses this right in the context of the education of indigenous people as a right to education without discrimination (Article 14.2) that also embeds recognition of their rights as national and linguistic minorities "to establish and control their educational systems and institutions providing education in their own languages, in a manner appropriate to their cultural methods of teaching and learning" (Article 14.1). This wording also appears to reflect the Hague Recommendations regarding the Education Rights of National Minorities and Explanatory Note, published by the High Commissioner on National Minorities for the Organisation for Security and Co-operation in Europe (1996), that recognises the right of national minorities to "establish and manage their own private educational institutions in conformity with domestic law" including "schools teaching in the minority language" (see Recommendation 8).

For indigenous students with disability, their right to education manifests the intersection of their identity and attributes as people who are both indigenous and people with disability, and therefore includes the right not to be segregated on the basis of disability and to receive supports and accommodations in accordance with Article 24 of the CRPD, as well as the right to attend schools that provide for the transmission of their languages and culture alongside non-disabled indigenous peers as stated in Article 14 of UNDRIP. In Australia, which endorsed the UNDRIP in 2009, this means that schools and other education settings established on the basis of Indigenous culture and language are *also* required under Article 24 of the CRPD to be inclusive of students with disability, *and* that Indigenous students have the same right not to be segregated on the basis of disability (First Peoples Disability Network, 2022; see also Disabled Persons Organisations Australia, 2020).

Australian governments have not taken formal steps to implement the UNDRIP domestically beyond the *Closing the Gap* strategy and the *2019 National Partnership Agreement on Closing the Gap* (Australian Government, n.d.-a). Further, unlike ratified international treaties such as the CRPD, the UNDRIP does not have the status of a legally binding international treaty and the Australian Parliament is not required to consider compatibility with the UNDRIP when new legislation is introduced. Australia's support for the UNDRIP began tentatively when it voted with three other United Nations member States (Canada, New Zealand, and the United States) against the adoption of the declaration by the United Nations General Assembly, while 143 member States voted in favour of it and eleven abstained. This was only one of several controversies related to Aboriginal and Torres Strait Islander affairs during the decade-long conservative government led by Prime Minister John Howard (Robbins, 2007) that ended with the election of the Labor government under Kevin Rudd in November 2007 and led to a change of position on the issue, at least in principle.

The federal election in 2022 brought a commitment by the newly elected Labor government to hold a referendum for the introduction of an Indigenous "Voice to Parliament" representative body to advise on policy matters with the potential to affect Indigenous Australians (Australian Government, n.d.-b). If the referendum is successful, this initiative has the potential to drive more substantial progress in the achievement of equality and better outcomes for Indigenous Australians (Davis & Williams, 2022). It will be important to ensure that the voices of Indigenous people with disability are also heard in any process adopted to shape future government policies that may affect Aboriginal and Torres Strait Islander people, including in education. It is also critical to ensure that intersectionalities are recognised in policy so that Indigenous students with disability receive accessible quality first teaching and relevant reasonable adjustments.

Conclusion

As a society, it is crucial to find ways to address the historical and social wrongs committed against people with disability. Returning to the inclusionary premise and right that all people with disability are equally entitled to participate in all aspects of society consistently with the core human-rights principle of equality first articulated in the UDHR (Article 1) and subsequently embedded through the CRPD, inclusive education is the gateway to accessing full social participation and equality in all areas of life. The CRPD is a legally binding instrument that has been ratified by the Australian government, committing all Australian education sectors to the realisation of the right to inclusive education. This cannot be achieved by 'tinkering' with existing systems—built on an educational binary between abled students and students with disability—which perpetuate and promote the segregation of the latter. It calls for the *transformation* of education so that educational provision for all students, including those with disability, is delivered through a universally accessible, quality, and *inclusive* education systems. The challenge for parents, educators and academics is how best to support this transformation to deliver on the educational rights of every child, now and into the future.

References

Australian Government. (n.d.-a). *Closing the gap: A new way of working together.* https://www.closingthegap.gov.au/

Australian Government. (n.d.-b). *Aboriginal and Torres Strait Islander voice.* https://voice.niaa.gov.au/

Australian Law Reform Commission. (n.d.). *Equality, capacity and disability in commonwealth laws.* https://www.alrc.gov.au/publication/equality-capacity-and-disability-in-commonwealth-laws-alrc-report-124/

Barlow, K., Abbott, T., Mendez, J., & Webb, D. (2015). The Prime Minister has dismissed another major report criticizing Australia's asylum seeker policies saying Australians are sick of being lectured to. *World News Australia.* https://search.informit.org/doi/10.3316/tvnews.tsm201503090045

Barta, T. (2001). Discourses of genocide in Germany and Australia: A linked history. *Aboriginal History, 25*(25), 37–56.

Benedict, S., Shields, L., & O'Donnell, A. J. (2009). Children's "euthanasia" in Nazi Germany. *Journal of Pediatric Nursing, 24*(6), 506–516. https://doi.org/10.1016/j.pedn.2008.07.012

Blatt, B. (1966). *Christmas in purgatory: A photographic essay on mental retardation.* https://www.canonsociaalwerk.eu/1966_Kerstmis/Xmas-Purgatory.pdf

Booth, T. (1996). A perspective on inclusion from England. *Cambridge Journal of Education, 26*(1), 87–99. https://doi.org/10.1080/0305764960260107

Byrnes, A. (2020). *Analysis of Article 24 of the Convention on the Rights of Persons with Disabilities and its relation to other international instruments.* Disability Royal Commission. https://disability.royalcommission.gov.au/system/files/2022-06/Public%20hearing%2024%20-F%20Andrew%20Byrnes%20%282020%29%20Analysis%20of%20Article%2024%20of%20the%20CRPD%20and%20note%20on%20the%20travaux%20pr%C3%A9paratoires_1.pdf

Carrington, S., Lassig, C., Maia-Pike, L., Mann, G., Mavropoulou, S., & Saggers, B. (2022). Societal, systemic, school and family drivers for and barriers to inclusive education. *Australian Journal of Education*, 66(3), 251–264. https://doi.org/10.1177/0004944122112528

Cisternas Reyes, M. S. (2019). Inclusive education: Perspectives from the UN Committee on the Rights of Persons with Disabilities. Part III—Implementation: B—Mechanisms', In G. de Beco, S. Quinlivan, & J. E. Lord (Eds.), *The right to inclusive education in international human rights law* (pp. 401–402). Cambridge University Press.

Council of Europe Commissioner for Human Rights. (2017). *Fighting school segregation in Europe through inclusive education: A position paper.* https://rm.coe.int/fighting-school-segregationin-europe-throughinclusive-education-a-posi/168073fb65

Cukalevski, E., & Malaquias, C. (2019). A CRPD analysis of NSW's policy on the education of students with disabilities–a retrogressive measure that must be halted. *Australian Journal of Human Rights*, 25(2), 232–247. https://doi.org/10.1080/1323238X.2019.1609720

Davidson, H. (2019, October 8). UN human rights commissioner rejects 'attack on "internationalist bureaucracy"'. *The Guardian Australian Edition.* https://www.theguardian.com/australia-news/2019/oct/08/un-human-rights-commissioner-rejects-morrisons-attack-on-internationalist-bureaucracy

Davis, M., & Williams, G. (2022). *Everything you need to know about the Uluru Statement from the heart.* NewSouth Publishing.

de Bruin, K. (2022). Learning in the shadow of eugenics: Why segregated schooling persists in Australia. *Australian Journal of Education*, 66(3), 218–234. https://doi.org/10.1177/00049441221127765

Deloitte Access Economics. (2017). *Review of education for students with disability in Queensland state schools.* Deloitte Access Economics. https://education.qld.gov.au/student/Documents/disability-review-report.pdf

Disability Discrimination Act 1992 (Cth).

Disabled Persons Organisations Australia. (2020). *Segregation of people with disability is discrimination and must end: Position statement.* https://dpoa.org.au/wp-content/uploads/2020/11/Segregation-of-People-with-Disability_Position-Paper.pdf

Dreyfus, M. (2022). *Restoring a human rights-based approach: Castan Centre Speech of the Hon Mark Dreyfus QC MP Attorney-General 22 July 2022.* https://www.markdreyfus.com/media/speeches/restoring-a-human-rights-based-approach-castan-centre-speech-mark-dreyfus-qc-mp/

Duranti, M. (2012). The Holocaust, the legacy of 1789 and the birth of international human rights law: Revisiting the foundation myth. *Journal of Genocide Research*, 14(2), 159–186. https://doi.org/10.1080/14623528.2012.677760

Evans, S. E. (2004). *Forgotten crimes: The Holocaust and people with disabilities.* Ivan R. Dee.

First Peoples Disability Network. (2022). *Response to the Disability Royal Commission Chair's published opening statement on Inclusive Education from Public Hearing 24.* https://fpdn.org.au/response-to-the-disability-royal-commission-chairs-published-opening-statement-on-inclusive-education-from-public-hearing-24/

Forbes, F. (2007). Towards inclusion: An Australian perspective. *Support for Learning*, 22(2), 66–71. https://doi.org/10.1111/j.1467-9604.2007.00449.x

Foth, T. (2014). Changing perspectives: From "euthanasia killings" to the "killing of sick persons". In S. Benedict, & L. Shields (Eds.), *Nurses and midwives in Nazi Germany: The 'euthanasia programs'* (pp. 218–242). Routledge.

Gallagher, H. G. (2008). Holocaust: The genocide of disabled peoples. In S. Totten, & W. S. Parsons (Eds.), *Century of genocide: Critical essays and eyewitness accounts* (pp. 170–192). Routledge.

Galliott, N., & Graham, L. J. (2014). A question of agency: Applying Sen's theory of human capability to the concept of secondary school student career "choice." *International Journal of Research & Method in Education, 37*(3), 270–284. https://doi.org/10.1080/1743727X.2014.885010

Graham, L. J., Medhurst, M., Malaquias, C., Tancredi, H., De Bruin, C., Gillett-Swan, J., . . . & Cologon, K. (2023). Beyond Salamanca: A citation analysis of the CRPD/GC4 relative to the Salamanca Statement in inclusive and special education research. *International Journal of Inclusive Education, 27*(2), 123–145. https://doi.org/10.1080/13603116.2020.1831627

Hodal, K. (2017, October 11). Revealed: The 10 worst countries for girls to get an education. *The Guardian.* https://www.theguardian.com/global-development/2017/oct/11/revealed-the-10-worst-countries-for-girls-to-get-an-education-international-day-girl

Hudson, L. (2011). From small beginnings: The euthanasia of children with disabilities in Nazi Germany: Nazi euthanasia of children. *Journal of Paediatrics and Child Health, 47*(8), 508–511. https://doi.org/10.1111/j.1440-1754.2010.01977.x

International Disability Alliance. (2020). *What an inclusive, equitable, quality education means to us: Report of the international disability alliance.* https://www.internationaldisabilityalliance.org/sites/default/files/ida_ie_flagship_report_english_29.06.2020.pdf

Jenkin, E., Spivakovsky, C., Joseph, S., & Smith, M. (2018). *Improving educational outcomes for children with disability in Victoria: Final report.* Monash University, Castan Centre for Human Rights Law. https://www.monash.edu/__data/assets/file/0016/1412170/Castan-Centre-Improving-Educational-Outcomes-for-Students-with-Disability.pdf

Kayess, R. (2019). Drafting Article 24 of the Convention on the Rights of Persons with Disabilities. In G. de Beco, S. Quinlivan, & J. E. Lord (Eds.), *The right to inclusive education in international human rights law* (pp. 122–140). Cambridge University Press.

Lee, Y. (2010). Communications procedure under the Convention on the Rights of the Child: 3rd Optional Protocol. *The International Journal of Children's Rights, 18*(4), 567–583. https://doi.org/10.1163/157181810X527239

Levesque, R. J. R. (1994). International children's rights grow up: Implications for American jurisprudence and domestic policy. *California Western International Law Journal, 24*(2), 193–240.

Loreman, T., Forlin, C., Chambers, D., Sharma, U., & Deppeler, J. (2014). Conceptualising and measuring inclusive education. In C. Forlin, & T. Loreman (Eds.), *Measuring inclusive education* (pp. 3–17). Emerald Publishing.

Maguire, A. (2022, March 30). Budget cuts to the Australian Human Rights Commission couldn't have come at a worse time. *The Conversation.* https://theconversation.com/budget-cuts-to-the-australian-human-rights-commission-couldnt-have-come-at-a-worse-time-180308

Mazower, M. (2004). The strange triumph of human rights, 1933–1950. *The Historical Journal, 47*(2), 379–398. https://doi.org/10.1017/S0018246X04003723

McGregor, R. (2002). "Breed out the colour" or the importance of being white. *Australian Historical Studies, 33*(120), 286–302. https://doi.org/10.1080/10314610208596220

Miles, S., & Singal, N. (2010). The Education for All and inclusive education debate: Conflict, contradiction or opportunity? *International Journal of Inclusive Education, 14*(1), 1–15. https://doi.org/10.1080/13603110802265125

Morsink, J. (1999). *The Universal Declaration of Human Rights: Origins, drafting & intent.* University of Pennsylvania Press.

Mostert, M. P. (2002). Useless eaters: Disability as genocidal marker in Nazi Germany. *The Journal of Special Education, 36*(3), 157–170. https://doi.org/10.1177/00224669020360030601

Murray, J. J., De Meulder, M., & le Maire, D. (2018). An education in sign language as a human right? The sensory exception in the legislative history and ongoing interpretation of Article 24 of the UN Convention on the Rights of Persons with Disabilities. *Human Rights Quarterly, 40*(1), 37–60. https://doi.org/10.1353/hrq.2018.0001

Naraian, S. (2013). Dis/ability, agency, and context: A differential consciousness for doing inclusive education. *Curriculum Inquiry, 43*(3), 360–387. https://doi.org/10.1111/curi.12014

Organisation for Security and Co-operation in Europe. (1996). *The Hague Recommendations regarding the education rights of national minorities.* https://www.osce.org/hcnm/hague-recommendations

Poed, S., Cologon, K., & Jackson, R. (2017). *Gatekeeping and restrictive practices with students with disability: Results of an Australian Survey.* Paper presented to the 2017 Inclusive Education Summit, University of South Australia. https://allmeansall.org.au/wp-content/uploads/2017/10/TIES-4.0-20172.pdf

Queensland Department of Education. (2018). *Inclusive education policy.* https://ppr.qed.qld.gov.au/pp/inclusive-education-policy

Robbins, J. (2007). The Howard Government and Indigenous rights: An imposed national unity? *Australian Journal of Political Science, 42*(2), 315–328. https://doi.org/10.1080/10361140701320042

Roe, I. (2018). Human Rights Commission denies new QLD trains exemption for disability access faults. *ABC News.* https://www.abc.net.au/news/2018-03-02/qld-rail-train-not-granted-exemption-disability/9502556

Royal Commission into Violence, Abuse, Neglect and Exploitation. (2022). *Transcript of Day 3 of Public Hearing 24–witness appearance of Mary Sayers for children and young people with disability in Australia.* https://disability.royalcommission.gov.au/system/files/2022-06/Transcript%20Day%203%20-%20Public%20hearing%2024%2C%20Canberra.docx

Srivastava, M., de Boer, A., & Pijl, S. J. (2015). Inclusive education in developing countries: A closer look at its implementation in the last 10 years. *Educational Review, 67*(2), 179–195. https://doi.org/10.1080/00131911.2013.847061

Tomlinson, S. (1982). A sociology of special education. Routledge.

United Nations. (n.d.-a). *Convention on the Rights of the Child: Ratification by country.* https://treaties.un.org/Pages/ViewDetails.aspx?src=TREATY&mtdsg_no=IV-11&chapter=4&clang=_en

United Nations. (n.d.-b). *United Nations decade of disabled persons 1983–1992.* https://www.un.org/development/desa/disabilities/united-nations-decade-of-disabled-persons-1983-1992.html

United Nations. (1948). *Universal Declaration of Human Rights.* https://www.un.org/en/about-us/universal-declaration-of-human-rights

United Nations. (1959). *Geneva Declaration of the Rights of the Child.* http://www.un-documents.net/gdrc1924.htm

United Nations. (1989). Convention on the Rights of the Child. https://www.ohchr.org/sites/default/files/crc.pdf

United Nations. (2006a). *Convention on the Rights of Persons with Disabilities (CRPD).* https://www.un.org/disabilities/documents/convention/convoptprot-e.pdf.

United Nations. (2006b). *Optional Protocol to the Convention on the Rights of Persons with Disabilities* (A/RES/61/106). https://www.un.org/development/desa/disabilities/convention-on-the-rights-of-persons-with-disabilities/optional-protocol-to-the-convention-on-the-rights-of-persons-with-disabilities.html

United Nations (2007). *Declaration on the Rights of Indigenous Peoples* (A/RES/61/295). https://www.un.org/development/desa/indigenouspeoples/wp-content/uploads/sites/19/2018/11/UNDRIP_E_web.pdf

United Nations. (2016). *General Comment No. 4, Article 24: Right to Inclusive Education.* (CRPD/C/GC/4). https://digitallibrary.un.org/record/1313836?ln=en

United Nations. (2018a). *General Comment No. 6 on Equality and Non-discrimination* (CRPD/C/GC/6). https://documents-dds-ny.un.org/doc/UNDOC/GEN/G18/119/05/PDF/G1811905.pdf?OpenElement

United Nations. (2018b). *Spain must ensure inclusive education for persons with disabilities, UN human rights experts say.* https://www.ohchr.org/en/press-releases/2018/05/spain-must-ensure-inclusive-education-persons-disabilities-un-human-rights

United Nations. (2022). *Views adopted by the Committee under article 5 of the Optional Protocol, concerning communication No 56/2018* (CRPD/C/27/D/56/2018). https://docstore.ohchr.org/SelfServices/FilesHandler.ashx?enc=6QkG1d%2FPPRiCAqhKb7yhsgVpk09EpSkE0Cpmp9l0dXtZYHcnimy07Fm41%2BZGw9vWp0%2F5AyizH%2FA4O5fWOdfhmaOdV2chKT%2BnJPZElK3PQ46ckD8tzn%2B5oCGyrDGVsUc929Lb24dCoA9FMOrI1fkG9g%3D%3D

United Nations. (2023). *Convention on the Rights of Persons with Disabilities (CRPD).* https://www.un.org/development/desa/disabilities/convention-on-the-rights-of-persons-with-disabilities.html

United Nations Educational, Scientific and Cultural Organisation. (1990). *World Conference on Education for All.* https://unesdoc.unesco.org/ark:/48223/pf0000085625

United Nations Educational, Scientific and Cultural Organisation. (1994). *The Salamanca Statement and Framework for Action on Special Needs Education.* https://unesdoc.unesco.org/ark:/48223/pf0000098427

Waltz, S. (2002). Reclaiming and rebuilding the history of the Universal Declaration of Human Rights. *Third World Quarterly, 23*(3), 437–448. https://doi.org/10.1080/01436590220138378

World Health Organisation. (2022). *Global report on health equity for persons with disabilities.* https://www.who.int/publications/i/item/9789240063600

Young, S. (2013, April 26). The politics of exclusion. *Ramp Up.* https://www.abc.net.au/rampup/articles/2013/04/26/3745990.htm

Chapter 4

Fundamental concepts of inclusive education

Linda J. Graham, Marijne Medhurst, Haley Tancredi, Ilektra Spandagou, & Elizabeth Walton

The first chapter of this book defined inclusive education with reference to *General Comment No. 4* (GC4; United Nations, 2016), a document that articulates the human right to inclusive education provided through Article 24 of the *Convention on the Rights of Persons with Disabilities* (CRPD; United Nations, 2006). Since the early 1990s, and before being defined in GC4, the meaning of inclusion was enacted through an assumed shared understanding of the philosophies, principles and concepts underpinning inclusive education. However, this assumption left meaning vulnerable to misinterpretation and misappropriation, resulting in an untenable situation that GC4 was designed to address. As noted in Chapter 2, there is still some danger that the GC4 definition will be similarly misunderstood because some of the words and phrases it uses carry implicit meaning and are informed by concepts far more significant than is implied by the words themselves. The second chapter of this book therefore unpacks the GC4 definition and briefly explains those words and phrases that are imbued with implicit meaning.

Among those is the phrase "overcome barriers" (United Nations, 2016, para 11). This phrase references the social model of disability; however, knowledge of the social model is necessary to comprehend the subtext of the phrase being used. Knowledge of the social model is also necessary to correctly identify and address those barriers. If the social model is not well understood, then the process of identifying and dismantling barriers—a practice that is at the foundation of inclusive education—becomes corrupted and ultimately fails. Understanding the fundamental concepts underpinning inclusive practice is therefore critical for anyone involved with education, whether they be principals, teachers, or other support staff in early-childhood education through to tertiary education, for the human right to an inclusive education applies to *all* students.

What Must Educators Know and Be Able to Do for Effective Inclusive Education?

For inclusive education to succeed, educators need a deep understanding of both curriculum content *and* learner diversity. This knowledge enables them to anticipate and eliminate (e.g., 'overcome') barriers in:

- what they teach (curriculum),
- the ways they teach it (pedagogy), and
- how learning is to be demonstrated (assessment).

DOI: 10.4324/9781003350897-5

Educators cannot achieve this if they believe that the barriers reside within the student and that *the student* must overcome those barriers. And educators will not do it if they believe that equity means that everyone should be taught the same way, get the same resources, or do the same assessment. And, even if barriers are addressed, students are still not genuinely included if they are stigmatised by educators' use of deficit language or if students are singled out for 'special' treatment. This is where the fundamental concepts of inclusive education come in and why they are so important. Deep understanding of these concepts provides teachers with the knowledge they need to enact inclusive practices with sensitivity, authenticity, and fidelity. The five most important concepts underpinning inclusive education are:

1. ableism,
2. the social model of disability,
3. the concept of equity,
4. the dilemma of difference, and
5. inclusive language.

This chapter explains each of the five, beginning with ableism.

Ableism

Ableism is a term used to describe a way of thinking produced through able-bodied experience. If left unexamined and unchallenged, able-bodied experience leads to narrow or ableist perceptions that can result in unlawful indirect discrimination (see Chapter 5). In other words, ableism has real-world effects; yet it is subtle, which means that its existence often goes unnoticed until too late. For example, architects who design public buildings without ramps or with doorways that are too narrow to enable wheelchair access are inadvertently engaging in ableist thinking. The recent experiences of Australian Greens Senator Jordon Steele-John provide a real-life example of the effects of ableism.

In 2017, Jordon Steele-John made history by becoming Australia's youngest ever senator (Worthington, 2018). He was also the parliament's first wheelchair user. The barriers to access and participation he experienced during his first years in Parliament House in Canberra are striking examples of the effects of ableism. Although described in the media as "having the loneliest seat in the Senate" (Worthington, 2018), because the floor of the Senate was only accessible by stairs, this was not the only barrier facing the new senator. Until the routes between his office and the Senate chamber were widened, Senator Steele-John was injured daily when his knuckles would scrape against the doorframes. This was not the only accessibility barrier. Although his office was on the ground floor, it was the furthest from the Senate chamber and the closest toilets were not wheelchair accessible.

Parliament House opened just over 30 years ago in 1988, and its architect clearly thought that no one with a mobility impairment would work there. This mindset is described by the term 'ableism'. Ableism has far-reaching impacts that go well beyond the design of public buildings and spaces, for it impacts beliefs about people with disability and limits what others think is possible for them to achieve. Senator Jordon Steele-John's daily encounter with structural barriers arising from the ableist thinking underpinning 20th-century architecture highlights the importance of different models of disability, as these models conceive of barriers in better and worse ways. One of these models underpins inclusive education, as it provides the necessary conceptual understanding for educators to enact inclusive practices. Knowing the difference between it and other models is essential for educators to avoid ableism.

Models of Disability

Over time, four models of disability have been discussed in the research literature, and these have formed the basis of political activism, legislation, and policy at different points in history. These four models of disability are: the medical model, the social model, the biopsychosocial model, and the human-rights model. In the following subsections, we discuss the affordances and limitations of each of these four models, as well as their implications for inclusive practice. We then explain why the social model of disability is fundamental to inclusive education, despite its limitations.

The Medical Model

The medical model of disability arose from the biomedical sciences and views impairments as the source of disability. These impairments are perceived as 'deviations' from the 'norm' that require remediation through intervention or medical treatment (Berghs et al., 2016). This view affects the perceived 'locus of change' (Burbules et al., 1982) or site of intervention. The medical model privileges medical intervention and focuses on adapting the person to suit an environment modelled on able-bodied experience, while the environment itself is viewed as natural. People with disability also refer to this as the 'individual deficit model' (Oliver, 2013), and they have criticised it for ignoring the richness of human diversity and for pathologising difference. The medical model perpetuates ableism, because it neglects the social structures and environmental factors that can result in barriers to access and participation for people with disability (Oliver, 2013; Terzi, 2005).

Criticising the medical model is not the same as criticising medicine or medical intervention. For example, assistive technologies such as hearing aids, glasses, targeted language interventions, and of course wheelchairs are all important contributions that can make the lives of people with impairments easier. The problem with the medical model—as a way of conceptualising disability—is that it directs focus purely on the limitations of the individual and ignores the environment in which that individual is forced to live. Let us return to our earlier example detailing Senator Jordon Steele-John's recent experiences in Parliament House. If viewed through the lens of the medical model, a mobility impairment may be the only 'problem' perceived. A solution to this problem might be fashioning some form of brace to enable the senator to walk from place to place, or taking the senator out of parliament for a daily physical-therapy session in the hope that this might improve his mobility and prevent the doorways from having to be widened. Such a solution would be an example of the medical model in practice, because ableist thinking only highlights one aspect of the problem: the individual, and what they can and cannot do within an environment that was never designed with them in mind.

Just as Parliament House was designed by able-bodied architects who never envisaged the need for wheelchair accessibility, school learning environments are largely run by able-bodied educators who generally liked school and did well at it. If the medical (individual deficit) model predominates in learning environments, educators are only encouraged to think about how a student's impairment is limiting their access, participation, and learning, not how the education system's own design and methods of delivery might be disabling the student. We see this thinking in pedagogical practices that align with the medical model of disability, such as when 'special' or remedial education is provided in segregated settings. This perpetuates the assumption that 'the problem' is the child and not the quality or accessibility of curriculum, pedagogy, assessment, or school/classroom environments. The mode of thinking perpetuated by the medical model is outdated and inconsistent with inclusive education, which instead endorses the social model of disability, even though the social model also has limitations.

The Social Model

The social model of disability arose from critique of the medical model and through the activism and scholarship of disabled scholars like Professor Michael (Mike) Oliver (1945–2019). The social model distinguishes disability from impairment, in that impairment is perceived as the individual characteristic (e.g., hearing impairment), whereas disability is the disadvantage or restriction of activity caused by societal barriers to the participation of people with such impairments (Oliver, 2013). In a classroom setting, such barriers include poor classroom acoustics, poor quality audio recordings, and lack of captions, teachers who do not project their voices, who turn away when they talk, and/or who talk too fast, and noisy group learning activities. The social model frames disability as 'socially constructed' because it arises from the interaction between a person with impairment(s) and the barriers that prevent them from going about their lives. In educational terms, barriers might arise from teachers' attitudes to and knowledge about teaching students with disability, which may influence the ways in which lessons are designed and taught. It may also arise from ableist thinking which can be detected in comments like "Grade 10 students should be able to . . ." and "that's just how I teach" (see Chapter 11). Other barriers extend from the ways that schooling is organised and timetabled through to the location and design of classrooms.

According to the social model, it is the barriers that are responsible for disablement, not the impairment itself. Taking our earlier example of Parliament House, Senator Jordon Steele-John has an impairment that affects his mobility, for which he uses a wheelchair. He is not 'disabled' until he meets a set of stairs or a narrow doorway. An intangible (but no less real) barrier is created by latent assumptions about the (im) possibility of participation in political life by people with disability. These assumptions result in a tangible barrier: the design of a public building that is inaccessible to wheelchair users and which 'disables' people with a mobility impairment. The value of the social model is that it focuses attention on identifying and eliminating the barriers to access and participation, as opposed to focusing only on individual remediation. In the United Kingdom, where the social model of disability first gained political traction, the term 'disabled person' is used to illustrate that disablement is something *done to* a person, not something that is within them. Note that this language is not used in Australia, where person-first language is more common (e.g., people with disability). We explain more about inclusive language later in this chapter.

The social model has had far-reaching impact for people with disability. As noted earlier with reference to the phrase 'overcome barriers' in GC4 (United Nations, 2016, para 11), the social model constitutes the philosophical basis of the CRPD, the first legally binding instrument articulating the human right to inclusive education (see Chapter 3). Well before the CRPD, however, enactment of the social model benefited everyone, not just those with disability. For example, in 1945 in Kalamazoo, Michigan, in the United States, the first 'kerb cuts' in street kerbs were installed. The existing city streets were inaccessible to hundreds of World War II veterans who used mobility aids, such as wheelchairs or crutches, so the City Commission modified the existing street kerbs to enable these veterans to safely access the city's shops and services (Brown, 1999). The success of the newly installed kerb cuts was immediate. Access to the city for people with disability improved access for *all* members of the community, including the elderly, small children, and mothers pushing prams. The existence of kerb cuts (also known as kerb ramps) is something that is easily taken for granted in modern society but represents an early example of the social model's impact through universal design. This ground-breaking initiative has since been followed by the universal application of assistive technologies (e.g., visual, auditory, and sensory walk/stop alerts) at traffic lights, footpaths and public doorways, and closed captioning on YouTube videos and television. Consider how often you rely on the little green symbol and/or the buzzer at the traffic lights, or when you might 'read' the news on a television while waiting at a doctor's surgery or in an airport terminal. Think of how much easier it is to open doors that have levers, rather than knobs that must be twisted, when you are carrying groceries or a small child. These are just some of the contributions that the social model of disability has made to all our lives.

Despite the positive impact of the social model, it has not been without criticism. For example, disability-studies scholar Professor Tom Shakespeare has pointed to several limitations. Shakespeare's (2006) main criticism is that the social model denies the reality of impairment. He argues that people with disability often live with limited functioning, fatigue, and discomfort and sometimes pain. Shakespeare and other critics maintain that the social model risks denying the impact of impairment, with the possible outcome that people with disability are not provided with the support or adjustments that they need or want. Some authors have also argued that disabilities impacting cognition and language are not well described within the social model, which is said to 'privilege' physical impairment (Shakespeare, 2006; Terzi, 2005).

The Biopsychosocial Model

The biopsychosocial model of disability attempts to integrate the medical and social models of disability. First discussed in the literature by Dr George L. Engel (1977), the biopsychosocial model considers biological factors (such as genetic predisposition), psychological factors (such as personality, and social factors (such as cultural and familial background). Engel's early description of the biopsychosocial model was not clearly defined (Shakespeare et al., 2017). However, the concept of disability as the result of interaction between health conditions (such as disorders, disease, or injury) and environmental and personal factors has since been extended and internationally accepted through the World Health Organisation's framework for health and disability: the *International Classification of Functioning, Disability and Health* (ICF; World Health Organisation, 2001). The primary function of the ICF is to standardise terminology, data collection, and assessment, particularly for eligibility for disability and health-support funding. For example, the National Disability Insurance Scheme (NDIS) in Australia is informed by the ICF. The biopsychosocial model is used more frequently in the fields of psychology, allied health, and modern medicine, and has not been broadly adopted in education. It is important to note that the language used within the biopsychosocial model is heavily influenced by the medical model. The biopsychosocial model has been promoted in education (Cooper, 2008); however, the model has not matured enough to be useful in inclusive education, mainly because it focuses too much on individual impairment and not enough on the barriers that can be adjusted.

The Human-Rights Model

The human-rights model of disability is a relatively new development described as a tool for implementing the CRPD (Degener, 2017). Central to the human-rights model are human dignity and the centrality of the person with disability in decision-making. As Quinn et al. (2002) write:

> Human dignity is the anchor norm of human rights. Each individual is deemed to be of inestimable value and nobody is insignificant. People are to be valued not just because they are economically or otherwise useful but because of their inherent self-worth . . . The human rights model focuses on the inherent dignity of the human being and subsequently, but only if necessary, on the person's medical characteristics. It places the individual centre stage in all decisions affecting him/her and, most importantly, locates the main 'problem' outside the person and in society (p. 14).

The human-rights model opposes the belief that impairment can hinder human-rights capacity. Within this model, impairment is valued as part of human diversity and disability-identity politics is explicitly acknowledged. For example, within the human-rights model, the unique contribution of Deaf culture is acknowledged and celebrated as part of the richness of human diversity. Of most significance is the centrality of social justice inherent in the human-rights model (Degener, 2017). The human-rights model is an important conceptual framework that can help educators and education systems to realise the human right to an inclusive education (United Nations, 2016); however, it requires further development to be of practical value in education.

Which Model Is Most Useful in Educational Terms?

The four models each have their merits and limitations. Viewing disability through the medical model risks stigmatisation and segregation, which are inconsistent with inclusive education. However, an extreme adoption of the social model may make it difficult to evaluate the impact of impairment and disability on individuals (Terzi, 2005). While the biopsychosocial model attempts to harvest the merits of both the medical and social models, its main function is to classify health and disability, which does not contribute to the everyday work of teachers. Similarly, the human-rights model has an important function in the implementation of the CRPD, but it does not offer practical applications to teachers for the design of inclusive teaching and assessment practices.

The social model of disability offers a conceptual lens with practical applications for the development of inclusive schools. Educators can use the social model to consider the barriers:

- faced by students due to the environment (e.g., noisy, cluttered, and visually busy classrooms, narrow corridors, and doorways; stairs),
- restricting students' access to the curriculum (e.g., when assistive technologies are not used or when students cannot navigate e-books),
- existing within teachers' pedagogical practices (e.g., when teachers talk too fast, use complex sentences, and deliver multipart instructions), and
- limiting a student's ability to demonstrate learning through assessment (e.g., when students are required to demonstrate learning through restrictive modalities, such as oral presentations).

These are all barriers that can be examined and adjusted by educators and school leaders if they understand and apply the social model to reflect on practice. To achieve this, educators must move from thinking about how a student's impairment limits their access and participation (the medical model perspective) to instead consider the barriers that surround the student (the social model perspective). Once identified, these barriers can be removed. Ideally, this occurs proactively in the planning and design phase using inclusive practices informed by universal design principles (see Chapter 11), although some students will require further adjustments, as modelled in Chapter 12. The social model provides a clear conceptual model to assist teachers in the process of identifying barriers and designing/implementing reasonable adjustments for students with disability.

The importance of educators understanding the social model of disability was recently emphasised by the Australian Government Productivity Commission's (2022) *Review of* the *National School Reform Agreement* (NSRA), with the Final Report recommending that parties should "implement commitments from *Australia's National Disability Strategy*, in particular application of a social model of disability in education systems", as part of the next intergovernmental school reform agreement (see Recommendation 4.3, p. 37). Building capability in the delivery of inclusive education to improve educational outcomes for school students with disability is a focussed policy priority in the NSRA, with new Targeted Action Plans being commissioned. This is a pleasing development, one that could be supported nationally by quality professional learning aligned with the content of this book (see Chapter 8). Another important concept for educators to understand is equity for it can help them work out and justify who gets what in terms of support in schools.

Equity vs. Equality

Within a human-rights framework, education is a right that, at the same time, provides opportunities to access other rights (for example, the right to work and be employed). Access to and participation in education are essential for independence in adult life; however, not all educational settings offer the sufficient conditions to realise these entitlements and offer the full benefits of the right to education. For this reason, and as outlined in the CRPD, education must be inclusive. The following discussion of equity is based on this premise, as it is important when we discuss issues of justice and fairness to clearly articulate the purpose of education for which we strive as a society. In educational settings (such as schools), teachers, parents, and students engage with what is 'fair' and appropriate to give everyone 'his or her due'; these are places where conceptions of justice and fairness are negotiated and acted upon. Which principles should drive these decisions, especially when resources are scarce, and the potential losses or gains are high? The underlining principle of distribution justice that goes back more than 2000 years to Greek philosopher Aristotle is to "treat equals equally and unequals unequally" (Graham, 2007, p. 535). Burbules et al. (1982) argue that the first part—*to treat equals equally*—refers to an equality principle, and the second part—*to treat unequals unequally*—refers to a fairness principle. These two principles are complementary, and their relevance is always contextual. Further, it means that both equality *and* equity are needed to achieve the fair distribution of resources. However, the distinction between the two is not always clear, and there is much confusion as to how equality and equity are understood and used.

Understanding Equality

Equality is based on an egalitarian understanding of the commonalities among human beings. As a human-rights principle, equality affirms that all people are born free and equal, and that they should not be discriminated against because of their personal characteristics. A narrow conception of equality, called universal sameness (Arnardottir, 2009) or *formal equality*, assumes that treating everybody the same achieves equality, but this approach focuses on equality in inputs and not outcomes.

Legislation and policy from the 1950s to the 1970s drew on the idea of formal equality when, for example, access to higher education expanded but without any provisions to ensure equal participation. As Professor Michael Oliver describes in a YouTube video, *Kicking Down the Doors: From Borstal Boy to University Professor* (University of Kent, 2018), students with disability had to navigate inaccessible buildings and exam conditions and prove themselves on 'merit'. The use of assistive technology of any kind during exams was considered an 'unfair advantage', a perception that still exists today (Osborne, 2019). The justification of such an approach to equality has been reinforced by internalised ableism and the inability to perceive the commonalities of different technological tools used to record information, regardless of whether these are a pencil or pen, a typewriter, a computer, speech-to-text software, or a braille writer. As noted earlier in our discussion of both ableism and the medical model, the practices of and assistive technologies used by people without disability were perceived as the norm, and anything else was seen as a deviation. Within an equality framework that merely provides the 'opportunity' to participate, some individuals 'excel', but the comparative effort to overcome barriers is an unjustifiable and additional burden that causes many more to fail.

Burbules et al. (1982) use the helpful metaphor of a race to illustrate this problem. Consider the following scenario. A group of runners competing in a timed race up a notoriously steep hill is split into two smaller groups. Each of these groups is running the same timed race and up the same mountain, but each group's route is different. Due to concerns about route congestion, one group is allocated the tarred road up the mountain. The other group must navigate the natural topography, as well as ancient stiles that were built to divide crop shares. The first person to make it over the threshold is the winner. Now, most people would agree that this is not fair. Nor is it equal. So, let us torture this metaphor a little further. What if the original group was not split, and all runners got the opportunity to run the tarred-road route? Would this be fair? Put even more simply, does *everyone* then have an equal chance of winning? Formal equality would say yes—but what about the person with a mobility impairment? As noted by Burbules et al. (1982), they have been given an opportunity to compete but have no opportunity to win. In this case, a formal-equality approach perpetuates disadvantage.

We have described the formal-equality approach as being in the past in terms of policy, but it still informs educators' beliefs and behaviours. Consider, for example, the current attitudes of many educators towards the provision of adjustments in relation to senior-school assessment. In many states in Australia, students with disability in Years 11 and 12 are routinely denied adjustments in the false belief that they must compete 'on a level playing field' with other students. This is no different to forcing athletes with mobility impairment to run under the same conditions as athletes without disability, as outlined in our metaphorical mountain race. In some schools, the concept of a level playing field is mistaken to mean that every student must complete the same assessment task, typically under the same conditions. When an adjustment *is* made, it is usually in the form of extra time (Cumming et al., 2013); however, extra time is of no value when the assessment itself is inaccessible or when time is not the barrier (Graham et al., 2018).

Adjustments are measures taken to level the playing field by dismantling barriers to access and participation. The fear preventing some educators from making adjustments is that this will somehow make a high-stakes competition easier for some students, disadvantaging others (Cumming et al., 2013). However, this would only be the case if the academic integrity of the assessment were affected, if navigating inaccessibility were an assessable item, or if the accessible version was only provided to some students and not others. While there is usually no argument against the provision of assessment tasks written in braille, there is less understanding when it comes to other aspects of accessibility, such as the visual, linguistic, and procedural complexity of the task description (Graham et al., 2018). Key to solving this problem is determining whether the perceived barrier is integral to the task; in other words, is students' ability to decipher a task description the objective of the assessment? Usually, it is not. Proactively designing assessment for accessibility through the application of universal design principles is one way to ensure fairness, accessibility, and academic integrity, because the same clearly worded, logically presented assessment task is made available to *all* (Graham et al., 2018).[1]

Achieving 'Equity' Through Substantive Equality

The concept of equality has thus evolved and expanded to incorporate the concept of equity. *Substantive equality* recognises the need for the removal of barriers through affirmative action. This involves policies that aim to increase the participation of specific groups through the provision of reasonable adjustments, which are changes to what is usually available to provide equal opportunity for participation. Substantive equality requires us to treat groups differently. A number of these changes are designed and implemented at the group level and become standards of provision, such as in the proactive assessment-design example provided earlier. And, although Parliament House does not provide a good example, architecture has led the way in inclusive design and the principles of universal design are now embedded in legislation and building codes. These are now core principles that apply to any public building, regardless of who the architect imagines will use it. For example, the accessibility of school buildings is based on building standards, regardless of whether a student, parent, or member of staff with mobility restrictions will be using them at any given time.

The notion of reasonable adjustments in the Australian *Disability Standards for Education 2005* (Cth) or reasonable accommodations (CRPD) (see Chapter 5) straddles both the concepts of equality and equity. While equality focuses mainly on groups, equity focuses on individuals and responding to their specific characteristics, demands, and

---

1 See Chapter 11 to learn more about current research showing that accessibility in assessment and pedagogy improves academic achievement for *all* students.

interests in a specific context. This can be achieved through the provision of reasonable adjustments but, in this case, they are tailored to the individual. Using our assessment example above, substantive equality is reflected in the design and provision of accessible assessment using universal design principles to *all* students. Equity would entail the provision of an assessment task written in braille—as one example of educational adjustment—to an *individual* student. Through this understanding, equity is about individual differences and how unequal treatment in specific circumstances is necessary to ensure equality of opportunity. This may have implications beyond the individual who requires the unequal treatment, and this is what concerns different stakeholders in schools in terms of ensuring 'fairness'.

Equity: To Each Their 'Just Desserts'

Deborah Stone (2001) uses the analogy of a chocolate cake to discuss equitable distribution. She has a delicious chocolate cake to share with one of her public-policy classes. She goes through the different challenges of distributing the cake equally: some students in the class do not like chocolate, while others are allergic to chocolate or do not have the gene that enables them to digest it. These students themselves propose that they get tiny slices of the cake (to be polite and just taste it), but that other students get bigger ones, resulting in unequal slices that are of equal value to recipients. In all of Stone's scenarios, the essence of the cake remains the same, even in a scenario where there is only enough cake mix to bake one cupcake to share. Stone discusses the different dimensions that challenge equity: *who* is going to get the cake (recipients), *what* the actual cake is (item), and *how* the cake is going to be shared (process). In the context of education, a key issue is to identify the actual experience that matters: using the cake analogy, *why* are we having cake? Is it about tasting chocolate, familiarisation with the texture of the cake, sharing celebratory food, or to engage in the social experience of relaxed, informal conversation? Depending on which elements of this experience are essential to equally partake in it, we can then redesign the experience, provide supports to access the cake, provide additional alternatives to the cake, and—if it does not really matter—even replace the chocolate cake with other options. One question to answer is whether these changes to the experience are 'fair' to the 'other' students, if they must miss out on this delicious cake. But, if the learning experience is, for instance, to teach fractions, replacing the cake with a vegan pizza does not detract from the learning objective.

The cake analogy has been used to describe equity ever since political philosopher and economist John Rawls published his theory of justice in 1971 (Coleman, 1976). His theories, and those of other political philosophers—such as Nobel Prize-winner Amartya Sen—have all influenced public policy, particularly taxation policy. Yet the question of how much of what should go to whom does not necessarily take other important questions or what we might call 'downstream issues' into account. One very important downstream issue with relevance to education is known as the 'dilemma of difference'.

The Dilemma of Difference

The obligation to make reasonable adjustments for students with disability requires educators to do something different for and/or provide something additional to some students and not others. Some educators feel anxious about doing this, because they have been brought up to believe that 'fair' means an equal share; however, as we explain above, fairness or 'equity' is achieved by each student receiving what they need. Nevertheless, providing something different or additional introduces another problem, which is that people with disability may be singled out as different. This can lead to stigmatisation, and the threat of stigmatisation prevents many educators, parents and even students from pursuing adjustments. Without adjustments, however, barriers remain in place. Legal scholar Martha Minow describes this predicament as the 'dilemma of difference'. To illustrate the "damned if you do and damned if you don't" nature of the dilemma, Minow (1990, p. 20) asks two questions:

1. When does treating people *differently* emphasise their differences and stigmatise or hinder them on that basis?
2. When does treating people *the same* become insensitive to their difference and likely to stigmatise or hinder them on that basis?

To explain this dilemma in practice, Minow (1985) discusses the legal cases brought by two different groups of parents in the United States during the 1970s. One group of parents was arguing *for* separate (bilingual) education, and the other group of parents was arguing *against* separate (special) education. The first legal case was brought because the language of instruction in the United States during the 1970s was English, and this was a major barrier for immigrant students who could not understand what was being taught, negatively affecting their access to the curriculum and, through this, their educational achievement and employment outcomes. Minow describes this case to present one outcome of what she calls 'the dilemma of difference', which is that treating people the same can result in discrimination and the denial of difference (readers will recognise this as a result of formal equality). To illuminate the other side of the dilemma, Minow then describes the case brought by parents of children with disability who were being provided with 'special' education in segregated settings. These parents argued that their children were being discriminated against because they *were* being treated differently, and that this different treatment resulted in stigmatisation and substandard outcomes. Translating this dilemma to educational settings today, the conundrum remains the same: "doing something different for some children and not others, *still* risks stigmatising those perceived as *different* [emphasis added]" (Graham & Tancredi, 2019, p. 2). The challenge then, for educators, is how to identify and address barriers to enable access and participation for individual students without stigmatising them in the process.

Stigmatisation is a result of society's use of categorisation. Minow (1990) argues that when individuals are categorised as belonging to a certain group, participation in society (including education) is enabled, or restricted, by their allocated category. In the current education climate, the identification of students who require additional support—a form of diagnostic categorisation—is often necessary to decide on the adjustments that should be made to ensure equitable access and participation in education (Graham & Tancredi, 2019). The dilemma of difference appears in this process as well: are we emphasising, and possibly stigmatising, students' impairments in our efforts to provide them access to education? As Minow (1985) stated, "making difference matter re-creates difference and its associated hierarchy of status" (p. 169). However, the opposite is true as well, for if we do not take students' differences into consideration, those differences are denied and adjustments are not made, leaving barriers to access and participation in place. This represents what Norwich (2008) called the "identification dilemma", where both the identification and non-identification of students with disability present a problem. But if labelling students leads to stigmatisation, why is it so commonplace?

We use labels to reach common understanding. To achieve this, educators need to use "certain words, terms and categories" (Graham & Macartney, 2012, p. 190) to convey specific meaning in relation to students' learning profiles. Besides being a form of communication, labels are a starting point from which to design curriculum, pedagogy, and assessment to enable students with disability to access and participate in education on the same basis as their peers. For example, in considering the dangers and affordances of diagnosis for Attention Deficit Hyperactivity Disorder (ADHD) and Developmental Language Disorder (DLD), Graham and Tancredi (2019) conclude that diagnostic labels provide teachers with valuable initial information to help them anticipate and prevent barriers in curriculum, pedagogy and assessment for students in these two groups. Teachers can use the information to determine aspects of a task that students with ADHD or DLD might find difficult to do and then ensure access and participation by removing that aspect, where possible. They note that working memory is an area of weakness for students in both groups, and that teachers can support these students by making sure that they avoid using complex sentences and multipart instructions, by catching and maintaining attention, supporting information processing through intentional pauses, and by providing visual supports (see Chapter 11). Importantly, these practices are beneficial for *all* students.

Although labels can provide teachers with useful information, they should not be an endpoint (Graham & Macartney, 2012). As noted by Wenger (1998), words are useful when people recognise their meaning through previous engagement with those words in similar situations, but they are also ambiguous: they can be used differently in different situations to convey a different meaning and purpose. It is therefore important that the use of language in inclusive education serves the purpose it was intended to serve.

Inclusive Language

Language matters. And language is particularly important in inclusive education, which is concerned with the expression and realisation of human rights, dignity, and freedom from discrimination. Our language is inherited from our past, and it changes over time but seldom quickly enough to prevent residual damage. Nowhere is this more evident than in relation to disability. Many words that have been used to describe people with disability in the past have been abandoned because they have acquired pejorative meanings over time. While many people know that certain words are offensive and avoid using them, these same words can remain stuck in place, even in official documents and laws. In these instances, activism and political leadership are required to bring about change. An example is *Rosa's Law*, which was enacted in 2010 by Barack Obama when he was President of the United States. Rosa was a young woman with Down syndrome, and the law that was named in her honour removed the term "mentally retarded" from the health and education code in the state of Maryland. In his speech, Obama quoted Rosa's brother, Nick, who said, "What you call people is how you treat them. If we change the words, maybe it will be the start of a new attitude towards people with disabilities" (The White House, 2010). Obama recognised the power of language to entrench or change attitudes about people with disability, and he acted to make a difference for people with intellectual disability. More work is clearly needed to remove the word 'retarded' from popular discourse, but laws and official documents are a good start.

Inclusive language is important. Language not only reflects beliefs, values, and attitudes, but it also plays a role in constructing the world (Walton & Marais, 2022). Classification is a natural cognitive function that enables humans to process information quickly and make sense of the world. The problem comes when classification categories are not useful or valid or are harmful. This is particularly evident in the use of labels for people who are deemed to be different. As we noted earlier, some labels represent diagnostic categories and can be useful for understanding conditions, promoting awareness, and securing appropriate educational and other support (Graham & Tancredi, 2019). They also might provide a social identity through belonging to a group of people with a similar diagnostic label. Often, though, labels lead to stigmatisation, bullying and low self-esteem. Labels can reinforce an individual, deficit view of children and young people in educational settings and can result in lowered expectations (Lauchlan & Boyle, 2007). It is crucial that those working in educational contexts are conscious of the effects of the language they use (Walton, 2016) and that they avoid terminology that is considered offensive by people with disability and other marginalised identities.

Language is subtle and ableism, racism, and sexism are insidious. Sometimes we 'other' certain groups, not by using specific words, but by using words in a particular way. For example, have you ever thought about the different ways the term 'diverse learners' is used? It is a tricky term because it can do either of two things, depending on the context in which it is being used. If used correctly, it means *all* students, and this is the way it is meant in Queensland University of Technology's (QUT) initial teacher education programs. This is the correct meaning of the term 'diverse' which means a great deal of variety. However, the term 'diverse learners' is often used as shorthand for difference; a euphemism for 'special needs'. But you can't have diversity if there's only one group, right? Diversity is the result of *many* groups; not just the result of some groups that are 'different' to the 'average' group. So, creating Heads of Diverse Learning in schools—where that person is responsible only for students with disability and not *all* students—is simply replacing the term 'Heads of Special Education Services' with another, equally divisive term. There are many words imbued with this type of cultural subtext and we need to be aware of them, so that we don't unknowingly engage in marginalisation. Another that is unconsciously used to mark others as 'different' is the word 'ethnic'. People from minority ethnic groups are continually referred to as 'ethnics' in the media and popular discourse but this again is a bastardisation of the term. We are *all* ethnics because every single one of us has an ethnicity. Describing people of Middle Eastern appearance as 'ethnics' (as was the case during the 2005 Cronulla Riots, see Graham & Slee, 2008) is racist for it marks out a minority group as different because they have "an ethnicity" (that is different to the norm), while portraying the majority as natural (and somehow without ethnicity). The word 'multicultural' is also often used as shorthand for 'other culture different to the norm' (see Graham & Slee, 2008), and this careless use of language serves to continually marginalise non-dominant groups who are reminded that they are the 'them' and not the 'us'.

Many terms that people use in reference to disability are similarly negative and offensive (Arciuli & Shakespeare, 2023). They reveal historical and stereotypical beliefs about the abnormality and inferiority of people with disability, and they are not acceptable terms. They include words such as "retarded" (which *Rosa's Law* sought to eliminate), "moron", "imbecile", and "idiot". While these words were once medical terms, they were discontinued and are now unlikely to be found in modern health and educational texts. Yet they often appear as insults in popular discourse. Spend time in any high school (and some primary schools), and you will hear students call each other "retards". Read a newspaper, attend a sporting event, or scroll through Twitter, and it does not take long for the word "idiot" to surface. These words have become so ubiquitous that users may not be fully aware of their origins or, even if they are aware, they may not realise their effect or who they are really insulting. To criticise an idea as "lame" or "insane" is to use a negative perspective of disability to show disapproval. Similarly, to criticise a politician's views using terms such as "blind" or "moronic" is to reinforce a negative view of disability. This is deemed ableist language: language that devalues people with disability. People might not realise they are being ableist and may use these terms inadvertently (Broderick & Lalvani, 2017). But, like racist and sexist language, ableist language needs to be identified and avoided.

Sometimes the words we use stereotype people with disability as deficient, needy, or pitiful, and disability is often portrayed as a tragedy. An example is when it is said that someone "suffers from" a disability. This phrase comes from an outdated and medicalised 'charity view' of disability that is both patronising and ableist, because it presumes that impairment must result in suffering and that the lives of people with disability must be awful. So, too, the expression that someone is "wheelchair bound" or "confined to a wheelchair". Such phrases privilege able-bodied experience and frame people with disability as objects to be pitied. Other terms that signal deficit can be more difficult to identify and avoid, because they are found in official policy and couched in the language of support. The term 'special needs' is one such example, and it has an interesting linguistic history. It was coined by Baroness Warnock in England in 1978 to try to shift the emphasis of difficulties with learning from individual deficit to the inadequacies of the schooling system (Thomas & Vaughan, 2004). But instead of the system changing, 'special needs' has become another label that signals deficit and legitimates segregation into 'special' provision. Cátia Malaquias is the mother of a young man with Down syndrome called Julius, and a co-author of Chapter 3 in this book. In a blog called, "He ain't special, he's my brother", Cátia says that she would like to see "this damaging phrase [special needs], and the mentality that goes with it . . . put on the scrapheap" (Malaquias, n.d.). She explains further that:

> The label of 'special needs', serving by definition to segregate or exceptionalise people with disability, is inconsistent with recognition of disability as part of human diversity. In that social framework, none of us is 'special' as we are all equal siblings in our diverse family of humanity.

Research confirms that people tend to be seen in a more negative light when they are described as having "special needs" than when they are described as having a disability (Gernsbacher et al., 2016). People with disability know this and are increasingly campaigning against the term. Every year, the national association of people with Down syndrome in Italy releases a video on World Down Syndrome Day to inform public knowledge and understanding. Their 2017 video was titled "Not Special Needs" and featured young people with Down syndrome satirising the concept of special needs. They illustrated how inappropriate the term really is by acting out needs that would be special if they were true, such as people with Down syndrome needing to be massaged by cats or fed dinosaur eggs. Their point was that people with disability have the same *needs* as everyone else and that the term '*special* needs' peculiarises them in inappropriate and offensive ways. But special is not the only problematic word in this phrase, meaning it cannot simply be replaced with 'additional'. That is because there is a problem with 'needs' as well.

Being such a ubiquitous term, especially in special education, it can be difficult for non-disabled people to understand why this term receives so much criticism. It is complex, but essentially the word 'needs' portrays people with disability as dependent on the largesse of others to provide them with the support and adjustments they 'need'. This can contribute to a perception that people with disability are weak and a burden on others, which is a perception that has had devastating consequences. These consequences have included—at different times in history—the extermination, sterilisation, institutionalisation, exclusion, and segregation of children with disability (see Chapter 3). The language of 'needs' also obfuscates the fact that inclusive education is a human right, and that education providers are obligated to provide adjustments under legislation. In other words, students with disability don't have needs that they are waiting on us to fulfil, they have rights that we have agreed to (and, in most cases, are paid to) provide.

Other terms carry similarly negative associations, contributing to perceptions of individual deficit and the belief that barriers are located within individuals. An example is when students' identities become conflated with official processes of categorisation or support provision, as reflected in the use of terms such as "EHSCP[2] student" or "wheelchair girl". In some cases, the person becomes the category, as children are referred to as "IMs", "IOs", or "ISs", reflecting the three levels of classification[3] of intellectual disability in New South Wales, Australia: mild (IM), moderate (IO), or severe (IS) (Graham & Macartney, 2012). And, although the ATSI acronym is still used to refer to Aboriginal and Torres Strait Islander peoples in many public documents, it is considered offensive by Indigenous Australians. The concern about these and other terms is that they deny the humanity within individuals, efface the diversity between groups, reflect individual deficit constructions of disability and difference, and are deeply disrespectful.

What Language Should We Use?

Educators often want to know what language is acceptable when talking about disability and difference in the context of inclusive education. While there is general agreement about offensive language, as illustrated by the numerous examples provided above, there are different opinions about preferred terminology. The key issue is that people with disability (or disabled people) get to decide on the language they as individuals or as groups prefer. Generally, the person or group of people should remain present in the terminology, so groups of people should not be referred to by a disability category. Terms such as "the blind", "the disabled", and "the epileptic" should not be used. Having secured the person in the terminology, there are two positions; each has proponents and opponents.

Person-First Language. Person-first language is often used to foreground the individual and signal that the individual is more than their disabled identity. This language would favour terms such as "person with a disability", "student with epilepsy", or "child with vision impairment". These terms focus on the person or student and are a reminder not to essentialise people in terms of their disability or imagine that because the disability is known, the person is known. It also recognises the intersectionality of identity, in that people have multiple identities assigned by their gender, sexuality, ethnicity, and nationality and occupational/relational roles. Person-first language serves as a useful way to resist the tendency of schools to prejudge, sort and separate students based on the low expectations associated with certain disability labels. It is also the approach used in the CRPD and, for these reasons, the approach adopted throughout this book. Despite the potential affordances of person-first language, many people in the disability community

---

2   In England, an Education, Health and Social Care Plan is drawn up to describe the 'special' needs that a child or young person has and outlines the support that will be given to meet these needs. It is intended to access support that would not normally be provided in 'mainstream' schools.

3   This reflects the New South Wales classification of intellectual impairment.

reject this construction on the grounds that disability is not incidental or an add-on to identity; it is inherent to the way identity is defined. Person-first language is seen by some as making disability separate from identity, and this is only done because disability continues to be framed negatively. Critics of person-first language note that other aspects of identity, such as race, gender, sexuality, and ethnicity, are never expressed in terms of a person *with* something, such as a person with "gayness" or a person with "femaleness". On these grounds, identity-first language is preferred by some.

Identity-First Language. Identify-first language puts the disability or other aspect of difference before the person and is seen as a way of affirming disability identity and rejecting negative connotations. Identity-first language talks of "disabled people" or "autistic students" or "deaf children". The Autistic community has been particularly active in promoting identity-first language by asserting #AutisticPride and celebrating the contribution that neurodiversity makes to the world. One criticism of the argument for identity-first language is that it is being made by people who can speak in the absence of the voices of people with complex learning profiles who might be non-speaking (otherwise described as non-verbal). For this reason, it is important that educators consult students (or their associates) to determine whether they prefer person-first or identity-first language, and the preferences of individuals should be respected. Finally, it is ableist to refuse to acknowledge someone's disability by saying "I don't see you as disabled". This might be well-intentioned and meant to mean "I don't see you in a negative light". But it is not a compliment and negates disability as an integral part of a disabled person's identity. It also risks people's disabilities being mis-or unrecognised, which can result in a lack of necessary support or adjustments.

Language will change. Terms that are currently acceptable may fall from favour. Previous taboo words (such as "cripple") will continue to be reclaimed by some scholars and activists, as in the derivative "crip". New terms will come into use. Scholars, practitioners, and students in the field of inclusive education will need to embrace a "life of alertness" (Walton, 2016, p. 155), maintaining a critical awareness of the power and effects of language. This makes three demands on educators. The first is a willingness to engage in critical self-reflection to identify and reject ableist thinking, beliefs and language. Second, it demands the sensitivity and courage to call out ableist, offensive and otherwise derogatory language when used in private and public spaces. Finally, it requires respectful dialogue to understand and affirm others' right to name and identify.

This right of individuals to name and identify themselves also applies to gender. It is important for educators to be aware of, and to use gender-inclusive language. Gender-inclusive language involves a few considerations. First, it means not using language that perpetuates gender stereotypes, like "Can I get a strong boy to help me carry these boxes?" or "I need some girls to volunteer to decorate the venue". Second, it means not using words associated with one gender (like the masculine 'guys') when speaking to or about a mixed-gender group. The third adjustment is the important acknowledgement of non-binary and transgender identities. Educators should not make assumptions about people's gender identities based on their appearance or name. Instead, educators should offer opportunities for students and colleagues to share their preferred pronouns. An inclusive environment can be created by adopting the practice of sharing one's own preferred pronouns, in email signatures, introductions, and on-line profiles. Once others have shared their pronouns, their preferences should be respected. Misgendering, that is, referring to someone in a way that does not match their own gender identity is harmful to the person. If this happens unintentionally, sincere apologies should be given, and efforts made not to do this again. Transgender or non-binary people should not be called by their birth or given names, or names used before transitioning. This is called deadnaming, and it invalidates a person's identity. Instead, the person's new or affirmed name should be used. With attention given to gender-inclusive language, classrooms can promote gender equality, diminish stereotypes, and model mutual respect.

Conclusion

To ensure that inclusive education is implemented with fidelity, educators, and support staff across all levels of education must understand the fundamental concepts that underpin it. The concept of ableism and the social model of disability clarify the external nature of barriers; these are barriers that students face, *not* individual deficits that they must overcome. Educators and other stakeholders must work with students to identify and address these barriers. Only then can they be dismantled so that *all* students can access and participate in education on an equitable basis. When the social model of disability is understood in partnership with the concepts of equity and the dilemma of difference, educators can shift their thinking from achieving equality in the form of inputs to focus instead on what is needed to achieve equity in outcomes. Engaging with these fundamental concepts, reconceptualising disability and realigning practice are all necessary to implement inclusive education effectively and with authenticity. This shift in thinking must be accompanied by a shift to inclusive language to avoid the dilemma of difference and to support inclusive practice. Together, these concepts invite educators to reflect on their beliefs, language, and practices. At times, the process of reflection can be jarring. This is a natural consequence of reflection and learning from which we all grow. With knowledge of the fundamental concepts of inclusive education, educators are well-equipped to enact genuine inclusive practices.

References

Arciuli, J., & Shakespeare, T. (2023). Language matters: Disability and the power of taboo words. In M. S. Jeffress, J. M. Cypher, J. Ferris, & J-A. Scott-Pollock (Eds.), *The Palgrave Handbook of Disability and Communication* (pp. 17–29). Springer.

Arnardottir, O. M. (2009). A future of multidimensional disadvantage equality? *The UN Convention on the Rights of Persons with Disabilities: European and Scandinavian Perspectives.* https://doi.org/10.1163/ej.9789004169715.i-320.19

Australian Government Productivity Commission. (2022). *Review of the National School Reform Agreement, Study Report.* https://www.pc.gov.au/inquiries/completed/school-agreement/report/school-agreement.pdf

Berghs, M., Atkin, K., Graham, H., Hatton, C., & Thomas, C. (2016). Implications for public health research of models and theories of disability: A scoping study and evidence synthesis *Public Health Research*, 4(8), 1–166. https://doi.org/10.3310/phr04080

Broderick, A., & Lalvani, P. (2017). Dysconscious ableism: Toward a liberatory praxis in teacher education. *International Journal of Inclusive Education*, *21*(9), 894–905. https://doi.org/10.1080/13603116.2017.1296034

Brown, S. E. (1999). *The curb ramps of Kalamazoo: Discovering our unrecorded history*. https://kb.osu.edu/bitstream/handle/1811/85717/DSQ_v19n3_1999_203.pdf

Burbules, N. C., Lord, B. T., & Sherman, A. L. (1982). Equity, equal opportunity, and education. *Educational Evaluation and Policy Analysis*, *4*(2), 169–187. https://doi.org/10.2307/1164011

Coleman, J. S. (1976). Rawls, Nozick, and educational equality. *The Public Interest*, *43*, 121–128.

Cooper, P. (2008). Like alligators bobbing for poodles? A critical discussion of Education, ADHD and the biopsychosocial perspective. *Journal of Philosophy of Education*, *42*(3-4), 457–474. https://doi.org/10.1111/j.1467-9752.2008.00657.x

Cumming, J., Dickson, E., & Webster, A. (2013). Reasonable adjustments in assessment: Putting law and policy. *International Journal of Disability, Development, and Education*, *60*(4), 295–311. https://doi.org/10.1080/1034912X.2013.846467

Degener, T. (2017). A new human rights model of disability. In V. Della Fina, R. Cera, & G. Palmisano (Eds.), *The United Nations Convention on the Rights of Persons with Disabilities: A commentary* (pp. 41–59). Springer.

Disability Standards for Education 2005 (Cth).

Engel, G. L. (1977). The need for a new medical model: A challenge for biomedicine. *Science (American Association for the Advancement of Science)*, *196*(4286), 129–136. https://doi.org/10.1126/science.847460

Gernsbacher, M. A., Raimond, A. R., Balinghasay, M. T., & Boston, J. S. (2016). "Special needs" is an ineffective euphemism. *Cognitive Research: Principles and Implications*, *1*(1), 29–29. https://doi.org/10.1186/s41235-016-0025-4

Graham, L. J. (2007). Towards equity in the futures market: Curriculum as a condition of access. *Policy Futures in Education*, *5*(4), 535–555. https://doi.org/10.2304/pfie.2007.5.4.535

Graham, L. J., & Macartney, B. (2012). Naming or creating a problem? The mis/use of labels in schools. In S. Carrington, & J. MacArthur (Eds.), *Teaching in inclusive school communities* (pp. 187–208). Wiley.

Graham, L. J., & Slee, R. (2008). An illusory interiority: Interrogating the discourse/s of inclusion. *Educational Philosophy and Theory*, *40*(2), 277–293. https://doi.org/10.1111/j.1469-5812.2007.00331.x

Graham, L. J., & Tancredi, H. (2019). In search of a middle ground: The dangers and affordances of diagnosis in relation to Attention Deficit Hyperactivity Disorder and Developmental Language Disorder. *Emotional and Behavioural Difficulties*, *24*(3), 287–300. https://doi.org/10.1080/13632752.2019.1609248

Graham, L. J., Tancredi, H., Willis, J., & McGraw, K. (2018). Designing out barriers to student access and participation in secondary school assessment. *Australian Educational Researcher*, *45*(1), 103–124. https://doi.org/10.1007/s13384-018-0266-y

Lauchlan, F., & Boyle, C. (2007). Is the use of labels in special education helpful? *Support for Learning*, *22*(1), 36–42. https://doi.org/10.1111/j.1467-9604.2007.00443.x

Malaquias, C. (n.d.). "He ain't special, he's my brother"—Time to ditch the phrase "special needs". *Starting with Julius*. https://www.startingwithjulius.org.au/he-aint-special-hes-my-brother-time-to-ditch-the-phrase-special-needs

Minow, M. (1985). Learning to live with the dilemma of difference: Bilingual and special education. *Law and Contemporary Problems*, *48*(2), 157–211. https://doi.org/10.2307/1191571

Minow, M. (1990). *Making all the difference: Inclusion, exclusion, and American law*. Cornell University Press.

Norwich, B. (2008). *Dilemmas of difference, inclusion and disability: International perspectives and future directions*. Routledge.

Oliver, M. (2013). The social model of disability: Thirty years on. *Disability & Society, 28*(7), 1024–1026. https://doi.org/10.1080/09687599.2013.818773

Osborne, T. (2019). Not lazy, not faking: Teaching and learning experiences of university students with disabilities. *Disability & Society, 34*(2), 228–252. https://doi.org/10.1080/0968759 9.2018.1515724

Quinn, G., Degener, T., Bruce, A., Burke, C., Castellino, J., Kenna, P., Kilkelly, U., & Quinlivan, S. (2002). *Human rights and disability: The current use and future potential of United Nations human rights instruments in the context of disability*. United Nations Publications. https://digital library.un.org/record/477534

Shakespeare, T. (2006). The social model of disability. In L. J. Davis (Ed.), *The disability studies reader* (2nd ed., pp. 197–204). Routledge.

Shakespeare, T., Watson, N., & Alghaib, O. A. (2017). Blaming the victim, all over again: Waddell and Aylward's biopsychosocial (BPS) model of disability. *Critical Social Policy, 37*(1), 22–41. https://doi.org/10.1177/0261018316649120

Stone, D. (2001). *Policy paradox: The art of political decision making* (3rd ed.). W.W. Norton & Company.

Terzi, L. (2005). A capability perspective on impairment, disability and special needs: Towards social justice in education. *Theory and Research in Education, 3*(2), 197–223. https://doi. org/10.1177/1477878505053301

The White House. (2010). *Remarks by the President at the signing of the 21st Century Communications and Video Accessibility Act of 2010*. https://obamawhitehouse.archives.gov/ the-press-office/2010/10/08/remarks-president-signing-21st-century-communications-and-video-accessib

Thomas, G., & Vaughan, M. (2004). *Inclusive education: Readings and reflections*. Open University Press.

United Nations. (2006). *Convention on the Rights of Persons with Disabilities (CRPD)*. https://www. un.org/disabilities/documents/convention/convoptprot-e.pdf.

United Nations. (2016). *General Comment No. 4, Article 24: Right to Inclusive Education (CRPD/C/ GC/4)*. https://digitallibrary.un.org/record/1313836?ln=en

University of Kent. (2018). *Professor Mike Oliver: Kicking down the doors: From Borstal boy to University Professor*. https://www.youtube.com/watch?v=NMfvoh-j9qw

Walton, E. (2016). *The language of inclusive education*. Routledge.

Walton, E., & Marais, C. (2022). Language matters. In K. Black-Hawkins and A. Grinham-Smith (Eds.), *Expanding possibilities for inclusive learning* (pp. 14–29). Routledge.

Wenger, E. (1998). *Communities of practice: Learning, meaning, and identity*. Cambridge University Press.

World Health Organisation. (2001). *International Classification of Functioning, Disability and Health (ICF)*. https://www.who.int/standards/classifications/international-classification-of-fun ctioning-disability-and-health

Worthington, B. (2018, April 2). Jordon Steele-John has the loneliest seat in the Senate, and it's locking him out of the parliamentary process. *ABC News*. https://www.abc.net.au/ news/2018-04-02/senator-jordon-steele-john-disability-access-parliament-house/9587308

Chapter 5

The legal foundations of inclusion

Elizabeth Dickson

All school students, regardless of ability, are entitled to an inclusive education in their local school (United Nations, 2006, 2016). More broadly, *inclusion* may be regarded as an education approach which welcomes all students regardless not only of ability, but also of gender, gender identity, sexuality, race, or religion. In countries like Australia, the human right to inclusive education is underpinned by domestic legislation designed to implement "as far as practicable" those rights (see, e.g., *Disability Discrimination Act 1992* section 3(b)). Legislation prohibits discrimination against students by education institutions on the ground of *protected attributes*. This chapter will explain how legislation supports inclusion by prohibiting discrimination by schools "as far as possible" (see DDA section 3(a)). The chapter will then consider two controversies that have arisen in the context of the management of inclusion, and which test the limits of the law. The first concerns reasonable adjustments for students with disability related challenging behaviour; and the second concerns accommodation of students who identify as transgender and/or non-binary. While the primary focus will be on Australian Commonwealth anti-discrimination legislation and related case law, some examples from anti-discrimination legislation and case law from the United Kingdom will also be given to illuminate alternative approaches to those adopted in Australia.

Australian Anti-Discrimination Law

Australia is a federation which means that it has a central government, the Commonwealth government, and a series of state and territory governments. Legislative power is shared between the Commonwealth and the states and territories, regulated by the *Australian Constitution*. Both Commonwealth laws and state and territory laws provide overlapping protection for students against discrimination by schools and affected students may commence legal action under either Commonwealth or state and territory laws. This chapter will focus on Commonwealth anti-discrimination laws as they apply uniformly throughout Australia. Moreover, if schools are compliant with their obligations under Commonwealth laws, they are likely compliant with state and territory laws, such is the level of similarity between them.

DOI: 10.4324/9781003350897-6

Commonwealth Legislation and Discrimination in Education

Four Commonwealth Anti-Discrimination Acts operate together to prohibit discrimination by schools: the *Racial Discrimination Act 1975* (RDA; Cth), the *Sex Discrimination Act 1984* (SDA; Cth), the *Disability Discrimination Act 1992* (DDA; Cth), and the *Age Discrimination Act 2004* (ADA; Cth). The RDA prohibits discrimination on the ground of race, colour, ethnicity, and nationality. Where race and religion coincide, such as for people of Jewish ethnicity, the RDA may also protect discrimination on the ground of religion (see *Miller v Wertheim*, 2002). Case law concerning racial discrimination in education in Australia has determined that it is lawful to provide targeted benefits to students because of their race where those benefits are 'special measures' intended to reduce historical disadvantage and promote participation in education (see RDA section 8; *Bruch v Commonwealth of Australia*, 2002). While there is no relevant Australian Commonwealth case law, the important United Kingdom case, *Mandla v Dowell Lee* (1983), demonstrates the potential for strictly enforced uniform codes to have a discriminatory impact upon students from some racial or ethnic groups. In that case, a Sikh boy was found to have been discriminated against when he was required by the respondent school to remove his turban in order to comply with the school's uniform policy. An Australian case decided under state law (*Anti-Discrimination Act 1991* (Qld)) and citing *Mandla v Dowell Lee*, found, similarly, that requiring a young boy of Cook Islander and Niuean descent to cut his hair, which had been kept long according to cultural tradition, was discrimination on the basis of race (*Australian Christian College Moreton Ltd & Anor v Taniela*, 2022).

The SDA prohibits discrimination on the ground of sex, sexual orientation, gender identity, intersex status, pregnancy, breastfeeding, and relationship status. Education cases brought under the SDA have been rare. An influential case brought under the *Anti-Discrimination Act 1977* (NSW), however, indicates the discrimination risks inherent in gendered curriculums. In *Haines v Leves* (1987), a girl was found to have been treated less favourably in that the elective subject options available to her at her all-girls state school were different from that the subject options available to her brother at his all-boys school. She had wanted to study industrial design subjects which was available only at the boys' school—her school offered home economics subjects instead. The SDA allows single sex schools (see section 21(3)). The Act is currently the subject of some controversy in that it allows religious schools to discriminate against students on the ground of sexual orientation, gender identity, marital or relationship status, or pregnancy (see section 38(3)). This controversy will be addressed further, below.

The DDA prohibits discrimination on the ground of disability which is very broadly defined to cover physical, intellectual, sensory, psychiatric, and behavioural impairments which are current or past, temporary, or on-going or intermittent (see section 4). It also obliges the making of reasonable adjustments for people with disabilities (see sections 5 and 6). The *Disability Standards for Education 2005* (DSE; Cth) were enacted with the aim of providing clarity for education institutions about the scope of reasonable adjustments. They articulate access rights in respect of the delivery of key aspects of education: enrolment, participation, curriculum development, delivery and assessment, and services and facilities. They oblige reasonable adjustments in relation to those key aspects so that students with disability can enjoy education rights "on the same basis" as students without disability (para 3.3).

The DDA has had some success in compelling schools to adapt their facilities to support inclusion of students with mobility impairments (e.g., *Hills Grammar School v Human Rights and Equal Opportunity Commission*, 2000; *Travers v New South Wales*, 2001; *Burns v Director General of the Department of Education*, 2015). Deaf students have also brought successful claims compelling the provision of Auslan interpretation at mainstream schools (e.g., *Clarke v Catholic Education Office*, 2003; *Hurst and Devlin v Education Queensland*, 2005; *Hurst v State of Queensland*, 2006). Where students have been excluded because their disability causes challenging behaviour which may disrupt the learning environment or pose a safety risk, however, Australian courts have consistently denied a remedy (Dickson, 2022a). The approach of the courts in these cases is explained further below. It should be noted that separate schools for students with disability, antithetical to inclusion, are currently tolerated in the Australian education system, and students with disability related challenging behaviour who are excluded from mainstream schools may be required to be enrolled in these segregated schools instead (e.g., *Minns v State of New South Wales*, 2002; *Purvis v New South Wales*, 2003).

The ADA prohibits discrimination on the ground of age but, in the context of education, allows education bodies to set age thresholds for enrolment during the compulsory phases of education (section 26(3)). In the case *Gupta v State of South Australia* (2014), this section was available to the state to authorise the refusal to enrol an academically 'advanced' student at primary school at the age of four. It appears that the ADA will not require schools to be *inclusive* to the extent that they must create class groups based on objective ability rather than age.

Varieties of Discrimination

Discrimination is prohibited by all four Acts in the protected area of education: RDA section 9, SDA section 21, DDA section 22, and ADA section 26. All Acts contemplate that unlawful discrimination may arise via failure to enrol, exclusion, or denial of educational benefits or opportunities. The Acts prohibit two varieties of discrimination: direct and indirect. Other varieties of offensive behaviour which may erode inclusion, such as harassment and victimisation, are also be prohibited (e.g., DDA sections 37 and 42).

Direct discrimination is, essentially, unequal treatment: a student, because of their protected attribute, is treated 'less favourably' than a student without that protected attribute. A different formula is used in the RDA—treatment must have "the purpose or effect of nullifying or impairing the recognition, enjoyment or exercise, on an equal footing, of any human right or fundamental freedom in the political, economic, social, cultural or any other field of public life" (section 9). The International *Convention on the Elimination of All Forms of Racial Discrimination* (CERD; United Nations, 1965) is attached as a schedule to the RDA and, relevantly, sets out the right to equality before the law and allied political, civil, and economic rights. A straightforward example of direct discrimination would be to refuse enrolment to a student because they are Asian, gay, transgender, or because they have a disability—when students who are not Asian, gay, transgender, or who do not have a disability are offered enrolment. Such a refusal would, prima facie, be less favourable treatment, and for the RDA, it would also impair the right to education as articulated in CERD Article 5(e)(v).

By contrast, indirect discrimination occurs when all students are unreasonably treated in the same way, but that treatment has a disparate, negative impact on a student because of their protected attribute. Inflexible policies and procedures may thoughtlessly manifest as indirect discrimination. If a school building is accessible only by steps, for example, a student who uses a wheelchair may be denied appropriate access. If students are required to use 'girls' or 'boys' toilets based on their sex assigned at birth, students who identify as transgender may be disadvantaged.

As noted above, in the context of disability discrimination, schools have an obligation not only to avoid discrimination but also to make 'reasonable adjustments' for students (DSE). A failure to make reasonable adjustments may result in either direct or indirect discrimination. For example, failure to make reasonable adjustments to a school campus to facilitate wheelchair access for a student with mobility impairment may result in de facto less favourable treatment of that student in that they are excluded from the school—this is direct discrimination. It may also result in an unreasonable condition being imposed that the student must be able to climb steps in order to attend the school—this is indirect discrimination.

Exemptions

Legislation does not guarantee inclusion or a freedom from discrimination. It may have a stipulated aim of protecting rights to equality, but it does not guarantee that such rights will always be respected. Indeed, to give an example from the DDA (as noted, above), the legislation aims to eliminate discrimination only "as far as possible" (section 3(a)) and to protect rights "as far as practicable" (section 3(b)). As such, there is an upfront acknowledgment that discriminatory treatment and a breach of education rights may, in some circumstances, be tolerated as lawful. In the context of indirect discrimination, for example, the discrimination must be "not reasonable" before it will be unlawful (DDA, section 6). The legislation also allows exemptions from liability for discrimination in certain contexts. If maintaining the enrolment of a student with disability would cause "unjustifiable hardship" to a school, for example, exclusion will be lawful (DDA, sections 11 and 29A). 'Reasonableness' and 'hardship' are *rubbery* terms and are determined according to the individual facts of individual cases. Matters relevant to proof of either or both can overlap. The impact of the discrimination on the student and whether it could be avoided by alternative action are relevant. So too are impact on others in a school community if the discrimination is removed and the cost of removing the discrimination would cause hardship. It should be noted that unjustifiable hardship is an exemption limited to disability discrimination. Reasonableness is currently most contentious in that context. Not only because of the reasonableness limit on indirect discrimination, but also because of the obligation placed on schools to make reasonable adjustments for students with disability. As will be discussed in more detail, below, reasonableness criteria may also be of emerging significance in the context of the inclusion of students who identify as transgender.

The Exclusion of Students with Disability Related Challenging Behaviour

It could be argued that the DDA has been successful in protecting the education rights of students with 'uncontroversial' disabilities such as the students who brought successful claims based on mobility impairment in *Hills Grammar School v Human Rights and Equal Opportunity Commission* (2000) and *Travers v New South Wales* (2001). Such students now do not often need to go to court to secure non-discriminatory treatment at school. For the last 20 years, most litigation arising under the DDA has concerned students whose disability manifests as challenging behaviour. For the students in these cases, the DDA has been less successful. Even the DSE with its promise of reasonable adjustments has not improved their prospects of inclusion.

The seminal case in respect of challenging behaviour is *Purvis v State of New South Wales* (*Purvis*, 2003). That case concerned a 12-year-old boy, Daniel Hoggan, who had been enrolled in year 7 at a regular high school. Daniel had sustained brain damage after contracting encephalitis as a baby. The damage manifested, relevantly, as dis-inhibited behaviour with Daniel, from time to time, lashing out physically at others in the school community and at their property. After a series of suspensions for violence, Daniel was notified that his enrolment would be terminated, and he would be enrolled instead at a segregated school. At first instance, the Human Rights and Equal Opportunity Commission (HREOC), which heard the matter, found that Daniel had been the victim of direct discrimination. He had been treated less favourably than a student without his disability would have been treated. The Commission also found that the school could have done more to support school staff to support Daniel, minimising triggers to violent behaviour (see *Purvis v New South Wales Department of Education (No 2)*, 2000). The case was appealed up the federal court hierarchy to the High Court of Australia. A majority of the High Court found that there had been no less favourable treatment of Daniel. Two key constructions of the legislation supported this finding. First, in order to prove "less favourable treatment", a comparison of the treatment of the complainant and a person without the complainant's disability must be conducted in "circumstances which are not materially different". HREOC had accepted that the relevant comparison should be made with a person without Daniel's disability, and without the problematic behaviour that was caused by the disability. The High Court majority judges found, however, that in order to render the circumstances "not materially different", the comparison should be made with a person without the disability but with the challenging behaviour. Because that comparator would also have been excluded, the majority judges found, there was no less favourable treatment of Daniel. This comparison ignores, of course, the fact that while Daniel's behaviour was intrinsic to his disability, the comparator's bad behaviour would be a choice and controllable.

Secondly, the High Court majority found that for discrimination to be "on the ground of disability", disability must be the cause of the discrimination, its "true basis". In Daniel's case, the majority judges found that the school principal's decision to exclude was caused by the risk Daniel's violence posed to others and not his disability. The principal had a legal duty to protect others from Daniel. Once again, this construction of the terms of the DDA ignores the fact that Daniel's behaviour was intrinsic to his disability. Chief Justice Gleeson made the clear point, however, that the *Purvis* case concerned a clash between competing rights:

> The present case [*Purvis*] illustrates that rights, recognised by international norms, or by domestic law, may conflict. In construing the Act [the DDA], there is no warrant for an assumption that, in seeking to protect the rights of disabled pupils, Parliament intended to disregard Australia's obligations to protect the rights of other pupils. (p. 98)

The minority judges in *Purvis*, like HREOC, thought that the school could have done more to support Daniel, to mitigate the violence. The *Purvis* decision was a prompt to the insertion of the obligation to make reasonable adjustments in the DDA. But the scope of reasonable adjustments has also been affected by narrow construction of the relevant provisions by the courts (Dickson, 2022a). Under the *Equality Act 2010 United Kingdom* (EAUK), an equivalent obligation to make reasonable adjustments is created as a stand-alone duty (section 20), supplementing prohibitions on direct (section 13), and indirect discrimination (section 19). However, the obligation in the DDA was retrofitted to the Act in 2009 (*Disability Discrimination and Other Human Rights Legislation Amendment Act 2009*; Cth) and requires for a remedy that the failure to make reasonable adjustments results in either direct or indirect discrimination. In the case *Sklavos v Australasian College of Dermatologists* (2017), the Full Federal Court found, counter intuitively, that for a failure to make reasonable adjustments to result in direct discrimination, the failure must have been on the ground of the disability. Such a failure, of course, would typically be because of cost or inconvenience and not on the ground of a student's disability. Further, the Full Court found that, in respect of indirect discrimination, if a potentially discriminatory condition was found to be 'reasonable', there was no need to even consider whether reasonable adjustments had been made. Under the EAUK, failure to make reasonable adjustments is of itself a variety of discrimination, independent of direct or indirect discrimination (sections 21 and 22). The DDA should be amended to adopt a similar approach.

It is noteworthy that the High Court was not able to rely on the unjustifiable hardship exemption to authorise Daniel's exclusion in the *Purvis* case. Like the obligation to make reasonable adjustments, availability of the unjustifiable hardship exemption post enrolment had initially been 'left out' of the DDA. Post *Purvis*, in 2009, that deficiency was also remedied. Despite the 2009 amendments, however, challenging behaviour cases continue to fail because issues of hardship and reasonableness are redundant when courts, applying the *Purvis* construction of the comparator and causation, find there has been no discrimination in the first place.

An indirect discrimination case concerning challenging behaviour was litigated at around the same time as *Purvis*. In that case, the Court rejected a finding of indirect discrimination in that it was 'reasonable' to impose a condition that students comply with a school behaviour code modified for the student's disability. In *Minns v State of New South Wales* (2002), the school had adjusted the code to account for the effects of the student's neurodiversity and the Court found that nothing further was required of the school. Once again, the rights of the majority trumped the complainant's right to inclusion. Federal Magistrate Raphael said in that case:

> I am of the view that the requirement that was placed upon Ryan to comply with each of the school's disciplinary policies as modified was reasonable in all the circum-stances. The classes in which Ryan was placed would be unable to function if he could not be removed for disruptive behaviour. The students could not achieve their poten-tial if most of the teachers' time was taken up with handling Ryan. The playgrounds would not be safe if Ryan was allowed free rein for his aggressive actions. (para 263)

The "reasonableness" enquiry for indirect discrimination, and since 2005 for the DSE, and since 2009 for "reasonable adjustments", requires a balancing of the competing interests of the student with disability and the interests of other students and staff. Where a safety risk is demonstrated, or even a disruption to the learning environment, repeated cases since *Purvis* and *Minns* have found that the balance will tip against the student with disability (e.g., *Walker v State of Victoria*, 2011; *Abela v State of Victoria*, 2013; *Kiefel v State of Victoria*, 2013; *Connor v State of Queensland*, 2020). Courts have proved unwilling to make decisions which would disrupt traditional teaching methods, and some judges have explicitly rejected the proposition that the courts should be used to compel changes to the education system, which may better support students with complex behavioural issues caused by disability (*Hurst and Devlin v Education Queens-land*, 2005; Dickson, 2022b). Students with disability in the United Kingdom may ben-efit from the fact that allegations of discrimination in education in that jurisdiction are heard by a specialist tribunal, the Special Educational Needs and Disability Tribunal, where, unlike Australian federal judges, the decision makers have education expertise (Dickson, 2022b).

Gender Identity and Discrimination

How the educational rights and welfare of students who identify as transgender and/or non-binary are protected at school is an emerging inclusion issue. Australian youth mental health research institute, Orygen (2022), has reported that:

> [f]eeling unsafe or uncomfortable in educational settings can directly impact school attendance: almost two-thirds of transgender women, more than half of transgender

men, and 45% of non-binary participants reported missing day/s at their educational setting in the past 12 months for this reason.

Discrimination on the basis of "gender identity" is prohibited in Australia by the SDA (section 5B). Gender identity is defined broadly to "mean the gender-related identity, appearance or mannerisms or other gender-related characteristics of a person (whether by way of medical intervention or not), with or without regard to the person's designated sex at birth" (section 4). As such, the definition covers people who identify as transgender and/or non-binary as their gender does not align with their "designated sex at birth". The relevant protected attribute in the EAUK, gender reassignment, is defined differently as applying to anyone who "is undergoing, has undergone or is proposing to undergo a process [or part of a process] of reassigning their sex by changing physiological or other attributes" (section 7). Note that both definitions are broad enough to cover students who have socially transitioned but who have not yet confirmed that transition medically or legally.

There is currently no Australian federal case law arising from claims alleging discrimination by schools against students on the ground of gender identity. This position may change. In the same way as women, and students with disability, and racial minority groups have done before them, people who identify as transgender are beginning to press their rights to education inclusion. Several students and ex-students of Brisbane's Citipointe School, for example, have reportedly launched legal action against that school over its policies in relation to gay and students who identify as transgender (Smee, 2022). At the time of writing, a transgender girl is awaiting hearing of her complaint that the all-girls Brisbane school, Carinity Education Southside, refused her application for enrolment (Wang, 2022). While both these cases have reportedly been brought under state legislation, the *Anti-Discrimination Act 1991* (Qld), it may be inferred that cases brought under the SDA are likely to emerge too. Although there is a current paucity of relevant case law, the legislation underpinning the rights of people who identify as transgender, and how it may be applied, can be explained.

Enrolment of Transgender and Non-Binary Students

It seems clear that for a co-educational school to refuse enrolment to a student who identifies as transgender because they identify as transgender would constitute direct discrimination on the basis of gender identity. Issues potentially arise for transgender students, however, in the context of single sex schools. The SDA allows a school to refuse enrolment if it "is conducted solely for students of a different sex from the sex of the applicant" (section 21(3)(a)). Subject to any available exemption (see religious exemptions addressed, below), it would likely be unlawful direct discrimination on the ground of gender identity to refuse to enrol a transgender girl at an all-girls school, or a transgender boy at an all-boys school, in that the student's gender identity aligns with the *sex* of the school. There is a possibility that a cynical statutory interpretation argument might be derived from the fact that "sex" is not defined in the SDA.

In conjunction with the use of the phrase "different sex" (section 21(3)(a)) the argument could, perhaps, be made that for the SDA "sex" is not confined to a binary male/female choice, and a student who identifies as transgender is a different "sex" for the purpose of enrolment at school. The equivalent exemption in the EAUK uses the terminology "opposite sex" (schedule 11) adopting a binary understanding of sex. For that Act, it would be more difficult to argue that a transgender girl was not a girl for the purpose of the single sex exemption. Ironically, when gender identity was inserted as a protected attribute into the SDA, by the *Sex Discrimination Amendment (Sexual Orientation, Gender Identity and Intersex Status) Act 2013*, section 21(3)(a) of the SDA was amended to change "opposite sex" to "different sex". Indeed, it was stipulated in the *Explanatory Memorandum to the Act* (2013), that the amendment was made to "ensure" the provision recognition that "a person may be, or identify as, neither male nor female" (para 61). The position of a student seeking enrolment at a single sex school who identifies as non-binary is, as such, similarly complicated. If a student identifies as neither a boy nor a girl, then it could also be argued, for the purpose of section 21(3)(a) of the SDA, that they are "of a different sex". In that situation, should the applicant wish to continue with the enrolment, they may need to consider making the uncomfortable decision to rely on their "sex designated at birth".

Curiously, if a student identifies as transgender and/or non-binary after being enrolled at an Australian single sex school, such that their gender identity no longer aligns with the sex of the school, the SDA single sex school exemption will not apply—it is limited by the terms of section 21(3)(a) to the point of enrolment. This is despite the fact that transitioning post-enrolment is potentially more problematic for a school as it may now have to make rapid and reactive adjustments to its facilities and protocols to accommodate the student who identifies as transgender and/or non-binary. The equivalent exemption in the EAUK is similarly limited to 'admission'. The only potential exemption that may apply here is the religious schools' exemption, addressed below.

Discrimination Against Students Who Identify as Transgender and/or Non-Binary Arising from School Policies and Facilities

Issues may arise during their enrolment which threaten the inclusion of a student who identifies as transgender and/or non-binary. Unfortunately, there is not room in this chapter to consider all the ways students who identify as transgender may encounter discrimination at school. While it should be acknowledged that careless use of pronouns, and school sport and uniform requirements are all potentially problematic, this chapter will focus on one issue which seems to have garnered significant controversy in Australian schools—toilets and change facilities (Stark, 2017; Bennett et al., 2019; Baker, 2022; Davis, 2022). A school policy that requires students who identify as transgender to use facilities that align with their birth sex may amount to unlawful indirect discrimination. In any enquiry into the 'reasonableness' of such a requirement, a dominant consideration would clearly be the objective anguish caused to students who identify as transgender by that requirement. On that basis such a policy would likely be found by a court to be unreasonable. That does not mean, however, that a court would automatically find that a student who identifies as transgender must be able to use facilities which align with their gender. Because of age limits on the opportunity to medically affirm a sex change, many transgender female school students will still be 'biologically male'. Traditionally, segregated spaces like toilets and change rooms have been a focus of controversy more broadly than the school context, with high profile 'feminists' such as J. K. Rowling making an argument that allowing transgender women in "women only" spaces raises a safety risk for "natal girls and women" (Rowling, 2020). Such an analysis positions transgender women as cynically manipulating their own gender to threaten "real women". Legal proof of risk would require objective evidence and not mere speculation driven by misunderstanding, misinformation, or prejudice. In analogous disability discrimination cases concerning risks posed by student behaviour, for example, there has been evidence adduced of the detrimental impact of that behaviour on others in the school community (e.g., *Minns v State of New South Wales*, 2002; *Purvis v State of New South Wales*, 2003; *Connor v State of Queensland*, 2020).

A 'solution' may be to provide gender-neutral facilities, available to all students but mandatory for students who identify as transgender and/or non-binary. This may still be discriminatory, however, as male and female students would each have two options, while students who identify as transgender and/or non-binary would be treated less favourably in that they have only the gender-neutral option. Universal design is likely the best 'solution'—make all facilities gender-neutral, incorporating private, single person toilet stalls and change rooms. Unfortunately, even this approach has been criticised. The Queensland Government, for example, abandoned plans for such facilities at a new school as "a recipe for disaster" after concerns were raised about "bullying" if girls and boys were required to share "unisex" toilets (Bennett et al., 2019). Surely, clever design can deliver safe spaces to be shared by all?

"Gender Dysphoria" and the DDA

Whether transgender identity is emergent evidence of a fundamental, historical misunderstanding of gender as limited to the binary choice, male or female, or a manifestation of an underlying gender dysphoria, remains contested. "Gender dysphoria" is included, however, in the *Diagnostic and Statistical Manual of Mental Disorders*, 5th Edition (American Psychiatric Association, 2013, 302.85). While the "diagnosis and treatment of gender dysphoria" are the subject of "emerging debate" (*Imogen (No. 6)*, 2020), the condition is likely within the scope of paragraph (g) of the definition of disability in section 4 of the DDA: it may be positioned as "a disorder, illness or disease that affects a person's thought processes, perception of reality, emotions or judgment or that results in disturbed behaviour". Further, students who identify as transgender attending high school may have commenced gender transition treatment consistent with the *Australian Standards of Care and Treatment Guidelines: For Transgender and Gender Diverse Children and Adolescents* (Telfer et al., 2020). There is also significant evidence that people who identify as transgender and/or non-binary are more likely to be affected by mental health issues such as anxiety and depression, compounding their vulnerability (Orygen, 2022). While people who identify as transgender and/or non-binary may object to being characterised as 'having a disability', there are some potential protections which flow from being within the scope of both the DDA and the SDA. At a minimum, schools will be required to be proactive about making reasonable adjustments for students who identify as transgender and/or non-binary consistent with the DSE. As noted above, "reasonable adjustments" compel proactive rather than merely reactive changes to policy and practice.

Religion and Discrimination

The SDA allows "[e]ducational institutions established for religious purposes" to discriminate against students on the ground of sexual orientation, gender identity, marital or relationship status, or pregnancy, where the discrimination is in "good faith in order to avoid injury to the religious susceptibilities of adherents of that religion or creed" (section 38(3)). This exemption is likely broad enough to allow a school to discriminate against a student who identifies as transgender and/or non-binary, if that gender status is not compatible with the religious beliefs promulgated by the school, by refusing enrolment, exclusion, and in the delivery of education during enrolment. By contrast, the equivalent exemption in the EAUK, is stated more narrowly and exempts religious schools from prohibitions on discrimination only "in relation to anything done in connection with acts of worship or other religious observance organised by or on behalf of a school" (schedule 11, clause 6).

At the time of writing, this section of the SDA has never been litigated in the context of discrimination against students. This does not mean, however, that schools have not used it as a weapon to refuse enrolment. Not every victim of discrimination has the will or the means to complain let alone to take their complaint to court (Dickson, 2022b). The exemption is controversial in that it privileges the protection of religious belief above the education rights of children. In 2018, a private members bill which would have repealed the exemption was abandoned (see *Sex Discrimination Amendment (Removing Discrimination Against Students) Bill 2018*; Cth).

Balancing Rights

Concerns about the appropriateness of the exemption have been caught up in an ongoing debate in Australia about whether and how Australia should legislate to protect religious freedom. Freedom of religion legislation put before parliament by the previous Australian government (*Religious Discrimination Bill 2022*; Cth) was abandoned by that government because it would not accept a majority view in the House of Representatives that section 38(3) of the SDA should be repealed. The current Australian government has, however, signaled an intention to repeal that section in that they have referred it to the Australian Law Reform Commission for consultation (see *Australian*

Law Reform Commission, Religious Educational Institutions and Anti-Discrimination Laws, Consultation Paper, 2023, Proposition B).

Conclusion

This chapter has covered two situations where inclusion tests the limits of the law: the accommodation of students with disability related challenging behaviour, and the accommodation of students who identify as transgender and/or non-binary. What many may not realise, however, is that while the law may allow exclusion in these situations, it does not mandate it. Schools are free to enrol students with challenging behaviour and to develop strategies to support inclusion. Religious schools are free to enrol students who identify as transgender and/or non-binary and to provide adjustments to their policies and practices to support them. Moreover, social change may occur more rapidly than legislative change delivering a misalignment between what is expected by society and what the law tolerates. Calls for law reform to address the erosion of the obligation to make reasonable adjustments delivered by the decision in the *Sklavos* case have not yet been actioned by government. Calls for the religious exemption in the SDA to be repealed are only now being actioned by government.

Public outcry over the Citpointe school case, referred to above, shows that people power can sometimes work more effectively than the law to deliver education rights. The school maintained that their approach to students who identify as gay and transgender was consistent with what the law allowed, and whether that is correct will be determined only when and if the matter proceeds to hearing. Nevertheless, community outrage compelled the school to retreat from its hardline position informed by religious doctrine and the principal of the school resigned.

References

Abela v State of Victoria [2013] FCA 832.
Age Discrimination Act 2004 (Cth).
American Psychiatric Association. (2013). *Diagnostic and statistical manual of mental disorders* (5th ed., 302.85). https://doi.org/10.1176/appi.books.9780890425596
Anti-Discrimination Act 1977 (NSW).
Anti-Discrimination Act 1991 (Qld).
Australian Christian College Moreton Ltd & Anor v Taniela, 2022 [2022] QCATA 118.
Australian Constitution (Cth).
Australian Law Reform Commission. (2023). *Religious educational institutions and anti-discrimination laws: Consultation paper.* https://www.alrc.gov.au/inquiry/anti-discrimination-laws/
Baker, J. (2022, February 11). Uniforms and toilets: How single-sex schools respond to transgender students. *Sydney Morning Herald.* https://www.smh.com.au/national/nsw/uniforms-and-toilets-how-single-sex-schools-respond-to-transgender-students-20220210-p59vfw.html
Bennett, S., Marszalek, J., & Ball, R. (2019, December 8). "Ridiculous": Unisex toilets for students at new Brisbane high school. *The Courier Mail.* https://www.couriermail.com.au/news/

queensland/ridiculous-unisex-toilets-for-students-at-new-brisbane-high-school/news-story/0f
ee2f3c7931dcaf8e979d34dea1617c

Bruch v Commonwealth of Australia [2002] FMCA 29.

Burns v Director General of the Department of Education [2015] FCCA 1769.

Clarke v Catholic Education Office [2003] FCA 1085.

Connor v State of Queensland [2020] FCA 455.

Davis, M. (2022, March 11). Angry parents slam Sydney primary school after it installs a gender-neutral toilet and say it's an attempt to encourage transgender transitioning. *Daily Mail*. https://www.dailymail.co.uk/news/article-10599977/Parents-slam-Mona-Vale-Public-School-new-gender-mixed-toilets-prompting-Mark-Latham-weigh-in.html

Dickson, E. (2022a). Barriers to inclusion embedded in the Disability Discrimination Act 1992 (Cth). *Australian Journal of Education, 66*(3), 265–280. https://doi.org/10.1177/0004944 1221127708

Dickson, E. (2022b). Legal system barriers to the effectiveness of the Disability Discrimination Act 1992 (Cth) as a support for the inclusion of students with disability. Australian Journal of Education, 66(3), 281–291. https://doi.org/10.1177/00049441221127706

Disability Discrimination Act 1992 (Cth).

Disability Discrimination and Other Human Rights Legislation Amendment Act 2009 (Cth).

Disability Standards for Education 2005 (Cth).

Equality Act 2010 (United Kingdom).

Gupta v State of South Australia [2014] FCCA 414.

Haines v Leves (1987) 8 NSWLR 442.

Hills Grammar School v Human Rights and Equal Opportunity Commission (2000) 100 FCR 306.

Hurst and Devlin v Education Queensland [2005] FCA 405.

Hurst v State of Queensland [2006] FCAFC 100.

Imogen (No. 6) [2020] FamCA 761.

Kiefel v State of Victoria [2013] FCA 1398.

Mandla v Dowell Lee (1983) 2 AC 548.

Miller v Wertheim [2002] FCAFC 156.

Minns v State of New South Wales [2002] FMCA 60.

Orygen. (2022). *Mental health and suicide risk in trans and gender-diverse young people*. https://www.orygen.org.au/About/News-And-Events/2022/Mental-health-and-suicide-risk-in-trans-and-gender#:~:text=Indeed%2C%20the%20Trans%20Pathways%20study,attempted%20suicide%20or%20self%2Dharmed

Purvis v New South Wales Department of Education (No 2) [2000] HREOCA 47.

Purvis v State of New South Wales [2003] 217 CLR 92.

Racial Discrimination Act 1975 (Cth).

Religious Discrimination Bill 2022 (Cth).

Rowling, J. K. (2020, June 10). *J. K. Rowling writes about her reasons for speaking out on sex and gender issues*. https://www.jkrowling.com/opinions/j-k-rowling-writes-about-her-reasons-for-speaking-out-on-sex-and-gender-issues/

Sex Discrimination Act 1984 (Cth).

Sex Discrimination Amendment (Removing Discrimination Against Students) Bill 2018 (Cth).

Sex Discrimination Amendment (Sexual Orientation, Gender Identity and Intersex Status) Act 2013 (Cth).

Sex Discrimination Amendment (Sexual Orientation, Gender Identity and Intersex Status) Bill 2013 (Cth) Explanatory Memorandum.

Sklavos v Australasian College of Dermatologists [2017] 256 FCR 247.

Smee, B. (2022, May 26). Citipointe College referred to Human Rights Commission over withdrawn student enrolment contracts. *The Guardian.* https://www.theguardian.com/australia-news/2022/may/26/citipointe-college-referred-to-human-rights-commission-over-withdrawn-student-enrolment-contracts

Stark, J. (2017, April 1). For some transgender students, the school bathroom is a battleground. *ABC News.* https://www.abc.net.au/news/2017-04-01/transgender-students-bathroom-battle-ground/8395782

Telfer, M. M., Tollit, M. A., Pace, C. C., & Pang, K. C. (2020). *Australian Standards of Care and Treatment Guidelines: For trans and gender diverse children and adolescents Version 1.3.* The Royal Children's Hospital. https://www.rch.org.au/uploadedFiles/Main/Content/adolescent-medicine/australian-standards-of-care-and-treatment-guidelines-for-trans-and-gender-diverse-children-and-adolescents.pdf

Travers v New South Wales [2001] FMCA 18.

United Nations. (1965). *International Convention on the Elimination of All Forms of Racial Discrimination* (CERD). https://www.ohchr.org/sites/default/files/cerd.pdf

United Nations. (2006). *Convention on the Rights of Persons with Disabilities (CRPD).* https://www.un.org/disabilities/documents/convention/convoptprot-e.pdf.

United Nations. (2016). *General Comment No. 4, Article 24: Right to Inclusive Education.* (CRPD/C/GC/4). https://digitallibrary.un.org/record/1313836?ln=en

Walker v State of Victoria [2011] FCA 258.

Wang, J. (2022, August 18). Carinity Education Southside: Mum of transgender girl slams school for discrimination. *News.com.* https://www.news.com.au/lifestyle/parenting/school-life/carinity-education-southside-mum-of-transgender-girl-slams-school-for-discrimination/news-story/0ea22e44ddb8eea945c725a2a13fcedc

Chapter 6

Inclusive education

A review of the evidence

Kate de Bruin

At its heart, the rationale for transforming education systems away from a dual track of mainstream and segregated settings is based in binding international human-rights obligations under the *Convention on the Rights of Persons with Disabilities* (CRPD; United Nations, 2006), which has been signed and ratified by 186 countries, including Australia (Chapter 3). However, the case for inclusive education is also grounded in research evidence which is outlined within this chapter and shows that inclusion is both achievable and desirable. It is this evidence which forms the focus of this chapter. In the sections that follow, I first examine some of the assumptions that inform popular beliefs about the need for segregation. I then present an updated summary of research findings based on the literature investigating outcomes from segregated and regular education environments and examine whether these assumptions hold up under scrutiny. I conclude by summing up the key lessons from research about how to provide quality teaching and personalised support for students with disability in regular schools and classrooms to support optimal academic, social, and post-school outcomes. I also offer some of the key implications arising from the review regarding teacher preparation and educational policy.

What Are the Assumptions about Segregated Special Education?

Assumption 1: Segregated Settings Can Be Inclusive

One assumption that often underpins arguments about segregated special education settings such as special schools and classrooms is that these can be inclusive by virtue of the fact that they specifically cater for and/or do not exclude students with disabilities. Proponents of this view, often those with interests in the maintenance of segregated education, draw on an old motto from the integration era that "inclusion is a process, not a place". As discussed in Chapter 2, this term was originally coined by inclusive education scholars and disability activists to protest the effects of the integration movement. It was never the intention of those who coined the phrase to imply that place does not matter, but rather that it is not sufficient. Integration (otherwise known as mainstreaming) failed students with disability because while physical access may have been provided, there was little change in school and classroom environments, and this left major attitudinal and pedagogical barriers in place. The "process, not place" phrase

DOI: 10.4324/9781003350897-7

has since been misappropriated by special education lobby groups to claim that segregated schools *can* be inclusive, for if "inclusion is not a place" then any place can be an inclusive one provided "they are inclusive in their nature" (Forbes, 2007, p. 68).

This ambiguity has recently been addressed through the move to explicitly define inclusive education in *General Comment No. 4* (GC4; United Nations, 2016). As discussed in Chapter 3, GC4 explains the right to inclusive education as per Article 24 of CRPD. Not only is inclusive education now defined within international human-rights law, but GC4 has also made it very clear that segregation and inclusion are fundamentally incompatible. No longer is it possible to claim that special schools and classes are inclusive, and nor does mere placement within regular schools constitute an inclusive education, although it *is a necessary precondition* for inclusive education to take place (de Bruin, 2019).

Assumption 2: Segregation Is Better for Children with Disability

Another common belief is that segregated special education is better for students with a disability. This is often accompanied by anecdotes to suggest that:

(1) students with disability cannot thrive in regular schools (e.g., Lawrenson, 2022),
(2) access to appropriately targeted teaching, support, and resources is only feasible in segregated settings (e.g., Bita, 2022), and
(3) students with disability impede teachers in mainstream settings from providing a quality education to non-disabled students, or hold other students back (e.g., Gilmour, 2017; Secret Teacher, 2015).

Such beliefs generate anxiety about the fairness and/or feasibility of inclusion and the capacity of teachers in regular schools and classrooms to teach students with disabilities effectively at the same time as teaching the whole class. Importantly, these beliefs are founded on a set of unspoken and unexamined presumptions that the needs of students with disability are special and fundamentally different from those of non-disabled students. These are used to justify the specialness of special segregated education as a benevolent, nurturing form of intensive care or treatment that is provided by teachers with specialist training.

What Is the Evidence for Segregated Special Education?

Some argue that the evidence for inclusion is an ideological position without strong foundation and is not sufficiently convincing or methodologically robust to warrant a change (e.g., Kemp 2022a, 2022b; Stephenson & Ganguly, 2022). Those espousing this view tend to adopt a rhetorical stance demanding that those advocating for change should bear the burden of proof and must meet a high threshold for the quality of that evidence before change can be justified. Robust evidence in favour of the status quo is seldom offered, and the maintenance of segregation is argued on the basis that the case for change is not strong (e.g., Stephenson & Ganguly, 2022), in lieu of providing evidence that segregation produces good outcomes.

A similar conclusion was reached in a recent scoping review of academic and social outcomes from mainstream and segregated placements for the *Disability Royal Commission*. The authors, McVilly et al. (2022), reviewed a set of studies limited to those published post 2006 (p. 114). The McVilly et al. study was a not a full systematic review of mainstream and segregated outcomes, as it focused solely on outcomes for students with "profound/severe disability", which was defined as:

> a broader category than low-incidence disability which, in the US, is defined as occurring in less than 1% of the population. It consists of vision or hearing impairment or simultaneous vision and hearing impairment; significant cognitive impairment; or any impairment for which a small number of personnel with highly specialised skills and knowledge are needed for children with that impairment to receive an appropriate education (p. 85).

This review, limited in both breadth and scope, concluded that "no greater academic benefit attaches to either setting", and that "we have not achieved reliable enough results from interventions for general recommendations to be made" (p. 114). Concerningly, this equivocal finding could well be mistaken as justifying the maintenance of the status-quo in Australia of a dual-track system of mainstream and special, even though it did not find definitive benefits to justify segregating students with profound/severe disability.

Readers of this book will know this group of students as those with complex learning profiles,[1] and those reading Chapter 12 will know how these students can be included in grade-level academic curriculum. These practices are not as widespread as they need to be for research to detect the positive benefits of authentic inclusive education where relevant extensive adjustments are made and students are provided with the supports they require to learn alongside their same-age peers. McVilly et al. emphasised the need for further high-quality research to provide a more comprehensive evidence base to support the inclusion of students with complex learning profiles. It is important for such research to be conducted by using rigorous methods to minimise bias and produce robust findings to guide policy and practice. As such research takes time to come to fruition, it is important to continue looking to findings internationally. I provide an updated review of the evidence for all students, including those with complex learning profiles where that evidence is available.

---

1 The term complex learning profile is defined in the glossary at the beginning of this book. It is worth noting that much of the literature specifically addressing these students can use ableist terms such as *educable mentally retarded*, *low functioning*, or *severe*, e.g., *severely autistic* or *severe intellectual disability*. Typically, these terms refer to the categorisation of students using adaptive or IQ scores, which are documented to be highly problematic, based on assessments developed during the peak of eugenics, and bearing little relevance to instruction, communication, mobility, or social support requirements. For a longer explanation of this, see de Bruin (2022a). From this point onwards in the chapter, the term 'complex learning profiles' will be used as an umbrella term to collectively refer to students requiring support across multiple domains or requiring intensive support within a single domain, both of which are variously referred to as severe or complex disabilities in research literature.

Review Methods

The summary of research findings presented in this chapter is not a systematic re-view, however, every effort was made to ensure that the search was as comprehensive as possible, and that data extraction preserved the findings and minimised bias. The studies were located by searching in ERIC via ProQuest (which is the largest educa-tion database) and A+ education via Informit (which focuses on Australian content). A hand-search was conducted using Google Scholar to check for missed records and an ancestral search of the reference list of included studies was conducted. Where needed, search terms used truncations (word roots ending in *) to capture variations such as differences in spelling, as well as plurals or suffixes. The search began by locating rel-evant studies from the highest level of evidence using the terms 'meta-analysis' and 'sys-tematic review' combined with inclus*, general education, regular, special*, segregat*, student*, learner*, school*, classroom*, impact, effect*, outcome*. An initial set of studies was located using these terms and mined for additional terms that should be added. Through an iterative process, further search terms/synonyms were extracted and added to the search strings, such as: academic, social, wellbeing, bullying, abuse, progress, long-term, and post-school.

Studies were included if the context of interest was general education classrooms within regular schools where students with and without disability were educated to-gether. Studies were excluded if the context of interest was a withdrawal or resource room, or a segregated special education setting such as classrooms, units, or schools that restrict placements to students meeting criteria defined by disability status. Studies were included if the phenomenon of interest was the inclusion of school students with disability and if the population of interest were school students either with or without disability. No date limits or methodological limits were applied and searches for grey lit-erature (e.g., doctoral dissertations, commissioned research, government reports) were conducted to minimise publication bias. A total of 78 items including empirical studies, reviews, and reports were included in the final set of studies for data extraction and review. The findings of 61 of these studies published between 1980 and 2021 were com-bined for reporting in this chapter, and a summary is provided below. They are indicated within the reference list with an asterisk to indicate that they are part of this set. The findings of the remaining 17 studies are not reported here as they focused on topics with more tangential relevance such as funding or enrolment patterns that lay beyond the scope of the chapter, or they reported duplicated findings.

What Is the Impact of Inclusive Education for Students with Disability?

Inclusive education is multidimensional and goes beyond merely accepting the enrol-ment of students with disabilities. Inclusion requires students with and without disabil-ity to be co-located and actively engaged in *learning together* with *appropriate support* and *reasonable adjustments* when and where needed. Because these aspects of any schools involved in research are not always known, I have chosen to refer to the settings cited in studies examining the inclusion of students as *regular schools* and *general education classrooms* as this captures that they are not segregated special education environments but makes no assumptions on their inclusiveness. I report specifically on the *outcomes* examined in these studies. For example, some studies examine social outcomes, including students' self-concept, anxiety, wellbeing, and safety. Others examine academic outcomes such as students' achievement on general tests of achievement such as state tests, within specific curriculum areas such as mathematics, or in specific skills such as reading. Yet other studies examine long-term outcomes arising from the provision of inclusive education, such as school completion rates, participation in post-school education, relationships with others, and engagement in community life. Where possible, I note the relevance of the findings from the research as it applies to students with complex learning profiles as there have been historical assumptions that they are simply too disabled to be included and this has been used to justify segregated education (de Bruin, 2022b). I outline separate summaries of the evidence relating to social outcomes, academic outcomes, and long-term outcomes below.

Impact of Inclusion on Social and Wellbeing Outcomes for Students with Disabilities

Multiple meta-analyses have shown that, in general, educating students with disability within regular schools and classrooms alongside their non-disabled peers results in *improved social and developmental outcomes* (Baker, 1994; Carlberg & Kavale, 1980; Oh-Young & Filler, 2015). These studies from the highest level of evidence show a range of social benefits for students with disability being educated in regular schools and classrooms, such as improved social competence, self-concept, and attitudes to school (Baker, 1994; Carlberg & Kavale, 1980). The early work by Carlberg and Kavale (1980) suggested that while many students with disability benefited socially from being included, students with more complex learning profiles did not. However, the negative finding for this group has not been replicated by another meta-analysis since. Subsequent meta-analyses have suggested that the social outcomes for students with disability are the same in either setting (e.g., Krämer et al., 2021; Wang & Baker, 1985) or better in regular schools (e.g., Baker, 1994), although they do not always disaggregate findings for students with complex learning profiles. Given that this finding by Carlberg and Kavale's (1980) has not been *consistently* supported by other meta-analyses, a reasonable conclusion that can be drawn from this collective body of evidence is that inclusion produces better social outcomes for students with disability in general, and *the same or better* social outcomes for students with complex learning profiles. Clearly there is a need for more high-quality empirical research to be conducted with this population.

Survey research conducted with young people suggests, unsurprisingly, that merely enrolling students with disability into regular schools and classrooms without the support to ensure their inclusion is ineffective on its own in achieving improved outcomes (Nepi et al., 2013). Rather, studies and reviews examining school and classroom practices suggest that the social benefits of including students with disability arises from *positive interactions* between these students and their wider peer group (McGregor &

Vogelsberg, 1998; Oh-Young & Filler, 2015). Importantly, studies show that this also holds true for students with complex learning profiles (e.g., Foreman et al., 2004; Hunt, Farron-Davis, et al., 1994; Kennedy et al., 1997).

Genuine social interactions between students with and without disability have been found to result in improved social competencies, communication skills, and even motor skills (Fisher & Meyer, 2002; Katz et al., 2002; McGregor & Vogelsberg, 1998). The skills for positive interaction are teachable and several effective practices can be employed to teach these in regular schools and classrooms where students with and without disability learn alongside each other. A systematic review by Garrote et al. (2017) identifies these effective practices as including explicitly teaching positive interaction skills to *all* students, as well as modelling examples and providing structured opportunities for purposeful practice to refine and rehearse these skills. This review highlights that it is also important to provide students with disability with access to supplementary and targeted supports for social learning, when appropriate, and to ensure that teaching assistants are well-trained to facilitate and support this positive interaction in the classroom.

Beyond the benefits for discrete social skill development, research also indicates that including students with disability in regular schools and classrooms is associated with improved social outcomes more broadly. For example, studies show that including students with disability in these settings can result in richer and more diverse social networks that include peers both with and without disability, as well as positive and enduring lasting friendships between students with and without disability (Avramidis, 2010; Kennedy et al., 1997; McGregor & Vogelsberg, 1998). These studies include students with complex learning profiles (e.g., Kennedy et al., 1997), and the observed benefits extend to *all* students with disabilities, not just some. Importantly, studies comparing the quality of everyday life for students educated in segregated and regular schools concluded that the increased interaction and stronger social networks in inclusive schools produced meaningful improvements in students' social lives beyond school (Finnvold, 2018; Zurbriggen et al., 2018). Specifically, these studies found that students with disabilities who were included in their local school spent more of their leisure time outside school socialising with their wider peer group, in comparison to their peers in special education settings who largely spent their leisure time with their families (Finnvold, 2018; Zurbriggen et al., 2018). Indeed, a qualitative study exploring the quality of school life of students with disabilities in segregated and regular education settings found that students in the segregated settings were lonelier (Wiener & Tardif, 2004). This is not to say that students with disabilities do not experience loneliness or isolation at school, but rather that loneliness and isolation can be equally as common for both students with and without disabilities (Avramidis, 2010), pointing to the need for educators to actively foster learning environments that facilitate friendship and belonging for students (Chapter 15).

The studies summarised above point to the potential for including students with disability in their local schools to facilitate their connection to their local community. This connection to the local community is vital for building an inclusive society and for improving the quality of life of young people with disability. Research shows that this is also vital for improving these students' safety. While there exists a popular belief that segregated schools and classrooms are safer places for students with disability, studies show that segregation can actually increase the risk of abuse as these restrictive environments separate and isolate children with disability from their local communities and wider society, leaving them more vulnerable to abuse from peers and adults, rather than less (Caldas & Bensy, 2014; Rose, Monda-Amaya, & Espelage, 2011; Royal Commission into Institutional Responses to Child Sexual Abuse, 2017). These studies point to the protective benefits of including students with disability in their local school by reducing that isolation and increasing their connection to peers and visibility within their community.

Moreover, studies indicate that segregation does not protect students from bullying and indeed can increase its likelihood (Norwich & Kelly, 2004; Rose, Monda-Amaya & Espelage, 2011). This is not to say that bullying and abuse do not occur in regular schools. Rather, studies on bullying and the safety of students with disability highlight the importance of fostering their connection to their non-disabled peers and local communities by including them in regular schools and classrooms and establishing environments that minimise the victimisation of any students, particularly those at increased risk (Rose, Espelage, et al., 2011). This points to the importance of building the capacity of teachers in regular schools to create such safe and welcoming environments, and actively facilitate positive interactions and relationships between *all* students in the classroom (Chapter 15).

An important point to be reiterated from the research discussed above is that integrating students with disability into unreconstructed mainstream settings does not lead to improved social outcomes. As discussed in Chapter 2, the term *mainstream* school remains widely used as shorthand to mean 'not a special school' and is frequently used as a synonym for an *inclusive* school; however, the terms are far from synonymous. Mainstream schools are those which have existed since the development of compulsory schooling, and they were not designed with students with disability in mind (de Bruin, 2022a). Inclusion, therefore, must occur at the whole school level. For example, the organisational grouping of students with disabilities should not result in them being grouped into classrooms together for scheduling convenience as this may see the social benefits of inclusion lost (Gottfried, 2014).

Academic Impact of Inclusion for Students with Disabilities

A number of studies, including meta-analyses and cohort analyses, have shown consistently over time that inclusion results in multiple academic benefits for students with disabilities (Baker, 1994; Carlberg & Kavale, 1980; Cole et al., 2021; Cosier et al., 2013; Hehir et al., 2012; Krämer et al., 2021; Oh-Young & Filler, 2015; Ruijs & Peetsma, 2009; Szumski & Karwowski, 2014; Wang & Baker, 1985). Several studies reported improved outcomes from inclusive education for students with disability in terms of general academic achievement on state or national testing (Cole et al., 2021; Hehir,

2012; Krammer et al., 2021; La Salle et al., 2013; Rea et al., 2002). Other studies examined outcomes through measures such as standardised assessments that were skill or discipline-specific, such as reading and mathematics (Cole et al., 2004; Cosier et al., 2013; Dessemontet et al., 2012; Krämer et al., 2021; Oh-Young & Filler, 2015; Ruijs et al., 2010; Szumski et al., 2017). A mix of systematic reviews, cohort and comparative studies have yielded particularly consistent and strong findings on the benefits of inclusion on students' literacy and language skills (Cole et al., 2004; Cosier et al., 2013; Dessemontet et al., 2012; Hehir et al., 2012; Kim et al., 2018; Rea et al., 2002). The findings are also positive for skills in other subjects including mathematics (Cole et al., 2004; Cosier et al., 2013; Hehir et al., 2012; Rea et al., 2002), and extends to broader cognitive skill development (Kim et al., 2018).

Importantly, research suggests that it is the quality of classroom teaching and the inclusive pedagogies implemented that is likely to lead to the superior outcomes for students with disabilities noted above. For example, one key element of such quality inclusive teaching is to ensure that students with disabilities receive explicit instruction and strategy instruction to support their success in acquiring skills and concepts, and to then be able to apply these fluently and accurately (Swanson, 2001). Other studies emphasise the importance of having access to age- and grade-appropriate content from the general academic curriculum (Helmstetter et al., 1998; Hunt & Farron-Davis, 1992; Kurth & Mastergeorge, 2012, Kurth et al., 2021), as well as to core academic content area instruction (Hollowood et al., 1994; Joshi & Bouck, 2017).

Research also suggests that improved academic outcomes in inclusive settings result from teachers providing increased opportunities for students with disabilities to actively engage and participate in learning activities and with their peers (Morningstar et al., 2017). This is particularly clear in relation to active engagement and participation in collaborative learning with non-disabled peers, which is associated with improved outcomes on individualised learning goals (Hunt & Farron-Davis, 1992; Katz et al., 2002), and the acquisition of basic skills for students with complex learning profiles (Hunt, Staub, et al., 1994). Studies demonstrate that collaborative learning arrangements are more common in inclusive settings than in segregated education settings which typically see students engaged in more solitary activities in the classroom (Helmstetter et al., 1998; Kurth & Mastergeorge, 2012). These findings build on and extend the findings of the social benefits arising from collaborative interactions between all students in inclusive classrooms outlined earlier and highlight that these pedagogies provide both social and academic benefits. Together they present a compelling case for using high-quality collaborative pedagogies to support all students working in heterogeneous groups in inclusive classrooms.

These findings about effective and collaborative instructional practices are mirrored for students with complex learning profiles. Studies on the impact of being included for this group of students found that their communication and motor skills were more effectively supported when the opportunities to learn these are connected and embedded within regular classroom teaching that provides natural learning opportunities and opportunities for skills to generalise (Hunt & Farron-Davis, 1992; Katz et al., 2002).

Evidence suggests that this learning is particularly beneficial when embedded within structured interaction through small group activities where students were learning together, such as in cooperative learning activities (Hunt, Staub, et al., 1994). This is in stark contrast to the findings relating to segregated settings where students with complex learning profiles are less likely to have access to the general academic curriculum, or interact with their peers, and are more likely to be offered a life skills curriculum focusing on 'basic' or 'self-care skills' (Causton-Theoharis et al., 2011; Kurth et al., 2021).

Individual Education Plans and Inclusive Education

An important component of inclusive education is the provision of appropriately targeted and individualised academic support, including reasonable adjustments, to ensure students with disability make good progress in their learning (Chapter 12). Evidence of how this is provided is revealed through research on Individual Education Plans (IEPs) for students with disability and their progress against the goals. The quality of IEPs is particularly important for students with complex learning profiles who are the canaries in the coal mine for IEP quality. This is because they are likely to need IEPs that cover more curriculum domains and require more extensive adjustments and are thus more reliant upon the quality of these plans to ensure access to learning and effective instruction is provided. Evidence has identified that high-quality individualised learning and support can indeed be implemented for these students in regular schools and general education classrooms and indeed that IEP quality is generally higher for students educated in regular schools than for those in segregated settings (Hunt et al., 1986; Hunt & Farron-Davis, 1992; Hunt, Farron-Davis, et al., 1994; Kurth et al., 2021). Evidence also suggests that students with disability make greater gains against their IEP goals when they are educated in regular schools and classrooms (Katz et al., 2002).

Just how the quality of an IEP is conceptualised has shifted over decades and Kurth et al.'s (2021) analysis of IEP foci shows how these have evolved and expanded over time with a gradual and perceptible increase in expectations for students with complex learning profiles. This study demonstrated that during the 1970s and 1980s, IEP philosophy tended to emphasise developmental (self-care) goals or functional (life-skills) goals. During the 1980s, this expanded to emphasise social inclusion (communication, social interaction, and behaviour) goals, as well as self-determination (choice-making) goals and functional academic goals required for adult life (e.g., working with money, clocks, or public transport). Kurth et al. (2021) note that it is only since the turn of the 21st century that IEP philosophy for students with complex learning profiles has expanded to focus on their access to the general curriculum with grade-aligned content and standards in reading, mathematics, science, and humanities.

It is interesting that at each historical time point in which IEP quality has been evaluated, and regardless of how quality in these was best understood at that time, IEPs have at each time been found to be superior in quality for students with complex learning profiles educated in regular schools and classrooms (Hunt et al., 1986; Hunt & Farron-Davis, 1992; Hunt, Farron-Davis, et al., 1994; Kurth et al., 2021). Only one study on

IEP quality suggested the quality did not vary between regular and segregated settings (La Salle et al., 2013). Taken collectively, these studies show very clearly that it is not necessary to segregate students to provide students with disability appropriately tailored and individualised support, and that this is more likely to be provided in a regular school. This challenges one of the popular assumptions about segregation outlined at the start of this chapter in which it is assumed that students cannot receive such individualised planning in regular schools and shows that this assumption is not supported by research.

Long-Term Impact of Inclusion for Students with Disabilities

Inclusive education does not only offer academic and social benefits for students with disabilities. In addition to these important advantages, multiple longitudinal studies have also found improved long-term outcomes for students with disability when they are educated in regular schools and classrooms. These improved outcomes include higher rates of engagement in in postsecondary employment, further education, or living independently (Haber et al., 2016; Lombardi et al., 2013; Test et al., 2009; Theobald et al., 2019). Improved outcomes also include a higher likelihood of enrolling in and graduating from higher education (Lombardi et al., 2013; Rojewski et al., 2015). Longitudinal data also indicates that students with disability educate in regular schools and classrooms have higher rates of post-school employment, earn higher wages, are more likely to be actively engaged within their community, and are more likely to be involved in long-term and stable relationships (Mazzotti et al., 2016; Test et al., 2009; White & Weiner, 2004). These findings clearly refute the presumption that special segregated education is required to prepare students with disabilities for adult life, although the employment and earnings of adults with disabilities remain stubbornly below that of the wider population.

What Is the Impact of Inclusive Education for Students Without Disability?

As discussed earlier, one of the assumptions made by those arguing that segregation is necessary or preferable is that the presence of students with disabilities in regular education schools and classrooms negatively affects students without disabilities. This belief is clearly refuted by a range of studies that found positive effects of inclusive education for students without disabilities in both social and academic domains as outlined below.

Social Benefits for Students Without Disabilities

Research examining the impact of inclusive education for non-disabled students has found a range of social and personal benefits. These benefits are largely attitudinal in nature. For example, students without disabilities tend to hold fewer prejudices about people with disabilities and are more open to socially interacting with them (Ruijs & Peetsma, 2009). Non-disabled students also develop improved social competencies as well as improving their own self-concept (McGregor & Vogelsberg, 1998). However, research suggests that the benefits do not arise from merely being in the same school or classroom but rather it is the *nature* of that contact that makes an impact. Studies suggest that the social benefits of inclusion for non-disabled students may be a consequence of positive interpersonal experiences through from genuine and involvement in the classroom and routine activities of the school (McGregor & Vogelsberg, 1998), such as working jointly on learning activities (Schwab, 2017), or engaging in peer tutoring (Ruijs & Peetsma, 2009). Such contact develops school and classroom climates in which the membership of all students is valued. It is vital to note that these benefits do not hold when the proportion of students with disabilities rises unduly with research noting that teachers report that the benefits appear to drop as the number of students rises (Gottfried, 2014).

This brings us back to a point made earlier, which is that inclusion is not *just* a place but *also* a process. Inclusive environments are necessarily heterogeneous places, whereby students both with and without disabilities are educated together. Yet inclusive environments are also *more* than that. Importantly, inclusive education environments are places in which teachers actively facilitate positive interpersonal contact between students with and without disabilities. This is key in establishing an environment that is conducive to valuing all students, regardless of their personal characteristics, which, in turn, is key to creating a society in which everybody is also valued.

Academic Impact of Inclusion for Students Without Disabilities

The academic impact of educating students with disabilities in regular classrooms alongside their non-disabled peers has been extensively studied. The evidence is strong, arising from meta-analytic reviews (Kalambouka et al., 2005; Krämer et al., 2021; Szumski et al., 2017), as well as very large cohort studies (Krammer et al., 2021) and narrative reviews (McGregor & Vogelsberg, 1998; Ruijs & Peetsma, 2009). The overwhelming consensus is that the impact of being educated in schools and classrooms alongside students with disability ranges from neutral to slightly positive. This challenges the belief that students without disabilities are necessarily held back or have their education compromised by the presence of students with disabilities. The most recent and compelling evidence regarding this came through a meta-analysis by Szumski et al. (2017). This study engaged directly with the question of the impact of the inclusion of students with disabilities on students without disability. It covered a total sample of almost 4.8 million students worldwide and found a positive and statistically significant academic benefit of inclusive education for students without disabilities, even when students with complex learning profiles were included.

This research base also addresses several variants on the assumptions made about the impact of inclusive education on students without disabilities. One assumption is that students with particular types of disabilities, such as those with emotional or behavioural disorders, or those with complex learning profiles, are more likely to have a detrimental effect on their non-disabled peers due to their potential disproportionate claim on teachers' time and attention. Both the Szumski et al. (2017) meta-analysis and a large-scale study from across an entire national school sector in the Netherlands

(Ruijs, 2017) found no differential impact due to disability type, and these findings extended to the inclusion of students with emotional and behavioural difficulties, and those with multiple and profound disabilities. Another assumption challenged is that the presence of students with disabilities in the classroom is likely to have a particularly negative impact on high-attaining students. This is not supported by research which finds no significant difference on academic progress regardless of attainment status of the non-disabled students (Dessemontet & Bless, 2013; Ruijs et al., 2010).

Two important caveats exist in the research on academic achievement like that found in the studies exploring the social benefits of inclusion. One is that the benefits of inclusion may be lost when the proportion of students with disabilities in a class rises beyond their natural distribution in the student population (Szumski et al., 2017). This situation may occur in schools with higher proportions of students with disabilities are grouped together in classrooms due to administrative attempts to concentrate resources (such as teaching assistants, Chapter 19) or when students with disabilities are segregated into support classes and special units. These practices are inconsistent with inclusive education and are not supported by research as producing good outcomes for students and are thus best avoided. An additional caveat is that the positive outcomes reported in the sections above rely on effective and inclusive teaching practices being used to teach the most diverse cohort. Inclusive schools must have more than inclusive enrolment policies, although these are important. If the benefits of genuine inclusive education are to be realised, schools must *also* have inclusive scheduling and effective teaching designed to support learning and positive interactions within a diverse student cohort (see Chapters 9, 11, 12).

Implications for Professional Practice

The empirical research reviewed in this chapter has provided clear evidence of the benefits that can be realised for students with and without disability, as well as instructional practices that are recommended for use to realise these benefits. The research reviewed here also highlights the errors within the assumptions that are often made about the need for segregation. It is neither necessary nor desirable to segregate students with disability either for their benefit or for the benefit of non-disabled students. Provided instruction is both accessible and optimal, access to an inclusive education is socially and academically beneficial for students with and without disability and it is both feasible and advantageous for schools to do this. Interestingly, in addition to these findings, two very clear themes ran through this research literature that are worth emphasising here about their implications for teacher professional practice. These provide evidence to support the proposition that inclusion is *both* a place and a process.

Inclusion Is a "Place"

There was a consistent finding that ran through the research regarding *where* inclusive education takes place, emphasising that students must be co-located within the same schools and classrooms. In other words, students with and without disability must access core classroom instruction within the same *place* for the benefits to be obtained. Heterogeneous classrooms are thus a necessary precondition for inclusive education (de Bruin, 2019). This does not mean that no additional support or tiered interventions may be required for some students, but as discussed in Chapters 9, 11, and 12, these rely on that strong foundation of core instruction in the general education classroom.

Another common thread that ran through the research acts as a qualifier to this first finding above. That is, inclusive classrooms are most beneficial when the proportion of students with disabilities does not rise above a certain threshold (Gottfried, 2014). While that threshold was hypothesised by some researchers to plausibly sit at around five students per class (Szumski et al., 2017), other studies indicated that there was substantial empirical evidence to support a *natural proportions* hypothesis; that is, that inclusive classrooms should have proportions of students with disabilities that roughly reflect their prevalence in the wider population (McGregor & Vogelsberg, 1998). This is readily achievable if schools enrol students from their local communities, in line with students' entitlements under international human rights and national legislation (see Chapters 3 and 5).

Inclusion Is a "Process"

The research reviewed for this chapter indicated that the benefits of inclusion flow because of the *processes* that take place within heterogeneous classrooms and schools. Specifically, the processes raised as important for these benefits were for teachers to use highly effective instructional practices for academic and social skills acquisition and practice that are designed with a highly diverse cohort in mind. Pedagogies emphasised as important for these included explicit teaching and strategy instruction for skills acquisition and mastery, as well as collaborative and cooperative learning to facilitate authentic and positive interactions within routine teaching and learning activities in the classroom.

One implication that can be drawn from these findings is that these effective pedagogies are vital to include in the curriculum for initial teacher education as well as teacher professional learning. Importantly, these pedagogies are not *special* education strategies, they are simply *effective teaching* (Donker et al., 2014; Hattie, 2008; Johnson et al., 2000; Slavin, 1991). This shows the outdated but persistent idea that students with disabilities require special teachers who hold special knowledge about special pedagogies or teaching a special curriculum to be patently untrue. Students with disability need and benefit from the same high-quality and evidence-based practices that benefit non-disabled students and benefit from accessing the same general academic curriculum (Chapter 12). While some students may need reasonable adjustments or additional layers of targeted intervention by educators with the requisite expertise (Chapter 9), all students benefit from a strong foundation of quality instruction in the general education classroom (Chapter 11).

Conclusion

As this chapter is going to print, the *Royal Commission into Violence, Abuse, Neglect and Exploitation of People with Disability* is collating its evidence and writing the final recommendations. There is much to be hoped that this may bring about the kind of systemic change that is so sorely needed in Australian school systems and that this change will inspire other systems of education worldwide. For too long people with disability, advocates, and academics have been calling for change and, while change has come, the pace has been glacial. What is needed is a more rapid trajectory if Australian education systems are to become inclusive, and to end the dual track of special and mainstream.

This call for change should not be interpreted as a culture war against special schools and classes, although advocacy for inclusive education has been perceived that way by some. What has perhaps been missed in the messaging about inclusive education is that people with disability, advocates, and academics are calling for an end to *both* mainstream and special. We are calling for the creation of a single inclusive system in which students with disability can have their requirements met, while learning alongside their siblings and their grade-level peers. The evidence shows that this is both desirable and possible for *all* students. A national transition plan, like that described in Chapter 7, is needed to achieve it.

There is both a moral imperative and a clear case in research evidence to transform the current dual-track system to a single inclusive one. Students educated in segregated settings graduate to inhabit the same society as students without disabilities; there is no special universe for them to graduate into. The outcomes from current systems of education for people with disability are indefensible, with substantially lower rates of school completion, post-school study, employment, and community participation, as well as higher rates of poverty experienced by this group (Australian Institute of Health and Welfare, 2022). These outcomes are a damning indictment on the current dual-track system and provide compelling evidence for change. The current system is simply not delivering the outcomes that it should be.

It is essential to cultivate an inclusive culture within schools if we wish to create an inclusive society. To achieve this, we must build the capacity of our pre-service and in-service teachers to implement high-quality inclusive and evidence-based practices that support positive academic, social, and post-school adult outcomes for a diverse cohort that includes students with and without disability. The transformation of the school system required to create genuinely inclusive schools begins, then, with teachers ensuring that their classroom practice is as high in quality as possible, maximising the learning of the most diverse cohort of students and designing instruction so that all students are learning together. While these practices may achieve benefits such as improved academic and social outcomes, they also enact the grand moral purpose of education itself: to create well-developed citizens who are freely accepted and are valued without exception as members of our society. The chapters in this book have been written to achieve this outcome.

References

(Asterisked references are those obtained through database searches for this chapter.)

Australian Institute of Health and Welfare. (2022). *People with disability in Australia.* https://www.aihw.gov.au/reports/disability/people-with-disability-in-australia/contents/about

*Avramidis, E. (2010). Social relationships of pupils with special educational needs in the mainstream primary class: peer group membership and peer-assessed social behaviour. *European Journal of Special Needs Education, 25*(4), 413–429. https://doi.org/10.1080/08856257.2010.513550

*Baker, E. (1994). Meta-analytic evidence for non-inclusive educational practices: Does educational research support current practice for special needs students? [Unpublished Dissertation]. *Temple University.* https://www.proquest.com/dissertations-theses/meta-analytic-evidence-noninclusive-educational/docview/304136939/se-2

Bita, N. (2022). Taking the special from special needs. *The Weekend Australian.* https://www.theaustralian.com.au/

*Caldas, S. J., & Bensy, M. L. (2014). The sexual maltreatment of students with disabilities in American school settings. *Journal of Child Sexual Abuse, 23*(4), 345–366. https://doi.org/10.1080/10538712.2014.906530

*Carlberg, C., & Kavale, K. (1980). The efficacy of special versus regular class placement for exceptional children: A meta-analysis. *The Journal of Special Education, 14*(3), 295–309. https://doi.org/10.1177/002246698001400304

Causton-Theoharis, J., Theoharis, G., Orsati, F., & Cosier, M. (2011). Does self-contained special education deliver on its promises? A critical inquiry into research and practice. *Journal of Special Education Leadership, 24*(2), 61–78.

*Cole, C. M., Waldron, N., & Majd, M. (2004). Academic progress of students across inclusive and traditional settings. *Mental Retardation, 42*(2), 136–144. https://doi.org/10.1352/0047-6765(2004)42<136:APOSAI>2.0.CO;2

*Cole, S. M., Murphy, H. R., Frisby, M. B., Grossi, T. A., & Bolte, H. R. (2021). The relationship of special education placement and student academic outcomes. *The Journal of Special Education, 54*(4), 217–227. https://doi.org/10.1177/0022466920925033

*Cosier, M., Causton-Theoharis, J., & Theoharis, G. (2013). Does access matter? Time in general education and achievement for students with disabilities. *Remedial and Special Education, 34*(6), 323–332. https://doi.org/10.1177/0741932513485448

de Bruin, K. (2019). The impact of inclusive education reforms on students with disability: An international comparison. *International Journal of Inclusive Education, 23*(7–8), 811–826. https://doi.org/10.1080/13603116.2019.1623327

de Bruin, K. (2022a). Learning in the shadow of eugenics: Why segregated schooling persists in Australia. *The Australian Journal of Education, 66*(3), 218–234. https://doi.org/10.1177/00049441221127765

de Bruin, K. (2022b). Multi-tiered systems of support: A roadmap for achieving an inclusive education system. In J. Banks (Ed.), *The inclusion dialogue: Debating issues, challenges and tension with global experts* (pp. 36–53). Routledge.

*Dessemontet, R. S., & Bless, G. (2013). The impact of including children with intellectual disability in general education classrooms on the academic achievement of their low-, average-, and high-achieving peers. *Journal of Intellectual & Developmental Disability, 38*(1), 23–30. https://doi.org/10.3109/13668250.2012.757589

*Dessemontet, R. S., Bless, G., & Morin, D. (2012). Effects of inclusion on the academic achievement and adaptive behaviour of children with intellectual disabilities. *Journal of Intellectual Disability Research, 56*(6), 579–587. https://doi.org/10.1111/j.1365-2788.2011.01497.x

Donker, A. S., De Boer, H., Kostons, D., Van Ewijk, C. D., & van der Werf, M. P. (2014). Effectiveness of learning strategy instruction on academic performance: A meta-analysis. *Educational Research Review, 11*, 1–26. https://doi.org/10.1016/j.edurev.2013.11.002

*Finnvold, J. E. (2018). School segregation and social participation: the case of Norwegian children with physical disabilities. *European Journal of Special Needs Education, 33*(2), 187–204. https://doi.org/10.1080/08856257.2018.1424781

*Fisher, M., & Meyer, L. H. (2002). Development and social competence after two years for students enrolled in inclusive and self-contained educational programs. *Research and Practice for Persons with Severe Disabilities, 27*(3), 165–174. https://doi.org/10.2511/rpsd.27.3.165

Forbes, F. (2007). Towards inclusion: An Australian perspective. *Support for Learning, 22*(2), 66–71. https://doi.org/10.1111/j.1467-9604.2007.00449.x

*Foreman, P., Arthur-Kelly, M., Pascoe, S., & King, B. S. (2004). Evaluating the educational Eexperiences of students with profound and multiple disabilities in inclusive and segregated classroom settings: An Australian perspective. *Research and Practice for Persons with Severe Disabilities, 29*(3), 183–193. https://doi.org/10.2511/rpsd.29.3.183

*Garrote, A., Sermier Dessemontet, R., & Moser Opitz, E. (2017). Facilitating the social participation of pupils with special educational needs in mainstream schools: A review of school-based interventions. *Educational Research Review, 20*, 12–23. https://doi.org/10.1016/j.edurev.2016.11.001

Gilmour, A. (2017). Has inclusion gone too far? Weighing its effects on students with disabilities, their peers, and teachers. *Education Next, 18*(4), 1–9.

*Gottfried, M. A. (2014). Classmates with disabilities and students' noncognitive outcomes. *Educational Evaluation and Policy Analysis, 36*(1), 20–43. https://doi.org/10.3102/0162373713493130

*Haber, M. G., Mazzotti, V. L., Mustian, A. L., Rowe, D. A., Bartholomew, A. L., Test, D. W., & Fowler, C. H. (2016). What works, when, for whom, and with whom: A meta-analytic review of predictors of postsecondary success for students with disabilities. *Review of Educational Research, 86*(1), 123–162. https://doi.org/10.3102/0034654315583135

Hattie, J. (2008). *Visible Learning: A synthesis of over 800 meta-analyses relating to achievement.* Routledge.

*Hehir, T., Grindal, T., & Eidelman, H. (2012). Review of special education in the Commonwealth of Massachusetts. *Massachusetts Department of Elementary and Secondary Education.* http://www.doe.mass.edu/sped/hehir/2012-04sped.docx.

*Helmstetter, E., Curry, C. A., Brennan, M., & Sampson-Saul, M. (1998). Comparison of general and special education classrooms of students with severe disabilities. *Education and Training in Mental Retardation and Developmental Disabilities, 33*(3), 216–227.

*Hollowood, T. M., Salisbury, C. L., Rainforth, B., & Palombaro, M. M. (1994). Use of instructional time in classrooms serving students with and without severe disabilities. *Exceptional Children, 61*(3), 242–252. https://doi.org/10.1177/001440299506100304

*Hunt, P., & Farron-Davis, F. (1992). A preliminary investigation of IEP quality and content associated with placement in general education versus special education classes. *Journal of the Association for Persons with Severe Handicaps, 17*(4), 247–253. https://doi.org/10.1177/154079699201700406

*Hunt, P., Farron-Davis, F., Beckstead, S., Curtis, D., & Goetz, L. (1994). Evaluating the effects of placement of students with severe disabilities in general education versus special classes. *Journal of the Association for Persons with Severe Handicaps, 19*(3), 200–214. https://doi.org/10.1177/154079699401900308

*Hunt P., Goetz L., Anderson J. (1986). The quality of IEP objectives associated with placement on integrated versus segregated school sites. *Journal of the Association for Persons with Severe Handicaps, 11*(2), 125–130. https://doi.org/10.1177/154079698601100206

*Hunt, P., Staub, D., Alwell, M., & Goetz, L. (1994). Achievement by all students within the context of cooperative learning groups. *Journal of the Association for Persons with Severe Handicaps, 19*(4), 290–301. https://doi.org/10.1177/154079699401900405

Johnson, D. W., Johnson, R. T., & Stanne, M. E. (2000). *Cooperative learning methods: A meta analysis.* University of Minnesota, Minneapolis: Cooperative Learning Center. http://www.co-operation.org/pages/cl-methods.html.

*Joshi, G. S., & Bouck, E. C. (2017). Examining postsecondary education predictors and participation for students with learning disabilities. *Journal of Learning Disabilities, 50*(1), 3–13. https://doi.org/10.1177/0022219415572894

*Kalambouka A., Farrell P, Dyson A, Kaplan I (2005). The impact of population inclusivity in schools on student outcomes: Review conducted by the Inclusive Education Review Group. *Research Evidence in Education Library, EPPI-Centre.* http://eppi.ioe.ac.uk/cms/Default.aspx?tabid=287

*Katz, J., Mirenda, P., & Auerbach, S. (2002). Instructional strategies and educational outcomes for students with developmental disabilities in inclusive "multiple intelligences" and typical inclusive classrooms. *Research and Practice for Persons with Severe Disabilities, 27*(4), 227–238. https://doi.org/10.2511/rpsd.27.4.227

Kemp, C. (2022a). What does it mean to be included? *InSped Insights.* https://www.insped.org.au/wp-content/uploads/2022/09/What_does_it_Mean_to_be_Included_September_2022.01.pdf

Kemp, C. (2022b). Inclusion: A research and practice conundrum. *Learning Difficulties Australia Bulletin 54*(2), 15–17.

*Kennedy, C. H., Shukla, S., & Fryxell, D. (1997). Comparing the effects of educational placement on the social relationships of intermediate school students with severe disabilities. *Exceptional Children, 64*(1), 31–47. https://doi.org/10.1177/001440299706400103

*Kim, S. H., Bal, V. H., & Lord, C. (2018). Longitudinal follow-up of academic achievement in children with autism from age 2 to 18. *Journal of Child Psychology and Psychiatry, 59*(3), 258–267. https://doi.org/10.1111/jcpp.12808

*Krämer, S., Möller, J., & Zimmermann, F. (2021). Inclusive education of students with general learning difficulties: A meta-analysis. *Review of Educational Research, 91*(3), 432–478. https://doi.org/10.3102/0034654321998072

*Krammer, M., Gasteiger-Klicpera, B., Holzinger, A., & Wohlhart, D. (2021). Inclusion and standards achievement: the presence of pupils identified as having special needs as a moderating effect on the national mathematics standards achievements of their classmates. *International Journal of Inclusive Education, 25*(7), 795–811. https://doi.org/10.1080/13603116.2019.1573938

*Kurth, J., Lockman-Turner, E., Burke, K., & Ruppar, A. L. (2021). Curricular philosophies reflected in individualized education program goals for students with complex support needs. *Intellectual and Developmental Disabilities, 59*(4), 283–294. https://doi.org/10.1352/1934-9556-59.4.283

*Kurth, J., & Mastergeorge, A. M. (2012). Impact of setting and instructional context for adolescents with autism. *The Journal of Special Education, 46*(1), 36–48. https://doi.org/10.1177/0022466910366480

*La Salle, T. P., Roach, A. T., & McGrath, D. (2013). The relationship of IEP quality to curricular access and academic achievement for students with disabilities. *International Journal of Special Education, 28*(1), 135–144.

Lawrenson, D. (2022). Children like my daughter need special schools to blossom. *The Sydney Morning Herald.* https://www.smh.com.au/national/children-like-my-daughter-need-special-schools-to-blossom-20220505-p5aitn.html

*Lombardi, A., Doren, B., Gau, J. M., & Lindstrom, L. E. (2013). The influence of instructional settings in reading and math on postsecondary participation. *Journal of Disability Policy Studies, 24*(3), 170–180. https://doi.org/10.1177/1044207312468766

*Mazzotti, V. L., Rowe, D. A., Sinclair, J., Poppen, M., Woods, W. E., & Shearer, M. L. (2016). Predictors of post-school success: A systematic review of NLTS2 secondary analyses. *Career Development and Transition for Exceptional Individuals, 39*(4), 196–215. https://doi.org/10.1177/2165143415588047

*McGregor, G., & Vogelsberg, R. T. (1998). Inclusive *schooling practices*: Pedagogical and *research foundations*. A synthesis of the literature that informs best practices about inclusive schooling. Brookes Publishing.

McVilly, K., Ainsworth, S., Graham, L., Harrison, M., Sojo, V., Spivakovsky, C., Gale, L., Genat, A., & Zirnsak, T. (2022). Outcomes associated with 'inclusive', 'segregated' and 'integrated' settings: Accommodation and community living, employment and education. *A research report commissioned by the Royal Commission into Violence, Abuse, Neglect and Exploitation of People with Disability, University of Melbourne, Australia.* https://disability.royalcommission.gov.au/publications/outcomes-associated-inclusive-segregated-and-integrated-settings-people-disability

*Morningstar, M. E., Kurth, J. A., & Johnson, P. E. (2017). Examining national trends in educational placements for students with significant disabilities. *Remedial and Special Education, 38*(1), 3–12. https://doi.org/10.1177/0741932516678327

*Nepi, L. D., Facondini, R., Nucci, F., & Peru, A. (2013). Evidence from full-inclusion model: The social position and sense of belonging of students with special educational needs and their peers in Italian primary school. *European Journal of Special Needs Education, 28*(3), 319–332. https://doi.org/10.1080/08856257.2013.777530

*Norwich, B., & Kelly, N. (2004). Pupils' views on inclusion: moderate learning difficulties and bullying in mainstream and special schools. *British Educational Research Journal., 30*(1), 43–65. https://doi.org/10.1080/01411920310001629965

*Oh-Young, C., & Filler, J. (2015). A meta-analysis of the effects of placement on academic and social skill outcome measures of students with disabilities. *Research in Developmental Disabilities, 47*, 80–92. https://doi.org/10.1016/j.ridd.2015.08.014

Rea, P. J., McLaughlin, V. L., & Walther-Thomas, C. (2002). Outcomes for students with learning disabilities in inclusive and pullout programs. *Exceptional Children, 68*, 203–222. https://doi.org/10.1177/001440290206800020

*Rojewski, J. W., Lee, I. H., & Gregg, N. (2015). Causal effects of inclusion on postsecondary education outcomes of individuals with high-incidence disabilities. *Journal of Disability Policy Studies, 25*(4), 210–219. https://doi.org/10.1177/1044207313505648

*Rose, C. A., Espelage, D. L., Aragon, S. R., & Elliott, J. (2011). Bullying and victimization among students in special education and general education curricula. *Exceptionality Education International, 21*(3), 2–14. https://doi.org/10.5206/eei.v21i3.7679

*Rose, C. A., Monda-Amaya, L. E., & Espelage, D. L. (2011). Bullying perpetration and victimization in special education: A review of the literature. *Remedial and Special Education, 32*(2), 114–130. https://doi.org/10.1177/0741932510361247

*Royal Commission into Institutional Responses to Child Sexual Abuse. (2017). https://www.royalcommission.gov.au/child-abuse/final-report

*Ruijs, N. (2017). The impact of special needs students on classmate performance. *Economics of Education Review, 58*, 15–31. https://doi.org/10.1016/j.econedurev.2017.03.002

*Ruijs, N. M., & Peetsma, T. T. D. (2009). Effects of inclusion on students with and without special educational needs reviewed. *Educational Research Review, 4*(2), 67–79. https://doi.org/10.1016/j.edurev.2009.02.002

*Ruijs, N. M., Van der Veen, I., & Peetsma, T. T. D. (2010). Inclusive education and students without special educational needs. *Educational Research (Windsor), 52*(4), 351–390. https://doi.org/10.1080/00131881.2010.524749

*Schwab, S. (2017). The impact of contact on students' attitudes towards peers with disabilities. *Research in Developmental Disabilities, 62*, 160–165. https://doi.org/10.1016/j.ridd.2017.01.015

Secret Teacher. (2015). Secret teacher: I am all for inclusion in principle, but it doesn't always work. *The Guardian.* https://www.theguardian.com/teacher-network/2015/may/23/secret-teacher-support-inclusion-but-not-at-any-cost

Slavin, R. E. (1991). Synthesis of research on cooperative learning. *Educational Leadership, 48*(5), 71–82.

Stephenson, J., & Ganguly, R. (2022). Analysis and critique of the advocacy paper "Towards inclusive education: A necessary process of transformation." *Australasian Journal of Special and Inclusive Education, 46*(1), 113–126. https://doi.org/10.1017/jsi.2021.23

*Swanson, H. L. (2001). Searching for the best model for instructing students with learning disabilities. *Focus on Exceptional Children, 34*(2), 1–15. https://core.ac.uk/download/pdf/162643941.pdf

*Szumski, G., & Karwowski, M. (2014). Psychosocial functioning and school achievement of children with mild intellectual disability in Polish special, integrative, and mainstream schools. *Journal of Policy and Practice in Intellectual Disabilities, 11*(2), 99–108. https://doi.org/10.1111/jppi.12076

*Szumski, G., Smogorzewska, J., & Karwowski, M. (2017). Academic achievement of students without special educational needs in inclusive classrooms: A meta-analysis. *Educational Research Review, 21*, 33–54. https://doi.org/10.1016/j.edurev.2017.02.004

*Test, D. W., Mazzotti, V. L., Mustian, A. L., Fowler, C. H., Kortering, L., & Kohler, P. (2009). Evidence-based secondary transition predictors for improving postschool outcomes for students with disabilities. *Career Development for Exceptional Individuals, 32*(3), 160–181. https://doi.org/10.1177/0885728809346960

Theobold, R., Goldhaber, D., Gratz, T., & Holden, K. (2019). Career and technical education, inclusion, and postsecondary outcomes for students with learning disabilities. *Journal of Learning Disabilities, 13*(4), 251–258. https://doi.org/10.1177/0022219418775121

United Nations. (2006). *Convention on the Rights of Persons with Disabilities (CRPD).* https://www.un.org/disabilities/documents/convention/convoptprot-e.pdf.

United Nations. (2016). *General Comment No. 4, Article 24: Right to Inclusive Education. (CRPD/C/GC/4).* https://digitallibrary.un.org/record/1313836?ln=en

*Wang, M. C., & Baker, E. T. (1985). Mainstreaming programs: Design features and effects. *The Journal of Special Education, 19*(4), 503–521. https://doi.org/10.1177/002246698501900412

*White, J., & Weiner, J. S. (2004). Influence of least restrictive environment and community based training on integrated employment outcomes for transitioning students with severe disabilities. *Journal of Vocational Rehabilitation, 21*(3), 149–156.

*Wiener, J., & Tardif, C. Y. (2004). Social and emotional functioning of children with learning disabilities: Does special education placement make a difference? *Learning Disabilities Research and Practice, 19*(1), 20–32. https://doi.org/10.1111/j.1540-5826.2004.00086.x

*Zurbriggen, C. L. A., Venetz, M., & Hinni, C. (2018). The quality of experience of students with and without special educational needs in everyday life and when relating to peers. *European Journal of Special Needs Education, 33*(2), 205–220. https://doi.org/10.1080/08856257.2018.1424777

Implementing Systemic Inclusive Education Reform

Part II

Implementing Systemic Inclusive
Education Reform

Chapter 7

Learning from international experience

Suzanne Carrington, Carly Lassig, Lara Maia-Pike, Glenys Mann, Sofia Mavropoulou, & Beth Saggers

Addressing equity in schools is a challenge because "exclusion resides deep in the bones of education" (Slee, 2018, p. 11), where there is a longstanding connection between schooling and divisions due to race, social class, ethnicity, gender, geography, sexuality, religion, ability, and disability. Developing a unified system of education, where all students are included in their local school, is legally, philosophically, and empirically justified and there is evidence of major international efforts to develop more inclusive schools (Ainscow, 2020). To date, 186 countries have ratified the *Convention of the Rights of Persons with Disabilities* (CRPD; United Nations, 2006, 2023), which clearly outlines a legally binding obligation for States parties to implement inclusive education rather than maintaining a binary system of mainstream and special schools. *General Comment No. 4* (GC4) on Article 24: Right to Education states:

> States parties have a specific and continuing obligation *to move as expeditiously and effectively as possible* [emphasis added] towards the full realization of article 24. This is not compatible with sustaining two systems of education: a mainstream education system and a special/segregated education systems . . . States parties are encouraged to redefine budgetary allocations for education, including by transferring part of their budgets to the development of inclusive education.
>
> (United Nations, 2016, para. 39)

Australia ratified the CRPD in 2008, however, we are still not meeting our commitments (Poed et al., 2020; De Bruin, 2019), despite significant national collaborative effort in the education sector. There is little evidence of progressing a national inclusive education system in Australia and countries around the world are also struggling with systemic transformation for inclusion (Ainscow, 2020). Achieving an inclusive education system is challenging because it requires policy, organisational, and philosophical change. Therefore, it is appropriate that we consider how several countries have progressed inclusive education and diminished special education. Transformation of a system requires strong leadership at both the systems and school levels. In this chapter, we report on policy implementation for a more unified system in Canada, Italy, and Portugal and consider what other jurisdictions can learn to progress inclusive education. The discussion of enablers and barriers to progressing inclusive education in the three

DOI: 10.4324/9781003350897-9

countries is organised using a framework structure of society, system, school, and community (Carrington et al., 2022).

- *Societal level enablers and barriers* include the impact of widespread attitudes and beliefs about disability, and laws and policies that facilitate or hinder moves to progress inclusive education.
- *System level enablers and barriers* encompass education reform, bureaucratic processes, approaches to funding, and the collaborative partnering of various stakeholders who contribute to the transformation required for inclusion. It is important to note in the cases of Canada, Italy, and Portugal how the society level laws and policies impacted implementation at the system and school levels.
- *School level enablers and barriers* include teacher attitudes, teacher skills, roles of specialist teachers, and the gap between policy and practice.
- *Community level (including family) enablers and barriers* include parent choice and advocacy for their schooling preference of inclusive or special school.

Canada

Canada is recognised internationally for the inclusive way it responds to diversity (Köpfer & Óskarsdóttir, 2019). While the experience of Canadian students is not singular and has differed depending on contextual features such as community location and size (Irvine et al., 2010), it is generally recognised that more progress has been made in some Canadian provinces in inclusive education than in many other jurisdictions (AuCoin at al., 2020). Canada, then, is a good direction in which to turn when investigating factors impacting school inclusion (Sider et al., 2022).

Enablers of Inclusive Education Progress in Canada

Key enablers of inclusive education can be found at a societal level. For example, changes in societal attitudes towards diversity have underpinned changes in schools. Significant trends include Normalization (Wolfensberger, 1972), the Human Rights movement, and the Community Living movement. These movements all promoted the valued participation of individuals with disability in typical—rather than 'special'—community places and activities. Additionally, schools were increasingly seen as instruments for equitable societies (Porter, 2008) and a prior belief in segregation eventually gave way to positive perceptions of inclusive schools. Change in attitudes coincided with changes in laws; Canada's *Charter of Rights and Freedom* (1982) is consistently referenced as critical to legislation underpinning inclusive reforms and the enactment of *New Brunswick's Bill 85* four years later led to significant changes in how students with disability were educated. For example, *Bill 85* represented a clear mandate that students with disability were to be taught in mainstream classes alongside peers without disability (AuCoin et al., 2020).

Key enablers have also occurred at the system level. These include, in some provinces, the move away from a dual system of mainstream and special schools to a unified education system that caters to all students. In the province of New Brunswick, *Policy 322* (2013) was foundational to the changes required for such a move and was an inclusive education directive that provided "clarity on programs and procedures to every public school in the province" (AuCoin et al., 2020, p. 316). *Policy 322* requires a common learning environment for all students that is appropriate to their age, applies student-centred learning principles, and implements appropriate accommodations. Flexible, non-categorical support systems were developed in New Brunswick, for example, the re-envisioning of special education support to encompass a variety of tasks facilitating mainstream classroom practice (Köpfer & Óskarsdóttir, 2019). The cost and inefficiency of maintaining two systems were increasingly questioned (Porter, 2008) and funding models were developed that redirected money from special to inclusive schools. Finally, collaboration has been a critical component of inclusive education progress. The work needed to transition to an inclusive system has taken time, planning, and the commitment of all stakeholders.

At the school level, leadership has been significant to inclusive education reform. For example, in New Brunswick, school leaders provided the values, direction, and energy needed for change (MacKay, 2006). Flexibility and innovation in classrooms were also important, such as increasing use of strength-based approaches (AuCoin et al., 2020). In the province of Ontario, teacher support and skill development were enablers of inclusive reform (Killoran et al., 2013), and the reframing of the work of teachers was key, for example, special education teachers upskilled to teach in mainstream classes (Somma, 2020). Similarly, general classroom teachers have assumed responsibility for all students (Köpfer & Óskarsdóttir, 2019). Finally, at the community level, independent advocacy has played a critical role in how some Canadian schools have responded to diversity. Parents and community allies have held systems and schools accountable for their actions and have exerted pressure both individually and collectively for an end to segregated schooling.

Barriers to Inclusive Education Progress in Canada

As is true internationally, inclusive reform in Canada has unfolded alongside a tenacious resistance to desegregation. To learn from Canada, it is important, then, to also be conscious of barriers to progress. A key obstacle at the societal level has been inconsistency between inclusive rhetoric and high-level decision-making, for example, litigation ruling for segregation despite laws mandating inclusive practice (Loreman, 2014), and performative efforts rather than ongoing investment in equitable practices (Sider et al., 2022). Another key barrier has been the lack of national power to dictate policy in the provinces, resulting in inconsistency in how inclusive education has been implemented across Canada (Sokal & Katz, 2015).

At the system level, difficulties with operationalising inclusive reform have been a barrier, for example, disassembling systemic structures of the dual system (Sokal & Katz, 2015). Establishing an alternative system to ensure students receive the support they need (without diagnostic categorisation) has proven difficult (Köpfer & Óskarsdóttir, 2019). A particularly significant hurdle has been the complex question of funding; for example, how to divide funding fairly (Porter & AuCoin, 2012), and concerns about the cost of a unified education system (Irvine et al., 2010).

Similarly, in schools, implementation has proven to be challenging, perhaps as a result of school leaders who have not fully understood their responsibilities for students with disability (van Walleghem et al., 2013) and a lack of accountability for inclusive practice (Killoran et al., 2013). Other barriers in schools have included apprehension that specialist knowledge would be lost (Lupart, 2012), the reluctance of some teachers to change (Lupart, 1998), and fears for the wellbeing of students should special schools close (Porter, 2008). And, finally, while parental advocacy has been a critical enabler of inclusive education progress, alongside parental voices for inclusion have been equally powerful voices for maintaining segregated provision (MacKay, 2006). It is widely recognised that the preference of some parents for special schooling is a significant barrier to progressing the move to a unified education system for all students.

Italy

Italy is recognised as one of the first countries to lead the inclusive education movement within the European continent (Lauchlan & Fadda, 2012). However, despite closure of public special schools in the 1970s and continuing progress in inclusive practices in mainstream schools, regional variation in how inclusion is implemented has been documented, and private segregated settings still exist for students with complex and multiple disabilities (Giangreco et al., 2012). Arguably, while Italy has made considerable progress in inclusion, particularly in relation to inclusive policy, consideration of the enablers and barriers to inclusive education within the Italian educational system can offer insights into how inclusive education for all can be achieved.

Enablers of Inclusive Education Progress in Italy

Since the 1970s, cultural debates, institutional reforms, and several new national policies and government initiatives have been significant enablers at the societal level in Italy. The movement towards inclusive education followed psychiatric reform in the 1960s that led to the closure of institutions and the establishment of de-centralised community services enforced by the *Basaglia Law* (1978) (Mura et al., 2020). This reform coincided with an intense critique of Italian schools as being class-conscious and excluding students unable to follow the same pace as their peers, together with a grass-roots movement to eliminate segregation, discrimination, and inequality in health and education in Italy (Canevaro & de Anna, 2010; Nota et al., 2014). Consequently, a national policy (e.g., *National Law 517*, 1977) mandated the closure of 'special schools' and supported all students with disability to enter mainstream schools for the first time in Italy (described as "wild integration") (Vitello, 1994, p. 62). Inclusive practice for students with disability was strengthened through the provision of individualised learning support and the allocation of support teachers in mainstream schools under *National*

Framework Law 104, 1992). Following the ratification of the CRPD in 2009, Italy's national strategy for full inclusion was delineated in a Ministerial Directive in 2012, and a National Observatory on the Status of Persons with Disabilities was established to provide support and advice on policy development for inclusion. *Law 107* (2017) provided specific guidance for employing support teachers to ensure full inclusion for students with disability in regular public schools.

Example system enablers resulting from *Law 170* (2010) include a strong emphasis on consultation, collaboration, communication, and cooperation (the 4Cs) between families and schools, and clearly defined roles and responsibilities of parents in this partnership (European Agency for Special Needs and Inclusive Education, 2016). Furthermore, there was a shift from a medical to a pedagogical approach to the education of students with disability, enforcing the provision of individualised supports by learning support teachers in mainstream schools (reflecting *Law 107*, 2015). This shift led to the allocation of more funding in mainstream schools to enable an increased number of learning support teachers in schools and reforms in their professional development training (Ianes et al., 2020; Shevchenco et al., 2020).

By examining the literature on key stakeholders' (e.g., teachers', parents', and students') perspectives on how national and school policies have been viewed and translated into practice, we identified teacher attitudes and school factors as enablers to inclusion 'on the ground'. Recent research documented that classroom and learning support teachers in Italian schools hold positive attitudes and high commitment to the inclusion of students with disability (Saloviita & Consegnati, 2019; Sharma et al., 2018). The allocation of learning support teachers to the whole class and their shared responsibility to prepare adjustments for all children facilitated successful inclusive practice (Devecchi et al., 2012). Students' self-reported experiences of inclusion focused on their strong sense of belonging and peer acceptance as being two of the most important enablers to their success and positive experiences in school (Vianello & Lanfranchi, 2011). Following the ratification of the CRPD, parents of children with disability took legal action against schools with allegations of discriminatory and exclusionary practices, which represented violations of their children's rights to inclusive education (Ferri, 2008). These pressures coupled with the Educational Cooperation Movement called for the provision of education for all students, without discrimination (Nota et al., 2014).

Barriers to Inclusive Education Progress in Italy

Despite the major legislative steps for the closure of special schools in Italy and encouragement for students with disability to enrol in their neighbourhood school, the term inclusion had not been explicitly defined in national policy until after Italy ratified the CRPD in 2009. Until then, the erroneous use of the term 'integration' as a synonym for inclusion was being used in several national laws to describe the progressive transition of students with disability into mainstream schools and contributed to the confusion about what genuine inclusive education involves (Mura et al., 2020). In addition, the national policy on inclusive education has been effective only for public schools, thereby allowing the continuing operation of private special schools for students with complex learning profiles (Giangreco et al., 2012).

The existence of private special schools has hindered the progress towards inclusion of *all* children with disability in mainstream schools in Italy. Following legislation mandating the closure of public special schools, the number of students with intellectual and sensory disabilities in private special schools increased considerably (Abbring & Meijer, 1994). Even though almost none of the students with disability were placed in special schools in Italy (United Nations Educational, Scientific and Cultural Organisation [UNESCO], 2021), micro-exclusion of those students in mainstream schools (Ianes et al., 2014) was still widely evident (D'Alessio, 2013). One of the reasons for this phenomenon is that special school closure occurred abruptly in Italy and general education teachers were not adequately prepared for supporting students with disability in mainstream classrooms (Giangreco et al., 2012). Lack of extra funding and a shortage of specialist school staff for students with disability requiring additional learning support in mainstream schools have been indicated as additional system barriers to inclusion for all students (D'Alessio et al., 2013).

Research on teachers', parents', and students' experiences of inclusion, as well as classroom observations in mainstream schools, have revealed critical school level barriers to genuine inclusion for students with disability. Classroom teachers have reported challenges in collaborating with support teachers and allied health professionals, and coordinating support for inclusion (Ghedin & Aquario, 2020). Large class sizes in regular schools (Saloviita & Consegnati, 2019) and high teacher workload (Devecchi et al., 2012) create additional challenges to the provision of adequate instructional support to students with disability. Support teachers are, in some schools, assigned to individual students and the supports for students with disabilities are not considered as classroom resources but linked specifically to individuals (Devecchi et al., 2012). Teachers' perceptions of inclusion as a threat to their expert role and professional interests, combined with their beliefs that 'special educational needs' require support by 'specialists' (rather than by all teachers), have been identified as reasons for their resistance to inclusion (Soresi et al., 2013). Changing these mindsets and practices will be important for further progressing inclusion in Italy.

Portugal

Portugal's progress in developing an inclusive education legislative framework has gained international attention. Over the past few decades, the Portuguese educational system has been transformed, despite implementation challenges and economic setbacks.

Enablers to Inclusive Education in Portugal

With the end of Salazar's dictatorship in the 1970s, Portugal experienced extensive political and social transformations, with a new constitution offering universal access to public health and social security systems. In 1986, Portugal joined the European Union, receiving substantial funds to support initiatives promoting equality in employment and vocational training for disadvantaged groups, including people with disability (Pinto, 2011). In the same year, the *Portuguese Education Act* was introduced promoting equal opportunity and the right to education for *all students* (Amatori et al., 2020). In 1991, *Decree-Law 319* established the right of children with disability to be educated in mainstream schools and introduced the pedagogical criteria *special education needs*, replacing medical disability categories (Alves, 2019). The term inclusion was introduced in legislation in 1997 (Najev Čačija et al., 2019) with successive Acts and Bills influenced by the social model of disability. Disability was first expressed as a human-rights issue in the *First Action Plan for the Integration of Persons with Disabilities and Impairments 2006–9* (Pinto, 2011), which was followed by the *National Accessibility Plan 2006–15*. These plans aimed to reduce discrimination and exclusion, considering the vast accessibility issues that continued to exist in the Portuguese society (Pinto, 2018). Progressively, disability issues were no longer seen as a matter of welfare, but rather a human-rights issue, leading to Portugal's signature and ratification of the CRPD in 2007 and 2009, respectively.

The introduction of *Decree-Law* 3 (2008) brought significant changes to the education system. Based on equal opportunity principles, the law prescribed the implementation of adequate supports to enable the full participation of students with disability in mainstream educational settings (Alves, 2019). The introduction of this legislation forced the closure of special schools and prohibited discrimination against students with disability both in the public and private sectors (Pinto, 2018). Further legislation changes were introduced in 2018 with the *Inclusive Education Act* (*Decree-Law 54*, 2018)). The Act brought further alignment with the CRPD, introducing a pedagogical model based on universal design and a multilevel approach to support students' access to the curriculum (Alves, 2019; Alves et al., 2020; Amatori et al., 2020). Similarly, the Act determined that support for all students was identified, managed, and implemented at the school level by teachers and multidisciplinary teams (Alves, 2019; Alves et al., 2020). The use of Individual Education Plans became compulsory and Learning Support Centres replaced former Specialised Units. Aligned with the Act was *Decree-Law 55* (2018), which introduced new curriculum policies offering more flexibility and autonomy in curriculum and assessment to ensure that all students had opportunity to reach the targets presented in the Student Profile at the end of compulsory schooling (Alves, 2020). The Student Profile is grounded in principles around freedom of choice, responsibility, excellence, self-awareness, citizenship, and participation (Martins et al., 2017). Professional development for teachers was made widely available by the Portuguese Ministry of Education, focusing on developing teachers' knowledge of policy context, inclusion concepts, and Universal Design for Learning (Alves, 2020).

The closure of special schools and their subsequent transformation into Resource Centres for Inclusion successfully retained specialised knowledge about adjustments and provided specialised support to mainstream schools (Alves, 2019). Changes in schools were monitored and evaluated through school inspections, effectively making schools accountable for the active implementation of changes whilst disseminating good practices (Alves, 2020). Many schools were invited to participate in experimental projects (e.g., *Project Autonomy and Curriculum Flexibility* and *Pilot Project of Pedagogical Innovation*), leading to the development of new curriculum policies that brought flexibility to curriculum and assessment, and consequently increased teacher agency and school autonomy (Alves, 2020). Recently, Portugal has been one of the five European countries participating in a trial of a new model called "Inclusive Inquiry", which involves primary teachers and students having dialogues to explore how lessons can become more inclusive (Ainscow, 2020). Another significant step towards inclusive education is the use of progressive assessment practices for all learners (UNESCO, 2021).

Policy reform in Portugal was accompanied by a series of initiatives open to educational professionals and the wider community to raise awareness about inclusive education and the need for change. These involved free public discussions, conferences, presentations, and seminars examining exclusionary practices and the need for change (Alves, 2020). Public consultations also took place before and after legislative changes to support policy development.

Barriers to Inclusive Education Progress in Portugal

Despite great success in developing a more inclusive legislative framework, legislation changes were accompanied by conceptual and/or definitional issues. For example, *Decree-Law 3* (2008), which resulted in the closure of special schools, had its implementation contested as a 'step back' into the medical categorisation because of its links to the *International Classification of Functioning, Disability and Health* (Alves, 2019). Similarly, the *Inclusive Education Act*, issued nearly ten years after Portugal's ratification of the CRPD, provided a vague definition of inclusion, resulting in a broad interpretation of policies (Alves et al., 2020). Additionally, low levels of understanding of disability rights, coupled with "forms of subtle and indirect discrimination" (Pinto, 2018, p. 137), indicate that people with disability continue to be excluded and marginalised in Portuguese society.

The lack of clarity of definitions in some pieces of legislation and policies led to inconsistent implementation of practices, with instances of integration being characterised as inclusion. Concerns around the availability of human resources to implement the changes mandated by legislation were also widespread (Bonança et al., 2022). Bonança et al. (2022) highlighted the lack of transition between legislative changes to allow effective implementation of inclusive practices and the lack of teacher preparation as barriers to successful system reform. Lack of success in implementing some changes has also been linked to the bureaucratic nature of the education system and the existence of competing agendas (more specifically, neoliberal, marketised, competitive school cultures) (see Alves, 2020; Alves et al., 2020). European indicators point to higher school dropout rates for students with disability than for students without disability in Portugal

(Pinto, 2018), suggesting that some students might not be receiving the support they need to complete their compulsory education.

Implementing inclusive practices at the school level has been peppered with financial and human resourcing issues. For example, during the Portuguese debt crisis, staffing numbers were inadequate, specialised pedagogical materials were scarce, and vocational training support was reduced (Pinto, 2018). Concerns around the quality of professional development opportunities provided by the government, coupled with teacher dissatisfaction with the introduction of new practices, and lack of clear guidelines around the role of multidisciplinary staff and classroom teachers, also constituted a barrier to implementation (Alves, 2020; Alves et al., 2020). Despite many students with disability formally being included in regular schools, those with complex learning profiles are still spending most of their time segregated from the rest of their class (Alves et al., 2020).

The lack of human and material resources to implement the changes mandated by legislation was an ongoing concern for many parents and meant that some students, particularly those with more complex profiles, have yet to be effectively included in their school (Alves et al., 2020). Disagreement between different interest groups and potential challenges with implementing the new policies, particularly regarding resourcing and interpretation, has obstructed the progression and consistent implementation of inclusive education initiatives.

Recommendations

Education systems around the world are developing policy frameworks to support the implementation of inclusive education informed by the CRPD, including in Canada, Italy, and Portugal. Education and policy leaders in these three countries have a long history of progressing equity and inclusion in schooling; however, there is a need for ongoing review and improvement in each country. Our discussion highlighted the enablers and barriers to progressing inclusive education using the domains of society, system, school, and community. The following section presents five lessons and a list of recommendations for system reform:

Lesson One: Need for Society and System Legislation, Policy, and Positive Perceptions about Inclusive Schools

A national commitment to, and understanding of, social justice and inclusion, and operationalisation of a clear definition of inclusive education, will impact legislation and policy that mandates inclusion for all students. Such enablers can lead to the closure of special schools and influence a positive change in understanding of human rights and attitudes to inclusion. Evidence from New Brunswick, Canada (*Bill 85*, 1986), Italy (*National Law 517*, 1977), and Portugal (*Decree-Law 3*, 2008) illustrates commitment at the legislative level to progress and support commitment to inclusive education in each country.

Lesson Two: Funding a Unified Education System

The second lesson is that funding from segregated provisions is redirected to the unified system (Canada, Italy), including funding for student support through a non-categorical (needs-based) approach (New Brunswick, Canada), for specialist and support staff to be hired in all schools (Italy), for inclusive education capacity building of educators and school leadership (Canada, Italy), and for trialling projects aimed at improving inclusive practice (Portugal).

Lesson Three: Accountability for Policy to Practice

A third lesson is around ensuring school accountability to uphold students' rights, for example through developing accountability measures to evaluate progress towards inclusion (Portugal) and safeguarding independent advocacy options for families (Canada). The procedures, such as school inspections in Portugal, ensure schools are accountable for implementing the policy. Italy's lack of consistent collection of data on student outcomes and teaching practices also highlights the need for systematic data collection to evaluate inclusive practice.

Lesson Four: Supporting Teachers to Implement Inclusive Evidence-Based Practice

The fourth lesson is around implementing evidence-based practices, such as a tiered model of support (see Chapter 9). There is evidence in all countries about how teachers are expected to learn about inclusive pedagogies to support policy implementation. Support for research and teacher inquiries to support collective advocacy for inclusion and equity would support an evidence-based approach for implementing inclusive education in other jurisdictions.

Lesson Five: Leadership, Reframing Roles, Collaboration, and Time

Effective leadership is instrumental in education reform and change in an education system (see Chapter 8). The success reported in Canada, Italy, and Portugal required strong leadership at both the systems and school level, as well as collaborative teamwork. Evidence from each country documents how the roles of special educators, learning support teachers, and classroom teachers had to be reframed to support an inclusive approach to education. Progressing a systemic approach to inclusive education requires leaders at all levels to influence others, but it is the school leaders who play critical roles in promoting and creating values and conditions that facilitate and support inclusion (DeMatthews et al., 2020). Reading about the progress to inclusive education in Canada, Italy, and Portugal also reinforces the need for time for dialogue with stakeholders and planning actions to meet the goal of a unified system for all students.

These five lessons inform a suite of recommendations for State parties to progress inclusive education and move away from special education. The example below focuses on Australia; however, these actions are not specific to this context and can be adjusted as necessarily to be applicable to other jurisdictions.

Recommendations

1. Develop a national inclusive education policy, with a clear definition of inclusion, consistent with the definition outlined in CRPD/GC4.
2. Ensure each Australian State and Territory has an inclusive education policy, with a clear definition of inclusion, consistent with the CRPD/GC4 definition.
3. Draw on The Australian Coalition for Inclusive Education (2020) road map for achieving inclusive education, which explicitly details plans for phasing out segregation while building inclusive education.
4. Implement evidence-based inclusive practices across all schools, supported by ongoing professional development for educators, and reframing of special education and mainstream classroom teachers' roles and responsibilities.
5. Develop and implement clear measures for evaluating national inclusive school practices and collect data outcomes for all students, including students with disability.
6. Develop more explicit detail in content and accountability in *The Australian Professional Standard for Principals and the Leadership Profiles* (Australian Institute for Teaching and School Leadership, 2014) regarding obligations under the *Disability Standards for Education* (Cth).
7. Provide national funding support for family organisations advocating for inclusive education.
8. Conduct further research to fill current gaps in the literature. For example, evidence of effective practices for particular cohorts of students with disability, studies of student and parent voice, and large-scale, uniform collection of data across stakeholders and contexts.

Conclusion

Inclusive education is a means for achieving social, economic, and cultural inclusion for individuals, and for achieving an inclusive society more broadly. Learning about the enablers and barriers that contributed to the implementation of more unified and inclusive education systems in Canada, Italy, and Portugal will support other countries, like Australia, to mobilise a shared commitment across society, systems, school, and community levels to enact change. The recommendations in this chapter are designed to help achieve realisation of the systemic reform required for States Parties to meet their human-rights obligations as signatories to the CRPD. As stipulated in Article 24: Education, those obligations include provision of an inclusive education to all students, including those with disability. An extensive roadmap for implementation has been provided in GC4 to assist States Parties to implement genuine inclusion, as this results in better outcomes and a better life (see Chapter 3). As expressed recently by Dr Kerri

Mellifont, Lead Counsel Assisting the Royal Commission into Violence, Abuse, Neglect and Exploitation of People with Disability in Australia:

> Getting education right is the starting point for the prevention of violence, abuse, neglect, and exploitation . . . it is . . . [a] starting point for creating an inclusive society.
>
> (Disability Royal Commission, 2020, p. 7)

References

Abbring, I., & Meijer, C. J. (1994). Italy. In C. Meijer, S. Pijl, & S. Hegarty (Eds.), *New Perspectives in Special Education: A Six-Country Study of Integration* (pp. 9–24). Routledge.

Ainscow, M. (2020). Promoting inclusion and equity in education: Lessons from international experiences. *Nordic Journal of Studies in Educational Policy, 6*(1), 7–16, https://doi.org/10.1080/20020317.2020.1729587

Alves, I. (2019). International inspiration and national aspirations: Inclusive education in Portugal. *International Journal of Inclusive Education, 23*(7–8), 862–875. https://doi.org/10.1080/13603116.2019.1624846

Alves, I. (2020). Enacting education policy reform in Portugal–the process of change and the role of teacher education for inclusion. *European Journal of Teacher Education, 43*(1), 64–82. https://doi.org/10.1080/02619768.2019.1693995

Alves, I., Campos Pinto, P., & Pinto, T. J. (2020). Developing inclusive education in Portugal: Evidence and challenges. *Prospects, 49*(3–4), 281–296. https://doi.org/10.1007/s11125-020-09504-y

Amatori, G., Mesquita, H., & Quelhas, R. (2020). Special Education for inclusion in Europe: Critical issues and comparative perspectives for teachers' education between Italy and Portugal. *Education Sciences & Society, 11*(1). https://doi.org/10.3280/ess1-2020oa9443

AuCoin, A., Porter, G. L., & Baker-Korotkov, K. (2020). New Brunswick's journey to inclusive education. *Prospects, 1*–16. https://doi.org/10.1007/s11125-020-09508-8

Australian Coalition for Inclusive Education. (2020). *Driving change: A roadmap for achieving inclusive education in Australia.* https://acie105204494.files.wordpress.com/2020/04/acie-roadmap-final_july-2020.pdf.

Australian Government Department of Social Services. (2023). *Disability and Australia's Disability Strategy 2021–2031.* https://www.dss.gov.au/disability-and-australias-disability-strategy-2021-2031

Australian Institute for Teaching and School Leadership. (2014). *Australian Professional Standard for Principals and the Leadership Profiles.* https://www.aitsl.edu.au/docs/default-source/national-policy-framework/australian-professional-standard-for-principals-and-the-leadership-profiles.pdf?sfvrsn=c07eff3c_24

Basaglia Law (1978).

Bonança, R., Castanho, M., & Morgado, E. (2022). Decree-Law 54/2018: A challenge for inclusion. *Brazilian Journal of Education, Technology and Society, 15*(1), 135–143 https://doi.org/10.14571/brajets.v15.nse1.135-143

Canevaro, A., & de Anna, L. (2010). The historical evolution of school integration in Italy: Some witnesses and considerations. *ALTER, European Journal of Disability Research, 4*, 203–216. https://doi.org/10.1016/j.alter.2010.03.006

Carrington, S., Lassig, C., Maia-Pike, L., Mann, G., Mavropoulou, S., & Saggers, B. (2022). Societal, systemic, school and family drivers for and barriers to inclusive education. *The Australian Journal of Education, 66*(3), 251–264. https://doi.org/10.1177/00049441221 125282

Charter of Rights and Freedom (1982).

D'Alessio, S. (2013). Inclusive education in Italy: A reply to Giangreco, Doyle, and Suter. *Life Span and Disability, 16*(1), 95–120.

De Bruin, K. (2019). The impact of inclusive education reforms on students with disability: An international comparison. *International Journal of Inclusive Education, 23*(7–8), 811–826. https://doi.org/10.1080/13603116.2019.1623327

Decree-Law 3 (2008).

Decree-Law 319 (1991).

DeMatthews, D., Billingsley, B., McLeskey, J., & Sharma, U. (2020). Principal leadership for students with disabilities in effective inclusive schools. *Journal of Educational Administration, 58*(5), 539–554. https://doi.org/10.1108/JEA-10-2019-0177

Devecchi, C., Dettori, F., Doveston, M., Sedgwick, P., & Jament, J. (2012). Inclusive classrooms in Italy and England: the role of support teachers and teaching assistants. *European Journal of Special Needs Education, 27*(2), 171–184. https://doi.org/10.1080/08856257.2011. 645587

Disability Royal Commission. (2020). *Royal Commission into violence, abuse, neglect and exploitation of people with disability. Interim Report.* Canberra: Australian Government. https://disability. royalcommission.gov.au/system/files/2020-10/Interim%20Report.pdf

Disability Standards for Education 2005 (Cth).

European Agency for Special Needs and Inclusive Education. (2016). *Country Policy Review and Analysis: Italy.* Odense, Denmark. https://www.european-agency.org/activities/ country-policy-review-and-analysis

Ferri, B. (2008). Inclusion in Italy: What happens when everyone belongs. In S. L. Gabel & S. Danforth, (Eds.), *Disability and the politics of education: An international reader* (pp. 41–52). Peter Lang.

First Action Plan for the Integration of Persons with Disabilities and Impairments 2006–09.

Ghedin, E., & Aquario, D. (2020). Collaborative teaching in mainstream schools: Research with general education and support teachers. *International Journal of Whole Schooling, 16*(2), 1–34.

Giangreco, M. F., Doyle, M. B., & Suter, J. C. (2012). Demographic and personnel service delivery data: Implications for including students with disabilities in Italian schools. *Life Span and Disability, 15*(1), 97–123.

Ianes, D., Demo, H., & Dell'Anna, S. (2020). Inclusive education in Italy: Historical steps, positive developments, and challenges. *Prospects, 49*(3–4), 249–263. https://doi.org/10.1007/s11125-020-09509-7

Ianes, D., Demo, H., & Zambotti, F. (2014). Integration in Italian schools: teachers' perceptions regarding day-to-day practice and its effectiveness. *International Journal of Inclusive Education, 18*(6), 626–653. https://doi.org/10.1080/13603116.2013.802030

Inclusive Education Act (Decree-Law 54 (2018)).

Irvine, A., Lupart, J., Loreman, T., & McGhie-Richmond, D. (2010). Educational leadership to create authentic inclusive schools: The experiences of principals in a Canadian rural school district. *Exceptionality Education International, 20*(2), 70–88. https://doi.org/10.5206/ eei.v20i2.7664

Killoran, I., Zaretsky, H., Jordan, A., Smith, D., Allard, C., & Moloney, J. (2013). Supporting teachers to work with children with exceptionalities. *Canadian Journal of Education, 36*(1), 240–270.

Köpfer, A., & Óskarsdóttir, E. (2019). Analysing support in inclusive education systems: A comparison of inclusive school development in Iceland and Canada since the 1980s focusing on policy and in-school support. *International Journal of Inclusive Education, 23*(7–8), 876–890. https://doi.org/10.1080/13603116.2019.1624844

Lauchlan, F., & Fadda, R. (2012). The "Italian Model" of full inclusion: Origins and current directions. In C. Boyle & K. Topping (Eds.), *What works in inclusion?* (pp. 31–40). Open University Press.

Law 107 (2015).

Law 107 (2017).

Law 170 (2010).

Loreman, T. (2014). Special education today in Canada. In A. Rotatory, J. P. Bakken, S. Burkhardt & F. E. Obiakor, *Special education international perspectives: Practices across the globe* (pp. 33–60). Emerald Group Publishing Limited.

Lupart, J. L. (1998). Setting right the delusion of inclusion: Implications for Canadian schools. *Canadian Journal of Education/Revue Canadienne de l'education, 23*(3), 251–264. https://doi.org/10.2307/1585938

Lupart, J. L. (2012). Toward a unified system of education: Where do we go from here? *Exceptionality Education International, 22*(2), 3–7. https://doi.org/10.5206/eei.v22i2.7691

MacKay, A. W. (2006). *Connecting care and challenge: Tapping our human potential-inclusive education: A review of programming and services in New Brunswick.* New Brunswick Department of Education and Early Childhood Development.

Martins, G., Gomes, C., Brocardo, J., Pedroso, J., Camilo, J., Silva, L., Encarnação, M., Horta, M., Calçada, M., Nery, R., & Rodrigues, S. (2017). *Perfil dos Alunos à Saída da Escolaridade Obrigatória.* Ministério da Educação, Direção-Geral da Educação. http://www.dge.mec.pt/noticias/perfil-dos-alunos-saida-da-escolaridade-obrigatoria

Mura, G., Olmos, A., Aleotti, F., Ortiz Cobo, M., Rubio Gomez, M., & Diamantini, D. (2020). Inclusive education in Spain and Italy: Evolution and current debate. *Journal of Inclusive Education in Research and Practice, 1*(1), 1–23.

Najev Čačija, L., Bilač, S. & Džingalašević, G. (2019). Benchmarking education policies and practices of inclusive education: Comparative empirical research—The case of Croatia, Italy and Portugal. In Á. H. Ingþórsson, N. Alfrević, J. Pavičić & D. Vican (Eds.), *Educational leadership in policy: Challenges and implementation within Europe* (pp. 117–134). Palgrave Macmillan.

National Accessibility Plan 2006–15.

National Framework Law 104 (1992).

National Law 517 (1977).

New Brunswick's Bill 85 (1986).

Nota, L., Soresi, S., & Ferrari, L. (2014). What are emerging trends and perspectives on inclusive schools in Italy? In J. McLeskey, F. Spooner, B., Algozzine, & N. L. Waldron (Eds.), *Handbook of Effective Inclusive Schools: Research and Practice* (pp. 531–544). Taylor & Francis.

Pinto, P. C. (2011). At the crossroads: Human rights and the politics of disability and gender in Portugal. *Alter, 5*(2), 116–128. https://doi.org/10.1016/j.alter.2011.02.005

Pinto, P. C. (2018). From rights to reality: Of crisis, coalitions, and the challenge of implementing disability rights in Portugal. *Social Policy and Society: A Journal of the Social Policy Association, 17*(1), 133–150. https://doi.org/10.1017/S1474746417000380

Poed, S., Cologon, K., & Jackson, R. (2020). Gatekeeping and restrictive practices by Australian mainstream schools: Results of a national survey. *International Journal of Inclusive Education, 26*(8), 766–779. https://doi.org/10.1080/13603116.2020.1726512

Policy 322 (2013).

Porter, G. L. (2008). Making Canadian schools inclusive: A call to action. *Education Canada, 48*(2), 62–66.

Porter, G. L., & AuCoin et al., A. (2012). *Strengthening inclusion, strengthening schools: Report of the review of inclusive education programs and practices in New Brunswick Schools: An action plan for growth.* New Brunswick Department of Education and Early Childhood Development.

Portuguese Education Act.

Saloviita, T., & Consegnati, S. (2019). Teacher attitudes in Italy after 40 years of inclusion. *British Journal of Special Education, 46*(4), 465–479. https://doi.org/10.1111/1467-8578.12286

Sharma, U., Aiello, P., Pace, E. M., Round, P., & Subban, P. (2018). In-service teachers' attitudes, concerns, efficacy and intentions to teach in inclusive classrooms: An international comparison of Australian and Italian teachers. *European Journal of Special Needs Education, 33*(3), 437–446. https://doi.org/10.1080/08856257.2017.1361139

Shevchenko, Y. M., Dubiaha, S. M., Melash, V. D., Fefilova, T. V., & Saenko, Y. O. (2020). The Role of Teachers in the Organization of Inclusive Education of Primary School Pupils. *International Journal of Higher Education, 9*(7), 207–216.

https://doi.org/10.5430/ijhe.v9n7p207

Sider, S., Beck, K., Eizadirad, A., & Morvan, J. (2022). Performative commitments to diversity and inclusion in Canadian educational institutions: Considerations for equity efforts in comparative and international education. *Global Comparative Education: Journal of WCCES, 6*(1), 15–28.

Slee, R. (2018). *Inclusive education isn't dead, it just smells funny.* Taylor & Francis.

Sokal, L., & Katz, J. (2015). Oh, Canada: Bridges and barriers to inclusion in Canadian schools. *Support for Learning, 30*(1), 42–54. https://doi.org/10.1111/1467-9604.12078

Somma, M. (2020). From segregation to inclusion: special educators' experiences of change. *International Journal of Inclusive Education, 24*(4), 381–394. https://doi.org/10.1080/13603116.2018.1464070

Soresi, S., Nota, L., Ferrari, L., Sgaramella, T. M., Ginevra, M. C., & Santilli, S. (2013). Inclusion in Italy: From numbers to ideas . . . that is from "special" visions to the promotion of inclusion for all persons. *Life Span and Disability, 16*(2), 187–217.

United Nations. (2006). *Convention on the Rights of Persons with Disabilities (CRPD).* https://www.un.org/disabilities/documents/convention/convoptprot-e.pdf.

United Nations. (2016). *General Comment No. 4, Article 24: Right to Inclusive Education (CRPD/C/GC/4).* https://digitallibrary.un.org/record/1313836?ln=en

United Nations. (2023). *Convention on the Rights of Persons with Disabilities (CRPD).* https://www.un.org/development/desa/disabilities/convention-on-the-rights-of-persons-with-disabilities.html

United Nations Educational, Scientific and Cultural Organisation. (2021). *Global Education Monitoring Report 2021, Central and Eastern Europe, the Caucasus and Central Asia—Inclusion and education: All means all.* UNESCO. https://unesdoc.unesco.org/ark:/48223/pf0000375517

Van Walleghem, J., Lutfiyya, Z. M., Braun, S., Trudel, L. E., Enns, C., Melnychuk, B. J., Mitchell, T., Park, Y-Y., & Zaretsky, J. (2013). Inclusive special education in Manitoba: 2001–2012.

Manitoba Education Research Network (MERN) Monograph Series, 6, 1–20. https://charlottejenns.weebly.com/uploads/3/0/7/7/30778141/mcle_mern_book_eng_pages_223368.pdf

Vianello, R., & Lanfranchi, S. (2011). Positive effects of the placement of students with intellectual developmental disabilities in typical class. *Life Span and Disability, 14*(1), 75–84.

Vitello, S. J. (1994). Special education integration: The Arezzo Approach. *International Journal of Disability, Development, and Education, 41*(1), 61–70. https://doi.org/10.1080/0156655940410106

Wolfensberger, W. (1972). *The principle of normalization in human services.* National Institute on Mental Retardation.

Chapter 8

Leading inclusive education reform

*Linda J. Graham, Callula Killingly, Haley Tancredi, &
Theresa Bourke*

All nations that are signatories to the *Convention on the Rights of Persons with Disability* (CRPD; United Nations, 2006), and especially those that have ratified the Optional Protocol, are required to ensure the "right of persons with disabilities to education through an inclusive education system at all levels . . . and for all students, includ-ing persons with disabilities, without discrimination and on equal terms with others" (United Nations, 2016, para 8). As discussed in Chapters 2 and 3, this is to be achieved through systemic inclusive education reform. Systemic inclusive education reform re-quires change throughout, not just operationally and not just at one level of an organisa-tion. It requires strong leadership that cascades from the centre of an education system through many and varied conduits to reach the epicentre for inclusion: the classroom.

Research on education reform most often focuses on school leaders (otherwise known as principals or head teachers) but the success of systemic inclusive education reform is dependent, first and foremost, on the leaders at the centre of an organisation; those who set the priorities to which all others respond. Success is then progressively dependent on those next to take the reform baton. In the case of Queensland—the most north-eastern state of Australia—those staff are regional directors, then education leadership teams, regional support teams, school leaders, middle leaders, and finally, classroom teachers. It is not a fast or simple process, but it is one that can be supported by leaders who invest in themselves and in others. In this chapter, we outline how systemic inclu-sive education reform is being achieved collaboratively through research-based profes-sional learning with system and school leaders in Central Queensland (CQ) Region. Their journey began some years ago when the Queensland government developed an inclusive education policy and implementation strategy.

Queensland's Inclusion Journey

In June 2016, after an incident involving the use of restrictive practices to manage a student on the autism spectrum, the Queensland Minister of Education announced an independent review into education for students with disability in Queensland state schools. The final report from what became known as the *Deloitte Disability Review* was released in March the following year (Deloitte Access Economics, 2017). The report in-cluded 17 largely system-level recommendations for reform, all of which were accepted

DOI: 10.4324/9781003350897-10

by the Queensland government for implementation by the Queensland Department of Education and Training. One of the department's first actions in response to the recommendations was to collaboratively develop an inclusive education policy and implementation strategy. The Department's Inclusive Education Policy was released in 2018 and is the first in Australia to adopt the definition of and nine core principles for inclusive education outlined in *General Comment No. 4* on Article 24 (GC4; United Nations, 2016) of the CRPD.

Leadership and school leaders are referenced in two of the nine core principles. Principle 2 describes 'Committed Leaders' as those who "commit to and are accountable for implementing inclusive education" and who "promote a culture and shared values that remove barriers and support inclusion" (Queensland Department of Education, 2018, p. 2). Principle 6 refers to school leaders as members of a "Confident, Skilled and Capable Workforce" who "build on their expertise to implement inclusive education practices", who share good practice "based on evidence" and who "mentor" and "engage in continuous professional learning" (p. 2). In 2021, the Policy received international recognition through an award from the Zero Project (2021), an initiative of the Essl Foundation aimed at recognising implementation of the CRPD. However, policy development is an easier task than policy implementation, for policy intent is interpreted, adapted, or even transformed by many varied policy actors (Braun et al., 2011), each with different beliefs, knowledges, and capabilities.

Implementing Policy

The intent of education policy is rarely to prescribe what needs to happen to solve a problem. Rather, policy can be understood as a process designed to create the circumstances to enact change (Braun et al., 2011). Policy enactment has been described as "creative processes of interpretation and translation" (Braun et al., 2011, p. 586), where the abstract ideas laid out in policy are contextualised in creative ways to take local contexts into account. Contextual factors—like people/staffing, ethos/culture, resources, and budgets—can therefore enable or constrain the realisation of policy intent. In the case of systemic inclusive education reform implementation in Queensland, system and school leaders' knowledge of inclusion may act as an enabler or a constraint (Bai & Martin, 2015), because knowledge is critical to the successful enactment of inclusive practices.

Although much of the research literature speaks to the central role of school leaders in the implementation of inclusive education, they are but one person and their ability to meet these obligations is dependent on the knowledge and capability of many other staff, including their own supervisors, some of whom may not be fully on board with the reform direction. Policy enactment, continuous school improvement, and high-quality practice in schools must also be stewarded by system leaders, who have been described as "important intermediaries between broader national and provincial policies, and the work and learning of those in schools" (Hardy & Melville, 2018, p. 160). To support the alignment of policy intent and enactment, system leaders also require opportunities for professional learning, which can occur with school leaders (Bai & Martin, 2015). When shared opportunities to build knowledge and skills are available, a network of support is built around school s and can drive a cascade from policy intent to policy enactment. A network of support for leading inclusion can also support leaders to drive adoption of school-wide frameworks like Multi-Tiered Systems of Support (MTSS) through to the use of inclusive practices in the classroom (see Chapters 9, 11, and 12).

Leading sustainable change in inclusive education practice can be challenging for school leaders (DeMatthews & Mawhinney, 2014; Kugelmass & Ainscow, 2004), for they must negotiate competing organisational priorities—some of which may not be compatible—and these intersections must be reconciled to progress inclusive education for all (DeMatthews, 2015). School leaders may also experience push-back from members of their school community, including teachers and parents. Some teachers do not support inclusion due to the belief that it creates additional workload (Saloviita, 2020), and while parents of students without disability are generally positive or neutral towards inclusive education (Paseka & Schwab, 2020), principals can experience opposition from competitively oriented parents when attempting to close segregated settings or abandon academic streaming. School leaders report that these challenges are difficult to overcome due to lack of knowledge of genuine inclusion, particularly in relation to including students with disability, which some leaders attribute to the quality of their preparation programs (Billingsley et al., 2014; Osterman & Hafner, 2009). Successful enactment of inclusive education policy intent requires that *both* system and school leaders have knowledge about what genuine inclusion is, why they should be implementing it and how it can be achieved, so that they have the confidence to uphold and progress their vision, even when faced with competing priorities and beliefs.

Researching Leadership for Inclusion

A scan of the literature from the turn of the century reveals that various types of leadership are aligned with inclusion, including distributed, transformational, ethical, and social justice leadership. For example, Ryan (2006) defines inclusive leadership as a form of leadership that promotes inclusive education by identifying and transforming multiple and diverse forms of exclusion endemic to current schooling. This goes beyond strategic and operational leadership, to leadership focused on values of equity and social justice (Ryan, 2006). More recently, the Supporting Inclusive School Leadership (SISL; European Agency, 2018) project team advocated for the integration of three leadership approaches—transformational, distributed, *and* instructional—to ensure the successful implementation of inclusive practices in schools (Óskarsdóttir et al., 2020).

Drawing on the work of Caroline Shields, Carrington (2022) describes *transformational leadership* as "a critical approach that is linked to promoting equity and inclusion with a focus on beliefs and values . . . to address inequity and foster an inclusive school culture" (p. 20). This requires building a shared vision, inspiring positive change in others, and taking measures to build a collaborative culture (Óskarsdóttir et al., 2020). Carrington (2022) also notes that transformative leaders make ethical decisions based on moral reasoning which requires them to resist perverse incentives to segregate and exclude, practices that are associated with school accountability measures like high stakes testing and competitive school markets. Shields (2005) herself refers to the importance of 'the why', which she describes as the moral purpose of the work, in enabling leaders to make decisions about the "who, what, where and when of schooling" (p. 110).

Carter and Abawi (2018) investigated the work of principals who worked with staff in leadership roles to establish a culture of inclusion. They determined that principals who successfully led inclusion in their school had a clear vision, established supportive processes and procedures that were monitored and reviewed using data-based decision making, and who empowered others to lead. This is described in the literature as *distributed leadership*. One principal interviewed in their study spoke to the need to "have the right people in the right places" (p. 57), while another described the need to make "tough decisions of 'shutting down or moving on' those who do not share an inclusive philosophy" (p. 56).

A consistent theme was the importance of principals engaging in *instructional leadership*. This involves the communication of expectations for pedagogical practice, investing in teachers' knowledge and capacity through modelling of practice and professional learning. Importantly, secondary analysis of data from the Teaching and Learning International Survey (TALIS) 2013 completed by 121,173 teachers found that teaching staff are less likely to require separate professional development related to inclusive practice in schools with higher levels of instructional leadership, compared with schools where instructional leadership is low (Cooc, 2019). System-level investment in instructional leaders, where these leaders take an active role in developing teachers' capabilities to teach students with disability, has positive effects on teachers and professional development gaps are reduced (Cooc, 2019).

Members of the SISL team argued that school leaders require knowledge of all three of these leadership theories to successfully lead inclusive schools (Óskarsdóttir et al., 2020), for together they encompass 'the why' (transformational), 'the who' (distributed), and 'the how' (instructional). More important than knowledge of leadership theories, however, is knowledge of genuine inclusive education and inclusive practice because principals cannot lead confidently, effectively or courageously without this knowledge. As noted earlier, moral courage is necessary for leadership for inclusion (Carrington, 2022) as it requires leaders to do what is right, not what is popular or expedient. The inclusion of *all* students means including those that some teachers might find hard to teach and students whom other students and their parents may not understand and/or like. It means engaging in practices that promote equity, and this might not always be appreciated in communities where parents are looking for a competitive edge for their children. It means staring down stakeholders who seek to limit the rights of some children because they perceive those rights to impinge on their own (Gillett-Swan & Lundy, 2022). The courage, confidence, and ability to do this is contingent on the conviction forged by knowledge; knowledge of genuine inclusive education, knowledge of its positive impact on student outcomes, knowledge of one's legal obligations, knowledge of effective practice, and knowledge of the frameworks that can make it all work. But how are systems to develop that knowledge in their leaders when those leaders have so many competing responsibilities at an unprecedented time of disruption to schooling?

Enhancing Leadership for Inclusion

Research on methods of enhancing leaders' knowledge of inclusive education and inclusive practice to enable them to lead inclusive schools and pedagogy is even rarer than research on leadership for inclusion. The only relevant large-scale study that we could find is the Ohio Leadership for Inclusion, Implementation, and Instructional Improvement (OLi) project, which was led by Wordfarmers Associates LLC, a research consultancy, together with researchers from Ohio University and the University of Cincinnati in the United States. Using a quasi-experimental design, the OLi team attempted to change school leaders' attitudes towards the inclusion of students with disability and to enhance instructional leadership practices through participation in a two-year professional development (PD) program (Howley et al., 2019). Two hundred and fifty-seven Ohio school leaders participated in the study with 56 engaging in the PD program and 201 in a matched control. All participants completed two scales tapping attitudes to the inclusion of all students and instructional leadership practices at the end of the study. Analyses revealed a statistically significant difference in attitudes towards the inclusion of students with disability between the program and control groups, suggesting that the PD program had some positive impact for the program group. However, no significant difference was observed between groups in the use of instructional leadership practices.

Two years is a significant investment of time on the part of school leaders, who have many and varied responsibilities that require them to learn continuously to stay abreast of changing legislation, government priorities, school curriculum, and workplace relations best practice. Such a level of time investment is akin to undertaking a Master's degree which some systems, including Queensland, have supported their principals to do through scholarships that subsidise course fees. While engaging in assessment helps postgraduate degree students to retain and consolidate their learning, it can be very challenging for school principals to manage that load given the complexity of their roles, even with the study leave provided. This presents a challenge for systems embarking on systemic inclusive education reform: how to provide leaders with the required knowledge—at scale—in a way that is responsive to the needs of busy professionals who are charged with running complex environments in which anything can happen and often does? And how can that be done across a system that has the added challenge of geographical distance between schools? We put our heads together with leaders in CQ Region to accomplish that exact task.

CQ Region: Leading Inclusive Education Reform

Central Queensland encompasses a vast area (497,714 square kilometres) that accounts for 26.9% of the north-eastern state of Queensland, Australia's second largest state. CQ region extends from towns like Gayndah at its southernmost tip to Birdsville in the west, all the way up to Bloomsbury just north of Mackay. It is famous for the crystal blue waters and idyllic beaches off Great Keppel Island, together with the massive mineral deposits in Moranbah, Middlemount, and Emerald, and is home to some of Australia's largest cattle stations. While the majority of CQ's 230,000 people live in regional cities like Rockhampton, Emerald, Gladstone, and Mackay, a large minority resides well beyond, posing challenges for the provision of education. CQ Region educates 48,327 students across 190 schools. Most of these (142) are primary schools, 26 are secondary schools, 16 are Prep to Grade 10, and two are schools of Distance Education. There are only four special schools.

The tyranny of distance is both a boon and a challenge for inclusion. As in other regional centres of Australia, regional and remote schools in country towns often have a strong civic culture where every child is welcomed as a member of the local community. With no alternative 'down the road', small country schools have always had to make inclusion work. The tyranny of distance, however, also brings isolation, making it difficult for educators to share knowledge and to learn from each other. High turnover of staff is a known challenge in large regional areas, as educators seek to return to the cities for family and employment reasons. This is the reality for many Australian education providers, one that is experienced by geographically large and predominantly rural regions in some other countries—like Wyoming in the United States—but not in others, like England, which has an area quarter that of Central QLD.[1]

In 2020, CQ system and school leaders conducted an Inclusion Scan, a process of inquiry to identify what is working well and can provide a foundation for further growth, and what is not working so well and which would benefit from refinement. The process, which was conducted with the input of school leaders, identified three challenges: (1) changing staff mindsets, (2) building inclusion capabilities of staff, and (3) principals' knowledge of inclusion. A key recommendation of the Inclusion Scan report was that the region: "Invest in providing a suite of universally accessible professional learning opportunities for the Education Leadership Team and School Leaders to build their knowledge of inclusion". In December 2021, CQ system leaders and researchers from the Centre for Inclusive Education at the Queensland University of Technology (QUT) embarked on a collaborative project to enhance knowledge of genuine inclusion and practice across the region through an evidence-based program of learning that could be delivered responsively and flexibly.

In early December 2021, the research team visited Rockhampton to conduct the co-design phase of the project. The aim of the regional visit was to meet members of the regional leadership and support teams, learn about the Central Queensland context, establish a common goal for the project, and to co-design the project

---

1 Although population density has its own challenges, these metrics speak for themselves: England has 406.9 people per square kilometre, whereas Central QLD has 0.5 people per square kilometre.

design. On day one of the visit, the QUT team attended the Central Queensland Region Education Leadership Team meeting to gauge the ELT team's knowledge of inclusive education, perceptions of the challenges/barriers influencing school leaders, views on what changes in leadership/teaching are necessary, and what it would "look like" if genuine inclusion was embedded in all Central Queensland schools. Day two of the visit comprised a series of meetings with stakeholders from the Inclusion and Disability team, the Aboriginal and Torres Strait Islander Education and Youth Transitions team, Early Childhood Education and Care (ECEC) team, and the Centre for Learning and Wellbeing (ClaW) team and Principal Advisors, Teaching and Learning Support (PATL). On the third day, the QUT discussed initial observations with members of the Education Leadership Team and canvassed project design options.

A common goal with two objectives was established for the project during the co-design process. The first objective was to enhance school and system leaders' knowledge *of* inclusion, beginning with the fundamental concepts that underpin it, the history and moral imperatives that sit behind it, and the laws, legislation, and standards that guide it. The second objective was to enhance their knowledge *for* inclusion by introducing them to frameworks and approaches that they could implement in their school or context. In the remaining sections of this chapter, we describe the processes undertaken to complete the project and then present its outcomes.

What Did We Do?

The team employed a traditional pre-post design which entailed the use of a purpose-built survey instrument *before* (Time 1) and *after* (Time 2) participation in a program of learning developed to identify and address the inclusive education knowledge needs of system and school leaders in CQ Region.

The Survey Instrument

The QUT team drew on the research literature to purposefully develop a survey instrument. The final 64-item questionnaire was organised into three domains distinguished by their purpose. The first domain (16 items) tapped participants' beliefs by asking participants to rate their agreement to a range of statements using a 5-point Likert scale from "Strongly Disagree" to "Strongly Agree". The second domain (26 items) assessed participants' foundational knowledge on the background to inclusion, including human rights and legislation, and concepts fundamental to inclusive practice, such as the social model of disability, with items requiring a variety of response types: open-ended, multiple-choice, closed response, or ratings on a five-point scale. The third domain (22 items) tapped perceptions of participants' capacity to lead inclusion, and included items rated on a five-point scale. The Time 2 instrument repeated these domains with the addition of one other to gauge participants' perception of knowledge growth, their reflections on the learning gained, and how they anticipated putting their learning into practice.

The Program of Learning

The research team devised a rigorous program of learning with three components: (i) full-day face-to-face introductory professional learning workshops, (ii) an online module designed to support self-paced 'anytime' learning, and (iii) four live webinars that were delivered at key junctures in the 12-week program to complement the online module.

Component 1: Regional Workshops

Seventy-two system and school leaders across four regional cities attended full-day face-to-face workshops. Each workshop was split into three sessions aimed at helping leaders to re-familiarise themselves with the Australian Standards for principals and teachers, learn about the history, development, and concepts of inclusive education, establish a shared vision for inclusive education within the region, discuss challenges in implementation, and determine both personal and inclusive education goals to be worked toward during the program of learning. A copy of the first edition of this book was provided to each participant to support their learning.

Component 2: Online Module

The online module offered a self-paced experience and comprised eight elements that were progressively released to participants at regular intervals (Table 8.1). In line with the principles of adult learning, the online module was designed to be interactive, engaging, and informative. Written materials were designed to activate participants' prior knowledge and encouraged reflection, and were presented in a variety of modes, including sub-module readings, short videos, interactive practice scenarios, quizzes, and academic readings, which included selected chapters from the first edition of this book (Graham, 2020).[2]

Together, these connected components provide the foundation for leaders to lead inclusive education in their schools and systems.

Component 3: Live Webinars

Four live webinars were designed to complement the online module and delivered across the three months of program delivery. Each 60-minute webinar was designed to both reiterate and extend key concepts and practices covered in the online module, and to encourage discussion between participants about the real-world application of these concepts and practices in CQ state schools. All webinars were recorded to enable participants to engage at their convenience.

---

2 Notably, this 2nd Edition includes new chapters that directly correspond with elements of this program of learning; see, for example, Chapters 9, 11, and 12.

Table 8.1 Eight Elements of the Leading Inclusive Education Reform Online Module

Element	Focus Area
1. *What is inclusive education?*	Provides participants with foundational knowledge about what genuine inclusive education is and how it came about over time.
2. *Fundamental concepts*	Explains the concepts that are fundamental to inclusive education philosophy and practice.
3. *The legal foundations*	Explains educators' obligations under relevant Australian legislation: the *Disability Discrimination Act 1992* (DDA; Cth) and the *Disability Standards for Education 2005* (DSE; Cth).
4. *Understanding inclusion/exclusion*	Considers exclusionary discipline data patterns with the aim of understanding factors driving those patterns in terms of possible barriers that can be eliminated or reduced.
5. *Transforming school cultures*	Focuses on implementation of inclusive education and the critical nature of school culture and teacher-student relationships in facilitating successful inclusive education reform.
6. *Transforming pedagogy*	Explains tiered systems of support, and the meaning of 'universal' within them, with a focus on Accessible Pedagogies as the first universal tier in a Multi-Tiered System of Support model.
7. *Transforming learning*	Unpacks the importance of evidence-based early reading instruction implemented within MTSS, wherein all students benefit from high quality classroom instruction (Tier 1), while screening and progress monitoring of reading skills enable the provision of further targeted supports as required (Tiers 2 and 3).
8. *Bringing it all together*	Focuses on how the elements explored across the Program of Learning can work in synergy to achieve systemic inclusive education reform.

How Did We Do It?

After receiving approval from the QUT Human Research Ethics Committee and the Queensland Department of Education, the project was advertised in the CQ Region newsletter. Invitations were sent via email to all school principals, and regional support team and region leadership team members. Participation in the research was voluntary. Of the 230 system and school leaders in CQ Region, 128 consented to participate. Of these, 100 elected to participate in the program of learning and 28 consented to participate in the control group. Participants had access to the online content for just over three months between the Time 1 and Time 2 surveys. Sixty-one of the 102 program group participants (61.0%), and 12 of the 29 control group participants (42.86%) completed the Time 2 survey. Due to response attrition, the number of participants in the control group who completed the Time 2 survey was too small to allow for group comparisons. This chapter therefore provides descriptive analyses comparing Time 1 and

Time 2 responses by the 73 participants who completed both surveys. Key questions relevant to the core aims of the program of learning are presented in the following section.

What Was the Result?

Increased Knowledge

Seventy-three of the 102 participants who enrolled in the program of learning completed the Time 2 survey.[3] We asked these 73 participants to indicate the extent to which they felt their knowledge of inclusive education had increased as a result of the program of learning. On average, participants provided a rating of 64 (on a scale of 0–100) for this question, with responses ranging from three to 100, and the most common response being in the 70–80 range.

Participants' perception of increased knowledge was evident in changes in responses between Time 1 and Time 2. These questions were based on the program content and readings. Some were intuitive, some were 'Googleable', and others were not. The aim was two-fold: to assess the effectiveness of the program of learning *and* to prompt participants to think about concepts they may not be familiar with. The results of some questions, for example, were used during the program of learning as 'conversation starters' or as attentional hooks in the survey to which more substantive content could be anchored. The survey began with items tapping participants' knowledge of inclusive education and how it came to be.

Background to Inclusion

Participants were asked—via a short-response question—who the first victims of the Holocaust were, with the correct answer being children or persons with a disability. Responses were thematically coded according to five categories (see Figure 8.1).

Approximately half of the program group participants (52.46%) provided the correct response at Time 1, increasing to 81.67% at Time 2. For the Control group, the same proportion of participants provided the correct response at each timepoint (41.67%).

Later in the survey, participants were asked to rate as true or false the statement: "Article 24 of the Convention on the Rights of Persons with Disabilities (CRPD) provides people with disability the human right to an inclusive education". Most participants in both the Program and Control groups responded correctly, that this was true, at both timepoints (> 90% in both groups each time). However, as indicated by responses to questions about other human-rights instruments, for example, the Universal Declaration of Human Rights (UDHR), their responses suggested the need for further development. For example, in the Time 1 survey, just under one in 10 participants in

---

3 Two additional participants completed engagement questions only; their responses are included for those questions.

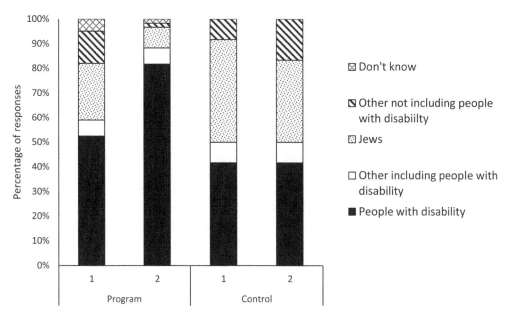

Figure 8.1 Responses to the question: "Who were the first victims of the Holocaust?".

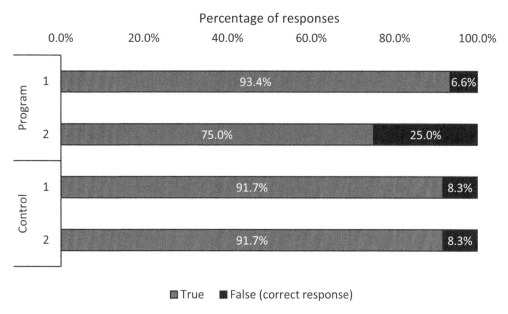

Figure 8.2 True/false responses on whether the UDHR provides the right to an inclusive education.

the program of learning (6.56%) selected 'false' (the correct answer) to this statement: "The Universal Declaration of Human Rights (UDHR) provides people with disability the human right to an inclusive education". By Time 2, this result had improved to 25% (see Figure 8.2). In contrast, the proportion of correct responses in the Control group was the same at both timepoints (8.33%).

Participants were also asked to rate the statement that "Integrating students with a disability into mainstream classes is a human right in accordance with the Convention on the Rights of Persons with Disabilities (CRPD)", as true or false. The correct response to this question is false, yet at Time 1, most of the Program and Control groups responded in the affirmative (see Figure 8.3), demonstrating a lack of understanding of the distinction between the terms 'inclusion' and 'integration', as well as the meaning of 'mainstream'; a problematic term discussed in Chapter 2 of both editions of this book.

Correct responses from the Program group increased from 13.11% to 21.67%, following the intervention, in which these definitions were explicitly taught; however, no participants in the Control group provided correct responses at Time 2.

The Social Model of Disability

In what might have seemed a slightly bizarre question, participants were asked if they knew why Senator Jordon Steele-John had grazed knuckles (see Figure 8.4). Four answer choices were provided in multiple choice format. The proportion of participants

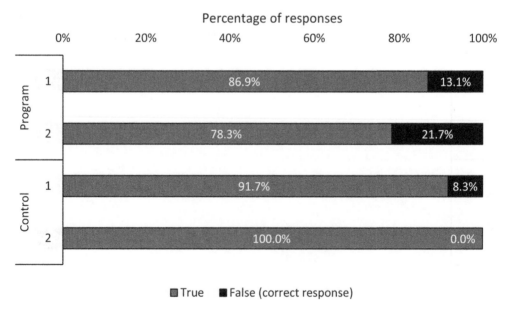

Figure 8.3 True/false responses to whether integrating students with a disability into mainstream classes is a human right in accordance with the CRPD.

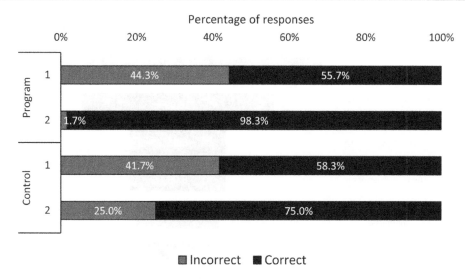

Figure 8.4 Responses to the question: "Why did Senator Jordon Steele-John have grazed knuckles?"

selecting the correct response—that the door to his office was not wide enough—increased from 55.74% to 98.33% in the Program group, while the Control group increased from 58.33% to 75.00%.

A more difficult question, because it cannot be 'Googled', tapped knowledge of the social model through another true/false statement: "Disability creates barriers to learning for which teachers need to make adjustments" (Figure 8.5). The correct response

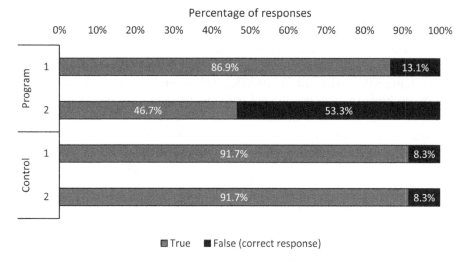

Figure 8.5 True/false responses to whether disability creates barriers to learning.

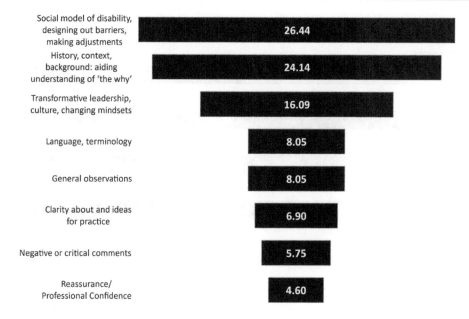

Figure 8.6 Participants' reflections about their learning grouped by theme.

to this statement is 'false' because disability is the outcome of barriers, it does not 'create' them. Few participants (<15% in both groups) selected false at Time 1. Following the program of learning, the proportion of Program participants providing the correct response increased from 13.11% to 53.33%, while the proportion of Control group participants was the same at each timepoint (8.33%).

Participant Reflections on Their Learning

Participants were invited to share their reflections on what they had learned from the program of learning. This open-ended question resulted in a range of reflections that pointed to changes in participants' knowledge, beliefs, and practices. As some responses touched on multiple themes, we divided individual comments into 89 statements and then grouped these into eight themes. As shown in Figure 8.6, the most dominant theme related to the social model of disability and associated concepts and practices, including the difference between impairment and disability and the impact of barriers, as well as how these can be designed out by implementing universal principles or minimised through the provision of reasonable adjustments.

Participants' reflections clearly demonstrated greater appreciation of the social model after engaging in this program of learning:

"The idea that there is no disability until a barrier has been put in place really opened my eyes". (Primary school principal)

"Social model isn't scary; it is common sense. Micro exclusions matter". (Education Leadership Team Member)

"Understanding about the difference forms of inclusion/exclusion. How we can make adjustments to make education accessible for all, clearer understanding about barriers for our learners". (Primary school principal)

"Moving from the social model to an understanding of seeing barriers to learning that can be removed". (Region Support Team)

The next most dominant theme—accounting for just under one-quarter (24.14%) of statements—was represented by participants' reflections on having learned about the background to inclusion.

"I broadened my scope of inclusion to include different participant groups with a strong theoretical understanding of *why*". (Primary school principal)

"More technical understanding of the history/evolution of inclusive mentalities and perspectives". (Primary school principal)

Exposure to this content enabled some participants to understand the moral imperative guiding inclusion or what several participants called "the why". It is essential for transformational leaders to have conviction, especially if the reform work is complex or difficult.

"I have reinforced my commitment to supporting all learners. I have developed a greater understanding of the necessity and complexity of the work". (Secondary school principal)

"As system leaders, this gave us a shared language and more consistent understanding of inclusion and '*the why*'". (Primary school principal)

Although the program of learning was only 12 weeks in length and delivered during a very challenging year affected by COVID-19 and floods, some participants' reflections suggested they were beginning to make important connections between concepts and that it had positively impacted their thinking:

"I think the biggest learning was around the change of thinking and ways. Understanding the background and violation of human rights was very confronting and I believe shows we are on the right path. The problem isn't how the student learns; it is the with the barriers that are stopping the learning". (Primary school principal)

"I have learned to think differently, to challenge my own perceptions about inclusive education, to recognise conversations that are biased and go against human rights and feel more equipped to be able to call out such behaviours and bring a different research-based perspective. We are definitely on the right track with this piece of work, but there is such a long way to go in changing the status quo". (Region Support Team)

The third most dominant theme—with 16.09% of statements—relates to participants' reflections on their enhanced capacity to lead inclusive education reform either in their region or in their school.

> "A transformational approach is required to ensure that as leaders we cultivate a positive, inclusive school culture that privileges the development of relationships as key to success". (Primary school principal)
>
> "Transformation of school culture, learning, pedagogy to drive inclusive reform in education". (Region Support Team)

Participant responses relating to this theme also indicated consolidation between ideas and concepts covered separately in the program of learning.

> "I've learned how extremely important it is to make sure that everyone is on the same page especially around inclusive practices. That teaching staff are ensuring that in their planning, lesson implementation and reflections on their lessons that they take the time to really look through the student lens and how to improve the learning outcomes for each student (reduce the barrier to learning for each student)". (Primary school principal)

Just under one in 10 statements referred to better recognition of the importance of language and/or terminology relating to inclusion. While some participants reflected that they had acquired new terminology or now better understood key terminology—such as learning the difference between equity and equality—one participant noted "my perception has changed and therefore my language has changed". (Region Support Team)

The last three themes together accounted for just over one in six statements. These were, in descending order, clarity about and ideas for practice, negative or critical comments, and reassurance/professional confidence. Only five participants provided reflections that might be perceived as negative or critical. Fewer again were specifically about the program or about inclusion—one was a secondary school principal—who gave a relatively low self-rating for engagement and learning gain (30 and 31, respectively), acknowledged that they could have benefited more but for barriers to participation that they described as 'time and space'. Prioritisation of time is potentially affected by perceptions of relevance and value. The reflection below is long but important, for while this participant acknowledges that they need to develop a clearer vision, they also foreground their need to learn 'the how'.

> "I was hoping this course would focus on more of the how to be inclusive rather than the legalities associate with it. I suspect this is the case and that the sessions that I have engaged with probably were the only ones that had this focus. Personally, the history nor legislation motivate me, and I know my staff put up a wall if I ever mention the legal requirements to do something and the gains made are through pulling teeth. What I need to learn more about is the how and the very small incremental

steps that I can assist my staff to be more inclusive. I also need to develop a clearer vision that I can paint for my staff. The vision of students learning beside their same age peer is too vague. I need to be able to articulate how the focused and intensive supports work, how quality differentiation occurs for this child, and what the next step for a teacher to achieve this". (Secondary school principal)

This perspective was not universal, and most participants indicated that they appreciated the opportunity to learn more about the legal requirements as well as the background that led to those requirements.

"Understanding the disability standards and historical origins of where we have come, was great". (P-10 Principal)

The smallest proportion of participant responses (4.60%, Fig. 8.8) referred to the reassurance/professional reinforcement that some participants experienced by engaging in Program of Learning. For example, one primary school principal noted that the Program of Learning afforded "greater clarity and reassurance that my leadership was moving in the right direction", while a regional support team member noted, "it has assisted me to consolidate my existing knowledge and engage in conversation with colleagues to broaden understanding".

Putting the Program of Learning into Practice

Lastly, participants were invited to share how they plan to use the knowledge they had gained. Again, some responses touched on multiple themes, so individual comments were divided into 75 statements, and these were grouped into five themes. As shown in Figure 8.7, the greatest proportion of responses related to participants' plans to use

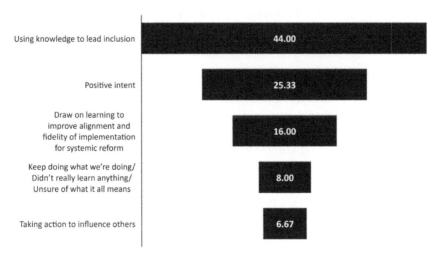

Figure 8.7 Participants' reflections on putting knowledge into practice.

knowledge to lead inclusion in their context by sharing information and collaborating with their respective teams. An example was provided by one primary school principal who was already working with their team to disseminate learning from the Program of Learning: "Have already started mirroring the webinar sessions with staff". Other participants were connecting with peers through their leadership networks to engaged in deeper discussions about inclusive leadership, particularly where all parties were involved in the Program of Learning, "I will continue to work with my principals, particularly those who have engaged in the program to further enhance collective knowledge and understanding" (Education Leadership Team).

Some participants indicated they would use what they had learnt to engage in instructional leadership:

> "Build capability of staff to ensure teaching and learning is aligned to same aged peer content and remove barriers for all students to access learning and show learning growth". (Special school principal)
>
> "Use my knowledge to help teachers make adjustments for learners in our school, so that they can access the curriculum". (Primary school principal)

Some participants identified that when engaging as an instructional leader, conversations about what genuine inclusion is may arise, which may challenge the thinking and practices of their colleagues. A range of participants indicated that they felt the Program of Learning empowered them to challenge thinking, assumptions, and implicit biases:

> "Continue to work with schools to develop an inclusive nature to the work that they do every day. Supporting principals to challenge long held beliefs about segregation and integration instead of genuine inclusive practices will be important for a range of the schools that I work with". (Education Leadership Team)
>
> ". . . to challenge teacher thinking about truly inclusive learning opportunities for students". (Primary school principal)
>
> "Be prepared to call or challenge hidden bias/subtle discriminations". (Education Leadership Team)

One-quarter of participants (25.33%) shared positive reflections on the Program of Learning and indicated that they would continue reading and learning.

> "I plan to continue gaining knowledge and understanding in this space". (Education Leadership Team)
>
> "I will continue my inclusion journey, reviewing and refining whilst still accessing evidence-based research to support us where we are in our journey". (Primary school Principal)
>
> "Stay on top of current research and use pedagogical practice that is individualised for all to achieve their best". (Primary school principal)

A reflection from a member of the Region Support Team encapsulated the intended learning of the program and the central ideas with which it engaged:

"I have gained a fuller understanding of: * the history behind the rights/policies, and via reading the textbook, a very clear definition of Differentiation and how to implement it practically at school level. *the MTSS model—clarity around what it entails and the importance of each component in the overall development and support of our students. *it has consolidated my previously held belief that reading is the 'key' to successful, inclusive learning practices".

Why Did We Do It Like This?

Inclusion has—for decades—been derided by special education interest groups as a 'fad' or an 'ideological bandwagon' (Brantlinger, 1997). As explained in Chapter 2 of this book, members of those groups have at the same time appropriated the language of inclusion. This has muddied the waters and confused educators worldwide who have enacted practices that they believed in good faith were compatible with inclusive education, but which were antithetical with its core ideas and intent. The only way that educators can avoid implementation errors is to know what genuine inclusion *is*. Without this, integration will continue to be the dominant form of education provision, the implementation challenges that educators experience will frustrate and exhaust them, and students will continue to be excluded by barriers and experiences that could otherwise be avoided.

It is for this reason that this book and this program of learning begin with 'the why': the historical, conceptual, and legal foundations of inclusion. It is also why the questionnaire featured questions on human rights and the long history behind those rights with specific reference to the civil and disability rights battles that resulted in desegregation and deinstitutionalisation (Cornett & Knackstedt, 2020) and which influenced education through mainstreaming (integration) and finally, inclusive education. Even if they 'Googled' the answer, the survey questions will have provided participants with the opportunity to learn by exposing them to knowledge that they may not previously have been aware. These questions also provided scaffolding for other salient items. For example, early in the survey, participants were asked—in a short-response question—who the first victims of the Holocaust were, with the correct answer being children or persons with a disability. Wrapped up within this theme is realisation of what can happen when children and people with disability are devalued, and their personhood is denied (see Chapter 3). Knowing that the entire framework of human rights emerged because of the Holocaust and the treatment of refugees during World War II, which led to the deaths of more than six million people, generates new awareness of a human-rights framework that has perhaps lost salience due to its longevity. This background knowledge is critical for educators to recognise that inclusion is neither 'fad' nor 'ideological bandwagon'

(Brantlinger, 1997), that its central purpose has indeed been around for a long time, and that it is the outcome of battles hard fought by people with disability, together with their families and advocates, who simply wanted the same opportunities as everyone else.

While it is common for educators to want to know 'the how', knowing 'the why' is a prerequisite for effective practice. Without it, educators cannot select the right practice at the right time for individual students. This capability is core to effective educational leadership (Shields, 2005) and is the result of consolidating ideas and concepts that may first appear distinct and understanding the connections between them. Time-poor people understandably want answers so that they can initiate action and, although a very small number of participants did not find the moral and legal imperative compelling, many others appreciated knowing more about their obligations. Even though they make for dry reading, the legal requirements underpinning inclusive education cannot be glossed over and concerns over the depth of educators' knowledge of their obligations have consistently been raised in each five-yearly review of the *Disability Standards for Education 2005* (DSE; Cth), as well as in the current Royal Commission into Violence, Abuse, Neglect and Exploitation against People with Disability (n.d.). Whether staff like it or not, they are legally obligated to enact these provisions, but they cannot succeed in that task if they do not know what their obligations are. Educators also cannot enact those obligations effectively, if they think the student is the focus of adjustments.

The social model of disability is an extremely important conceptual model for it helps educators to redirect focus from the student to attitudinal, pedagogical, or environmental barriers that are more within educators' power to control (see Chapter 4). In other words, the social model changes how we view disability. The social model was explained in the online module with reference to Senator Jordon Steele-John and his experiences navigating Parliament House, a structure that was built without wheelchair users in mind and which resulted in injury to the Senator's knuckles due to narrow doorways. A large increase in the number of correct responses in the Time 2 survey indicate that his story resonated with program participants. Knowledge of concepts like the social model of disability might seem unimportant, but they are fundamental to successful implementation of inclusive practice.

Educators cannot design relevant or effective adjustments if they misperceive what they are meant to be adjusting. Understanding that disability is the outcome of barriers to the access and participation of someone with an impairment directs focus to adjusting the barriers and not the person. By contrast, believing that disability resides within the individual will direct focus towards the individual, leaving the disabling barrier in place. This misperception is ubiquitous and is why we still see students on the autism spectrum integrated into noisy 'mainstream' classrooms and provided with ear defenders to cope—or worse segregated into 'autism specific' special schools—when really the focus needs to be on changing the routines and acoustics in everyday *inclusive* classrooms so that all students benefit, whether they be on the autism spectrum or not.

Conclusion

There is great diversity in what is put forward as inclusive practice across universities, by education departments and sectors, by education consultants, and in the huge variety of professional development educators experience at conferences. Deep knowledge of what inclusion is (and what it is not) is necessary for educators to critically appraise the messages they are receiving and adopt or discard accordingly. This collaborative project has been a valuable first step towards achieving this goal in Central Queensland region. Participants themselves reflected on the value of a common vision and acquiring a common language and have indicated that they will repay this investment in their knowledge and capacity by sharing and adopting what they have learnt in their context. Participants also indicated that they were better equipped to defend that vision when being dissuaded from doing the 'right work'. These are core beliefs and capabilities that enable leaders to engage in transformational, distributed, and instructional leadership; all three of which are considered necessary for successful inclusive education reform. Our research indicates that it is possible not only to enhance the knowledge of system and school leaders but also to (re)ignite their passion in pursuit of a common vision at the same time. We have also demonstrated that this is achievable in a three-month timeframe using a mixture of online technologies with some face-to-face components.

Before anyone runs off to replicate what we did, there were several 'secret herbs and spices' that aided along the way. The first was the knowledge and passion of the research team, who are leaders in inclusive education and highly experienced at teaching this content both online and face-to-face. The second was the commitment of CQ system leaders who decided that of the many important priorities competing for investment, this would be the one. The third was the genuine good will and commitment of participants who gave up their precious time to engage in this work. Perhaps one of the most important herbs or spices was the sense that we were all in this together, and that CQ Region was doing something brave and innovative. Lastly, we cannot claim that the program itself achieved all of what it did; rather, we suspect that it simply validated and amplified an existing moral purpose: to do the best for *all* students, no matter what.

Contrary to reports that school leaders hold negative attitudes towards inclusion— especially when it comes to students with complex learning profiles and/or challenging behaviour—responses to our survey suggested that the will to include was already strong among CQ system and school leaders. Analyses of attitudinal items will be presented in a future publication, but we were heartened by the positive skew towards inclusion. The work that has been happening in Queensland since the release of the 2018 Inclusive

Education Policy may have had an impact, but it is likely that these system and school leaders have always wanted the best for their students. The investment by CQ Region in the knowledge of staff responsible for implementing the policy couldn't have come at a better time because the best will in the world will falter without deep knowledge of 'the why' for this informs everything else: not just 'the how', but also 'the when', 'the who', and for 'how long'.

Positive outcomes from this project are incredible, given the period in which it was conducted. December 2021 to September 2022 was extremely challenging for all involved. While 2020 and 2021 COVID-19 lockdowns have featured large in the media and in public memory, this work coincided with the decision to abandon a strategy of elimination and instead transition to 'living with the virus'. This severely impacted education systems nationally at a time of national teacher shortages and resulted in the start of the Queensland school year being put back by two weeks. In the months following, schools across Queensland grappled with staffing due to the spread of COVID among students and teachers. These impacts have been particularly acute in the regions, which do not have the same level of access to ITE graduates and supply teachers that metropolitan areas do, even at the best of times. It is testament to the commitment and tenacity of CQ system and school leaders that this project got off the ground in the first place. CQ's commitment and tenacity was matched by the QUT team, who were forced by COVID/flood disruptions to juggle data collection for two large projects—which were meant to unfold successively—in unison. That there has been a positive impact on the knowledge of so many, be that through the acquisition of new knowledge or the extension and affirmation of existing knowledge, is remarkable given that the only similar study we could find was two years in duration: *four times the length of this project*.

We salute all the system and school leaders who participated in this project and encourage other regions, sectors, and systems to join with us and follow their lead!

References

Bai, H., & Martin, S. M. (2015). Assessing the needs of training on inclusive education for public school administrators. *International Journal of Inclusive Education*, 19(12), 1229–1243. https://doi.org/10.1080/13603116.2015.1041567

Billingsley, B., McLeskey, J., & Crockett, J. B. (2014). *Principal leadership: Moving toward inclusive and high-achieving schools for students with disabilities* (Document No. IC–8). University of Florida, Collaboration for Effective Educator, Development, Accountability, and Reform Center. http://ceedar.education.ufl.edu/tools/innovation-configurations/

Brantlinger, E. (1997). Using ideology: Cases of nonrecognition of the politics of research and practice in special education. *Review of Educational Research*, 67(4), 425–459. https://doi.org/10.3102/00346543067004425

Braun, A., Ball, S. J., Maguire, M., & Hoskins, K. (2011). Taking context seriously: Towards explaining policy enactments in the secondary school. *Discourse: Studies in the Cultural Politics of Education*, 32(4), 585–596. https://doi.org/10.1080/01596306.2011.601555

Carrington, S. (2022). Transformative leadership for equity and inclusion. *The Learning Difficulties Australia Bulletin*, 54(2), 36–38. https://ldaustralia.org/publications/bulletin-vol-54-no-2-sep-2022/

Carter, S., & Abawi, L. A. (2018). Leadership, inclusion, and quality education for all. *Australasian Journal of Special and Inclusive Education, 42*(1), 49–64. https://doi.org/10.1017/jsi.2018.5

Cooc, N. (2019). Teaching students with special needs: International trends in school capacity and the need for teacher professional development. *Teaching and Teacher Education, 83,* 27–41. https://doi.org/10.1016/j.tate.2019.03.021

Cornett, J., & Knackstedt, K. M. (2020). Original sin(s): Lessons from the US model of special education and an opportunity for leaders. *Journal of Educational Administration, 58*(5), 507–520. https://doi.org/10.1108/JEA-10-2019-0175

DeMatthews, D. (2015). Making sense of social justice leadership: A case study of a principal's experiences to create a more inclusive school. *Leadership and Policy in Schools, 14*(2), 139–166. https://doi.org/10.1080/15700763.2014.997939

DeMatthews, D., & Mawhinney, H. (2014). Social justice leadership and inclusion: Exploring challenges in an urban district struggling to address inequities. *Educational Administration Quarterly, 50*(5), 844–881. https://doi.org/10.1177/0013161X1351444

Deloitte Access Economics. (2017). *Review of education for students with disability in Queensland state schools.* https://education.qld.gov.au/student/Documents/disability-review-report.pdf

Disability Discrimination Act 1992 (Cth).

Disability Standards for Education 2005 (Cth).

Gillett-Swan, J. K., & Lundy, L. (2022). Children, classrooms and challenging behaviour: Do the rights of the many outweigh the rights of the few? *Oxford Review of Education, 48*(1), 95–111. https://doi.org/10.1080/03054985.2021.1924653

Graham, L. (Ed.). (2020). *Inclusive education for the 21st century: Theory, policy and practice.* Routledge.

Hardy, I., & Melville, W. (2018). The activation of epistemological resources in epistemic communities: District educators' professional learning as policy enactment. *Teaching and Teacher Education, 71,* 159–167. https://doi.org/10.1016/j.tate.2017.12.019

Howley, C., Howley, A., Yahn, J., VanHorn, P., & Telfer, D. (2019). Inclusive instructional leadership: A quasi-experimental study of a professional development program for principals. *Mid-Western Educational Researcher, 31*(1), 3–23.

Kugelmass, J., & Ainscow, M. (2004). Leadership for inclusion: A comparison of international practices. *Journal of Research in Special Educational Needs, 4*(3), 133–141. https://doi.org/10.1111/j.1471-3802.2004.00028.x

Óskarsdóttir, E., Donnelly, V., Turner-Cmuchal, M., & Florian, L. (2020). Inclusive school leaders—their role in raising the achievement of all learners. *Journal of Educational Administration, 58*(5), 521–537. https://doi.org/10.1108/JEA-10-2019-0190

Osterman, K. F., & Hafner, M. M. (2009). Curriculum in leadership preparation: Understanding where we have been in order to know where we might go. In M. D. Young, G. M. Crow, J. Murphy, & R. T. Ogawa (Eds.), *Handbook of research on the education of school leaders* (pp. 269–318). Routledge.

Paseka, A., & Schwab, S. (2020). Parents' attitudes towards inclusive education and their perceptions of inclusive teaching practices and resources. *European Journal of Special Needs Education, 35*(2), 254–272. https://doi.org/10.1080/08856257.2019.1665232

Queensland Department of Education. (2018). *Inclusive education policy.* https://ppr.qed.qld.gov.au/pp/inclusive-education-policy

Royal Commission into Violence, Abuse, Neglect and Exploitation against People with Disability. (n.d.). https://disability.royalcommission.gov.au/

Ryan, J. (2006). Inclusive leadership and social justice in schools. *Leadership and Policy in schools*, 5(1), 3–17. https://doi.org/10.1080/15700760500483995

Saloviita, T. (2020). Teacher attitudes towards the inclusion of students with support needs. *Journal of Research in Special Educational Needs*, 20(1), 64–73. https://doi.org/10.1111/1471-3802.12466

Shields, C. M. (2005). School leadership in the 21st century. In W. K. Hoy, & C. Miskel (Eds.), *Educational leadership and reform* (pp. 77–116). Information Age Publishing.

United Nations. (2006). *Convention on the Rights of Persons with Disabilities (CRPD)*. https://www.un.org/disabilities/documents/convention/convoptprot-e.pdf.

United Nations. (2016). *General Comment No. 4, Article 24: Right to Inclusive Education*. (CRPD/C/GC/4). https://digitallibrary.un.org/record/1313836?ln=en

Zero Project. (2021). *A rights-based approach for young people to have a place in mainstream classrooms*. https://zeroproject.org/view/project/17e4c70d-9317-eb11-a813-000d3ab9b226

Chapter 9

Multi-Tiered Systems of Support

What are they, where did they come from, and what are the lessons for Australian schools?

Kate de Bruin, Callula Killingly, & Linda J. Graham

The History of MTSS

Tiered support frameworks were originally developed in the United States in response to legislation, funding, and practice reforms aimed at supporting the inclusion of students with disability. These developments began in the latter half of the 20th century and gained pace in 1975 with the US federal government passage of *Public Law 94–142* (see Chapter 2), which legislated the right of all children to a free and appropriate education in the least restrictive environment (de Bruin, 2019). With many more children with disability enrolling in their local schools, new models of funding and service delivery were needed to cater to rising demand for student support. However, these early models were underpinned by a deficit view of student learning and behaviour (Ysseldyke & Marston, 1999). An early model, based on disability categories and the use of IQ-achievement discrepancy to diagnose learning disabilities (Danforth, 2009), was predicated on the assumptions that students in the same disability category would share the same support needs, that these needs were 'special' (and therefore different to those of nondisabled students), and that these 'special needs' would be most efficiently addressed by pulling students out of general education classes and grouping them together for the delivery of 'special' education in a separate location grouped by their disability category (Germann, 2010).

Although well-intended, categorical models have resulted in a huge increase in the number of students being identified and segregated (Germann, 2012; Graham & Sweller, 2011). It also soon became apparent that students in segregated settings tended to be provided with basic, functional, or life skills curriculum (Zigmond & Sansone, 1986), which served to increase, rather than narrow, learning gaps, lowering the likelihood of school completion (Tindal et al., 1987). Further, categorical models generated delays and gaps in service delivery, as funding was contingent on establishing student eligibility through medical and allied health assessments (de Bruin et al., 2020). The assessment process itself relied on documentation of students' sustained underachievement compared to their peers, resulting in delays of at least two to three years before services would be provided. The categorical model has therefore been described as a "wait to fail model" (Yell, 2018, p. 28), and this is why many systems internationally have implemented or are in the process of implementing needs-based approaches to the

DOI: 10.4324/9781003350897-11

allocation of funding based on teachers' professional judgement (de Bruin et al., 2020; Graham & Jahnukainen, 2011). The allocation of funding, however, is only one component of service delivery and a tiered system of funding allocation based on levels of intensity of adjustment—such as those in the Nationally Consistent Collection of Data on Students with Disability (NCCD) in Australia—or tiers of targeted disability funding (such as in Tasmania, Victoria, and South Australia) do not equate to a full-scale model of service delivery.

Tiered Approaches to Service Delivery

The mandate to educate students in the least restrictive environment in the United States required educators to devise effective methods of support service identification and provision. In 2003, the United States federal government created six research centres, charged with the task of drawing on a three-tiered framework for prevention and intervention popular in public health, and investigating how this approach might be translated into education (Chard, 2012; Sailor et al., 2018). The six commissioned research centres leveraged previous decades of research innovation to develop tiered frameworks for use in education, paying particular attention to reading and behaviour, as the two fastest-growing areas of diagnosis and categorical support funding. The work at Vanderbilt and Kansas universities focused on assessment and intervention within the academic domain, leading to the three-tiered framework that became known as Response to Intervention (RTI). The work from University of Oregon resulted in the three-tiered approach known as Positive Behaviour Interventions and Supports (PBIS).

RTI is a framework designed to enable the early identification of students with learning difficulties, through universal screening assessments, ongoing progress monitoring, and a tiered approach to instruction and intervention (Fuchs & Fuchs, 2006). Similarly, PBIS is a tiered framework that focuses on delivering support and intervention to address behaviour (Horner et al., 2005). Both frameworks are characterised by a preventative, proactive approach to supporting students, emphasising high quality classroom instruction and universal supports to benefit all students (Tier 1). RTI and PBIS both make use of student data to inform support and intervention, and are underpinned by a collaborative, problem-solving approach. Students identified as experiencing difficulties, either academically (RTI) or behaviourally (PBIS) are provided targeted small-group support (Tier 2) where required, with those who continue to experience difficulties being evaluated to receive more individualised intensive support at Tier 3.

In 2004, the United States federal government re-authorised *Public Law 94–142*, at which point it became known as the *Individuals with Disabilities Education Act* (IDEA). States were permitted to opt-out of using the IQ-achievement discrepancy approach for identifying students with learning disabilities and to opt-in on the use of RTI for assessing students' need for intervention, representing a clear shift away from the categorical approach. In response to the IDEA reforms, many states wrote policies and guidelines for implementing RTI and PBIS and partnered with universities to provide professional learning and technical assistance to schools and districts to shift their practice. In the two decades since RTI was legislated, it has become one of the most widely scaled-up reforms in United States education, with a 2016 estimate that 68% of schools were engaging in a district-wide scaling of RTI and 24% of schools embedding RTI within their routine school practice (McIntosh & Goodman, 2016). PBIS has been implemented in some 26,000 (~22.5%) schools in the United States (Pas et al., 2019).

From RTI and PBIS to MTSS

The two frameworks of RTI and PBIS have matured and developed over time, generating significant reforms to the way that schools identify and support students in learning and behaviour, respectively. A particularly valuable contribution of research in RTI and PBIS has been the standardised and problem-solving protocols for determining which students might require support at higher tiers and what those supports or interventions might be. These protocols represented a dramatic improvement in how students were identified for education support and support services. However, while these frameworks and their protocols are valuable, their foci have increasingly been viewed as narrow. For example, too often, RTI and PBIS systems have focused most closely on academic or behavioural assessment and intervention, with less attention to the Tier 1 component of quality core instruction (see Chapter 11). While this focus is perhaps a logical consequence of these frameworks' origin in special education, there is evident need for a concerted effort to meet the original intent of the RTI reforms, which was to ensure foundational quality instruction is provided to each child without exception (Hughes & Dexter, 2011). Further, while RTI and PBIS remain important specific tiered frameworks for academic and behavioural learning, using either in isolation impedes the provision of holistic and comprehensive support for students at school. Over time, this recognition has led a shift away from the separate implementation of these systems to an expanded integrated framework under the term Multi-Tiered Systems of Support (MTSS). This framework, which includes both the academic and behavioural domains, with the added domain of social-emotional development (see Chapter 14), is now evident in most states throughout the United States (Berkeley et al., 2020).

Characteristics of MTSS

MTSS is a comprehensive framework that addresses academic, social-emotional, and behavioural domains through a coordinated system of universal and targeted supports, delivered through culturally appropriate and trauma-informed approaches (American Institutes for Research, 2023). MTSS is underpinned by inclusive philosophy where all students are presumed capable of learning and thriving with the right level of support. Unlike RTI and PBIS, which are both represented by tiered pyramids, MTSS is represented differently to emphasise its holistic focus. Most often, an umbrella image is used to signify the preventative/protective intent and the packaging of support under a unifying framework. Also common is a Venn diagram representing the three developmental domains with the child at the centre. Figure 9.1 features an image in the latter tradition,

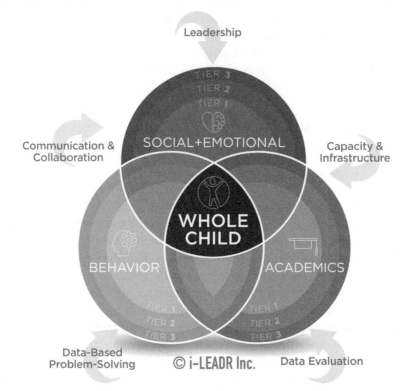

Figure 9.1. The three developmental domains with the child at the centre.

used with permission from a United States educational consultancy, i-LEADR Inc. We have chosen this image because it illustrates the tiers within the three domains, as well as the core operational elements that make this delivery system work.

Key to successful MTSS implementation is working out how much and what type of support each student requires and providing the correct support in a timely manner to ensure learning gaps do not open or widen. To achieve this, MTSS places emphasis on the use of evidence-based practices that have been documented in multiple well-designed experimental evaluations to result in improved outcomes for students. The framework is characterised by a coordinated system of support across a tiered continuum with the type of provision—including frequency, intensity, and duration—determined through data-based decision making.

Coordinated Supports Across a Tiered Continuum

An important component of MTSS is coordination across three tiered domains. These tiers operate as a continuum that increases in intensity, depending on individual student need. This coordinated system is designed to maximise the number of students making progress through universal instruction at Tier 1, and to provide just the right amount of additional support for those who need it at Tiers 2 and 3.

Tier 1 refers to classroom-level instruction and supports for 100% of students. At Tier 1, effective instruction and support is provided universally within core instruction to maximise the number of students who succeed and to prevent the need for any supplementary support in as many cases as possible. Research suggests that in a typical school where core universal instruction at Tier 1 is highly effective and consistent, approximately 80% of students will make good progress. Research shows that use of practices that are well-established as effective for a wide range of students leaves fewer students needing support at higher tiers (Stoiber & Gettinger, 2016).

Tier 2 refers to targeted supports provided to small groups. Up to 15% of students may require appropriately targeted high-quality Tier 2 intervention to support their academic, social-emotional, and/or behavioural development. Rather than supplanting classroom instruction, Tier 2 provides additional opportunities and time for students to acquire and practise underdeveloped skills, increasing the intensity of instruction (Stoiber & Gettinger, 2016). Students also have more opportunities to respond, their progress is assessed more frequently, and they receive corrective feedback more quickly and more often.

Tier 3 refers to more intensive individualised supports. Students who continue to experience difficulties despite receiving effective evidence-based support at Tier 2 may benefit from Tier 3 support. At Tier 3, instruction is typically provided in a highly individualised and intensive mode and is often more prolonged. Students' progress is monitored more frequently through assessment to enable adjustment of instruction where needed. Tier 3 interventions may be carried out by a specialist teacher, speech-language pathologist, or educational psychologist. Fewer than 5% of students should require intensive and sustained support at Tier 3 (Burns & Symington, 2002; Burns et al., 2005).

Importantly, the percentages relating to each tier—Tier 1, 100/80%; Tier 2, 15%; Tier 3, 5%—should be used as a guide to audit system performance. If, for example, more students are progressing to Tiers 2 and/or 3 in any domain, this should prompt urgent evaluation of practice in the tiers below, especially the quality and accessibility of Tier 1 instruction (see Chapter 11). Also, the three tiers are not locations where students are placed, nor are they descriptors of students themselves; rather, the tiers are descriptors for levels of support intensity, and this is always considered within a time frame with an exit criterion. Interventions offered at a higher tier of support contain the same instructional content as offered in the Tier 1 academic or general capabilities curriculum, but in a form that is intensified, more frequent, and/or of a longer duration. In other words, intervention and support offered at a higher tier should supplement and complement rather than replace Tier 1. This is an approach best achieved when schools work collaboratively using a whole-school vision with strong leadership at the helm, and when educators use robust evidence to make decisions about support provision.

Data-Driven Decision-Making

Using data to make decisions about whether students are making progress and what support is needed to ensure they succeed is a hallmark of MTSS. Such decisions require a dedicated team to meet regularly and to inspect and use data collected using validated assessments to inform decision-making (Eagle et al., 2015). Teams may include classroom teachers, school leaders, and administrative support, as well as allied health professionals with expertise in language and literacy, such as educational speech pathologists or school psychologists (see Chapter 18). Determining whether students require support at higher tiers is a high-stakes decision with implications for resourcing and scheduling as well as student progress and engagement at school. For this reason, decisions should be based on data gathered from assessments that are reliable and efficient to implement. Such assessments need to be technically adequate, sensitive enough to pick up all students who are not making adequate progress, and specific enough that they only pick up those students without misidentifying others as underachieving. These assessments also need to be feasible to implement multiple times per year to identify issues in a timely fashion, meaning that they should be very quick to administer and not overly burdensome for teachers or stressful for students. Care also needs to be taken that assessments are used for the purpose they have been developed and that they are not being used diagnostically when inappropriate to do so, nor administered with a frequency that invalidates the test, potentially resulting in practice effects. Further, they also need to have predictive power, meaning that they are accurate forecasters of student achievement on more general outcomes of academic, social, or behavioural success.

Universal Screening. Universal screening at Tier 1 should occur across academic, social-emotional, and behavioural domains for all students. Screening provides schools with a primary data source, enabling identification of patterns of students who are/ are not making expected progress through the academic curriculum, and/or who may be experiencing mental health or behavioural difficulties. Many measures have been evaluated for their technical adequacy, and these are summarised in the academic and screening tools charts from the National Center for Intensive Intervention (n.d.). Of note are those assessments known as curriculum-based measures (CBM). These are quick (typically 1–5 minutes per student), easy to administer, and suitable for making decisions about academic progress. Some of the more well-known CBM batteries include the Dynamic Indicators of Basic Early Literacy Skills 8th Edition (DIBELS; University of Oregon, 2023a), AIMSWeb (Pearson, 2017), and easyCBM (Anderson et al., 2014). A recent suite of DIBELS materials has been released for Australia (University of Oregon, 2023b).

Universal screening data from CBM and other measures can be used to inform Tier 1 academic instruction. For example, trends in data can be examined by grade-level data teams at the level of the class, as well as the individual student, and gaps can be identified, e.g., low progress in decoding or basic maths facts. This process—known as 'problem analysis'—is undertaken in teams to understand if there is an issue at the whole-class level or individual level, what the category of the issue is, and what aspect of the environment (social or instructional) might need to be adjusted and/or intensified. If the problem is a class-wide issue, with less than 80% of students making expected progress, Tier 1 teaching should be adjusted to align with the principles of accessible quality teaching with adjustments for students with disability (see Chapters 11 and 12). Closer monitoring of the class would then be undertaken weekly or biweekly, typically for a 12-week period to determine whether further adjustments should be made to Tier 1 instruction. Universal screening data can also be used to identify individuals who would benefit from additional support at Tier 2, once the quality and accessibility of initial instruction at Tier 1 has been ruled out as a contributing factor. The point at which intervention should be considered is typically determined by the use of a cut score, by which students are classified as at risk/not at risk of poor academic and/or social outcomes.

Diagnostic Assessments. Screening assessments can help to indicate the presence of underlying difficulties; however, they are not always sensitive enough to identify precisely what that difficulty is. Diagnostic assessments, such as the Test of Word Reading Efficiency—Second Edition (TOWRE-2; Torgesen et al., 2012), can provide information to understand the category of the issue and to align students to appropriate intervention. For example, the TOWRE-2 is used to assess students' skills in sounding out words (phonemic decoding) and their recognition of well-known words. Lower scores on these measures may indicate that intervention should focus on building a student's skills in word-level reading. These diagnostic instruments are normed on large, representative samples, therefore providing an age-relevant criterion against which an individual student's academic skills and competencies can be compared. Diagnostic assessments can be conducted with qualified teachers or allied health professionals, with the results used to inform the target for, as well as the intensity of, intervention.

Progress Monitoring. Data-based decision-making also includes progress monitoring for students receiving academic, social, or behavioural interventions to ensure that progress toward the desired outcome is being made. Student progress within intervention should be monitored closely, typically monthly, to measure growth over time and to ensure that the additional resource-intensive interventions and supports being offered are having the desired impact. Such monitoring should also be used to ensure that interventions are faded out when students meet the exit criteria for intervention.

Benefits of MTSS

MTSS offers a comprehensive framework of universal support and early intervention across academic, social-emotional, and behavioural domains, underpinned by a proactive and preventative approach to supporting students (Lane et al., 2013). Within this model, the learning and wellbeing of all students is prioritised through the emphasis placed on high quality instruction and support at the classroom-level with methods to identify when that support is not enough for individual children and/or when classroom-level teaching may itself need intervention. Undetected learning difficulties can often snowball as students' progress through school (Graham, White, et al., 2020), resulting in learning gaps that continue to widen over time, and which become increasingly difficult to address. MTSS provides a school-wide mechanism for identifying these difficulties early, using universal screening and ongoing progress monitoring. Through this combined emphasis on high quality universal support and the provision of timely intervention, tiered systems of support are effective in reducing the number of special educational placements (Burns et al., 2016).

While MTSS is gaining traction, particularly in the United States, existing research has focused predominantly on the outcomes associated with RTI or PBIS through which academic and behavioural domains tend to be addressed in isolation. For example, Burns et al. (2005) meta-analytic review of the impacts of RTI on student outcomes demonstrated that tiered frameworks to support academic achievement: (1) enhanced academic skills, time on task and task completion, and (2) reduced grade retention, special education placement, and time spent in special education services. Similarly, in a randomised control trial of 58 schools (Bradshaw et al., 2021), a tiered behaviour support system significantly reduced teachers' reactive behaviour management. These benefits of first-generation tiered systems of support notwithstanding, school systems are increasingly adopting comprehensive integrated MTSS due to the recognition that behaviour, academic outcomes, and social-emotional development are intricately connected. There is now copious evidence showing that externalising behaviours are reciprocally associated with difficulties in academic domains, such as reading (Halonen et al., 2006; Morgan et al., 2008). Similarly, longitudinal research shows that early reading difficulties at age seven are predictive of poor emotional health outcomes (e.g., depression, anxiety) at ages 9 to 11 (McArthur et al., 2022). There is therefore strong potential for co-occurring difficulties or for one problem to mask another, making the case for integrated identification and delivery systems. Tiered frameworks that focus solely on behaviour or emotional wellbeing have no mechanism for identifying and addressing underlying learning difficulties, and vice versa. By contrast, MTSS enables more accurate identification and targeted supports by screening for difficulties across all three developmental domains.

Research also shows that interventions and supports that target one area tend to produce positive effects that extend into other domains, due to the connectedness between these three developmental domains. For example, interventions that target academic skills have been shown to have a positive impact on behaviour (Warmbold-Brann et al., 2017). Similarly, research shows that strengthening students' social emotional learning through high quality universal supports enhances not only students' skills in that domain, but also their academic performance (see Chapter 14). Further, implementation of trauma-informed MTSS—in which universal screening was undertaken to identify students at risk for social, academic, and emotional difficulties, and where teachers received professional coaching—reduced suspensions and disciplinary infractions (von der Embse et al., 2019). These findings showcase the need for systems and schools to invest in MTSS implementation to allow the delivery of relevant intervention and support for the whole child.

Implementing MTSS

In the two decades since the reauthorisation of IDEA, there has been a substantial uptake in the adoption of MTSS in many states across the United States, with Kansas hailed as a pioneer (Berkeley et al., 2020). Implementation was further galvanised in 2014 by the joint issuance of Guiding Principles by the Obama Administration and the Office of Civil Rights reminding education providers of their obligations under federal law to reduce racial disparities in the use of exclusionary discipline. Later that same year, the United States Department of Health and Human Services, and the United States Department of Education (2014), jointly issued a statement strongly discouraging the use of exclusionary discipline with young children—due to its known ill-effects on children's academic, social-emotional, and behavioural development—and explicitly recommending the use of tiered intervention frameworks to support social-emotional and behavioural development (Graham et al., 2023). This joint statement was followed a year later by the Obama Administration's reauthorisation of the *Every Student Succeeds Act* (ESSA, 2015), which defines MTSS as "a comprehensive continuum of evidence-based systematic practices to support a rapid response to students' needs, with regular observations to facilitate data-based instructional decision making" (Yell, 2018, p. 36). ESSA also allows the use of federal funds to support MTSS implementation, which has helped to fuel implementation in the United States.

Some states, like Kansas (Ysseldyke & Marston, 1999), were involved in early innovations which meant that MTSS implementation was already well underway in that state (Kansas Technical Assistance System Network, 2021). By 2014, 18 Kansas public-school districts had adopted a district-wide approach to implementation, nearly half (48%) of Kansas schools had received formal training in MTSS, and 43% of students (approx. 224,000) were attending schools that had participated in training (Reedy & Lacireno-Paquet, 2015). Importantly, the integrated MTSS model in use by Kansas is explicitly distinguished from both special education and RTI (Berkeley et al., 2020). In a state-wide survey assessing the impacts of MTSS implementation on school outcomes, the majority of participating schools indicated that MTSS had increasedhttps://connectqutedu-my.sharepoint.com/personal/killingl_qut_edu_au/Documents/Education/2023 Publications/MTSS chapter.docx - _msocom_4 the number of students reaching academic benchmarks and proficiency on state assessments, as well as reducing the number of office disciplinary referrals and special education placements (Reedy & Lacireno-Paquet, 2015).

In the US state of Vermont, there has also been a shift toward comprehensive MTSS, for which extensive implementation guidelines are provided on the Vermont Agency of Education website (State of Vermont, 2019). Bohanon et al. (2016) describe how MTSS has been enacted within one secondary school in this region. The school had a high percentage of students with disability (14% in Grades 6–8; 24% in Grades 9–12) and many students came from low socioeconomic backgrounds (39%). Implementation was guided through a dedicated team spanning administrative staff and educators, meeting on a weekly basis. Universal screening of social, behavioural, and academic outcomes was conducted, and data were collated in spreadsheets colour-coded to allow for quick and easy interpretation of which students would benefit from more targeted supports. These screening outcomes were reviewed by the implementation teams regularly, enabling the provision of timely and relevant supports across a range of domains. Fidelity of implementation was continually monitored by verifying whether students were responding to the universal and targeted supports provided. The school observed positive impacts in reading and maths during the years of implementation, with a higher percentage of students meeting proficiency levels in both areas following one year of implementation. Similarly, there was a reduction in suspensions and office disciplinary referrals with rates decreasing by 44% between the first and third year of implementation.

MTSS has also been implemented in schools across the state of California, through the California Scale-up of MTSS Statewide Initiative (CAMTSS). This initiative involved 610 schools participating within a two-year window from 2017–2019. A retrospective study examined the impacts for 42 elementary schools, comparing these schools with a matched control group of schools that had not implemented MTSS (Choi et al., 2022). Schools involved in the initiative were observed to have statistically significant improvements in test scores in English Language Arts and Mathematics across the two years, with medium effect sizes, while scores for the control schools did not significantly increase. Results also indicated that, for the participating schools, the extent of improvement in academic results was positively associated with fidelity of implementation.

Conclusion

MTSS represents a coordinated system of tiered supports that traverse academic, behavioural, and social-emotional domains, providing a comprehensive framework through which to support the whole child. Single domain tiered models, whether they direct support delivery or funding allocation, do not achieve such comprehensive results, as each domain is addressed in isolation and the tiers associated with each model do not build on one another. Successful outcomes require programs and instruction—across all three tiers and all three domains—to be high quality, accessible, and evidence-based and their impact needs to be monitored with robust measures to make educated decisions for intensifying or decreasing support for students. Importantly, MTSS provides schools and systems with a unified and evidence-based approach to service delivery that meets the needs of *all* students within *one* setting. It is an inherently inclusive model for the aim is to bring services *to* students, in their local school. Importantly, and contrary to common misinformation about inclusive education, Tier 2 and 3 supports may be delivered in a variety of ways. Where feasible, these supports may be provided in the classroom, but also outside it. This brings us to an important point that needs to be clarified.

It has been claimed, as recently as this year, that "for some, inclusion means no separation at any time" (McVilly et al., 2023, p. 89). One of the citations used to support this statement is a paper written by many of the authors of chapters this book (Graham, Medhurst, et al., 2020),[1] however, the paper did not say anything to warrant citation in support of the McVilly et al. statement about "no separation at any time". It *did* explain the GC4 definitions of inclusion, exclusion, segregation, and integration, but McVilly et al. have misinterpreted both those definitions and our reference to them. As discussed in Chapter 3, segregation *based on disability* is discrimination; but this should not be extrapolated to mean "no separation at any time". If that were truly the case, why would MTSS have first taken flight in inclusive education (see Sailor et al., 2018) and why would *we* (of all people) be proposing its implementation?

To be crystal clear, separation of students for the provision of support is acceptable *if* (but only if) it is time limited, flexible, and based on the specific skill to be learnt, e.g., not based on disability category, not fixed, and not singling one group out (for an example of what not to do, think of the 'inclusion class' and Daniel's experience in Chapter 2). Key to an inclusive approach to providing targeted or intensive supports is for *all* students to be separated into groups and for *all* groups to travel, not just one. For example, in a visit to a Kansas primary school in Abilene County, Kate and Linda witnessed students go on their daily 'Reading Walk'. Every student went to join a designated group that was working on a particular reading skill. Some were focusing on decoding, others vocabulary, others fluency, and some extension. Importantly, the constitution of groups changed fluidly, based on recorded gains using robust progress measures. A similar process was in operation for mathematics and again the groups were constituted by discrete skills to be learnt and not by disability category.

Sadly, there are many misnomers about inclusive education, and this "full inclusion 100% of the time, no separation at any time, for any reason, never ever!" misrepresentation of inclusive education and its advocates is just one. We hope that this chapter has provided you with greater clarity, so that you can make inclusive evidence-based decisions while implementing MTSS in your system or school. We leave you with a checklist to provide you with ideas for where to begin. In the academic domain, we have chosen to focus on reading due to its protective benefits for academic, social-emotional, and behavioural outcomes. Note that these are recommendations for where to get started, and there are many more options across the domains. We have therefore also provided trusted sources to help educators identify evidence-based programs and measures when selecting those options.

---

1 The Graham, Medhurst et al. (2023) paper longitudinally analyses citation patterns in published research on inclusive education to investigate whether academics in this field are aware of the *Convention on the Rights of Persons with Disabilities* (CRPD; United Nations, 2006) and/or *General Comment No. 4* (GC4; United Nations, 2016) and whether and how they are using these documents in their published research. Our analysis found that citation of the CRPD and GC4 is increasing, relative to the Salamanca Statement, but sadly, many scholars who claim to be in the field still appear to be unaware of this legally binding human-rights instrument articulating the right to inclusive education.

MTSS IMPLEMENTATION CHECKLIST

Establish several dedicated teams to oversee implementation:

– One team should oversee MTSS implementation and others should focus on each tier. Teams should include people holding decision-making and resourcing positions as well as a variety of expertise in subject areas and data literacy (e.g., school leaders, teachers, specialists, administrative staff, and allied health professionals such as speech-language pathologists).

– Develop shared understanding of MTSS elements and goals for school (short- and long-term).

– Engage in quality ongoing professional learning to support implementation fidelity.

Create a schedule to coordinate times for:

– Collecting screening assessments and progress monitoring.

– Frequent meetings of MTSS team, Tier 1, 2 and 3 teams, and grade-level teams to examine data universal screening and progress monitoring data and evaluate current instruction and supports.

– Professional learning opportunities for staff.

DATA-BASED DECISIONS

Use an accessible and sustainable tool for collating and monitoring data:

– Develop a spreadsheet (e.g., Bohanon et al., 2016) or use electronic data storage facilities that permit secure data storage and easily visualisation of trends (for an overview, see Runge et al., 2016)

– Include outcomes on relevant screening measures for academic skills (e.g., reading and numeracy), measures of social and emotional learning, school attendance, and school disciplinary absences.

Implement universal screening measures for each domain each year (frequency depends on measure):

Academic	Social and Emotional	Behaviour
Sample measures:	*Sample measures:*	*Sample measures:*
• Curriculum-based measures, e.g., DIBELS-8 (Grade 1–8 reading)	• Devereux Student Strengths Assessment (DESSA; Grade K-8)	• Attendance data (including late slips)
• In middle/secondary, academic history can be used to determine need for higher tier supports, and fluency can be used as a quick screener upon entry to the school for reading	• Social Skills Improvement System Rating Forms (SSIS; Grade 3–12)	• Nurse/sick bay and school counsellor visits
	• The Collaborative for Social and Emotional Learning (CASEL) provides an assessment guide on their website Connectedness to school and teachers (Graham et al., 2022)	• Failure to submit assignments.
		• Office Discipline Referrals (ODRs or Incident reports)
		• School disciplinary absences.

Monitor progress of students in Tiers 2 and 3 to determine effectiveness of intervention:

– Many of the above measures can also be used to monitor progress, with frequency dependent on intensity of intervention. See also the US National Center for Intensive Intervention website for further measures.

Monitor implementation fidelity:

– Audit percentages of students in Tiers 2 and 3 across domains to determine adequacy of Tier 1.

– Monitor progress of individual students receiving Tier 2 and 3 supports to make decisions about the appropriateness of the support and any adjustments needed.

TIER 1

TIER 1: Deliver high quality instruction and supports to benefit all students across all 3 domains:

– Employ universal design principles to reduce barriers and increase accessibility of classroom instruction (Chapter 11)

Academic	Social and Emotional	Behaviour
High-leverage and evidence-based instructional practices, such as explicit instruction and teaching metacognitive strategies, should be used to ensure student success across the curriculum. The curriculum itself should also be aligned with research evidence, for example reading should be taught explicitly using a structured literacy approach, encompassing these five key areas: • phonemic awareness • phonics • vocabulary • fluency • comprehension In secondary years, teachers can continue to foster reading proficiency and disciplinary literacy across different subject areas by explicitly teaching relevant subject vocabulary, building fluency through providing reading opportunities, and teaching comprehension strategies.	Incorporate Social and Emotional Learning (SEL) at a classroom level: • Use evidence-based programs (e.g., Social Skills Improvement System (SSIS) Classroom Intervention Program; more listed on CASEL website). • Plan lessons with reference to the Personal and Social Capability (see Chapter 14). Key SEL competencies include: • self-awareness • self-management • social awareness • relationship skills • responsible decision-making.	School values and rules should be collaboratively developed and expected behaviours modelled and taught explicitly. *Example practices at Tier 1 include:* • Student-voice initiatives • Predictable classroom routines • Explicit teaching of expectations and the skills required to meet them (e.g., hands up vs. calling out in class) • Modelling of prosocial habits (e.g., respectful communication) • System to regularly acknowledge, reward, and promote prosocial behaviour.

TIER 2

TIER 2: Provide targeted interventions for areas identified through screening (~15% of students):

- Typically provided in small groups.
- Instruction is more intensive, providing more opportunities to practise skills with teacher feedback.
- Tier 2 must not replace Tier 1 classroom instruction in that area (e.g., students receiving reading intervention should not be removed from reading and writing whole-class instruction)

Academic	Social and Emotional	Behaviour
Determine specific areas where intervention is required through diagnostic measures, e.g., TOWRE-2 (Torgesen et al., 2012).	*Example practices:* • Further explicit instruction of Tier 1 SEL programs in small group to solidify understanding.	Students requiring more support should be identified through careful analysis of data to understand how they can be supported to be successful. Particular attention should go to the possibility of disability and whether relevant adjustments are being provided.
Based on results, provide targeted intervention in subcomponent skills such as phonics. Instruction should be delivered by an instructor with appropriate expertise (typically a teacher with specific training but may also be a Teaching Assistant with specific training). Interventions should be robust and use evidence-based instructional strategies to intensively teach concepts, skills and strategies students need. Some commercial programmes exist for this purpose e.g., MultiLit; Corrective Reading). Tier 2 is typically at a frequency of 3–5 times per week in 20–40-minute sessions.	• Supporting student to implement strategies in the classroom in area of difficulty, e.g., self-management. • Targeted skill building in small groups (e.g., play and social skills, conflict resolution, emotional regulation; Skeen et al., 2019)	*Example practices at Tier 2 include:* • Chill out cards and token systems • Check in/Check out • Breaks are Better • Functional Behavioural Assessment Observations and Interviews • Role playing restorative conferences (Vincent et al., 2021).

TIER 3

TIER 3: Provide individualised intervention for those not making progress at Tier 2 (~5% of students):

- Typically provided one-on-one but can be in very small groups.
- Longer duration and/or frequency (e.g., more time per session or more times per week).

Academic	Social and Emotional	Behaviour
Includes:	*Includes:*	*Includes:*
• Intervention to be implemented by a trained specialist, typically a teacher with specific training but may also be a Teaching Assistant with specific training.	• One-on-one intervention reinforcing SEL curriculum content and building SEL competencies.	• Functional Behavioural Assessment Analysis
• Monitor progress frequently using appropriate and robust mastery measures to inform ongoing intervention (Klingbeil et al., 2015).	• Individualised supports developed in collaboration with school-based (or external) psychologist.	• Intensive individualised skill-building (e.g., video modelling)
		• Collaborative & Proactive Solutions (Stetson & Plog, 2016).

SCHOOLWIDE

- Consistent proactive and function-based approach to behaviour
- Foster positive teacher-student relationships
- Partner with families
- Trauma-informed practice
- Culturally appropriate pedagogy
- Inclusive instructional practices
- **Consult students with a disability and/or their associate to identify and deliver relevant reasonable adjustments.** For example, use of a chill out card to support self-regulation and prevent overwhelm; one-on-one presentation of summative assessment to teacher instead of whole class; completion of individual instead of group assessment.
  - o Chapter 11 describes quality accessible teaching as the baseline for quality Tier 1 instruction.
  - o Chapter 12 describes an evidence-based process for making adjustments to include students with complex learning profiles in grade-level curriculum.
- Eliminate harassment and victimisation through schoolwide implementation of evidence-based programs aimed at building positive school culture, preventing bullying, and promoting prosocial behaviours (Gaffney et al., 2021)

References

American Institutes for Research. (2023). *Trauma-sensitive schools.* https://mtss4success.org/special-topics/trauma-informed-care

Anderson, D., Alonzo, J., Tindal, G., Farley, D., Irvin, P. S., Lai, C.-F., Saven, J. L., & Wray, K. A. (2014). *Technical Manual: easyCBM. Technical Report #1408.* Behavioral Research and Teaching. https://files.eric.ed.gov/fulltext/ED547422.pdf

Berkeley, S., Scanlon, D., Bailey, T. R., Sutton, J. C., & Sacco, D. M. (2020). A snapshot of RTI implementation a decade later: New picture, same story. *Journal of Learning Disabilities, 53*(5), 332–342. https://doi.org/10.1177/0022219420915867

Bohanon, H., Gilman, C., Parker, B., Amell, C., & Sortino, G. (2016). Using school improvement and implementation science to integrate multi-tiered systems of support in secondary schools. *Australasian Journal of Special Education, 40*(2), 99–116. https://doi.org/10.1017/jse.2016.8

Bradshaw, C. P., Pas, E. T., Debnam, K. J., & Johnson, S. L. (2021). A randomized controlled trial of MTSS-B in high schools: Improving classroom management to prevent EBDs. *Remedial and Special Education, 42*(1), 44–59. https://doi.org/10.1177/0741932520966727

Burns, M. K., Appleton, J. J., & Stehouwer, J. D. (2005). Meta-analytic review of responsiveness-to-intervention research: Examining field-based and research-implemented models. *Journal of Psychoeducational Assessment, 23*(4), 381–394. https://doi.org/10.1177/073428290502300406

Burns, M. K., Jimerson, S. R., VanDerHeyden, A. M., & Deno, S. L. (2016). Toward a unified response-to-intervention model: Multi-tiered systems of support. In S. R. Jimerson, M. K. Burns, & A. M. VanDerHeyden (Eds.), *Handbook of response to intervention: The science and practice of multi-tiered systems of support* (pp. 719–732). Springer.

Burns, M. K., & Symington, T. (2002). A meta-analysis of prereferral intervention teams: Student and systemic outcomes. *Journal of School Psychology, 40*(5), 437–447. https://doi.org/10.1016/S0022-4405(02)00106-1

Chard, D. J. (2012). A glass half full: A commentary on the special issue. *Journal of Learning Disabilities, 45*(3), 270–273. https://doi.org/10.1177/0022219412442169

Choi, J. H., McCart, A. B., Miller, D. H., & Sailor, W. (2022). Issues in statewide scale up of a multi-tiered system of support. *Journal of School Leadership, 32*(5), 514–536. https://doi.org/10.1177/10526846211067650

Danforth, S. (2009). *The incomplete child: An intellectual history of learning disabilities* (Vol. 6). Peter Lang.

de Bruin, K. (2019). The impact of inclusive education reforms on students with disability: An international comparison. *International Journal of Inclusive Education, 23*(7–8), 811–826. https://doi.org/10.1080/13603116.2019.1623327

de Bruin, K., Graham, L. J., & Gallagher, J. (2020). What is the NCCD and what does it mean for my practice? In L. J. Graham (Ed.), *Inclusive education for the 21st century: Theory, policy and practice* (1st ed., pp. 122–155). Routledge.

Eagle, J. W., Dowd-Eagle, S. E., Snyder, A., & Holtzman, E. G. (2015). Implementing a multi-tiered system of support (MTSS): Collaboration between school psychologists and administrators to promote systems-level change. *Journal of Educational and Psychological Consultation, 25*(2–3), 160–177. https://doi.org/10.1080/10474412.2014.929960

Every Student Succeeds Act 2015, Pub. L. No. 114–95.

Fuchs, D., & Fuchs, L. S. (2006). Introduction to response to intervention: What, why, and how valid is it? *Reading Research Quarterly, 41*(1), 93–99. https://doi.org/10.1598/RRQ.41.1.4

Gaffney, H., Ttofi, M. M., & Farrington, D. P. (2021). Effectiveness of school-based programs to reduce bullying perpetration and victimization: An updated systematic review and meta-analysis. *Campbell Systematic Reviews, 17*(2), e1143. https://doi.org/10.1002/cl2.1143

Germann, G. (2010). Thinking of yellow-brick roads, emerald cities and wizards. In M. R. Shinn & H. M. Walker (Eds.), *Interventions for achievement and behavior problems in a three-tier model including RtI* (pp. 13–36). National Association of School Psychologists.

Germann, G. (2012). Implementing data-based program modification: Big ideas. In C. A. Espin, K. L. McMaster, S. Rose, & M. M. Wayman (Eds.), *A measure of success: The influence of curriculum-based measurement on education* (pp. 79–87). University of Minnesota Press.

Graham, L. J., Gillett-Swan, J., Killingly, C., & Van Bergen, P. (2022). Does it matter if students (dis)like school? Associations between school liking, teacher and school connectedness, and exclusionary discipline. *Frontiers in Psychology, 13*, 1–13. https://doi.org/10.3389/fpsyg.2022.825036

Graham, L. J., & Jahnukainen, M. (2011). Wherefore art thou, inclusion? Analysing the development of inclusive education in New South Wales, Alberta and Finland. *Journal of education policy, 26*(2), 263–288. https://doi.org/10.1080/02680939.2010.493230

Graham, L. J., Killingly, C., Laurens, K. R., & Sweller, N. (2023). Overrepresentation of Indigenous students in school suspension, exclusion, and enrolment cancellation in Queensland: Is there a case for systemic inclusive school reform? *The Australian Educational Researcher, 50*, 167–201. https://doi.org/10.1007/s13384-021-00504-1

Graham, L. J., Medhurst, M., Malaquias, C., Tancredi, H., De Bruin, C., Gillett-Swan, J., Poed, S., Spandagou, I., Carrington, S., & Cologon, K. (2020). Beyond Salamanca: A citation analysis of the CRPD/GC4 relative to the Salamanca Statement in inclusive and special education research. *International Journal of Inclusive Education, 27*(2), 123–145. https://doi.org/10.1080/13603116.2020.1831627

Graham, L. J., & Sweller, N. (2011). The inclusion lottery: Who's in and who's out? Tracking inclusion and exclusion in New South Wales government schools. *International Journal of Inclusive Education, 15*(9), 941–953. https://doi.org/10.1080/13603110903470046

Graham, L. J., White, S. L., Tancredi, H. A., Snow, P. C., & Cologon, K. (2020). A longitudinal analysis of the alignment between children's early word-level reading trajectories, teachers' reported concerns and supports provided. *Reading and Writing, 33*(8), 1895–1923. https://doi.org/10.1007/s11145-020-10023-7

Halonen, A., Aunola, K., Ahonen, T., & Nurmi, J. E. (2006). The role of learning to read in the development of problem behaviour: A cross-lagged longitudinal study. *British Journal of Educational Psychology, 76*(3), 517–534. https://doi.org/10.1348/000709905X51590

Horner, R. H., Sugai, G., Todd, A. W., & Lewis-Palmer, T. (2005). School-wide positive behavior support. In L. M. Bambara & L. Kern (Eds.), *Individualized supports for students with problem behaviors: Designing positive behavior plans* (pp. 359–390). Guilford Publications.

Hughes, C. A., & Dexter, D. D. (2011). Response to intervention: A research-based summary. *Theory into Practice, 50*(1), 4–11. https://doi.org/10.1080/00405841.2011.534909

i-LEADR Inc. (2020). *MTSS | Beyond the textbook.* https://ileadr.com/mtss-beyond-the-textbook/ *Individuals with Disabilities Education Act 2004.*

Kansas Technical Assistance System Network. (2021). *Timeline of the development of the Kansas multi-tier system of supports and alignment.* https://ksdetasn.org/resources/1269

Lane, K. L., Menzies, H. M., Ennis, R. P., & Bezdek, J. (2013). School-wide systems to promote positive behaviors and facilitate instruction. *Journal of Curriculum and Instruction, 7*(1), 6–31. https://doi.org/10.3776/joci.2013.v7n1p6-31

McArthur, G., Badcock, N., Castles, A., & Robidoux, S. (2022). Tracking the relations between children's reading and emotional health across time: Evidence from four large longitudinal studies. *Reading Research Quarterly, 57*(2), 555–585. https://doi.org/10.1002/rrq.426

McIntosh, K., & Goodman, S. (2016). *Integrated multi-tiered systems of support: Blending RTI and PBIS.* Guilford Publications.

McVilly, K., Ainsworth, S., Graham, L., Harrison, M., Sojo, V., Spivakovsky, C., Gale, L., Genat, A., & Zirnsak, T. (2023). *Outcomes associated with 'inclusive', 'segregated' and 'integrated' settings: Accommodation and community living, employment and education.* A research report commissioned by the Royal Commission into Violence, Abuse, Neglect and Exploitation of People with Disability. University of Melbourne, Australia. https://apo.org.au/node/321761

Morgan, P. L., Farkas, G., Tufis, P. A., & Sperling, R. A. (2008). Are reading and behavior problems risk factors for each other? *Journal of Learning Disabilities, 41*(5), 417–436. https://doi.org/10.1177/0022219408321123

National Center for Intensive Intervention. (n.d.). *Academic screening tools chart.* https://intensiveintervention.org/resource/academic-screening-tools-chart

Pas, E. T., Ryoo, J. H., Musci, R. J., & Bradshaw, C. P. (2019). A state-wide quasi-experimental effectiveness study of the scale-up of school-wide positive behavioral interventions and supports. *Journal of school psychology, 73,* 41–55. https://doi.org/10.1016/j.jsp.2019.03.001

Pearson. (2017). AIMSwebplus technical manual. Pearson.

Public Law 94–142, 1975.

Reedy, K., & Lacireno-Paquet, N. (2015). *Implementation and outcomes of Kansas multi-tier system of supports: Final evaluation report 2014.* WestEd. https://www.wested.org/resources/kansas-multi-tier-system-of-supports-final-evaluation-report-2014/#

Runge, T. J., Lillenstein, D. J., & Kovaleski, J. F. (2016). Response to intervention and accountability systems. In S. R. Jimerson, M. K. Burns, & A. M. VanDerHeyden (Eds.), *Handbook of response to intervention: The science and practice of multi-tiered systems of support* (pp. 103–120). Springer.

Sailor, W., McCart, A. B., & Choi, J. H. (2018). Reconceptualizing inclusive education through multi-tiered system of support. *Inclusion, 6*(1), 3–18. https://doi.org/10.1352/2326-6988-6.1.3

Skeen, S., Laurenzi, C. A., Gordon, S. L., du Toit, S., Tomlinson, M., Dua, T., Fleischmann, A., Kohl, K., Ross, D., Servili, C., Brand, A. S., Dowdall, N., Lund, C., van der Westhuizen, C., Carvajal-Aguirre, L., Eriksson de Carvalho, C., & Melendez-Torres, G. J. (2019). Adolescent mental health program components and behavior risk reduction: A meta-analysis. *Pediatrics, 144*(2), 1–13. https://doi.org/10.1542/peds.2018-3488

State of Vermont. (2019). *Vermont Multi-Tiered Systems of Support.* Vermont Agency of Education. Available from: https://education.vermont.gov/student-support/vermont-multi-tiered-system-of-supports

Stoiber, K. C., & Gettinger, M. (2016). Multi-tiered systems of support and evidence-based practices. In S. R. Jimerson, M. K. Burns, & A. M. VanDerHeyden (Eds.), *Handbook of response to intervention: The science and practice of multi-tiered systems of support* (pp. 121–141. Springer.

Tindal, G., Shinn, M., Walz, L., & Germann, G. (1987). Mainstream consultation in secondary settings: The Pine County model. *The Journal of Special Education, 21*(3), 94–106. https://doi.org/10.1177/0022466987021003

Torgesen, J. K., Wagner, R. K., & Rashotte, C. A. (2012). *Test of word reading efficiency (2nd ed.) examiner's manual.* Pro-Ed.

United Nations. (2006). *Convention on the Rights of Persons with Disabilities (CRPD)*. https://www. un.org/disabilities/documents/convention/convoptprot-e.pdf.

United Nations. (2016). *General Comment No. 4, Article 24: Right to Inclusive Education (CRPD/C/ GC/4)*. https://digitallibrary.un.org/record/1313836?ln=en

United States Department of Health and Human Services & United States Department of Education. (2014). *Policy statement on expulsion and suspension policies in early childhood settings*. https://www.acf.hhs.gov/sites/default/files/documents/ecd/expulsion_suspension_fi nal.pdf

University of Oregon. (2023a). *8th Edition of Dynamic Indicators of Basic Early Literacy Skills (DI-BELS®): Administration and scoring guide* (2023 edition). https:// dibels.uoregon.edu

University of Oregon (2023b). DIBELS 8th Edition: Australasian Materials. https://dibels. uoregon.edu/materials/dibels-australasian

Vincent, C., Inglish, J., Girvan, E., Van Ryzin, M., Svanks, R., Springer, S., & Ivey, A. (2021). Introducing restorative practices into high schools' multi-tiered systems of support: successes and challenges. *Contemporary Justice Review, 24*(4), 409–435. https://doi.org/10.1080/102825 80.2021.1969522

von der Embse, N., Rutherford, L., Mankin, A., & Jenkins, A. (2019). Demonstration of a trauma-informed assessment to intervention model in a large urban school district. *School Mental Health: A Multidisciplinary Research and Practice Journal, 11*(2), 276–289. https://doi. org/10.1007/s12310-018-9294-z

Warmbold-Brann, K., Burns, M. K., Preast, J. L., Taylor, C. N., & Aguilar, L. N. (2017). Meta-analysis of the effects of academic interventions and modifications on student behavior outcomes. *School Psychology Quarterly, 32*(3), 291–305. https://doi.org/10.1037/spq0000207

Yell, M. L. (2018). Response to intervention, multi-tiered systems of support, and federal law: Analysis and commentary. In *Handbook of response to intervention and multi-tiered systems of support* (pp. 26–39). Routledge.

Ysseldyke, J., & Marston, D. (1999). Origins of categorical special education services in schools and a rationale for changing them. In D. J. Reschly, W. D. Tilly, & J. P. Grimes (Eds.), *Special education in transition: Functional assessment and noncategorical programming* (pp. 1–18). Sopris West.

Zigmond, N., & Sansone, J. (1986). Designing a program for the learning disabled adolescent. *Remedial and Special Education, 7*(5), 13–17. https://doi.org/10.1177/074193258600700504

Chapter 10

The critical importance of language

Jennifer Alford & Haley Tancredi

Almost all social, cognitive, and literacy-based tasks that take place at school are grounded in language (Ukrainetz & Fresquez, 2003). Language therefore is at the heart of learning. As highly structured systems for communication, languages enable humans to use and understand specified numbers of sounds (phonemes) to create words and those words are combined into trillions of sentences to communicate meaning (Berwick & Chomsky, 2016). In this chapter, we focus on the centrality of language in the enactment of inclusive education, drawing on our experience with two groups of learners, often labelled as 'diverse',[1] and who are entitled to full participation and success in inclusive education. These learners are students from language backgrounds other than English, sometimes known as English as an Additional Language/Dialect (EAL/D), and students with language disorders.

While our respective backgrounds as practitioners and researchers are different—Jennifer from EAL/D education, and Haley from speech pathology—we share a common interest in understanding the critical role of language in teaching and learning for all young people. Writing this chapter has provided a platform for thinking through some of the language-related issues teachers face, both theoretically and practically. Our positions, respectively, represent student and context-responsive approaches to education, aimed at supporting the myriad of ways that learners present in classrooms. Within this approach, students and their learning are placed at the centre and a social model is adopted, rather than a traditional medically informed approach that pathologises young people. Our intention is to focus on the possibilities for converging knowledge and practices from both of our traditions to identify and engage with "productive discursive gaps" (Simmie et al., 2019, p. 68) in the messiness of teaching, without conflating the two traditions.

As discussed in Chapter 4, terms like 'diverse learners' are problematic, so we want to make our position on this clear at the outset. All young people, regardless of dis/abilities, ethnicities, socio-economic backgrounds, sexualities, etc., are diverse and different *from each other*. This includes so-called 'regular' learners who are constructed as middle class, white, able-bodied, dominant language speaking social groups. However, education policy

---

1 See Chapter 4 to understand why this term is problematic.

DOI: 10.4324/9781003350897-12

and practices have yet to fully embrace these understandings. In maintaining the focus on those who deviate from the mythical mainstream, we perpetuate the practice of 'othering' (Said, 1978), which creates unhelpful distance between groups and reifies those in the mainstream as the reference point. Our interest in this chapter is therefore to (i) help teachers understand students from language backgrounds other than English, and students with language disorder, (ii) assist teachers to make decisions that avoid stereotypes and stigmatisation, and instead use Minow's dilemma of difference (1990) and inclusive language, and (iii) to support teachers to enact high quality and accessible language-related pedagogy to enhance inclusive education practices for *all* students.

The Students in Focus

Students from language backgrounds other than English are those who were born here or who have migrated here, and who know and use languages other than English, or dialects of English other than standard varieties used in schooling. English *as an additional language* (EAL) is significant, because it acknowledges that students may use and understand a number of languages other than English with their family, at school, and in the broader community (e.g., Aboriginal Kriol, Mandarin, Arabic, among others). Therefore, the acronym EAL gives breadth to the languages that students might use and learn at school and highlights that English should be viewed as "adding to students' capacities as bilingual or multilingual learners, rather than displacing the language/s that students may have acquired earlier" (Bracken et al., 2016, p. 6). English as an additional *dialect* refers to the fact that Australian students may speak regional or social variants of the English language, including:

- Aboriginal and Torres Strait Islander students,
- immigrants and temporary visa holders who have come to Australia from non-English speaking countries,
- students who have a refugee background,
- children with migrant heritage who were born in Australia, but where English is not the language spoken at home,
- students who are English-speaking and have returned to Australia after living for extended periods in non-English speaking countries,
- children of Deaf parents who use Auslan as their first language, and
- international students from non-English speaking countries. (Australian Curriculum, Assessment and Reporting Authority [ACARA], n.d.-a)

Approximately 25% of school students learn English as an additional language or dialect. In some schools, depending on location, the number can be as high as 90%.

Students with language disorder are those with a common but under-identified neurodevelopmental disorder that impacts use and comprehension of spoken and written language, despite adequate language exposure. Language disorder is an overarching term that encompasses (i) language disorder associated with a biomedical condition that is known to impact language development (e.g., autism or hearing impairment), and

(ii) Developmental Language Disorder (DLD), which refers to language impairment that cannot be attributed to biomedical causes and impacts around 7% of the population (Bishop et al., 2017; Norbury et al., 2016). Language disorder has a functional impact on learning, social interactions, and other everyday activities, and is lifelong (Bishop et al., 2017). Despite the wide-ranging impacts of language disorder, it has been described as "hiding in plain sight" (Tancredi, 2020, p. 203), meaning it is poorly understood and often under-supported. As a result, students with language disorder often experience reduced academic outcomes, low school attendance, and social and emotional concerns (Conti-Ramsden et al., 2018; Durkin et al., 2012; Graham & Tancredi, 2019; Merrell et al., 2017).

Students with language disorder are a heterogeneous group, and it is therefore possible for these students to *also* be from a language background other than English. The prevalence of language disorder in multilingual populations is thought to be comparable to monolingual populations (Hunt et al., 2022; Stow & Dodd, 2005). However, disentangling multilingualism from language disorder is complex and risks misidentification, particularly with young and primary school aged children (Li'el et al., 2019). For example, the use of monolingual assessment with multilingual children can result in over-identification and incorrect classification of language disorder. More common, however, is under-identification of co-occurring multilingualism and language disorder, which can result in inappropriate responses to students' learning requirements and/or the failure to provide any kind of support (Morgan et al., 2015). Importantly, it is a myth that speaking more than one language causes language disorder (Paradis et al., 2011). When culturally diverse, monolingual students who have had lifelong English exposure display language and/or literacy difficulties, the possibility of a language disorder must be considered. Speech-language pathologists can collaborate with students, their families, educators, and specialist EAL/D educators to undertake careful assessment using case history information, standardised language assessment and/or dynamic assessment of children's language-learning skills, and language processing tasks (Li'el et al., 2019). A range of sources are essential to unpack a student's profile adequately and accurately. This information can then inform the design and implementation of appropriate educational supports based on data, not assumptions.

Unintended Consequences of the Current Policy Landscape

In Australia, state education authorities have created broad inclusive education policies that seek to include students who are considered *different* from 'regular' students. These include:

> Aboriginal and Torres Strait Islander students, students from culturally and linguistically diverse backgrounds, students who identify as LGBTIQ+, students living in out-of-home care, students from rural and remote communities, students with disability, students with mental health needs, and gifted and talented students.
>
> (Queensland Government, 2022, p. 2)

One of the consequences of this recent shift to all-encompassing inclusive education policies in Australia is that the specific requirements of certain groups, for example students who use English as an additional language or dialect, are subsumed with little direction for classroom teachers as to how to cater for their language requirements, as Creagh et al. (2022) note:

> The devolution of EAL/D support to individual schools through autonomous targeted funding results in policy 'everywhere', distributed across broad portfolios dedicated to ensuring schools provide quality education services for all learners, but also 'nowhere', lacking systemic support and detail on how inclusion should be enacted for EAL/D and with no accountability placed on schools to demonstrate that they are addressing EAL/D learner needs. The co-location of EAL/D policy with a broad systemic policy of inclusion, the absence of systemic professional support, combined with devolution to school sites has had real effects on the policy in practice (p. 1).

We also know from research that some students who use English as an additional language or dialect, if not supported well with specific practices, can take all of primary school to achieve reading parity with their same age English speaking peers, and that newly arrived high school learners can take five to nine years to acquire academic language for schooling success and some from refugee-backgrounds with interrupted education may never reach this goal in the time they have at school (Creagh et al., 2019; Slama, 2012). In the current context, therefore, there is an urgent need to look closely at what this group of learners requires, in terms of language support, for success in school.

Similarly, Australian research has shown that teachers often have limited knowledge of language disorder and teacher professional development is required to support teachers to teach these students in inclusive classrooms (Glasby et al., 2022). Current policy mandates further reinforce the urgent need to make information and professional learning about responsive language-relevant pedagogies available to teachers, to encompass many varied types of learners. Given the high prevalence of students with language disorder and possibility of language disorder in the context of students' speaking English as an additional language/dialect it is imperative that teachers are supported to have deep knowledge of these students and confidence to support them. Without this understanding, there is a risk that students who speak English as an additional language/dialect and/or those with language disorder will experience stereotypes, stigmatisation, and barriers to accessing the curriculum, teachers' pedagogical practices, and in assessment.

A Return to Two Fundamental Concepts: The Dilemma of Difference and Inclusive Language

On the surface, similarities regarding the education of students from language backgrounds other than English and students with language disorder may not be immediately apparent. And yet, educators and school leaders regularly grapple with complex decision making to meet the learning requirements of these students within inclusive settings. An important contribution in this field is that of legal scholar Martha Minow, whose work was introduced in Chapter 4. Minow (1990) posed an important question, which she termed "the dilemma of difference", asking: "when does treating people differently emphasise their differences and stigmatise or hinder them on that basis? And when does treating people the same become insensitive to their difference and likely to stigmatise and hinder them on that basis?" (Minow, 1990, p. 20). She interrogated this question by drawing on two examples of United States case law from the 1970s, which demonstrated the risks these students face relating to stigmatisation, assumptions, and discrimination. The experience of these two groups of students in present day Queensland provide an excellent example to understand Minow's point in context.

To briefly recap from the discussion in Chapter 4, all students attending San Francisco Public Schools in the US during the 1960s received their instruction in English, regardless of students' language backgrounds. In the early '70s, a group of families from language backgrounds other than English collectively identified that English-only instruction was impacting their children's academic progress. These families took their case to the United States Supreme Court,[2] arguing that monolingual instruction in English, with no regard for the fact these students were still developing proficiency in English, violated these students' educational access (Minow, 1990). In this particular case, the courts found that 'equal' treatment was inherently unequal. The result encouraged multilingual education programs, where students who were developing English proficiency could access separate instruction, either for part of the school day or for extended periods, in specialised settings.

Almost concurrently to the case of English language learners in San Francisco, US parents of children with disability were progressing a legal challenge against the provision of separate, segregated education provision for their children, both in Washington D.C. and in the state of Pennsylvania.[3] These claimants drew on the precedent set by *Brown v Board of Education* (1954), which stipulated that separate educational facilities were incompatible with equality. These parents argued that their children were entitled to a free, public education, alongside their peers who did not have a disability in non-segregated settings, where accommodations were available to meet students' learning requirements. The courts ruled in favour of the children and their families, and *Mills v Board of Education* and Pennsylvania Association for Retarded Children v Commonwealth of Pennsylvania were the legal predecessors to the *Education for All Handicapped Children Act* (1975), now known as the *Individuals with Disabilities Education Act* (IDEA; Katsiyannis et al., 2001).

---

2 E.g., *Lau v Nichols* (1974) 414 U.S. 563.
3 E.g., *Mills v Board of Education* (D.D.C. 1972) 348 F. Supp. 866 and *Pennsylvania Association for Retarded Children v Commonwealth of Pennsylvania* (1971) 334 F. Supp. 1257.

An important distinction here is that while *Brown v Board of Education* was concerned with *who* was allowed past the school gate, *Lau v Nichols* (1974) brought into question the regulation of what goes on *inside* the school gate; in other words, how instruction and support is provided, and to whom (Sugarman & Widess, 1974). However, the way support has been provided over time has continued to be reviewed and refined. For example, in Australia, the 'withdrawal' approach for students who speak English as an additional language/dialect was later found to be wanting as it denied students access to regular education settings, curriculum content, materials, social relationships, and other opportunities. Thus 'mainstreaming' was introduced in the 1980s as a way of strengthening "multiculturalism by bringing welfare, educational and government servicing needs from the margins into the central concerns of core social institutions" (Castles et al., 1986, p. 2). Despite the significant gains over the past 40 years, the dilemma of difference still holds importance, because students from language backgrounds other than English and students with language disorder continue to be perceived as 'different', risking assumptions and stigmatisation. At the same time, if these learners' learning profiles and requirements go unrecognised, there is a risk that they are not provided responsive supports. This is the crux of the dilemma for these learners and their teachers.

Issues Surrounding Language in Practice

We now turn to three issues that exemplify the critical importance of language in schools. First, we discuss how "school talk"—the terms used in education policy, staffroom chat, and verbal references to students—can create unhelpful or helpful discourses around them. We then turn our attention to how language variety can be used in the school environment to build inclusive whole-school cultures. Finally, we discuss how teachers can include an explicit focus on language in their pedagogy to help learners increasingly master academic English while still utilising their existing language experiences.

"School Talk": Pointing to or Denying Difference Through Language Use

The terms educators use to refer to learners, or the 'labels' used to identify areas of strength and difficulty have the potential to either (i) deny difference, or (ii) risk stigmatisation. Here, we interrogate some frequently used and pervasive terms that risk positioning students as 'different'. Such terms may also send a message to the student, their family, or other students and teachers that a students' background or learner characteristics require support that cannot be achieved in a 'regular' setting. For example, some authors have pointed to the use of terms such as "at risk" (Alford & Woods, 2017). This term has the potential to evoke negative associations about learners' capabilities and may thereby limit educators' expectations (Valencia, 2012). This attitude is enduring, with Macaulay (2022) reporting on a study of South Sudanese refugee-background learners in Australian high schools that these youth experienced negative student-teacher relationships and low academic expectations from their teachers.

Such attitudes are influenced by deficit discourse which "locates its explanation of the underperformance or underachievement of non-dominant students in the nonalignment of the cultural practices of the home and school" (Gutiérrez et al., 2009, p. 218), providing a convenient excuse for not examining the causes of non-alignment elsewhere: in curriculum expectations, text choices, and pedagogies adopted. However, it does not have to be this way as Alford and Woods (2017) show in their study of a high school teacher who demonstrated a more positive and generative way of talking about English learners as more than just 'needing help' and potentially 'at risk'. They couched descriptions of learners in relation to *second/additional* language learning trajectories (not comparing them to first language users of English), to policy influences on curriculum and pedagogy, and possible future pathways.

As evidenced by the examples above, inclusive language is important. The words we use can serve to include, exclude, point to, or deny difference, or have a positive impact on a young person's school experience. Language evolves over time and while some highly offensive racist and ableist terms have been rejected outright by the community at different points in time, some persist (see Chapter 4). Sometimes educators, support staff, and/or members of school communities may use terms that inadvertently position students as 'different' or less capable. Knowing what these terms are, feeling confident to reject them, and knowing with what to replace them, can help foster inclusion (Walton, 2015). Table 10.1 presents an overview of a range of terms often used to reference students who speak English as an additional language or dialect and students with language disorder, indicating where terms are not inclusive (and why), and providing more inclusive alternatives.

For students with language disorder, diagnostic terms carry both dangers and affordances, and this is particularly the case for language disorder (Graham & Tancredi, 2019). In a small-scale study conducted in Australia where students with previously unidentified language disorder were supported alongside their families and teachers to understand students' language profiles and to design appropriate educational adjustments, teachers reflected on their initial lack of awareness (Tancredi, 2018). One teacher noted her changed in perspective, following an awareness of 'Michael's' underlying language difficulties, saying:

> I guess it's all down like with the way that I had sort of pegged 'Michael', just from you know sort of assessing him early in the year, I just thought okay he's just a kid who doesn't really like school and he probably just needs a bit of a push to get started but he actually needed help to figure out how to get started (p. 93).

This teacher's insights give rise to some of the risks that arise when students' underlying profiles of strength and difficulty are not identified, and where assumptions may potentially lead to inappropriate educational responses. However, this example also points to the dilemma of difference, where there is a risk that diagnostic labels can lead to stigmatisation. Therefore, information about a student and their profile/diagnosis should only be viewed as a starting point. The broader aim is to support teachers to use

Table 10.1 Inclusive Language

For students from language backgrounds other than English		For students with language disorder	
Non-inclusive	**More inclusive**	**Non-inclusive**	**More inclusive**
Non-English speaking background (NESB) ☒ Deficit view referencing English use only.	English as an *Additional* Language/Dialect (EAL/D) ☑ Acknowledges that English does not replace the first language/s but adds to their repertoire.	"My DLD student" ☒ Focus here is on the disability, not the student. ☒ This language dehumanises the student and must be avoided.	Student with DLD ☑ Terminology must focus on the person rather than the disability.
English as a *Second* Language learners ☒ Ignores the fact they may already speak two or three (or more) other languages as is the case for many.	Language Background other than English (LBOTE) ☑ Acknowledges diversity in language backgrounds among families.	"James is afflicted with language disorder" ☒ This terminology presumes the student is "suffering" or is to be pitied. Do not use this language.	☑ Replace with strengths-based language, where the focus is on students' strengths and language that highlights the similarities and commonalities between all students, rather than differences.
English language learners ☒ Positions English as the language reference point.	Multilingual speakers/learners ☑ Celebrates their rich linguistic repertoire.	"Language needs" ☒ Language that positions the student in a deficit view.	Language requirements ☑ Adopts a human-rights lens.
Refugee ☒ Ignores the fact that they have been granted asylum and are no longer seeking refuge.	Students from a *refugee-background* ☑ Acknowledges they are no longer seeking refuge.	"Student with special needs" "Special needs students" ☒ "Special needs" has been rejected by people with disability.	Student with disability* ☑ Person first *Unless the person self-identifies using identity-first language. If in doubt, use person first language.
"At risk" ☒ Positions them as failing only in relation to English use when they may be very capable in other languages.	☑ While the intentions here are often admirable—to identify students who may be at risk of failing—it is also a stigmatising label that can lock some young people out of achieving in other ways.	☒ Avoid any terminology that sends a message that students with disability are inherently "different" or do not belong e.g., do not use "them", "they", "those kids", "students like that".	☑ Students should all be spoken about as a group of children/young people who belong, unless there is an express need to identify difference.

information about students to design and implement pedagogical responses, rather than jumping to more generic, diagnoses-led approaches.

When students experience intersectionality (e.g., learners who have language disorder and have a language background other than English), the dangers of assumptions become even more apparent. Limited opportunities may be available to share information about students and their learning, which may contribute to assumptions, stereotypes, and possible discrimination. However, appropriate support provision can be achieved through knowledge of what language disorder, EAL/D, and intersectionality are, and how teachers can teach in ways that maximise learning for these students. The literature on the topic of intersectionality and how teachers can best respond is scant. However, in current doctoral research being undertaken by the second author of this chapter, a Grade 10 student revealed her experience of the negative consequences of educator assumptions and the resulting support offerings. 'Samantha' was born in Australia, has Asian heritage, speaks both English and Japanese, and has attended only English-speaking schools. Despite life-long English exposure, she experiences language difficulties. During an interview that focused on experiences of English subject lessons, Samantha shared an experience from a high school classroom:

Interviewer: Does your teacher do anything for you that they don't do for other students?
Samantha: Uh, yes.
Interviewer: Okay, tell me about that.
Samantha: Um, I think he misunderstood that I don't speak English well, when I can. So, he treated me like (laughs) I was a foreigner.
Interviewer: Oh, Samantha. I'm so sad to hear that. You speak very good English. Have you always spoken English?
Samantha: Uh, yes. I was born here . . . I understand and can write normally . . . But like "it's okay I understand that you speak Japanese so it's okay, it's okay". He never tells people to read books but he's like "Read this book, read this book. I will give you books to read".

As this exchange demonstrates, assumptions about students' learning strengths and difficulties that do not accurately reflect students' learner characteristics risk the provision of inappropriate educational support. While well-intentioned, this teacher's offer to provide additional reading materials is unlikely to adequately support Samantha's underlying language difficulties. There are, however, evidence-based, whole-class language-focused pedagogies that can support students like Samantha to understand the language of the classroom and to build her language skills, relevant to curricular content. We discuss some of these pedagogies in the next section.

Making Language Variety Visible to Build Whole-School Inclusive Culture

Schools with signs in multiple languages—at the tuckshop, in classrooms, in the reception/administration area, in newsletters, during assemblies, at special events and so on—reflect a commitment to linguistic diversity. Inclusive practices such as these extend a welcome to students who speak other languages fluently and who are now learning English. If you never hear or see your mother tongue in your school environment, it sends a clear message that it, and by extension, you, are not welcome. Such practices should be common in Australian schools given that more than one in five Australians (22.3%) report speaking a language other than English at home (Australian Bureau of Statistics, 2021). Visible and audible recognition of learners' languages is especially important for students from language minority groups, which can include students from Aboriginal and Torres Strait Islander language backgrounds. However, it is crucial that this is not done tokenistically but with a solid understanding of the role language plays in social identity-making and enhancing school connectedness. Visible and audible recognition of learners' languages, as normalised elements of learning, can make a positive difference to students' sense of belonging and connectedness to school (Miller, 2003).

In a study of belonging in an intensive language school for migrant and refugee-background youth, Schweitzer et al. (2021) found that support through the students' home languages (or first languages), provided by bilingual staff members, helped to cushion some of the challenges of adjusting to school in Australia. The home languages were respected and leveraged, not ignored, to enable a smoother transition to schooling. Being inclusive of learners' home languages is important because it recognises the role that language plays in constructing and negotiating identities and relationships, especially amongst diaspora communities (Canagarajah & Silberstein, 2012). Saubich and Guitart (2011) note that all learners have "funds of identity"—the banks of knowledge they themselves consider important to their identity and self-understanding. It stands to reason that a learners' first language could be an important identity marker and a gateway to making learning more personally meaningful. Critically, using language that is clear and unambiguous can contribute to whole-school language inclusive cultures. Students and teachers must share meaning and teachers have an important role in making continuous adaptations to meet the language requirements of students (Titsworth et al., 2015). In validating language as a source of learner knowledge, it then becomes a resource for building new knowledge.

Models of Language Influencing Practice in Schools

Before moving to classroom pedagogical applications, we provide a brief overview of the different but related views of language that have historically influenced the teaching of students who speak English as an additional language or dialect and students with language disorder. Teachers who work with students who speak English as an additional language or dialect in Australia have been guided in much of the pedagogic literature towards a functional model of language, or Systemic Functional Linguistics (see Halliday, 1978; Halliday & Hasan, 1985; Halliday & Matthiessen, 2004; Martin & Rose, 2013) which also underpins the Australian Curriculum. A functional view of language centres the role of language in achieving purposeful social and cultural goals, and the employment of specific language features (grammar, vocabulary, and text structures) to achieve these goals (e.g., ordering a meal at a restaurant, or writing a Science report). Bartlett and Bowcher (2021) note that "a general and accepted view across social approaches to the study of language (is) that understanding *context* and its relation to language is of paramount importance to understanding the communicative role of language in social life" (p. 243). For example, the informal context of ordering a meal at a restaurant creates the contextual conditions for certain language use over others, although there can be variation depending on the nature of the restaurant, the event, and who is present. The formal context and purpose of writing a scientific report, however, requires quite different language features. Treating language as a holistic social system, embedded within cultural and situational contexts (Halliday, 1978, 1985), allows teachers to explore with their learners the reasons why language varies at the moment of production (Hasan, 1992, 2009).

A second and related model of language was conceptualised in the communication sciences. The multi-component theoretical model developed by Bloom and Lahey (1978) includes three interconnected domains: language form, language content, and language use.

- *Language form* is the phonological, morphological, and syntactic structures of language (Bloom & Lahey, 1978). Examples of skills related to language form are the ability to combine sounds into words, sentences, and texts, express/comprehend sequences of events, and make connections between ideas.
- *Language content* refers to meaning components: vocabulary, conceptual understanding, flexibility of word meanings/uses, and knowledge related to objects and events. During the school years, students exponentially increase the number of words they know and use (Nippold, 2016), both for curricular content (e.g., 'societies' and 'classifications') and academic tasks (e.g., 'annotate' and 'thematic devices'). Some suggest that language content is the most fundamental aspect of academic success (Sparks et al., 2014).
- *Language use* refers to how we use and understand language in social contexts and to adjust communication to suit the task and communication partners' requirements. At school, students must understand the social codes of communication and use and adjust language for a variety of functions (e.g., greeting versus questioning or retelling a story).

Synergies exist between the models presented by Derewianka (2011) and Bloom and Lahey (1978), whereby the granular components of language (syntax, semantics, and pragmatics) are nested within a contextual frame, relevant to the student's local environment and the language relevant to that environment and/or the learning tasks at hand. While the importance of cultural and social context is made explicit in Derewianka's (2011) model, the social, educational, and linguistic contexts of language development and learning are somewhat 'hidden' assumptions in Bloom and Lahey's (1978) model. Positioning language within the cultural, social, and instructional contexts are essential in ensuring that appropriate word, language structures, and textual features are explored, taught, and practised.

Including an Explicit Focus on Language (English and Other Languages) in Lessons

In the following section, we discuss classroom approaches that are relevant to both student groups, plus distinct adjustments and/or supports that may be differentially required. An explicit focus on language is central to the learning success of both groups. Language-focused classrooms foreground and celebrate language through embedded opportunities for students to participate in oral language tasks, contain explicit language instruction and discussion, and make language accessible for all students. An explicit focus on language aims to help students who speak English as an additional language or dialect to increasingly master academic English—the language of schooling and powerful genres—while utilising their first languages as learning resources. Meanwhile, teachers' use of Accessible Pedagogies (see Chapter 11) optimises comprehension of classroom instructional language and consolidation of curricular concepts, new word learning, structuring of oral and written texts, and assessment success for *all* students, including those who speak English as an additional language or dialect and/or those with language disorder.

Focus on Language in Classroom Exchanges

Drawing on Bernstein's notion of pedagogic discourse, Martin and Rose (2013) argue that 'inclusion' equates to:

> Active engagement in the curriculum *genres* of the school, building identities as authoritative members of a community of learners. This requires enabling all students to respond successfully in classroom *exchanges* [emphasis added], to be continually affirmed, and so benefit equally from pedagogic activities (p. 256).

Genres and exchanges involve specific, pedagogic attention to language in all semiotic forms—written, spoken, multimodal, gestural, embodied. Classroom exchanges consist of more than the default IRE pattern—Initiation, Response, Evaluation (Cazden, 1988)—where substantive conversation can flourish. However, students who speak English as an additional language or dialect and/or students with language disorder require additional structure to enable them to participate in these exchanges. Structural supports may include the provision of sentence starters or prompt questions for use during group work, which aim to support all students to participate and to sustain interactions. For example, if groups are required to identify evidence for a certain point of view within historical sources, sentence starters that the group might use include:

- "I know that the author is trying to persuade us because they said . . .", or
- "I think the author is saying X, do you agree? Why/why not?"

Another strategy that can support students to practise the language needed to create a written response is an oral rehearsal. Structured approaches to oral rehearsal have been shown to have positive impacts on students' writing quality (Traga Philippakos et al., 2020), however, unstructured approaches have shown mixed results (Gillies & Khan, 2009).

Clarity in Instructional Language

Verbal and written instruction is an important and frequently utilised medium in classrooms. Importantly, the pedagogical practices that teachers employ to explain tasks and teach content relevant to classroom tasks must be clear and accessible (Ketterlin-Geller & Jamgochian, 2011). Accessible Pedagogies, discussed in Chapter 11 of this book, focus specifically on the evidence-based, instructional practices that teachers can use in inclusive classrooms to avert the presence of barriers arising from complex instructional language and/or cognitive load. Linguistic Accessibility is one dimension of Accessible Pedagogies, which encompasses instructional clarity, vocabulary, and comprehension checking. These dimensions are described in detail in Chapter 11. Here, we discuss explicit vocabulary instruction, which is important for students who speak English as an additional language or dialect *and* students with a language disorder, because both are at risk of not understanding the words used by teachers in the classroom (Graham et al., 2018; Starling et al., 2012).

Vocabulary Instruction

Vocabulary is concerned with the categorisation of words, the features and depth of knowledge that we have about words, and the associations we make between words (McKeown et al., 2018). An effective vocabulary system is *broad* (that is, we know and use a variety of words) and *deep* (that is, we have a deep understanding of the words we know and use; McGregor et al., 2013). Explicit new-word teaching is critical for students who speak English as an additional language or dialect and/or students with language disorder but is important for *all* students to succeed at school. However, research indicates that classroom-based vocabulary instruction is often brief—only five minutes per day on average—which may not be enough to facilitate deep, broad, and long-term new word learning (Connor et al., 2014; Snow et al., 2009). Similarly, in-the-moment and contextual word learning can help with real-time comprehension, but this strategy is often deployed for words that students already know and rarely facilitates long-term vocabulary retention (Beck et al., 2013).

Conceptual models of vocabulary delineate between four 'vocabularies' for listening, speaking, reading, and writing (Pikulski & Templeton, 2004). The listening vocabulary develops from infancy and is the largest of the four vocabularies. The speaking vocabulary forms the foundation for growth in the other vocabularies and is the most dynamic, with words coming and going with the times (for example, no one knew what a smartphone was in the 1980s, but everyone was talking about their Walkman). The reading vocabulary develops as children become literate and over time helps build vocabulary for speaking, listening, and writing. The written vocabulary is the smallest and requires integration of both word meaning and orthography to spell words and convey meaning. Therefore, within this model, it is possible to use our listening vocabulary to understand a word that we hear in context (e.g., "The host was generous and efficient, but not to the point of being *obsequious*") without having sufficient word knowledge to define a word or use it in an independently crafted written text. However, the goal of vocabulary instruction is deep word knowledge that enriches the spoken and written language that students' use.

Of course, it is impossible to teach every word in a language. However, evidence-based approaches to targeted vocabulary instruction can be effectively provided through whole-class instruction, with positive outcomes (Murphy et al., 2017). The three-tier framework for vocabulary instruction (Beck et al., 1987) offers a way forward. *Tier 1* words are the most frequently occurring, basic terms that are commonly used, such as exam, write, speech, and science. *Tier 2* words are high-frequency, rich, and descriptive terms that can be used across a range of subject areas and in many situations, such as articulate, convey, radiate, and colossal. *Tier 3* words are fewer in number, and are the subject-specific, technical words that belong to particular fields of study or activities, and includes term such as rubric, electrostatics, and literary devices.

Within the three-tier framework, Tier 2 words are the focus of instruction as these are the words that bring depth and richness to our language. They are most often found in written texts but less often used in verbal conversations. Beck et al. (2013) suggest three main criteria to choose which words to teach: (i) the importance of the word/s and how frequently they appear or could be used, (ii) the teach-ability of a new word that has nuanced meaning, but is similar to other words known by the student/s, and (iii) the instructional potential of the word and array of opportunities for deep word learning.

Effective instruction includes frequent and multiple encounters with target words, provision of a broad range of examples that demonstrate how a word can be used, and an approach that begins with context (e.g., using literature) and extends use of the word into other texts and into everyday examples relevant to the student's lived experience (Beck et al., 2013). This means going beyond word definitions and encouraging structured opportunities to use target words, build connections between target words and other words, understand the various parts of the word (e.g., root word, suffix/prefix), and see how the word can be used in different sentences and texts. An instructional sequence could include:

(i)   co-creating a student-friendly word definition with students,
(ii) generating synonyms and antonyms for the word and developing a visual semantic web or word cline to show connections/non-connections based on meaning,
(iii) sharing examples of the word in context and supporting students to create their own sentences using the word,

(iv) drawing, acting out or finding real-world or online materials that show examples of the word, and

(v) keeping a record of what has been learned about the word/s through a word wall, poster, PowerPoint or OneNote file or online repository (Beck et al., 2013).

Approaches to Support Students from Language Backgrounds Other Than English

This third dimension is perhaps where significant differences exist between the two groups of learners on which this chapter focuses. When it comes to language, students who speak English as an additional language or dialect are a distinct group in their profiles, experiences, assets, and learning requirements. It is tempting to think that the need for vocabulary teaching is the same for all learners, however, Nation (2008) points out three important differences between first language users of English and those learning it as a second or additional language. These are:

(i) By the age of five, most first language speakers of English have a vocabulary of around 3,000-to-4,000-word families. Those just beginning their study of English know few English words. Because high-frequency words are so important for language use—around 2,000–3,000 words—it is feasible to directly teach them, over time, especially if learners are entering school in mid-upper primary or secondary year levels.

(ii) First language speakers of English have plentiful opportunities to learn from varied input (e.g., listening, reading, viewing) and to produce output (e.g., speaking and writing) in English. Those learning English do not have the same opportunities. Classrooms need to provide these opportunities to maximise the language input and output available. Direct vocabulary teaching can bridge the gap between second language learners' current proficiency level and the level needed to understand and learn from the unsimplified input they will encounter outside the classroom.

(iii) Students who speak English as an additional language or dialect, especially those in secondary school, do not have the luxury of just being exposed to language. Direct teaching of vocabulary[4] can speed up the process.

Teaching students who speak English as an additional language or dialect means focussing on the explicit teaching of language *as an additional language* to the one the learner already speaks, writes, reads at home. English is often a totally different language to the main language used at home, with a new script (e.g., Arabic, Hindi,

---

4 Direct teaching of vocabulary means not leaving it up to chance that the words will be learned incidentally, although much vocabulary is learned incidentally as well. This is not to be confused with what is known as "Direct Instruction" based on behaviourist models of education.

Hebrew, Greek, Chinese, etc.), directionality on the page (right to left or left to right), set of syntax rules, phonological system, grapho-phonic relationship, and sociocultural norms around use. Compare, for example, English with Arabic, a language increasingly present in Australia. All sentences in English must have a verb, however, in Arabic, there are nominal sentences that do not include verbs. Arabic does not have a present perfect tense (e.g., "I *have been* . . ."). Arabic does not have a vowel sound for the letter 'e' or 'o'. Arabic has fewer consonant clusters than English (e.g., sh, sp, spr). In English, stress placed on different syllables can change the word category and meaning (e.g., record (noun) and record (verb)). In Arabic, regular stress is used and any stress does not change the word's meaning (Racoma, 2022). Learner's knowledge and experience of their first language structure and features and how it is used in context will have an influence on their acquisition and learning of subsequent languages. This can present challenges to both teacher and learner, but it also offers possibilities to leverage their experience as a competent language user of another set of meaning-making resources. In this way, these learners are thus seen through an asset lens, as having "funds of knowledge" (Moll et al., 1992, p. 133), and not through a deficit lens.

Focussing on language in teaching also means paying careful and regular attention in everyday lessons to the structure, linguistic features, and sociolinguistic and sociocultural aspects of Standard Australian English (SAE). This involves delving into a range of dimensions of language including phonological features, non-verbal language features, orthographic features, lexical competence (e.g., low frequency and highly technical terms in the curriculum), grammatical competence, semantic competence, and sociolinguistic understanding of language use in context.[5]

Context-embedded teaching, where teachers recreate contexts for teaching unfamiliar content, is another powerful approach for culturally diverse students who speak English as an additional language or dialect. Decontextualised presentation of concepts and content presents a significant barrier to learning for students who speak English as an additional language or dialect as they have nothing on which to 'hang' the content learning. Experience, as Dewey (1938) notes, occurs on a continuum where past and present experiences impact the future. If no experience has gone before, it needs to be generated at some point for learners to be able to access an initial experience. For instance, when teaching about rainforests with young people from arid regions such as Syria or central Australia, teachers can recreate the rainforest in the classroom with plants, forest soundscapes, objects, fauna specimens, photos and books from the library, rolling video footage, or VR if possible. This creates "message abundancy" (Gibbons, 2003, p. 259) through a range of modes which enhances experiential immersion in the content and associated *language*. It amplifies, rather than simplifies, the input making language more available for uptake.

5 For more detail on each of these, see the Language Table (ACARA, n.d.-b).

Finally, in their extensive work on scaffolding lessons with additional language learners, Hammond and Gibbons (2005) suggest what they call appropriating and recasting. This involves taking the learners' contributions in whatever language they can produce and reshaping it into the academic language and concepts of the unit. For example, if the learner offers the word "round" to describe the globe, since that is the only vocabulary item at their disposal at that point in their language learning trajectory, the teacher could spell 'r-o-u-n-d' on the whiteboard, to reinforce spelling and phonological awareness, and also explain and use the word "spherical" (and "sphere") to build low-frequency, curriculum-specific vocabulary knowledge.

Conclusion

In this chapter, we have highlighted the centrality of language in the enactment of successful inclusive education by drawing on our experience with students from language backgrounds other than English and students with language disorder. While different models of language have historically shaped practice for these two groups, there are generative synergies between the two that teachers can explore. The chapter unpacks the dilemmas of difference that teachers grapple with daily and reminds us all that inclusive practice needs to be holistic and responsive to individual learner profiles and characteristics. A range of whole-of-school and classroom pedagogical approaches, that specifically foreground language, have been offered to enable teachers to cater for these two groups of learners at a time when varied groups of learners have been subsumed under one policy.

References

Alford, J., & Woods, A. (2017). Constituting "at risk" literacy and language learners in teacher talk: Exploring the discursive element of time. *The Australian Journal of Language and Literacy, 40*(1), 7–15. https://doi.org/10.1007/BF03651980

Australian Bureau of Statistics. (2021). *2021 Census Data.* https://www.abs.gov.au/statistics/people/people-and-communities/cultural-diversity-census/latest-release

Australian Curriculum, Assessment and Reporting Authority (ACARA). (n.d.-a). *Meeting the needs of students for whom English is an additional language or dialect.* https://www.australiancurriculum.edu.au/resources/student-diversity/meeting-the-needs-of-students-for-whom-english-is-an-additional-language-or-dialect/

Australian Curriculum, Assessment and Reporting Authority (ARARA). (n.d.-b). *Language table.* https://www.australiancurriculum.edu.au/senior-secondary-curriculum/english/english-as-an-additional-language-or-dialect/language-table/

Bartlett, T., & Bowcher, W. (2021). Context in systemic functional linguistics: Principles and parameters. *Functions of Language, 28*(3), 243–259. https://doi.org/10.1075/fol.20017.bar

Beck, I. L., McKeown, M. G., & Kucan, L. (2013). *Bringing words to life: Robust vocabulary instruction.* Guilford Press.

Beck, I. L., McKeown, M. G., & Omanson, R. C. (1987). The effects and uses of diverse vocabulary instructional techniques. In M. G. McKeown, & M. E. Curtis (Eds.), *The nature of vocabulary acquisition* (pp. 147–163). Erlbaum.

Berwick, R. C., & Chomsky, N. (2016). *Why only us: Language and evolution.* MIT press.

Bishop, D. V. M., Snowling, M. J., Thompson, P. A., Greenhalgh, T., Adams, C., Archibald, L., Baird, G., Bauer, A., Bellair, J., Boyle, C., Brownlie, E., Carter, G., Clark, B., Clegg, J., Cohen, N., Conti-Ramsden, G., Dockrell, J., Dunn, J., Ebbels, S., . . . Grist, M. (2017). Phase 2 of CAT-ALISE: A multinational and multidisciplinary Delphi consensus study of problems with language development: Terminology. *Journal of Child Psychology and Psychiatry, 58*(10), 1068–1080. https://doi.org/10.1111/jcpp.12721

Bloom, L., & Lahey, M. (1978). *Language development and language disorders.* Wiley.

Bracken, S., Driver, C., & Kadi-Hanifi, K. (2016). English as an additional language: What does it mean, who is it for and how is it acquired? In S. Bracken, C. Driver, & K. Kadi-Hanifi (Eds.), *Teaching English as an additional language in secondary schools: Theory and practice* (pp. 5–30). Routledge.

Brown v Board of Education [1954] 347 U.S. 483.

Canagarajah, S., & Silberstein, S. (2012). Diaspora identities and language. *Journal of Language, Identity, and Education, 11*(2), 81–84. https://doi.org/10.1080/15348458.2012.667296

Castles, S., Kalantzis, M., & Cope, B. (1986). *The end of multiculturalism?* Australian Society.

Cazden, C. (1988). *Classroom discourse: The language of teaching and learning.* Heinemann.

Connor, C. M., Spencer, M., Day, S. L., Giuliani, S., Ingebrand, S. W., McLean, L., & Morrison, F. J. (2014). Capturing the complexity: Content, type, and amount of instruction and quality of the classroom learning environment synergistically predict third graders' vocabulary and reading comprehension outcomes. *Journal of Educational Psychology, 106*(3), 762–778. https://doi.org/10.1037/a0035921

Conti-Ramsden, G., Durkin, K., Toseeb, U., Botting, N., & Pickles, A. (2018). Education and employment outcomes of young adults with a history of developmental language disorder. *International Journal of Language & Communication Disorders, 53*(2), 237–255. https://doi.org/10.1111/1460-6984.12338

Creagh, S., Hogan, A., Lingard, B., & Choi, T. (2022). The 'everywhere and nowhere' English language policy in Queensland government schools: A license for commercialisation. *Journal of Education Policy.* Advance online publication. https://doi.org/10.1080/02680939.2022.2037721

Creagh, S., Kettle, M., Alford, J., Comber, B., & Shield, P. (2019). How long does it take to achieve academically in a second language? Comparing the trajectories of EAL students and first language peers in Queensland schools. *The Australian Journal of Language and Literacy, 42*(3), 145–155. https://doi.org/10.1007/BF03652034

Derewianka, B. (2011). *A new grammar companion for teachers.* Primary English Teachers' Association.

Dewey, J. (1938). *Experience and education.* Macmillan.

Durkin, K., Conti-Ramsden, G., & Simkin, Z. (2012). Functional outcomes of adolescents with a history of specific language impairment (SLI) with and without autistic symptomatology. *Journal of Autism and Developmental Disorders, 42*, 123–138. https://doi.org/10.1007/s10803-011-1224-y

Education for All Handicapped Children Act (1975).

Gibbons, P. (2003). Mediating language learning: Teacher interactions with ESL students in a content-based classroom. *TESOL Quarterly, 37*(2), 247–273. https://doi.org/10.2307/3588504

Gillies, R. M., & Khan, A. (2009). Promoting reasoned argumentation, problem-solving and learning during small-group work. *Cambridge Journal of Education*, 39(1), 7–27. https://doi.org/10.1080/03057640802701945

Glasby, J., Graham, L. J., White, S. L. J., & Tancredi, H. (2022). Do teachers know enough about the characteristics and educational impacts of Developmental Language Disorder (DLD) to successfully include students with DLD? *Teaching and Teacher Education*, 119, 103868. https://doi.org/10.1016/j.tate.2022.103868

Graham, L. J., & Tancredi, H. (2019). In search of a middle ground: the dangers and affordances of diagnosis in relation to Attention Deficit Hyperactivity Disorder and Developmental Language Disorder. *Emotional and Behavioural Difficulties*, 24(3), 287–300. https://doi.org/10.1080/13632752.2019.1609248

Graham, L. J., Tancredi, H., Willis, J., & McGraw, K. (2018). Designing out barriers to student access and participation in secondary school assessment. *The Australian Educational Researcher*, 45(1), 103–124. https://doi.org/10.1007/s13384-018-0266-y

Gutiérrez, K. D., Morales, P. Z., & Martinez, D. C. (2009). Re-mediating literacy: Culture, difference, and learning for students from nondominant communities. *Review of Research in Education*, 33(1), 212–245. https://doi.org/10.3102/0091732X08328267

Halliday, M. A. K. (1978). *Language as social semiotic: The social interpretation of language and meaning*. Arnold.

Halliday, M. A. K., & Hasan, R. (1985). *Language, Context and Text: Aspects of Language in a Social-Semiotic Perspective*. Geelong.

Halliday, M. A. K., & Matthiessen, C. (2004). *An Introduction to Functional Grammar* (3rd ed.). Arnold.

Hammond, J., & Gibbons, P. (2005). Putting scaffolding to work: The contribution of scaffolding in articulating ESL education. *Prospect*, 20(1) 6–30.

Harper, H., & Feez, S. (2021). Learning and teaching English as an additional language or dialect in mainstream classrooms. In H. Harper & S. Feez (Eds.), *An EAL/D handbook* (pp. 1–15). PETA.

Hasan, R. (1992, 2009). Rationality in everyday talk: From process to system. In J. J. Webster (Ed.), *Semantic Variation: Meaning in Society and in Sociolinguistics* (pp. 309–352). Equinox.

Hunt, E., Nang, C., Meldrum, S., & Armstrong, E. (2022). Can dynamic assessment identify language disorder in multilingual children? Clinical applications from a systematic review. *Language, Speech, and Hearing Services in Schools*, 53(2), 598–625. https://doi.org/10.1044/2021_LSHSS-21-00094

Individuals with Disabilities Education Act.

Katsiyannis, A., Yell, M. L., & Bradley, R. (2001). Reflections on the 25th Anniversary of the Individuals with Disabilities Education Act. *Remedial and Special Education*, 22(6), 324–334. https://doi.org/10.1177/074193250102200602

Ketterlin-Geller, L. R., & Jamgochian, E. M. (2011). Instructional adaptations: Accommodations and modifications that support accessible instruction. In S. N. Elliot, R. J. Kettler, P. A. Beddow, & A. Kurz (Eds.), *Handbook of accessible achievement tests for all students: Bridging the gaps between research, practice, and policy* (pp. 131–146). Springer.

Lau v Nichols [1974] 414 U.S. 563.

Li'el, N., Williams, C., & Kane, R. (2019). Identifying developmental language disorder in bilingual children from diverse linguistic backgrounds. *International Journal of Speech-Language Pathology*, 21(6), 613–622. https://doi.org/10.1080/17549507.2018.1513073

Macaulay, L. (2022). "She Just Saw Me—She Didn't Teach Me": The perspectives of Australian Sudanese and South Sudanese youth on the student/teacher relationship in Australian schools. *Australian Educational Researcher*. Advance online publication. https://doi.org/10.1007/s13384-022-00554-z

Martin, J., & Rose, D. (2013). Pedagogic discourse: Contexts of schooling. *RASK: International Journal of Language and Communication, 38*, 219–264.

McGregor, K. K., Oleson, J., Bahnsen, A., & Duff, D. (2013). Children with developmental language impairment have vocabulary deficits characterized by limited breadth and depth: Vocabulary deficits. *International Journal of Language & Communication Disorders, 48*(3), 307–319. https://doi.org/10.1111/1460-6984.12008

McKeown, M. G., Crosson, A. C., Moore, D. W., & Beck, I. L. (2018). Word knowledge and comprehension effects of an academic vocabulary intervention for middle school students. *American Educational Research Journal, 55*(3), 572–616. https://doi.org/10.3102/0002831217744181

Merrell, C., Sayal, K., Tymms, P., & Kasim, A. (2017). A longitudinal study of the association between inattention, hyperactivity and impulsivity and children's academic attainment at age 11. *Learning and Individual Differences, 53*, 156–161. https://doi.org/10.1016/j.lindif.2016.04.003

Mills v Board of Education [D.D.C. 1972] 348 F. Supp. 866.

Miller, J. (2003). *Audible difference: ESL and social identities in schools*. Multilingual Matters.

Minow, M. (1990). *Making all the difference: Inclusion, exclusion, and American law*. Cornell University Press.

Moll, L. C., Amanti, C., Neff, D., & Gonzalez, N. (1992). Funds of knowledge for teaching: Using a qualitative approach to connect homes and classrooms. *Theory into Practice, 31*(2), 132–141. https://doi.org/10.1080/00405849209543534

Morgan, P. L., Farkas, G., Hillemeier, M. M., Mattison, R., Maczuga, S., Li, H., & Cook, M. (2015). Minorities are disproportionately underrepresented in special education: Longitudinal evidence across five disability conditions. *Educational Researcher, 44*(5), 278–292. https://doi.org/10.3102/0013189X15591157

Murphy, A., Franklin, S., Breen, A., Hanlon, M., McNamara, A., Bogue, A., & James, E. (2017). A whole class teaching approach to improve the vocabulary skills of adolescents attending mainstream secondary school, in areas of socioeconomic disadvantage. *Child Language Teaching and Therapy, 33*(2), 129–144. https://doi.org/10.1177/0265659016656906

Nation, I. S. P. (2008). *Teaching vocabulary: Strategies and techniques*. Heinle Cengage Learning.

Nippold, M. A. (2016). *Later language development: School-aged children, adolescents, and young adults* (4th ed.). Pro-Ed.

Norbury, C. F., Gooch, D., Wray, C., Baird, G., Charman, T., Simonoff, E., Vamvakas, G., & Pickles, A. (2016). The impact of nonverbal ability on prevalence and clinical presentation of language disorder: Evidence from a population study. *Journal of Child Psychology and Psychiatry, 57*(11), 1247–1257. https://doi.org/10.1111/jcpp.12573

Paradis, J., Genesee, F., & Crago, M. (2011). *Dual language development and disorders: A handbook on bilingualism & second language learning*. Brookes Publishing.

Pennsylvania Association for Retarded Children v Commonwealth of Pennsylvania [1971] 334 F. Supp. 1257.

Pikulski, J. J., & Templeton, S. (2004). Teaching and developing vocabulary: Key to long-term reading success. *Current Research in Reading/Language Arts, 1*, 1–12.

Queensland Government. (2022). *Inclusive Education Policy*. https://ppr.qed.qld.gov.au/attach ment/inclusive-education-policy.pdf

Racoma, B. (2022). *Arabic interpreting: Major differences between English and Arabic*. https://www. daytranslations.com/blog/interpreting-english-arabic/

Said, E. (1978). *Orientalism*. Pantheon Books.

Saubich, X., & Guitart, M. E. (2011). Bringing family funds of knowledge to school: The living Morocco project. *Multidisciplinary Journal of Educational Research, 1*(1), 79–103.

Schweitzer, R. D., Mackay, S., Hancox, D., & Khawaja, N. G. (2021). Fostering belonging in a CALD school environment: learning from a research collaboration with a refugee and migrant school community in Australia. *Intercultural Education, 32*(6), 593–609. https://doi.org/10.10 80/14675986.2021.1985803

Simmie, G. M., Moles, J., & O'Grady, E. (2019). Good teaching as a messy narrative of change within a policy ensemble of networks, superstructures and flows. *Critical Studies in Education, 60*(1), 55–72. https://doi.org/10.1080/17508487.2016.1219960

Slama, R. B. (2012). A longitudinal analysis of academic English proficiency outcomes for adolescent English language learners in the United States. *Journal of Educational Psychology, 104*(2), 265–285. https://doi.org/10.1037/a0025861

Snow, C. E., Lawrence, J. F., & White, C. (2009). Generating knowledge of academic language among urban middle school students. *Journal of Research on Educational Effectiveness, 2*(4), 325–344. https://doi.org/10.1080/19345740903167042

Sparks, R. L., Patton, J., & Murdoch, A. (2014). Early reading success and its relationship to reading achievement and reading volume: Replication of "10 years later." *Reading & Writing, 27*(1), 189–211. https://doi.org/10.1007/s11145-013-9439-2

Starling, J., Munro, N., Togher, L., & Arciuli, J. (2012). Training secondary school teachers in instructional language modification techniques to support adolescents with language impairment: A randomized control trial. *Language, Speech and Hearing Services in Schools, 43*(4), 474–495. https://doi.org/10.1044/0161-1461(2012/11-0066)

Stow, C., & Dodd, B. (2005). A survey of bilingual children referred for investigation of communication disorders: A comparison with monolingual children referred in one area in England. *Journal of Multilingual Communication Disorders, 3*(1), 1–23. https://doi. org/10.1080/14769670400009959

Sugarman, S. D., & Widess, E. G. (1974). Equal Protection for Non-English-Speaking School Children: Lau v. Nichols. *California Law Review, 62*(1), 157–182. https://doi.org/10.2307/ 3479823

Tancredi, H. (2018). *Adjusting language barriers in secondary classrooms through professional collaboration based on student consultation* [Master's thesis, Queensland University of Technology]. Queensland University of Technology ePrints. https://eprints.qut.edu.au/122876/

Tancredi, H. (2020). Meeting obligations to consult students with disability: methodological considerations and successful elements for consultation. *The Australian Educational Researcher, 47*(2), 201–217. https://doi.org/10.1007/s13384-019-00341-3

Titsworth, S., Mazer, J. P., Goodboy, A. K., Bolkan, S., & Myers, S. A. (2015). Two meta-analyses exploring the relationship between teacher clarity and student learning. *Communication Education, 64*(4), 385–418. https://doi.org/10.1080/03634523.2015.1041998

Traga Philippakos, Z. A., & MacArthur, C. A. (2020). Integrating collaborative reasoning and strategy instruction to improve second graders' opinion writing. *Reading & Writing Quarterly, 36*(4), 379–395. https://doi.org/10.1080/10573569.2019.1650315

Ukrainetz, T. A., & Fresquez, E. F. (2003). "What isn't language?": A qualitative study of the role of the school speech-language pathologist. *Language, Speech, and Hearing Services in Schools, 34*(4), 284–298. https://doi.org/10.1044/0161-1461(2003/024)

Valencia, R. R. (2012). Conceptualizing the notion of deficit thinking. In R. R. Valencia (Ed.). *The evolution of deficit thinking* (pp. 1–12). Routledge.

Walton, E. (2015). *The language of inclusive education: Exploring speaking, listening, reading and writing*. Routledge.

Chapter 11

Accessible Pedagogies™

Linda J. Graham & Haley Tancredi

An increased level of attention has turned to the quality of teaching in recent decades with the aim of enhancing teachers' practice through professional development involving standardised observation and feedback cycles (Singh et al., 2019). A variety of pedagogical frameworks and observational tools have been developed with the most well-known and commonly used emerging from the United States. These include the Danielson Framework for Teaching (FFT; Danielson, 2007), the Classroom Assessment Scoring System (CLASS; Pianta et al., 2008), and the Art and Science of Teaching (ASoT; Marzano, 2007). Frameworks that have originated elsewhere include the International Comparative Analysis of Learning and Teaching (ICALT) from The Netherlands (van der Grift, 2007), and Load Reduction Instruction (LRI; Martin & Evans, 2018), Productive Pedagogies (Lingard et al., 2003), and Quality Teaching Framework from Australia (QTF; New South Wales Department of Education, 2003). Each of these frameworks defines key elements of teaching important for student learning and provide a means to recognise and enhance teachers' proficiency through observation, coaching and/or professional learning communities. However, as argued elsewhere (Graham, Tancredi, et al., 2022), each framework is broad, and none—aside from perhaps the ICALT—goes to the level of granularity necessary to identify and promote practices that represent quality for students with common disabilities, like Attention Deficit Hyperactivity Disorder and Developmental Language Disorder, who are present in everyday classrooms (Graham & Tancredi, 2019). This is a core weakness of measures of quality teaching more broadly, which we suspect is due to common assumptions about who is being taught in everyday classrooms and what 'quality' means for them.

Research on teaching quality is typically conducted in mainstream schools by general education researchers, using broad measures derived from large-scale observational studies, which are themselves a product of the students, teachers, and interactions within those environments (Brownell et al., 2020). While studies conducted in these classrooms will have had students with learning difficulties or disabilities within them, no study that we know of has disaggregated for students with and without these differences to determine whether quality for *most* equals quality for *all*. This point was recently made by Morris-Mathews et al. (2021) who questioned the relevance of Danielson's FFT (Danielson, 2007) to all learners, as well as the assumptions underlying the framework. For example, Morris-Mathews et al. (2021) argue that, in privileging

DOI: 10.4324/9781003350897-13

constructivist teaching practices, such as inquiry learning, Danielson's FFT assumes that "all students have the expertise necessary to design and direct their own learning" (p. 74). Equally salient for inclusive educators is their observation that "practices known to reduce cognitive load . . . appear rarely in the rubrics", and that "teacher-directed instruction" is relegated to "the unsatisfactory and basic levels of performance" (p. 72). While the battle between constructivist and traditional models of teaching have been somewhat reconciled by Load Reduction Instruction (LRI)[1], there remains a perception that teacher-directed instruction is only necessary for students with learning difficulties or disabilities, and that 'average' (and especially 'bright') students will become bored and disengaged without the stimulation afforded by group activities and inquiry learning. Readers of this book may find an interesting parallel in the arguments made in favour of 'balanced literacy' versus structured literacy instruction. The well-worn trope goes something like this:

> Some children learn to read without explicit teaching of the alphabetic code. Said teaching is boring for those children and risks killing the joy of literature. There-fore, only those who need explicit instruction should be subjected to it.

While this might be a somewhat polemical representation of the balanced literacy position, this trope is what we—as researchers in inclusive education—read in the sub-text about *some* versus *all* children. This subtext linking structured literacy instruction to 'the needs' of 'some' children (those not born into a book-loving family and who supposedly have not been read quality literature and sung lullabies from birth) is evident in the 2018 report funded by the New South Wales Teachers Federation, *Exploding some of the myths about learning to read: A review of research on the role of phonics* (Ewing, 2018). Included alongside children from socially disadvantaged backgrounds in the "*some* children" group are those with "difficulties and disabilities" (p. 29), for whom something different or extra is apparently warranted:

> To improve reading for *all* Australian children, it is not constructive to assert undue pressure on educators (and teacher educators) to adopt only one way of teaching reading, as if it must and will answer all the difficulties that *some* students face in learning to read (emphasis added, p. 7).

And: "While determining how to best help students struggling with the reading process is an important area of research, it is highly inappropriate to suggest its relevance for *all* children" (emphasis added, p. 32).

---

1 LRI is a research-based model for teaching that begins by supporting novice learners through teacher directed instruction that transitions to guided discovery learning as learners' knowledge and capacity increases (Martin & Evans, 2018).

This trope is also strongly evident in the affirmative side's rhetoric in *The Great Literacy Debate* held by the Australian College of Educators later that year. You can watch the debate on YouTube and decide for yourself, as well as read more about evidence-based approaches to reading instruction in Chapter 9 of this book. The reason we have raised this parallel is to highlight the difference in approach between mainstream (+special) education and inclusive education. Mainstream and special are interdependent; you can't have a *mainstream*, unless there are other streams, right? Inclusion is different. At this point, it is worth recalling the definition of inclusion from *General Comment No. 4* (GC4) on Article 24 of the *Convention on the Rights of Persons with Disabilities* (CRPD; United Nations, 2006) provided in Chapter 2 of this book, which describes inclusion as "a process of systemic reform embodying changes and modifications in content, teaching methods, approaches, structures and strategies in education to overcome barriers" (United Nations, 2016, para 11).

Many educators will read this definition and believe that what they are doing is, in fact, 'inclusion'. But, if this process is conducted mainly through the provision of adjustments[2] to business-as-usual teaching, the result tends to be what we call 'teaching to the middle' with add-ons for students with identified disabilities. This all-too-common approach not only requires students to encounter barriers before those barriers are removed but also carries the high risk of those barriers remaining in place, particularly when it comes to students with less 'visible' disabilities, like Attention Deficit Hyperactivity Disorder (ADHD) or Developmental Language Disorder (DLD; Graham & Tancredi, 2019). Incidentally, this process of teaching to the middle with add-ons is how we have ended up with integration by default in 'mainstream' schools, as described in Chapter 2, despite the significant and sustained effort of so many educators, activists, parents, and scholars. It is in recognition of this problem that the CRPD Committee stipulated (now seven years ago) in GC4 that States parties apply Universal Design for Learning (UDL; United Nations, 2016, para 25), an approach to teaching that involves the proactive removal of barriers and provision of supports.

UDL is a comprehensive multidimensional pedagogical framework that draws on the principles of universal design. The framework was designed to guide flexibility in educational practices by optimising how learners are engaged, how information is presented during the teaching process, and how learners can demonstrate their learning (CAST, 2018). Like many other pedagogical frameworks, including the Accessible Pedagogies framework outlined in this chapter, it comprises three domains of practice (termed "principles", see Table 11.1), each with three dimensions that unite to achieve a key goal (Rose & Meyer, 2006).

Within each dimension are multiple checkpoints to guide practice within that specific area. The *Executive Functions* dimension, for example, includes practices and strategies

2 Adjustments are the Australian equivalent to 'modifications'.

Table 11.1 Universal Design for Learning Guidelines

	Principle 1: Multiple Means of Engagement	Principle 2: Multiple Means of Representation	Principle 3: Multiple Means of Action and Expression
Access	Recruiting interest	Perception	Physical action
Build	Sustaining effort and persistence	Language and symbols	Expression and communication
Internalise	Self-regulation	Comprehension	Executive Functions
Goal	*Purposeful and motivated*	*Resourceful and knowledgeable*	*Strategic and goal directed*

Adapted from CAST (2018).

to (i) guide appropriate goal setting, (ii) support planning and strategy development, (iii) facilitate managing information and resources, and (iv) enhance capacity for monitoring progress. The first of these, goal setting, includes recommendations that teachers:

- embed prompts to 'stop and think' before acting,
- embed prompts to 'show and explain your work',
- provide checklists and project planning templates for understanding the problem, setting up, prioritisation, sequences, and schedules of steps,
- embed coaches or mentors that model think-alouds of the process, and
- provide guides for breaking long-term goals into reachable short-term objectives. (CAST, 2018)

UDL has been developed from the perspective of including all students from the outset, especially those with disability. However, from our observation and experience, it has not yet been widely adopted in schools and, due to its comprehensive nature, may be difficult to integrate with existing pedagogical frameworks, many of which *have* been widely adopted (Graham, Tancredi, et al., 2022). This leaves us with a conundrum:

> How do we move towards inclusive practice when schools have largely adopted pedagogical frameworks that are built on mainstream teaching practices, and when not all teachers have the individual capacity, awareness, and/or motivation to develop the depth of knowledge of the UDL framework required to enact UDL well?

Readers of the first edition of this book will notice that this new edition does not include a chapter on differentiation and UDL. Instead, we have a new chapter on Multi-Tiered Systems of Support, this chapter on Accessible Pedagogies, and a new chapter on including students with complex learning profiles in grade-level academic curriculum. We have done this because it is impossible to cover UDL adequately in the space of one unit of study, which is all that is mandated for initial teacher education in Australia.[3] We have also chosen to abandon differentiation in this book, not because it is false in premise, rather because it is poorly understood and enacted, both in research and in practice (Graham et al., 2021). Therefore, instead of agnostically describing two approaches to inclusive planning and teaching—as do many books, including the first edition of this book—this second edition of Inclusive Education for the 21st Century proposes a different way.

There are three reasons behind this decision. First, we don't think that inclusion needs to be complicated, and our view is that what is missing from existing pedagogical frameworks is a focus on accessibility. Second, we recognise that teachers tend not to have autonomy when it comes to the selection and adoption of pedagogical frameworks and that the decision to go with one framework or another is typically made by school leaders, who may or may not even be aware of UDL (or even their obligations under the *Disability Discrimination Act 1992* (Cth) and *Disability Standards for Education 2005* (Cth)). And third, we think that understanding the social model of disability and the principles of universal design are more valuable to classroom teachers than learning yet another pedagogical framework that exists in isolation from those that have already been adopted.

What Are the Principles of Universal Design?

The concept of universal design originated from the field of architecture with the aim of designing buildings and spaces that can be accessed by as many people as possible. To be accessible, a space must be useful, safe, and comfortable for all users, regardless of their size or mode of mobility. As explained in Chapter 4, universal design has brought many innovations to everyday life that we now take for granted. For example, have you ever used your elbow to open a door when carrying something? If you have, this was made possible by universal design. It inspired, among many other things, levered door handles, which were created to mitigate the need for a person with, let's say, arthritis to grip and twist a knob to open doors. A lever in place of a knob is simple but effective in addressing the barrier, right? Levered door handles are an innovation that helps everyone. This is the value of universal design.

The aim of universal design is to maximise access by anticipating and then designing out barriers from the outset and the principles apply just as much to *education* as they do to architecture. While UDL offers a framework, it has received criticism for being "seductively easy", leading to teachers claiming that they are "doing UDL", when they are not (Edyburn, 2010, p. 40). Edyburn and others have further cautioned that the

---

3 Note that we think that *at least two mandatory units should be required* and that we have tried to achieve this in our own university where space permits.

principles of UDL may serve as a distraction, when more attention needs to be paid to the complex interactions that take place in classrooms, involving instructional design, learning objectives, student characteristics, and learning outcomes. Therefore, to employ universal design principles successfully, educators must approach lesson planning, assessment design, and pedagogy with deep understanding not only of the content to be taught and how to teach and assess it—they must also "know students and how they learn" (Australian Institute for Teaching School Leadership [AITSL], 2017, p. 1). While this phrase is used in the Australian Professional Standards for Teachers, it is not defined and those of us in inclusive education know how dangerous lack of definition can be. The danger here is that "know students and how they learn" can be (and is being) innocently interpreted to mean knowing biographical details about students, like how many siblings Johnny has and whether he likes skateboarding, and which modality he prefers,[4] but this information does not tell educators anything about *why* Johnny has difficulty reading and could lead to the implementation of flawed theories, like letting Johnny act out his assessment response because 'he's a kinaesthetic learner'. In this book, we interpret "know students and how they learn" (AITSL, 2017, p. 1) to mean that educators must have deep understanding of students' individual learning profiles and the cognitive processes involved in learning.

How Does Learning Occur?

In the classroom, information is exchanged through oral and written language, and visual, auditory, and spatial media. For learning to take place, this information must first be adequately processed in working memory before it can be transferred to long-term memory (Cowan, 2014). Working memory can be thought of as a 'mental notepad', a time and capacity limited system that facilitates the temporary retention and use of small amounts of information (Baddeley, 2000). For example, to remember a phone number when we don't have a pen handy, we use our working memory to hold number strings in mind by mentally repeating the strings or thinking about what the numbers might look like when written down. Information stored in long-term memory can be transformational for learning because having a rich store of background knowledge to draw on boosts the performance of working memory (Baddeley, 1997; Gathercole & Alloway, 2004). However, because working memory has space limitations, it can easily become overloaded, resulting in students 'missing' crucial instructions and/or information, and consequently restricting their ability to participate and learn. Over time, students' repeated experiences of working memory overload will impact their ability to store information in long-term memory, with pervasive and far-reaching negative consequences for students' learning progress (Gathercole & Alloway, 2008).

---

4 Note that research has comprehensively debunked the notion that students learn better if information is presented via their preferred 'learning style', yet the theory is still influencing practice (Cuevas, 2015).

The limitations of students' working memory capacities has significant implications for instructional practice, yet teachers are often not provided with the deep grounding in language and cognition they need to guide practice. This knowledge is especially important for inclusive practice. While all students can be overwhelmed if they are confronted with too much information at once or when unnecessary demands or distractions are placed on the cognitive system during learning, this is especially the case for students with disabilities impacting language and information processing. Importantly, while it is sometimes said that all students are more alike than they are different in the way they learn (Willingham et al., 2015), we think this is a dangerously simplistic assertion. Rather, it is correct to say that all humans use the same cognitive system to learn, but the efficiency of processes within the cognitive system, such as working memory or attentional control, can be different and this has important implications for teaching.

Our research (and this chapter) principally focuses on students with disabilities impacting language and information processing, like ADHD and DLD. Students with ADHD and DLD learn using the same system to process auditory and visual information; however, they may not be able to do so at the same pace, they may need more frequent repetition, they may need more help to pay attention and to distinguish between important and unimportant information, and greater use of visual representations to make sense of abstract concepts. Another important difference between these students and those without ADHD or DLD is in the personal resources they have at hand to overcome instructional barriers. It is not the case that instructional barriers exist *only* for students with disabilities impacting language and information processing. All students experience barriers arising from extraneous language and cognitive load: the difference between groups is in the relative impact of those barriers. For students without disability, these barriers create additional cognitive burden and impede students' rate of learning. However, if left unaddressed these barriers will significantly impede—if not completely block—access to teachers' instruction for students with disability and through that their access to the curriculum.

Critically, the instructional barriers that impede access for students with disabilities impacting language and information processing will also seriously disadvantage English language learners, students on the autism spectrum, students with hearing impairment, and more. These instructional barriers can include:

- long, complex, and/or poorly sequenced instruction (Starling et al., 2012),
- use of unfamiliar vocabulary (Becker & McGregor, 2016),
- instructional strategies (e.g., questioning, feedback, worked examples) that confuse rather than support the message conveyed during teaching (Sweller et al., 2019), and/or
- fast-paced verbal instruction (Lapadat, 2002).

Each of these barriers tax working memory, impeding the transfer of information to long-term memory by overloading the cognitive system. To avoid cognitive overload, instruction needs to be designed in a way that ensures a logical structure to the delivery of verbal, written, and multimedia information (Martin et al., 2023; Sweller, 2012). This is important for all students but especially those with disabilities impacting language and information processing.

Two types of cognitive load are important for teachers to know about. These are *intrinsic cognitive load*—the load that exists due to the inherent complexity of the content,[5] and *extraneous cognitive load*—the load that is imposed by how information is presented via pedagogical practices (Sweller, 2012; Sweller et al., 2019). Classroom instruction that requires students to devote working memory resources to managing extraneous cognitive load will reduce their capacity to deal with intrinsic cognitive load and significantly impacts students' learning of new material (Sweller, 2010). While students may not use these same terms to describe the complexification of instruction, the original research from which we developed the idea for Accessible Pedagogies indicated that students really do know what they are talking about when it comes to practices that support learning.

What Did the Kids Say?

In a study funded by the *Queensland Government's Education Horizon Scheme* (2016–2018), we investigated student perspectives about effective teaching practice. The project had two phases. The first involved a large-scale survey of all consenting students in Grades 7–10 from three secondary schools serving disadvantaged communities (Graham, Gillett-Swan, et al., 2022), and the second involved in-depth semi-structured interviews with a 'brains trust' comprising 50 students with a history of disruptive and disengaged behaviour that included conflict with classroom teachers. These students were all nominated by the school leadership team based on OneSchool behaviour data.[6] We asked consenting students: "What makes an excellent teacher?" and "What do those teachers *do* and how does it help you to learn?" (Graham, Tancredi, et al., 2022). Students' responses to the first question were coded into three categories derived from the literature on quality teaching: emotional support, classroom organisation, and instructional support (Pianta & Hamre, 2009). We added a fourth category to capture students' statements about teachers' temperament and personality (see Table 11.2). Answers to the second question were used to confirm the validity of coding and to add context and description. It might be a surprise to some—given the popularity of the myth that students with disruptive and disengaged behaviour do not value education or learning—that the most dominant statements from these 50 'brains trust' kids were those relating to instructional support.

---

5 Hello Shakespeare!

6 In Queensland state schools, data are captured using OneSchool, a school performance and student management database. https://behaviour.education.qld.gov.au/supporting-student-behaviour/positive-behaviour-for-learning/data-informed-decision-making

Table 11.2 Descriptions of Coding Categories Used and Corresponding Responses

Category	Description	Percentage of Responses
Temperament/personality	Teachers' likeability, fun/bubbly nature, or relatability	16.1%
Classroom organisation	Teachers' use of behaviour management strategies, classroom productivity, and multi-modal teaching practices	18.3%
Emotional support	Teachers' responsiveness to students and their perspectives, positive classroom climate	24.7%
Instructional support	Practices that support students to learn, such as feedback, clear explanations of concepts, and modelling language	40.9%

Importantly, however, these students went beyond what is described in most quality teaching frameworks for this domain by specifically referring to practices that improve the accessibility of teaching and the comprehensibility of lesson content, particularly through clear explanation and providing examples. As we saw these patterns emerging early in the interviews with the first 35 students, we developed a visual resource featuring six practices:

(i)   teachers talking slower,
(ii) teachers explaining things more clearly,
(iii) teachers checking in with you more often,
(iv) having a buddy who can help explain,
(v)   teachers writing instructions on the board, and
(vi) teachers giving regular reminders of what you are meant to be doing.

The resource was used during interviews with the remaining students and all 15 agreed that these practices were helpful but also noted they were not routinely used. For example, when shown the visual support, one student stated: "If that all happened in every single class then I wouldn't have any issues" (Grade 9, School D, p. 9).

On concluding these interviews, we developed an observational matrix that included the instructional practices from the full list nominated by the 50 students and subjected it to a process of review in concordance with the research literature. We then piloted the refined matrix with nine classroom teachers in 2018, noting gaps or redundancies to enable further refinement. In 2019, we received funding from the Australian Research Council Linkage Projects scheme (LP180100830). The Accessible Assessment Linkage Project, as it became known, had two main objectives. The first was to test whether re-designing assessment task sheets for accessibility makes a positive impact on students' task comprehension, and achievement.[7] The second objective was to test whether improving the accessibility of everyday classroom teaching does the same. The Accessible Assessment Linkage Project commenced in 2020 and, despite a global pandemic, devastating floods, and a cyber-attack on our university, we have worked hard to:

(1) identify a core set of evidence-based instructional practices to optimise student engagement with and comprehension of everyday classroom teaching,
(2) investigate their frequency and effectiveness of use in teachers' general instructional practice, and
(3) devise ways to help teachers adopt these practices so that they *do* happen in every single class *and* that they happen for every single student.

The result is Accessible Pedagogies.

What Are Accessible Pedagogies?

Accessible Pedagogies comprise a set of evidence-based, instructional practices that prevent barriers arising from extraneous language and cognitive load (Bussing et al., 2016; Gathercole & Alloway, 2004; Starling et al., 2012; Sweller et al., 2019). We have developed Accessible Pedagogies to complement and enhance existing pedagogical frameworks. Its structure is informed by the first author's deep familiarity with the Classroom Assessment Scoring System (CLASS; Pianta et al., 2008), and experience conducting standardised classroom observations using the CLASS throughout a six-year longitudinal study, as well as the second author's deep expertise as an educational speech pathologist with 15 years' experience working in collaboration with classroom teachers to adjust their pedagogy to meet the needs of students with disability. The CLASS is the most rigorously evidenced of existing pedagogical frameworks. It does not, however—and nor do many other pedagogical frameworks—go to the level of granularity that Accessible Pedagogies does, possibly because existing frameworks come from the general education sphere of research, and not inclusive education (Graham, Gillett-Swan, et al., 2022).

Accessible Pedagogies has three domains with seven dimensions of practice (see Table 11.3). The core focus of Accessible Pedagogies is the comprehensibility of instructional practice because classroom teaching occurs predominantly through spoken and written language. The seven dimensions of Accessible Pedagogies therefore focus on signature practices that will—if implemented frequently and effectively as part of everyday practice for *all* students—optimise students' engagement with and comprehension of classroom instruction.

---

7 Spoiler: it does, and we are currently publishing a second book with Routledge on the findings from the full project.

Table 11.3 A Brief Snapshot of the Domains and Dimensions of Accessible Pedagogies

Domains	Dimensions	Description
Linguistic Accessibility	Clarity of Language Structure and Expression	This dimension encompasses five indicators of accessible verbal instruction relating to the audibility, clarity, relatability, volume, and sequencing of explanation.
	Vocabulary	This dimension has three indicators of accessible instruction relating to the vocabulary use in the classroom, including scaffolding, modelling and extension.
	Comprehension Checking	This dimension has two indicators focusing on the use of strategies to monitor task initiation and engagement, and strategies to check and enhance student understanding.
Procedural Accessibility	Catching and Maintaining Attention	This dimension has three indicators relating to teachers' use of strategies to attract and maintain students' attention such as gesture, routines/cues, proximity, variation in tone/volume, and/or the use of students' names.
	Supporting Information Processing	This dimension has six indicators focused on strategies to support students' processing of language and concepts and minimise extraneous load. These include teaching pace, pausing, signposting, reiteration of lesson objectives/main points, and prioritisation of important concepts or instructions.
Visual Accessibility	Visual Supports	This dimension has three indicators relating to the provision of written instructions, images, diagrams, symbols, and/or video, and demonstration and/or worked examples to support instruction.
	Quality, Clarity and Alignment	This dimension has four indicators concerned with the quality, attractiveness, legibility and simplicity of visual supports, and their alignment with associated verbal instruction.

The first domain of Accessible Pedagogies is **Linguistic Accessibility**. This domain incorporates three dimensions of practice aimed at reducing barriers to students' comprehension of teachers' verbal instruction: (1.1) Clarity of Language Structure and Expression, (1.2) Vocabulary, and (1.3) Comprehension Checking.

The second domain of Accessible Pedagogies is **Procedural Accessibility**. This domain has two dimensions that focus on practices to ensure that students are ready to both receive and respond to teachers' instruction, and that they can easily and quickly process that instruction: (2.1) Catching and Maintaining Attention, and (2.2) Supporting Information Processing.

The third domain of Accessible Pedagogies is **Visual Accessibility**. This domain has two dimensions aimed at supporting working memory through the provision of written (indelible) instructions and visual resources (e.g., diagrams, worked examples) that can help students to make better conceptual sense of what they are hearing: (3.1) Visual Supports, and (3.2) Quality, Clarity and Alignment.

Measuring Accessible Pedagogies

We designed the Accessible Pedagogies Observational Measure (APOM) to measure the accessibility of classroom practice. Trained observers recorded evidence of explicit practice indicators for each dimension in 30-minute cycles and then rated that evidence using a seven-point scale (with 7 being the highest score and 1 being the lowest). Ratings of 1–2 are in the low range (no or minimal effective examples observed), ratings of 3–5 are in the mid-range (some examples of this practice were observed but inconsistent and/ or not always effective) and ratings of 6–7 are in the high range (consistent and effective examples of this practice observed and accessible teaching practice is consistently occurring in this area). Upon conclusion of at least four 30-minute cycles, an average score is calculated for each dimension. Optimal practice is indicated by dimension scores that are rated at 6 or above, indicating both consistency *and* effectiveness of practice.

Using the APOM to Improve Accessibility in Everyday Classrooms

The Accessible Assessment ARC Linkage project was conducted in partnership with three large Queensland state secondary schools together with the Queensland Curriculum Assessment Authority (QCAA), the Queensland Secondary Principals Association (QSPA) and Speech Pathology Australia (SPA). In the second year of the project, we implemented the Accessible Pedagogies Program of Learning with the aim of supporting classroom teachers to apply accessibility principles to everyday classroom teaching. Our focus was two-fold: first, we were interested to know whether and how secondary school teachers' practice could be made more accessible; and second, whether this made a difference to students with disabilities impacting language and information processing. In this chapter, we describe the program of learning and its effects on participating teachers' practice.[8]

---

8 Future editions of this book will include a chapter by Haley Tancredi on the impact of Accessible Pedagogies on students' classroom experiences, engagement, and academic output as this is the focus of her doctoral research.

Learning about Accessible Pedagogies

Twenty-one Grade 10 English teachers participated in the Accessible Pedagogies Program of Learning across Terms 2 (n = 11) and Term 3 (n = 10) of 2022. The program commenced with an introductory workshop that took participating teachers through the foundations of inclusive education with emphasis on the social model of disability, the concept of barriers, teachers' legislative obligations to provide reasonable adjustments, and the principles of universal design (see Figure 11.1). Teachers were then introduced to the foundations of cognitive load theory and the cognitive processes involved in learning with emphasis on language and information processing and working and long-term memory. A copy of the first edition of this book was provided to all participating teachers and each was given access to an online module with content to support their learning week to week.

Classroom Observations

Classroom observations were conducted in the first two weeks of term for each cohort and repeated in the final weeks of term. Two full lessons were observed for each participant resulting in a minimum of four observation cycles per classroom. Due to restrictions imposed by COVID-19, these observations were video-recorded, which was hugely beneficial for coding validity, as it allowed coders to replay the footage to catch any interactions they may have missed. Lessons were coded using the APOM by trained observers.

Online Module

The Accessible Pedagogies module was housed in QUT's online Learning Management System. The module comprised four parts, enabling participants to engage in self-directed learning to support and align with other aspects of the Program of Learning (outlined in Table 11.4). Each part began with an example of complexity (linguistic, procedural, or visual) and an explanation as to how this might affect students' learning.

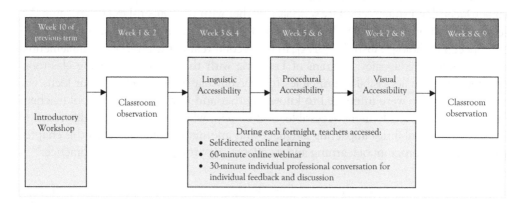

Figure 11.1 Structure of the accessible pedagogies program of learning.

Table 11.4 Components of the Accessible Pedagogies Online Program of Learning

Part 1	**Understanding and Preventing Barriers to Learning** • Understanding barriers • Identifying and dismantling barriers • Barriers in the classroom • What are language and attentional difficulties? • Potential effects on student outcomes • Working memory
Part 2	**Linguistic Accessibility** • Unpacking linguistic complexity • Why is linguistic accessibility important for learning? • Success criteria: What are we looking for? • Linguistic Accessibility in Grade 10 English classrooms
Part 3	**Procedural Accessibility** • Unpacking procedural complexity • Why is procedural accessibility important for learning? • Success criteria: What are we looking for? • Procedural Accessibility in Grade 10 English classrooms
Part 4	**Visual Accessibility** • Unpacking visual complexity • Why is visual accessibility important for learning? • Success criteria: What are we looking for? • Visual accessibility in Grade 10 English classrooms

These examples were then related to the accessibility of pedagogy along with further concrete examples.

Webinars

The aim of the four webinars was to (i) share and discuss content related to Accessible Pedagogies, (ii) provide de-identified group feedback based on Time 1 observation data, and (iii) discuss classroom practice applications and pedagogic refinements. Webinar 1 followed the introductory workshop and served as a content re-cap on understanding and preventing barriers to learning. Webinars 2, 3, and 4 focused on Linguistic Accessibility, Procedural Accessibility, and Visual Accessibility, respectively. Graphs showing de-identified group means were shared to illustrate APOM rating patterns. Practice applications were shared with the aim of supporting teachers to consistently apply practices within the various dimensions. Following the webinar, an infographic was disseminated to all attendees, which summarised the practices discussed at the webinar.

Fortnightly Individual Summaries

Each fortnight, the research team prepared individual summaries for participants, based on the practices observed during the Time 1 observations. Summaries were shared in a staged approach, with preliminary data relevant to each part of the Accessible Pedagogies program of learning shared one domain at a time. This was done intentionally, to enable participant feedback to align with the program of learning and to support participants to receive feedback in manageable segments, which could be applied in their classrooms. In addition to Time 1 observation data, the summary described potential pedagogical refinements, relevant to the individual teacher and their classroom context, to enhance accessibility.

Professional Conversations

All participants were invited to participate in fortnightly, 30-minute professional conversations at a time of their choosing and conducted via Teams. Teachers participated in up to four conversations each, resulting in a total of 77 conversations overall. A coaching model was adopted, and professional conversations were an opportunity for participants and the researcher to share practices, refine current approaches, and share resources. Following each professional conversation, participants received a follow up email which summarised key discussion points and focus practices arising from the professional conversation.

What Did We Find?

Time 1: Before the Program of Learning

Dimension scores for all participants at Time 1 are displayed in Figure 11.2. Their distribution demonstrates a wide range in practice with most teachers scoring in the mid-range for accessibility, some teachers scoring in the high range, and some teachers scoring in the low range. As shown in Figure 11.2, there was also within-teacher variability across the seven dimensions, with some individuals scoring consistently across dimensions and others scoring both high and low. Scores in the high range (6–7) reflect consistent and effective use of practices that help students to pay attention, engage, comprehend, and learn. The high range is the bar for genuinely inclusive classrooms, so we will start there.

Examples of Practice Scoring in Higher Ranges

Participant 8 scored in the high-range for all dimensions. This teacher largely possessed the indicators of practice that we were looking for and needed only to elevate their frequency of use. For example, in the Catching and Maintaining Attention dimension, Participant 8 stood in a consistent classroom position when they were about to issue whole-class instructions. This routine meant that students had a clear cue for when to stop what they were doing and listen. Other cues supported students to maintain their focus on the task. For example, after setting students up to do independent reading, the teacher consistently gave verbal prompts, such as "alright one more minute and we will start our activity". This teacher also carefully monitored students' attention and engagement. When students were off task, the teacher used students' names and employed the proximity technique to silently bring them back to the task at hand.

By scoring in the high range across all seven APOM dimensions, Participant 8 demonstrates not only that greater consistency and effectiveness is achievable but that this is already present in some teachers' practice. However, this quality of practice was not

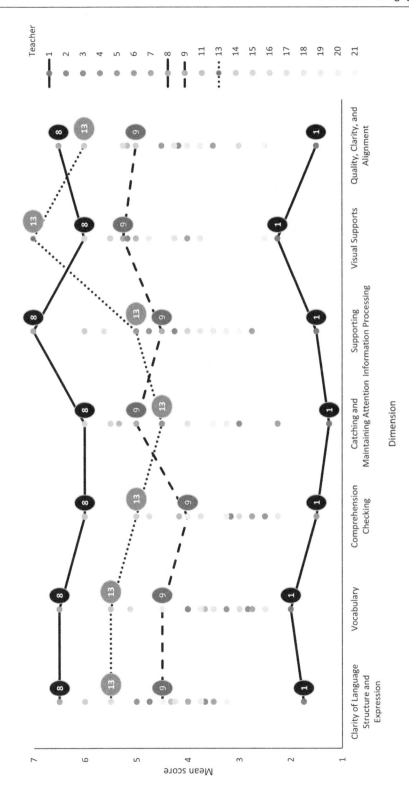

Figure 11.2 Dimension scores for all participants at Time 1.

the sole province of experienced teachers with early career teachers demonstrating the potential to reach the same level of quality and consistency. Participant 9, for example, was in their very first year of teaching and Participant 13 was in their third year. Both these teachers scored in the mid to upper-mid range for accessibility, whereas some teachers with many more years' experience performed in the low or low-mid range, e.g., Participant 1 had more than two decades teaching experience.

Examples of Practice Scoring in the Lower Ranges

Scores in the low range or lower end of the mid-range for Clarity of Language Structure and Expression reflected the use of long, complex sentences, and/or instruction that did not follow a logical sequence. These lessons were also characterised by deviations from the main point that interrupted the flow of the lesson. Scores in the low range for Vocabulary reflected the use of low-frequency or complex words that exceeded students' developmental stage, and which were not explained to support comprehension or to build students' vocabularies. For example, technical terms such as "aesthetic features" and "stylistic devices" were often assumed to be comprehensible by students, but deep word knowledge of these terms, as is required for application of such terms in classwork and assessment, cannot be assumed.

Scores in the low and low-mid ranges for Comprehension Checking occurred, not because teachers failed to check for understanding, but rather because they typically employed ineffective methods of doing so. A common example was the routine use of whole class statements, such as "Everyone got it? Okay, moving on!" Sometimes teachers would say this without scanning the room or waiting for students to respond. Similarly, scores in the low and low-mid ranges for Supporting Information Processing were also largely due to the ineffectiveness of routine practices, like explaining an important concept while students were completing a set task, causing students' attention to be split and possibly resulting in cognitive overload. Another common reason for low scores in this dimension was when teachers spoke too quickly, for too long, and without sufficient pauses to allow students to process what they were saying.

The Visual Supports dimension really needs to be considered alongside Quality, Clarity and Alignment. Ratings for Visual Support reflect whether teachers used visual aids, whereas Quality, Clarity and Alignment drills down into their legibility and relevance. When teachers scored in the low and low-mid-range for Visual Supports, it was generally because they relied on verbal instruction and did not augment their teaching with slides, written instructions, diagrams, video, OneNote, or handouts. When teachers scored in the low range for Quality, Clarity and Alignment, it was generally due to the use of old and poorly constructed slides, illegible images or text, and slides that had too much text, forcing students to try to read while their teacher was teaching, producing what is known as the "split attention effect" (Sweller et al., 2019). Importantly, practices in this dimension were negatively impacted by the resources available to teachers. Many of our participants had only small whiteboards in their classrooms with data projectors. For text to be legible, teachers would have to project an image in a size larger than their whiteboard which would at times distort the text, making it difficult to read. Similarly, many teachers were using whiteboard markers that were either old or poor quality which meant that their written instructions were faint or illegible. These are factors that are largely out of teachers' control, and this was accounted for in the scoring when it was clear the teacher had no other option.

Well within teachers' control, however, is the size and neatness of their writing on the board and whether they use a dark whiteboard marker. Some participants used neon yellows and pinks, which are difficult to see from the vantage point of students. Some participants wrote all over the board and then attempted to project documents and images on the board without removing their earlier writing. The lowest score in Quality, Clarity and Alignment was the result of one participant projecting Word documents (again over the top of handwritten text already on the whiteboard) through which they rapidly scrolled back and forth as they talked. These Word documents had sections that were highlighted in bright yellow, pink, and green which appeared to be some sort of code however the code was never explained to the class. This participant also had numerous documents open, some of which were not relevant to that Grade 10 class. At one point, the teacher projected an old version of the unit plan that had incorrect details (e.g., due dates). This created anxiety and confusion for students that the teacher's verbal explanations did not resolve.

Time 2: After the Program of Learning

Classroom observations were repeated late in the term for all participants and coded again by the authors and three trained observers. Results were analysed using paired samples *t* tests with 1000 bootstrap samples. Mean scores improved significantly between Time 1 (prior to participation in the program of learning) and Time 2 (towards completion of the program of learning) for all seven Accessible Pedagogies dimensions (see Figure 11.3).

As shown in Table 11.5, effect sizes for the Accessible Pedagogies dimensions ranged from moderate (0.5 to 0.8) for Clarity of Language Structure and Expression,

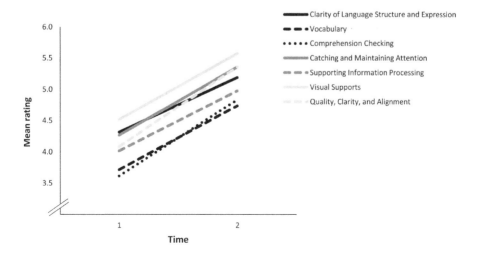

Figure 11.3 All teachers with both timepoints observed (n = 21), comparing Time 1 and 2.

Table 11.5 Effect Sizes and p-Values for Each Dimension of Accessible Pedagogies

Dimension	Cohen's d	p (bootstrapped)
Clarity of Language Structure and Expression	0.72	.007*
Vocabulary	0.67	.007*
Comprehension Checking	0.75	.002*
Catching and Maintaining Attention	1.09	.003*
Supporting Information Processing	0.74	.008*
Visual Supports	0.82	.007*
Quality, Clarity and Alignment	0.91	.002*

Note. * denotes significance at α = .05

Vocabulary, Comprehension Checking, and Supporting Information Processing to high (0.8 and above) for Catching and Maintaining Attention, Visual Supports; and Quality, Clarity and Alignment.

How Did Participants React to Observation and Feedback?

Teachers' responses to observation and feedback were as variable as the accessibility of practice observed. Most participants were unfamiliar with being observed and none was familiar with their practice being measured against explicit criteria. Some teachers found this confronting, but many welcomed the feedback. Participant 11 demonstrated a somewhat ambivalent response to the feedback provided, first stating: "A lot of the stuff that sort of, been given to me in terms of like, what you guys have highlighted and stuff, it's things that are like, it's nothing that I don't already know."

Despite this self-reported awareness, Participant 11 also reported using complex and developmentally inappropriate vocabulary in their teaching, even after completing the program of learning. Participant 11 acknowledged that this would impose extraneous cognitive load and would likely negatively impact students' comprehension, saying:

Like, I love, I love throwing in words like 'ultracrepidarian' in, just for fun. And just watching the kids go, "Huh?" Um, like, and it's part of that tension between like, we talked about the tension between like, wanting to have it as successful, as possible for the kids, but also broadening their vocabulary and their perspective around things.

As discussed earlier in this chapter, using rich vocabulary *is* important in secondary school classrooms. However, inaccessible vocabulary can come at the expense of or cause distraction from key learning objectives. Participant 11 extended on this idea, and reflected on recent classroom examples where students clearly had become lost during the lesson, saying:

So like, I'll like, sort of stop or like, it'll be the tail end of like, "And I've said a lot of words . . . did any of it make sense?" And they kind of like, "Yeah, mate." Okay, clearly it didn't. Let's go back. Um, so, being a little bit more conscious in terms of acknowledging when I'm not doing that accessibly.

Proactive and intentional measures to increase accessibility—like reducing verbosity, using developmentally appropriate vocabulary, and maintaining a logical instructional sequence—remain inconsistent in this teacher's practice, despite them acknowledging the accuracy and value of the feedback. Participant 1 offered some insight when they shared how some of their peers were reacting "behind closed doors", saying:

> I think some, like, senior teachers might be a bit annoyed with some of the, you know, being told "So, are you reiterating in your lessons and that sort of stuff?" "And do you have enough white space on your worksheets?"

Participant 1 intimated that teachers at their school were engaging in group talk and that it was disparaging:

> Um, you have to be a bit careful about doing that to like . . . if you have like a whole, especially once you get all teachers together . . . you know, you represent that in a big open forum and . . . and . . . yeah. That . . . some of them are just . . . That can be very nasty.

However, Participant 1 also acknowledged that while receiving feedback might be confronting and uncomfortable, on viewing video-recorded evidence of their own teaching, the evidence clearly demonstrated inaccessible practice:

> But yeah . . . but once you get tested in a classroom say, well, you're actually not doing that. You might think you are, but you're actually not. So, there's an idea that the, the perception of what I'm doing is different to the reality, but you've gotta have that battle with their mindset. Like you might well be right. But in their heads, uh, we say, "Oh, I've been teaching for 25 years. What do you mean?"

Most participants were trepidatious in the beginning due to the vulnerability that comes with one's teaching being observed, recorded, and assessed, but most warmed to the experience over time. Participant 1 intimated that one of their colleagues had found the graph displaying anonymised group means "very confronting and demoralising", and then shared that they felt the same.

> I actually felt . . . I felt that reaction too, 'cause I was . . . I was down at the bottom end of it and like, oh my God (laughs) that's . . . this is cruel business. I'm . . . I suck basically. That was the reaction I had. And I admit, I had a sleepless night.

Participant 3 also found the graph confronting, even though the data were deidentified and no teachers knew where others were placed. As individuals could recall their individual report data, some mentally estimated their own position in the group.

> Seeing my own data was, like, fine, even though it was like, "Ugh, mid." I'm li- . . . (laughs). It's like, ugh, it sucks, but, like, seeing it at . . . Seeing it with everyone else's,

I think, is, like, kinda sad. It was, like, it was fine. I didn't have, like, a breakdown or anything, but I was just like, "Oh shit, like, um, there's all these other teachers above me." I don't know who they are, but, like, they exist. If I was the person at the bottom and I knew that, like, that would be really, really crushing.

However, 3 also acknowledged that teachers would vary in their level of sensitivity and that some would respond differently to the process:

I mean, that depends on the person. And, and maybe that person was like, "Whatever, like, I don't care." But, like, if it was me and I was at the place where I was, like, that would be, like, "Oh sh- . . . I'm like a terrible teacher," which is not the message that you guys were sending at all, um, but that's something that someone can, like, interpret.

Participants 1 and 3 were not alone in finding the feedback confronting. Participant 18 found the constant intrusion of researchers disruptive and was "shirty" after receiving the initial feedback. On reflection, however, they decided that it was a fair assessment of their practice on that lesson and decided it was "game on".

Um, and I was a little bit kind of shirty, um, that the feedback was given on that, um, verbal dump lesson because I didn't produce a, a lesson, like, especially for observation. I thought I'm just gonna do like I have to do, because that's what I have to do. And, and then I got this [feedback], so like "your questioning was low and all this". And I went, "Oh, shit, I don't like the feedback. Wow. That really that's cutting." And then I thought, well, if that's all they could see, what are they gonna give me feedback on? So, I just thought, "Okay, I'll show you!"

Whether teachers accepted or rejected the feedback was strongly influenced by whether they engaged in the online program of learning and if they reflected on the APOM criteria as they viewed the recording of their own classroom. This was too confronting for a small group of teachers who began to quietly disengage from the program of learning early in the term, but a sizeable number found it a useful way of provoking reflection. For example, Participant 12 said:

When we got the email at the beginning of the term saying, oh, you need to watch yourself [teaching] and I, my first thought was like, oh God, but then I did and I was like, wait a minute, that's, like, this is actually helpful!

Participant 21 was similarly enthusiastic and spoke strongly in favour of a supportive feedback process that could highlight teachers' strengths, as well as indicate areas that might benefit from refinement.

I think we have a lot of self-criticism in how we teach and so having someone go "Actually you're doing pretty well. Like this is really great." It's really re-affirming.

I think sometimes you need that validation that what you're doing is good . . . because I think, yeah, we definitely don't hear that enough. Um, but also, if you're doing something wrong, I'd prefer to know.

The advances made when Participant 18 decided to embrace the challenge we had offered were worth the hard work by all involved. This teacher described the difference that greater accessibility had made for one student in their class who engaged for the first time: "like I was really stunned, and I thought 'Well, here's, here's a kid who, you know, really didn't like school, didn't wanna engage and [is now] actually trying his hardest'".

Although this teacher admitted to being very resistant at the beginning of the program, they finished with enthusiasm, saying: "So, I think it's been very worthwhile, and the opportunity's been great 'cause you often don't get these opportunities when teaching to do these things."

Conclusion

This chapter is the outcome of six years of research that began with the voices of 50 young people who experience difficulties in school and with learning. We listened to those voices and drew on the empirical evidence, as well as our research and professional expertise to develop Accessible Pedagogies: a set of practices that reduce instructional barriers and extraneous cognitive load to improve students' access to the taught curriculum. It is not a measure of quality teaching writ large but—from an inclusive education perspective—teaching is neither quality and nor are teachers really teaching, if their pedagogy is not accessible and if students cannot learn from their instruction. Along the way, we have received push-back, like "but that's just the way I teach" and "this is more for beginning teachers than it is for experienced teachers" and "but Grade 10 students should be able to . . . [understand those words, keep up when I talk fast, comprehend abstract concepts]". Notably, those comments came from the participants who most needed to improve the accessibility of their practice. However, until students with disability—or indeed any students with any form of difference—are seen as integral members of everyday classrooms and until Accessible Pedagogies are implemented systemically and at scale through formal systems of standardised observation, feedback, coaching and review, large numbers of students will continue to experience instructional barriers that lock them out of learning. While some teachers will find this confronting, our research with these 21 participants suggests that many will work through it and those who do will find it professionally rewarding and beneficial for their students. We hope that you will be one of those teachers!

Acknowledgments

This research was partially supported by the Australian Government through the Australian Research Council's *Linkage Projects* funding scheme (LP180100830) and our industry partners. The views expressed herein are those of the authors and are not necessarily those of the Australian Government or Australian Research Council or our industry partners. The statistical analyses and graphs were produced by Dr Callula Killingly and we acknowledge her incredible contribution to this project.

References

Australian Institute for Teaching and School Leadership (AITSL). (2017). *Australian Professional Standards for Teachers*. https://www.aitsl.edu.au/standards

Baddeley, A. (1997). *Human memory: Theory and practice*. Psychology Press.

Baddeley, A. (2000). The episodic buffer: A new component of working memory? *Trends in Cognitive Sciences, 4*(11), 417–423. https://doi.org/10.1016/S1364-6613(00)01538-2

Becker, T. C., & McGregor, K. K. (2016). Learning by listening to lectures is a challenge for college students with developmental language impairment. *Journal of Communication Disorders, 64*, 32–44. https://doi.org/10.1016/j.jcomdis.2016.09.001

Brownell, M. T., Jones, N. D., Sohn, H., & Stark, K. (2020). Improving teaching quality for students with disabilities: Establishing a warrant for teacher education practice. *Teacher Education and Special Education, 43*(1), 28–44.

Bussing, R., Koro-Ljungberg, M., Gagnon, J. C., Mason, D. M., Ellison, A., Noguchi, K., Garvan, C. W., & Albarracin, D. (2016). Feasibility of school-based ADHD interventions: A mixed-methods study of perceptions of adolescents and adults. *Journal of Attention Disorders, 20*(5), 400–413. https://doi.org/10.1177/1087054713515747

CAST. (2018). *Universal design for learning guidelines: Version 2.2.* http://udlguidelines.cast.org

Cowan, N. (2014). Working memory underpins cognitive Development, learning, and education. *Educational Psychology Review, 26*, 197–223. https://doi.org/10.1007/s10648-013-9246-y

Cuevas, J. (2015). Is learning styles-based instruction effective? A comprehensive analysis of recent research on learning styles. *Theory and Research in Education, 13*(3), 308–333. https://doi.org/10.1177/1477878515606621

Danielson, C. (2007). *Enhancing Professional Practice: A Framework for Teaching* (2nd ed.). Association for Supervision and Curriculum Development.

Disability Discrimination Act 1992 (Cth).

Disability Standards for Education 2005 (Cth).

Edyburn, D. L. (2010). Would you recognize universal design for learning if you saw it? Ten propositions for new directions for the second decade of UDL. *Learning Disability Quarterly, 33*(1), 33–41. https://doi.org/10.1177/073194871003300103

Ewing, R. (2018). *Exploding some of the myths about learning to read: A review of research on the role of phonics*. NSW Teachers Federation. https://www.nswtf.org.au/wp-content/uploads/2022/06/Exploding-some-of-the-myths-about-learning-to-read.pdf

Gathercole, S. E., & Alloway, T. P. (2004). Working memory and classroom learning. *Dyslexia Review, 15*, 4–9.

Gathercole, S. E., & Alloway, T. P. (2008). *Working memory and learning: A practical guide for teachers.* SAGE.

Graham, L. J., de Bruin, K., Lassig, C., & Spandagou, I. (2021). A scoping review of 20 years of research on differentiation: Investigating conceptualisation, characteristics, and methods used. *Review of Education, 9*(1), 161–198. https://doi.org/10.1002/rev3.3238

Graham, L. J., Gillett-Swan, J., Killingly, C., & Van Bergen, P. (2022). Does it matter if students (dis)like school? Associations between school liking, teacher and school connectedness, and exclusionary discipline. *Frontiers in Psychology, 13*, 1–13. https://doi.org/10.3389/fpsyg.2022.825036

Graham, L. J., & Tancredi, H. (2019). In search of a middle ground: the dangers and affordances of diagnosis in relation to attention deficit hyperactivity disorder and developmental language disorder. *Emotional and Behavioural Difficulties, 24*(3), 287–300. https://doi.org/10.1080/1363 2752.2019.1609248

Graham, L. J., Tancredi, H., & Gillett-Swan, J. (2022). What makes an excellent teacher? Insights from junior high school students with a history of disruptive behavior. *Frontiers in Education, 7*, 1–12. https://doi.org/10.3389/feduc.2022.883443

Lapadat, J. C. (2002). Relationships between instructional language and primary students' learning. *Journal of Educational Psychology, 94*(2), 278. https://doi.org/10.1037//0022-0663.94.2.278

Lingard, B., Hayes, D., & Mills, M. (2003). Teachers and productive pedagogies: contextualising, conceptualising, utilising. *Pedagogy, Culture, and Society, 11*(3), 399–424. https://doi.org/10.1080/14681360300200181

Martin, A. J., & Evans, P. (2018). Load reduction instruction: Exploring a framework that assesses explicit instruction through to independent learning. *Teaching and Teacher Education, 73*, 203–214. https://doi.org/10.1016/j.tate.2018.03.018

Martin, A. J., Ginns, P., Nagy, R. P., Collie, R. J., & Bostwick, K. C. (2023). Load reduction instruction in mathematics and English classrooms: A multilevel study of student and teacher reports. *Contemporary Educational Psychology*, 102147. https://doi.org/10.1016/j.cedpsych.2023.102147

Marzano, R. J. (2007). *The art and science of teaching: A comprehensive framework for effective instruction*. ASCD.

Morris-Mathews, H., Stark, K. R., Jones, N. D., Brownell, M. T., & Bell, C. A. (2021). Danielson's framework for teaching: Convergence and divergence with conceptions of effectiveness in special education. *Journal of Learning Disabilities, 54*(1), 66–78. https://doi.org/10.1177/0022219420941804

New South Wales Department of Education. (2003). *Quality teaching in New South Wales public schools: A discussion paper.*

Pianta, R. C., & Hamre, B. K. (2009). Conceptualization, measurement, and improvement of classroom processes: Standardized observation can leverage capacity. *Educational Researcher, 38*(2), 109–119. https://doi.org/10.3102/0013189X09332374

Pianta, R. C., La Paro, K. M., & Hamre, B. K. (2008). *Classroom Assessment Scoring System™: Manual K–3*. Brookes Publishing.

Rose, D. H., & Meyer, A. (2006). *A practical reader in universal design for learning*. Harvard Education Press.

Singh, P., Allen, J., & Rowan, L. (2019). Quality teaching: standards, professionalism, practices. *Asia Pacific Journal of Teacher Education, 47*, 1–4. https://doi.org/10.1080/1359866X.2019.1557925

Starling, J., Munro, N., Togher, L., & Arciuli, J. (2012). Training secondary school teachers in instructional language modification techniques to support adolescents with language impairment: A randomized control trial. *Language, Speech and Hearing Services in Schools, 43*(4), 474–495. https://doi.org/10.1044/0161-1461(2012/11-0066)

Sweller, J. (2010). Element interactivity and intrinsic, extraneous, and germane cognitive load. *Educational Psychology Review, 22*, 123–138. https://doi.org/10.1007/s10648-010-9128-5

Sweller, J. (2012). Human cognitive architecture: Why some instructional procedures work and others do not. In K. R. Harris, S. Graham, T. Urdan, C. B. McCormick, G. M. Sinatra, & J. Sweller (Eds.), *APA educational psychology handbook, Vol. 1. Theories, constructs, and critical issues* (pp. 295–325). American Psychological Association.

Sweller, J., van Merriënboer, J. J., & Paas, F. (2019). Cognitive architecture and instructional design: 20 years later. *Educational Psychology Review, 31*, 261–292. https://doi.org/10.1007/s10648-019-09465-5

United Nations. (2006). *Convention on the Rights of Persons with Disabilities (CRPD)*. https://www.un.org/disabilities/documents/convention/convoptprot-e.pdf.

United Nations. (2016). *General Comment No. 4, Article 24: Right to Inclusive Education (CRPD/C/GC/4)*. https://digitallibrary.un.org/record/1313836?ln=en

Willingham, D. T., Hughes, E. M., & Dobolyi, D. G. (2015). The scientific status of learning styles theories. *Teaching of Psychology, 42*(3), 266–271. https://doi.org/10.1177/0098628315589505

Chapter 12

Including students with complex learning profiles in grade-level curriculum

Loren Swancutt

Authentic and effective inclusion of the increasingly diverse range of students now enrolling in regular schools demands a high level of curriculum and instructional knowledge and skill from classroom teachers. Historically, inclusive education has been preoccupied with the provision of physical access and social participation with less attention on curriculum inclusion (Ballard & Dymond, 2017). This has resulted in students being present, but not genuinely engaged in and learning from rigorous curriculum provision drawn from grade-level academic standards. Including students in grade-level academic curriculum is challenging because it requires knowledge and understanding of curriculum design, as well as changes to common instructional strategies, values, and traditional ways of working. The demands of curriculum and instructional knowledge and skill increase further when including students with complex learning profiles.[1] While this group is diverse, students with complex learning profiles share common experiences of education.

Educational Experiences of Students with Complex Learning Profiles

Students with complex learning profiles are susceptible to perceptions that they cannot learn in and/or benefit from regular education classrooms. Such perceptions are rooted in societal prejudice said to be linked to the false binary of the productive/non-productive citizen (Agran et al., 2020; Jorgensen, 1998) and in associated beliefs and attitudes about the intellectual capacities and learning potential of individuals (Vandercook et al., 2020). The false binary of the productive/non-productive citizen frames people with disability, particularly those with complex learning profiles, as inferior and bereft of social, educational, and economic capacities (Agran et al., 2020; Biklen, 1992; Ferguson, 1986; Jorgensen, 1998). Common perceptions relating to intelligence and the learning potential of students with complex learning profiles have historically resulted in low expectations that prioritise a focus on basic functional and life skills training over academic knowledge and skills (Jorgensen et al., 2010). The result is

---

1 The term 'complex learning profiles' is defined in the glossary of this book.

DOI: 10.4324/9781003350897-15

students being categorised and placed together in segregated education settings, including special schools and special education units and classrooms.

This segregation of students with complex learning profiles is supported by practitioners and researchers the late Ellen Brantlinger (1997) referred to as 'traditionalists'. Traditionalists do not see a need for restructure or advancement of inclusive education provision. They believe that statistical norms and competitive school structures are neutral, fair, and expected, and that disabilities are innate conditions that are best served and remediated in segregated education settings (Brantlinger, 1997). Traditionalists maintain that segregated education settings benefit students with complex learning profiles through the provision of (i) smaller class sizes that better facilitate targeted teaching, (ii) instructional practices and modified curriculum content that are appropriate to the student, and (iii) timely access to highly specialised services and intensive supports that best respond to student needs. Traditionalists also believe that such provisions are not effective or achievable in regular schools and classroom settings (Kauffman et al., 2016).

Claims of the superiority of segregated education provision are exaggerated. On balance, the empirical evidence positions inclusive education as a more productive and impactful form of education for students with disability, including those with complex learning profiles (see Chapter 6). Some of the benefits of genuine inclusive education outlined in the literature are:

1. Greater growth in academic achievement and use of academic skills (Gee et al., 2020; Hudson et al., 2013; Kurth & Mastergeorge, 2009).
2. Increased communication competence and interaction with peers (Gee et al., 2020).
3. Increased self-determination skills (Hughes et al., 2013).
4. Enhanced access and engagement with grade-level academic content and contexts (Gee et al., 2020; Hudson et al., 2013; Kleinert et al., 2015; Ruppar et al., 2018).

Most experimental studies undertaken demonstrate that there is no additional benefit for students with complex learning profiles being taught in segregated classrooms (Agran et al., 2020; Cole et al., 2021; Cole et al., 2022; Gee et al., 2020). On the contrary, an increasing body of evidence demonstrates negative consequences of segregating students with complex learning profiles, particularly in terms of academic outcomes (Causton-Theoharis et al., 2011; Cole et al., 2021; Cole et al., 2022; Gee et al., 2020; Kurth et al., 2016; Ruppar et al., 2017; Saur & Jorgensen, 2016).

The negative impacts of segregation on academic outcomes are in part related to students' inconsistent exposure to and interaction with rigorous grade-level academic curriculum standards and content (Soukup et al., 2007; Walker et al., 2018; Wehmeyer et al., 2003). Students in segregated education settings are more likely to be learning functional and life skills goals over regular curriculum content (Lee et al., 2010; Walker et al., 2018; Wehmeyer et al., 2003). This is despite a focus from the early 2000s on increased equity and high-expectations across legislation and policy reform resulting in preferential expectations for students with complex learning profiles to access grade-level curriculum content with appropriate support (Ruppar et al., 2016). This expectation coincided with a surge of research highlighting that students with complex learning profiles are in fact capable of making progress in grade-level academic curriculum (McSheehan et al., 2006; Taub et al., 2017; Vandercook et al., 2020) and that critical thinking, problem solving, and cooperative and active learning are just as important for students with complex learning profiles as any other student (Wehmeyer et al., 2002).

Students with complex learning profiles can learn a variety of academic skills (Browder et al., 2006; Lee et al., 2010; Wehmeyer & Palmer, 2003), and their academic achievement accelerates when included in regular classrooms and curriculum (Cole et al., 2021; Cole e al., 2022; Gee et al., 2020; Kurth et al., 2012). Therefore, arguments that focus solely on the provision of and access to instruction and services, irrespective of their location, to justify the continuation of segregation fail to recognise that context does matter with respect to student learning (Agran et al., 2020). The targeted teaching, instructional strategies, and supports identified by traditionalists as being most effective and appropriately delivered in segregated settings can be replicated in inclusive education, with the added bonus of the inclusive context yielding significantly better outcomes (Cole et al., 2021; Cole et al., 2022; Gee et al., 2020; Vandercook et al., 2020).

Teaching Students with Complex Learning Profiles

There are several possible explanations for the paradox of continued segregation of students with complex learning profiles despite legislation and research evidence. Impediments to major reform measures at a system level that genuinely reflect advancements in legislation and research tell part of the story. However, the success of some schools in educating all students together—including students with complex learning profiles—would suggest there are also influential factors at the school level. One potential school-level factor is teacher confidence and capability. Research indicates variability in teacher competence relating to the inclusion of students with complex learning profiles in grade-level academic curriculum (Valle-Flórez et al., 2022). This variability exists even when units and specialisations have been undertaken throughout undergraduate initial teacher education (Barr & Mavropoulou, 2021), with only slight improvements when teachers have engaged in professional development opportunities and other professional exposures across the career span (Valle-Flórez et al., 2022). This reality poses a challenge as the implementation of inclusive education policy is largely dependent on classroom teachers (Pit-ten Cate et al., 2018), and robust evidence indicates that teacher competence plays a key role in instructional quality and ultimately student learning (Firestone et al., 2021). For students with complex learning profiles to have access to high-quality, rigorous curriculum provision, classroom teachers need to be able to effectively construct and enact curriculum that identifies and embeds individualised adjustments, whilst maintaining alignment to the grade-level academic curriculum content (Taub et al., 2017).

The importance of teacher competence in relation to the education of all students, including students with complex learning profiles, is captured across the Australian Professional Standards for Teachers (APST; Australian Institute for Teaching and School Leadership [AITSL], 2018). The APST describe the expected practice and expertise across four career stages in relation to the acquisition and application of professional knowledge, professional practice, and professional engagement. The expected competence relating to the teaching of students with disability can be found across all seven standards, with mention of teachers possessing specific proficiency in the following areas:

- Using strategies based on students' physical, social, and intellectual development and characteristics to improve learning (APST 1.1).
- Developing teaching activities that incorporate differentiated strategies that meet the specific learning needs of students across the full range of abilities (APST 1.5).
- Designing and implementing teaching activities that support the participation and learning of students with disability and address relevant policy and legislative requirements (APST 1.6).
- Setting explicit, challenging, and achievable learning goals for all students (APST 3.1).
- Establishing and implementing inclusive and positive interactions to engage and support all student in classroom activities (APST 4.1).

Although the expected competence of all teachers is identified in the Standards, the determination of responsibility for possessing sufficient knowledge and skills for the teaching of students with complex learning profiles remains a contentious and ambiguous debate. The debate is fuelled by professional competition and industrial interests, which has created a delineation between roles and responsibilities of special education teachers and classroom teachers.

Classroom teachers are considered to have subject-matter content knowledge expertise which extends to specialised subject-matter content knowledge in secondary schools, with a broad base of generalised and/or subject-specific pedagogical knowledge. Professional development for regular classroom teachers often has a heavy emphasis on subject matter pedagogy and on subject and grade level specific content, especially in secondary school settings with the increased complexity in specific academic content areas such as English, mathematics, and science. This, in combination with large class sizes, limitations on resources, and highly mobile student and staff populations results in the principle of including students with complex learning profiles in grade-level academic curriculum becoming lost in the multiple demands for teacher time and resources (Colley & Lassman, 2021). Classroom teachers feel underprepared to teach all students and are unsure of their roles, which instructional techniques to use and when, and to what extent they can break down and vary the pace and complexity of subject-matter content (King-Sears, 2008; Lancaster & Bain, 2019). Studies also demonstrate that regular classroom teachers have limited knowledge and understanding of evidence-based inclusive practices and their importance and application in promoting student learning (King-Sears, 2008; Lancaster & Bain, 2019).

The Critical Importance of Inclusive Classroom Teachers

Classroom teachers are important leaders in the development and implementation of curriculum programs and are tasked with providing the majority of instruction to students in inclusive classrooms (Theobold et al., 2019). However, a recent systematic review of 40 research studies indicates that classroom teachers have limited or peripheral roles in the planning and implementation of curriculum instruction for students with complex learning profiles (Kuntz & Carter, 2021). This often results in the responsibility for curriculum planning being deflected to special education teachers. However, when special education teachers plan curriculum for students with complex learning profiles without sufficient clarity of the grade-level curriculum goals and instructional tasks and activities, there is a risk that students will not be authentically included. For students with complex learning profiles to be included in grade-level academic curriculum, *all* teachers need to have sufficient competence and increased accountability to provide appropriate curricular and instructional opportunities that incorporate specific and personalised adjustments within inclusive classroom settings (Foley-Nicpon et al., 2013).

Increasing the leadership of classroom teachers in the design, implementation and evaluation of curriculum planning and instruction of students with complex learning profiles is critical and would better reflect recommended practice in inclusive education (Kurth et al., 2015; Ryndak et al., 2013). One means of increasing their leadership is through the facilitation of collaborative planning structures and job-embedded professional learning. This chapter describes the process underpinning my current doctoral study which involves the use of a research-informed curriculum framework with a complementary program of learning to support classroom teachers to include students with complex learning profiles in grade-level academic content.

Working with the Inclusive Academic Curriculum Framework

In the first 18 months of my doctoral studies, I drew on the research literature on evidence-informed practices to develop the Inclusive Academic Curriculum Framework (IACF, see Figure 12.1). The intent of the IACF is to provide classroom teachers with a systematic process to facilitate access and active participation in grade-level content and instruction in the regular classroom as the primary context for learning. Five values form the basis of its design and intention:

1. High-expectations of students with complex learning profiles and the presumption of competence to learn age-equivalent social and academic topics drawn from the regular grade-level curriculum.
2. Value the rights of all students to attend heterogenous, inclusive classrooms that foster belonging and learning for all.

3. Engage in collaborative and consultative practices to support professional knowledge, understanding and practice.
4. Prioritise grade-level academic curriculum content for students with complex learning profiles through the provision of curriculum adjustments.
5. Plan for and support full access and participation in grade-level academic instructional tasks and activities by engaging with universal design principles and inclusive practices.

I developed the IACF by drawing on and synthesising a range of existing literature and documented curriculum planning models relating to standards-based curriculum design and implementation, and inclusive curriculum provision for students with complex learning profiles internationally (Flowers et al., 2009; Hunt, 2012; Jorgensen, 2018; Jorgensen et al., 2010; Kurth, 2013; Root et al., 2021; Thompson et al., 2017; Wehmeyer et al., 2002). The IACF builds on this rich body of work to support teachers to address the challenges of interpreting and planning grade-level academic curriculum for students with complex learning profiles. It explicates and contextualises theory, policy, and conceptual orientations to produce a practical and forward-thinking approach to inclusive curriculum planning and implementation. It differs from existing models in that it is focused on the Australian context and the Australian Curriculum, it positions academic learning as the priority, and it aligns personalised supports and adjustments to grade-level content and contexts.

Furthermore, the IACF positions classroom teachers as being central to the process, recognising their critical role in leading curriculum planning and implementation for students with complex learning profiles. To support this, the IACF is grounded in classroom teachers engaging in professional learning that is job-embedded, including workshops, coaching, collaborative planning, and reflective practice, as part of the

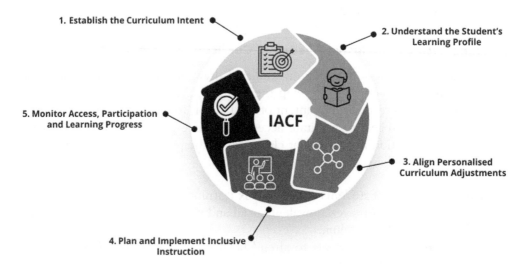

Figure 12.1 The five phases in the Inclusive Academic Curriculum Framework (IACF) Cycle.

framework's application. In doing so, the IACF questions a prevailing paradigm that positions the teaching and learning of students with complex learning profiles as being the responsibility and work of special education teachers over that of classroom teachers. Subscribing to this prevailing paradigm results in low-expectations and suboptimal educational opportunity and outcomes. The IACF aims to shift the paradigm by increasing the efficacy of classroom teachers to realise their potential as leaders of inclusion, student learning, and achievement. There are five iterative phases for successful implementation:

1. establishing the grade-level curriculum intent,
2. understanding the student's learning profile,
3. aligning personalised curriculum adjustments,
4. planning and implementing inclusive instruction, and
5. monitoring access, participation, and learning progress.

The remainder of this chapter provides a description of each of the IACF's phases, along with instructions, activities, and guiding questions for putting them into practice.

Phase 1: Establishing the Grade-level Curriculum Intent

Phase 1 of the IACF centres on determining the curriculum intent of the unit of study as drawn from the grade-level academic curriculum, using the Australian Curriculum as the example. This phase involves deconstructing the academic curriculum standards at grade-level to identify the core concepts and skills that will inform teaching and learning across the unit of study. Tasks undertaken in this phase draw on the flexible intent of standards-based curriculum design to inform the establishment of clear instructional goals denoting what students need to know and be able to do for success and translating academic content standards into their critical functions (Kleinert & Thurlow, 2001). Clearly identifying what concepts and skills students must know and be able to do at grade level ensures teachers understand the level of cognition and the standard of learning that is expected. Clarity of the grade-level curriculum intent also forms the foundation from which decisions regarding the inclusion of students with complex learning profiles in grade-level academic curriculum are made. Understanding what students need to know and be able to do at grade-level allows teachers to have high-expectations and to align personalised curriculum adjustments that enable access, participation, and meaningful progress across grade-level academic curriculum. This phase is operationalised in six steps.

Step 1: Identifying the Aspect(s) of the Grade-Level Achievement Standard That Are Forming the Focus of the Unit of Study

Details of what aspect(s) of academic curriculum standards are expected to be covered in identified units of study across a year are typically documented in a whole school/ grade level curriculum program or plan. These curriculum programs or plans are broken into subject areas and grade-levels and provide a matrix capturing the delineation of academic achievement standard coverage across a year of study. Teachers consult the school's curriculum work program to determine the aspect(s) of the grade-level achievement standard identified for the unit of study they will be teaching.

Step 2: Deconstructing the Identified Aspect(s) of the Achievement Standard to Determine What Concepts and Skills Are Required

Achievement standards are written as broad goal statements that articulate expected levels of achievement relating to the specific knowledge and skills a student should master within a subject area across a grade level (Ainsworth, 2003; Australian Curriculum, Assessment and Reporting [ACARA], n.d.-a; Bailey & Jakicic, 2018). The wording of an achievement standard can be complex, incorporating multiple skills and concepts within one statement. Therefore, teachers need to engage in a process of unpacking or deconstructing the achievement standard to clarify the specific knowledge and skills need to be addressed across a unit of study (Ainsworth, 2003; Many, 2020; Rao & Meo, 2016; Wiggins & McTigh, 2005). Ainsworth (2003) describes a process for deconstructing the aspect(s) of the achievement standard that involves breaking the wording down into component parts via a coding method. First, skills are identified within the aspect(s) of the achievement standard by highlighting words that denote what students must be able to do. Skills often correspond to the verbs contained within the statements as verbs define the actions required. Next, key knowledge and concepts that are required to perform the skills are identified. This is done by highlighting the nouns and descriptive phrases that correspond to the knowledge and concepts that students need to learn. A two-column table (Table 12.1) can then be used to separate and organise the statements into their component parts. This table can be later used as the basis for defining instructional goals relating to what students need to know and be able to do to be successful (Morgan et al., 2013).

Coding Method (*Concepts*/*Skills*)

Students <u>use</u> <u>*appropriate metric units*</u> when <u>solving measurement problems involving</u> the *perimeter* and *area* of *composite shapes,* and *volume* of *right prisms* (ACARA n.d.-b).

Unit Analysis Table

Table 12.1 Example Table Deconstructing Statements into Component Parts for Year 8 Math

Concepts	Skills
Appropriate metric units Perimeter Area Composite shapes Volume Right prisms	Solve measurement problems involving: • Perimeter • Area • Composite shapes • Volume of right prisms Use appropriate metric units when solving measurement problems.

*Step 3: Identifying the Associated Content Descriptions and
Prioritising Grade-Level Content*

The purpose of this step is to identify and prioritise the essential grade-level content that
will contribute to the acquisition of sufficient knowledge and skills as dictated by the
achievement standard. This is achieved by consulting the content descriptions that are
aligned to the identified aspect(s) of the achievement standard. The identification and
prioritisation of grade-level content may require teachers to pinpoint the highest-leverage
content through professional reflection and collaboration (Ainsworth, 2003; Bailey &
Jakicic, 2018). This will involve making professional decisions regarding the extent that
each content description contributes to the development of knowledge and skills contained within the aspect(s) of the achievement standard and assessing the feasibility of
sufficiently covering the content in the timeframe provided. The content description
elaborations, level descriptions, and the glossary can be draw upon to support interpretation and understanding of the priority grade-level content. Once the grade-level content has been prioritised, the unit analysis table can be updated (as I have done in the
example below (Table 12.2)) to reflect additional contributions and refinements to the
concepts and skills that students need to learn across the unit of study.

Step 4: Refining Instructional Goals and Determining the Critical Function(s)

The deconstructed aspect(s) of the achievement standard and content descriptions
from Steps 2 and 3 form the basis for defining the instructional goals of the unit of
study. Teachers can complete further analysis of the identified concepts to determine
the nuanced aspects that students will need to know. To guide this process, teachers
can consider four main things that students must know about the specific concepts,
(i) what the concept is, (ii) what the concept looks like, (iii) how to identify the concept
through practical experience, and (iv) how the concept connects to other concepts that
students already know about (Morgan et al., 2013). Further analysis of the concepts
and skills can occur by considering the critical functions that denote what students

Table 12.2 **Example Year 8 Math Unit Analysis Table**

Concepts	Skills

• Appropriate metric units
• Perimeter
• Area
• Composite shapes
• Volume *and capacity*
• Right prisms
	1. Solve measurement problems involving:
	
	  o Perimeter *of irregular and composite shapes*
	  o Area *of irregular and composite shapes*
	  o Composite shapes
	  o Volume *and capacity* of right prisms
	
	2. Use appropriate metric units when solving measurement problems.
	3. *Use the 4 operations—choosing and using efficient strategies and tools.*

*Italics = addition of prioritised content.

will need to know and be able to do (Kleinert & Thurlow, 2001). Consideration of the critical functions of the identified skills requires teachers to look beyond the form of the academic content to its function. In other words, what is the key purpose of the knowledge and skills required?

The instructional goals are written by consolidating and translating the deconstructed concepts and skills, in combination with their additional analysis, into an articulation of what students need to know and be able to do to be successful (Table 12.3). Teachers should view this process as an opportunity to deepen their content knowledge and understanding of the constructs of the curriculum intent.

Step 5: Developing a Standards-Based Marking Criteria and Determining the Means of Summative Assessment

Once teachers have determined the instructional goals, the final step is to develop the standards-based marking criteria and the summative assessment task that will be used to evaluate student learning. The identified aspect(s) of the achievement standard articulate the satisfactory standard of learning, or the C level of achievement within a five-point scale (ACARA, n.d.-c). A range of performance is then articulated across the five-point scale by increasing and decreasing the level of sophistication and extent of the application of the concepts and skills (Guskey & Bailey, 2001; Tomlinson & McTigh, 2006). Increases and decreases in the sophistication of the application of the aspect(s) of the achievement standard are achieved by applying variations to the context, breadth, and depth of the satisfactory standard (Tomlinson & McTigh, 2006). Curriculum elements such as the general capabilities progressions, in combination with the level description and content descriptions and elaborations, can be used to identify specific variations in the range of performance (see example in Table 12.4). The extent of the aspect(s) of the achievement standard can also be increased/decreased in breadth and depth.

With consideration of the developed marking criteria, teachers should then create and/or review a summative assessment task that aligns with the aspect(s) of the achievement standard and priority grade-level content forming the focus of the unit of

Table 12.3 Example Year 8 Math Instructional Goals Table

Know	*Do*
Students need to know and understand:	Students will be successful when they can:

• What appropriate metric units are and how/when they are applied.
• The purpose of calculating perimeter, area, and/or volume, their associated formulas, and how to determine the required measurements for substitution.
• The properties of composite shapes and right prisms and how to calculate their perimeter, area, and/or volume and capacity.
	• Solve measurement problems involving:
	  o Perimeter of irregular and composite shapes
	  o Area of irregular and composite shapes
	  o Volume and capacity of right prisms
	• Use appropriate metric units when solving measurement problems.
	• Use the 4 operations to perform calculations using formulas—choosing and using efficient strategies and tools to do so.

Table 12.4 Example Year 8 Math Marking Criteria

A	B	C	D	E
Use appropriate metric units when solving *complex* measurement problems involving the perimeter and area of composite shapes (*cylinders, cones, pyramids*), and volume of right prisms *with dissection and rearrangement.*	Use appropriate metric units when solving measurement problems involving the perimeter and area of composite shapes (*cylinders, cones, pyramids*), and volume of right prisms *with rearrangement.*	Use appropriate metric units when solving measurement problems involving the perimeter and area of composite shapes (parallelograms, trapeziums, rhombuses, and kites), and volume of right prisms.	Use appropriate metric units when solving *simple* measurement problems involving the perimeter and area of ~~composite~~ shapes (rectangles and triangles)~~, and volume of right prisms.~~	Use appropriate metric units when *simple* solving measurement problems involving the perimeter ~~and area~~ of ~~composite~~ shapes (rectangles and triangles~~, and volume of right prisms.~~

* *Italics* and ~~strikethrough~~ represent the variation in sophistication and extant of concepts and skills across the five-point scale as informed by curriculum elements.

study. In this process, teachers should ensure that the assessment task provides opportunity for students to use varied methods and materials to authentically demonstrate their learning against the identified knowledge and skills of the curriculum intent. Importantly, assessment within standards-based curriculum is focused on judging student performance against the achievement standard, *not student against student*. As a result, there should be sufficient flexibility in the design of the summative assessment task to enable universal access and participation.

Phase 2: Understanding the Student's Learning Profile

Implementation of Phase 2 of the IACF includes a collaborative process for gathering informing data about the student to identify their background, capabilities, performance, and educational support requirements in the context of the learning area/subject and the unit of study they will be engaging with. A variety of activities are used to gather this information, including:

1. consultation with the student and/or their associate,
2. anecdotal comments and observations,
3. review of the student's educational records and school-based plans,
4. examples of the student's work and academic engagement and progress,
5. specialist reports provided by multi-disciplinary professionals, and
6. collaboration with relevant allied health professionals and stakeholders.[2]

---

2 Readers can learn more about consultation with students in Chapter 13, and collaboration with colleagues and allied health professionals in Chapter 18.

A team-based approach enables a variety of professional and personal perspectives for interpreting and evaluating the student's relevant characteristics, the anticipated and known barriers that may be experienced, and the appropriate and responsive adjustments as they apply to the learning area/subject and the specific unit of study being planned for. Teachers can use the instructional goals table and draw on the collation of informing data—in combination with relevant professional knowledge and consultation with the student and their associates—to synthesise information and document findings to inform shared decision-making regarding curriculum priorities, instructional strategies, and adjustments. Six essential questions frame the phase of understanding the student's learning profile:

1. What are the student's strengths, interests, preferences, and support requirements?
2. What are the student's communicative competencies and behaviours?
3. How does the student currently access and participate in this learning area/subject?
4. How does the student navigate the classroom environment and routines for this learning area/subject?
5. What barriers exist in relation to the curriculum and common instructional approaches applied in this learning area/subject?
6. What adjustments are needed for the student to engage in and learn from the grade-level academic curriculum of this learning area/subject?

Phase 3: Aligning Personalised Curriculum Adjustments

Phase 3 of the IACF centres on systematically aligning personalised curriculum adjustments to the unit of study as drawn from the grade-level academic curriculum. This process draws on information collated in Phases 1 and 2 to make evidence-informed decisions regarding the most appropriate and beneficial forms of curriculum adjustments. When engaging in this process, the grade-level academic curriculum content, or what students need to know and be able to do at grade level, forms the basis of instruction for all students (ACARA, n.d.-d). This means that adjustments are made to the grade-level academic content over that of providing alternate grade-level content or programs. Although instruction for all students is provided through grade-level content, adjustments to the complexity and extent of what is expected to be learnt can occur. Grade-level instructional methods, materials, marking criteria and assessment tasks can be adjusted based on the individualised needs of students with complex learning profiles. There can be a focus on adjusting the breadth, depth, and/or complexity of academic curriculum standards to ensure students are provided with meaningful opportunities to access, participate, and make progress through grade-level content.

The learning focus for students with complex learning profiles may need to focus on emergent knowledge and skills associated with earlier grade-level achievement standards or highly individualised goals informed by Level 1 of the Literacy, Numeracy, and/or Personal and Social General Capabilities. The IACF, however, is premised on teaching those emergent knowledge and skills using grade-level instructional tasks and activities with adjustment, thereby making it possible for all students to be engaged in the same learning experiences as their peers. For example, in English, students still at the beginning reader stage can be provided access to grade-level texts by adjusting the number of pages and amount of text, simplifying vocabulary and text complexity, engaging with text to speech applications, and including visual supports and graphic organisers to promote comprehension. This allows students to engage with and experience literature beyond the instructional level texts they are learning to independently decode. In math, a student's skill development may be focusing on earlier grade-level concepts such as counting, simple addition, grouping objects, and identifying shapes and amounts. For science, humanities, and social sciences, individualised adjustments can be made to the breadth, depth, and/or complexity of the content topic and levels of cognition, in combination with any necessary earlier year level achievement standards in the areas of subject skills, science inquiry, and science as a human endeavour.

If such concepts are considered prerequisites to moving on to more complex mathematics, then a student could be subjected to many years of learning the same skills in the same ways, often existing in parallel to their 'mainstream' classmates. Over time, the gap between their skills and those of their same-age peers grows wider and is later—particularly when it comes to secondary school—used as justification for that student to be segregated into a special school, unit, or support class. Readers will recall that this was the plight of 'Daniel' in Chapter 2 of this book, a student who had been placed on a P/1 level Individual Curriculum Plan, who was present in the classroom but not included in the content of the lesson. The IACF is intended to address this problem to ensure that the student is meaningfully included even when they are learning earlier grade-level skills. This can be achieved by identifying and addressing those skills in the teaching of grade-level academic content. This phase is operationalised in six steps.

Step 1: Identifying Competencies and Barriers Relating to the Grade-Level Unit of Study

When aligning personalised curriculum adjustments, teachers first need to analyse the grade-level curriculum content to identify competencies and barriers relating to access and participation. Analysis of the grade-level curriculum content occurs by drawing on the instructional goals table and marking criteria from Phase 1, and the student profile guiding questions from Phase 2. Any identification of personalised adjustments for students with complex learning profiles should be based on the individual characteristics and needs of the student in relation to the context of the unit of study. This means that decisions should not be based on what is easiest, what has been done before, or what is most convenient or available. Particular consideration should also be given to the student's communicative competencies and behaviours, which can vary in intentionality and convention. They can include pre-symbolic and informal behaviours (e.g., vocalisations, facial expressions, movement), communication with concrete symbols and conventional behaviours (e.g., words, gestures, pictorial representations), and use of a variety of abstract symbols and speaking (e.g., phrases, signs, communication systems; ACARA, n.d.-e).

The student's current level of communicative competence and behaviours will be a critical factor in the determination of personalised curriculum adjustments (Hunt, 2012; Jorgensen, 2018; Jorgensen et al., 2010). For example, a student who is learning that symbols have meaning might be engaged in learning to attend to pictures and concrete objects and responding to experiences with movement and gesture. A student using concrete symbols and conventional behaviours might respond to simple questions and requests by pointing to appropriate symbols/objects or using single words. They might similarly demonstrate anticipation of events by choosing symbols and objects and arranging pictures to demonstrate understanding. A student using a variety of abstract symbols and/or speaking might interact with and respond to learning opportunities through spoken phrases or alternate and augmentative communication methods. To support the identification of competencies and barriers relating to the grade-level unit of study, teachers can annotate the unit analysis table (Table 12.5) from Phase 1 to reflect strengths, challenges, and anticipated barriers.

In addition to the identification of strengths, challenges, and anticipated barriers relating to the academic content, consideration should also be made regarding the supplemental skills or demands that are involved in the teaching and learning process. For example, in math, students are often expected to read and comprehend questions, memorise, and write out formulas, draw diagrams, and use mental computation. These demands are not always present in the grade-level achievement standard and are therefore supplemental skills and demands that can be considered construct irrelevant (CAST, n.d.). Construct irrelevant demands can often result in significant barriers to

Table 12.5 Example Math Instructional Goals, Year 8

	Know	*Do*	
Currently working with informal units of measure.	Students need to know and understand:	Students will be successful when they can:	Solving basic problems with prompting and scaffolding.

Currently working with attributes such as visible size and capacity of concrete objects and pictures.	• What appropriate metric units are and how/when they are applied.
	• The purpose of calculating perimeter, area, and/or volume, their associated formulas, and how to determine the required measurements for substitution.
	• The properties of composite shapes and right prisms and how to calculate their perimeter, area, and/or volume and capacity.
		• Solve measurement problems involving:
		  o Perimeter of irregular and composite shapes
		  o Area of irregular and composite shapes
		  o Volume and capacity of right prisms
		• Use appropriate metric units when solving measurement problems.
		• Use the 4 operations to perform calculations—choosing and using efficient strategies and tools to do so.
			Familiar with regular shapes and can trace the distance around the outside and determine perimeter and area using informal units.
			
			Currently adding and subtracting with intermittent support of a number line.
			
			Can use a calculator for basic operations.

Familiar with properties of squares, rectangles, triangles, and circles.			
Knows how to do this informally—not yet exposed to formal units or formulas.			

a student proficiently learning and demonstrating the construct relevant knowledge and skills articulated in the achievement standards. Therefore, construct irrelevant demands should be identified and addressed through universal design principles and adjustments that eliminate such barriers; for example, providing a reader to support the reading and interpretation of math problems, and the use of a scribe or assistive technology to draw a diagram or write a formula.

Step 2: Determining the Origin/Cause of Barriers

This process involves the articulation of identified barriers relating to the grade-level academic content and the associated supplemental skills and demands that will exist in the instructional process. Determination is made regarding the status of each barrier as being construct relevant or construct irrelevant (Table 12.6).

Step 3: Determining How Best to Address the Identified Barriers

Having identified the barriers and their status as being construct relevant or irrelevant, attention can now turn to determining how best to address barriers. In this process teachers can draw on the three actions of the R^3 model, which I have developed for use in my doctoral study (see Figure 12.2).

Table 12.6 **Example Math Barriers Table, Year 8**

Demand	Barrier(s)	Construct Relevant or Irrelevant
What appropriate metric units are and how/when they are applied	Complexity of the concept	Construct Relevant
The purpose of calculating perimeter, area, and/or volume, and their associated formulas	Complexity of concept	Construct Relevant
The properties of composite shapes and right prisms	Complexity of the concept	Construct Relevant
Reading and interpreting math problems	Reading skills (decoding and comprehension)	Construct Irrelevant
Drawing accurate diagrams	Fine motor skills	Construct Irrelevant
Identifying the correct formula	Complexity of the skill	Construct Relevant
Writing the formula	Handwriting, tracking, copying error	Construct Irrelevant
Determining the required measurements and substituting them into the formula	Complexity of the skill	Construct Relevant
Calculating each step of the formula to determine perimeter, area, and/or volume and capacity	Applying and following a formula Mental computation Completing calculations involving multiplication Completing multi-step problems	Construct Relevant

Addressing Barriers using the R³ Model

R1. Remove   Engage universal design principles to remove barriers that can be completely avoided (e.g., removing a rigid time restriction from the conditions of a task).

R2. Reduce   Engage universal design principles to reduce the impact of barriers that cannot be completely removed (e.g., providing clear and concise visual supports to support whole-class verbal instruction).

R3. Respond   Provide adjustments to enable equitable access and participation (e.g., assistive technology, simplifying the complexity of a task).

Figure 12.2 R³ Model Actions.

Importantly, construct relevant demands cannot be removed from the teaching and learning process because they represent the concepts and skills demanded by the achievement standards. In this case, the reduce and respond actions can be applied together to reduce the impact of the barrier through universal design principles, whilst simultaneously providing an adjustment that increases access and participation (Table 12.7).

Step 4: Determining the Need for Alternate Achievement Standards

When determining actions to address barriers, it may be identified that the breadth, depth and/or complexity of the grade-level academic curriculum needs to be adjusted. In the Australian Curriculum, this level of adjustment can draw on knowledge and skills associated with earlier grade-level achievement standards (substantial curriculum adjustments) or highly individualised goals (extensive curriculum adjustments). The level of adjustment necessary is informed by the student's learning profile. When determining what alternate achievement standards or highly individualised goals to draw on, alignment to the concepts, skills, and critical functions of the grade-level academic curriculum should be maintained. For students requiring substantial curriculum adjustments, teachers can utilise the achievement standards and content descriptions scope and sequences to identify the grade-level concepts and skills requiring adjustment, and backward map to determine the student's current levels of performance and next steps in learning (see Table 12.8). For students requiring extensive curriculum adjustments, teachers can consult Level 1 (including the sublevels of 1a, 1b, and 1c) of the Literacy, Numeracy, and/or Personal and Social Capabilities (ACARA, n.d.-f) to determine elements that align to the grade-level academic curriculum content.

Table 12.7 Example Barriers Table with Relevant R³ Action, Year 8 Math

Demand	Barrier(s)	Relevance	R³ Action
What appropriate metric units are and how/when they are applied	Complexity of concept	Construct Relevant	Respond by varying the complexity, breadth, and depth of knowledge and skills.
The purpose of calculating perimeter, area, and/or volume, and their associated formulas	Complexity of concept	Construct Relevant	
The properties of composite shapes and right prisms	Complexity of concept	Construct Relevant	Reduce by adjusting the complexity of oral and written instructional language
Reading and interpreting math problems	Reading skills (decoding and comprehension)	Construct Irrelevant	Respond by providing a reader/assistive technology and monitoring of comprehension
Drawing accurate diagrams	Fine motor skills	Construct Irrelevant	Remove the barrier by providing completed diagrams
Identifying the correct formula	Complexity of the skill	Construct Relevant	Respond to the barrier by adjusting the complexity of knowledge and skills
Writing the formula	Handwriting, tracking, copying error	Construct Irrelevant	Reduce the barrier by providing scaffolds and promoting
Determining the required measurements and substituting them into the formula	Complexity of the skill	Construct Relevant	Respond to the barrier by adjusting the complexity of knowledge and skills
Calculating each step of the formula to determine perimeter, area, and/or volume and capacity	Applying and following a formula	Construct Relevant	Respond to the barrier by adjusting the complexity of knowledge and skills
	Mental computation	Construct Irrelevant	Remove the barrier by supplying a calculator
	Completing multi-step problems	Construct Relevant	Respond to the barrier by adjusting the complexity and breadth of problems to be solved

Table 12.8 Math Sequence of Achievement for the Strand of Measurement

	Foundation	Year 1	Year 2	Year 3	Year 4	Year 5	Year 6	Year 7	Year 8	Year 9	Year 10
Measurement	Identify the attributes of mass, capacity, length and duration. Use direct comparison strategies to compare objects and events. Sequence and connect familiar events to the time of day.	Compare and order objects and events based on the attributes of length, mass, capacity and duration, communicating reasoning. Measure the length of shapes and objects using uniform informal units.	Identify and represent part-whole relationships of halves, quarters and eighths in measurement contexts. Use informal units of measure and compare shapes and objects. Determine the number of days between events using a calendar and read time on an analog clock to the hour, half hour and quarter hour.	Make estimates and determine the reasonableness of financial and other calculations. Use familiar metric units when estimating, comparing and measuring the attributes of objects and events. Identify angles as measures of turn and compare them to right angles. Estimate and compare measures of duration using formal units of time. Represent money values in different ways.	Use scaled instruments and appropriate units to measure length, mass, capacity and temperature. Measure and approximate perimeters and areas. Convert between units of time when solving problems involving duration. Compare angles relative to a right angle using angle names.	Choose and use appropriate metric units to measure the attributes of length, mass and capacity, and to solve problems involving perimeter and area. Convert between 12- and 24-hour time. Estimate, construct and measure angles in degrees.	Interpret and use timetables. Convert between common units of length, mass and capacity. Use the formula for the area of a rectangle and angle properties to solve problems.	Apply knowledge of angle relationships and the sum of angles in a triangle to solve problems, giving reasons. Use formulas for the areas of triangles and parallelograms and the volumes of rectangular and triangular prisms to solve problems. Describe the relationships between the radius, diameter and circumference of a circle.	Use appropriate metric units when solving measurement problems involving the perimeter and area of composite shapes, and volume of right prisms. Use Pythagoras' theorem to solve measurement problems involving unknown lengths of right-angle triangles. Use formulas to solve problems involving the area and circumference of circles. Solve problems of duration involving 12- and 24-hour cycles across multiple time zones.	Apply formulas to solve problems involving the surface area and volume of right prisms and cylinders. Solve problems involving ratio, similarity and scale in two-dimensional situations. Determine percentage errors in measurements. Apply Pythagoras' theorem and use trigonometric ratios to solve problems involving right-angled triangles. Use mathematical modelling to solve practical problems involving direct proportion, ratio and scale, evaluating the model and communicating their methods and findings. Express small and large numbers in scientific notation.	Interpret and use logarithmic scales representing small or large quantities or change in applied contexts. Solve measurement problems involving surface area and volume of composite objects. Apply Pythagoras' theorem and trigonometry to solve practical problems involving right-angled triangles. Identify the impact of measurement errors on the accuracy of results. Use mathematical modelling to solve practical problems involving proportion and scaling, evaluating and modifying models, and reporting assumptions, methods and findings.

Current level of performance

Next step in learning

Adapted from the Year 8 Math Achievement Standard (ACARA, n.d.-b)

Step 5: Identifying Meaningful Instructional Goals

Having determined the variation in complexity as informed by an earlier grade-level achievement standard or via highly individualised goals derived from Level 1 of the Literacy, Numeracy, and/or Personal and Social Capabilities, the unit analysis table (Table 12.9) can be updated to reflect the alignment of meaningful instructional goals to the grade-level content and context.

Step 6: Adjusting the Marking Criteria and Assessment Task

Substantial adjustments to the breadth, depth, and/or complexity of grade-level academic achievement standards need to be reflected in the in the marking criteria. The same process of marking criteria creation detailed in Phase 1, Step 5 should be followed, with substitution of the aspect(s) of the grade-level achievement standard for those that have been identified from an earlier grade-level (Table 12.10). Alignment to the grade-level content and contexts should remain.

The grade-level summative assessment task should also be updated to reflect the identified adjustments to the breadth, depth, and/or complexity of content. Updates to the assessment task(s) and activities should be informed by the adjusted instructional goals and marking criteria. For students accessing extensive curriculum adjustments, teachers should use a competency based three-point scale (e.g., working toward, achieved, working beyond) to determine student performance in relation to their highly

Table 12.9 Adjusted Instructional Goals, Year 8 Math

Know	Do	Alternate Achievement Standard
Students need to know and understand:	Students will be successful when they can:	

• What appropriate metric units are and how/when they are applied.
• The purpose of calculating perimeter, area, and/or volume, their associated formulas, and how to determine the required measurements for substitution.
• The properties of composite shapes and right prisms and how to calculate their perimeter, area and/or volume and capacity.
	• Solve measurement problems involving:
	  o Perimeter of irregular and composite shapes
	  o Area of irregular and composite shapes
	  o Volume and capacity of right prisms
	• Use appropriate metric units when solving measurement problems.
	• Use the 4 operations to perform calculations using formulas—choosing and using efficient strategies and tools to do so.
		• Solve measurement problems involving:
		  o Comparison of objects using familiar metric units to determine length, mass and capacity.
		• Use familiar metric units when estimating, comparing and measuring the attributes of everyday objects.
		• Use single-digit addition and related subtraction facts and apply additive strategies to model and solve perimeter problems.

Table 12.10 Adjusted Marking Criteria, Year 8 Math

A	B	C	D	E
Use familiar metric units when estimating, comparing and measuring the *perimeter* ~~attributes~~ of everyday objects and *two-dimensional shapes* with labelled markings.	Use familiar metric units when estimating, comparing and measuring the attributes of *two-dimensional shapes* and everyday objects with labelled markings.	Use familiar metric units when estimating, comparing and measuring the attributes of everyday objects with labelled markings.	Use familiar metric units when estimating ~~comparing and~~ measuring the attributes of everyday objects ~~with labelled markings~~.	Use informal ~~familiar metric~~ units when ~~estimating, comparing and~~ measuring the attributes of everyday objects ~~with labelled markings~~.

individualised goals. The formal summative assessment task can also be replaced with less formal data collection methods including portfolios of work, observations, and annotated photographs and videos.

Phase 4: Plan and Implement Inclusive Instruction

Phase 4 of the IACF aids translation of the grade-level academic curriculum and the alignment of personalised curriculum adjustments into an instructional plan. This involves taking the articulated instructional goals from Phase 1, in combination with the student profile data in Phase 2, and the aligned personalised curriculum adjustments from Phase 3, to plan inclusive instructional tasks for implementation across the unit of study. This process draws on the anticipation of the personalised learning requirements of the student with a complex learning profile, in combination with the content and contexts of the grade-level academic curriculum to proactively plan instructional methods, materials, and tasks that will ensure flexible and engaging ways for the student to be included.

Six essential questions frame the instructional tasks planning phase:

1. Which instructional tasks, methods, and materials will be used to teach the grade-level academic curriculum?
2. What adjustments to the breadth, depth, and/or complexity of tasks are required?
3. Which key supports and scaffolds will assist with access and participation in tasks?
4. What evidence of learning will be collected to monitor progress?
5. What personalised resources, materials, and equipment are needed?

The IACF Weekly Overview has been provided as a tool for thinking about and documenting instructional decisions across a weekly plan (Table 12.11).

Table 12.11 Example Weekly Overview using the IACF

Teacher: Mrs Jones	Year Level: 8		Learning Area: Math	Unit: Measurement		Week: 2
Learning Intention	Success Criteria	Lesson	Monitoring	Adjustments	Supports
Students are learning to...	*Students will be successful when they can...*	*Overview of the lesson sequence and the key instructional methods, tasks, and activities*	*Evidence of learning— what to look for and/ or what formative assessment data will be collected/reviewed*	*Changes or actions that enable equitable access, participation, and progress in learning*	*Materials/ resources/ measures to facilitate access and participation*
1 Understand the application of perimeter and area to triangles and parallelograms.	• Find the perimeter of a triangle and parallelogram. • Find the area of a triangle and parallelogram. • Select appropriate linear and square units.	1. Revise properties of triangles and parallelograms—discussing similarities and differences. 2. Calculate perimeter of triangles and parallelograms—use a variety of methods and materials. Start with teacher modelling followed by a partner activity. 3. Calculate area of triangles and parallelograms using a variety of methods and materials— discuss how the area of parallelograms and triangles is linked, and how their formulas extend on this link. 4. Students practice calculating the area of triangles and parallelograms using formulas—incorporate a range of activities, provide scaffolds and opportunities for extended teacher modelling and guided practice.	Samples of work that show the application of formulas and calculations to determine the perimeter and area of triangles and parallelograms. Ensure students are: • Selecting the right formula for perimeter vs. area • Applying appropriate linear and square units • Using the perpendicular height when calculating the area of triangles and parallelograms	Estimating the size of the sides of triangles and parallelograms— concrete, on paper, and in the environment. Measuring the length of the sides of triangles and parallelograms using a ruler and measuring tape. Supporting the teacher to measure the attributes of scaled shapes used during teacher modelling of perimeter and area calculations.	• Concrete shapes • Ruler • Measuring tape • Identified shapes in the environment

Left margin: *Lesson*

Phase 5: Monitoring Access, Participation and Learning Progress

Phase 5 of the IACF centres on monitoring and reflecting on the student's access, participation and learning progress across the course of the unit of study. This involves gathering and analysing data to consider what is working well and what could be improved to ensure the student is authentically included in the grade-level academic curriculum. The process of monitoring and reflecting occurs through two forms of data collection: (i) formative data that monitors progress from lesson to lesson, and (ii) summative data that captures what the student has learned at the completion of the unit of study. Both forms of data provide opportunity to evaluate the impact of curriculum priorities, instructional strategies, and adjustments.

Six essential questions frame the monitoring and reflecting on access, participation and learning progress phase:

1. When will formative data be collected, and what flexible methods of data collection will be used?
2. What learning progress has occurred and what impact have instructional strategies and adjustments had?
3. Are there any additional barriers that are posing a challenge and how can they be addressed?
4. What level of achievement has the student demonstrated?
5. What curriculum priorities, instructional strategies, and adjustments need to be changed or sustained into the next unit of study?
6. What further professional learning and/or collaboration is needed to build capability?

The IACF provides a systematic and practical approach to working toward the vision for all students, including those with complex learning profiles, to be included in grade-level academic curriculum. The chapter has stepped through each of the IACF phases to help achieve this vision in practice. In doing so, it provides readers with a comprehensive guide to 'the how' of inclusion, knowledge that educators keen to do the 'right work' need and want (see Chapter 8). Critical to the success of this practice in action are classroom teachers. While they need to be supported by knowledgeable leaders, specialist colleagues and allied health professionals (see Chapter 18), classroom teachers can use the ideas and tools in this chapter to lead the process of identifying and aligning curriculum adjustments to ensure all students learn together.

Conclusion

Inclusive education demands access to grade-level classrooms and curriculum with genuine opportunities for learning and participation. This requires teachers to respect and respond to difference through curriculum and instructional practices that extend what is ordinarily available, instead of providing something that is additional or different (Florian & Black-Hawkins, 2011). To effectively include students with complex learning profiles, teachers need access to viable practices that result in educational opportunity in grade-level academic curriculum and regular classroom contexts. This is particularly necessary when a student's present level of academic performance is substantially below their grade level (Giangreco, 2020). If teachers do not have the confidence and capacity to address this ongoing challenge, the segregation of students with complex learning profiles is likely to continue (Agran et al., 2020; Kleinert, 2019).

To provide meaningful opportunities for students with complex learning profiles to access grade-level academic curriculum, expectations about students' competence and capabilities need to be higher. Rather than using perceived student deficits and assumptions about potential as the driving force for educational programs, attention needs to shift to how curriculum content, instruction, and materials can be manipulated to create a context in which all students can access and participate in grade-level academic standards. There needs to be a shift in focus from what students *currently* do (in a mainstream context replete with curricular and instructional barriers), to what students *could* do when provided with appropriately designed instruction, adjustments, and support. The IACF exemplifies strategies for universally designing grade-level academic curriculum and instruction in ways that enables all students to meaningfully engage in academic content alongside peers. It is not just a presentation of practices or an illustration of what is possible, but a challenge to all educators to be reflective of and pay attention to how knowledge and practices have evolved. When educators focus on rigorous curriculum provision and responsive instruction, they can raise expectations and influence the educational experiences and outcomes of <u>all</u> students. We want you to be that educator!

References

Agran, M., Jackson, L., Kurth, J. A., Ryndak, D., Burnette, K., Jameson, M., Zagona, A., Fitzpatrick, H., & Wehmeyer, M. (2020). Why aren't students with severe disabilities being placed in general education classrooms: Examining the relations among classroom placement, learner outcomes, and other factors. *Research and Practice for Persons with Severe Disabilities*, 45(1), 4–13. https://doi.org/10.1177/1540796919878134

Ainsworth, L. (2003). *"Unwrapping" the standards: A simple process to make standards manageable.* Lead + Learn Press.

Australian Curriculum, Assessment and Reporting Authority. (n.d.-a). *F-10 Curriculum: Structure.* https://www.australiancurriculum.edu.au/f-10-curriculum/structure/

Australian Curriculum, Assessment and Reporting Authority. (n.d.-b). *F-10 Curriculum: Math.* https://v9.australiancurriculum.edu.au/f-10-curriculum/learning-areas/mathematics/year-8

Australian Curriculum, Assessment and Reporting Authority. (n.d.-c). *F-10 Curriculum: Learning areas.* https://www.v9.australiancurriculum.edu.au/f-10-curriculum/f-10-curriculum-overview/learning-areas

Australian Curriculum, Assessment and Reporting Authority. (n.d.-d). *F-10 Curriculum: Meeting the needs of students with disability.* https://www.australiancurriculum.edu.au/resources/student-diversity/meeting-the-needs-of-students-with-a-disability/

Australian Curriculum, Assessment and Reporting Authority. (n.d.-e). *F-10 Curriculum: Literacy—Understand this general capability.* https://v9.australiancurriculum.edu.au/teacher-resources/understand-this-general-capability/literacy

Australian Curriculum, Assessment and Reporting Authority. (n.d.-f). *General capabilities.* https://www.australiancurriculum.edu.au/f-10-curriculum/general-capabilities/

Australian Institute for Teaching and School Leadership. (2018). *Australian professional standards for teachers.* https://www.aitsl.edu.au/standards

Bailey, K., & Jakicic, C. (2018). *Make it happen: Coaching with the four critical questions of PLCs at work.* Solution Tree Press.

Ballard, S. L., & Dymond, S. K. (2017). Addressing the general education curriculum in general education settings with students with severe disabilities. *Research and Practice for Persons with Severe Disabilities, 42*(3), 155–170. https://doi.org/10.1177/1540796917698832

Barr, F., & Mavropoulou, S. (2021). Curriculum accommodations in mathematics instruction for adolescents with mild intellectual disability educated in inclusive classrooms. *International Journal of Disability, Development and Education, 68*(2), 270–286. https://doi.org/10.1080/1034912x.2019.1684457

Biklen, D. (1992). *Schooling without labels: Parents, educators, and inclusive education.* Temple University Press.

Brantlinger, E. (1997). Using ideology: Cases of nonrecognition of the politics of research and practice in special education. *Review of Educational Research, 67*(4), 425–459. https://doi.org/10.3102/0034654306700442

Browder, D. M., Spooner, F., Wakeman, S., Trela, K., & Baker, J. N. (2006). Aligning instruction with academic content standards: Finding the link. *Research and Practice for Persons with Severe Disabilities, 31*(4), 309–321. https://doi.org/10.1177/154079690603100404

CAST (n.d.). *UDL on campus.* http://udloncampus.cast.org/page/assessment_udl

Causton-Theoharis, J., Theoharis, G., Orsati, F., & Cosier, M. (2011). Does self-contained special education deliver on its promises? A critical inquiry into research and practice. *Journal of Special Education Leadership, 24*(2), 61–78.

Cole, S. M., Murphy, H. R., Frisby, M. B., Grossi, T. A., & Bolte, H. R. (2021). The relationship of special education placement and student academic outcomes. *The Journal of Special Education, 54*(4), 217–227. https://doi.org/10.1177/0022466920925033

Cole, S. M., Murphy, H. R., Frisby, M. B., & Robinson, J. (2022). The relationship between special education placement and high school outcomes. *The Journal of Special Education.* Advance online publication. https://doi.org/10.1177/00224669221097945

Colley, K. E., & Lassman, K. A. (2021). Urban secondary science teachers and special education students: A theoretical framework for preparing science teachers to meet the needs of all students. *Insights into Learning Disabilities, 18*(2), 159–186.

Ferguson, P. M. (1986). The social construction of mental retardation. *Social Policy, 18*(1), 51–56.

Firestone, A. R., Aramburo, C. M., & Cruz, R. A. (2021). Special educators' knowledge of high-leverage practices: Construction of a pedagogical content knowledge measure. *Studies in Educational Evaluation, 70*, 100986. https://doi.org/10.1016/j.stueduc.2021.100986

Florian, L., & Black-Hawkins, K. (2011). Exploring inclusive pedagogy. *British Educational Research Journal, 37*(5), 813–828. https://doi.org/10.1080/01411926.2010.501096

Flowers, C., Wakeman, S., & Browder, D. M. (2009). Links for Academic Learning (LAL): A conceptual model for investigating alignment of alternate assessments based on alternate achievement standards. *Educational Measurement: Issues and Practice, 28*(1), 25–37. https://doi.org/10.1111/j.1745-3992.2009.01134.x

Foley-Nicpon, M., Assouline, S. G. & Colangelo, N. (2013). Twice-exceptional learners: Additional disabilities. *RE:View, 28*, 25–32.

Gee, K., Gonzalez, M., & Cooper, C. (2020). Outcomes of inclusive versus separate placements: A matched pairs comparison study. *Research and Practice for Persons with Severe Disabilities, 45*(4), 223–240. https://doi.org/10.1177/1540796920943469

Giangreco, M. F. (2020). "How can a student with severe disabilities be in a fifth-grade class when he can't do fifth-grade level work?" Misapplying the least restrictive environment. *Research and Practice for Persons with Severe Disabilities, 45*(1), 23–27. https://doi.org/10.1177/1540796919892733

Guskey, T. R., & Bailey, J. M. (2001). *Developing grading and reporting systems for student learning.* Corwin Press.

Hudson, M. E., Browder, D. M., & Wood, L. A. (2013). Review of experimental research on academic learning by students with moderate and severe intellectual disability in general education. *Research and Practice for Persons with Severe Disabilities, 38*(1), 17–29. https://doi.org/10.2511/027494813807046926

Hughes, C., Agran, M., Cosgriff, J. C., & Washington, B. H. (2013). Student self-determination: A preliminary investigation of the role of participation in inclusive settings. *Education and Training in Autism and Developmental Disabilities, 48*(1), 3–17. http://www.jstor.org/stable/23879882

Hunt, P. (2012). Reconciling an ecological curricular framework focusing on quality of life outcomes with the development and instruction of standards-based academic goals. *Research and Practice for Persons with Severe Disabilities, 37*(3), 139–152. https://doi.org/10.2511/027494812804153471

Jorgensen, C. M. (1998). *Restructuring high schools for all students: Taking inclusion to the next level.* Brookes Publishing.

Jorgensen, C. M. (2018). *It's more than 'just being in': Creating authentic inclusion for students with complex learning needs.* Brookes Publishing.

Jorgensen, C. M., McSheehan, M., & Sonnenmeier, R. M. (2010). *The beyond access model.* Brooks Publishing.

Kauffman, J. M., Anastasiou, D., Badar, J., Travers, J. C., & Wiley, A. L. (2016). Inclusive education moving forward. In J. P. Bakken, F. E. Obiakor, & A. Rotatori (Eds.), *General and special education in an age of change: Roles of professionals involved* (Vol. 32, pp. 153–178). Emerald Group.

King-Sears, M. E. (2008). Facts and fallacies: Differentiation and the general education curriculum for students with special educational needs. *Support for Learning, 23*(2), 55–62. https://doi.org/10.1111/j.1467-9604.2008.00371.x

Kleinert, H. L. (2019). Students with the most significant disabilities, communicative competence, and the full extent of their exclusion. *Research and Practice for Persons with Severe Disabilities, 45*(1), 34–38. https://doi.org/10.1177/1540796919892740

Kleinert, H. & Thurlow, M. (2001). An introduction to alternate assessment. In H. Kleinert & J. Kearns (Eds.), *Alternate assessment: Measuring outcomes and supports for students with disabilities* (pp. 1–15). Brookes Publishing.

Kleinert, H., Towles-Reeves, E., Quenemoen, R., Thurlow, M., Fluegge, L., Weseman, L., & Kerbel, A. (2015). Where students with the most significant cognitive disabilities are taught. *Exceptional Children, 81*(3), 312–328. https://doi.org/10.1177/0014402914563697

Kuntz, E.M., & Carter, E. W. (2021). General educators' involvement in interventions for students with intellectual disability. *Inclusion, 9*(2), 134–150. https://doi.org/10.1352/2326-6988-9.2.134

Kurth, J. A. (2013). A unit-based approach to adaptations in inclusive classrooms. *Teaching Exceptional Children, 46*(2), 34–43. https://doi.org/10.1177/004005991304600204

Kurth, J. A., Born, K., & Love, H. (2016). Ecobehavioral characteristics of self-contained high school classrooms for students with severe cognitive disability. *Research and Practice for Persons with Severe Disabilities, 41*(4), 227–243. https://doi.org/10.1177/1540796916661492

Kurth, J., Gross, M., Lovinger, S., & Catalano, T. (2012). Grading students with significant disabilities in inclusive settings: Teacher perspectives. *The Journal of International Association of Special Education, 12*(1), 41–57. http://hdl.handle.net/1808/29916

Kurth, J., & Mastergeorge, A. M. (2009). Individual education plan goals and services for adolescents with autism: Impact of age and educational setting. *The Journal of Special Education, 44*(3), 146–160. https://doi.org/10.1177/0022466908329825

Kurth, J. A., Morningstar, M. E., & Kozleski, E. B. (2015). The persistence of highly restrictive special education placements for students with low-incidence disabilities. *Research and Practice for Persons with Severe Disabilities, 39*(3), 227–239. https://doi.org/10.1177/1540796914555580

Lancaster, J., & Bain, A. (2019). Designing university courses to improve pre-service teachers' pedagogical content knowledge of evidence-based inclusive practice. *Australian Journal of Teacher Education, 44*(2), 51–65. https://doi.org/10.14221/ajte.2018v44n2.4

Lee, S.-H., Wehmeyer, M. L., Soukup, J. H., & Palmer, S. B. (2010). Impact of curriculum modifications on access to the general education curriculum for students with disabilities. *Exceptional Children, 76*(3), 213–233. https://doi.org/10.1177/001440291007600205

Many, T. W. (2020). Unwrapping the standards: A priceless professional development opportunity. *Texas Elementary Principals & Supervisors Association's TEPSA News, 77*(6).

McSheehan, M., Sonnenmeier, R. M., Jorgensen, C. M., & Turner, K. (2006). Beyond communication access: Promoting learning of the general curriculum by students with significant disabilities. *Topics in Language Disorders, 26*(3), 266–290.

Morgan, J. J., Brown, N. B., Hsiao, Y.-J., Howerter, C., Juniel, P., Sedano, L., & Castillo, W. L. (2013). Unwrapping academic standards to increase the achievement of students with disabilities. *Intervention in School and Clinic, 49*(3), 131–141. https://doi.org/10.1177/1053451213496156

Pit-ten Cate, I. M., Markova, M., Krischler, M., & Krolak-Schwerdt, S. (2018). Promoting inclusive education: The role of teachers' competence and attitudes. *Insights into Learning Disabilities, 15*(1), 49–63.

Rao, K., & Meo, G. (2016). Using Universal Design for Learning to design standards-based lessons. *SAGE Open, 6*(4). https://doi.org/10.1177/2158244016680688

Root, J. R., Jimenez, B., & Saunders, A. (2021). Leveraging the UDL framework to plan grade-aligned mathematics in inclusive settings. *Inclusive Practices, 1*(1), 13–22. https://doi.org/10.1177/2732474521990028

Ruppar, A. L., Afacan, K., Yang, Y., & Pickett, K. J. (2017). Embedded shared reading to increase literacy in inclusive English/language arts class: Preliminary efficacy and ecological validity.

Education and Training in Autism and Developmental Disabilities, 52, 51–63. https://www.jstor.org/stable/26420375

Ruppar, A. L., Allcock, H., & Gonsier-Gerdin, J. (2016). Ecological factors affecting access to general education content and contexts for students with significant disabilities. *Remedial and Special Education, 38*(1), 53–63. https://doi.org/10.1177/0741932516646856

Ruppar, A. L., Fisher, K. W., Olson, A. J., & Orlando, A. M. (2018). Exposure to literacy for students eligible for the alternate assessment. *Education and Training in Autism and Developmental Disabilities, 53*(2), 192–208. https://www.jstor.org/stable/26495269

Ryndak, D., Jackson, L., & White, J. M. (2013). Involvement and progress in the general curriculum for students with extensive support needs: K–12 inclusive-education research and implications for the future. *Inclusion, 1*(1), 28–49. https://doi.org/10.1352/2326-6988-1.1.028

Saur, J., & Jorgensen, C. M. (2016). Still caught in the continuum: A critical analysis of least restrictive environment and its effect on placement of students with intellectual disability. *Inclusion, 4*(2), 56–74. https://doi.org/10.1352/2326-6988-4.2.56

Soukup, J. H., Wehmeyer, M. L., Bashinski, S. M., & Bovaird, J. A. (2007). Classroom variables and access to the general curriculum for students with disabilities. *Exceptional Children, 74*(1), 101–120. https://doi.org/10.1177/001440290707400106

Taub, D. A., McCord, J. A., & Ryndak, D. L. (2017). Opportunities to learn for students with extensive support needs: A context of research-supported practices for all in general education classes. *The Journal of Special Education, 51*(3), 127–137. https://doi.org/10.1177/0022466917696263

Theobold, R., Goldhaber, D., Gratz, T., & Holden, K. (2019). Career and technical education, inclusion, and postsecondary outcomes for students with learning disabilities. *Journal of Learning Disabilities, 13*(4), 251–258. https://doi.org/10.1177/0022219418775121

Thompson, J. R., Shogren, K. A., & Wehmeyer, M. L. (2017). Supports and support needs in strengths-based models of intellectual disability. In M. L. Wehmeyer, & K. A. Shogren (Eds.), *Handbook of research-based practices for educating students with intellectual disability* (pp. 31–49). Routledge.

Tomlinson, C., & McTighe, J. (2006) *Integrating differentiated instruction & understanding by design: Connecting content and kids.* Association for Supervision and Curriculum Development.

Valle-Flórez, R.-E., de Caso Fuertes, A. M., Baelo, R., & Marcos-Santiago, R. (2022). Inclusive culture in compulsory education centers: Values, participation and teachers' perceptions. *Children, 9*(6), 813–834. https://doi.org/10.3390/children9060813

Vandercook, T., Taub, D., Loiselle, T., & Shopa, A. (2020). Why students with severe disabilities are not being placed in general education classrooms: Using the frame of a basic change model to expand the discussion. *Research and Practice for Persons with Severe Disabilities, 45*(1), 63–68. https://doi.org/10.1177/1540796919895970

Walker, P. M., Carson, K. L., Jarvis, J. M., McMillan, J. M., Noble, A. G., Armstrong, D. J., Bissaker, K. A., & Palmer, C. D. (2018). How do educators of students with disabilities in specialist settings understand and apply the Australian Curriculum framework? *Australasian Journal of Special and Inclusive Education, 42*(2), 111–126. https://doi.org/10.1017/jsi.2018.13

Wehmeyer, M. L., Lance, D. G., & Bashinski, S. (2002). Promoting access to the general curriculum for students with mental retardation: A multi-level model. *Education and Training in Mental Retardation and Developmental Disabilities, 37*(3), 223–234. https://www.jstor.org/stable/23880001

Wehmeyer, M. L., Lattin, D. L., Lapp-Rincker, G., & Agran, M. (2003). Access to the general curriculum of middle school students with mental retardation: An observational study. *Remedial and Special Education*, 24(5), 262–272. https://doi.org/10.1177/07419325030240050201

Wehmeyer, M. L., & Palmer, S. B. (2003). Adult outcomes for students with cognitive disabilities three years after high school: The impact of self-determination. *Education and Training in Developmental Disabilities*, 38(2), 131–144. https://www.jstor.org/stable/23879591

Wiggins, G. P., & McTighe, J. (2005). *Understanding by design.* Association for Supervision and Curriculum Development.

Developing an Inclusive School Culture

Chapter 13

Putting *all* students at the centre

Jenna Gillett-Swan, Haley Tancredi, & Linda J. Graham

Putting *all* students at the centre of the learning and teaching process requires a shift from the way we currently perceive and deliver school education. It is a mindset that conceives of each student as an individual with unique talents and aspirations, and as the holder of personal insights that can help teachers to better craft their teaching. It signals a departure from traditional ideas about schooling and students (like, you know, they "should be seen and not heard") and is consistent with recent calls for personalisation of curriculum, pedagogy, and assessment to improve outcomes for all students (Gonski et al., 2018). Putting *all* students at the centre requires teachers and school leaders to think about students as individuals and to consult them about their learning; however, genuine consultation requires teachers and school leaders to both enable and listen to student voice in all its forms. These practices of enabling and respecting voice, and consulting and communicating with students, are embedded in the *United Nations Convention on the Rights of the Child* (UNCRC; United Nations, 1989) and the *Australian Professional Standards for Teachers* (Standards 3.5 and 3.6; Australian Institute for Teaching and School Leadership, 2018), both of which have a bearing on educational practice. Teachers have additional responsibilities for students with disability for whom consultation is a human right under the *Convention on the Rights of Persons with Disabilities* (CRPD; United Nations, 2006), and there is also a requirement for educators to consult in order to meet their obligations under the *Disability Standards for Education 2005* (DSE; Cth; see Chapters 3 and 5). No longer is it a question of *whether* students should be consulted about their education; rather, the question is *how* to consult students—including those with disability—in authentic and meaningful ways. This chapter explores methods of eliciting and responding to students' voices that are inclusive of students with disability, including those with communication difficulties.

Hearing and Responding to the Voices of All Students

All students are unique and, as their experiences and perceptions are often far removed from those of their teachers, their perspectives cannot be intuited by adults. To fully understand students' points of view, all voices need to be heard and acted upon. Eliciting and listening to student voice, however, may feel threatening for teachers and school

DOI: 10.4324/9781003350897-16

leaders who are charged with the responsibility of managing classrooms and schools that to this day still rely on a compact of adult authority and student compliance. The adoption of democratic processes, such as voice-inclusive practice (Gillett-Swan & Sargeant, 2018), can feel risky in such environments. Teachers and school leaders may feel that they are inviting anarchy and/or that they will not like what they hear back. It takes courage to allow students to speak back to power, and even greater courage to listen to and act on their views. Yet it is a necessary step to achieve Goal 2 of the *Alice Springs (Mparntwe) Education Declaration on Educational Goals for Young Australians* (Australian Government Department of Education, Skills and Employment, 2019) which aims for "all young Australians to become confident and creative individuals, successful lifelong learners, and active and informed members of the community" (p. 6). The ability to communicate, to act with moral and ethical integrity, to commit to national values of democracy, and to participate in civic life are all listed as essential elements of active and informed citizenship in the *Alice Springs (Mparntwe) Declaration.* Yet despite an almost identical goal articulated in the Declaration's predecessor Declaration, which was in place for over a decade (the *Melbourne Declaration*; Ministerial Council on Education, Employment, Training and Youth Affairs, 2008), children and young people are still infrequently provided with an opportunity to have input into what happens to them at school, or they are offered only tokenistic involvement opportunities. While tokenistic involvement is better than nothing, providing it is on the pathway to full realisation, it is still a far cry from what is required to achieve involvement obligations (Lundy, 2018).

Research has documented clear benefits from student-centred approaches to education, which have been shown to contribute positively to academic and social outcomes, foster student agency, and position students as competent social actors with the ability to enact or participate in change (Cook-Sather, 2020; Ruddock & Fielding, 2006). However, such approaches, starting with the elicitation of student voice, must be conducted carefully to mitigate known risks. One risk is that some voices may dominate, drowning out less dominant yet equally valid views. This raises another risk, which is that the most common preferences and the environment they produce may be alienating to other students. For example, very sociable students may express a desire for common areas and group learning, whereas introverts will experience significant stress in such environments. It may also be the case that only some students are comfortable expressing their views, and that what might appear to be the majority view is simply the view of those who are confident enough to make their voice heard. Students on the autism spectrum (Saggers et al., 2016), students with communication difficulties (McLeod, 2011) and students with emotional and behavioural difficulties (Cefai & Cooper, 2010) are at particular risk of not being heard. This can occur because students in these groups can find it difficult to communicate verbally, and their behaviour—which is a form of non-verbal communication—becomes the indicator of meaning. Not surprisingly, they are often misunderstood and punished when they are trying to convey their distress.

Effort must be made to include the perspectives of students in these groups; however, educators must also take care to not coerce students, as the choice to remain silent should also be considered an expression of voice (Gillett-Swan & Sargeant 2018; Hanna, 2022; Lundy, 2007). To be inclusive of all students' voices, and to respect the valuable contribution that their voices can offer, time and space must be allocated for the purpose of listening and responding to students within curriculum planning, pedagogical practices, and classroom interactions. However, seeking and responding to the voices of students are not ad hoc processes, nor are they easy (Rudduck & Fielding, 2006). In the next section, we present a well-known model that schools can use as a framework to seek and respond to student voice, along with a case-study example of how this was adopted with considerable success in a large secondary school serving a diverse disadvantaged community in south-east Queensland.

Fostering Participation through Student Consultation

The Lundy model of participation (Lundy, 2007) provides a useful starting point for the application of children's participatory rights in educational practice and is being increasingly used as the basis of Government youth participation and engagement strategies, such as the Government of Ireland's *National Framework for Children and Young People's Participation in Decision-making* (Government of Ireland, 2021). The Lundy Model is one of the most influential models of child participation, with impact across the three domains of policy, research, and practitioner practice. In pulling together the four spheres of *space, voice, audience,* and *influence,* the model provides a clear, practical, and sequential process to foster participation through student consultation. It does this in a way that respects the indivisibility and interrelatedness of different rights affordances. In other words, it does not pit rights against one another (Gillett-Swan & Lundy, 2022). Instead, the process shows the interrelatedness of different rights in enactment. The process as conceptualised through the four spheres is as follows.

Sphere 1: Space

Adults must first provide a safe space for students to express their views, and they should encourage them to do so without coercion or consequence. Adults need to proactively and intentionally provide these spaces, rather than only seeking student input in response to predetermined agendas. A proactive pursuit of student perspectives would include eliciting input on exactly what matters affect them, and to what extent they would like to be involved in conversations and decisions about these matters (Lundy, 2007). It is important to remember that if students indicate they do not wish to be involved in consultation about a particular matter at one point in time, this does not automatically exclude them from future conversations or consultations about their involvement. Nor does it mean that students should be forced to participate when they do not want to. Space alone is not sufficient, however, as children may require assistance and support in expressing their views—particularly if these opportunities have not been provided to them previously.

Sphere 2: Voice

Meaningful voice opportunities require adequate time provisions, appropriate information, and adult receptiveness to listening to and acting upon children's expressed views (Lundy, 2007). Some students may respond with scepticism about intention or be wary of sharing their perspectives. As we discuss later in this chapter, initial hesitancy can be addressed through the building of trust, the development of rapport, the minimisation of power relations, and the provision of multiple opportunities for students to express their views. If students choose to remain silent despite these provisions, their silence should be respected as an expression of voice (Gillett-Swan & Sargeant, 2018; Hanna, 2022). We all know how loud silence can be!

Sphere 3: Audience

Adults must also listen to students' expressed views and opinions, and take their perspectives seriously, providing an *audience* for their perspectives. Lundy (2007) describes the need for adult attentiveness to verbal and non-verbal 'voice' expressions and how this may require additional training in active listening skills. Audience also requires students' voice expressions to be communicated to those with the power to enact change or action.

Sphere 4: Influence

Students' perspectives must also be acted upon. This enables *influence* of their expressed views to enact the provision of the right for their opinions to be given 'due weight' in accordance with the UNCRC. A common misunderstanding about acting on children's views is that a child's expressed preference automatically outweighs the views of other stakeholders—but this is not the case. The UNCRC provides *all* children with the right to express their views in *all* matters affecting them, and for their views to be taken seriously and acted upon by adults. However, this right does not extend to children's views vetoing or overriding the views of others. Instead, it emphasises the importance of ensuring that children are provided with the opportunity to have a 'seat at the table', and to have their views and opinions considered, incorporated, and taken seriously (Gillett-Swan, 2022). Children's perspectives must be sought and incorporated in the same way that adults consult with other stakeholders, and decisions must be based on careful integration and consideration of all perspectives. This practice supports the multiple representations of perspective and experience, even when they are diverse or divergent. While some adults may be resistant to involving students, "respecting children's views is not just a model of good pedagogical practice (or policy making), but a legally binding obligation . . . [that] applies to all educational decision making" (Lundy, 2007, p. 930). In some cases, this may also require a disruption to the beliefs of some adults about children's capabilities.

Voice-Inclusive Practice

Voice-inclusive practice builds on Lundy's model of participation by putting student views and opinions at the centre of educational activity (Gillett-Swan & Sargeant,

2019). In this way, voice-inclusive practice initiates educational partnerships between adults and children so that voice may be authentically and meaningfully integrated into everyday educational practice. These partnerships need to value and embrace student contributions to their educational experience by "engaging with the child as both a recipient *and* as a key participant in the learning process" (Sargeant & Gillett-Swan, 2019, p. 127). Seeking and including the perspectives of *all* stakeholders across *all* matters affecting them through voice-inclusive practice maintains close alignment to student-centred educational principles, cultivating multistakeholder collaborative partnerships built on shared interests. One matter of increasing educational interest and relevance to multiple stakeholders is student wellbeing. Few schools or systems, however, genuinely consult students on what wellbeing means to *them* or what *they* think will help to improve their wellbeing at school.

A Queensland Case Study

The following case study of a large secondary school in south-east Queensland, Australia provides an example of how student-voice initiatives helped guide reform to improve school belonging and student wellbeing (Gillett-Swan & Graham, 2017; Gillett-Swan et al., 2019). The participating school was situated just outside Brisbane.

The school's leadership team had been driving reform for several years, and the school had developed a reputation for excellence, especially in sport. Enrolments had increased due to improving student outcomes, such that the school had become one of the largest in the state. At the time of the study, more than a third of its students were from a language background other than English, with a large proportion of students from Pacific Islander families. Almost one in ten students were Indigenous. With increased size and student diversity, however, comes greater complexity. When faced with these challenges, together with performance indicators set and monitored by both regional and central offices, leadership teams may feel pressure to exert control through homogenising practices that affirm the hierarchical order.

Putting all students at the centre and encouraging them to express their views is the antithesis of hierarchical control. This, however, is what schools must do to discover what really affects students, and where reform is needed and will have the most leverage. Genuine engagement with students takes courage and leadership from educators who not only listen with an open mind but who also actively respond to student feedback in ways that will lead to genuine change. Key staff at this school had already identified student wellbeing as the next goal in their school improvement journey, and they saw this project as an opportunity to help realise their reform objectives.

The research project on which this case study is based began in 2018 with a survey that asked students in Years 7–10 about their wellbeing at school and used the responses to identify opportunities for change (Phase 1). A similar survey was distributed to school staff, with the aim of determining similarities and differences in the conceptualisation of wellbeing and perceptions between groups. This phase had the added benefit of providing a wellbeing 'temperature gauge' that could act as a measure to assess the impact of the initiatives developed in subsequent phases (see Figure 13.1). Focus groups were then conducted with students across Years 7–10 to discuss the survey responses. Care was taken to include a variety of students to test the salience of survey themes.

Phases 2 and 3 occurred concurrently. Following initial integrative analysis of the Phase 1 data, a staff working party was developed to support interpretation and further exploration of the key issues identified by both students and staff (Phase 2). The staff working party consisted of 11 staff members (the wellbeing coordinator, a deputy principal, the facilities manager, the business manager, five heads of year, and two guidance officers) plus the university project team. At the same time, a multi-year-level student inquiry group was formed to investigate the findings emerging from the student survey and focus groups in more depth (Phase 3). The student inquiry group comprised 21 students (thirteen females and eight males) from Years 7–10. These students then formed seven smaller 'wellbeing inquiry project' groups with two to five students in each.

The student inquiry groups each examined the Phase 1 findings, identified a topic of relevance to their group and then conducted a student inquiry project to learn more about their chosen issue through research with their peers. Connections between the student inquiry groups and the staff working party were created by the university project team and school wellbeing coordinator, who acted as intermediaries between both groups. Information about the activities of the groups was continually fed forwards and

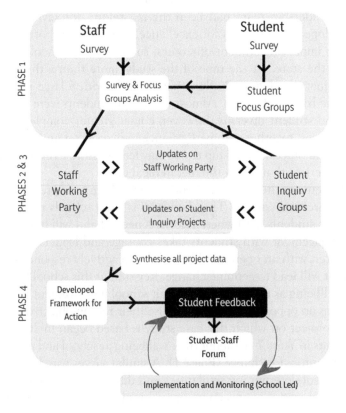

Figure 13.1 Research approach.

backwards between the staff working party and student inquiry groups, demonstrating to students that school staff valued their perspectives. This process also supported the further development of positive staff–student relationships.

In the final integrative phase of the project, the student inquiry groups presented their findings and key implications to the school leadership via a student forum, where both students and staff had the opportunity to seek further information and provide additional insight. Concurrently, the staff working party used the interpretations and data generated through all phases of the research to determine actionable ways to address and/or improve the issues identified. These actionable strategies (including policy review, streamlining of processes, and inclusion of extra support, resources, and passion classes) were then taken back to the whole student body for further input.

These processes were compatible with each component of Lundy's model of participation (Lundy, 2007). For example, Phases 1 and 2 provided direct opportunities for multiple *spaces* and opportunities for *voice*. Opportunities for meaningful student participation at the centre of the project were further enabled through the provision of time and regular opportunities for direct student engagement. For example, as most of the project activities occurred over a period of almost a year, this act of 'giving time' helped fortify student contributions. Further, the frequency of their involvement over the duration of the project provided multiple opportunities for students to develop a considered and informed view. Phase 3 enabled *audience* and *influence*, while also providing opportunities for adults at the school with the power to act upon matters raised by the students to examine and adjust their own perspectives about students' capabilities, with support from the researchers who acted as critical friends. Students were at the centre of subsequent decision-making, as those with the power to act upon and instigate change took students' expressed views and opinions seriously. Working *with* students in considering appropriate actions also enabled opportunities for consulting with students to become sustainable practice.

What Did the Students and Staff Say?

Findings from Phase 1 revealed that overall, staff members were more positive than students about what staff were doing (for example, in the quality and quantity of support provision). Conversely, students were generally more positive than staff about what students were doing, particularly in relation to their attitudes and effort; however, there was also a lot of variability within student responses. Trends in the data were synthesised into five 'areas of need' relating to students' perspectives on: (i) the value of education, (ii) respect and recognition, (iii) relationships, (iv) support provision, and (v) equality and fairness.

The Value of Education. Staff had a lower opinion of student commitment to school than the students, and this was statistically significant. For example, while students liked that there were a lot of different opportunities provided for them, and that the school prepared them for their future, they did not like the pressure to achieve or that assessment was seen as high stakes. They felt that the school paid too much attention to sport and physical appearance, and not enough to student socio-emotional needs. Students also felt that there was inconsistency in the practices and support provided by teachers, and that the current approach to behaviour management was ineffective.

Respect and Recognition. Staff thought that students were being treated with respect more than the students felt that they were being respected, and this was statistically significant. In considering voice and participation specifically, just over 38% of the student participants felt that adults at the school did not often *listen* to student concerns, and just over 42% felt that adults at the school did not often *act* on student concerns. Thirty-one per cent of participants felt that they did not often have opportunities to make decisions at school. In thinking about the importance of seeking *and* acting upon children's views, these findings are particularly revealing.

Relationships. Staff and student perceptions were generally the same in their perceptions of relationships, although there was a significant difference between male and female teachers in that males were more likely than females to say that they told students when they did a good job. In general, students liked that most teachers tried their best and felt that there were some good teachers at the school. However, students also felt as though there were not many teachers that they could trust, and not many who cared. They felt that there was a lack of follow-up when students did go to teachers with problems and that there was a long response time before action. Students also identified a lack of rapport and relationship-building opportunities with teachers.

Support Provision. Staff had a higher opinion of the support available to students than students did, and this was statistically significant. Students appreciated having additional academic and non-academic support available and felt that there were genuine teachers and staff. Even so, they felt that there was a lack of support for problems, and there was perception of different support and treatment for different students. Students expressed a lack of confidence in seeking help and thought that there were not enough support options available. They also felt that there was a need for changes in the way that support in class is provided. They also questioned the effectiveness of the current support programs available at the school.

Equality and Fairness. Students predominantly agreed that the rules at the school were fair, that all racial and ethnic groups were respected, and that the school would respond in an emergency. However, there were some differences by year level, with Year 7 responses being more positive about the fairness of school rules than the Year 8s and Year 10s. This was a statistically significant result. Overall, students felt that they were treated differently based on behaviour or stream (e.g., mainstream versus excellence programs), that the rules were not applied consistently, and that, in some cases, students or groups were targeted in rule implementation. They felt that there was a lack of inclusivity of mainstream (as opposed to 'excellence') students and the support received.

How Did Staff and Students Respond to the Findings?

Staff Response. Some of these findings were understandably confronting for staff, particularly when staff and student perspectives diverged or if there was an apparent misunderstanding about the different provisions or processes available. Initially, there was resistance from some members of the working party, who challenged or dismissed students' feedback. After approximately three weeks of weekly working-party meetings, which involved discussions between staff and the researchers who acted as critical friends, all staff on the working party could appreciate that—although divergent from their own—students' perspectives had merit. By this time, the researchers had developed some rapport and trust with members of the staff working party. This, together with the leadership demonstrated by the wellbeing coordinator and a deputy principal, reassured staff and ensured that they engaged with the process and with the data in good faith.

The working party's analysis of the data highlighted several areas for action. Each area involved different levels of complexity, and some issues were able to be addressed relatively easily. For example, there was general confusion and variability in student perspectives of support provisions. In discussing student experiences of obtaining support, and staff understandings of the same processes, it became clear that this confusion was not limited to the student experience. Staff initially considered some of the support concerns highlighted by the students as already addressed through existing provisions; however, it soon emerged that the pathway to *access* this support lacked clarity. While students may have expressed this issue in terms of identifying a lack of support provision, it may have instead been that the support was there, but they did not know about it or how to access it. Therefore, in addition to revisiting and streamlining processes for support services and provisions, the school created an infographic and flowchart for clarity and ease of reference for staff and students alike. This is just one example of how student perspectives enabled greater insight into the student experience of wellbeing at the school and opportunities for further refinement and enhanced provision. It also emphasises the importance of collaborative interrogation of information to ensure that reactive changes are not made on adult and/or surface interpretations of what has been said.

Student Response. Students were initially sceptical that the project would result in meaningful change. However, the authenticity with which the school sought, incorporated, and respected student involvement and insight shows that students and staff can work together for school improvement. This is despite some of the student feedback being initially quite confronting for some staff. Responses to the follow-up survey suggested that some students appreciated that school staff were taking the time to listen and to find out more about the issues affecting students, and that they were trying to find ways to better support students and improve the school: "My reason [for indicating that my wellbeing is better this year compared to last year] is that the school listened to these surveys last year and improved on wellbeing" (Year 8 male, 2019 survey). This was not universal, however, with others indicating that staff could go further. Students' responses were insightful, demonstrating their understanding of the tensions that accompany change and the difficulty that staff face when engaging with student perspectives.

> Listen more. With an open mind at that. I think you're all used to the structure we've had for such a long time that you may not understand the change we are making. I understand it takes time to interpret. But please, listen with open ears and an open mind (Year 11 female, 2019 survey).

Students also acknowledged that some desired changes are out of the school's control, but still valued the effort and genuineness of the staff as they strived to do their best.

Both the students and the staff reflected on the consultation process better enabling each group to see things from the other's perspective, in turn supporting greater levels of mutual respect and relationship development. Despite the project focusing on student wellbeing, it was clear that some students were also conscious of and concerned about staff wellbeing.

> I do understand that sometimes not everyone can be heard, but it would be really good if we are able to be heard as students and I'm sure that the teachers would like to be heard as well (Year 9 female, inquiry group, 2018 survey).

Student consultation and involvement in this project enhanced the school's reform efforts, as the initiatives developed through the process were based on students' lived realities and were targeted at students' identified needs. While some members of the staff working party were initially resistant and inclined to dismiss students' views, the value of seeking and listening to students' perspectives was roundly endorsed by project end. For some, it was clear that a school-reform agenda is better realised with the participation of and buy-in from students.

> [A]lthough [principal] sort of says, this is your brief, this is the excellence I want to happen, I can't see how we're going to achieve that excellence without having that balance between the research and the student voice. It's gotta stay. The way that we hear the student voice, and the way that it's articulated might change . . . Those things could probably change, but that dynamic needs to continue to inform our teaching and learning practices, that's for sure (Participant, staff working party, 2019).

Why Should Schools Embed Student Voice into Inclusive School Reform?

This case study provides one example of the way that direct and meaningful consultation with students can contribute to school improvement. In consulting with students, adults are placing students at the centre of their educational experiences and positioning them as key stakeholders. In doing so, positive staff–student relationships may be further developed and fortified through mutual respect and a shared understanding that the student experience matters. Consulting students is also cost-effective. There is no need for funding other than the time required for students, teachers, and others to engage in the process. Taking the time to engage with students to understand different aspects of their experience may also contribute to lessening misunderstandings within adult and student perspectives. These views may initially appear divergent but could, in fact, be advocating for the same thing, as illustrated by our example of the sufficiency and suitability of support provisions. However, consulting meaningfully with students is not without its challenges.

The elevation of student voice and value associated with its relative power can be confronting for some adults, especially those who see it as a disruption to more 'traditional' approaches to education that position students as subordinate (Quinn & Owen, 2016). Even in contexts where staff members are receptive to direct student contributions, they may still place limits on the scope of student involvement—allowing the adults to venture slightly out of their comfort zones but ultimately still maintaining the status quo. In this way, the process of engaging with students may be considered tokenistic or inauthentic by the students. This can lead to their reluctance to engage in consultation opportunities in the future, or scepticism regarding adult intention. By contrast, embedding voice-inclusive practice into everyday practice, as illustrated in this case study, supports the enactment of children's participatory rights, rather than seeing direct student consultation as an add-on or additional burden (Sargeant & Gillett-Swan, 2019). Finally, seeking student perspectives and placing them at the centre of the teaching and learning process also offer practical benefits (to teachers especially) by enabling and supporting adults to provide more focused and effective support to better meet student need. There is, however, no 'one size fits all' approach to voice elicitation and practice, and voice-inclusive practices need to be different for different students in different contexts. This is particularly relevant to students with disability with whom educators are legally obliged to consult.

Inclusive Education, Student Consultation, and Reasonable Adjustments

As discussed in Chapter 3, the right to an inclusive education for all students, including those with disability, without discrimination and based on equal opportunity has been in place for over a decade, and was clarified recently through *General Comment No. 4* (GC4), which makes clear the legal obligations of States parties that have ratified the CRPD. GC4 also states that educators are required to provide "participatory learning experiences" and that students must be consulted, and their voices respected:

> States parties must consult with and actively involve persons with disabilities, including children with disabilities . . . in all aspects of planning, implementation, monitoring, and evaluation of inclusive education policies. Persons with disabilities and, when appropriate, their families, must be recognised as partners and not merely recipients of education (United Nations, 2016, para 7).

Further, the need to provide accessible consultative processes for people with disability, including children, has been mandated through *General Comment No. 7* to the CRPD:

> States parties should also ensure that consultation processes are accessible—for example, by providing sign language interpreters, Braille and Easy Read—and must provide support, funding and reasonable accommodation as appropriate and requested, to ensure the participation of representatives of all persons with disabilities in consultation processes (United Nations, 2018, para 45).

Of note is the clear direction provided in the statement "States parties should also ensure that consultation *processes* [emphasis added] are accessible". Accessible consultation means that students can understand the content of a consultative conversation, can comprehend the questions that are posed to them, and are able to communicate a response that reflects their perspective. As authentic consultation requires effective, two-way communication, the consultation process may also need to be adjusted to ensure genuine participation of students with disability.

In Australia, the DSE provides guidance for educators and education systems as to their obligations under the *Disability Discrimination Act 1992* (DDA; Cth), as per Table 13.1. As discussed in Chapter 5, the DSE outlines the national legal obligations for education providers, which include the obligation to make *reasonable adjustments* for students with disability, as well as the obligation to *consult* students (or their associate) during the process of designing and implementing adjustments. The third review of the DSE took place in 2020 and for the first time included a Young People's Advisory Group. The Advisory Group was established to directly hear students' voices and put the lived experience of people with disability at the centre of the review (Australian Government Department of Education, 2020). Recommendation 2 of the *2020 DSE Review* was "That the Australian Government amend the Standards to *include principles on consultation* [emphasis added], issues resolution and complaints handling processes" (Australian Government Department of Education, 2020, p. vii). This recommendation shows promise for real change to the support available to students with disability and their families in knowing their rights and increasing educator knowledge of the obligations to consult.

Table 13.1 Educators' Obligations under International Law and Australian Legislation

Document	Obligations for Educators and Education Systems	Context
Universal Declaration of Human Rights (United Nations, 1948)	Everyone has the right to education Everyone has the right to hold and freely express their opinions	International
Convention on the Rights of the Child (United Nations, 1989)	All children have a right to education *all children have a right to express an opinion about issues that affect them*	International
Disability Discrimination Act 1992 (Cth)	Students with disability are entitled to reasonable adjustments	Australia
Disability Standards for Education 2005 (Cth)	Students with disability are entitled to reasonable adjustments	Australia
	Students with disability are to be consulted about adjustments	
Convention on the Rights of Persons with Disabilities (United Nations, 2006)	Students with disability have the right to inclusive and accessible education Students with disability have the right to equal and full participation	International
General Comment No. 4 (United Nations, 2016)	Students with disability have the right to an inclusive education Students have the right to be consulted	International
General Comment No. 7 (United Nations, 2018)	Consultation processes must be accessible	International

Testimonies provided by students with disability and their families to the *Royal Commission into Violence, Abuse, Neglect and Exploitation of People with Disability* have revealed ongoing gaps between the obligation to consult as per the DSE and what often happens in Australian schools. For example, in Public Hearing 24: The experience of children and young people with disability in different education settings, Ms Kimberly Langcake and her son Mitch gave witness testimony about Mitch's school experiences (Royal Commission into Violence, Abuse, Neglect and Exploitation of People with Disability, 2022). Kimberly described a tricycle riding program that was instigated by Mitch's school when he was in Grade 11, for which students received a certificate. However, Kimberly shared in her evidence that Mitch had been independently riding two-wheeled BMX bikes outside of school from the age of eight:

> I was totally frustrated that they hadn't asked about his capacity to ride a bike and he was put on a trike. Like, this kid can ride a bike. Why did you not ask? Why did we not have a two-wheeler bike? . . . "I chose to buy trikes" was what I was told by the principal of the Disability Unit (Disability Royal Commission, 2022).

This example demonstrates the consequences of failing to consult and making assumptions instead. Because Mitch and his family were not consulted about his skills and previous experiences, a program of support was implemented that was not appropriate or relevant to Mitch. This resulted in an inappropriate resource allocation and time spent on a task of limited value. However, if consultation had occurred, a program could have been designed to extend Mitch's skills and/or provide relevant and enriching new learning experiences.

Providing educators and education providers with tools to support them to enact consultation may reverse some of the myths about and inhibitors to consultation. For example, research has pointed to educators' varying perceptions about the relative credibility of students (McLeod, 2011), assumptions about the capacity and value of the perspectives of children with disability, the costs and (assumed) difficulties associated with enabling their participation, the potential for student perspectives to undermine teacher authority, and the assumption 'that they have no views to express; [or] . . . that their interests and experiences will always be best articulated by adult caretakers' (Byrne & Kelly, 2015, p. 197; see also Byrnes & Rickards, 2011). These assumptions are significant barriers to students' legislative and human right to be consulted on matters that impact them. Students with a disability that impacts communication are at particular risk of not being consulted.

Consulting Students with Communication Difficulties

Figures from Australia, the United Kingdom, and United States estimate that the prevalence of communication disability among school-aged students is around 10% (Black et al., 2015; McLeod & McKinnon, 2007; Norbury et al., 2016). This broad group can include—but is not restricted to—students with Developmental Language Disorder (DLD), speech sound disorder, hearing impairment, cerebral palsy, epilepsy, intellectual disability, and/or students on the autism spectrum. Australian educators are obligated as per the DSE to make reasonable adjustments *and* to consult these students about the adjustments prior to them being designed and implemented.

Students with communication difficulties may experience barriers in the consultation process (Tancredi, 2020). For example, consultative conversations require students to engage in high-level reflection, negotiation, and problem-solving. There is also a requirement to express ideas and opinions, prioritise and share information, and contribute to a plan of action or goal. The pace, linguistic complexity, level of complex and abstract content, and demands on working memory all represent possible barriers for a student with communication difficulties (Graham et al., 2018). Research shows that teachers are already less likely to consult students, because they are not adults, and their propensity to consult further decreases when students have a disability, especially one involving communication difficulties (McLeod, 2011). Similar arguments are made to justify the exclusion or lack of consultation with any student due to assumptions around their relative capacities and potential contribution (United Nations, 2009), however, teachers also report not having an adequate understanding of communication difficulties (Glasby et al., 2022). In practice, this may mean that teachers overestimate a student's communicative competence, may not anticipate or address barriers in the consultation process, and/or provide inadequate adjustment to the consultation process. The hidden nature of communication difficulties highlights the need for teachers to both *ask* students about the barriers they encounter, and to *use* that information to proactively design curriculum and assessment that is accessible to *all* (Tancredi, 2020). In the following section, we provide evidence-based suggestions to support teachers to meet their obligations to consult students with disability, with an emphasis on strategies that assist students with communication difficulties.

Approaches and Strategies for Student Consultation

Different situations will call for different approaches to student consultation, and some common examples are outlined in Table 13.2. While individual discussions or interviews are the most commonly adopted approach, focus groups can offer a naturalistic discussion platform for students to share their insights. A group situation will, however, require the facilitator to ensure that all students can contribute and have a genuine voice in the discussion. For students who have an established support network or team within their school, consultation may take place at regular intervals with members of the Student Support Team (SST). For each of these approaches to student consultation, additional strategies may be needed to ensure that students can genuinely engage in the process. The strategies discussed below have been shown to support students to engage in the process of consultation and share their thoughts and opinions.

These strategies can be used with all students, but they are particularly important for students with disability and communication difficulties. A first principle for any accessible consultation process, however, is accessible language.

Table 13.2 Example Approaches to Student Consultation

Approach	People Involved	Activity	Considerations
Interview	Student Interviewer A support person may be present for the student	Can comprise: • a set series of questions (a structured interview); • an open discussion (an unstructured interview); or • both structured questions and unstructured discussion (a semi-structured interview). • Interviews can combine both verbal interaction and multiple means of students constructing and sharing their message.	Interview should be transcribed verbatim to facilitate an objective record of what the student has shared. This reduces the risk that the student's words are paraphrased, and the student's intended meaning is diluted or changed.
Focus group	A group of six to eight students Facilitator(s)	An opportunity for discussion and innovative ideas that arises through interaction between the group members.	Strategies may need to be put in place to allow all students to have the opportunity to contribute.
Student Support Team (SST)	Student Parent(s) and/or caregiver(s) Educator(s) Case manager School principal or principal's delegate	• Student attends all meetings. • Student's perspective is foregrounded in the design and implementation of adjustments or decisions regarding education provision.	Student and their family are provided written feedback based on group discussions and action plans/ outcomes.

The Critical Importance of Accessible Language

Student consultation typically involves the use of written or spoken language. Most teachers are proficient language users, making it difficult for them to understand the inherent language demands of the curriculum and their own subject discipline and how this impacts their own teaching, as well as the assessments they create (see Chapters 10 and 11). As adult language users, teachers are also developmentally different to the students they teach. Mutual understanding is therefore affected by teachers' ability to match their vocabulary to their students' ages, as well as their socio-economic, cultural and language backgrounds. Given that students' responses are determined by the questions that are asked, it is essential for teachers to think carefully about the words and phrases they use to construct questions and frame consultative conversations. This is important because the challenges imposed by language are more subtle than they might appear.

For example, research with 96 students aged 9–16 years in Sydney, Australia found significant differences in the receptive and expressive vocabulary of students both *with* and *without* a history of behavioural difficulties (Graham et al., 2020). Anticipating that students in the behaviour difficulties group would *also* have difficulties with language, the researchers carefully developed a range of interview questions that would be accessible to all students. Most questions were short, concrete, and direct; however, a couple were not. Subsequent analyses found significant differences between groups both in terms of expressive vocabulary and in their responses to the different types of questions. For instance, in response to the question, "What do you think your teacher thinks of you?", students *with* a history of behavioural difficulties were significantly more likely to say something like, "I dunno, I don't ask them" than students *without* language and behavioural difficulties. The researchers had deliberately included this question even though they knew it was abstract, because it required "sophisticated linguistic reasoning in addition to the ability to compare one's perception of self in relation to the perceived perceptions of others" (Graham et al., 2020, p. 4). In other words, to answer this question students needed to interpret abstract language and impute mental states, then articulate that in a verbal response. Imputing mental states is a skill otherwise known as Theory of Mind, which is a less developed skill in students with disability affecting social communication, such as Autism. Notably, concrete questions such as "Do you like school?" and "What happened to make you start disliking school?" resulted in more definitive responses and fewer non-responses from this group of students (Graham et al., 2016). Using accessible language is a mandatory first step in consulting students with disability, but for students with communication difficulties, it will be insufficient on its own. For these students, a range of practical strategies can be employed.

Multiple Methods and Means of Participation/Engagement

While accessible language is critical to support genuine participation, language has its own limitations. This is where using multiple methods for engaging students in consultation can minimise the barriers imposed by language. To ensure that students can fully participate in consultation, we need to think about *how* students' views are sought, as this impacts *what* they say (Lyons et al., 2022). Carefully developed visual supports and activities can assist students to comprehend a consultative discussion and to articulate their thoughts (Lyons & Roulstone, 2018). The information generated can also provide non-verbal data, which is helpful when interpreting meaning for students with complex communication difficulties (Clarke et al., 2001). In addition to building rapport, the use of multiple methods and opportunities to consult students can improve the student's understanding of both the process and the questions raised during consultation. In some instances, the student may prefer to be interviewed by a person who acts as a broker of information between the student and their teacher. When used collaboratively, these approaches can help to build trust, address power imbalances, and ensure mutual understanding of the student's intended message (Merrick & Roulstone, 2011).

Visual Supports and Activities. Visual supports and activities provide a supplementary mode for both parties to communicate information in a consultative conversation. This is necessary because the information exchange that takes place in a verbal conversation is transient (for more on this topic, see Chapter 11). That is, once words are spoken, they must be comprehended quickly and accurately by the listener. If this process is disrupted, the listener may forget or misinterpret what has been said by their communication partner, which can impact the listener's response. Consultative conversations also require students to reflect on their experiences, share their opinions and express their views. The high-level and complex nature of this task risks students not understanding what has been asked, and students might not always have the vocabulary to explain the ideas they have. Visual supports and activities address both issues by providing a concrete, tangible addition to conversations, which can support all students to participate in consultation.

Visual supports can be pre-prepared (created ahead of the conversation) or produced in situ (created during the conversation). An example of a pre-prepared visual support is a list that uses text, images or a combination of text and images, which outlines options that are available for a task. When pre-prepared visual supports are used, it is important that students are given the opportunity to also contribute to the options that are available. This kind of visual aid can help students to understand the options that are available, support them to express their choice and facilitate brainstorming of other options. Drawing and mind-mapping are examples of visual aids that are created in situ. This strategy can help the student to organise and expand their thoughts by creating a static, visual record of ideas and insights. It can also enable the adult to clarify the student's ideas in real time and can help the student to expand their thinking (Tancredi, 2020).

Activities can include arts-based approaches and interactive tasks. In one study, Merrick and Roulstone (2011) encouraged students to share their experiences by giving an adult a tour of their school. During the tour, students took the adults to particular places and discussed events that were meaningful to them. Students were encouraged to take photos of places and objects during the tour. These pictures were then used as visual supports to prompt reflection and storytelling during the consultative conversation that followed. More recently in Queensland, Kucks and Hughes (2019) worked with young primary-school students to redesign their play spaces. Students were asked to create collages and models that represented their idea of a fun, sensory garden. In combination with the ideas suggested by the teaching team, these young students' suggestions were used by the educational landscaper to create a new play space. As these examples show, hands-on activities can enable all students to express their ideas and opinions.

Multiple Interviews. Asking students to share their stories requires the development of trust, as well as the active consideration and minimisation of power differentials (Lyons et al., 2022). Conducting multiple short interviews provides opportunities for trust and rapport to be built, thereby reducing the potential of a power imbalance between student and interviewer. Lyons and Roulstone (2018), for example, investigated the ways that students with speech, language, and communication difficulties constructed their identities, using a narrative-inquiry approach. By conducting five or six short, semi-structured interviews with each student, the interviewers built rapport which helped convince the students to trust the adults with their stories. Interviewing students on multiple occasions has other benefits as well. Through multiple interviews, students are provided with enough time and exposure to become familiar with the process of consultation, and students are provided multiple opportunities to share their insights.

Given that not all students will have had the experience of consultation, particularly in relation to things that happen at school, multiple interviews can also help students to understand the unique nature of consultative conversations. This strategy helps to increase the student's participation but also mitigates any potential biases that the interviewer may bring to the interview situation. This is particularly important for students with communication difficulties, as the student's intended message may be misinterpreted by the interviewer. For example, Tancredi (2020) interviewed students with language difficulties on two or three occasions about the adjustments that they believed helped them to learn. In the final interview, she asked students to prioritise their preferred adjustments by numbering their top three preferences (where 'one' indicated the most helpful adjustment). This process revealed that what the students said in initial interviews, and the frequency of discussion about a particular adjustment, did not necessarily match the student's stated level of preference for the adjustments used by their teachers.

Engaging an Impartial Information Broker. In some circumstances, the power relationship between students and teachers may make students reluctant to share their insights about what works for them at school with their teacher. Depending on the topic and situation, it may be inappropriate for a teacher to seek feedback from students about their own practice. This can place students in a difficult position, and they may withhold important feedback to protect their teacher's feelings. By engaging a trusted third party in the consultative process and having students' permission to feed their insights back to the teaching team, students may feel more comfortable about sharing their ideas and experiences (both positive and negative). This person may be another teacher, a school counsellor, a speech pathologist, or a specialist teacher. Alternatively, teachers can use anonymous classroom feedback systems, such as a suggestion box into which students can submit tips for what their teachers should keep doing, stop doing and start doing to further enhance students' learning.

Conclusion

All students have the right to an inclusive education and the right to express opinions. Internationally, these rights are provided through the UNCRC and the CRPD, and they represent a student-centred approach to education. For students with disability in Australia, additional protections exist, where teachers are obligated to provide reasonable adjustments and to consult students about the adjustments that are designed and implemented, as per the DSE. As we have discussed in this chapter, students who are placed at the centre of their education experience are active participants, are consulted on issues that affect them, and are positioned as agents who can contribute to decisions and processes that take place at school. When students have a genuine voice at school, they are developing the skills of a democratic citizen. Their unique insights and reflections are valuable sources of information, which may provide innovative and dynamic solutions or outcomes. Without careful attention to the consultation process, however, students may go unheard.

To maximise success, the consultation process must be well planned to ensure that students can understand the questions posed during consultation and express their true ideas and opinions. The approach also needs to be considered and chosen based on the situation and context. A range of evidence-based strategies exists to support all students to express their views. These strategies include visual supports and activities to support verbal interaction, as well as asking clear questions that students will be able to comprehend and respond to with ease. Engaging in multiple interviews with students and engaging a third party to support the transfer of information between students and teachers can provide a supportive environment for participation and engagement. Putting students at the centre is essential for student participation and wellbeing, but its success depends on the enactment of a planned and intentional process. This may seem like a lot of work to time-poor teachers and principals, but by consulting students about their education and responding to their voices, educators are both upholding their obligations and contributing to each student's personal and social development.

References

Australian Government Department of Education. (2020). *Review of the Disability Standards for Education 2005.* https://www.education.gov.au/disability-standards-education-2005/2020-review-disability-standards-education-2005

Australian Government Department of Education, Skills and Employment. (2019). *The Alice Springs (Mparntwe) Education Declaration.* https://www.education.gov.au/alice-springs-mparntwe-education-declaration/resources/alice-springs-mparntwe-education-declaration

Australian Institute for Teaching and School Leadership. (2018). *Australian Professional Standards for Teachers.* https://www.aitsl.edu.au/docs/default-source/teach-documents/australian-professional-standards-for-teachers.pdf

Black, L. I., Vahratian, A., & Hoffman, H. J. (2015). Communication disorders and use of intervention services among children aged 3–17 years: United States, 2012. *NCHS Data Brief, 205,* 1–8.

Byrne, B., & Kelly, B. (2015). Special issue: Valuing disabled children: Participation and inclusion. *Child Care in Practice, 21*(3), 197–200. https://doi.org/10.1080/13575279.2015.1051732

Byrnes, L. J., & Rickards, F. W. (2011). Listening to the voices of students with disabilities: Can such voices inform practice? *Australasian Journal of Special Education, 35*(1), 25–34. https://doi.org/10.1375/ajse.35.1.25

Cefai, C., & Cooper, P. (2010). Students without voices: The unheard accounts of secondary school students with social, emotional and behaviour difficulties. *European Journal of Special Needs Education, 25*(2), 183–198. https://doi.org/10.1080/08856251003658702

Clarke, M., McConachie, H., Price, K., & Wood, P. (2001). Views of young people using aug-mentative and alternative communication systems. *International Journal of Language & Communication Disorders, 36*(1), 107–115. https://doi.org/10.1080/13682820150217590

Cook-Sather, A. (2020). Student voice across contexts: Fostering student agency in today's schools. *Theory into Practice, 59*(2), 182–191.

Disability Discrimination Act 1992 (Cth).

Disability Standards for Education 2005 (Cth).

Gillett-Swan, J. K. (2022). *Student-driven school change: A practical guide for educators and other professionals.* The Centre for Inclusive Education. https://research.qut.edu.au/c4ie/wp-content/uploads/sites/281/2022/02/Practice-Guide-Student-Driven-School-Change.pdf

Gillett-Swan, J. K., & Graham, L. J. (2017). *Wellbeing matters: A collaborative approach to harnessing student voice to develop a Wellbeing Framework for Action in the middle years.* Department of Education (Queensland) Education Horizon Competitive Grant Scheme Project, ref: 2017000734

Gillett-Swan, J. K., Graham, L. J., Cayas, A., & Crisp, N. (2019). *A wellbeing framework for action to support student voice implementation in schools.* Queensland University of Technology. https://eprints.qut.edu.au/203858/

Gillett-Swan, J. K., & Lundy, L. (2022). Children, classrooms and challenging behaviour: Do the rights of the many outweigh the rights of the few? *Oxford Review of Education, 48*(1), 95–111. https://doi.org/10.1080/03054985.2021.1924653

Gillett-Swan, J., & Sargeant, J. (2018). Assuring children's human right to freedom of opinion and expression in education. *International Journal of Speech Language Pathology, 20*(1), 120–127. https://doi.org/10.1080/17549507.2018.1385852

Gillett-Swan, J. K., & Sargeant, J. (2019). Perils of perspective: Identifying adult confidence in the child's capacity, autonomy, power and agency (CAPA) in readiness for voice-inclusive practice. *Journal of Educational Change, 20*(3), 399–421. https://doi.org/10.1007/s10833-019-09344-4

Glasby, J., Graham, L. J., White, S. L., & Tancredi, H. (2022). Do teachers know enough about the characteristics and educational impacts of Developmental Language Disorder (DLD) to successfully include students with DLD?. *Teaching and Teacher Education, 119*, 103868. https://doi.org/10.1016/j.tate.2022.103868

Gonski, D., Arcus, T., Boston, K., Gould, V., Johnson, W., O'Brien, L., Perry, L., & Roberts, M. (2018). *Through growth to achievement: Report of the review to achieve educational excellence in Australian schools.* Australian Government Department of Education and Training. https://www.education.gov.au/quality-schools-package/resources/through-growth-achievement-report-review-achieve-educational-excellence-australian-schools

Government of Ireland. (2021). *National framework for children and young people's participation in decision-making.* https://www.gov.ie/en/publication/9128db-national-strategy-on-children-and-young-peoples-participation-in-dec/

Graham, L. J., Sweller, N., & Van Bergen, P. (2020). Do older children with disruptive behaviour exhibit positive illusory bias and should oral language competence be considered in research? *Educational Review (Birmingham), 72*(6), 752–769. https://doi.org/10.1080/00131911.2018.1549536

Graham, L. J., Tancredi, H., Willis, J., & McGraw, K. (2018). Designing out barriers to student access and participation in secondary school assessment. *Australian Educational Researcher, 45*(1), 103–124. https://doi.org/10.1007/s13384-018-0266-y

Graham, L. J., Van Bergen, P., & Sweller, N. (2016). Caught between a rock and a hard place: disruptive boys' views on mainstream and special schools in New South Wales, Australia. *Critical Studies in Education, 57*(1), 35–54. https://doi.org/10.1080/17508487.2016.1108209

Hanna, A. (2022). Silent epistemologies: Theorising children's participation rights. *International Journal of Children's Rights*. Advance online publication. https://doi.org/10.1163/15718182-30040003

Kucks, A., & Hughes, H. (2019). Creating a sensory garden for early years learners: Participatory designing for student wellbeing. In H. Hughes, J. Franz, & J. Willis (Eds.), *School spaces for student wellbeing and learning* (pp. 221–238). Springer.

Lundy, L. (2007). "Voice" is not enough: Conceptualising Article 12 of the United Nations Convention on the Rights of the Child. *British Educational Research Journal, 33*(6), 927–942. https://doi.org/10.1080/01411920701657033

Lundy, L. (2018). In defence of tokenism? Implementing children's right to participate in collective decision-making. *Childhood, 25*(3), 340–354. https://doi.org/10.1177/0907568218777292

Lyons, R., Carroll, C., Gallagher, A., Merrick, R., & Tancredi, H. (2022). Understanding the perspectives of children and young people with speech, language and communication needs: How qualitative research can inform practice. *International Journal of Speech Language Pathology, 24*(5), 547–557. https://doi.org/10.1080/17549507.2022.2038669

Lyons, R., & Roulstone, S. (2018). Listening to the voice of children with developmental speech and language disorders using narrative inquiry: Methodological considerations. *Journal of Communication Disorders, 72*, 16–25. https://doi.org/10.1016/j.jcomdis.2018.02.006

McLeod, S. (2011). Listening to children and young people with speech, language and communication needs: Who, why and how? In S. Roulstone & S. McLeod (Eds.), *Listening to children and young people with speech, language and communication needs* (pp. 23–40). J and R Press.

McLeod, S., & McKinnon, D. H. (2007). Prevalence of communication disorders compared with other learning needs in 14,500 primary and secondary school students. *International Journal of Language & Communication Disorders, 42*(S1), 37–59. https://doi.org/10.1080/13682820601173262

Merrick, R., & Roulstone, S. (2011). Children's views of communication and speech-language pathology. *International Journal of Speech Language Pathology, 13*(4), 281–290. https://doi.org/10.3109/17549507.2011.577809

Ministerial Council on Education, Employment, Training and Youth Affairs. (2008). *Melbourne Declaration on Educational Goals for Young Australians.* http://www.curriculum.edu.au/verve/_resources/National_Declaration_on_the_Educational_Goals_for_Young_Australians.pdf

Norbury, C. F., Gooch, D., Wray, C., Baird, G., Charman, T., Simonoff, E., Vamvakas, G., & Pickles, A. (2016). The impact of nonverbal ability on prevalence and clinical presentation of language disorder: Evidence from a population study. *Journal of Child Psychology and Psychiatry, 57*(11), 1247–1257. https://doi.org/10.1111/jcpp.12573

Quinn, S., & Owen, S. (2016). Digging deeper: Understanding the power of 'student voice'. *The Australian Journal of Education, 60*(1), 60–72. https://doi.org/10.1177/0004944115626402

Royal Commission into Violence, Abuse, Neglect and Exploitation of People with Disability. (2022). *Public Hearing 24 transcript of proceedings.* https://disability.royalcommission.gov.au/system/files/2022-06/Transcript%20Day%201%20-%20Public%20hearing%2024%2C%20Canberra.pdf

Rudduck, J., & Fielding, M. (2006). Student voice and the perils of popularity: The potential of listening to pupils. *Educational Review, 58*(2), 219–231. https://doi.org/10.1080/00131910600584207

Saggers, B. R., Klug, D., Harper-Hill, K., Ashburner, J., Costley, D., Clark, T., Bruck, S., Trembath, D., Webster, A. A., & Carrington, S. B. (2016). *Australian autism educational needs analysis: What are the needs of schools, parents and students on the autism spectrum?*. Cooperative Research Centre for Living with Autism. https://www.autismcrc.com.au/sites/default/files/inline-files/Educational%20Needs%20Analysis%20-%20Final%20report%20Version%202.pdf

Sargeant, J., & Gillett-Swan, J. K. (2019). Voice-Inclusive Practice (VIP): A charter for authentic student engagement. *The International Journal of Children's Rights, 2019*(1), 122–139. https://doi.org/10.1163/15718182-02701002

Tancredi, H. (2020). Meeting obligations to consult students with disability: Methodological considerations and successful elements for consultation. *Australian Educational Researcher, 47*(2), 201–217. https://doi.org/10.1007/s13384-019-00341-3

United Nations. (1948). *Universal Declaration of Human Rights*. https://www.un.org/en/universal-declaration-human-rights

United Nations. (1989). *Convention on the Rights of the Child*. https://www.ohchr.org/sites/default/files/crc.pdf

United Nations. (2006). *Convention on the Rights of Persons with Disabilities (CRPD)*. https://www.un.org/disabilities/documents/convention/convoptprot-e.pdf.

United Nations. (2009). *General Comment No. 12: The Right of the Child to be Heard (CRC/C/GC/12)*. https://www2.ohchr.org/english/bodies/crc/docs/AdvanceVersions/CRC-C-GC-12.pdf

United Nations. (2016). *General Comment No. 4, Article 24: Right to Inclusive Education (CRPD/C/GC/4)*. https://digitallibrary.un.org/record/1313836?ln=en

United Nations. (2018). *General Comment No. 7, Article 4.3 and 33.3: Participation of Persons with Disabilities, including Children with Disabilities, through their Representative Organizations, in the Implementation and Monitoring of the Convention (CRPD/C/GC/7)*. https://documents-dds-ny.un.org/doc/UNDOC/GEN/G18/336/54/PDF/G1833654.pdf?OpenElement

Chapter 14

What is Social and Emotional Learning (SEL) and why is it important?

Melissa Close, Callula Killingly, Amy S. Gaumer-Erickson, and Patricia M. Noonan

There is a growing understanding of the need for schools to provide more than just academic instruction to prepare students for life during and beyond the school years (Organisation for Economic Co-operation and Development [OECD], 2018; Weissberg et al., 2015). Young people today are faced with rapid and profound social, economic, and environmental changes from globalisation and advancements in technology (OECD, 2018), which have caused significant shifts in knowledge, skills, and the information environment (Graham et al., 2017). With the steep rise in mental health challenges in recent years (Brennan et al., 2021), young people are at increased risk of poor educational outcomes, such as lower academic performance, absenteeism, school drop-out, interpersonal challenges, unemployment, substance abuse, and self-harm and suicide (Lawrence et al., 2015). Schooling can itself be a source of anxiety for young people due to the marginalisation of difference, along with increases in both traditional and cyber bullying, as well as practices that promote competition and comparison, which together create hierarchies of student worth (Chapters 13 and 15).

Given increasing recognition that mental health and wellbeing is both protective of and indivisible from academic achievement and behavioural development, schools are expected to also attend to students' mental health and wellbeing. This can be achieved through implementation of Multi-Tiered Systems of Support (MTSS), a framework that considers the whole child through equal focus on all three developmental domains: academic, social-emotional, and behavioural (see Chapter 9). Social and emotional learning (SEL) is a key practice within the social-emotional domain in MTSS. SEL is an approach through which students are explicitly taught the skills they need to understand and manage their emotions, show empathy for others, establish positive relationships, and make responsible decisions (Collaborative for Academic, Social, and Emotional Learning [CASEL], 2023a; Meyers et al., 2019; Zins et al., 2004). The empirical evidence suggests that SEL not only improves students' social and emotional development, wellbeing, and academic outcomes, but also prevents and reduces mental health and behavioural challenges (Durlak et al., 2011; Sklad et al., 2012; Taylor et al., 2017; Wigelsworth et al., 2016).

SEL and Its Origins

Although research on social and emotional learning has been progressing since the late 1960s, led by foundational work emanating from the United States (e.g., Comer,

DOI: 10.4324/9781003350897-17

1980; Weissberg et al., 1981), the term Social and Emotional Learning (SEL) was first introduced in 1994 by a group of researchers, educators, and child advocates, as a strategy to support the psychological, developmental, academic, and general wellbeing needs of children (Elias et al., 1997). In the same year, the Collaborative for Academic, Social, and Emotional Learning (CASEL) was established. CASEL is an organisation aimed at advancing evidence based SEL as an essential part of preschool to high school education in the United States. In its most widely applied definition (CASEL, 2023a), SEL is described as:

> an integral part of education and human development. SEL is the process through which all young people and adults acquire and apply the knowledge, skills, and attitudes to develop healthy identities, manage emotions and achieve personal and collective goals, feel and show empathy for others, establish and maintain supportive relationships, and make responsible and caring decisions.

Developing students' capacity in SEL competencies is most effectively achieved through high quality instruction and student-centred learning environments (CASEL, 2023a), within school and classroom cultures and climates that are safe, supportive, well-managed, and participatory (Zins et al., 2004). Such environments encourage students' thoughts, feelings, and voice, and highlight the positive contribution students can have towards their school, family, and communities (Weissberg et al., 2015). Systemic schoolwide SEL begins at the classroom and school levels and is enhanced through partnerships with families and community members, and the support of local, state, and federal governments (Meyers et al., 2012).

Reform progress for systemic, evidence based SEL is most advanced in the United States, largely due to the sustained efforts of CASEL (Bowles et al., 2017). CASEL has also played a leadership role in strengthening international interest in schoolwide SEL. In addition to expanding the science of SEL, the organisation has established best-practice guidelines for implementing evidence-based programs in the United States, while further influencing broader SEL-related efforts within other international jurisdictions. For example, several countries, including Australia, the United Kingdom, Canada, and Japan, have put forward national initiatives to improve the wellbeing of school students through the expansion of their own SEL programs and frameworks. Today, SEL is recognised as a global priority that continues to gain momentum worldwide (Collie et al., 2017).

A Framework for Systemic SEL in Education

CASEL's framework presents the parameters of a systemic approach to SEL (Weissberg et al., 2015). According to the framework, SEL encompasses five competencies, spanning cognitive, affective, and behavioural domains. These include self-awareness, self-management, social awareness, relationship skills, and responsible decision making.

- *Self-awareness* refers to the ability to recognise one's emotions, goals, and values. This includes understanding one's strengths and limitations, having a positive mindset, and a good sense of self-efficacy. It also involves understanding how thoughts, feelings, and behaviours are interconnected.

- *Self-management* is the capacity to effectively regulate one's emotions and behaviours. This includes the ability to manage stress, control impulses, delay gratification, and persist through challenges to achieve personal and educational goals.
- *Social awareness* involves the ability to take the perspective of, and to empathise, with others from diverse cultures and backgrounds. Competence in this domain also includes understanding social norms for behaviour, and recognising external resources and supports in family, school, and community.
- *Relationship skills* refers to the ability to form and maintain high quality relationships through clear communication, active listening, cooperation, and negotiation. It also involves resisting inappropriate social pressure and seeking and offering help when required.
- *Responsible decision making* is the ability to make respectful and constructive choices about personal behaviour and social interactions. Making responsible decisions also reflects one's ability to consider ethical standards, social norms, consequences, and the wellbeing of oneself and others.

Students' proficiency in the five competencies is foundational to achieving short- and long-term attitudinal and behavioural outcomes. In addition to the five competencies, these outcomes are further supported through the implementation of systemic schoolwide SEL that considers the various contexts and relationships in which students live and learn (Weissberg et al., 2015). This means that SEL should be promoted through daily classroom practices, conducted schoolwide, provide opportunities to include family and community members, and be adequately supported by the broader systems in which schools operate, such as local, state, and federal government (Oberle et al., 2016). SEL competencies can also be informally developed through student-centred interpersonal interactions between adults and students throughout the school day (Weissberg et al., 2015). This means nurturing positive student-teacher relationships that allow students to feel safe, valued, engaged, and challenged as learners (see Chapter 16). Such contexts enhance opportunities for teachers to model and embody social-emotional competencies and promote skills in students that can mitigate against the effects of stress, adversity, and trauma (Osher et al., 2020).

At the school level, SEL should be delivered through policies, practices, and structures that promote a safe and supportive school climate, and a culture that positively affects students' academic, behavioural, and mental health outcomes (Meyers et al., 2019). A positive school environment starts with developing clear social, emotional, and behavioural norms, values, and expectations for all students and staff (Oberle et al., 2016). It also involves establishing inclusive and equitable discipline policies, anti-bullying practices that provide students with opportunities to effectively manage conflict and repair relationships, and high quality professional learning opportunities for teachers and staff (Weissberg et al., 2015). SEL-focused professional learning should include enhancing theoretical understandings, pedagogical capacity, personal social-emotional competence, and access to ongoing feedback to improve practice (Patti et al., 2015).

Finally, SEL is most successful when implemented and sustained through priorities that align with and are supported by local, state, and federal governments. At the local level, SEL is facilitated through leadership that communicates a vision of SEL, partnerships with stakeholders to cultivate organisational support towards SEL, and advocates for policies, practices, and supports the provision of systemic SEL (Mart et al., 2015). The state and federal levels play a broader role in the ecological context of SEL and are the foundation for advancing evidence-based interventions. These levels shape what is prioritised in schools through defining age-appropriate learning standards and setting expectations for student outcomes across different learning areas (Dusenbury et al., 2015; Oberle et al., 2016; Weissberg et al., 2015). Federal and state policies that provide clear goals and developmental standards are foundational to the implementation of evidence-based interventions, SEL-related professional learning opportunities for teachers and staff, and assessment to monitor students' progress (Dusenbury et al., 2015).

Benefits of SEL

Social and emotional competency is predictive of a range of positive outcomes, such as enhanced wellbeing, increased prosocial behaviours, increased school engagement, and better academic performance (Durlak et al., 2011; Dix et al., 2020; Yang et al., 2018). Social and emotional skills serve an important protective function (Domitrovich et al., 2017; Taylor et al., 2017), being associated with reduced involvement in violence and bullying (Polan et al., 2013), and fewer behavioural problems (Durlak et al., 2011). Conversely, lower competency in this area is associated with negative impacts across the lifetime, such as poorer employment outcomes, increased risky behaviour, and involvement with the justice system (Hessler & Katz, 2010; Jones et al., 2015).

Importantly, social and emotional skills can be taught and enhanced with extensive research highlighting the short- and long-term benefits of programs targeting competencies across interpersonal, intrapersonal, and cognitive domains (Durlak et al., 2011; Mertens et al., 2022; Pandey et al., 2018). Analogous to a public health approach, where population level intervention is undertaken to mitigate risk of disease, universal approaches to building SEL skills reduce the need for more intensive intervention by taking a proactive, preventative approach to supporting students' social-emotional learning (Greenberg et al., 2017). Beyond individual student outcomes, there is mounting evidence that implementation of SEL programs shapes the climate of the school and classroom itself and promotes positive relationships between teachers and students (Brown et al., 2010; Charlton et al., 2021). Given variation in children's skills and developmental trajectories and the beneficial impacts of social-emotional learning, the provision of universal school based SEL programs can serve to 'level the playing field', providing more equitable educational and life outcomes for all children.

Several meta-analyses have been conducted in recent years to investigate the effectiveness of universal school based SEL programs, commencing with the foundational work of Durlak et al. (2011), which included studies conducted between 1955 to 2007. This meta-analysis examined 213 programs, ranging from kindergarten through to the end of high school, and included a total of 270,034 students. Results showed that not only did SEL programs enhance students' social-emotional skills, as compared to the skills of non-participating students, but these programs also promoted widespread improvements across behavioural outcomes, manifesting in increased prosocial behaviours, reduced conduct problems, and improved academic outcomes, as reflected in an 11-percentile gain in standardised test results across a subset of the programs. These positive impacts, while reduced in magnitude, were sustained when followed up six or more months following the program's implementation.

Similarly beneficial findings have been produced in subsequent meta-analyses, including analysis of short-term impacts (Wigelsworth et al., 2016) and those which show that the benefits of SEL programs appear to be sustained over time (Sklad et al., 2012; Taylor et al., 2017). Taylor and colleagues' (2017) meta-analysis of follow-up outcomes in 82 interventions found significant effects of SEL programs on multiple indicators, measured on average between 1.1 years and 3.75 years after program implementation. Participation in SEL programs enhanced SEL skills and attitudes, academic performance, and positive behaviour, while simultaneously reducing the likelihood of subsequent substance use, emotional distress, and conduct problems, thereby conferring protection against negative outcomes. Importantly, the strongest predictor of wellbeing at follow-up was the extent to which students had gained social-emotional skills following program implementation.

The wide array of benefits offered by SEL programs is thus well-established with research shifting to a focus on what factors drive the success of program effectiveness (Lawson et al., 2019). In their meta-analysis of 89 studies, Wigelsworth et al. (2016) found evidence for the positive effects of SEL programs on student outcomes, but the main focus of their analysis was the potential reasons differentiating effective and ineffective programs, such as stage of evaluation, involvement of program developers, and whether the programs were conducted in the country where they had been developed. SEL programs are developed within particular cultural contexts; hence, transferring programs to other countries can result in reduced effectiveness (Wigelsworth et al., 2016). It is therefore critically important to evaluate how successful evidence-based programs originating from the United States, for example, may be adapted to better suit the cultural context of Australian schools, and for research to monitor the effectiveness of these programs.

SEL in Australia

While attention to students' social and emotional development in Australian schools has increased in recent years, SEL is still in its infancy with education systems tending to focus on and direct resources to behaviour management, principally through Positive Behaviour Intervention Supports (PBIS), even when implementation of MTSS and SEL has specifically been recommended to address increases in the use of exclusionary discipline (Graham et al., 2020; Graham et al., 2022). PBIS has already been widely used in Australian schools to foster positive student behaviour and reduce the incidence of challenging behaviours (Poed & Whitefield, 2020). PBIS places emphasis on the creation of safe and supportive learning environments through the setting of clear expectations, providing positive reinforcement, and offering supportive corrective feedback to students (Horner & Sugai, 2015). Despite sharing similar features, such as creating a safe and supportive learning environment, the explicit goals of PBIS and SEL differ (Bear et al., 2015). PBIS is primarily aimed at promoting positive behaviour, while the SEL framework has a broader focus on empowering students and promoting equitable outcomes through explicit teaching of the critical skills and competencies students need to navigate the world effectively. The two approaches are therefore complementary, although SEL is not subordinate to PBIS, for it helps children to develop the competencies necessary for children and young people to successfully respond to behavioural expectations.

Since 2010, the importance of developing students' social-emotional competencies with academic learning has been recognised in the Australian Curriculum through the inclusion of the Personal and Social Capability strand in the General Capabilities (Gilbert, 2019). Four of the five core competencies outlined by CASEL are incorporated in the Personal and Social Capability strand, including self-awareness, self-management, social awareness, and social management (also referred to as relationship skills; Australian Curriculum, Assessment and Reporting Authority [ACARA], 2023). The final competency, responsible decision-making, is not included as a separate competency, and is instead integrated as a subset of the social management domain. Unlike literacy, which is assessed through four of the five domains in the National Assessment Program in Literacy and Numeracy (NAPLAN), competencies within the Personal and Social Capability strand are not assessed, which in the busy lives of schools can also mean that they are not taught.

While the General Capabilities section of the Australian Curriculum is widely accepted by educators (Donnelly & Wiltshire, 2014), the matrix approach to curriculum design presents certain limitations. The matrix approach, which aims to incorporate the General Capabilities (e.g., Literacy, and Personal and Social Capabilities) into different subject areas, is perceived to make curriculum planning more complex, and the linking of capabilities to subject areas something of a 'forced process', rendering these capabilities to the status of afterthought (Gilbert, 2019). Skourdoumbis (2016) found, in his study of four secondary schools, that while most teachers were familiar with the General Capabilities, their understanding of them was not always thorough. The study also revealed that teachers were not consistent in incorporating the General Capabilities into their planning and instruction. This was particularly pronounced when teachers felt that the capabilities did not have an immediate connection to subject learning raising concerns around the extent to which social and emotional competencies are being effectively addressed in the taught curriculum.

Despite various initiatives aimed at promoting student mental health and wellbeing in Australia, many schools face challenges in implementing policies, practices, cultures, and resources to support students' social and emotional wellbeing and development (Powell & Graham, 2017). The diverse provision of educational services by states and territories, as well as government and non-government organisations, has led to a proliferation of policies and practices governing student mental health and wellbeing (Laurens et al., 2022). This has left schools with a lot of flexibility, but also the burden of navigating a wide range of programs and services. While schools should have flexibility to choose mental health and wellbeing programs appropriate to their cultural and contextual needs, the large number of programs available can be overwhelming for educators who do not have the time or research knowledge to intentionally select evidence-based programs (Humphrey, 2013; Laurens et al., 2022).

Consequently, the need for a 'hub' of evidence-based programs that can be enacted in Australian schools has been identified, like what is available in the United States through CASEL's Program Guide (CASEL, 2023b; Laurens et al., 2022). One of the main sources of information about SEL programs for Australian school leaders is *Be You*, a national directory of programs and information, across all schooling levels; however, this collection is not restricted to programs with evidence of effectiveness (Laurens et al., 2022). A review of over 200 school-based mental health and wellbeing programs available in the *Be You* directory revealed that a majority of the programs (56%) had a low-quality evidence base (Dix et al., 2020), in which a theoretical framework for the approach was presented, yet there were no published studies examining whether the program was effective. The same authors also conducted a meta-analysis of 75 international intervention research studies examining effective student wellbeing in schools and their academic outcomes (Dix et al., 2020). Of the studies included in the review, only one was conducted in Australia, indicating the scarcity of high-quality research on SEL programs within Australian schools. Moreover, only two of the programs listed on the *Be You* website were evaluated in this meta-analysis with the remainder of the 200+ programs considered to lack "sufficient quality of evidence" to merit inclusion (Dix et al., 2020, p. 5).

Laurens et al. (2022) conducted a survey of 598 NSW primary school principals from both government and non-government schools to investigate and assess the range of school-based mental health programs being adopted in Australia's most populous state. Programs targeting SEL competencies were implemented by nearly 60% of the principals surveyed, albeit these programs had varying degrees of evidence behind them. Of the 569 programs delivered across the different schools, 33.6% were found to have little or no supporting evidence. Only 57.2% of the programs provided the formal structure and facilitation instructions requisite to effective implementation or provided opportunities for students to practise at least four of the five competencies specified by CASEL (self-awareness, self-management, social awareness, social management, and responsible decision making). These results indicate both inconsistencies and deficiencies in the implementation of evidence-based programs in Australia.

There are increasing calls to address this implementation gap within Australian schools. The promotion of social and emotional development in school children was identified as a priority area for reform in the recent *Productivity Commission Inquiry into*

Mental Health Report (Productivity Commission, 2020), in which it was recommended that student wellbeing be placed on an equal footing with literacy and numeracy with clear, measurable outcome targets and measures to ensure accountability. It was also recommended in the report that national guidelines be developed for the accreditation of social-emotional learning programs for implementation in schools. The report of the *National Children's Mental Health Strategy* (National Mental Health Commission, 2021) similarly calls for the delivery of evidence-based mental health and wellbeing programs within schools, specifically articulating the need for psychosocial supports and programs that "support healthy peer relationships" and "assist with the prevention of bullying and racism" (p. 75). Another priority action specified in the report relates to the need to collect student wellbeing data as an accountability measure and to inform best practice. Implementation evaluation was also recommended to be "a core component of programs delivered in schools and early childhood learning settings to identify what is required to ensure fidelity" (p. 13).

Most recently, the final report from the Productivity Commission's (2023) *Review of the National School Reform Agreement* further highlighted the need for teacher training in the implementation of SEL curriculum. The report also noted the confusion arising from overlapping and unclear wellbeing policies, in addition to recommending that student wellbeing become a key priority area in the next *National School Reform Agreement*. These reports and the evident gaps in research and practice underscore the need for effectively monitored, evidence-based SEL programs, implemented with fidelity and with appropriate training to foster positive social-emotional development and wellbeing in Australian schools.

Implementing SEL Within the Context of MTSS

High quality SEL instruction and supports are best implemented through MTSS, a framework that simultaneously addresses academic, social-emotional, and behavioural domains (see Chapter 9). MTSS is a tiered framework, providing universal supports for all students (Tier 1) and more targeted, intensive supports as required (Tier 2 and 3). SEL delivered through MTSS includes the following critical elements: curriculum, instruction, assessment, data-based decision making, collaboration, and family engagement. All six elements are addressed and overseen by a leadership committee that works to continually improve implementation and student outcomes.

Curriculum Delivered Through a Tiered Approach

To reach all students, SEL competency instruction should be provided within and as part of core classroom instruction at Tier 1. Tier 1 refers to instruction and support provided to *all* students, and not simply supports that are available to students through elective or related services. As students demonstrate differing responsiveness to core instruction in social and emotional competencies, the provision of support can be intensified based on need, with more targeted support provided at Tiers 2 and 3. Student movement between tiers of support should be fluid and seamless with decisions regarding levels of needed supports based upon multiple sources of data.

As schools begin implementing systematic SEL instruction, focus should be on delivering effective Tier 1 instruction with high feedback and ample reinforcement. A structured curriculum with clear learning targets, formative measures, family-engagement mechanisms, and scenario-based activities is necessary for consistent schoolwide instruction that yields positive student outcomes. This curriculum must be evidence-based and appropriate for the student population. CASEL provides guidelines on their website for evaluating the quality of SEL curricula (2023b). For SEL to be effective, alignment between the different tiers is critical, as well as across different grade levels (Weissberg et al., 2015). When tiers are well-aligned, students receive the support they need at the right time, based on their individual needs and progress. Such an approach helps to create a supportive learning environment that fosters students' social-emotional development and enhances their overall academic success. In addition, aligned tiers and grades make it easier for teachers to implement SEL instruction in a way that is consistent with students' developmental needs across the school years (Jackson et al., 2021).

Instruction

SEL is delivered through instructional approaches that are developmentally and culturally appropriate and which provide ongoing and consistent opportunities for students to build and reinforce social-emotional competence and positive behaviours (Hecht & Shin, 2015; Rimm-Kaufman & Hulleman, 2015). SEL skills can be taught through direct instruction (e.g., evidence-based intervention programs), as well as through infused integration into core academic subjects. The former is notably the main approach by which schools are choosing to deliver SEL and is supported by an extensive body of evidence (e.g., Durlak et al., 2011). As an example of the latter, an English lesson may provide opportunities for students to engage in SEL by drawing on the experiences of characters, through being directed to consider and explore the relationships, emotions, and behaviours presented in the text (Oberle et al., 2016; Zins et al., 2004).

For SEL to be effective, educators need a shared understanding of the specific competencies being taught (e.g., assertiveness, conflict management, self-efficacy, self-regulation, or responsible decision-making). Educators then need to determine context-specific application opportunities for these skills in an environment that includes constructive feedback. For example, for students to learn self-efficacy, it is important that the adults in the school have a common understanding of this competency, as well as knowledge of specific research-based strategies to support students' self-efficacy development. Educators explicitly teach and prompt students to apply these strategies and thereby increase students' confidence in their abilities. Example self-efficacy strategies include viewing mistakes as essential to the learning process, remembering past successes when facing a challenging task, and focusing on growth over time rather than making comparisons to others (Heger et al., 2022).

Assessment

There are numerous formative methods to measure students' growth in intrapersonal and interpersonal SEL skills. These include the assessment of students' perceptions, knowledge, skills, performance, and outcomes. According to the *CASEL Assessment Guide* (CASEL, 2023c), the most common type of SEL assessment is self-report, prompting students to reflect on their application of, for example, assertiveness and conflict management practices, and their use of intrapersonal strategies in self-efficacy and self-regulation. The triangulation of assessment data is necessary when determining tertiary and intensive supports, analysing the effectiveness of universal instruction and prioritising students' practice opportunities with constructive feedback.

Perception measures assess whether students are increasing their self-awareness and accurately analysing their own social-emotional development. After students have thoroughly learned a competency, they are better able to critically appraise their behaviours; therefore, perception measures should not be used for pre/post comparisons. Instead, the primary purpose of questionnaires should be to promote student reflection and guide practice opportunities and feedback.

Knowledge measures are curriculum-based and focus on the specific competency being taught. These measures help educators determine students' prior knowledge and their gains in knowledge. Knowledge assessments show whether students understand the concepts, but they do not measure students' application of their knowledge.

Skills measures provide an assessment of whether students are increasing their skills by demonstrating specific social-emotional learning strategies. Skills can be measured through situational judgement assessments in which students are asked to determine the best course of action in specific situations.

Performance-based measures are used to assess application of skills and can be completed by the student or the teacher. For students, these measures may look like a reflection, for example, asking them which self-efficacy strategies they applied in association with a challenging academic task (Noonan et al., 2021). Teachers complete performance-based observations for which they rate each student's intrapersonal or interpersonal behaviours based on observations across time or in specific situations.

Outcome measures provide an indication of the impact of students' social and emotional learning in other areas. Schools collect numerous indicators of academic and social-emotional behaviours. For example, a research-based outcome of learning self-regulation is that students improve their overall school performance (Dignath et al., 2008; Gaumer Erickson & Noonan, 2022), but to measure this impact, specific short-term and long-term indicators should be monitored. Schoolwide long-term indicators include grade point average, suspension/exclusion rates, graduation rates, and post-school outcomes. Proximal outcomes include attendance, reduction in tardiness, on-time assignment submission, and improved regulation of emotional reactions resulting in reduced office disciplinary referrals. Teachers can also monitor students' effective use of class time, quality of work, engagement in collaborative learning, and demonstration of learning through tests and projects.

Table 14.1 outlines some commonly used strength-based assessment tools that assess SEL competencies and monitor the effectiveness of interventions and growth in skills over time. These measures include self-report assessments for older students where developmentally appropriate (i.e., Grade 3 or above), or teacher- or parent-rated measures, or measures that allow triangulation of responses across all three. Schools should consider factors such as cost, administrative and analytic capabilities, scalability, and reporting requirements when selecting a suitable assessment tool. Additionally, it is important for schools to acknowledge the various terms used to depict SEL competencies, particularly in relation to how they align with Personal and Social Capabilities.

Data-Based Decision Making

Effective data-based decision making is not a singular event. It is a continuous, but not necessarily linear, cycle. There are four phases of the data-based decision-making cycle: (i) gathering or collecting data; (ii) analysing, interpreting, and discussing data; (iii) planning improvement; and (iv) enacting change and monitoring progress. As teachers develop and deliver competency instruction, they gather data to determine the impact of instruction, refine their instruction, and identify ways to continually reinforce

Table 14.1 Example Assessment Tools to Measure Students' SEL Competencies

Name of Assessment Tool	Grade Level/Age Range	Respondent Format	Competencies Addressed	Time	Source
The Social Skills Improvement System Rating Forms (SSIS SEL Rating Forms) – Student	Grades 3–12	Student self-report	Self-awareness, self-management, social awareness, relationship skills, responsible decision-making	10–15 min	Gresham et al., 2020
Devereux Student Strengths Assessment (DESSA)	Grades K–8	Teacher/staff, Family	Decision-making, goal-directed behaviour, optimistic thinking, personal responsibility, relationship skills, self-awareness, self-management, social awareness, and social-emotional composite	10 min or less	LeBuffe et al., 2014
Social-Emotional Assets and Resilience Scales (SEARS)	Ages 5–18 years	Multi-informant: Child/ adolescent self-report, Teacher, Parent	Self-regulation, responsibility, social competence, and empathy	20 min	Merrell, 2011

learning. This same cycle can be used to increase competency instruction schoolwide by determining common data points and continually improving a collaborative culture of data-based decision-making regarding students' competency development. Data-based decision making is an ongoing process of gathering, interpreting, and sharing data to understand trends and inform decisions. The use of data guides improvements at all levels of the education system from data regarding the instructional needs for a single student to schoolwide data that inform Tier 1 universal instruction.

Collaboration

When a school adopts SEL curriculum, teachers, counsellors, special educators, related service providers, and administrators learn common instructional practices often through ongoing professional development and coaching. Each educator, regardless of their role, learns how to teach specific strategies and provide practice with feedback for students. SEL is also incorporated into other initiatives and systems, such as schoolwide disciplinary protocols or behaviour expectations. All students benefit from this instruction and guided practice. Through collaboration, data are gathered, interpreted, and shared to understand trends and inform important decisions. In this process, educators, administrators, and other stakeholders use data to collaboratively set goals and create plans to enact change and monitor progress (see Chapter 18). Instruction and practice are then systematised into ongoing classroom activities, becoming a standard way of work and a part of daily school life. SEL becomes fully embedded in school culture, and parents and community members are aware of and included in a common vision.

Family Engagement in SEL

Family and community partnerships strengthen SEL through extending learning to the home and neighbourhood. Families may not be able to support their children in learning advanced content, but throughout their child's education, they continue to be the primary guides for their children's development of intrapersonal and interpersonal skills (Chapter 17). Families can foster students' SEL by modelling and engaging in effective parenting strategies, including through promoting appropriate behaviours, positive relationships, clear and consistent boundaries, and structure and routine (Garbacz et al., 2015). Families can also be instrumental in schoolwide competency development efforts. Community members can support SEL through affording opportunities for students to refine and apply social-emotional skills within diverse environments, such as during after-school activities and through community programs and events (Fagan et al., 2015; Garbacz et al., 2015).

Examples of SEL Implementation Within MTSS

The following section provides three examples of how SEL can be implemented using MTSS. The first example demonstrates how SEL can be universally integrated into academic instruction at Tier 1, after which fictionalised exemplars are then provided to illustrate how targeted supports can be provided at Tiers 2 and 3.

Tier 1 SEL: Lesson plan

The exemplar lesson plan, as seen in Table 14.2, shows the integration of SEL into academic instruction at Tier 1. The lesson structure draws on multiple frameworks, including the Gradual Release of Responsibility (GRR) model (Fisher & Frey, 2008). The GRR model is effective in informing lesson plans related to SEL because it provides a structured approach to student development and transfer of responsibility. The model starts with teacher-led instruction ('I do'), followed by collaborative learning ('we do'), and concludes with student-led independent work ('you do'). In addition to the GRR model, the lesson structure also draws on the SEL-integrated lesson plan template outlined in the *CASEL Guide to Schoolwide SEL* (CASEL, 2023d), while also integrating the Personal and Social Capabilities in the Australian Curriculum (ACARA, 2023).

The SEL-integrated lesson plan begins by articulating both the academic and social-emotional goals for the lesson, which correspond with the learning standards outlined in Version 9.0 of the Australian Curriculum. While not all content descriptions across all learning areas directly address Personal and Social Capabilities, teachers can still foster these skills throughout the teaching and learning process. Teachers can also highlight SEL-related goals that reflect the social-emotional demands of the tasks students will perform during the lesson. For example, activities and experiences such as pair or group work, turn-taking, and class discussions promote SEL competencies including self-management, relationship skills, and responsible decision making.

Further to articulating appropriate academic and social-emotional goals, the lesson plan considers several teaching strategies that have been widely recognised and commonly used across a range of SEL programs (American Institute of Research, 2023; CASEL, 2023d). In the 'opening' stage of the lesson, students are instructed to work in pairs and reflect on how they plan to communicate and collaborate with each other. This step establishes the foundation for cooperative structures that foster interdependence, as students contribute individually and negotiate terms to complete the task. As the lesson progresses, cooperative learning is reinforced, particularly during the 'we do' stage, where students engage in dialogue in their pairs and then during a whole-class discussion. The use of open-ended questions, discussion prompts, and facilitative questions are emphasised in the lesson to promote reflection and the development of social-emotional skills like empathy, active listening, and effective communication. In addition, the lesson plan incorporates cultural responsiveness and reflection opportunities, through linking academic learning to students' personal experiences throughout (therefore addressing the Personal and Social Capability sub-component skill, empathy). As with the beginning of the lesson, the 'wrap up' focuses on a reflection period where students discuss both academic and social-emotional skills learned.

Table 14.2 Tier 1 Lesson Plan Exemplar

Date:	Class: Year 1	Subject: English
Personal and Social Capability addressed[1]: *Social awareness—Empathy* Students will understand similarities and differences between the needs, emotions, cultures and backgrounds of themselves and others		**Academic focus:** Students will discuss literary texts and share responses by making connections to their own experiences
Personal and Social Capability Success Criteria: Students will: • Put themselves in another's shoes to examine other people's points of view, experiences, and feelings • Interpret cues that indicate how other people may feel		**Academic Success Criteria:** Students will: • Examine the literature and take the perspective of characters and their lived experiences • Discuss similarities and differences between the lived experiences of characters and themselves

Resources: (1) "I'm Australian Too" by Mem Fox; (2) Worksheet for students to indicate partner responses; (3) Materials for 'cultural drawing'.

Lesson Structure

Stage	Teacher	Student
Opening	Introduce the lesson. Explain that today the class will be reading a book. The class will work in pairs, and will then share their partner's thinking during the class discussion. Provide students with options to record and communicate their partner's thinking. Note. Try not to interrupt pairs as they discuss. Only intervene if partners are having challenges that they cannot resolve on their own.	Work in pairs to discuss the reflection questions: • *How will you make sure that your partner understands you clearly when you are talking to them?* • *How will you make sure you are prepared to share your partner's thinking with the group?*

1 Other SEL competencies addressed include self-management, relationship skills, responsible decision making.

I do *Modelled*	Recap on vocabulary discussed in previous lesson: culture, background, emotions. Read "I'm Australian Too" aloud, slowly and clearly (twice). Ensure the text is accessible to all students (e.g., project it onto the board). On the second read, give students the option to close their eyes and picture the story in their minds.	Review vocabulary as a class Listening and viewing
We do *Guided/Shared*	Provide questions on a worksheet for students to fill out with their partner. Have students discuss the book in pairs. Once they have recorded each other's responses, ask 1–2 students to share their partner's thinking with the class. Record key words and ideas from their responses in large print on the board. Encourage students to use the discussion prompts. Display the prompts in the classroom and reinforce them daily. • I agree with _____ because. . . . • I have a different idea because . . . . • In addition to what _____ said, I think. . . . Ask facilitative questions during pair and class discussions: • What do you think about what _____ just said? • Do you agree or disagree with what _____ just said? Why? • What questions can we ask _____? What can you add to what _____ just said? Note. During the class reflection, teach listening by saying, "_____ is going to share now. Let's turn and give him/her our attention". Have students reflect on their own culture, background, and emotions through making a 'cultural drawing'.	Students answer: • What do you think the book is about? • Who are the characters in the book? Describe some of their experiences. • How do you think those experiences made the characters feel? • How are the characters in the book similar to you? How are they different? • Can you think of any people you know who might have different backgrounds and cultures to you? • Why do you think it is important to understand the similarities and differences between people?
You do *Independent*		Work on their cultural drawing

(Continued)

Table 14.2 (Continued)

Date:	Class: Year 1	Subject: English

Lesson Structure

Stage	Teacher	Student
Closing	Have students display their cultural drawing in the classroom. Provide an opportunity for students to walk around and see what other students have done. Ask facilitative questions while students walk around and view other students' work. • *What do you like about _____'s cultural drawing?* • *What do you notice about what _____ has included in their drawing?* • *Can you see any cultural similarities/differences in _____'s drawing to yours?*	Display cultural drawing for other students to view
Wrap up	Have students reflect on the lesson as a class. Call on 1–2 students to respond to each question during the whole class reflection. Note: During the class reflection, teach listening by saying, "_____ is going to share now. Let's turn and give him/her our attention".	Students answer: • *What did we learn today?* • *What was easy or challenging for you today?* • *What did you do to be a good partner?* • *Did you have any problems working together? How did that affect your work? What can you do next time to avoid that problem?*

Tier 2 SEL: A Creative Exemplar about Mary

Mary, who could be a Grade 5 student at just about any primary school, has a passion for reading books and spending time outdoors. She enjoys schoolwork, particularly creative writing. However, her teachers have noticed that she has difficulties forming friendships and becomes frustrated and angry when faced with challenging tasks or social situations. In the classroom, Mary often exhibits disruptive behaviours, interrupts others, and engages in verbal altercations with classmates. She is also frequently excluded from peer activities in the classroom and during breaks. Recently, these incidents have escalated, as Mary and another classmate became involved in a heated argument, resulting in Mary being issued with a detention.

While Mary's classroom teacher, Mr. Smith, regularly incorporates SEL into classroom instruction, and is working through the 'Bounce Back!' program with his class to address SEL skills (Axford et al., 2010), he feels that Mary might benefit from some further targeted support, along with several other students who are struggling with emotional regulation. Mr. Smith consults with Mrs. Maria, the school psychologist, and decides to administer an assessment of social-emotional skills to these identified students. He uses the student report version of the Social Skills Improvement System Rating Form (SSIS SEL), which measures each of the five CASEL competencies and takes appropriately 10–15 minutes to complete. This assessment provides a summary identifying areas of strength and difficulty in relation to a normed sample (Gresham et al., 2020).

After reviewing Mary's profile and identifying the primary difficulties she faces, in the areas of self-awareness, self-management, and relationship skills, Mr. Smith works with Mrs. Maria to initiate a small-group, classroom-based intervention lasting 20–40 minutes, three times per week. This targeted support, as seen in Table 14.3, provides Mary and three other students, who have comparable social-emotional profiles, with an opportunity to receive more focused instruction that aligns with the Tier 1 classroom content. Further to incorporating targeted strategies into academic instruction (as demonstrated in the exemplar below), Tier 2 interventions can also be provided through small group SEL programs.

As seen above, Tier 2 involves targeted support and additional prompts to help guide social-emotional development, supplementing, rather than replacing Tier 1 classroom instruction, consistent with the principles of MTSS (see Chapter 9). The 'check-in' activity at the beginning of the lesson allows the students to identify and express their emotions and needs, fostering a greater sense of connection and support. Additionally, having coping strategies in place helps with emotion regulation and reduces the likelihood of disruptive behaviours (Weingarten et al., 2020). Students in the group are provided with opportunities to engage in reflection, including

Table 14.3 Targeted Strategies to Support SEL Instruction at Tier 2

Stage	Tier 2 Intervention Strategies	Targeted Competencies
Opening	Have the student 'check-in' before the lesson. Ask: • *How are you feeling?* (Provide a visual check-in chart on the student's desk.) • *What do you need to prepare yourself for today's lesson?*	Self-awareness/ Self-management
	Have the student identify any triggers or challenges that might arise. Have coping strategies in place and available to the student if they feel overwhelmed or dysregulated. Develop these strategies in consultation with the student.	
	Have the student participate in the pair reflection, providing additional prompts. For example: • *What does your body look like when you are listening to your partner?* • *How can you make sure you are ready to listen to your partner?* • *How do you plan to record your partner's thinking?*	Self-awareness/ Relationship skills
I do *Modelled*	After reading the book to the class, have the student record their performance on a self-monitoring recording form based on their listening skills. Inform the student that you are also recording their performance. The form should include a list of specific listening skills (e.g., identifying main ideas, understanding details, making inferences), and a scale for the student to rate themself on each skill (e.g., 1–5 or "needs improvement", "satisfactory", "excellent").	Self-awareness/ Self-management
We do *Guided/ Shared*	Have the student fill out the worksheet with their partner. Use more prompting and structure as needed (e.g., include sentence stems and visuals on the worksheet). Display the discussion prompts on the student's desk and reinforce how they can be used when interacting with their partner. Have them actively practise them as they discuss their thinking with their partner. Note. Remind the student that if they are feeling dysregulated, they can signal for a movement break or can retreat to the 'calm corner' in the classroom (use a timer to set an expectation if needed).	Relationship skills/ Self-management
You do *Independent*	Have the student participate in reflecting on their own culture, background, and emotions through either making a 'cultural drawing' or through role play. Have the student practice recognising the strengths in others and offer compliments as they view their peer's work.	Self-awareness/ Social awareness
Wrap Up	Have the student 'check-out' at the end of the lesson. Ask: • *How are you feeling after the lesson?* Go back to the visual check-in chart on the student's desk. • *What was your highlight of the lesson?* • *What was a challenge for you during the lesson?*	Self-awareness/ Self-management
	Have the student reflect on either academic or social-emotional highlights and challenges, with the option to share reflection with their peers.	

Adapted from Weingarten et al. (2020).

partner reflection, self-monitoring, and reflection on overall learning (Weingarten et al., 2020). These reflective activities help students to become more self-aware of their emotions, thoughts, and behaviours. By engaging in partner reflection, students can develop empathy and perspective-taking skills. The session is supported by teachers using accessible verbal, visual, and written instructions and prompts (Chapter 11), and students are given the opportunity to make choices where possible, promoting autonomy over learning.

To track Mary's progress toward her social-emotional goals, Mr Smith and Ms Maria determine a learning goal to work towards based on Mary's baseline SSIS scores (Filderman et al., 2022). They establish timepoints and frequency at which to re-assess Mary, data which allows them to provide ongoing feedback for improvement and make adjustments to Mary's Tier 2 support plan as needed.

Tier 3 SEL: A Creative Exemplar about Dylan

Dylan, who could be a 13-year-old grade 8 student at just about any high school, is a talented artist who is passionate about creating comic books in his spare time. Dylan has struggled with social-emotional skills since he was in middle school. He often finds it difficult to connect with peers, engage in perspective-taking, express his feelings in healthy ways, and regulate his emotions. As a result, he has become isolated, severely anxious, and prone to explosive outbursts. Based on the outcomes of screening assessments and several months of observation, Dylan's teachers determine that he requires Tier 3 support in SEL. To assess his social-emotional competencies, the teacher/staff report version of the Social Skills Improvement System Rating Form (SSIS SEL) is used, as Dylan feels anxious about participating in a self-assessment. Dylan's assessment reveals substantial difficulties in several key areas of social-emotional development, including self-awareness, self-management, social awareness, and relationship skills. Based on these results, his teachers and the school counsellor, Mr. Hart, develop an intensive and individualised support plan that addresses the specific SEL areas identified.

Dylan's support plan involves several components. First, in consultation with Dylan and his support team (e.g., his parents, teachers, and school counsellor), an Individual Behaviour Plan (IBP) is developed based on the results from the SSIS SEL Rating Form. The IBP is used to inform Dylan's developing SEL skills and infused throughout every interaction and setting that he encounters inside and outside of the classroom. Second, Dylan begins seeing a psychologist outside of school. The psychologist liaises with Dylan's support team to ensure a coordinated approach to supporting his social-emotional development. Third, Dylan participates in small group sessions with the school counsellor, Mr. Hart, for three lessons per week over a period of 15–20 weeks, with progress monitored regularly. Finally, Dylan's parents attend regular meetings with the school to discuss their son's progress, and to receive guidance on how to continue to reinforce the skills he is learning. This wrap-around approach (the collaboration and communication of a variety of support people) ensures that the support plan is coordinated and appropriate for Dylan.

Recommendations

Fostering students' social and emotional skills and wellbeing has become increasingly recognised as a priority in recent years. An extensive body of evidence highlights the effectiveness of universal and targeted school based SEL programs in equipping students with these pivotal skills and strategies, and further serving to enhance their academic and behavioural outcomes. In Australia, the importance of developing students' capacities in this area is recognised in the national curriculum; yet challenges to consistent and effective delivery of SEL remain at the level of the system through to classroom instruction. In this section, we outline key recommendations for enhancing the effective implementation of SEL with the aim of promoting systemic inclusive education reform.

1. Developing a National Approach to the Implementation of SEL

Effective implementation of SEL depends on clear and consistent direction and support, from the broadest level of establishing a schoolwide approach to social-emotional wellbeing to the specifics of selecting effective SEL programs and service-providers. At present, schools everywhere, including Australia, are faced with numerous overlapping policies in this area, due to the development of policies across government and non-government sectors and within different states, along with varying degrees of guidance regarding the delivery of social and emotional learning curriculum (Laurens et al., 2022; Productivity Commission, 2023).

Therefore, and in accordance with the recommendations from numerous recent national reports (National Mental Health Commission, 2021; Productivity Commission, 2020, 2023), it is recommended that a coherent national strategy be developed to support the embedding of SEL in schools across the country, to stipulate the means by which SEL progress is monitored at the school- and student-level, and to provide schools and educators with guidance, including a high-quality evidence-base of programs and resources. In addition to including the Personal and Social Capability in the Australian Curriculum, a method of assessing these skills needs to be developed and used in schools to ensure the curriculum is being enacted effectively and that students are acquiring desired social and emotional skills. Finally, it is highly recommended that this national approach stipulates the implementation of SEL in a framework such as MTSS (see Chapter 9), which employs a tiered approach to supporting students at the universal, targeted, and intensive levels, and which simultaneously addresses academic and behavioural domains. Stronger, more effective collaborations between schools and families may be fostered through explicit enumeration of such collaboration in relevant policy, and through the provision of guidance and support to schools in identifying opportunities and implementation strategies to involve parents and/or families (Chapter 17).

2. Supporting Educators to Implement SEL Through ITE and Professional Learning

Greater attention needs to be paid to Initial Teacher Education (ITE) and the provision of ongoing professional learning to deepen knowledge of SEL skills and instruction and strengthen capacity to effectively establish SEL in schools (Freeman & Strong, 2017). The teaching of social and emotional skills and capacities is recognised in the Australian Curriculum through the inclusion of the Personal and Social Capability, which addresses four of the five CASEL competencies, yet barriers to genuinely integrating these competencies into instruction include difficulties in identifying the connections between the component skills and the content area, such that the endeavour can seem forced, or become something of a box-ticking exercise (e.g., Gilbert, 2019; Skourdoumbis, 2016). Space needs to be created within the already crowded ITE curriculum to include specific training on how this general capability can be embedded into curriculum, how to explicitly teach SEL competencies, and how to identify students at risk of poor social and emotional outcomes, so that students can be provided with timely and appropriate supports. Similar ongoing professional learning opportunities should be developed for school leaders and educators.

In the absence of mandated approaches to SEL curriculum in Australia, schools have autonomy in determining the delivery of social-emotional learning content; however, this latitude also places the onus on school leaders and educators to sift through an extensive and continually expanding range of programs and service providers (Laurens et al., 2022). Moreover, the development of schoolwide, multi-tiered frameworks for delivering SEL entails considerable investment in terms of acquiring the requisite knowledge and thinking through the implementation at a practical level. Training opportunities, particularly for school leaders and other relevant school personnel, should be provided to deliver knowledge and support on the use of frameworks such as MTSS, give direction on where to source high-quality programs to foster SEL and wellbeing, and guidance on how to evaluate the quality of SEL programs.

3. Establishing SEL at a School-Wide Level

Social and emotional learning and instruction is best enacted through a schoolwide, tiered approach. All students benefit from SEL embedded in the curriculum at a universal level (i.e., Tier 1), by purposeful integration of the Personal and Social capability of the Australian Curriculum into content areas. Students who may benefit from more targeted or intensive SEL instruction (i.e., Tier 2 and 3) can be identified through screening assessments of all students, while students' progress in acquiring skills can be monitored using student-level indicators (e.g., academic achievement, attendance) and standardised measures of social-emotional skills. Importantly, SEL instruction should be evidence-based and aligned across tiers and grade levels to ensure a consistent approach that addresses the subcomponent skills in each competency. It is highly recommended that schools adopting this approach establish a dedicated school team to support implementation and monitor fidelity, considering and coordinating the resourcing required to sustain these practices over time. Schools should also foster social and emotional health through establishing a wider school culture that places value on student-teacher relationships, a positive and safe school climate, and restorative approaches to addressing behaviour (Chapters 13, 15, and 16).

Conclusion

The school years represent a pivotal developmental window during which social and emotional skills can be acquired and practiced. An extensive and rapidly growing body of evidence attests to the benefits of school based SEL programs, both those which are universal in their delivery as well as more targeted or intensive approaches. As outlined in this chapter, the drive for SEL implementation is increasing in Australia, and it is crucial to consider how these efforts may be directed and sustained, by developing a national approach to SEL instruction that is underpinned by high-quality evidence, enacted through consistent policy, and that prioritises the dissemination of clear guidance and training opportunities for schools and educators, as well as effective assessment and monitoring of student learning. Such an approach is essential not only to promoting equitable educational outcomes in Australian schools, but to providing all students with the opportunity to acquire critical life skills and thrive in and beyond the classroom.

References

American Institute of Research. (2023). *SEL coaching toolkit.* https://mtss4success.org/resource/sel-coaching-toolkit

Australian Curriculum, Assessment and Reporting Authority. (2023). *Australian Curriculum v9: Personal and Social Capability.* https://v9.australiancurriculum.edu.au/f-10-curriculum/general-capabilities/personal-and-social-capability/

Axford, S., Blyth, K., & Schepens, R. (2010). *Can we help children learn coping skills for life? A study of the impact of the Bounce Back programme on resilience, connectedness and wellbeing of children and teachers in sixteen primary schools in Perth and Kinross, Scotland.* https://www.pearsonschoolsandfecolleges.co.uk/asset-library/pdf/Primary/Scotland/bounce-back-case-study.pdf

Bear, G. G., Whitcomb, S. A., Elias, M. J., & Blank, J. C. (2015). SEL and schoolwide positive behavioural interventions and supports. In J. A. Durlak, R. P. Weissberg, & T. P. Gullotta (Eds.), *Handbook of social and emotional learning: Research and practice* (pp. 453–467). Guilford Press.

Bowles, T., Jimerson, S., Haddock, A., Nolan, J., Jablonski, S., Czub, M., & Coelho, V. (2017). A review of the provision of social and emotional learning in Australia, the United States, Poland, and Portugal. *Journal of Relationships Research*, 8, E16. https://doi.org/10.1017/jrr.2017.16

Brennan, N., Beames, J. R, Kos, A., Reily, N., Connell, C., Hall, S., Yip, D., Hudson, J., O'Dea, B., Di Nicola, K., & Christie, R. (2021). *Psychological distress in young people in Australia: Fifth biennial youth mental health report: 2012–2020*. https://www.missionaustralia.com.au/publications/youth-survey/2061-psychological-distress-in-young-people-in-australia-fifth-biennial-youth-mental-health-report-2012–2020/file

Brown, J. L., Jones, S. M., LaRusso, M. D., & Aber, J. L. (2010). Improving classroom quality: Teacher influences and experimental impacts of the 4rs program. *Journal of Educational Psychology*, 102(1), 153–167. https://doi.org/10.1037/a0018160

Charlton, C. T., Moulton, S., Sabey, C. V., & West, R. (2021). A systematic review of the effects of schoolwide intervention programs on student and teacher perceptions of school climate. *Journal of Positive Behavior Interventions*, 23(3), 185–200. https://doi.org/10.1177/1098 30072094016

Collaborative for Academic, Social, and Emotional Learning. (2023a). *Fundamentals of SEL.* https://casel.org/fundamentals-of-sel/

Collaborative for Academic, Social, and Emotional Learning. (2023b). *Program guide.* https://pg.casel.org/

Collaborative for Academic, Social, and Emotional Learning. (2023c). *Assessment Guide.* https://measuringsel.casel.org/

Collaborative for Academic, Social, and Emotional Learning. (2023d). *The CASEL guide to social and emotional learning.* https://schoolguide.casel.org/

Collie, J. R., Martin, J. A., & Frydenberg, E. (2017). Social and emotional learning: A brief overview and issues relevant to Australia and the Asia-Pacific. In E. Frydenberg, A. J. Martin, & R. J. Collie (Eds.), *Social and emotional learning in Australia and the Asia-Pacific: Perspectives, programs and approaches* (pp. 1–13). Springer.

Comer, J. (1980, June 5). *The New Haven school intervention project* [Paper presentation]. Strategies for Urban School Improvement Workshop Series, Washington, DC, United States.

Dignath, C., Buettner, G., & Langfeldt, H-P. (2008). How can primary school students learn self-regulated learning strategies most effectively?: A meta-analysis on self-regulation training programmes. *Educational Research Review*, 3(2), 101–129. https://doi.org/10.1016/j.edurev.2008.02.003

Dix, K., Kashfee, S. A., Carslake, T., Sniedze-Gregory, S., O'Grady, E., & Trevitt, J. (2020). *A systematic review of intervention research examining effective student wellbeing in schools and their academic outcomes.* Evidence for Learning. https://evidenceforlearning.org.au/education-evidence/evidence-reviews/student-health-and-wellbeing

Domitrovich, C. E., Durlak, J. A., Staley, K. C., & Weissberg, R. P. (2017). Social-emotional competence: An essential factor for promoting positive adjustment and reducing risk in school children. *Child Development*, 88(2), 408–416. https://doi.org/10.1111/cdev.12739

Donnelly, K. & Wiltshire, K. (2014). *Review of the Australian Curriculum final report.* https://apo.org.au/sites/default/files/resource-files/2014-10/apo-nid41699.pdf

Durlak, J. A., Weissberg, R. P., Dymnicki, A. B., Taylor, R. D., & Schellinger, K. B. (2011). The impact of enhancing students' social and emotional learning: A meta-analysis of school-based universal interventions. *Child Development*, 82(1), 405–432. https://doi.org/10.1111/j.1467-8624.2010.01564.x

Dusenbury, L., Newman, J. Z., Weissberg, R. P., Goren, P., Domitrovich, C. E., & Mart, A. K. (2015). The case for preschool to high school state learning standards for social and emotional learning. In J. A. Durlak, C. E. Domitrovich, R. P. Weissberg, & T. P. Gullotta (Eds.), *Handbook of social and emotional learning: Research and practice* (pp. 532–549). Guilford Press.

Elias, M. J., Zins, J. E., Weissberg, R. P., Frey, K. S., Greenberg, M. T., & Haynes, N. M. (1997). *Promoting social and emotional learning: Guidelines for educators.* Association for Supervision & Curriculum Development.

Fagan, A. A., Hawkins, D. J., & Shapiro, V. B. (2015). Taking SEL to scale in schools: The role of community coalitions. In J. A. Durlak, C. E. Domitrovich, R. P. Weissberg, & T. P. Gullotta (Eds.), *Handbook of social and emotional learning: Research and practice* (pp. 468–481). Guilford Press.

Filderman, M. J., McKown, C., Bailey, P., Benner, G. J., & Smolkowski, K. (2022). Assessment for effective screening and progress monitoring of social and emotional learning skills. *Beyond Behavior, 32*(1), 15–23. https://doi.org/10.1177/10742956221143112

Fisher, D., & Frey, N. (2008). *Better learning through structured teaching: A framework for the gradual release of responsibility.* Association for Supervision and Curriculum Development.

Freeman, E., & Strong, D. (2017). Building teacher capacity to promote social and emotional learning in Australia. In E. Frydenberg, A. J. Martin, & R. J. Collie (Eds.), *Social and emotional learning in Australia and the Asia-Pacific: Perspectives, programs and approaches* (pp. 413–435). Springer.

Garbacz, A. S., Swanger-Gagné, M. S., & Sheridan, S. M. (2015). The role of school-family partnership programs for promoting student SEL. In J. A. Durlak, C. E. Domitrovich, R. P. Weissberg, & T. P. Gullotta (Eds.), *Handbook of social and emotional learning: Research and practice* (pp. 244–259). Guilford Press.

Gaumer Erickson, A. S., & Noonan, P. M. (2022). *Teaching self-regulation: 75 instructional activities to foster independent, proactive students, grades 6–12.* Solution Tree Press.

Gilbert, R. (2019). General capabilities in the Australian Curriculum: Promise, problems and prospects. *Curriculum Perspectives, 39,* 169–177. https://doi.org/10.1007/s41297-019-00079-z

Graham, A., Powell, M. A., Thomas, N., & Anderson, D. (2017). Reframing 'well-being' in schools: The potential of recognition. *Cambridge Journal of Education, 47*(4), 439–455. https://doi.org/10.1080/0305764X.2016.1192104

Graham, L. J., Killingly, C., Laurens, K. R., & Sweller, N. (2022). Overrepresentation of Indigenous students in school suspension, exclusion, and enrolment cancellation in Queensland: Is there a case for systemic inclusive school reform? *The Australian Educational Researcher,* 1–35. https://doi.org/10.1007/s13384-021-00504-1

Graham, L. J., McCarthy, T., Killingly, C., Tancredi, H., & Poed, S. (2020). *Inquiry into suspension, exclusion and expulsion processes in South Australian Government schools.* The Centre for Inclusive Education. https://www.education.sa.gov.au/documents_sorting/docs/support-and-inclusion/engagement-and-wellbeing/student-absences/report-of-an-independent-inquiry-into-suspensions-exclusions-and-expulsions-in-south-australian-government-schools.pdf

Greenberg, M. T., Domitrovich, C. E., Weissberg, R. P., & Durlak, J. A. (2017). Social and emotional learning as a public health approach to education. *The Future of Children 27*(1), 13–32. http://www.jstor.org/stable/44219019

Gresham, F., Elliott, S., Metallo, S., Byrd, S., Wilson, E., Erickson, M., Cassidy, K., & Altman, R. (2020). Psychometric fundamentals of the social skills improvement system: social–emotional learning edition rating forms. *Assessment for Effective Intervention, 45*(3), 194–209. https://doi.org/10.1177/1534508418808598

Hecht, M. L., & Shin, Y. (2015). Culture and social and emotional competencies. In J. A. Durlak, C. E. Domitrovich, R. P. Weissberg, & T. P. Gullotta (Eds.), *Handbook of social and emotional learning: Research and practice* (pp. 50–64). Guilford Press.

Heger, E., Haught, T., Noonan, P. M., & Gaumer Erickson, A. S. (2022). *Teaching self-efficacy in elementary classrooms K–2.* [Teacher lessons and student workbook]. College & Career Competency Framework. https://www.cccframework.org/competency-lessons-and-student-workbooks/

Hessler, D. M., & Katz, L. F. (2010). Brief report: Associations between emotional competence and adolescent risky behavior. *Journal of Adolescence, 33*(1), 241–246. https://doi.org/10.1016/j.adolescence.2009.04.007

Horner, R. H., & Sugai, G. (2015). Schoolwide PBIS: An example of applied behavior analysis implemented at a scale of social importance. *Behavior Analysis in Practice, 8,* 80–85. https://doi.org/10.1007/s40617-015-0045-4

Humphrey, N. (2013). *Social and emotional learning: A critical appraisal.* SAGE.

Jackson, D., Wolforth, S., Airhart, K., Bowles, A., & Conner, P. (2021). *SEL MTSS toolkit for state and district leaders.* Council of Chief State School Officers. https://753a0706.flowpaper.com/CCSSOSELMTSSToolkit/#page=1

Jones, D. E., Greenberg, M., & Crowley, M. (2015). Early social-emotional functioning and public health: The relationship between kindergarten social competence and future wellness. *American Journal of Public Health, 105*(11), 2283–2290. https://doi.org/10.2105/AJPH.2015.302630

Laurens, R. L., Graham, L. J., Dix, K. L., Harris, F., Tzoumakis, S., Williams, K. E., Schofield, J. M., Prendergast, T., Waddy, N., Taiwo, M., Carr, V. J., & Green, M. J. (2022). School-based mental health promotion and early intervention programs in New South Wales, Australia: Mapping practice to policy and evidence. *School Mental Health, 14*(3), 582–597. https://doi.org/10.1007/s12310-021-09482-2

Lawrence, D., Johnson, S., Hafekost, J., De Haan, K. B., Sawyer, M., Ainley, J., & Zubrick, S. (2015). *The mental health of children and adolescents: Report on the second Australian child and adolescent survey of mental health and wellbeing.* https://apo.org.au/sites/default/files/resource-files/2015-08/apo-nid56473.pdf

Lawson, G. M., McKenzie, M. E., Becker, K. D., Selby, L., & Hoover, S. A. (2019). The core components of evidence-based social emotional learning programs. *Prevention Science, 20*(4), 457–467. https://doi.org/10.1007/s11121-018-0953-y

LeBuffe P. A., Shapiro V., Naglieri J. (2014). *The Devereux Student Strengths Assessment (DESS). Assessment and technical manual and user's guide.* Apperson.

Mart, A. K., Weissberg, R. P., & Kendziora, K. (2015). Systemic support for social and emotional learning in school districts. In J. A. Durlak, C. E. Domitrovich, R. P. Weissberg, & T. P. Gullotta (Eds.), *Handbook of social and emotional learning: Research and practice* (pp. 482–499). The Guilford Press.

Merrell, K. (2011). *Social and Emotional Assets Scale (SEARS).* Psychological Assessment Resources.

Mertens, E. C. A., Deković, M., van Londen, M., Spitzer, J. E., & Reitz, E. (2022). Components related to long-term effects in the intra-and interpersonal domains: A meta-analysis of universal school-based interventions. *Clinical Child and Family Psychology Review, 25,* 627–645. https://doi.org/10.1007/s10567-022-00406-3

Meyers, D. C., Domitrovich, C. E., Dissi, R., Trejo, J., & Greenberg, M. T. (2019). Supporting systemic social and emotional learning with a schoolwide implementation model. *Evaluation and Program Planning, 73,* 53–61. https://doi.org/10.1016/j.evalprogplan.2018.11.005https://doi.org/10.1016/j.evalprogplan.2018.11.005

Meyers, D. C., Durlak, J. A., & Wandersman, A. (2012). The quality implementation framework: A synthesis of critical steps in the implementation process. *American Journal of Community Psychology, 50*(3–4), 462–480. https://doi.org/10.1007/s10464-012-9522-x

National Mental Health Commission. (2021). *National Children's Mental Health and Wellbeing Strategy.* National Mental Health Commission. https://www.mentalhealthcommission.gov.au/getmedia/9f2d5e51-dfe0-4ac5-b06a-97dbba252e53/National-children-s-Mental-Health-and-Wellbeing-Strategy-FULL

Noonan, P. M., Gaumer Erickson, A. S., & Maclean, T. L. (2021). *Self-efficacy performance-based reflection.* From P. M. Noonan, & A. S. Gaumer Erickson (2018), *College and Career Competency Sequence.* College & Career Competency Framework. https://www.cccframework.org/

Oberle, E., Domitrovich, C. E., Meyers, D. C., & Weissberg, R. P. (2016). Establishing systemic social and emotional learning approaches in schools: a framework for schoolwide implementation. *Cambridge Journal of Education, 46*(3), 277–297. https://doi.org/10.1080/0305764X.2015.1125450

Organisation for Economic Co-operation and Development. (2018). *The future of education and skills: Education 2030.* https://www.oecd.org/education/2030/

Osher, D., Cantor, P., Berg, J., Steyer, L., & Rose, T. (2020). Drivers of human development: How relationships and context shape learning and development. *Applied Developmental Science, 24*(1), 6–36. https://doi.org/10.1080/10888691.2017.1398650

Pandey, A., Hale, D., Das, S., Goddings, A. L., Blakemore, S. J., & Viner, R. M. (2018). Effectiveness of universal self-regulation–based interventions in children and adolescents: A systematic review and meta-analysis. *JAMA Pediatrics, 172*(6), 566–575. https://doi.org/10.1001/jamapediatrics.2018.0232

Patti, J., Senge, P., Madrazo, C., & Stern, S. (2015). Developing socially, emotionally, and cognitively competent school leaders and learning communities. In J. A. Durlak, R. P. Weissberg, & T. P. Gullotta (Eds.), *Handbook of social and emotional learning: Research and practice* (pp. 438–452). Guilford Press.

Poed, S., & Whitefield, P. (2020). Developments in the implementation of positive behavioral interventions and supports in Australian schools. *Intervention in School and Clinic, 56*(1), 56–60. https://doi.org/10.1177/1053451220910742

Polan, J. C., Sieving, R. E., & McMorris, B. J. (2013). Are young adolescents' social and emotional skills protective against involvement in violence and bullying behaviors? *Health Promotion Practice, 14*(4), 599–606. https://doi.org/10.1016/j.jadohealth.2009.11.156

Powell, M. A., & Graham, A. (2017). Wellbeing in schools: Examining the policy–practice nexus. *The Australian Educational Researcher, 44,* 213–231. https://doi.org/10.1007/s13384-016-0222-7

Productivity Commission. (2020). *Mental health, inquiry report.* Commonwealth of Australia. https://www.pc.gov.au/inquiries/completed/mental-health/report/mental-health.pdf

Productivity Commission. (2023). *Review of the National School Reform Agreement: Study report.* Commonwealth of Australia. https://www.pc.gov.au/inquiries/completed/school-agreement/report

Rimm-Kaufman, S. E., & Hulleman, C. S. (2015). SEL in elementary school settings: Identifying mechanisms that matter. In J. A. Durlak, C. E. Domitrovich, R. P. Weissberg, & T. P. Gullotta (Eds.), *Handbook of social and emotional learning: Research and practice* (pp. 151–166). Guilford Press.

Sklad, M., Diekstra, R., Ritter, M. D., Ben, J., & Gravesteijn, C. (2012). Effectiveness of school-based universal social, emotional, and behavioral programs: Do they enhance students' development in the area of skill, behavior, and adjustment?. *Psychology in the Schools, 49*(9), 892–909. https://doi.org/10.1002/pits.21641

Skourdoumbis, A. (2016). Articulations of teaching practice: A case study of teachers and "general capabilities". *Asia Pacific Education Review, 17,* 545–554. https://doi.org/10.1007/s12564-016-9460-7

Taylor, R. D., Oberle, E., Durlak, J. A., & Weissberg, R. P. (2017). Promoting positive youth development through school-based social and emotional learning interventions: A meta-analysis of follow-up effects. *Child Development, 88*(4), 1156–1171. https://doi.org/10.1111/cdev.12864

Weingarten, Z., Brown, C., & Marx, T. (2020). *Social and emotional learning and intensive intervention.* National Center on Intensive Intervention, Office of Special Education Programs, United States Department of Education.

Weissberg, R. P., Durlak, J. A., Domitrovich, C. E., & Gullotta, T. P. (2015). Social and emotional learning: Past, present, and future. In J. A. Durlak, R. P. Weissberg, & T. P. Gullotta (Eds.), *Handbook of social and emotional learning: Research and practice* (pp. 3–19). Guilford Press.

Weissberg, R. P., Gesten, E. L., Rapkin, B. D., Cowen, E. L., Davidson, E., Flores de Apodaca, R., & McKim, B. J. (1981). Evaluation of a social-problem-solving training program for suburban and inner-city third-grade children. *Journal of Consulting and Clinical Psychology, 49*(2), 251. https://doi.org/10.1037/0022-006X.49.2.251

Wigelsworth, M., Lendrum, A., Oldfield, J., Scott, A., Ten Bokkel, I., Tate, K., & Emery, C. (2016). The impact of trial stage, developer involvement and international transferability on universal social and emotional learning programme outcomes: A meta-analysis. *Cambridge Journal of Education, 46*(3), 347–376. https://doi.org/10.1080/0305764X.2016.1195791

Yang, C., Bear, G. G., & May, H. (2018). Multilevel associations between schoolwide social–emotional learning approach and student engagement across elementary, middle, and high schools. *School Psychology Review, 47*(1), 45–61. https://doi.org/10.17105/SPR-2017-0003. V47-1

Zins, J. E., Weissberg, R. P., Wang. M. C., & Walberg, H. J. (2004). *Building academic success on social and emotional learning: What does the research say?* Teachers College Press.

Chapter 15

Supporting a sense of belonging and peer relationships

Beth Saggers, Marilyn Campbell, & Glenys Mann

A sense of belonging is important for the success of all learners. Students may feel they do not belong in school when they are not well connected socially, resulting in students experiencing a sense of loneliness, social anxiety and being vulnerable to bullying. This can lead to increased risk of marginalisation and result in poor long-term wellbeing and quality of life outcomes. Educators and the school environment play a critical role in promoting a sense of belonging for all children that facilitates the development of secure, respectful peer relationships. In this chapter, we first examine the link between belonging and peer relationships and their effects over time. We then consider the risks associated with not belonging, such as bully victimisation, loneliness, and social anxiety, as well as the interrelations between these risks. We then provide a range of strategies that educators can use to enhance students' sense of belonging and build peer relationships.

The Link Between Belonging and Peer Relationships

While different constructs have been used to describe a sense of belonging, one of the most cited definitions is that of Goodenow and Grady (1993) who define belonging as "the extent to which students feel personally accepted, respected, included, and supported by others in the school social environment" (p. 80). There is, therefore, a bi-directional relationship between belonging and relationships with others, including peers. Nurturing a sense of belonging can help to facilitate peer relationships, while peer relationships can in turn help nurture a stronger sense of belonging. Students' sense of belonging has an important role to play in their success at school with previous research identifying belonging as a key protective factor, one that is associated with student academic and emotional wellbeing and resilience (Korpershoek et al., 2020). A positive sense of belonging across the school years has also been associated with longer-term positive post-school and quality of life outcomes (Scorgie & Forlin, 2019). In contrast, a poorer sense of belonging has been identified as contributing to mental health concerns, school attrition, academic underachievement, maladaptive and risk-taking behaviours in both the short term and across the lifespan (Slaten et al., 2018). Within the school context, a student's sense of belonging can provide opportunities for prosocial engagement, which facilitates positive peer relationships and reduces feelings

DOI: 10.4324/9781003350897-18

of marginalisation and loneliness (Allen et al., 2018). In turn, the nurturing of peer relationships and opportunities for prosocial engagement can create a stronger sense of belonging to peers and the school community.

Amplifying Effect of Belonging and Peer Relationships Over Time

It is important for schools to be aware of the bi-directional amplifying effect over time between a sense of belonging and peer relationships. This means that a sense of belonging and positive relationships generally develop and grow stronger over time and across the school years while in contrast a poor sense of belonging can result in a further deterioration and reduction in peer relationships over time (Raufelder et al., 2015). This amplifying effect suggests that investment in peer relationships and developing a sense of belonging over time for students is a worthwhile goal for educators and draws attention to the critically important role schools play in achieving this.

Marginalised Students' Groups at Risk of Poor Sense of Belonging in Schools

Historically, some groups of students have been at increased risk of feeling like they do not belong and being marginalised at school. These may include students with a disability, those with mental health concerns, students from culturally and linguistically diverse groups, and gifted and talented or gender diverse students (Scorgie & Forlin, 2019). Marginalisation often focuses on individual differences, behaviours or traits that are used to justify exclusion from the group (Scorgie & Forlin, 2019). Four interrelated components originally described by Link and Phelan (2001) have been identified as contributing to marginalisation and exclusion including: labelling an individual as different, stereotyping or attributing a negative perception to a characteristic of an individual that is then used to create and 'us' and 'them' status within a group, and allocating a lower place within the social hierarchy of the group for an individual. Therefore, critical to nurturing inclusive school communities is reducing this sense of difference and promoting social inclusion through developing a strong sense of belonging, positive peer and teacher-student relationships (Chapter 16), and the active participation and engagement of all students within the school community (Chapter 13). With social inclusion comes opportunities for shared experience and commonality amongst students rather than difference. Inclusive school communities that are supportive of diversity, focus on similarities rather than difference and give equity, agency, and voice to all within the community build a sense of belonging and promote peer relationships (Scorgie & Forlin, 2019).

Exclusion by Bullying Victimisation

There are many negative consequences, as mentioned previously, of not feeling connected to school. Low school connectedness may lead to social relationship problems such as being victimised by peer bullying, loneliness, and social anxiety, all of which are inextricably linked (Campbell, 2013). One behaviour which contributes greatly to exclusion is being bullied by peers. Bullying is a behaviour where there is an intent to hurt by the perpetrator(s), with the behaviour usually being repeated, and where the person who is being victimised cannot get the bullying to stop and thus is powerless. Bullying can be categorised into four different forms. These four forms can be split into two types: (i) traditional or school bullying, and (ii) bullying via technology. Traditional bullying includes physical, verbal, and relational (or exclusion) bullying. Bullying via technology is cyberbullying. While the prevalence of bullying victimisation varies greatly in studies because of definitional and methodological differences, it is generally thought to affect 20–33% of the student population (Jadambaa et al., 2019). However, it has been shown that young people who are the most different from the student population—because they have a disability, are gender diverse, racially, or ethnically different or have learning difficulties, mental health difficulties, or are gifted and talented—experience more bullying victimisation than others (Lebrun-Harris et al., 2019). All forms of bullying have negative consequences for victimised students with the most serious being suicidal ideation or behaviour, and self-harm (Ahmad et al., 2023). Mental health problems such as anxiety, depression, psychosomatic symptoms, and academic underachievement as well as loneliness are consequences of bullying victimisation (Singham et al., 2017).

Loneliness

One of the consequences of not being connected to one's peers is the feeling of loneliness. Most adults would not consider that children could be lonely, especially when they are at school, surrounded by other students. However, being alone does not necessarily mean that a student is lonely and conversely being in crowd does not necessarily mean one will not experience loneliness. Loneliness is not an absence of other people but an absence of fulfilling social relationships. Being alone can be a relief, a creative solitude but being lonely is a subjective distressing experience because it is a feeling of disconnectedness from a desired belongingness to a group or for an important friendship (Campbell, 2013). Loneliness has a social stigma of failure to connect to others.

Most young people will feel lonely at some time during their school years usually because of situational factors such as changing schools and leaving their friends behind, parental separation disrupting their friendships, or conflicts with peers. These situations often resolve themselves over a period of time. However, for some young people loneliness is chronic and a long-lasting aversive state of feeling. The prevalence of chronic loneliness has been estimated to affect 9–15% of young people (Pengpid & Peltzer, 2021), however there are group differences and most marginalised students usually report more loneliness compared to their peers. For example, children with Attention Deficit Hyperactivity Disorder (ADHD) were perceived as lonelier by their parents than their peers and children with mild intellectual disability tend to experience limited acceptance and increased rejection from peers with about half of these children reporting they are lonely (Papoutsaki et al., 2013). Students who find difficulty with academic work also report higher levels of loneliness than their peers (Heiman & Olenik-Shemesh, 2020). The negative consequences of chronic loneliness in young people include depression and anxiety, social difficulties and not wanting to go to school (Stickley et al., 2016). Some theorists think that young people with low social skills experience feelings of loneliness, which then produces social withdrawal and this in turn inhibits practice in social relationship skills (Rubin et al., 2010). Social anxiety is therefore considered by some to be a consequence of loneliness.

Social Anxiety

As with other connectedness problems in school many young people experience social anxiety. While for most students this is episodic, there are some individuals whose fear of social situations is continuous and chronic. Social phobia or social anxiety is where students fear social situations in which they are worried about being negatively evaluated by others. These situations are usually everyday occurrences of eating in front of other people, having a conversation, or using a public toilet. They therefore try to avoid these situations for fear they might act in an embarrassing way and be humiliated in front of others.

Anxiety disorders are the most common psychological disorder in young people. Although some adults think that social anxiety only starts in adolescence, onset can also begin in childhood (Campbell, 1996). Social anxiety disorder is one of the most common disorders among adolescents with prevalence rates of about 8% (Kessler et al., 2012). As with bullying victimisation, marginalised children experience more social anxiety than their peers and this is especially so for students on the autism spectrum and those with high autistic traits (Salazar et al., 2015). This association has been shown by both cross-sectional and longitudinal studies (Campbell et al., 2017).

The consequences of social anxiety can include school avoidance resulting in irregular attendance, early school leaving, and poor relationships with family and friends. Depression, other anxiety disorders, and substance abuse have also been found to be associated with social anxiety (American Psychiatric Association, 2013). Somatic symptoms, such as headache and stomach aches, as well as ADHD and selective mutism, have also been found to be associated with social anxiety (Rao et al., 2007). More loneliness than their peers is also reported even by children as young as seven and eight who are socially anxious (Weeks et al., 2009).

Interrelations Between Bullying, Loneliness, and Social Anxiety

Bullying victimisation, loneliness, and social anxiety are all separate and distinct concepts (Maes et al., 2019). However, it has been shown that they are inextricably linked in very complex ways. Not only are these concepts associated with one another, but they can both cause and be a consequence of one other, often creating a negative circle or loop (Kochenderfer-Ladd & Wardrop, 2001). In addition, victimisation, loneliness, and social anxiety might affect each other or may affect other factors that have a role in the linking of bullying victimisation, loneliness, and social anxiety. For instance, lonely students are often selected to be victimised because they are seen as vulnerable. A major consequence of being bullied is increased loneliness as the children withdraw socially to avoid bullying which increases their vulnerability to victimisation even further. Thus, loneliness can also be both an antecedent and a consequence of bullying victimisation. In fact, the chance of loneliness grows as bullying victimisation increases (Due et al., 2005). In a similar way, excessively anxious students who are also victimised experience even more anxiety. Children who have experienced bullying victimisation have been found to be at increased risk of social anxiety at the age of 13 years (Pickard et al., 2018). Relational or exclusion victimisation has been shown to be even more strongly associated with the development of social anxiety in adolescents.

Loneliness has been found to be a correlate of social anxiety (Shanahan et al., 2008), an antecedent, as loneliness precedes being victimised and a consequence of social anxiety (Shanahan et al., 2008). These constructs are also interactional and bi-directional with bullying victimisation preceding social anxiety and loneliness and loneliness preceding social anxiety and bullying victimisation (Heinrich & Gullone, 2006). It is therefore imperative that those students who do not experience good social connectedness are supported in all aspects of their lives. As it has been shown, the social problems of bullying, loneliness, and social anxiety all contribute to and are consequences of each other. Therefore, interventions need to be cognisant of the interrelationships and bidirectionality of these phenomena in prevention and intervention efforts.

How Can a Sense of Belonging and Peer Relationships Be Supported in School Environments?

Now that the importance of belonging and peer relationships for all students has been established, the following sections focus on what educators and their collaborators can do to support a sense of belonging in schools, particularly for students at increased risk of experiencing poor social relationships. Framing these suggestions, is a model for understanding loneliness developed by Gilmore and Cuskelly (2014). Given the interconnectedness between loneliness, social anxiety and bullying, the model has implications beyond its original intent. Although the focus of Gilmore and Cuskelly's model of loneliness vulnerability was individuals with intellectual disability, there is value in considering the model for all students who have increased vulnerability to loneliness and disconnection. The model provides a useful framework for holistic support for positive peer relationships rather than just focusing on 'fixing' individual students.

Gilmore and Cuskelly's theoretical model of loneliness vulnerability has three reciprocal domains: (i) attitudes and expectations, (ii) opportunity and experiences, and (iii) individual skills. While these domains do highlight characteristics of individuals that make it more difficult for them to form relationships (e.g., difficulties with communication or social understanding), the authors also argue that social attitudes and expectations comprise the most influential of the domains. The final domain focuses on opportunities for and past experiences of social connection. These three domains are now discussed in more detail, starting with attitudes and expectations, then opportunity and experiences, and finishing with individual skills.

Domain 1. Attitudes and Expectations

Too often, social exclusion is explained simply as a product of student capacity (e.g., deficits in communication skills, social skills, motivation). In other words, teachers can inadvertently 'blame the victim' for their social plight and focus their interventions solely on skills development. Instead, Gilmore and Cuskelly argue that student experiences of belonging and peer relationships are *not* just a product of their own capacities and skills but are, in fact, highly dependent on the attitudes and expectations of those around them. Individual student characteristics can make students more vulnerable to loneliness, however social disconnection is not inevitable. Low expectations by educators are known to predict students' academic outcomes (Price & Slee, 2021) but they are just as serious a barrier for social outcomes. When educators do not believe that friendships with peers are possible or desirable for students with disability, vital opportunities to facilitate a sense of belonging and/or peer relationships go unnoticed and unactioned. If educators think students—for whatever reason—*cannot* form relationships with others, then it can too easily be assumed that adults have no role to play in supporting relationship building. The least dangerous assumption we can make then, is that *all* students want to belong and that social relationships are possible for everyone. When educators are driven by such an assumption, they are more likely to contribute to possibilities for connection. The beauty of thinking this way is that positive attitudes and high expectations for peer relationships can feed into a loop. For example, teachers' intentional facilitation of positive contact between students with and without disabilities can help to break down negative attitudes towards students with disability (Scior, 2011), and when negative attitudes are broken down, ongoing positive relationships are more likely (Carter et al., 2016).

Strategies for Facilitating Attitudes and Expectations That Support a Sense of Belonging and Peer Relationships

School leadership and whole school universal approaches that build community are essential to attitudes and expectations that will promote connections in the school environment. When students feel included and connected to school, they are more likely to participate and engage in the school community, achieve academic success, and develop skills that promote resilience and wellbeing (Allen et al., 2018). This starts with school policies and practices that create a positive learning environment reflected by attitudes and expectations where all community members feel included, valued, and supported and set the scene for respectful communication and relationships. These safe and caring environments ensure there are whole school social emotional learning approaches (see Chapter 14), positive approaches to behaviour support and clearly defined anti-bullying policies and practices that provide opportunities to interact with others in positive ways that nurture individual difference. School leadership can support this whole school approach by implementing Multi-Tiered Systems of Support (Chapter 9), and through the ongoing provision of professional development and support for teachers and other school staff that focus on inclusive policy and practices and nurture belonging across the whole school community.

Within the smaller environment of the classroom, the teacher is pivotal to promoting positive attitudes and expectations through class wide approaches that ensure a sense of belonging and positive relationships with peers can be nurtured, and that provide opportunities for social success for all students. How the classroom teacher works to develop positive relationships with their students (Chapter 16) and to promote relationships between students is central to social success for all students (Kilday et al., 2022). Critical to these relationships is how the classroom teacher engages with students through the 4 Cs: Consultation, Collaboration, Communication, and Cooperation (Griffiths et al., 2021).

Domain 2. Opportunity and Experiences

It is easy to see the strong link between high expectations for peer relationships and the subsequent opportunities that educators create or seize. When thinking about their role in facilitating opportunities for social connection, it is helpful if educators consider how relationships typically develop. Sharing experiences, over time, plays a critical role. Educators constantly make decisions about how students are grouped, where students spend time, and what students are doing. When these decisions are underpinned by a commitment to social inclusion, they are more likely to facilitate the presence and meaningful participation of marginalised students in the life of the school and classroom. For example, the most significant decisions for the social lives of students with disability (who are highly vulnerable to social isolation and disconnection) are decisions about segregated provision. If students are separate from each other, and not learning and 'playing' together in school spaces, it is highly unlikely they will form relationships that might go that step further to become friendships. Friendships are often related to the degree of inclusion in a school; they need proximity and presence in the same space to flourish (Therrien et al., 2022). It is for this reason that the weight of evidence shows inclusion leads to better social experiences and outcomes (Chapter 6). Similarly, Miller et al. (2022) found that while specialised learning environments developed the skills and knowledge of students from refugee backgrounds in the short term, those learning environments did little to facilitate social inclusion. Educators cannot make friendship happen, but they can play a key role in setting the ground for relationships, along with parents who also enable social opportunities for their children (Lindner et al., 2022).

Strategies for Facilitating Opportunities for Social Connections

While the skills and competencies used to interact with others are often taken for granted, it is important to understand that rather than being a static skill set, social interactions require a complex, flexible, dynamic, ever-evolving set of social problem-solving skills that are responsive to the context in which they are being used. Critical to promoting a sense of belonging and positive peer relationships in the school environment are the opportunities provided to students to connect with each other and develop these skills. Loomis' (2008) framework for providing social opportunities for students with developmental disability has application for providing social opportunities for all students. This framework outlines ten key factors that are useful for teachers to consider when planning for and providing social opportunities in their classroom and across the school environment. These factors are described in the Table 15.1 below.

Table 15.1 Factors Influencing Social Opportunity

Factor	*Considerations*
Factor 1: Predictability	The more predictable/familiar/routine the activity/context or people are in the social exchange the easier it is to facilitate opportunities for social success.
Factor 2: Clear explanations/ expectations	Linked to predictability are the importance of social opportunities that have clear explanations, structure, and expectations that will help facilitate success and reduce stress.
Factor 3: Communication	The conventions of social communication need to be understood and clear to the those involved in the interactions. Opportunities to learn about and practice these are important for all students to help them understand and utilise them in social situations. Opportunities to use communication to facilitate clear explanations and expectations are also important.
Factor 4: Hidden curriculum/social conventions/ demands	There are often unstated rules, assumptions or expectations when interacting with others that if not understood can be a barrier to social success. Opportunities to learn about and understand these 'hidden' elements of the curriculum are important to provide.
Factor 5: Number of people **Factor 6:** Type of People **Factor 7:** Length of Time	Generally, the less people involved in an interaction, the less social challenging it is. In addition, the more familiar the person or people are in the social situation reduces the social challenge and the shorter the time you engage with them the less challenges there are. When providing opportunities for social success therefore consideration to how many people are involved, who is involved and for how long will reduce social challenge and increase success. Also engaging with adults, older or younger peers can have less challenge than same aged peers initially and may be a good first step for opportunities to engage. Critical to interacting with same aged peers is providing the skills and understanding all peers need to support them socially.

(Continued)

Table 15.1 (Continued)

Factor	Considerations
Factor 8: Sensory demands Factor 9: Physical environmental demands	The sensory and environmental demands can influence the stress levels of those involved e.g., crowds, noise, temperature, large open spaces, small, enclosed spaces can all add stress and need to be factors that are considered in providing social opportunities.
Factor 10: Physiological Factors	Internal to individual students are physiological factors that need to be considered when providing opportunities for engagement with others such as fatigue, hunger or illness to ensure they can maximise their success. Reducing factors that increase social challenge are important to consider if these physiological factors are evident.

Adapted from Loomis (2008).

Each of these 10 factors can increase or reduce social challenge and need to be considered when planning opportunities to support a sense of belonging and positive peer relationships. When teachers plan, deliver, and evaluate opportunities to connect in their everyday teaching activities, they will need to think about how they might adjust the frequency and intensity of the social events they provide. Taking into consideration the context, with whom the interactions occur and how they occur.

Domain 3. Individual Skills

The intersection between the three domains in Gilmore and Cuskelly's (2014) theoretical model of loneliness vulnerability are clear. Opportunities for connection help to build an individual's skills, and when individual skills are developed, opportunities for connection are more likely to be successful. Challenges faced by individual students do make a difference to social connection, for example, students who find communication difficult either because of disability or because the school and home languages differ, are more likely to also struggle socially. Similarly, students who do not understand the social rules will also struggle. On their own, however, individual interventions to address these difficulties are unlikely to be enough. Norm Kunc, a man with cerebral palsy and significant difficulties with speech, described how in his early years in a segregated school, he realised that regular speech therapy made no sense without friends to speak clearly to. It was only when he insisted on going to his local regular high school that he was able to seize the many opportunities to be with his peers to put his speech therapy strategies into practice.

By the end of my first year at the regular school, I would meet family friends and relatives who hadn't seen me since I left the segregated school. Astonished by the improved clarity of my speech, they would invariably say, "Norman, you're talking so much more clearly. What did you do?" I'd say, "I quit speech therapy!" I usually get prolonged laughter when I tell this story in conference keynotes. But when I told this story to an audience of speech therapists . . . they somehow missed the humour. In fact, some felt I discounted the importance of speech therapy. This isn't true. What I learned in speech therapy was useful. My *ability* to talk clearly was important. But it was the *opportunity* to attend a regular school that allowed me to put what I learned into practice.

(Van der Klift & Kunc, 2017, p. 5)

Educators must beware that when they focus too heavily on a student's individual 'problems' (even with good intentions), this is unlikely to be fuel for social connections. A focus on commonality is much more likely to be fruitful. Shared interests and experiences can be productive ground for peer connection and the development of skills in meaningful contexts. It is also helpful to think about the roles that students play. Other students are more likely to want to connect with those in typical, valued roles (e.g., fellow team or choir or drama club members) than those in devalued roles (e.g., the disabled 'buddy'). Skill building, then, must mean more than just social skills programs. Rather, teachers can help students to build the competencies they need to authentically participate alongside their peers in day-to-day school and classroom roles.

Considerations for Facilitating Individual Skill Development

Getting to know individual students, is critical to teachers supporting their skills in connecting with others. Teacher knowledge of a student's personal attributes, strengths, likes, interests, and individual needs will ensure a nuanced and dynamic approach to teaching opportunities and instructional strategies is in place. This will take into consideration knowledge of the student that informs the implementation of suitable adjustments to maximise success, promote social networks and positive experiences, and inform the opportunities you provide for your students.

Conclusion

For school to be an enjoyable experience for all learners, requires more than just a focus on academic learning—children must feel socially connected and experience a sense of belonging. For some children though, through no fault of their own, school is *not* a place where they have a sense of belonging or experience positive relationships with peers. Can you imagine what it would be like to have to go, every day, to a place where you have no friends, where you feel lonely, anxious, and/or bullied? School would be a nightmare from which there is no escape. Just as school is about more than literacy and numeracy, inclusive education is more than making adjustments to curriculum and pedagogy; inclusive educators also promote the social lives of their students and their role as teachers, through facilitating a sense of belonging, encouraging the development of positive peer relationships, and by helping all students to feel welcome and wanted. Educators that have positive attitudes and expectations promote an inclusive school community. Opportunities for social connection that are informed by getting to know the students and their individual needs and strengths can promote positive interactions and pathways for success.

References

Ahmad, K., Beatson, A., Campbell, M. A., Hashmi, R., Keating, B. W., Mulcahy, R., Riedel, A., & Wang, S. (2023). The impact of gender and age on bullying role, self-harm and suicide: Evidence from a cohort study of Australian children. *PLOS One, 18*(1), e0278446. https://doi.org/10.1371/journal.pone.0278446

Allen, K., Kern, M. L., Vella-Brodrick, D., Hattie, J., & Waters, L. (2018). What schools need to know about fostering school belonging: A meta-analysis. *Educational Psychology Review, 30*(1), 1–34. https://doi.org/10.1007/s10648-016-9389-8

American Psychiatric Association. (2013). *Diagnostic and Statistical Manual of Mental Disorders* (5th ed.). https://doi.org/10.1176/appi.books.9780890425596

Campbell, M. A. (1996). Does social anxiety increase with age? *Australian Journal of Guidance and Counselling, 6*(1), 43–52. https://doi.org/10.1017/S1037291100001485

Campbell, M. A. (2013). Loneliness, social anxiety and bullying victimization in young people: A literature review. *Psychology and Education, 50*(3/4), 1–10.

Campbell, M. A., Hwang, Y., Whiteford, C., Dillon-Wallace, J., Ashburner, J., Saggers, B., & Carrington, S. (2017). Bullying prevalence in students with autism spectrum disorder. *Australasian Journal of Special Education, 41*(1), 101–122. https://doi.org/10.1017/jse.2017.5

Carter, E. W., Asmus, J., Moss, C. K., Biggs, E. E., Bolt, D. M., Born, T. L., Brock, M. E., Cattey, G. N., Chen, R., Cooney, M., Fesperman, E., Hochman, J. M., Huber, H. B., Lequia, J. L., Lyons, G., Moyseenko, K. A., Riesch, L. M., Shalev, R. A., Vincent, L. B., & Weir, K. (2016). Randomized evaluation of peer support arrangements to support the inclusion of high school students with severe disabilities. *Exceptional Children, 82*(2), 209–233. https://doi.org/ 10.1177/0014402915598780

Due, P., Holstein, B. E., Lynch, J., Diderichsen, F., Gabhain, S. N., Scheidt, P., & Currie, C. (2005). Bullying and symptoms among school-aged children: International comparative cross-sectional study in 28 countries. *European Journal of Public Health, 15*(2), 128–132. https://doi.org/10.1093/eurpub/cki105

Gilmore, L., & Cuskelly, M. (2014). Vulnerability to loneliness in people with intellectual disability: An explanatory model. *Journal of Policy and Practice in Intellectual Disabilities, 11*(3), 192–99. https://doi.org/10.1111/jppi.12089

Goodenow, C., & Grady, K. E. (1993). The relationship of school belonging and friends' values to academic motivation among urban adolescent students. *Journal of Experimental Education, 62*(1), 60–71. https://www.jstor.org/stable/20152398

Griffiths, A. J., Alsip, J., Hart, S. R., Round, R. L., & Brady, J. (2021). Together we can do so much: A systematic review and conceptual framework of collaboration in schools. *Canadian Journal of School Psychology, 36*(1) 59–85. https://doi.org/10.1177/0829573520915368

Heiman, T., & Olenik-Shemesh, D. (2020). Social-emotional profile of children with and without learning disabilities: The relationships with perceived loneliness, self-efficacy and well-being. *International Journal of Environmental Research and Public Health, 17*(20), article7358. https://doi.org/10.3390/ijerph17207358.

Heinrich, L. M., & Gullone, E. (2006). The clinical significance of loneliness: A literature review. *Clinical Psychology Review, 26*(6), 695–718. https://doi.org/10.1016/j.cpr.2006.04.002

Jadambaa, A., Thomas, H. J., Scott, J. G., Graves, N., Brain, D., & Pacella, R. (2019). Prevalence of traditional bullying and cyberbullying among children and adolescents in Australia: A systematic review and meta-analysis. *Australian & New Zealand Journal of Psychiatry, 53*(9), 878–888. https://doi.org/10.1177/0004867419846393

Kessler, R. C., Petukhova, M., Sampson, N. A., Zaslavsky, A. M., & Wittchen, H.-U. (2012). Twelve-month and lifetime prevalence and lifetime morbid risk of anxiety and mood disorders in the United States. *International Journal of Methods in Psychiatric Research, 21*(3), 169–184. https://doi.org/10.1002/mpr.1359

Kilday, J., Brass, N., Ferguson, S., Ryan, A., & Pearson, M. (2022). Teachers' management of peer relations: Associations with fifth grade classroom peer ecologies. *The Journal of Experimental Education, 91*(2), 278–297. https://doi.org/10.1080/00220973.2022.2039890

Kochenderfer-Ladd, B., & Wardrop, J. L. (2001). Chronicity and instability of children's peer victimization experiences as predictors of loneliness and social satisfaction trajectories. *Child Development, 72*(2), 134–151. https://doi.org/10.1111/1467–8624.00270

Korpershoek, H., Canrinus, E. T., Fokkens-Bruinsma, M., & de Boer, H. (2020). The relationships between school belonging and students' motivational, social-emotional, behavioural, and academic outcomes in secondary education: A meta-analytic review. *Research Papers in Education, 35*(6), 641–680. https://doi.org/10.1080/02671522.2019.1615116

Lebrun-Harris, L. A., Sherman, L. J., Limber, S. P., Miller, B. D., & Edgerton, E. A. (2019). Bullying victimization and perpetration among U.S. children and adolescents: 2016 National Survey of Children's Health. *Journal of Child and Family Studies, 28*(9), 2543–2557. https://doi.org1007/10./s1082 6-018-1170-9

Lindner, K. T., Hassani, S., Schwab, S., Gerdenitsch, C., Kopp-Sixt, S., & Holzinger, A. (2022). Promoting factors of social inclusion of students with special educational needs: Perspectives of parents, teachers, and students. *Frontiers in Education, 7.* https://doi.org/10.3389/feduc.2022.773230

Link, B. G., & Phelan, J. C. (2001). Conceptualizing stigma. *Annual Review of Sociology, 27*(1), 363–385. https://doi.org/10.1146/annurev.soc.27.1.363

Loomis, J. W. (2008). *Staying in the game: Providing social opportunities for children and adolescents with autism spectrum disorders and other developmental disabilities.* Autism Asperger Pub Co.

Maes, M., Nelemans, S., Danneel, S., Fernández-Castilla, B., Van den Noortgate, W., & Goossens, L. (2019). Loneliness and social anxiety across childhood and adolescence: Multilevel meta-analyses of cross-sectional and longitudinal associations. *Developmental Psychology, 55*(7), 1548–1565. https://doi.org/10.1037/dev0000719

Miller, E., Ziaian, T., de Anstiss, H., & Baak, M. (2022). Practices for inclusion, structures of marginalisation: Experiences of refugee background students in Australian secondary schools. *The Australian Educational Researcher, 49,* 1063–1084. https://doi.org/10.1007/s13384-021-00475-3

Papoutsaki, K., Gena, A., & Kalyva, E. (2013). How do children with mild intellectual disabilities perceive loneliness? *Europe's Journal of Psychology, 9*(1), 51–61. https://doi.org/10.5964/ejop.v9i1.489

Pengpid, S., & Peltzer, K. (2021). Prevalence and associated factors of loneliness among national samples of in-school adolescents in four Caribbean countries. *Psychological Reports, 124*(6), 2669–2683. https://doi.org/10.1177/0033294120968502

Pickard, H., Happe, F., & Mandy, W. (2018). Navigating the social world: The role of social competence, peer victimisation and friendship quality in the development of social anxiety in childhood. *Journal of Anxiety Disorders, 60,* 1–10. https://doi.org/10.1016/j.janxdis.2018.09.002

Price, D., & Slee, R. (2021). An Australian curriculum that includes diverse learners: The case of students with disability. *Curriculum Perspectives, 41*(1), 71–81. https://doi.org/10.1007/s41297-021-00134-8

Rao, P. A., Beidel, D. C., Turner, S. M., Ammerman, R. T., Crosby, L. E., & Sallee, F. R. (2007). Social anxiety disorder in childhood and adolescence: Descriptive psychopathology. *Behaviour Research and Therapy, 45*(6), 1181–1191. http://dx.doi.org/10.1016/j.brat.2006.07.015

Raufelder, D., Sahabandu, D., Martínez, G. S., & Escobar, V. (2015). The mediating role of social relationships in the association of adolescents' individual school self-concept and their school engagement, belonging and helplessness in school. *Educational Psychology*, *35*(2), 137–157. https://doi.org/10.1080/01443410.2013.849327

Rubin, K., Root, A.K., & Bowker, J. (2010). Parents, peers, and social withdrawal in childhood: A relationship perspective. *New Directions for Child and Adolescent Development*, *127*(1), 79–94. https://doi.org/10.1002/cd.264

Salazar, F., Baird, G., Chandler, S. Tseng, E., O'Sullivan, T., Howling, P., Pickles, A., & Simonoff, E. (2015). Co-occurring psychiatric disorders in preschool and elementary school-aged children with Autism Spectrum Disorder. *Journal of Autism Developmental Disorde*rs, *45*(8) 2283–2294. https://doi.org/10.1007/s10803-015-2361-

Scior, K. (2011). Public awareness, attitudes, and beliefs regarding intellectual disability: A systematic review. *Research in Developmental Disabilities*, *32*(6), 2164–2182. https://doi.org/10.1016/j.ridd.2011.07.005

Scorgie, K., & Forlin, C. (Ed). (2019). *Promoting social inclusion: Co-creating environments that foster equity and belonging*. Emerald.

Shanahan, L., Copeland, W., Costello, E. J., & Angold, A. (2008). Specificity of putative psychosocial risk factors for psychiatric disorders in children and adolescents. *Journal of Child Psychology and Psychiatry*, *49*(1), 34–42. https://doi.org/10.1111/j.1469-7610.2007.01822.x

Singham, T., Viding, E., Schoeler, T., Arseneault, L., Ronald, A., Cecil, C. M., McCory, E., Rijskijk, F., & Pingault, J.-B. (2017). Concurrent and longitudinal contribution of exposure to bullying in childhood to mental health: The role of vulnerability and resilience. *Journal of the American Medical Association Psychiatry*, *74*(11), 1112–1119. https://doi.org/10.1001/jamapsychiatry.2017.2678

Slaten, C. D., Allen, K., Ferguson, J. K., Vella-Brodrick, D., & Waters, L. (2018). A historical account of school belonging: Understanding the past and providing direction for the future. In K. Allen & C. Boyle (Eds.), *Pathways to belonging: Contemporary perspectives of school belonging* (pp. 7–26). Brill.

Stickley, A., Koyanagi, A., Koposov, R., Blatný, M., Hrdlička, M., Schwab-Stone M., & Ruchkin, V. (2016). Loneliness and its association with psychological and somatic health problems among Czech, Russian and U.S. adolescents. *BMC Psychiatry*, *16*, 128. https://doi.org/10.1186/s12888-016-0829-2

Therrien, M., Rossetti, Z., & Ostvik, J. (2022). Augmentative and alternative communication and friendships: Considerations for speech-language pathologists. *Perspectives of the ASHA Special Interest Groups*. https://doi.org/10.1044/2022_PERSP-22-00105

Van der Klift, E., & Kunc, N. (2017). Ability and Opportunity in the Rearview Mirror. In K. Scorgie, & D. Sobsey (Eds.), *Working with families for Inclusive education: Navigating identity, opportunity and belonging* (pp. 3–10). Emerald.

Weeks, M., Coplan, R. J., & Kingsbury, A. (2009). The correlates and consequences of early appearing social anxiety in young children. *Journal of Anxiety Disorders*, *23*(7), 965–972. https://doi.org/10.1016/j.janxdis.2009.06.006

Chapter 16

Nurturing close student–teacher relationships

Penny Van Bergen, Kevin F. McGrath, Daniel Quin, &
Emma C. Burns

Close relationships between teachers and students are important for all classrooms at all stages of schooling. Close student–teacher relationships provide a critical foundation for learning and set the tone for the classroom climate (Hughes, 2011). Students who experience close and supportive relationships with their teachers are more likely to interact positively with other classmates, to excel academically, and to feel a positive sense of school belonging and adjustment (Endedijk et al., 2022; Pianta & Stuhlman, 2004). Close relationships are also powerfully predictive. Relationship quality in the early years of schooling predicts positive social and academic outcomes in high school (Hamre & Pianta, 2001; McGrath & Van Bergen, 2015), for example, while relationship quality in early high school predicts decreased disengagement (Burns et al., 2019) and increased intentions to complete school (Burns, 2020).

In developing close relationships with their students, educators face two inherent challenges. First, research shows that student–teacher relationship quality typically declines across the school years (Jerome et al., 2009), albeit with different trajectories and fluctuations for different groups of students (Lee & Bierman, 2018; Spilt, Hughes et al., 2012). This may be because reduced interactional opportunities in higher grades create conditions whereby teachers and students are less invested in student–teacher relationships, and more attentive to relationships with peers and colleagues. It is also possible that teachers' expectations of students change across time, as students grow older and as differences in student behaviour become entrenched. Finally, according to O'Connor and McCartney (2007), interactions are increasingly instruction-based and not relationship-based. Whatever the cause, strategies for ameliorating both reductions and fluctuations in relationship quality are important (Lee & Bierman, 2018).

Second, some students and some teachers are at greater risk of experiencing poor-quality relationships than others. For example, boys are more likely than girls to experience a negative student–teacher relationship, as are students in at-risk groups—including students from racial and ethnic minority groups, students from low-income families, students with disruptive behaviour, and students with learning difficulties (see McGrath & Van Bergen, 2015; Roorda et al., 2011 for reviews). Worryingly, it is these same at-risk groups who are most likely to benefit from close, supportive, and caring relationships with teachers (McGrath & Van Bergen, 2015).

DOI: 10.4324/9781003350897-19

For teachers, a host of different risk factors emerge. Teachers with low teaching self-efficacy and teachers who provide less emotional support in the classroom are each more likely to experience poor-quality relationships with their students, as are teachers with depression (Hamre et al., 2008; McGrath & Van Bergen, 2017). These results hold true even when student characteristics, such as disruptive behaviour, are taken into account (that is, statistically removed from the analyses such that the unique contributions of the teacher can be determined). Teachers with more years' experience might also be at greater risk of experiencing poor-quality student–teacher relationships (Brekelmans et al., 2005), although findings are equivocal (Hughes, 2011). Interestingly, despite evidence that student gender predicts relationship quality (McGrath et al., 2017), the findings for teacher gender are more complex. Gender *matching* appears important for female teachers, who report preferences for female students, but it is not vital for male teachers (Spilt, Koomen, et al., 2012).

In this chapter, we explore the characteristics of different student–teacher relationships and the contexts in which they develop. We also draw on available research evidence to identify the benefits of high-quality student–teacher relationships for all students. We conclude the chapter by considering the practices that can help teachers to nurture such relationships with their students. In doing so, we present a blueprint that teachers, teacher educators and researchers can use to drive new lines of questioning and troubleshoot interactional problems as they arise. We note that all students have the right to expect a close, supportive, and effective relationship with their teachers, irrespective of challenging learning, developmental, behavioural characteristics, or other individual characteristics (Spilt & Koomen, 2009).

Characterising the Student–Teacher Relationship

Research investigating student–teacher relationships in primary school typically considers three relational constructs: closeness, conflict, and dependency (Hughes, 2011; Murray & Murray, 2004; Pianta, 2001; Sabol & Pianta, 2012). While student–teacher closeness has been associated with positive adjustment, and conflict with poorer adjustment, the effects of dependency on student outcomes are less clear (Hughes, 2011; Murray & Murray, 2004; Solheim et al., 2012). This may be because dependency is both age-sensitive and culturally specific, with some cultures valuing independence and autonomy more than others (Solheim et al., 2012). Following these same lines of reasoning, we encourage teachers to view dependency not as an obstacle but as a much-needed opportunity to support the student's development of self-regulation and autonomy in a way that is developmentally and culturally appropriate (see McGrath & Van Bergen, 2015; Roorda et al., 2011). In high school, while closeness and conflict remain important, instructional support may become more pertinent than dependency (Ang, 2005; Ang et al., 2020; see also Burns et al., 2022). Applying these constructs, student–teacher relationships have traditionally been classified as being either positive or negative. A positive student–teacher relationship is high in closeness (and instructional support) and low in conflict (and dependency), while a negative relationship is low in closeness and high in conflict (Hughes, 2011; Pianta, 2001; Pianta & Stuhlman, 2004).

Towards a More Nuanced View of Student–Teacher Relationships

Although educational research has traditionally dichotomised student-teacher relationships as positive and negative, these relationships may be more nuanced in practice. For example, it is entirely possible for students and teachers who share warmth and closeness to also experience significant conflict (Spilt & Koomen, 2009). In recent research, McGrath and Van Bergen (2017, 2019) presented four relationship categories, based on bisections of both closeness and conflict data among primary school teachers who were asked to report their most 'well-behaved' and disruptive students in Kindergarten, Year 1, and Year 2. They found evidence that more than 40% of relationships in their study may be 'atypical', with either high closeness and high conflict (a *complicated* relationship), or low closeness and low conflict (a *reserved* relationship). Together, these atypical relationship types exceeded the number of purely negative relationships (see Table 16.1).

Building on this earlier work, Burns et al. (2022) used latent profile analysis–a statistical technique which enables different subgroups within a population to emerge–to examine different relationship types among high school students and their science teachers. More than 2000 Australian students were asked to report on emotional support, instructional support, and conflict with their science teacher. Four relationship profiles were identified: positive (20.7%), negative (16.6%), complicated (28.2%), and distant (34.5%; see Figure 16.1). These high school student profiles look very similar to the primary student profiles identified in McGrath and Van Bergen (2019), with the caveat that there were fewer positive relationships and more complicated relationships. As might be expected, students with negative student-teacher relationships also reported lower motivation in science.

The identification of multiple student–teacher relationship types, in primary and secondary school, highlights the need for teachers and researchers to broaden their discussions of relationships beyond the positive–negative dichotomy. This is important for two reasons. First, and despite benefiting strongly from relational closeness, students in complicated student–teacher relationships may still require support to improve prosocial behaviour and reduce aggression. As relational closeness may be less stable than conflict (Lee & Bierman, 2018), it is also possible that these same students will not experience the benefits of close relationships with other teachers. It is therefore vital that teachers do not overlook necessary behaviour supports, despite their own feelings of closeness towards the student. Similarly, it is important for teachers to remember that closeness is

Table 16.1 Characteristics of Four Student-Teacher Relationship Types

Relationship type	Characteristics	Incidence
Positive	High in closeness and low in conflict	41.2%
Complicated	High in closeness and high in conflict	15.7%
Reserved	Low in closeness and low in conflict	25.5%
Negative	Low in closeness and high in conflict	17.6%

Adapted from McGrath and Van Bergen (2019).

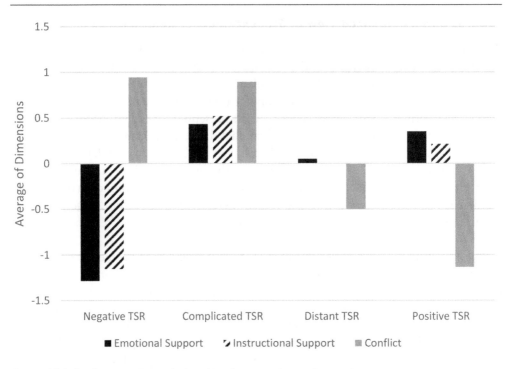

Figure 16.1 Student-teacher relationships in secondary science classrooms.

not necessarily the antidote to conflict, as they are not mutually exclusive interactions. Instead, teachers and school support staff may consider instructional strategies and behaviour supports that reduce conflict and sustain closeness (Burns et al., 2022).

Second, students with reserved or distant student–teacher relationships may be particularly vulnerable to negative academic and social outcomes. As reserved relationships are characterised by both low closeness and low conflict, these students may go unnoticed by teachers and receive considerably less attention, time, and support than students who experience other relationship types. Compounding this risk is a possible confound between reserved student–teacher relationships and shyness. Shy students often have great difficulty in forming positive relationships with their teachers, and therefore have relationships that are neither close nor conflictual (Coplan & Rudasill, 2016). Interestingly, however, they also tend to have higher levels of dependency on teachers (Arbeau et al., 2010). This dependency may be due to anxiety when interacting with peers, which leads the student to over-rely on teachers for social interaction (Arbeau et al., 2010). To ensure the development of close and supportive relationships with teachers and peers alike, such students must be identified and supported.

Student–Teacher Relationships in Context

When considering the characteristics of different student–teacher relationships, it is important to examine the broader contexts in which those relationships occur. These broader contexts have an impact on how close and effective student–teacher relationships are, and the influence of the student–teacher relationship on other developmental outcomes. For almost 40 years, Bronfenbrenner's seminal ecological systems theory (1979) has been used to describe how factors relating to the individual student, the student's family, the school, the peer group, and the broader community each have complex and interrelated influences on child and adolescent development. At the individual level, for example, prior educational experiences may influence a student's developmental outcomes and their relationships, while at the peer level, the educational values and antisocial behaviours of one's friends may be of influence. At the family level, socio-economic status and family conflict each play a role, and at the community level, student safety and community involvement are likely to be influential.

Drawing upon Bronfenbrenner's classic work (1979), relationship scholars have also developed ecological models of development to examine both the role of student–teacher relationships in development, and the processes and experiences that may influence relationship quality (O'Connor, 2010; Pianta & Walsh, 1996). Such research has identified important findings for student wellbeing, including that high-stakes testing negatively impacts close student–teacher relationships (Thompson, 2013) and that there is a bidirectional relationship between student–teacher relationship quality and peer liking (Endedijk et al., 2022; Hughes & Chen, 2011). For younger children, there are even early findings that a close student-teacher relationship can protect against the negative effects of a poor parent-child relationship (Hughes & Cavell, 1999).

Using ecological models of development, student–teacher relationships have increasingly been targeted as a mechanism for enhancing development for students at risk. Not only do student–teacher relationships have powerful outcomes, but they also are amenable to intervention. This means there is the potential for whole-school communities to implement initiatives designed to improve the quality of specific students' relationships with their teachers and, in doing so, also target other child and adolescent outcomes, such as peer relationships, academic achievement and student behaviour (Quin, 2017). Other contextual factors (e.g., school resourcing, family influences) that place students at risk of negative outcomes are less readily influenced by educators within the school community (Quin, 2017). It is important to remember that the outcomes of these relationship interventions are also likely to be influenced by other in-school factors, including academic climate, interpersonal safety, and institutional environment (Quin et al., 2018). Thus, other approaches might also be needed in specific cases. When relationship interventions are paired with these other approaches, the chance of positive student outcomes is high.

The Role of the Teacher: Emotional Labour, Relational Labour, and Instruction

Above we describe how individual student or teacher characteristics, peer and family relationships, and school and community structures might also influence student–teacher relationships and student outcomes. As many readers of this book are pre-service and existing teachers, there is a need to also consider the work of teachers specifically. Here, we focus on the role of the teacher in managing and building close and effective student–teacher relationships.

Teaching is often described as a type of *emotional labour*, requiring teachers to manage their emotions in accordance with professional rules and expectations (de Ruiter et al., 2021). This classification does not fully consider the longitudinal and interpersonal nature of classroom dynamics, however. Given the inherently relational work of teachers, we identify teaching as also being a kind of *relational labour*. In addition to being required to manage their emotions to conform to predetermined rules, teachers are expected to have superior relational skills that allow them to form close relationships with a diverse range of students. Hence, the teachers who are most likely to be considered 'effective' by colleagues, students and parents are those whom students can connect with and relate to on a personal level. In this chapter, we use the term 'relational labour' to frame the practices that promote relational closeness between teachers and students.

Of course, relational work is not a teacher's only task. Perhaps most prominent in popular discourse is the expectation that teachers should provide instruction that aligns with the prescribed academic curriculum. Yet relationships and instructional work are mutually dependent. When students struggle to understand a difficult concept, for example, those with close student–teacher relationships are likely to feel comfortable expressing frustration or difficulty in a safe and secure environment. The teacher is then afforded the opportunity to offer emotional support while simultaneously providing more nuanced instruction. When there is a mismatch between a student's psychological needs and learning, teachers who are close to that student may be better able to disentangle these competing motivations. For this reason, the overlap between relational and instructional work is critical (Nie & Lau, 2009).

Benefits of Close Student–Teacher Relationships for Students, Teachers, and Society

Just as student–teacher relationships are multifaceted, so too are their benefits. Below we highlight short- and long-term benefits for students, teachers, and society. We note that these benefits are long term and interlinked, with strong bodies of evidence to support them. We highlight the need for relationship-building to be prioritised in pre-service teacher training, whole-school interventions, and broader educational policies.

Benefits for Students. Close and supportive student–teacher relationships contribute to students' wellbeing and psychological engagement, academic performance, and peer relationships (Hamre & Pianta, 2001; McGrath & Van Bergen, 2015; Quin, 2017). In contrast, poor student–teacher relationships contribute to low academic achievement and greater disciplinary infractions, even when student behaviour is accounted for (Hamre & Pianta, 2001). High-quality student–teacher relationships are also protective (McGrath & Van Bergen, 2015), with students being less likely to be absent from school, to be suspended, or to drop out (Burns, 2020; De Wit et al., 2010; Rumberger, 2011).

The benefits of close and supportive student–teacher relationships are particularly important for students who are otherwise vulnerable. For example, Meehan et al. (2003) found evidence of reduced aggression in students with supportive teacher relationships, with particularly strong effects for students in minority groups. Close relationships with teachers can also buffer the detrimental effects of negative parent–child relationships (Hughes & Cavell, 1999). Indeed, students without other positive adult role models may be particularly likely to take notice of positive social processes and behaviours displayed by teachers in the classroom (Catalano et al., 2004). Although a legacy of successive close relationships is optimal (Lee & Bierman, 2018), just one teacher can make a powerful difference. McGrath and Van Bergen's (2015) review of 92 studies on student–teacher relationships revealed that a single close relationship can protect students who are at risk.

Benefits for Teachers. Although student–teacher relationships are typically discussed relative to student outcomes, they are also important for teachers. Teachers report considerable distress from managing disruptive classroom behaviours (Beaman et al., 2007), with long-term wellbeing and employment outcomes. In a large-scale study of 2569 Norwegian teachers, for example, Skaalvik and Skaalvik (2011) found that problems with student discipline left teachers feeling emotionally exhausted, and this exhaustion in turn predicted both lower job satisfaction and higher motivation to leave the teaching profession. If close and supportive student–teacher relationships can arrest these behaviours, as we show above, the benefits for teachers and their schools are enormous.

Closeness with students is also an important source of teacher wellbeing more broadly (Milatz et al., 2015), and teachers typically report finding the relational aspects of their work highly rewarding (Gallant & Riley, 2017). This was particularly evident during the COVID-19 remote learning period. The difficulties teachers faced in building relationships with students had negative impacts on their wellbeing (Van Bergen & Daniel, 2022). Given the benefits of closeness for students and teachers alike, strategies are needed to identify teachers who commonly experience lower levels of closeness. Although there is some counterintuitive evidence that low levels of closeness may protect teachers from emotional exhaustion (Milatz et al., 2015), this strategy is likely to backfire. Low closeness with students serves as a coping strategy in the short term but is also associated with teachers' feelings of helplessness (Spilt & Koomen, 2009). A more effective strategy, therefore, is to provide direct and indirect support for teachers as they engage in relationship-building and relational labour. We discuss this support in our final section.

Benefits for Society. Over and above the benefits of close student–teacher relationships for individual students, teachers, and schools, there are also significant flow-on benefits for society. We note above, for example, that close and supportive student–teacher relationships can significantly reduce students' aggressive behaviour. Given evidence that aggression at school predicts long-term unemployment and criminal activity (Kokko & Pulkkinen, 2000), these early relationships may have larger economic and social-justice benefits for individuals and communities. As above, students who experience close relationships with their teachers are also less likely to be truant, to be suspended, or to drop out of school. Such trends have important societal outcomes: truancy and dropout are associated with diminished physical and emotional health (and, thus, greater societal health burden), reduced academic opportunities, poor vocational opportunities, and increased mortality (Belfield & Levin, 2007). The greater engagement students have with school, the stronger the social benefits overall.

Nurturing Close and Supportive Student–Teacher Relationships

In the final section of this chapter, we consider what teachers can do to build strong relationships with their students. We draw on our own research conducted with collaborators in Australia, and on research conducted by other teams internationally. Consistent with the view that teaching is a kind of *relational labour*, we organise this section by strategies and approaches that can be used to build closeness, reduce conflict, and respond to dependency, as well as schoolwide approaches that can be taken to support teachers and create a positive school environment in which healthy relationships are prioritised. When considering these approaches, we recommend an overarching multi-tiered system of support: with ongoing data collection and evidence used to triage students who could benefit from whole school approaches, small group interventions, or intensive one-on-one strategies.

In considering how teachers can best build close relationships with their students, it is important to also consider how the student–teacher relationship changes over time. Research focusing on the progression of individual student–teacher relationships across the school year is limited, yet it suggests that there are multiple opportunities to renegotiate relationship boundaries. In a longitudinal case study of a disruptive student and his teacher, Newberry (2010) describes four relationship phases:

1. *an appraisal phase*, where the student and teacher gather information about one another,
2. *an agreement phase*, where routines, expectations and interactional styles are established,
3. *a testing phase*, where boundaries are explored and re-established, and
4. *a planning phase*, where the student and teacher reflect on their past experiences and establish expectations for the future.

Critically, each phase offers opportunities for individual or whole-school interventions. Put simply, therefore, it is never too late to enhance student–teacher relationship quality.

Building Closeness

Closeness within the student–teacher relationship is supported by care, warmth, and open communication (Pianta, 2001). Students are likely to feel closer to teachers who express an interest in their personal lives, who offer support when needed, and who care about their wellbeing. They are less likely to feel close to teachers with whom they clash.

Across the past ten years, a range of interventions has been developed to support the emergence of warm and supportive student–teacher interactions (Sabol & Pianta, 2012). These interventions typically enjoy moderate support. In the 'Banking Time' intervention for younger children, for example, teachers work one-on-one with a student they are worried about to observe the student's actions and emotions during play (Driscoll & Pianta, 2010). To demonstrate emotional sensitivity and care, the teacher then narrates the child's actions and emotions back to the student in an interested tone of voice. After just six weeks, teachers who participate in the Banking Time intervention report higher levels of closeness with the targeted student, increased frustration tolerance themselves, and more successful classroom interactions (Driscoll & Pianta, 2010). In the "My Teaching Partner—Secondary" intervention for secondary students, teachers are offered strategies to increase closeness and boost their instructional success simultaneously (Mikami et al., 2011). They may, for example, be encouraged to ask about students' extracurricular interests, and then to incorporate these interests into their teaching. Such interventions require the dedicated focus of a teacher on particular students yet are otherwise easy to implement.

Interestingly, and as alluded to in the Banking Time intervention, teachers' own attitudes and emotional responses are also important in facilitating relationship closeness. When students are disruptive, teachers who make external attributions for this disruption and who express high emotional competence are likely to experience closer and more enjoyable relationships than those who do not (McGrath & Van Bergen, 2019). Drawing on the notion of relational labour, such teachers may regulate their own emotional responses to frustration to nurture their ongoing relationships with students. They also appear to be more likely to express emotional self-efficacy: a belief that they can regulate their emotional reactions and supporting students to regulate theirs. For teachers who have lower emotional self-efficacy, engaging with psychologists (or other expert coaches) in emotion-reframing strategies and self-efficacy interventions may be beneficial for both themselves and their students.

Finally, when considering how best to build close and supportive relationships for at-risk groups, we encourage teachers not to forget about the students in their classes who are especially shy. Shy students do not typically experience high levels of conflict with their teachers, and, thus, they are more readily overlooked. Such students are highly likely to turn to teachers for emotional support when they are feeling anxious about interacting with peers, however, and there is good evidence that relational closeness with a teacher can protect shy students from peer rejection and school avoidance (Arbeau et al., 2010).

Reducing Conflict

In public discourse, student–teacher conflict is often attributed to disruptive and challenging student behaviours, such as calling out in class, shouting, hitting, and swearing. Consistent, systematic, and evidence-based behavioural interventions for students who exhibit disruptive and challenging behaviours are critically important. Students themselves often report a need for such support, with suspended students reporting that they would have been less likely to be suspended if they had learned alternative strategies to manage their behaviours, received additional assistance with schoolwork and been given support to manage stressors at home (Quin & Hemphill, 2014). Recent research also provides direction for interventions to minimise conflict. Graham and Walker (2021) reported that student self-regulation and oral language development had positive associations with classroom behaviour and subsequent relationships with teachers. Interestingly, however, research has shown that only half (53%) of the variance in teachers' ratings of conflict can be attributed to student behaviour (Hamre et al., 2008). Other factors include teachers' own mental health and self-efficacy, with teachers who feel less able to manage their classroom and less able to motivate students also reporting higher levels of conflict with the students in their class (Hamre et al., 2008). That these ratings of conflict exist over and above students' own disruptive behaviour suggests that initiatives and interventions to support teachers' own wellbeing and self-efficacy may have powerful implications for relational conflict, too. Even when particular students exhibit disruptive or challenging behaviour that is slow to change, teachers' beliefs and actions are powerful and important.

One mistake that teachers may make in an attempt to reduce potential conflict is to give a pre-emptive warning or reprimand. Yet our own research reveals that this approach may backfire. To better understand students' perceptions of their relationships with teachers, Van Bergen et al. (2020) conducted interviews with 96 Australian students in middle childhood and adolescence (Years 3 to 9). Some of the participants were enrolled in alternative school settings for students with behavioural difficulties, giving unique insight into the factors driving relationship quality for both mainstream and non-mainstream groups. Interestingly, although students themselves varied in age, school context, and propensity for disruptive behaviour, the factors underpinning their perceptions of high-and low-quality relationships were remarkably consistent. Students reported close, supportive relationships with teachers who they perceived as being kind, caring, helpful or humorous, and negative, conflictual relationships with teachers who they perceived as being hostile or unjust (Van Bergen et al., 2020). Importantly, reports of injustice highlighted pre-emptive discipline as a key source of conflict:

> Well, she always picked me out, as well, for misbehaving, so I got in a lot of trouble for that, but . . . like, a lot of people were just doing a lot worse than I was doing, but she was like, no, no, you've been bad before (Sean, aged 15).

One reason that pre-emptive discipline is so likely to contribute to relational conflict is that it conveys negative expectations. In related research, findings over several decades have also highlighted the detrimental effect of negative expectations on academic achievement and progression (Rubie-Davies et al., 2006). To support student behaviour, reduce relational conflict, and enhance other developmental outcomes, positive expectations and optimism are critical.

Supporting Teachers

Thus far, our recommendations for enhancing close relationships and reducing conflict have centred on strategies that individual teachers can use when interacting with students. Both in Australia and internationally, there has been a tendency to place responsibility for student outcomes on 'super' teachers without addressing broader, systemic issues (Mockler, 2014). Consistent with a multi-tiered system of support, however, it is the responsibility of the entire school community to create an environment in which close and nurturing relationships with all children are modelled, supported, and encouraged, and where conflictual and reserved relationships are addressed sensitively and urgently. An explicit whole-school approach is invaluable.

School leaders can play a vital role in creating a whole-school climate that is emotionally positive and supportive, and which promotes teacher efficacy (Wang & Degol, 2016). Among Australian teachers who had left the profession, for example, Gallant and Riley (2017) found evidence of significant stress and burnout due to a perception of poor support, excessive workloads, and short-term contracts. Although many of these stressors are structural, and beyond the control of any one school, leaders can provide emotional support to students, staff members and parents in the school community who are experiencing undue stress by addressing their concerns sensitively and directly. At an administrative level, school leaders should also seek to decrease those extraneous workload demands that are within their control, and to set clear behavioural expectations and values for the school community. Here we note it is also a responsibility of educational policy and funding bodies to offer adequate support and resources to make reducing workload viable for school leaders. Finally, leaders can demonstrate confidence in their teachers by allowing them greater autonomy where possible. Leaders who are effective in providing timely direction, intervention, and support will create opportunities for teachers to invest greater time and energy in building relationships with their own students.

It is also highly advantageous for teachers to have the support of a collaborative pastoral-care team that includes school psychologists and other specialist staff. Ideally, this pastoral-care team should work directly with school leaders to provide holistic support to the entire school community. For students, of course, psychological support is critical, and—as we note above—even highly disruptive students frequently identify this as a need (Quin & Hemphill, 2014). Yet teachers, too, need support, and this is particularly the case when they are charged with managing complex student behaviours. Worryingly, school psychologists typically have limited time in which to work with teachers and their students (Tegethoff et al., 2014). In many cases, this means that teachers must manage at least some complex student behaviours with limited support for their own psychological needs. To address this problem, we advocate for widespread increases in educational funding for qualified specialist school staff.

Conclusion

Across this chapter, we have identified the key characteristics of close student–teacher relationships and discussed the benefit for students who experience a close relationship with their teachers. Given the value of close student–teacher relationships for all students—irrespective of their learning, developmental and behavioural characteristics—we suggest that schools focus on relationships as an essential priority. To support this goal, we have reviewed a variety of interrelated strategies and approaches for building close relationships. We see, for example, that teachers can begin to build a close relationship with any student—even if the student is at risk in other ways—by simply expressing care and positive regard. This is an important finding, because it positions the quality of each student–teacher relationship within the teachers' sphere of influence. Of course, the expression of care can sometimes seem extremely challenging, particularly in the face of chronic misbehaviour. The research clearly shows that close and supportive relationships between students and their teachers are both necessary and valuable, however. Moreover, they also help to mitigate misbehaviour. Teachers who manage, develop, and pursue close and supportive relationships with their students are often adept at considering a variety of explanations for their students' behaviour and in regulating their own emotional reactions carefully. Schools and communities must look for ways to support teachers in this task, such that no students (or teachers) fall through the cracks.

References

Ang, R. P. (2005). Development and validation of the teacher-student relationship inventory using exploratory and confirmatory factor analysis. *The Journal of Experimental Education, 74*(1), 55–74. https://doi.org/10.3200/JEXE.74.1.55-74

Ang, R. P., Ong, S. L., & Li, X. (2020). Student version of the Teacher–Student Relationship Inventory (S-TSRI): Development, validation and invariance. *Frontiers in Psychology, 11,* 1724–1724. https://doi.org/10.3389/fpsyg.2020.01724

Arbeau, K. A., Coplan, R. J., & Weeks, M. (2010). Shyness, teacher-child relationships, and socio-emotional adjustment in grade 1. *International Journal of Behavioral Development, 34*(3), 259–269. https://doi.org/10.1177/0165025409350959

Beaman, R., Wheldall, K., & Kemp, C. (2007). Recent research on troublesome classroom behaviour: A review. *Australasian Journal of Special Education, 31*(1), 45–60. https://doi.org/10.1080/10300110701189014

Belfield, C. R. & Levin, H. M. (2007). *The price we pay: Economic and social consequences of inadequate education.* Brookings Institution Press.

Brekelmans, M., Wubbels, T., & van Tartwijk, J. (2005). Teacher–student relationships across the teaching career. *International Journal of Educational Research, 43*(1), 55–71. https://doi.org/10.1016/j.ijer.2006.03.006

Bronfenbrenner, U. (1979). *The ecology of human development: Experiments by nature and design.* Harvard University Press.

Burns, E. C. (2020). Factors that support high school completion: A longitudinal examination of quality teacher-student relationships and intentions to graduate. *Journal of Adolescence, 84*(1), 180–189. https://doi.org/10.1016/j.adolescence.2020.09.005

Burns, E. C., Bostwick, K. C. P., Collie, R. J., & Martin, A. J. (2019). Understanding girls' disengagement: Identifying patterns and the role of teacher and peer support using latent growth modeling. *Journal of Youth and Adolescence, 48*(5), 979–995. https://doi.org/10.1007/s10964-019-00986-4

Burns, E. C., Van Bergen, P., Leonard, A., & Amin, Y. (2022). Positive, complicated, distant, and negative: How different teacher-student relationship profiles relate to students' science motivation. *Journal of Adolescence, 94*(8), 1150–1162. https://doi.org/10.1002/jad.12093

Catalano, R. F., Oesterle, S., Fleming, C. B., & Hawkins, J. D. (2004). The importance of bonding to school for healthy development: Findings from the social development research group. *The Journal of School Health, 74*(7), 252–261. https://doi.org/10.1111/j.1746-1561.2004.tb08281.x

Coplan, R. J., & Rudasill, K. M. (2016). *Quiet at school: An educator's guide to shy children.* Teachers College Press.

de Ruiter, J. A., Poorthuis, A. M. G., & Koomen, H. M. Y. (2021). Teachers' emotional labor in response to daily events with individual students: The role of teacher–student relationship quality. *Teaching and Teacher Education, 107*, 103467. https://doi.org/10.1016/j.tate.2021.103467

De Wit, D. J., Karioja, K., & Rye, B. J. (2010). Student perceptions of diminished teacher and classmate support following the transition to high school: Are they related to declining attendance? *School Effectiveness and School Improvement, 21*(4), 451–472. https://doi.org/10.1080/09243453.2010.532010

Driscoll, K. C., & Pianta, R. C. (2010). Banking time in head start: Early efficacy of an intervention designed to promote supportive teacher-child relationships. *Early Education and Development, 21*(1), 38–64. https://doi.org/10.1080/10409280802657449

Endedijk, H. M., Breeman, L. D., van Lissa, C. J., Henickx, M. M. H., den Boer, L., & Mainhard, T. (2022). The teacher's invisible hand: A meta-analysis of the relevance of teacher–student relationship quality for peer relationships and the contribution of student behavior. *Review of Educational Research, 92*(3), 370–412. https://doi.org/10.3102/00346543211051428

Gallant, A., & Riley, P. (2017). Early career teacher attrition in Australia: Inconvenient truths about new public management. *Teachers and Teaching, Theory and Practice, 23*(8), 896–913. https://doi.org/10.1080/13540602.2017.1358707

Graham, L. J., & Walker, S. (2021). At risk students and teacher-student relationships: Student characteristics, attitudes to school and classroom climate. *International Journal of Inclusive Education, 25*(8), 896–913. https://doi.org/10.1080/13603116.2019.1588925

Hamre, B. K., & Pianta, R. C. (2001). Early teacher-child relationships and the trajectory of children's school outcomes through eighth grade. *Child Development, 72*(2), 625–638. https://doi.org/10.1111/1467-8624.00301

Hamre, B. K., Pianta, R. C., Downer, J. T., & Mashburn, A. J. (2008). Teachers' perceptions of conflict with young students: Looking beyond problem behaviors. *Social Development, 17*(1), 115–136. https://doi.org/10.1111/j.1467-9507.2007.00418.x

Hughes, J. N. (2011). Longitudinal effects of teacher and student perceptions of teacher-student relationship qualities on academic adjustment. *The Elementary School Journal, 112*(1), 38–60. https://doi.org/10.1086/660686

Hughes, J. N., & Cavell, T. A. (1999). Influence of the teacher-student relationship in childhood conduct problems: A prospective study. *Journal of Clinical Child Psychology, 28*(2), 173–184. https://doi.org/10.1207/s15374424jccp2802_5

Hughes, J. N., & Chen, Q. (2011). Reciprocal effects of student–teacher and student–peer relatedness: Effects on academic self-efficacy. *Journal of Applied Developmental Psychology, 32*(5), 278–287. https://doi.org/10.1016/j.appdev.2010.03.005

Jerome, E. M., Hamre, B. K., & Pianta, R. C. (2009). Teacher-child relationships from kindergarten to sixth grade: Early childhood predictors of teacher-perceived conflict and closeness. *Social Development, 18*(4), 915–945. https://doi.org/10.1111/j.1467-9507.2008.00508.x

Kokko, K., & Pulkkinen, L. (2000). Aggression in childhood and long-term unemployment in adulthood: A cycle of maladaptation and some protective factors. *Developmental Psychology, 36*(4), 463–472. https://doi.org/10.1037/0012-1649.36.4.463

Lee, P., & Bierman, K. L. (2018). Longitudinal trends and year-to-year fluctuations in student–teacher conflict and closeness: Associations with aggressive behavior problems. *Journal of School Psychology, 70*, 1–15. https://doi.org/10.1016/j.jsp.2018.06.002

McGrath, K. F., & Van Bergen, P. (2015). Who, when, why and to what end? Students at risk of negative student–teacher relationships and their outcomes. *Educational Research Review, 14*, 1–17. https://doi.org/10.1016/j.edurev.2014.12.001

McGrath, K. F., & Van Bergen, P. (2017). Elementary teachers' emotional and relational expressions when speaking about disruptive and well behaved students. *Teaching and Teacher Education, 67*, 487–497. https://doi.org/10.1016/j.tate.2017.07.016

McGrath, K. F., & Van Bergen, P. (2019). Attributions and emotional competence: Why some teachers experience close relationships with disruptive students (and others don't). *Teachers and Teaching, Theory and Practice, 25*(3), 334–357. https://doi.org/10.1080/13540602.2019.1569511

McGrath, K. F., Van Bergen, P., & Sweller, N. (2017). Adding color to conflict: Disruptive students' drawings of themselves with their teachers. *The Elementary School Journal, 117*(4), 642–663. https://doi.org/10.1086/691567

Meehan, B. T., Hughes, J. N., & Cavell, T. A. (2003). Teacher-student relationships as compensatory resources for aggressive children. *Child Development, 74*(4), 1145–1157. https://doi.org/10.1111/1467-8624.00598

Mikami, A. Y., Gregory, A., Allen, J. P., Pianta, R. C., & Lun, J. (2011). Effects of a teacher professional development intervention on peer relationships in secondary classrooms. *School Psychology Review, 40*(3), 367–385. https://doi.org/10.1080/02796015.2011.12087704

Milatz, A., Lüftenegger, M., & Schober, B. (2015). Teachers' relationship closeness with students as a resource for teacher wellbeing: A response surface analytical approach. *Frontiers in Psychology, 6*, 1949–1949. https://doi.org/10.3389/fpsyg.2015.01949

Mockler, N. (2014). Simple solutions to complex problems: moral panic and the fluid shift from "equity" to "quality" in education. *Review of Education, 2*(2), 115–143. https://doi.org/10.1002/rev3.3028

Murray, C., & Murray, K. M. (2004). Child level correlates of teacher-student relationships: An examination of demographic characteristics, academic orientations, and behavioral orientations. *Psychology in the Schools, 41*(7), 751–762. https://doi.org/10.1002/pits.20015

Newberry, M. (2010). Identified phases in the building and maintaining of positive teacher–student relationships. *Teaching and Teacher Education, 26*(8), 1695–1703. https://doi.org/10.1016/j.tate.2010.06.022

Nie, Y., & Lau, S. (2009). Complementary roles of care and behavioral control in classroom management: The self-determination theory perspective. *Contemporary Educational Psychology, 34*(3), 185–194. https://doi.org/10.1016/j.cedpsych.2009.03.001

O'Connor, E. (2010). Teacher–child relationships as dynamic systems. *Journal of School Psychology*, 48(3), 187–218. https://doi.org/10.1016/j.jsp.2010.01.001

O'Connor, E., & McCartney, K. (2007). Examining teacher-child relationships and achievement as part of an ecological model of development. *American Educational Research Journal*, 44(2), 340–369. https://doi.org/10.3102/0002831207302172

Pianta, R. C. (2001). *Student–teacher relationship scale: Professional manual*. Psychological Assessment Resources.

Pianta, R. C., & Stuhlman, M. W. (2004). Teacher-child relationships and children's success in the first years of school. *School Psychology Review*, 33(3), 444–458. https://doi.org/10.1080/02796015.2004.12086261

Pianta, R. C. & Walsh, D. J. (1996). *High-risk children in schools: Constructing sustaining relationships*. Routledge.

Quin, D. (2017). Longitudinal and contextual associations between teacher-student relationships and student engagement: A systematic review. *Review of Educational Research*, 87(2), 345–387. https://doi.org/10.3102/0034654316669434

Quin, D., Heerde, J. A., & Toumbourou, J. W. (2018). Teacher support within an ecological model of adolescent development: Predictors of school engagement. *Journal of School Psychology*, 69, 1–15. https://doi.org/10.1016/j.jsp.2018.04.003

Quin, D., & Hemphill, S. A. (2014). Students' experiences of school suspension. *Health Promotion Journal of Australia*, 25(1), 52–58. https://doi.org/10.1071/HE13097

Roorda, D. L., Koomen, H. M. Y., Spilt, J. L., & Oort, F. J. (2011). The influence of affective teacher-student relationships on students' school engagement and achievement: A meta-analytic approach. *Review of Educational Research*, 81(4), 493–529. https://doi.org/10.3102/0034654311421793

Rubie-Davies, C., Hattie, J., & Hamilton, R. (2006). Expecting the best for students: Teacher expectations and academic outcomes. *British Journal of Educational Psychology*, 76(3), 429–444. https://doi.org/10.1348/000709905X53589

Rumberger, R. W. (2011). *Dropping out: Why students drop out of high school and what can be done about it*. Harvard University Press

Sabol, T. J., & Pianta, R. C. (2012). Recent trends in research on teacher-child relationships. *Attachment & Human Development*, 14(3), 213–231. https://doi.org/10.1080/14616734.2012.672262

Skaalvik, E. M., & Skaalvik, S. (2011). Teacher job satisfaction and motivation to leave the teaching profession: Relations with school context, feeling of belonging, and emotional exhaustion. *Teaching and Teacher Education*, 27(6), 1029–1038. https://doi.org/10.1016/j.tate.2011.04.001

Solheim, E., Berg-Nielsen, T. S., & Wichstrøm, L. (2012). The three dimensions of the student–teacher relationship scale: CFA validation in a preschool sample. *Journal of Psychoeducational Assessment*, 30(3), 250–263. https://doi.org/10.1177/0734282911423356

Spilt, J. L., Hughes, J. N., Wu, J.-Y., & Kwok, O.-M. (2012). Dynamics of teacher-student relationships: Stability and change across elementary school and the influence on children's academic success. *Child Development*, 83(4), 1180–1195. https://doi.org/10.1111/j.1467-8624.2012.01761.x

Spilt, J. L., & Koomen, H. M. Y. (2009). Widening the view on teacher-child relationships: Teachers' narratives concerning disruptive versus nondisruptive children. *School Psychology Review*, 38(1), 86–101. https://doi.org/10.1080/02796015.2009.12087851

Spilt, J. L., Koomen, H. M. Y., & Jak, S. (2012). Are boys better off with male and girls with female teachers? A multilevel investigation of measurement invariance and gender match in teacher–student relationship quality. *Journal of School Psychology, 50*(3), 363–378. https://doi.org/10.1016/j.jsp.2011.12.002

Tegethoff, M., Stalujanis, E., Belardi, A., & Meinlschmidt, G. (2014). School mental health services: Signpost for out-of-school service utilization in adolescents with mental disorders? A nationally representative United States cohort. *PloS One, 9*(6), e99675–e99675. https://doi.org/10.1371/journal.pone.0099675

Thompson, G. (2013). NAPLAN, MySchool and accountability: Teacher perceptions of the effects of testing. *International Education Journal, 12*(2), 62–84.

Van Bergen, P., & Daniel, E. (2022). "I miss seeing the kids!": Australian teachers' changing roles, preferences, and positive and negative experiences of remote teaching during the COVID-19 pandemic. *Australian Educational Researcher,* 1–20. https://doi.org/10.1007/s13384-022-00565-w

Van Bergen, P., Graham, L. J., & Sweller, N. (2020). Memories of positive and negative student-teacher relationships in students with and without disruptive behavior. *School Psychology Review, 49*(2), 178–194. https://doi.org/10.1080/2372966X.2020.1721319

Wang, M.-T., & Degol, J. L. (2016). School climate: A review of the construct, measurement, and impact on student outcomes. *Educational Psychology Review, 28*(2), 315–352. https://doi.org/10.1007/s10648-015-9319-1

Chapter 17

Parents and teachers working together

Glenys Mann, Katarzyna Fleming, Jacqueline Specht, & Francis Bobongie-Harris

Facilitating positive parent-teacher partnerships is more than just common sense; the literature is clear that productive partnerships between parents and teachers consistently lead to better outcomes for students (Povey et al., 2016). This is so for both social-emotional skills and academic achievement (Smith & Sheridan, 2019) and is true for all students including those with a disability, and those from disadvantaged and/or Indigenous backgrounds. The concept of partnership has been described as a relationship in which all partners are equally valued and recognised for their knowledge, experience, and skills (Gascoigne, 1996). Recognition of the importance of this partnership is evidenced by the existence of many parent-teacher partnership frameworks (Department of Education and Training, 2017; Education Endowment Foundation, 2021; Ministry of Education, 2010). Parent participation in educational programming for students with disabilities, for example, is now mandated in Australia, Canada, and the United Kingdom, and there is an expectation that parents and schools work in partnership to create and review programming goals, accommodations, and modifications.

Parent-teacher partnerships, however, can be difficult. In Australia, working better with families has consistently been identified as a priority area for educators and feature in Priority Area 2 of the *National Teacher Workforce Action Plan* (Department of Education, 2022), Finding 4.7 of the *Review of the National School Reform Agreement* (Productivity Commission, 2022), and the findings of Hearing 7 of the *Disability Royal Commission into Violence, Abuse, Neglect and Exploitation of People with Disability* (2021). In Canada, ineffective communication with parents about the rights of their children has been identified as an ongoing barrier to accessible education (Ontario Human Rights Commission, 2018). Parent-teacher partnerships can be particularly difficult when children have disability and for Indigenous and disadvantaged families (Sianturi et al., 2022).

Why Are Parent-Teacher Partnerships So Challenging?

Parent-teacher partnerships come under pressure in several ways. Evidence suggests that diminished trust in public institutions has widened the gap between family and school (Lasater, 2019), and opportunities for parents and teachers to engage in meaningful dialogue are becoming rarer (Rusnack, 2018). Inadequate coverage of parent-teacher

DOI: 10.4324/9781003350897-20

partnerships in Initial Teacher Education (ITE) may also leave graduates underprepared for working with parents (Thompson et al., 2018). In the United Kingdom, ITE focuses on the functionality of exchanges with families rather than engaging with theories of parent-teacher partnership or fostering authentic partnerships with parents (Mutton et al., 2018).

The formality of mandated processes for working with parents also constrains the nature of parent-school collaboration. These formal processes are rooted in educational jargon that can be intimidating for parents. They can also narrow the scope of what the parental role could be, and often promote parent participation on paper but not in practice (Finn, 2019). Additionally, parents can be faced with conflicting messages. Schools will encourage parent perspectives, but often respond to parental concerns with frustration or criticism (Finn, 2019; Lai & Vadeboncoeur, 2012). Furthermore, collaboration often takes a school-centric approach, where school staff are viewed as experts and parents as having limited knowledge (Baxter & Kilderry, 2022). Another concern with current models of collaboration is that schools are placing the responsibility of inclusion on parents and families by expecting their intense involvement (Bendixsen & Danielsen, 2020; Rossetti, Burke, Hughes, et al., 2021), an expectation that creates additional barriers for marginalised families. This brings us to a core question: What can be done to facilitate, improve, and sustain positive parent-teacher partnerships?

This chapter focuses on what *educators* can do. Certainly, educators and parents both need to feel equipped to rise to the occasion if collaboration is going to be effective (McDermott-Fasy, 2009), however, as much of the literature is aimed at parents, this chapter looks to supporting educators in their partnership work with parents. We focus on three spheres: communication, school culture, and decision-making, and discuss both barriers and enablers in these spheres. The chapter also focuses on partnership work in the context of inclusive education and students who are at risk of marginalisation. It is a worldwide ambition to ensure equitable access to education for all, including those with disability, Indigenous students, and children in vulnerable situations (United Nations Educational, Scientific and Cultural Organization, 2017). International treaties like the *Convention on the Rights of Persons with Disabilities* (United Nations, 2006) and the *United Nations Declaration on the Rights of Indigenous Peoples* (United Nations, 2007), highlight the importance of working with families to protect the rights of children. While we do reference considerations that are important for specific groups of parents, overall, our focus is on general advice that will be relevant for working better with *all* parents.

Sphere 1: Communication

Parents have noted that communication difficulties tend to arise when general education teachers are seemingly unprepared to meet the learning needs of their children. Some research indicates that when parents try to advocate for their children, negativity arises (Burke & Hodapp, 2016; Rossetti, Burke, Rios, et al., 2021). Too often, our own biases can cloud the ways in which we interpret people's actions. This issue indicates a need for parents and schools to have a shared vision for the process and outcomes of their communication (VanValkenburgh et al., 2021). Epstein et al. (2019) indicate that there are benefits to both parents and educators when communication is improved. Perhaps indicating benefits for both is a good starting point in the drive to increase communication to the two-way street that Fullan (2015) deemed as so essential. Parents may learn more about the academic and social development of their children, have a better knowledge of school procedures and policies, and their interaction with teachers can increase. Advantages for teachers may include increased understanding of parents and their situations. Such understandings help to decrease personal bias that can interfere with communication.

To benefit from these advantages, both teachers and parents must learn how to improve their communication skills. Parent advocacy training is one way to increase positive communication outcomes (Rios & Burke, 2021). In their systematic review of literature on community-based parenting programs, Rios and Burke (2021) determined that teachers who included culturally sensitive approaches were more successful than those that did not. When thinking of culturally sensitive approaches, it is necessary to think about parental needs to participate. Providing information in the home language is very important as is providing opportunities for parents to meet others in similar situations. Parenting networks are key to supporting parents within the school. Furthermore, when parent networks have opportunities to advocate collectively for their children, this can have a powerful impact on school reform.

Educators' recognition of, and support for, parental advocacy is also critical. Rossetti, Burke, Hughes, et al. (2021) indicate that the most effective types of advocacy that parents can employ are aspirational advocacy and social capital advocacy. Aspirational advocacy involves a focus on children's strengths and viewing them as competent and capable. Teachers must encourage parents to advocate for their children's success. Social capital advocacy involves teachers recognising that parental advocacy for their own children has potential to change the school experiences for others.

Other research has investigated how teachers can increase positive communication with families. For example, Sisson et al. (2022) note the ways in which teachers can speak to parents to show true partnership. Rather than just telling parents what needs to be done, teachers can ask parents what they think and for suggestions they have regarding supporting their children. Parents know their children and their expertise should be respected. Whitley et al. (2022) interviewed Canadian parents during the initial school closures during COVID-19 and heard loud and clear that they were feeling stressed because their children were not getting the support that they needed to learn the material. Although parents tried to explain what accommodations their children required, some teachers continued to provide the same work for all the children.

One interesting way of engaging parents involved teachers being present on the playground 10 minutes before school started (Sisson et al., 2022). This opened times for casual conversations between teachers and parents. This school also changed the wording of parent-teacher 'interview' to parent-teacher 'conversation', and introduced other ways of communicating. For example, if their children were having a tough morning before school, parents would send a quick email to teachers alerting them to the issue. Teachers then knew that the student may need a little more care that day. Van-Valkenburgh et al. (2021) noted that digital methods of communication (e.g., flyers, newsletters, email) are great, but reminds schools that traditional routes are important for parents who do not have access to technology. These small changes helped erase the hierarchy of power that had schools leading the connection. Teachers reported that parents felt reciprocal communication was possible, rather than waiting for teachers to reach out. Good communication builds trust and when trust is there, students do better (Bachman et al., 2021).

In Practice: What Do Parents of Students with Disability Say?

I wasn't prepared for how hard they clung to their goals. As we worked through each goal, I stated why I thought certain ones were unnecessary. They politely listened and then stated why they wanted it included. And then I countered with my suggestions and concerns, and they countered again. It seemed like they were listening to what I was saying but it wasn't their language. I felt that to get more goals removed I would have to be irate, and I erred on the side of preserving relationships . . .

I'm proud of the tone I set—checking every detail, speaking my mind, and building working relationships. I do wish the percentage of inclusion for my child was higher. I wasn't prepared for feeling so mixed, but truly it is a preview of the next 15 years. The biggest takeaway is that my foremost challenge will be educating each team member individually, and in their own 'language' about how and why inclusion is truly best practice (George, 2022).

The experiences of parents provide critical insights into parent-teacher communication. Reflection on what parents say about interacting with teachers can highlight differences in the 'language' of parents and teachers, for example, the ways they understand disability and their priorities for students (Community Resource Unit, 2019). Parents' experiences, such as those described in the previous quote, are reminders that shared language is more than just the terminology used. They also give cause to consider how often parents feel they must become irate before they will be listened to, and the importance of both parents and teachers investing in constructive communication as a means of building and preserving individual relationships.

Sphere 2: School Culture

Positive communication between parents and teachers does not happen in a vacuum. It is facilitated by the culture of a school, that is, the "values [and] expected norms" which "influence the actions and patterns of behaviour of those in the organisation" (McKeon, 2020, p. 162). You do not have to look too far in the literature on parent-teacher partnerships to read about school qualities that are key to positive home-school relationships; qualities such as 'trust', 'welcome', and 'respect'. The literature also identifies aspects of school culture that hinder parent-teacher partnerships, for example, being overly bureaucratic, inaccessible school processes, and negative teacher attitudes. We will look at these barriers first, before moving on to a discussion of facilitative school qualities.

When a school culture is highly bureaucratic and focuses heavily on "procedural fidelity" (Love et al., 2017, p. 159) rather than meaningful relationships, efficiency boxes get ticked, but authentic connection is compromised. A parent described the effects of this type of exchange in a study by Gilmore et al. (2022), saying, "there are teachers I've never even met for more than five minutes in the parent-teacher interview" (p. 188). Parent experience suggests that sometimes procedures put in place to facilitate parent-teacher partnerships become obstacles to the very relationships they are meant to assist (Gilmore et al., 2022). Relational issues undermine parent-teacher partnerships (Garbacz et al., 2022), so it is a problem when schools undervalue family-school collaboration and prioritise system concerns over individuals (deFur, 2012).

Furthermore, school systems can be difficult for parents to navigate, particularly for those parents who are not white, middle class, and educated (Connor & Cavendish, 2018). Repeatedly we hear from parents about the inaccessibility of school processes. Parents can feel talked down to (O'Hare et al., 2021; Solvason & Proctor, 2021) and that they are not trusted, respected, and believed (O'Hare et al., 2021). Tensions arise between parents and teachers when home and school belief systems collide, rather than cohere (Lalvani, 2015).

Finally, a culture of trust and welcome is unlikely if educators view parents as troublemakers (Bennett et al., 2020) or blame them for students' struggles (e.g., due to aspirations that might be different to those of the teachers). Surprisingly, this view of parents is not uncommon in the literature (e.g., Lasater, 2019; Thompson et al., 2018; Solvason & Proctor, 2021). Schools will not feel welcoming to parents if parent-teacher partnerships are viewed by teachers as challenging, extra work or a source of potential conflict (Lasater, 2019). So, what part can school culture play in nurturing healthy parent-teacher partnerships? To answer that question, we first turn to the topic of trust.

Rautamies et al. (2021) define trust within parent-teacher partnerships, as "parents' confidence that educators will act in a manner that benefits the relationship, or the goals of the relationship, in seeking positive outcomes on behalf of the child and parents" (p. 3). Broomhead (2018) adds that trustworthiness is being able to depend on others to "behave in accordance with our expectation" (p. 441). Parents' trust of educators is consistently described as foundational to working in partnership with teachers, so it is essential that educators know how parental trust is engendered. The literature suggests a range of qualities associated with trusting relationships. For example, parents are more likely to trust educators who are reliable (do what they say they will do), safe (who are positive about their students and inform parents about what is happening at school), and discrete (keep parent-teacher interactions and family business confidential) (Rautamies et al., 2021). Furthermore, Leenders et al. (2019) found that characteristics important for trust included openness of educators, informal contact, and outreach to parents. Other important qualities for trust include non-judgment of parents (Broomhead, 2018; Leenders et al., 2019), teacher approachability and availability (Broomhead, 2018), and honest, rich, and frequent interactions (Lasater, 2019). When trust is present in partnerships, biases, and assumptions can more easily be dispelled and misunderstandings do not need to cause conflict (Rautamies et al., 2021).

Another key element for positive parent-teacher partnerships is a school culture of welcome and belonging. However, for parents to feel welcome in schools, it is fundamental that educators have a desire to connect with them (Lasater, 2019) and to listen and respond to their concerns (Broomhead, 2018; Solvason & Proctor, 2021). A culture of welcome is built around respectful (O'Hare et al., 2021), warm and caring relationships (Rautamies et al., 2021), and regular events that nurture connections with parents, particularly for those who feel like they do not fit in (Leenders et al., 2019). Sensitivity to family backgrounds and the perspectives of parents is a must, if parents are to feel like they belong. Runswick-Cole et al. (2018) refer to "sympathetic moral imagination" (p. 546), whereby educators do not necessarily *understand* the experiences of parents but do recognise that parents have different but equally valid perspectives to their own and actively elicit those perspectives.

Deeply connected to parental feelings of trust and welcome is a school community that recognises the contribution of all its many members and values the expertise of both teachers and parents. Bennett et al. (2020) highlight this point in relation to their work on parents' experiences with the school system. Parents in their study noted that the teacher and the principal were so important in the success and failure of their children. If these individuals can make all the difference, it is clear that the power lies within the school rather than within the shared partnership of school and family. In collaborative school communities, educators are willing to try something different (Hodges et al., 2020), to abandon their expert role, to solve challenges together with parents, and to admit when they do not know or make a mistake (Leenders et al., 2019).

Empowering parents facilitates better relationships and authentic partnerships (Lasater, 2019). Managing the varying and sometimes conflicting expectations of stakeholders, however, can be a complex task. In undertaking this task there is no room for criticism, blame, and defensiveness (Hodges et al., 2020), and the important role of school leaders in influencing school culture and setting appropriate examples about forming relationships is clear (Broomhead, 2018). Let's now look at specific cultural considerations that are important for fostering connections with Indigenous families. We will then move on to our next section which goes into the sphere of shared decision-making in more detail.

In Practice: School Cultures that Foster Connections with Indigenous Families

Indigenous students are expected to know and understand Western ways of learning and experiencing success, however, for Indigenous students, achievement is not only defined by academic standards, but by social and cultural survival. Partnerships between schools and students, families, and communities are important for student success and for navigating the cultural interface between a Western and Indigenous society.

For educators to engage with Indigenous families, and more broadly Indigenous communities, requires an understanding of Indigenous Knowledges, relationships and responsibilities that connect Indigenous students to place and knowing. Teacher connection with Indigenous families also requires an understanding of how history and policy have impacted on the people of the community where they live, learn, and work. There is an interconnectedness between place and people, and it is important to understand why they are important to Indigenous peoples. Understanding these relationships and connections provides a more inclusive educational environment.

First, Indigenous communities are deeply linked to place through language, music, history, and culture. Indigenous knowledges are sacred and are at the heart of identity. Identity is influenced by language and culture and belonging to a kinship system. These are all connected back to place.

Second, history and policy have played an important part in determining where Indigenous communities are situated and how their communities have evolved. Relationships to place and land tie Indigenous students and their families back to their ancestral lands and environments. Prior to colonisation, there was recognition of a family's connection to place and their responsibility to the land, sky, and water systems attached to that place. Because of colonisation these connections are not as strong in some communities. It is important for educators to know and understand why this is the case.

Third, Indigenous students rely on the support of their extended families and support networks. Their families are made up of grandparents, mothers, fathers, uncles, aunties, brothers, sisters, and cousins. Sometimes there is no biological connection at all. These relationships and connections may not make sense to educators, but they do make sense to Indigenous students.

It is the responsibility of educators to connect with their students, families, and communities. Developing and strengthening relationships with Indigenous students, families and communities takes time. Communities operate in different ways with different processes and protocols in each. Before you engage be sure to know and understand the principles around these processes and protocols as engagement with Indigenous students, families, and the broader Indigenous community must take place in a respectful way. Quinn and Bobongie-Harris (2021) provide a set of guidelines to consider for engagement between an educational setting and their community, which include:

- getting to know where students come from, their family connections, and the Traditional Custodians of the lands where schools are situated,
- engaging informally with Indigenous students and their families by attending community events and celebrations, and
- ensuring that the school curriculum is embedded with Indigenous knowledge and perspectives.

Sphere 3: Decision-Making

The divergence in lived experiences of parents and teachers can lead to assumptions, unsubstantiated judgments, or disagreements about the most effective decisions regarding educational provision (Graham et al., 2020). Although it is unrealistic for each educator to have a deep understanding of all familial circumstances (Seligman & Darling, 2007), some parents argue that without this familiarity, educators are unable to develop empathy (Broomhead, 2018). This dissonance in experience, and therefore explicitly suggested [mis]understanding of parental point of view by teachers, emphasises the need for teachers and parents to learn from each other (Hodge & Runswick-Cole, 2018) and to acknowledge the differing standpoints (Connor & Cavendish, 2018). However, the extensive focus on academic attainment and teachers' performativity measures can take priority over creating opportunities to engage with families' lived experiences (Hellawell, 2018).

This openness can be challenging as it requires a change in attitudes and entrenched ways of working together (Mittler, 2001; Glazzard et al., 2015). On the one hand, teachers who have, historically, held professional dominance in decision-making processes (Mann & Gilmore, 2021) may now have to adopt the position of a learner whose expertise is not all-encompassing. On the other hand, parents might struggle to rebuild trust in partnerships, especially if they previously encountered challenges or a lack of support from services (Seligman & Darling, 2007). Moreover, this increased demand for parental expertise and engagement may put additional pressure on parents to navigate complex systems without adequate training and remuneration for their input (Fleming & Borkett, 2023). One may argue that the best interest of children cannot have a price tag attached to it; however, parental capacity for commitments outside of school life can already be significantly impacted and therefore this recognition requires careful consideration.

Co-production is an approach that recognises the importance of inclusive dialogue with families (Todd, 2007), and is recognised in the United Kingdom as a way to enable joint decision-making within inclusive education (Department for Education and Department of Health and Social Care, 2022). Despite requiring time to build trusting and reciprocal relationships, multiple attempts where both sides of the partnership can express their point of view, and to reassure participants that their contributions are recognised, respected, and acted upon (Needham, 2007), co-production is fostered across public services worldwide. In education, however, co-productive partnerships require conceptualisation and research (Boddison & Soan, 2022). Underpinned by principles of social justice, Fleming's (2021) framework for co-productive partnerships in Table 17.1 begins to address this gap and conceptualises co-production by bringing together key ideas from Cahn's (2000) four pillars of co-production, parental recommendations, and practical considerations for partnership working.

Although the framework was intended to amplify the historically marginalised "voice of parents/carers" (Tomlinson, 1982), Fleming (2021) recognised the

Table 17.1 Fleming's Framework for Co-Productive Parent-Practitioner Partnerships

Co-production (Cahn's pillars, 2000)	Parental recommendations for inclusive partnerships	Practical considerations for co-productive practice
Pillar 1. Everycne is an asset Equal, reciprocal, and participatory partnership: • Respectful and not power based or condescending. • Parents as the first and foremost experts and educators of their children.	• Being recognised and treated as an equal and valued contributor to decisions. • Recognise everyone as an asset. • All work together to make the best decision with available resources.	• 'Open door policy'—all voices are welcomed into the discussion. • Co-production interwoven into school strategies and ethos. • Parents engaged in planning and delivery of provisions/ community events/training and learning. • A bigger sense of an ongoing journey of reflection and action.
Pillar 2. Reworking current structures Learning from parents to shape services: • Effective information exchange. • Shared decision-making that responds to complex families' needs.	• Shared stories (by practitioners and parents) to inform practice and practitioners' reflection. • Anonymised stories can help families feel they are not alone in their experience. • Practitioners to share/express their humanity/vulnerability. • Set ground rules as this can be very subjective. • Consider stories of parents who do not engage.	• Celebration of parental input; parents invited, supported and renumerated, to deliver training and raise awareness of practitioners. • Parents actively engaged in shaping provisions and making decisions. • Authentic co-production that shows real engagement and prevents cynicism/ failure.

(Continued)

Table 17.1 (Continued)

Co-production (Cahn's pillars, 2000)	Parental recommendations for inclusive partnerships	Practical considerations for co-productive practice
Pillar 3. Reciprocity		
Acknowledging and working through difference: • Building trust and communication between participants. • Allowing bureaucrats and citizens to explain their perspective and listen to others. • Revealing citizens' needs. • Identifying the main causes of delivery problems and negotiating effective means to resolve them.	• Parents to be recognised for their expertise on their child, and on educational practice and policy. • Parents to recognise the limitations of policy/practice, too. • Challenging the assumptions that parents' expectations are unrealistic—adopting the mantra of 'every parent wants their child's needs to be met'.	• Sharing the same values of reciprocity, equality, and respect by acknowledging the need to learn together and from each other. • The premise of 'everyone being imperfect' and the commitment to reflect on and learn from mistakes. • Clear channels of communication about systemic ramifications (e.g., budgets) to enable parents to understand them.
Pillar 4. Social capital		
Inclusion is everyone's business: • Staff on the frontlines are recognised to have a distinctive voice and expertise as a result of regular interaction with parents and, often, parents' experience of schools is shaped almost entirely by their interaction with frontline staff.	• Understanding of disability and lived experiences of families should inform inclusive principles for schools.	• All staff (support, administrative, and casual) to engage in training delivered by parents. • Co-produced multi-modal materials to be made available for school staff (e.g., visual, policies written in accessible language). • Mission statements to always explicitly refer to inclusion.

Adapted from Fleming (2021).

imperative role of practitioners in co-productive partnerships and engaged in further small-scale research with parents and practitioners in education, health, and social care sectors to develop the framework further. Despite varying lived experiences, the shared space enabled by this study allowed participants to take time to make space for human connections, to consider the mutual impact of systemic barriers on providing support, and to engage in, what some might consider, a difficult dialogue. All participants were willing to engage in potentially challenging conversations about partnerships and were eager to ignite change in their own thinking and practice. The findings demonstrate the potential of co-productive partnerships in educational settings as a more equitable way for shared decision-making between educators and families.

In Practice: What Do Educators Say?

We're trying to work around it and to make sure that we are always the faces of the process for the parents, because they're having to share such intimate details of their life and their child's life and what they can and can't do, and how that impacts the family and the family dynamics. They're talking about a really complex relationship, and the fact that sometimes, as a parent, they can't cope. That's, that's an immense thing to have to communicate, to have to do that within an impersonal email. I, I think this and the idea of co-production is so important and I'm really, really hoping that our local authority rethinks . . . contracts the next time it comes up for review, because we're all human and we're all vulnerable and people don't want to share with a form (educator; Fleming, co-production pilot, 2021 unpublished data).

To embed co-productive partnerships in school life, teachers can utilise the principles of co-production and consider how their own assumptions, beliefs, and values might impact their interactions. They can reflect on their language and its implication for collaboration with parents, for example, whether working with parents is viewed as a 'them and us' scenario or as 'us working together for a shared outcome'. Finally, teachers can proactively plan for opportunities to learn from families they work with to ensure an appreciation of their circumstances and acceptance of their point of view.

Conclusion

In summary, when families and educators work productively together, students experience better outcomes both socially and academically. Effective home-school partnerships are underpinned by warm and supportive school cultures and rely on positive communication and shared decision-making. A celebration of reciprocal relationships between the school and families further contributes to the development of an ethos where the varied lived experiences of all stakeholders inform partnerships and ensure more socially just ways of working together. This chapter has provided evidence-based ideas to support such ways of working. We encourage continued discussion to promote the wellbeing of all stakeholders in schools.

References

Bachman, H. F., Anderman, E. M., Zyromski, B., & Boone, B. (2021). The role of parents during the middle school years: Strategies for teachers to support middle school family engagement. *School Community Journal, 31*(1), 109–126.

Baxter, G., & Kilderry, A. (2022). Family school partnership discourse: Inconsistencies, misrepresentation, and counter narratives. *Teaching and Teacher Education, 109*, 103561. https://doi.org/10.1016/j.tate.2021.103561

Bendixsen, S., & Danielsen, H. (2020). Great expectations: Migrant parents and parent-school cooperation in Norway. *Comparative Education, 56*(3), 349–364. https://doi.org/10.1080/03050068.2020.1724486

Bennett, S., Specht, J., Somma, M., & White, R. (2020). Navigating school interactions: Parents of students with intellectual disabilities speak out. *Current Developmental Disorders Reports, 7*(3), 149–154. https://doi.org/10.1007/s40474-020-00203-z

Boddison, A., & Soan, S. (2022). The coproduction illusion: Considering the relative success rates and efficiency rates of securing an education, health and care plan when requested by families or education professionals. *Journal of Research in Special Educational Needs, 22*(2), 91–104. https://doi.org/10.1111/1471-3802.12545

Broomhead, K. E. (2018). Perceived responsibility for developing and maintaining home–school partnerships: The experiences of parents and practitioners. *British Journal of Special Education, 45*(4), 435–453. https://doi.org/10.1111/1467-8578.12242

Burke, M. M., & Hodapp, R. M. (2016). The nature, correlates, and conditions of parental advocacy in special education. *Exceptionality, 24*(3), 137–150. https://doi.org/10.1080/09362835.2015.1064412

Cahn, E. (2000). *No more throw-away people: The co-production imperative.* Edgar Cahn.

Community Resource Unit. (2019). *Families for Inclusive Education Project.* https://cru.org.au/our-work/inclusive-education/

Connor, D. J., & Cavendish, W. (2018). Sharing power with parents: Improving educational decision making for students with learning disabilities. *Learning Disability Quarterly, 41*(2), 79–84. https://doi.org/10.1177/0731948717698828

deFur, S. (2012). Parents as collaborators: Building partnerships with school and community-based providers. *Teaching Exceptional Children, 44*(3), 58–67. https://doi.org/10.1177/004005991204400307

Department of Education. (2022). *National Teacher Workforce Action Plan.* https://www.education.gov.au/teaching-and-school-leadership/resources/national-teacher-workforce-action-plan

Department of Education and Training. (2017). *Family-school partnerships framework: A guide for school and families.* https://www.education.gov.au/supporting-family-school-community-partnerships-learning/family-school-partnerships/family-school-partnerships-framework

Department for Education and Department of Health and Social Care (2022). *SEND review. Right support, right place, right time.* https://www.gov.uk/government/consultations/send-review-right-support-right-place-right-time

Education Endowment Foundation. (2021). *Working with parents to support children's learning.* https://educationendowmentfoundation.org.uk/education-evidence/guidance-reports/supporting-parents

Epstein, J. L., Sanders, M. G., Sheldon, S., Simon, B. S., Salinas, K. C., Jansorn, N. R., Van-Voorhis, F. L., Martin, C. S., Thomas, B. G., & Greenfield, M. D. (2019). *School, family, and community partnerships: Your handbook for action* (4th ed.). Corwin Press.

Finn, R. (2019). Specifying the contributions of parents as pedagogues: Insights for parent-school partnerships. *The Australian Educational Researcher, 46*(1), 879–891. https://doi.org/10.1007/s13384-019-00318-2

Fleming, K. (2021). *Exploring inclusive partnerships: Parents, co-production, and the SEND code of practice (2015)*. Doctoral dissertation, Sheffield Hallam University. https://doi.org/10.7190/shu-thesis-00419

Fleming K., & Borkett, P. (2023). The potential of co-production. In P. Thompson & H. Simmons (Eds.). *Partnerships with parents in Early Childhood—Today* (forthcoming 2023). SAGE.

Fullan, M. (2015). *The new meaning of educational change*. Teachers College Press.

Garbacz, A., Godfrey, E., Rowe, D., & Kittelman, A. (2022). Increasing parent collaboration in the implementation of effective practices. *Teaching Exceptional Children, 54*(50), 324–327. https://journals.sagepub.com/doi/pdf/10.1177/00400599221096974

Gascoigne, E. (1996). *Working with parents: As partners in special educational needs*. David Fulton Publishers.

George, R. (2022). *Brave, not perfect*. ABI Community. https://www.abicommunity.org/news/brave-not-perfect

Gilmore, L., Mann G., & Pennell, D. (2022). Inclusive secondary schooling: Challenges in developing effective parent-teacher collaborations. In C. Boyle, & K-A. Allen (Eds.), *Research for inclusive quality education. Sustainable Development Goals series* (pp. 183–192). Springer.

Glazzard, J., Stokoe, J., Hughes, A., Netherwood, A., & Neve, L. (2015). *Teaching and supporting children with special educational needs and disabilities in primary schools* (2nd ed.). Learning Matters.

Graham, L. J., Medhurst, M., Tancredi, H., Spandagou, I., & Walton, E. (2020). Fundamental concepts of inclusive education. In L. J. Graham (Ed.), *Inclusive education for the 21st century: Theory, policy and practice* (pp. 27–54). Routledge.

Hellawell, B. (2018). "There is still a long way to go to be solidly marvellous": Professional identities, performativity and responsibilisation arising from the send code of practice 2015. *British Journal of Educational Studies, 66*(2), 165–181. https://doi.org/10.1080/00071005.2017.1363374

Hodge, N., & Runswick-Cole, K. (2018). "You Say . . . I Hear . . .": Epistemic gaps in practitioner-parent/carer talk. In K. Runswick-Cole, T. Curran, & K. Liddiard (Eds.), *The Palgrave handbook of disabled children's childhood studies* (pp. 537–555). Palgrave Macmillan.

Hodges, A., Joosten, A., Bourke-Taylor, H., & Cordier, R. (2020). School participation: The shared perspectives of parents and educators of primary school students on the autism spectrum. *Research in Developmental Disabilities, 97*, 103550. https://doi.org/10.1016/j.ridd.2019.103550

Lai, Y., & Vadeboncoeur, J. A. (2012). The discourse of parent involvement in special education: A critical analysis linking policy documents to the experiences of mothers. *Educational Policy, 27*(6), 867–897. https://doi.org/10.1177/0895904812440501

Lalvani, P. (2015). Disability, stigma and otherness: Perspectives of parents and teachers. *International Journal of Disability, Development and Education, 62*(4), 379–393. https://doi.org/10.1080/1034912X.2015.1029877

Lasater, K. (2019). Developing authentic family-school partnerships in a rural high school: Results of a longitudinal action research study. *School Community Journal, 29*(2), 157–182. https://files.eric.ed.gov/fulltext/EJ1236596.pdf

Leenders, H., de Jong, J., Monfrance, M., & Haelermans, C. (2019). Building strong parent-teacher relationships in primary education: The challenge of two-way communication. *Cambridge Journal of Education, 49*(4), 519–533. https://doi.org/10.1080/0305764X.2019.1566442

Love, H. R., Zagona, A. L., Kurth, J. A., & Miller, A. L. (2017). Parents' experiences in educational decision making for children and youth with disabilities. *Inclusion, 5*(3), 158–172. https://doi.org/10.1352/2326-6988-5.3.158

Mann, G., & Gilmore, L. (2021). Barriers to positive parent-teacher partnerships: The views of parents and teachers in an inclusive education context. *International Journal of Inclusive Education*, 1–13. Advance online publication. https://doi.org/10.1080/13603116.2021.1900426

McDermott-Fasy, C. E. (2009). *Family-school partnerships in Special Education: A narrative study of parental experiences.* Doctoral dissertation, Boston College. https://dlib.bc.edu/islandora/object/bc-ir:101976

McKeon, D. (2020). 'Soft barriers'—The impact of school ethos and culture on the inclusion of students with special educational needs in mainstream schools in Ireland. *Improving Schools, 23*(2), 159–174. https://doi.org/10.1177/1365480219898897

Ministry of Education. (2010). *Parents in partnership: A parent engagement policy for Ontario schools.* Ontario. https://files.ontario.ca/edu-1_6/edu-parents-in-partnership-engagement-policy-en-2022-03-07.pdf

Mittler, P. (2001). From exclusion to inclusion. In P. Mittler (Ed.), *Working towards inclusive education: Social contexts.* David Fulton Publishers.

Mutton, T., Burn, K., & Thompson, I. (2018). Preparation for family-school partnerships within initial teacher education programmes in England. *Journal of Education for Teaching, 44*(3), 278–295. https://doi.org/10.1080/02607476.2018.1465624

Needham, C. (2007). Realising the potential of co-production: Negotiating improvements in public services. *Social Policy and Society, 7*(2), 221–231. https://doi.org/10.1017/S1474746407004174

O'Hare, A., Saggers, B., Mazzucchelli, T., Gill, C., Hass, K., Shochet, I., Orr, J., Wurfl, A., & Carrington, S. (2021). "He is my job": Autism, school connectedness, and mothers' roles. *Disability & Society*, 1–22. Advance online publication. https://doi.org/10.1080/09687599.2021.1976110

Ontario Human Rights Commission. (2018). *Accessible education for students with disabilities.* Government of Ontario. https://www.ohrc.on.ca/en/policy-accessible-education-students-disabilities

Povey, J., Campbell, A. K., Willis, L.-D., Haynes, M., Western, M., Bennett, S., Antrobus, E., & Pedde, C. (2016). Engaging parents in schools and building parent-school partnerships: The role of school and parent organisation leadership. *International Journal of Educational Research, 79*, 128–141. https://doi.org/10.1016/j.ijer.2016.07.005

Productivity Commission. (2022). *Review of the National School Reform Agreement: Study report.* https://www.pc.gov.au/inquiries/completed/school-agreement/report/school-agreement-overview.pdf

Quin, A., & Bobongie-Harris, F. (2021). Aboriginal and Torres Strait Islander education. In J. Allen, & S. White, (Eds.), *Learning to teach in a new era* (2nd ed., pp. 250–277). Cambridge University Press.

Rautamies, E., Vähäsantanen, K., Poikonen, P.-L., & Laakso, M-L. (2021). Trust in the educational partnership narrated by parents of a child with challenging behaviour. *Early Years 41*(4), 414–427. https://doi.org/10.1080/09575146.2019.1582475

Rios, K., & Burke, M. M. (2021). The effectiveness of special education training programs for parents of children with disabilities: A systematic literature review. *Exceptionality, 29*(3), 215–231. https://doi.org/10.1080/09362835.2020.1850455

Rossetti, Z., Burke, M. M., Rios, K., Tovar, J. A., Schraml-Block, K., Rivera, J. I., Cruz, J., & Lee, J. D. (2021). From individual to systemic advocacy: Parents as change agents. *Exceptionality, 29*(3), 232–247. https://doi.org/10.1080/09362835.2020.1850456

Rossetti, Z., Burke, M. M., Hughes, O., Schraml-Block, K., Rivera1, J. I., Rios. K., Tovar, J. A., & Lee, J. D. (2021). Parent perceptions of the advocacy expectation in special education. *Exceptional Children, 8*(4), 438–457. https://doi.org/10.1177/0014402921994095

Royal Commission into Violence, Abuse, Neglect and Exploitation of People with Disability. (2021). *Public hearing 7: Barriers experienced by students with disability in accessing and obtaining a safe, quality and inclusive school education and consequent life course impacts.* https://disability.royalcommission.gov.au/public-hearings/public-hearing-7

Runswick-Cole, K., Curran, T., & Liddiard, K. (2018). *The Palgrave handbook of disabled children's childhood studies* (1st ed.). Palgrave Macmillan.

Rusnack, M. (2018). "The oversensitive, demanding parent" vs. "the professional teacher"—the ongoing struggle for the common ground of parent-teacher collaboration in Poland. *International Journal About Parents in Education, 10*(1), 70–78.

Seligman, M., & Darling, R. B. (2007). *Ordinary families, special children: A systems approach to childhood disability.* Guilford Publications.

Sianturi, M., Lee, J-S., & Cumming, T. M. (2022). A systematic review of Indigenous parents' educational engagement. *Review of Education, 10*, e3362. https://doi.org/10.1002/rev3.3362

Sisson, J. H., Shin, A. M., & Whitington, V. (2022). Re-imagining family engagement as a two-way street. *The Australian Educational Researcher, 49*, 211–228. https://doi.org/10.1007/s13384-020-00422-8

Solvason, C., & Proctor, S. (2021). 'You have to find the right words to be honest': Nurturing relationships between teachers and parents of children with special educational needs. *Support for Learning, 36*(3), 470–485. https://doi.org/10.1111/1467-9604.12373

Smith, T. E., & Sheridan, S. M. (2019). The effects of teacher training on teachers' family-engagement practices, attitudes, and knowledge: A meta-analysis. *Journal of Educational and Psychological Consultation, 29*(2), 128–157. https://doi.org/10.1080/10474412.2018.1460725

Thompson, I., Willemse, M., Mutton, T., Burn, K., & De Bruïne, E. (2018). Teacher education and family-school partnerships in different contexts. *Journal of Education for Teaching, 44*(3), 258–277. https://doi.org/10.1080/02607476.2018.1465621

Todd, L. (2007). *Partnerships for inclusive education: A critical approach to collaborative working.* Routledge.

Tomlinson, S. (1982). *A sociology of special education.* Routledge.

United Nations. (2006). *Convention on the Rights of Persons with Disabilities (CRPD).* https://www.un.org/disabilities/documents/convention/convoptprot-e.pdf.

United Nations (2007). *Declaration on the Rights of Indigenous Peoples (A/RES/61/295).* https://www.un.org/development/desa/indigenouspeoples/wp-content/uploads/sites/19/2018/11/UNDRIP_E_web.pdf

United Nations Educational, Scientific and Cultural Organization. (2017). *Education for Sustainable Development Goals.* https://unesdoc.unesco.org/ark:/48223/pf0000247444/PDF/247444eng.pdf.multi

VanValkenburgh, J., Putnam, J., & Porter, M. (2021). Middle school parent involvement: Perceptions of teachers and parents. *Middle School Journal, 52*(4), 33–42. https://doi.org/10.1080/00940771.2021.1948299

Whitley, J., Specht, J., Matheson, I., & MacCormack, J. (2022). Holes, patches and multiple hats: The experiences of parents of students with special education needs navigating at-home learning during COVID-19. In R. Turok-Squire (Ed.) *COVID-19 and education in the global north* (pp. 61–81). Palgrave.

Chapter 18

Collaborating with colleagues and other professionals

Haley Tancredi, Gaenor Dixon, Libby English, & Jeanine Gallagher

Schools are working environments where interpersonal interactions are an essential component of the work life of teachers and other professionals. Harvesting the professional skills available within, as well as between, schools and external service providers through collaboration can contribute significantly to student learning success and participation in social and extracurricular activities within inclusive-school contexts. Collaboration in schools may take many forms and involves multiple stakeholders, including students, parents/carers, and teacher aides (see Chapters 13, 17, and 19, respectively). This chapter focuses on professional collaboration as the interaction between teachers and other professionals when engaged in collective problem-solving and joint action. After defining professional collaboration in the inclusive-school context, we will discuss the known benefits for both professionals and students, describe some of the ways that collaboration can be enacted, and explore factors that will add to its success. Finally, we will use a series of vignettes to show how professional collaboration may be enacted in inclusive schools, within a Multi-Tiered Systems of Support framework (MTSS).

Professional Collaboration in the Inclusive School Context

Professional collaboration is defined as a process where two or more professionals work towards a common goal by sharing responsibility and contributing professional expertise in the spirit of reciprocity and trust (D'Amour et al., 2005; Friend & Cook, 2010). Collaboration requires commitment and a planned approach by all parties involved. In the context of inclusive schools, professional collaboration can exist both between individuals from the same professional group (known as intra-professional collaboration) and between individuals who come from different professional backgrounds (known as inter-professional collaboration). Collaboration may also take place between professionals who share a workplace (for example, between staff from the same school or education system) or can take place across workplaces and/or services. An example of this is when a school partners with a health-services team on a project or to support a particular student or group of students. Professional collaboration can take place to directly support students and their learning and/or to facilitate professional development of the staff involved.

DOI: 10.4324/9781003350897-21

Teachers are keenly aware of the need to work with other teachers (such as other classroom teachers, curriculum leaders, and learning-support teachers) and with stakeholders from other professional groups to maximise their effectiveness in the classroom (Murawski & Hughes, 2009). Modern schools employ a range of professional staff. In Australia, guidance officers and/or educational psychologists routinely work as part of school teams. Increasingly, schools are recognising and using the services of allied health (speech pathologists, occupational therapists, and physiotherapists), health professionals (nurses and medical practitioners), and staff from external agencies including registered nurses, youth workers, social workers, and paediatricians (Shahidullah et al., 2019). School-based non-teaching professionals may be employed through a staffing schedule or as part of support services offered by the education system (Australian Psychological Society, n.d.; Speech Pathology Australia, 2022a). While allied health professionals are often referred to as "student support and services" (Queensland Government, n.d.), increasingly schools are engaging allied health services for collaboration on whole-school projects, teaming with teachers for professional development or working with school teams to progress systemic and cultural change in teaching practice in areas such as inclusive education and literacy (Christner, 2015; Foley et al., 2022; Tancredi, 2018).

The National Disability Insurance Scheme (NDIS) commenced in Australia in 2016 and has resulted in changes to funding arrangements and access to community-based support (which may include allied health services or specialist equipment) for people with disability. Some school-aged students with significant and permanent disability are eligible for funding through the NDIS to enable participation in activities of their choosing or to receive support to achieve their goals (National Disability Insurance Agency, 2019a). Clear guidelines have been provided by the National Disability Insurance Agency (National Disability Insurance Agency, 2019b) to delineate what the NDIS will and will not fund in schools. The NDIS *cannot* be used to fund education services (such as teaching assistants, Auslan interpreters, adjustments to buildings or therapy delivered within the school to support education, or curriculum-based teacher professional development). The NDIS *can* fund support for a student's equipment (such as mobility aids and speech-generating devices) that is used at school but is also used for community, social, and economic participation as well as in the school setting. For school teams, it is important to understand the parameters of the NDIS and how it intersects with education-support services. With this understanding, stakeholders can identify when NDIS-funded external agencies or supports can and cannot be engaged to support students. Furthermore, when students are accessing the NDIS, professional collaboration must consider and include NDIS-funded stakeholders as part of the student's collaborative team. It is important that all stakeholders are considerate of each other's responsibilities and that external professionals respect the policies and processes of the school, particularly when it comes to requests to withdraw students from the learning environment or requests for specific programs be implemented by school staff.

High-quality professional collaboration is fundamental to all students having access to high-quality learning, social and wellbeing experiences at school. Collaborative approaches are particularly important for some groups of students, including students from a language background other than English (Pardini, 2006), students with mental-health concerns (Mælan et al., 2020), students with complex medical or learning profiles (Shahidullah et al., 2019), and students in out-of-home care (Edwards et al., 2010). There is also extensive literature about the importance of professional collaboration in the education of students with disability (Murawski & Hughes, 2009; Scruggs et al., 2007; Tancredi, 2018). *General Comment No. 4* names professional collaboration as an essential component of supporting teachers to provide inclusive learning environments, stating "an inclusive culture provides an accessible and supportive environment that encourages working through collaboration, interaction and problem-solving" (United Nations, 2016, para 12).

Professional collaboration is explicitly named within a range of professional standards and clinical-guideline documents in Australia. For teachers, collaboration is named within the three domains of the Australian Professional Standards for Teachers (Australian Institute for Teaching and School Leadership, 2018): Professional Knowledge (e.g., Standard 2.1: Content and teaching strategies of the teaching area), Professional Practice (e.g., Standard 3.2: Plan, structure, and sequence learning programs), and Professional Engagement (e.g., Standard 6.3: Engage with colleagues and improve practice). Similarly, the importance of professional collaboration between speech pathologists and teachers was highlighted in a recent project investigating the role of speech pathologists in Australian schools (Speech Pathology Australia, 2017) and in the recently updated Speech Pathology in Education Practice Guideline and Position Statement (Speech Pathology Australia, 2022a; Speech Pathology Australia, 2022b). Professional collaboration is also outlined in the Australian occupational therapy competency standards (Occupational Therapy Board of Australia, 2019). Professional associations such as Australian Psychologists and Counsellors in Schools (APACS) and Learning Difficulties Australia (LDA) provide professional learning opportunities for members to develop skills and knowledge about collaborative practices. However, these professional associations do not have a role in professional registration, and therefore do not monitor the uptake of professional collaboration among their members.

Defining Professional Collaboration

From a conceptual basis, professional collaboration has been described as an evolving process, grounded in the concepts of equality, sharing, partnership, power, interdependence, and process (D'Amour et al., 2005). Conceptualising professional collaboration in schools in this way reminds us that when professionals work collaboratively, no team members are in the position of 'advice giving', but instead are equal partners in the everyday work that takes place in schools. Allied health and medical professionals may approach professional collaboration from a medical model, however, the power inequity inherent to the medical model and ideologies that oppose educational philosophy can be a barrier to effective and positive collaboration (Hartas, 2004). Essential to a shared partnership is a balance of power and interdependence, where all parties contribute unique but important knowledge, skills, and expertise. To avoid so-called 'turf wars', all participants must be positioned as contributors rather than competitors, where reciprocal relationships are the foundation for successful teamwork (D'Amour et al., 2005; McKean et al., 2017).

Gallagher et al. (2022) identify five key concepts from literature that can promote collaboration for allied health professionals and teaching teams:

- boundary crossing: the ability to take on new roles sometimes beyond traditional areas, for example, beyond the traditional remediation remit of an allied health professional,
- gaining entry: being invited and welcomed to the collaboration is essential for full participation,
- building relationships: to successfully collaborate,
- achieving action: the need for accountability and action for collaboration to be successful, which requires realistic and honest communication between all collaborators, and
- enduring belief: a commitment and belief that collaborative practice will benefit the student.

Collaboration is thus distinct from coordination (where stakeholders pursue individually assigned action, with a specific objective) and cooperation (where stakeholders work together in only specific situations, to achieve a shared objective) (Paju et al., 2022). We will further discuss the 'drivers' for successful collaboration and a spectrum of ways of working with other professionals, later in this chapter.

As outlined in Chapter 9, Multi-Tiered Systems of Support (MTSS) is an evidence-based unifying framework for the system-wide provision of high-quality instruction and intervention (Burns et al., 2016). MTSS is deployed within a three-tier structure, where Tier 1 (universal) is available to all students, Tier 2 (targeted support) is provided for some students who require additional monitoring and interventions, and Tier 3 (intensive support) is provided for a small number of students who require individualised monitoring and interventions. Collaborative problem-solving processes are an important element of MTSS, where educators, specialist teachers, school leaders, allied health professionals, parents, and students can work together to plan, design, and provide high-quality instruction and intervention that is responsive to students' learning progress and requirements, across three domains: (i) academic, (ii) social-emotional development, and (iii) behaviour (Adamson et al., 2019; Cirrin et al., 2003). The aim of collaboration within an MTSS is to minimise and prevent academic under-achievement and minimise disruptive or unsafe behaviour and support social-emotional learning. Importantly, MTSS is data driven and research evidence informs the selection of instructional approaches and interventions, with the type of support and complexity of decision making that is organised by tiers, as opposed to children belonging to tiers. This complex work is well-suited to a collaborative team approach, which can benefit both students and the professionals involved.

Benefits of Professional Collaboration

Professional collaboration takes place with two goals in mind: (i) enhance the school experience of students, and (ii) contribute to the professional development of the professionals involved. Research has demonstrated that collaborative approaches benefit both students and the professionals involved (McKean et al., 2017; Scruggs et al., 2007; Tancredi, 2018). By working together, teachers and other professionals can work with their colleagues to problem-solve and consider new methods and pedagogical approaches for implementation in the classroom (Scruggs et al., 2007). School-based professional collaboration has been shown to improve student achievement (Gore et al., 2021) and promoting positive peer interactions (Gregory et al., 2017). Further, collaboration has also been shown to create more accessible and inclusive learning programs for all students through consistent whole-school and year-level planning; explicit naming of content within the unit, and the concepts and vocabulary to be taught; as well as forward planning to determine how these elements will best be taught (Boudah et al., 2008).

Professional Collaboration: Ways of Working

Although the importance of professional collaboration within schools is well established, models that underpin related work and activities can vary significantly (Scruggs et al., 2007; Sileo, 2011). There are also some collaborative ways of working that are more conducive to upholding a student's right to an inclusive education than others (Tancredi, 2018). For example, while information sharing between professionals (e.g., teachers and paediatricians sharing information about a student's behaviour and learning profile) is important, without joint goal-directed action and contribution to outcomes, information sharing alone is not likely to harness the benefits of true professional collaboration (Shahidullah et al., 2019). In deciding on a model of collaboration and the activities that will take place, it is important that a variety of factors are considered:

- What is the goal and purpose of the collaboration?
- Is the collaborative work going to support a specific student, a group of students or a whole-school project?
- What data or information will inform decision-making and the activities undertaken?
- Are there any time, resourcing or logistical constraints to consider?
- Do the professionals involved have an existing relationship?
- Does my relationship with the team enable collaboration?

- What is my role in the team?
- How can I work towards more collaborative ways of working?

The answers to these questions may impact on the model that is chosen and how the collaborative work is enacted. In the following section, we outline some common ways of working within a collaborative team, beginning with collaborative consultation.

Collaborative Consultation

Collaborative consultation is an interactive process between professionals who work together to address complex issues in a student-centred framework (Idol et al., 1995). The collaborative-consultation model is commonly used by external allied health professionals who provide services to schools. Within the collaborative-consultation model, both the consultant and consultee share expertise and joint leadership to identify goals that will progress students' learning outcomes. Thus, the collaborative-consultation model may offer opportunities to professionals who are teaching students with disability, mental-health concerns, or complex medical and learning profiles. There has been some criticism of this model, as professionals working in this way often do not progress beyond information sharing, meaning true collaboration is unlikely to be taking place (Shahidullah et al., 2019; Villeneuve, 2009).

Collaborative Planning

While collaborative planning is an essential component of co-teaching, collaborative planning can also exist as a separate activity (Jitendra et al., 2002), involving only teachers (e.g., teachers from a year-level cohort or a classroom teacher working with a learning-support teacher) or teachers working with someone with a different professional background. Collaborative planning may focus on a unit of study, a series of lessons, or an individual lesson. Ideally, planning will foreground students' expected learning outcomes and utilise universal approaches to curriculum, pedagogy, and assessment (as discussed in Chapters 11 and 12). This will enable accessible learning experiences to be designed proactively for all students, reducing the need for retrofitted adjustments (Hinder & Ashburner, 2017). Collaborative planning between teachers and speech pathologists has been shown to enhance curricular and pedagogical access for all students, as well as increase teacher confidence and skill in accessible pedagogical practices and designing adjustments (Starling et al., 2012; Tancredi, 2018). Planning tools are an effective way to structure collaborative-planning discussions and to support teachers to identify and map the key concepts and vocabulary to be taught (e.g., see Boudah et al., 2000). By schematically mapping lessons, weekly plans, and/or curricular units using a planning tool, teachers can collaboratively agree on areas of teaching focus and the connections that they want their students to make in their learning. Planning tools can also form the basis of discussion and a platform for joint planning to identify and remove barriers that may exist within activities or assessment. When barriers are identified, teachers and other professionals can work to design and implement adjustments to ensure that all students, including those with disability, are able to participate fully (Jitendra et al., 2002).

Co-teaching

Co-teaching is often cited as a popular means for providing high-quality instruction in primary-and secondary-school classrooms (Friend et al., 1993; Scruggs et al., 2007). Friend and Cook (2010) define co-teaching as an instructional delivery approach where the classroom teacher and another professional share responsibility for planning, delivering, and reflecting on classroom instruction. In their meta-synthesis of the literature, Scruggs et al. (2007) identify five models of co-teaching: (i) one teach, one assist, where one professional (usually the classroom teacher) assumes teaching responsibilities and the other provides individual support as needed; (ii) station teaching, where learning stations are created and supported by professionals; (iii) parallel teaching, where professionals teach the same or similar content in groups; (iv) alternative teaching, where one professional takes a smaller group of students to a different location for different instruction; and (v) team teaching (or interactive teaching), where professionals equally share teaching responsibilities and are equally involved in leading classroom instruction. Sileo (2011) describes an additional model—one teach, one observe—where one professional is responsible for whole-class instruction, and the other observes students and gathers information (primarily about the students, but this may also be for professionals to learn about their co-teaching partner). The model most frequently used in co-teaching classrooms is *one teach, one assist* (King-Sears et al., 2021). This model often takes the form of a general classroom/subject teacher and learning-support teacher take on either of these roles when co-teaching in the classroom.

Where there is clarity about the roles and responsibilities of the professionals involved and co-teaching is an authentic partnership with equal contribution to the delivery of learning instruction, King-Sears et al. (2021) suggest that students recognise both teachers as equals. Criticisms of co-teaching reflect the pervasive confusion over what co-teaching is and how models of co-teaching are labelled and enacted. Specifically, the term 'co-teaching' is often used interchangeably with 'collaboration'. While the collaborative nature of co-teaching is not disputed, collaboration refers to how professionals interact more broadly, while co-teaching refers to a specific instructional activity. The efficacy of co-teaching has therefore been difficult to establish, due to the varying fidelity with which co-teaching models are applied (Solis et al., 2012). However, anecdotal evidence indicates that teachers feel that co-teaching has a positive impact on student achievement, particularly for students with disability (Scruggs et al., 2007). Friend et al. (2010) caution, however, that poorly enacted co-teaching can potentially increase segregation for students with disability or learning difficulties, where classroom teachers may, in fact, spend less time with some students, instead relying on the presence of a specialist teacher or other professional to assume the role of key teacher. Joint preparation and clarity in roles and responsibilities are essential elements of effective co-teaching (Friend et al., 2010).

Coaching

Coaching is a person-centred approach, which is defined as an "activity with classroom observation at its centre and professional learning as its aim" (van Nieuwerburgh, 2012, p. 7). It has the "potential to cross-pollinate good practices, and develop reflective, exploratory and metacognitive teachers" (Gallagher & Bennett, 2018, p. 20). Coaching is intentionally dialogic; therefore, coaches need to be skilled communicators and attentive listeners (Gallagher & Bennett, 2018; van Nieuwerburgh, 2012). When using coaching to improve learning outcomes for students with disability, Gore (2014) suggests that coaching should firstly focus on general teaching and then consider practices for specific students' learning needs. Coaching, in this context, would involve a colleague with professional expertise in a specific area taking on the role of coach, and the 'coachee' seeking to change something in their own practice (van Nieuwerburgh, 2012). This type of specialist coaching is predicated on the coachee choosing their coach, which may have practical implications to consider, such as the availability of an appropriate coach and adequate time to foster the coaching relationship.

Student Support Team Processes

The Student Support Team (SST) is a referral-based service that exists in many schools. SSTs engage in meetings and problem-solving processes that aim to collaboratively design adjustments and interventions for students who would benefit from an explicit team approach to support their learning progress. Engaging professionals with a shared vision and a willingness to be genuinely collaborative is essential for this team. In many schools, the SST core members include a member of the school-leadership team, a curriculum leader, a support teacher, a school counsellor, and a speech pathologist. Procedures that promote success of the SST include:

- having a well-defined student referral process (and sticking to it),
- managing the pace and focus of the SST meetings,
- scheduling SST meetings frequently enough to discuss referrals,
- disseminating meeting minutes to all relevant school staff,
- allowing enough time to discuss the student referral in detail (25 to 45 minutes),
- including the right people for student-referral discussion (including the class teacher and parents and/or caregivers), and
- developing a student support plan for implementation, which includes a review date. (Powers, 2001)

The SST is deliberately a collaborative solution-focused approach. There are some key roles and responsibilities that will contribute to the success of the group. For example, the classroom teacher is responsible for initiating the student referral and then coordinating the implementation plan. The SST coordinator is responsible for scheduling and chairing meetings, having the document ready for the meeting, and disseminating meeting outcomes.

Professional Learning Communities

A school-based Professional Learning Community (PLC) is a form of collaborative professional support where teachers, school leaders, and other stakeholders from within a school meet regularly to share knowledge, research, classroom practices, and reflect on teaching practices, with a focus is student learning and achievement (Australian Institute for Teaching and School Leadership, n.d.). Effective PLCs promote the professional growth of teachers and have positive impacts on student outcomes. Five defining characteristics of PLCs have been described in the literature: (i) that school leaders and teachers work collaboratively to design and lead the PLC; (ii) that PLC members have a shared vision, values, and goals; (iii) that there is a shared expectation that all members continuously apply the knowledge and skills gained through the PLC to enhance and expand their instructional practices over time; (iv) that PLC members engage in peer observation and feedback, building a culture of reflexivity and collective responsibility for the learning and teaching of both students and professionals; and (v) that supportive conditions are established to facilitate the operation of the PLC, such as time and space to meet and collaborate, shared decision-making and problem solving, trust, and respect (Schuster et al., 2021; Vangrieken et al., 2017).

Vangrieken et al. (2017) identified three main types of PLCs: formal, member-oriented with a pre-set agenda, and formative. Formal PLCs are often focused on national education standards and often originate from government initiatives. This type of PLC is more likely to include external attendees or experts who attend with the aim of upskilling teachers. Member-oriented PLCs that have a pre-set agenda typically have a pre-determined schedule and session objectives, which may focus on sharing practice, research, and/or to give/receive feedback. Formative PLCs have no pre-determined goals or agendas prior to the first meeting, but are developed through iterative cycles and learning requirements, as determined by participants and across sessions. Schuster et al. (2021) found in their research that less-structured PLC environments often resulted in teachers gravitating towards formation of groups that are relatively homogenous. Conversely, when well-established whole-school structures were in place to support PLCs, group members tended to more likely to be diverse. These findings further emphases the importance of school leaders creating safeguarded times and spaces for collaboration, so that PLCs can bring together groups of teachers with a breadth of backgrounds, characteristics, experiences, and areas of expertise (Schuster et al., 2021).

Quality Teaching Rounds

Professional development in schools has traditionally adopted a passive approach to learning, through single-session formats (Bowe & Gore, 2017). In recent years, collaboration as a means for professional development has grown in popularity, seeing the emergence of communities of practice and professional-learning communities within schools and professional groups (Vescio et al., 2008). A process known as 'Quality Teaching Rounds' has been cited as a pedagogically based, collaborative approach to professional development that focuses on teachers improving their practice (Bowe & Gore, 2017). Quality Teaching

Rounds combine collaborative discussion of a professional reading, classroom observation using the Quality Teaching Model (New South Wales Department of Education, 2023), reflective discussion about the learning and teaching that was observed, and coding and discussing a lesson using the Quality Teaching framework (Bowe & Gore, 2017). Significant positive effects on teaching quality have been found for Quality Teaching Rounds, with maintenance six months post-implementation (Gore et al., 2017).

Enablers for Successful Professional Collaboration

Several studies have identified factors that are likely to drive the success of collaborative partnerships. The strength of the interpersonal relationship that is formed between parties both prior to and during the professional collaboration is a critical factor in their success (Ploessl et al., 2010). Personal commitment to the collaborative work is required for longevity and sustained activities, and parties are more likely to engage with one another if they have learned about each other and built a relationship. Gallagher et al. (2022) discuss the need for allied health professionals to explain their role to teaching staff to facilitate collaborative work. In a recent study that trialled a process of collaboration between teachers and an external agency for students with mental-health concerns, initial whole-school initiatives provided positive opportunities for professionals to build interpersonal relationships, which later lay the foundation for more productive targeted professional collaborations (Gallagher et al., 2022). Simple steps such as learning about someone's professional background and their family or interests can form the basis of an interpersonal relationship, on which trust and collaboration can be built.

Provision of Time and Resources

Professionals require time and resources to develop skills in collaborative practice and to engage in the activities of collaborative work. School-leadership teams, external service leaders, and education systems must therefore support professional collaboration through education policy and school priorities that support this way of working (McKean et al., 2017). For example, supporting team members by providing additional planning time or resources to support access to professional learning may be required. Individual professionals can also prioritise the importance of professional collaboration by developing professional-learning goals that reflect a dedication to professional collaboration. For example, a professional-learning plan might include goals that focus on building a professional network or identifying skills that need to be developed to support effective collaborative-working relationships.

Clearly Defined Roles and Responsibilities

To support realistic and practical recommendations, team members need to take time to discuss their roles, their perspectives and how they can contribute to student outcomes (Rens & Joosten, 2014; Truong & Hodgetts, 2017). Recent research has identified that team members from different professional backgrounds may approach their work with different priorities or anticipated student outcomes in mind (Gallagher et al., 2019). For example, allied health professionals may wish to see students further develop their communication or motor skills, while teachers may focus on increased curricular content development. A lack of understanding of other collaborators' roles or the context of their work has been demonstrated to be a barrier to effective collaboration (Christner, 2015). One way of building the understanding of each team member's role is to work together with the student in the classroom or to observe each other in action. After a while, less time will need to be invested, as a shared understanding of each person's role and scope of practice will improve with experience and knowledge (Casillas, 2010). Given that at times there will be overlap between professionals' areas of expertise, it is also important to clarify where each person's professional skills begin and end, and where the boundaries meet and overlap. Table 18.1 summarises the professional skills that some key members of a professional collaboration may contribute in school settings.

It may also be important for each professional to examine their own beliefs about another profession. For example, Aguilar et al. (2014) found that occupational therapists and physiotherapists each attributed values and beliefs to the other's profession that were not held by the profession itself. By extension, a teacher may believe that a therapist's role is to withdraw students from the classroom to work with them, and that the allied health professional's role is to 'fix the student' so that they can learn better in the classroom. Similarly, allied health professionals may not understand the complexities of a teacher's role and the fact that teachers are more likely to apply strategies in the classroom that contribute to quality, whole class instructional practices and the provision of reasonable adjustments (Mælan et al., 2020).

Some authors have also stressed the importance of what has been termed 'boundary skill' (Akkerman & Bakker, 2011). This is described as the ability to negotiate the boundaries of one's professional role and the capacity to engage in dialogue with professionals from different backgrounds, while understanding the different perspectives and lenses through which they perceive situations and problems that arise. In other words, boundary skill reflects an understanding of the underlying philosophy of the profession, as well as the values and beliefs that drive the suggested actions, recommendations, and problem-solving approach of each professional. Boundary skill can only be fully realised when each professional involved in the collaboration has an understanding and appreciation of the professional identities of the other professionals involved in the collaboration. For example, a teacher's professional identity is deeply rooted in their pedagogical approaches and epistemological beliefs about teaching. Conversely, an allied health professional's identity may be grounded in the biopsychosocial model of disability (see Chapter 4). Gallagher et al. (2022) describe additional roles that collaborators may adopt, including "awareness builder" (understanding a student's needs), "knowledge translator", and "advocate".

Table 18.1 Collaborators and the Professional Skills They Contribute

Professional Skills: Areas of Knowledge and Understanding

Classroom Teacher	Understanding how students learn and the implications for pedagogical practice
	Curricular structure, content and concepts, and teaching strategies across teaching areas
	Leader in pedagogical practices
	Formative and summative assessment practices, and using data to progress students' learning
	Lesson planning and adjusting lessons to progress the learning goals of all students
	Leader in the classroom context
	Leads the classroom routines and culture
Learning-support teacher	Understanding how students learn and the implications for pedagogical practice
	Curricular structure, content and concepts, and teaching strategies across teaching areas
	Leader in pedagogical practices (such as Universal Design for Learning)
	Formative, summative, and diagnostic assessment practices, and using data to progress students' learning
	Collaborative lesson planning and adjusting lessons to progress the learning goals of all students and/or for specific students
	Explicit teaching processes, including task analysis
	Reviewing recommendations from other providers to identify relevant and specific adjustments for students, and how these adjustments can be incorporated into teacher planning
Guidance officer/school psychologist/school counsellor/ social worker	Understanding how students learn and the implications for pedagogical practice
	Diagnostic assessment and using data to progress students' learning
	Collaborative lesson planning and adjusting lessons to progress the learning goals for specific students
	Explicit teaching processes, including task analysis
	Reviewing recommendations from other providers to support class teachers to incorporate recommendations into teacher planning
	Providing recommendations for teachers to address specific learning/support needs of the student
	Developing and implementing specific intervention strategies directed at student engagement and/or student wellbeing
	Leader in the whole-of-school context for student and staff wellbeing
Speech pathologist	Typical communication development
	Identification of communication-based barriers to students' access to the curriculum, teachers' pedagogical practices, or demonstration of learning
	High-level understanding of the language and communication skills underlying the curriculum
	Observational, criterion-referenced and standardised assessments of language, speech, fluency, voice, literacy, and swallowing
	Able to support the design and provision of high-quality teaching practices and targeted adjustments that support communication and/or literacy competence and/or communication difficulties
	Advice on reasonable adjustments that enable access and participation in curriculum
	Diagnosis: communication, literacy, and swallowing disorders
	Therapeutic interventions: communication, literacy, and swallowing

	Professional Skills: Areas of Knowledge and Understanding
Occupational therapist	General child development and the functional impact of disability
	Knowledge and understanding of a range of areas of human function (e.g., motor skills, cognitive skills, processing sensory information, play skills, social interaction, using objects and tools)
	Task analysis: understanding the components or subskills involved in completing a task
	Identification of barriers within an environment or task that impact access or participation in school life
	Therapeutic interventions aimed at supporting the child's skill development, or adapting the task or environment to enable participation and independence

Educational psychologists and speech pathologists have been shown to have different perspectives on what should be prioritised as the focus of support for students with communication difficulties (McConnellogue, 2011). This variation stems from underlying professional values and beliefs, which need to be explicitly identified to minimise barriers that varying perspectives may have on effective collaborative information sharing and working. Forbes (2003) argues that effective collaboration needs to take the differences in discourses between allied health professionals and teachers into account. A teacher's discourse and beliefs may stem from a belief in the universal provision of education, a focus on provision of curriculum across a year, and a perspective of whole-class provision of supports. Therapists may come from a remediation and/or developmental perspective, with a focus on the rights and needs of individual students, and they may believe that delivery of therapy support is not a universal provision. Therefore, time needs to be taken to ensure that the perspective of each stakeholder is clarified and to enable reciprocal working relationships to be built.

Clear and Effective Communication

Effective communication skills underpin successful professional collaboration. During interactions, active listening by all stakeholders is required to enable each partner to share and receive all ideas and viewpoints. Approaching interactions in the spirit of trust and open communication also requires participating parties to understand that any ideas can be accepted, rejected, or adjusted. Regular in-person or written communication is required to review progress, make adjustments, and ensure forward planning. Meeting minutes or discussion summaries will support a goal-directed focus and can help to track the progress towards goal attainment over time. For collaboration to be successful, individuals must know how to resolve conflict, develop relationships, and plan and evaluate supports and progress, and they must be allowed the time for planning and implementation (Friend & Cook, 2010).

Goal Setting

A central tenant of effective professional collaboration is that clear goals are established between stakeholders. When discussing goals and how these goals will be met, it is important to consider *what* the goal and associated activities may be, as well as to develop a shared understanding between stakeholders about *why* the goal is important and *how* it may best be achieved. Given the school-based context of the collaboration, goals need to:

- align with information gathered through consultation with the student and their family,
- foreground every child's right to an inclusive education, and
- demonstrate respect and understanding for each professional's skills, working context, and capabilities.

For example, the teacher, student, and their family may identify achievement in maths as an area of focus. The school psychologist may suggest some teaching strategies identified from their cognitive assessment of the student that will assist their achievement. The speech pathologist may identify the specific linguistic concepts being taught in the maths curriculum in the semester and provide strategies for developing the student's vocabulary in those areas. The school team may work with the family (at their request) to provide some fun home-learning activities that will reinforce the concepts learned at school.

Professional Collaboration in Practice

The following vignettes provide practice-based examples of how school teams can effectively engage in a goal-directed process of professional collaboration. These examples outline a process of planning, joint decision-making, and reflection.

Example 1: Coaching in the Secondary-School Context

Lin, a Year 9 Home Economics teacher, is troubled about how the class is progressing. The students are not as engaged in lessons as Lin would like, and some students are not completing tasks. This is placing them at risk of failing the subject. Lin seeks out a colleague from within the faculty for support to problem-solve this issue.

As the coaching process commences, the coach works with Lin to identify the reality of the situation and tease out some of the key issues. In this situation, the coach explores the issues with Lin, who then concludes that the literacy demands of the workbook may be too complex for some students. They discuss ideas about how to make literacy tasks more accessible and consider the instructional language that Lin uses when teaching. Lin then seeks the support of the speech pathologist to discuss the literacy demands of the workbook and requests that the speech pathologist observe her teaching to give her specific feedback about instructional language. Through coaching, Lin has developed a deeper understanding of the language and learning profiles of the class students, and the pedagogical refine-ments needed, so that students can access instructional language in the classroom.

Using a MTSS lens to view this scenario, Lin has used data to identify the bar-riers that students are experiencing. Through coaching and collaborating with the speech language pathologist, Lin has identified the importance of first focusing on universal teaching practice, which are essential for some students in her class but useful for all. Making these changes, Lin continues to collect data on student out-comes, and identifies successful practices that are sufficient for most students to make appropriate progress. Lin continues to collaborate with the learning support team, including the speech language pathologist to identify students who require more intensive literacy interventions at a Tier 2 level.

As discussed in this chapter, coaching is a process that enables a person to identify a specific issue and to develop a plan to address this issue. A key tenet of coaching is that the solution lies within the coachee (van Nieuwerburgh, 2012). As this scenario shows, professional collaboration and coaching can support teachers in regular classrooms to refine practices and support all students.

Example 2: Collaborating for Universal Outcomes

When analysing Prep and Year 1 student-outcomes data, a principal notices that many students are struggling with early reading and spelling skills. She raises this with the early-years teachers in a cohort planning meeting, who agree with the pattern identified by their principal. The Prep and Year 1 teaching-team members self-identify that they would like further support to develop students' oral lan-guage and handwriting skills.

In this school, speech pathology and occupational therapy services are available through the education system. With the principal's support, a process of profes-sional collaboration between the Prep and Year 1 teachers, speech pathologist, and occupational therapist commences. The team engage in a process of joint planning and co-teaching, focused on the provision of universal high-quality whole class teaching for all students. At the initial meeting, team members clarify their role and what they can contribute to the shared goal of improving students' reading and spelling skills. Within the team, there are diverse perspectives on approaches to teaching literacy. Time is spent respectfully discussing these views and where they may be divergent. Through this discussion, team members agree on the scope of the collaboration, the purpose of the shared work, and the goals.

Members of the team agree to collaboratively plan and co-teach the Founda-tion level (prep or kindergarten) and Year 1 English curriculum with a review after four weeks. This collaborative planning includes discussion and use of evidence informed instructional strategies for supporting students' oral language access to the curriculum. The team members feel unsure about how students might react to activities with so many 'teachers' present and so debrief after the first lesson to make refinements to suit the classes better.

After four weeks, team members have meet to review student learning data and to develop a strategy for the remainder of the term. The team members agree that their goals have been met and decide that the ongoing role of the occupational therapists and speech pathologists will be to build teacher capacity for teaching vocabulary and handwriting, with focused allied health support to continue for students whose data suggests that they require a more intensive intervention. The teachers feel confident to continue the work and schedule less frequent allied health input for the following term.

As this example shows, through understanding roles and responsibilities, being open to negotiation, having shared goals, and addressing barriers as they arise, school teams can develop highly effective professional collaborations that can resulted in improved student learning outcomes.

Example 3: Working Together to Design Extensive Adjustments

Suzie is a Year 6 student in Mr Teal's class and she could be a student at just about any primary school. She loves watching YouTube, hanging out with her friends, and swimming. Suzie also has cerebral palsy and cortical vision impairment, which means that she uses a wheelchair to move around and requires support to transfer onto the toilet. To communicate, Suzie skilfully uses picture symbols and a voice-output device, which she has accessed through her NDIS package. Ever since she was small, Suzie's parents have made sure that she has an active and central role in her team, which also includes Mr Teal, her learning-support teacher (Ms Fey), her physiotherapist, and her speech pathologist. In October, all Year 6 students at Suzie's school will go on a camp, so in March, the team starts planning to ensure that Suzie is fully included at camp. The process commences with a collaborative-planning meeting, where Mr Teal asks Suzie what she is looking forward to most about camp. Suzie says that she can't wait to sleep in the same cabin as her friends and do all the activities. The team plans for a series of meetings to identify and design adjustments so that Suzie can participate fully at camp.

To support the collaborative-planning process, the deputy principal ensures that Mr Teal is released to attend all meetings. Ms Fey chairs the meetings and takes notes, recording the different tasks that each team member will take on and the actions that are required. Over the next two months, the team plans and arranges for the Year 6 students to travel, stay, and do a range of activities at camp that can be accessed by wheelchair. During the planning discussions, Suzie's parents explain that Suzie has supplementary nutrition and medication at night through PEG into her stomach. All Year 6 teachers receive training from a nurse to support Suzie with her night-time feeding and medication, and the team creates a health plan that includes protocols for when to contact Suzie's parents if needed and information about health and emergency services near the camp. All staff members going to the camp attend training by the physiotherapist to learn how to safely support Suzie's toilet transfers. To make sure Suzie can communicate with her friends and others about the activities at camp, the speech pathologist works with Mr Teal to ensure that Suzie's communication device has the camp-related vocabulary that she will need. In the week before camp, the team has a final meeting to plan check-ins with each other and Suzie's family throughout the camp.

Suzie has an awesome time at camp. She doesn't feel homesick once, and her favourite part is staying up late. At a debrief meeting the week after camp, the team reflects on the processes that made Suzie's experience of camp so positive. Everyone agrees that they are glad they started planning early and that open communication and shared decision-making allowed the team to anticipate and minimise any barriers to Suzie's full participation.

Conclusion

While many professionals in schools cooperate on a daily basis as part of their role, true collaboration requires that professionals share responsibility for working towards a common goal (D'Amour et al., 2005; Friend & Cook, 2010). Professional collaboration in schools provides teams with the opportunity to engage in shared decision-making, joint action, and localised professional development. Drawing on a breadth of expertise, classroom teachers, learning-support teachers, school counsellors and allied health professionals can engage in reciprocal working relationships, within a MTSS framework. Collaboration can happen within and across professional boundaries, with the potential to improve the inclusive-school experience of all students. As discussed in this chapter, effective collaborative work requires that time and space are allocated for collaborators to develop a working relationship, establish roles, and plan, implement, and reflect on their collaborative work. While there is a range of activities in which professionals may engage, certain factors can support or inhibit the collaborative relationship. For example, stakeholders need to ensure that roles and responsibilities are clear, and team members must engage in joint goal setting and reflection. These drivers for collaboration are enhanced when school leaders and education systems support professional collaboration through policy, school priorities, and resourcing. The importance of collaboration is supported across international and local legislation, policy, and professional standards, and the efficacy of professional collaboration has been documented in the research literature. All that remains is for education systems, schools, and individual professionals to ensure that professional collaboration is central in the enactment of inclusive education for all students, and particularly for students with disability.

References

Adamson, R. M., McKenna, J. W., & Mitchell, B. (2019). Supporting all students: Creating a tiered continuum of behavior support at the classroom level to enhance schoolwide multi-tiered systems of support. *Preventing School Failure: Alternative Education for Children and Youth*, *63*(1), 62–67. https://doi.org/10.1080/1045988X.2018.1501654

Aguilar, A., Stupans, I., Scutter, S., & King, S. (2014). Exploring how Australian occupational therapists and physiotherapists understand each other's professional values: Implications for interprofessional education and practice. *Journal of Interprofessional Care*, *28*(1), 15–22. https://doi.org/10.3109/13561820.2013.820689

Akkerman, S. F., & Bakker, A. (2011). Boundary crossing and boundary objects. *Review of Educational Research*, *81*(2), 132–169. https://doi.org/10.3102/0034654311404435

Australian Institute for Teaching and School Leadership. (2018). *Australian Professional Standards for Teachers*. http://www.aitsl.edu.au/docs/default-source/teach-documents/australian-professional-standards-for-teachers.pdf

Australian Institute for Teaching and School Leadership. (n.d.). *Professional learning communities*. https://www.aitsl.edu.au/docs/default-source/feedback/aitsl-professional-learning-communities-strategy.pdf

Australian Psychological Society. (n.d.). *Psychologists in schools*. http://www.psychology.org.au/for-the-public/about-psychology/What-does-a-psychologist-do/Psychologists-in-schools

Boudah, D. J., Lenz, B. K., Bulgren, J. A., Schumaker, J. B., & Deshler, D. D. (2000). Don't water down! Enhance content learning through the unit organizer routine. *Teaching Exceptional Children*, *32*(3), 48–56. https://doi.org/10.1177/004005990003200308

Boudah, D. J., Lenz, B. K., Schumaker, J. B., & Deshler, D. D. (2008). Teaching in the face of academic diversity: Unit planning and instruction by secondary teachers to enhance learning in inclusive classes. *Journal of Curriculum and Instruction*, *2*(2), 74–91. https://doi.org/10.3776/joci.2008.v2n2p74-91

Bowe, J., & Gore, J. (2017). Reassembling teacher professional development: The case for Quality Teaching Rounds. *Teachers and Teaching*, *23*(3), 352–366. https://doi.org/10.1080/13540602.2016.120652

Burns, M. K., Jimerson, S. R., Van Der Heyden, A. M., & Deno, S. L. (2016). Toward a unified response-to-intervention model: Multi-Tiered Systems of Support. In S. R. Jimerson., M. K. Burns., & A. M. Van Der Heyden, (Eds.), *Handbook of response to intervention* (pp. 719–732). Springer.

Casillas, D. (2010). Teachers' perceptions of school-based occupational therapy consultation: Part I. *Early Intervention & School Special Interest Section Quarterly*, *17*(1), 1–3.

Christner, A. (2015). Promoting the role of occupational therapy in school-based collaboration: Outcome project. *Journal of Occupational Therapy, Schools, & Early Intervention*, *8*(2), 136–148. https://doi.org/10.1080/19411243.2015.1038469

Cirrin, F., Bird, A., Biehl, L., Disney, S., Estomin, E., Rudebusch, J., Schraeder, T., & Whitmire, K. (2003). Speech-language caseloads in the schools: A workload analysis approach to setting caseload standards. *Seminars in Speech and Language*, *24*(3), 155–180. https://doi.org/10.1055/s-2003-42823

D'Amour, D., Ferrada-Videla, M., San Martín Rodríguez, L., & Beaulieu, M.-D. (2005). The conceptual basis for interprofessional collaboration: Core concepts and theoretical frameworks. *Journal of Interprofessional Care*, *19*(S1), 116–131. https://doi.org/10.1080/13561820500082529

Edwards, A., Lunt, I., & Stamou, E. (2010). Inter-professional work and expertise: New roles at the boundaries of schools. *British Educational Research Journal*, 36(1), 27–45. https://doi.org/10.1080/01411920902834134

Foley, K., D'Arcy, C., & Lawless, A. (2022). "There's been a huge change": Educator experiences of a whole-school SLP-led project to address developmental language disorder in three Australian secondary schools. *International Journal of Speech-Language Pathology*. Advance online publication. https://doi.org/10.1080/17549507.2022.2075467

Forbes, J. (2003). Grappling with collaboration: Would opening up the research "base" help? *British Journal of Special Education*, 30(3), 150–155. https://doi.org/10.1111/1467-8527.00301

Friend, M., & Cook, L. (2010). *Interactions: Collaboration skills for school professionals* (6th ed.). Pearson.

Friend, M., Cook, L., Hurley-Chamberlain, D., & Shamberger, C. (2010). Co-teaching: An illustration of the complexity of collaboration in special education. *Journal of Educational and Psychological Consultation*, 20(1), 9–27. https://doi.org/10.1080/10474410903535380

Friend, M., Reising, M., & Cook, L. (1993). Co-teaching: An overview of the past, a glimpse at the present, and considerations for the future. *Preventing School Failure: Alternative Education for Children and Youth*, 37(4), 6–10. https://doi.org/10.1080/1045988X.1993.9944611

Gallagher, A. L., Eames, C., Roddy, R., & Cunningham, R. (2022). The invisible and the non-routine: A meta-ethnography of intersectoral work in schools from the perspective of speech and language therapists and occupational therapists. *Journal of Interprofessional Care*. Advance online publication. https://doi.org/10.1080/13561820.2022.2108774

Gallagher, A. L., Murphy, C.-A., Conway, P., & Perry, A. (2019). Consequential differences in perspectives and practices concerning children with developmental language disorders: An integrative review. *International Journal of Language & Communication Disorders*, 54(4), 529–552. https://doi.org/10.1111/1460-6984.12469

Gallagher, T. L., & Bennett, S. M. (2018). The six "P" model: Principles of coaching for inclusion coaches. *International Journal of Mentoring and Coaching in Education*, 7(1), 19–34. https://doi.org/10.1108/IJMCE-03-2017-0018

Gore, J., Lloyd, A., Smith, M., Bowe, J., Ellis, H., & Lubans, D. (2017). Effects of professional development on the quality of teaching: Results from a randomised controlled trial of Quality Teaching Rounds. *Teaching and Teacher Education*, 68, 99–113. https://doi.org/10.1016/j.tate.2017.08.007

Gore, J. M., Miller, A., Fray, L., Harris, J., & Prieto, E. (2021). Improving student achievement through professional development: Results from a randomised controlled trial of Quality Teaching Rounds. *Teaching and Teacher Education*, 101, 103297. https://doi.org/10.1016/j.tate.2021.103297

Gore, M. (2014). The implementation of coaching to enhance the classroom practice of staff in teaching pupils with autism in a generic special school. *Good Autism Practice*, 15(1), 14–21. https://dx.doi.org/10.4135/9781526470409

Gregory, A., Ruzek, E., Hafen, C. A., Mikami, A. Y., Allen, J. P., & Pianta, R. C. (2017). My teaching partner-secondary: A video-based coaching model. *Theory into Practice*, 56(1), 38–45. https://doi.org/10.1080/00405841.2016.1260402

Hartas, D. (2004) Teacher and speech-language therapist collaboration: being equal and achieving a common goal? *Child Language Teaching and Therapy*, 20(1), 33–54. https://doi.org/10.1191/0265659004ct262oa

Hinder, E., & Ashburner, J. (2017). Occupation-Centred Intervention in the School Setting. In S. Roger & A. Kennedy-Behr (Eds.), *Occupation-centred practice with children: A practical guide for occupational therapists* (2nd ed., pp. 233–256). Wiley.

Idol, L., Paolucci-Whitcomb, P., & Nevin, A. (1995). The collaborative consultation model. *Journal of Educational and Psychological Consultation*, 6(4), 329–346. https://doi.org/10.1207/s1532768xjepc0604_3

Jitendra, A. K., Edwards, L. L., Choutka, C. M., & Treadway, P. S. (2002). A collaborative approach to planning in the content areas for students with learning disabilities: Accessing the general curriculum. *Learning Disabilities Research & Practice*, 17(4), 252–267. https://doi.org/10.1111/0938-8982.t01-1-00023

King-Sears, M. E., Stefanidis, A., Berkeley, S., & Strogilos, V. (2021). Does co-teaching improve academic achievement for students with disabilities? A meta-analysis. *Educational Research Review*, 34, 100405. https://doi.org/10.1016/j.edurev.2021.100405

Mælan, E. N., Tjomsland, H. E., Baklien, B., & Thurston, M. (2020). Helping teachers support pupils with mental health problems through inter-professional collaboration: A qualitative study of teachers and school principals. *Scandinavian Journal of Educational Research*, 64(3), 425–439. https://doi.org/10.1080/00313831.2019.1570548

McConnellogue, S. (2011). Professional roles and responsibilities in meeting the needs of children with speech, language and communication needs: Joint working between educational psychologists and speech and language therapists. *Educational Psychology in Practice*, 27(1), 53–64. https://doi.org/10.1080/02667363.2011.549354

McKean, C., Law, J., Laing, K., Cockerill, M., Allon-Smith, J., McCartney, E., & Forbes, J. (2017). A qualitative case study in the social capital of co-professional collaborative co-practice for children with speech, language and communication needs. *International Journal of Language & Communication Disorders*, 52(4), 514–527. https://doi.org/10.1111/1460-6984.12296

Murawski, W. W., & Hughes, C. E. (2009). Response to intervention, collaboration, and co-teaching: A logical combination for successful systemic change. *Preventing School Failure: Alternative Education for Children and Youth*, 53(4), 267–277. https://doi.org/10.3200/PSFL.53.4.267-277

National Disability Insurance Agency. (2019a). *What is the NDIS?* https://www.ndis.gov.au/understanding/what-ndis

National Disability Insurance Agency. (2019b). *Education.* https://www.ndis.gov.au/understanding/ndis-and-other-government-services/education

New South Wales Department of Education. (2023). *Quality Teaching Model.* https://education.nsw.gov.au/teaching-and-learning/professional-learning/quality-teaching-rounds#:~:text=The%20Quality%20Teaching%20Model%20can%20be%20used%20to,helps%20make%20learning%20meaningful%20and%20important%20to%20students

Occupational Therapy Board of Australia. (2019). *Australian Occupational Therapy Competency Standards.* https://www.occupationaltherapyboard.gov.au/Codes-Guidelines/Competencies.aspx

Paju, B., Kajamaa, A., Pirttimaa, R., & Kontu, E. (2022). Collaboration for inclusive practices: Teaching staff perspectives from Finland. *Scandinavian Journal of Educational Research*, 66(3), 427–440. https://doi.org/10.1080/00313831.2020.1869087

Pardini, P. (2006). In one voice: Mainstream and ELL teachers work side-by-side in the classroom, teaching language through content. *Journal of Staff Development*, 27(4), 20–25.

Ploessl, D. M., Rock, M. L., Schoenfeld, N., & Blanks, B. (2010). On the same page: Practical techniques to enhance co-teaching interactions. *Intervention in School and Clinic*, 45(3), 158–168. https://doi.org/10.1177/1053451209349529

Powers, K. M. (2001). Problem solving Student Support Teams. *The California School Psychologist*, 6(1), 19–30. https://psycnet.apa.org/doi/10.1007/BF03340880

Queensland Government. (n.d.). *Student support and services*. https://www.qld.gov.au/education/schools/student

Rens, L., & Joosten, A. (2014). Investigating the experiences in a school-based occupational therapy program to inform community-based paediatric occupational therapy practice. *Australian Occupational Therapy Journal*, 61(3), 148–158. https://doi.org/10.1111/1440-1630.12093

Schuster, J., Hartmann, U., & Kolleck, N. (2021). Teacher collaboration networks as a function of type of collaboration and schools' structural environment. *Teaching and Teacher Education*, 103, 103372. https://doi.org/10.1016/j.tate.2021.103372

Scruggs, T. E., Mastropieri, M. A., & McDuffie, K. A. (2007). Co-teaching in inclusive classrooms: A metasynthesis of qualitative research. *Exceptional Children*, 73(4), 392–416. https://doi.org/10.1177/001440290707300401

Shahidullah, J. D., Forman, S. G., Palejwala, M. H., Chaudhuri, A., Pincus, L. E., Lee, E., Shafrir, R., & Barone, C. (2019). National survey of chief pediatric residents' attitudes, practices, and training in collaborating with schools. *Journal of Interprofessional Education & Practice*, 15(1), 82–87. https://doi.org/10.1016/j.xjep.2019.02.008

Sileo, J. M. (2011). Co-teaching: Getting to know your partner. *Teaching Exceptional Children*, 43(5), 32–38. https://doi.org/10.1177/004005991104300503

Solis, M., Vaughn, S., Swanson, E., & McCulley, L. (2012). Collaborative models of instruction: The empirical foundations of inclusion and co-teaching. *Psychology in the Schools*, 49(5), 498–510. https://doi.org/10.1002/pits.21606

Speech Pathology Australia. (2017). *Speech pathology in schools*. https://www.speechpathologyaustralia.org.au/SPAweb/Resources_For_Speech_Pathologists/Speech_Pathologists_in_Schools/SPAweb/Resources_for_Speech_Pathologists/Speech%20Pathologists%20in%20Schools/Speech_Pathologists_in_Schools.aspx?hkey=f6a3b0ae-222f-491d-98a2-9df940018e1b

Speech Pathology Australia. (2022a). *Speech pathology in education clinical guideline*. https://www.speechpathologyaustralia.org.au/SPAweb/Members/Clinical_Guidelines/SPAweb/Members/Clinical_Guidelines/Clinical_Guidelines.aspx?hkey=0fc81470-2d6c-4b17-90c0-ced8b0ff2a5d

Speech Pathology Australia. (2022b). *Speech pathology in education position statement*. https://www.speechpathologyaustralia.org.au/SPAweb/Members/Clinical_Guidelines/SPAweb/Members/Clinical_Guidelines/Clinical_Guidelines.aspx?hkey=0fc81470-2d6c-4b17-90c0-ced8b0ff2a5d#edu

Starling, J., Munro, N., Togher, L., & Arciuli, J. (2012). Training secondary school teachers in instructional language modification techniques to support adolescents with language impairment: A randomized controlled trial. *Language, Speech, and Hearing Services in Schools*, 43(4), 474–495. https://doi.org/10.1044/0161-1461(2012/11-0066)

Tancredi, H. (2018). *Adjusting language barriers in secondary classrooms through professional collaboration based on student consultation* [Master's thesis, Queensland University of Technology]. QUT ePrints. https://eprints.qut.edu.au/122876/

Truong, V., & Hodgetts, S. (2017). An exploration of teacher perceptions toward occupational therapy and occupational therapy practices: A scoping review. *Journal of Occupational Therapy, Schools & Early Intervention*, 10(2), 121–136. https://doi.org/10.1080/19411243.2017.1304840

United Nations. (2016). *General Comment No. 4, Article 24: Right to Inclusive Education* (CRPD/C/GC/4). https://digitallibrary.un.org/record/1313836?ln=en

Vangrieken, K., Meredith, C., Packer, T., & Kyndt, E. (2017). Teacher communities as a context for professional development: A systematic review. *Teaching and Teacher Education*, 61, 47–59. https://doi.org/10.1016/j.tate.2016.10.001

van Nieuwerburgh, C. (2012). Coaching in education: An overview. In C. van Nieuwerburgh (Ed.), *Coaching in education: Getting better results for students, educators, and parents* (pp. 3–23). Karnac Books.

Vescio, V., Ross, D., & Adams, A. (2008). A review of research on the impact of professional learning communities on teaching practice and student learning. *Teaching and Teacher Education*, 24(1), 80–91. https://doi.org/10.1016/j.tate.2007.01.004

Villeneuve, M. (2009). A critical examination of school-based occupational therapy collaborative consultation. *Canadian Journal of Occupational Therapy*, 76(S1), 206–218. https://doi.org/10.1177/000841740907600s05

Chapter 19

Rethinking the use of teacher aides

Rob Webster & Peter Blatchford

Many schools in many jurisdictions worldwide employ additional adults (commonly called teacher aides or teaching assistants) to support the inclusion of children and young people with disability. Research, however, has raised questions about the educational effectiveness of this model of student support, particularly in the United Kingdom where the research has been sustained and rigorous. This chapter discusses the research findings on the impact of teacher aides/assistants (TAs) in inclusive classrooms. Further, we explore the evidence on the deployment, practice, and preparation of teachers and TAs, and explain why—based on our extensive collaborative and developmental work with schools—a reconceptualisation of the TA role around promoting student independence offers a potentially transformative, and impactful alternative model to TA utilisation.

Background

The long-term, international trend towards inclusion over the last 35 years has been accompanied and assisted by an increase in the number of support paraprofessionals in schools. Australia, Italy, Sweden, Canada, Finland, Germany, Hong Kong, Iceland, Ireland, Malta, New Zealand, South Africa, the United States, and the United Kingdom have all experienced large increases in this sector of their education workforces (Giangreco et al., 2014). Policies of inclusion and provision for students with learning difficulties and disability in regular settings in other OECD countries now rely heavily on this 'non-teaching' workforce (Navarro, 2015). These staff are known variously as teaching assistants, learning-support assistants, or classroom assistants in the United Kingdom, and paraeducators, teacher aides, education assistants, or school learning-support officers in the United States, Australia, and New Zealand. In this chapter we refer to all personnel with equivalent classroom-based support roles collectively as TAs.

No other education system in the world has expanded both the number and role of TAs to quite the same extent as England. Over the last 20 years, the number of TAs in mainstream schools in England has more than trebled. TAs comprise 28% of the school workforce in England (Department for Education, 2021). Australia has seen a comparatively small increase in TAs over the last ten years, with approximately 90,000 TAs employed in schools (Australian Government, n.d.). The most common model

DOI: 10.4324/9781003350897-22

of deployment internationally is for the TA to support students in regular classrooms, alongside the teacher. The second most common model is for TAs to deliver structured intervention (or catch-up) programs, which typically take place outside of the classroom, during and away from regular lessons. The third most common model is the use of TAs to support students' behavioural, emotional, and social development (Butt, 2016). However, the most common methods of deployment are not necessarily the most effective, and research evidence can provide critical guidance to maximise the effectiveness of this important resource.

The Impact of TAs

Investing in TAs seems to be a worthwhile investment, based on the not-unreasonable assumption that support from TAs leads to positive outcomes for students with learning difficulties and/or disability—the groups that TAs are shown to spend the most time working alongside. Until recently, there has been little research on the impact of TAs and the support they provide. What we have learned in the last decade challenges the veracity of the assumption that TA support always leads to positive outcomes. We now consider the evidence of the impact of TAs in terms of the three ways they are commonly used in schools, as summarised above.

Support from TAs in Regular Classrooms

Much of the research investigating the use of TAs in regular classroom environments is small-scale and describes what TAs do. Almost all of it has some focus on how TAs facilitate the inclusion of students with disability (Alborz et al., 2009; Sharma & Salend, 2016). Early research investigated teamwork between teachers and other adults, such as parent-helpers and TAs (Geen, 1985; Thomas, 1992), and led to a useful collaborative study with schools on alternative ways of organising classrooms (Cremin et al., 2005). Both the qualitative and quantitative work on impact relies principally on impressionistic data from school staff.

Large-scale systematic analyses investigating the effects of TAs on learning outcomes are rare. One experimental study in the United States found no differences in the outcomes for students in classes with TAs present (Finn et al., 2000). Longitudinal research in the United Kingdom has produced similar results (Blatchford et al., 2007). There are very few randomised control trials that investigate the impact of TAs in regular classrooms, but two conducted in Denmark have found mixed effects (Navarro, 2015). One of these two studies involved 125 schools and found no strong effect of TAs on student learning. It did, however, find positive impacts for TAs on teachers' job satisfaction and workload. A second randomised control trial involving 105 primary schools measured the impact of unqualified TAs and qualified teachers working as TAs, compared to a control group. There was a positive impact on reading for both types of aide, but no impact on maths. However, there was insufficient data on school leaders' decision-making and classroom practices to conclude what drove the effects. Secondary analyses of school expenditure have suggested that the expenditure on TAs is positively correlated with improved academic outcomes (Brown & Harris, 2010; Clotfelter et al., 2016; Nicoletti & Rabe, 2014). However, these analyses of TA impact do not adequately rule out the possibility that other school factors might explain the correlations found. The conclusions drawn are also not supported by the evidence collected; in particular, they do not include data on what actually happens in classrooms.

The largest and most in-depth study ever carried out on the use and impact of TA support in everyday classroom environments is our multi-method Deployment and Impact of Support Staff (DISS) project in the United Kingdom (Blatchford, Russell, & Webster, 2012). Unlike other studies, it linked what TAs actually do in classrooms to effects on student progress. The results show that TAs in the United Kingdom have a predominantly pedagogical role and spend much of their time supporting students with learning difficulties and/or disability. Teachers in the DISS project felt that deploying TAs in this way allowed them to devote time to the rest of the class, in the knowledge that the TAs were giving potentially valuable individual attention to the students in most need. There are additional benefits in terms of reductions in teacher workload. Importantly, however, the DISS project also found that there are *serious unintended consequences* of this model of support: a negative relationship existed between the amount of TA support received and the progress made by students, especially students with complex learning profiles (Webster et al., 2010). Put simply, the more support students received from TAs, the less progress they were found to make. This finding was not explained by student characteristics (such as prior attainment or social disadvantage), whether the student had a disability and whether the student was found consistently over seven different year groups in regular primary-and secondary-school settings. Later, we describe the explanatory factors in the relationship between TA support and academic outcomes.

Structured Intervention Programs

In contrast to in-class support, the evidence on the role of TAs in delivering structured interventions in one-to-one or small-group settings shows a much stronger, positive impact on student attainment. This research shows a consistent, moderate impact on attainment of approximately three to four additional months' progress over an academic year (Higgins et al., 2013; Nickow et al., 2020; Slavin et al., 2009; Slavin et al., 2011). The average impact of Tas delivering structured interventions is, perhaps unsurprisingly, less than that for interventions using experienced qualified teachers, which typically provide around six additional months' progress per year (Higgins et al., 2013; Slavin et al., 2011). That said, TA-led interventions generally produce better outcomes than volunteers who deliver interventions; effects for volunteer-led interventions are typically one to two months' additional progress (Slavin et al., 2011). The positive effects of TAs delivering structured interventions may challenge the assumption that only qualified teachers can provide effective one-to-one or small-group support; however, teacher-led interventions tend to be expensive to deliver, requiring additional and often specialist staff.

Crucially, though, the positive effects are only observed when adults work in structured settings with high-quality support and training. The research investigating TAs delivering interventions is small, but it is growing. The majority of this research has been conducted internationally and is small-scale work involving between 30 and 200 students. However, the emerging findings from larger-scale evaluations in the United Kingdom, funded by the Education Endowment Foundation (2022) are showing consistency with the international picture (Sharples, 2016). Overall, more research has been conducted on literacy interventions than for mathematics, although positive impacts are observed for both.

Studies showing positive impacts of TA-led interventions on learning outcomes tend to measure learning outcomes at the end of the intervention. Less is known about the extent to which any immediate, positive improvements translate into long-term learning and performance on national tests. Encouragingly, a recent evaluation of AB-RACADABRA, a 20-week literacy program delivered by trained Tas to small groups of students (aged five to seven years), showed that students who participated in the program continued to do better than their comparison-group peers a year after the intervention finished (Martell, 2018). Studies of a reading intervention for similar-aged students have also found residual impacts (Savage & Carless, 2005, 2008).

The evidence on TA-led structured interventions stands in contrast to the research on the effect of classroom deployment. Where Tas are used in more informal, unsupported instructional roles, there is little or no impact on student outcomes. In light of the DISS project, then, the most salient evidence gap is in terms of the impact of Tas in regular classrooms. Helpfully, a promising model called Maximising the Impact of Teaching Assistants (MITA)—developed through our collaborative work with schools (Webster et al., 2013, 2021), and subjected to further refinement and extensive professional validation through a 'research-into-practice' program in the United Kingdom—offers a way forward (more below).

Behavioural, Emotional, and Social Development

In addition to the effect of TAs on learning outcomes, the DISS project also assessed the effects of the amount of TA support in relation to students' behavioural, emotional and social development, which we called 'positive approaches to learning'. Support of this nature is provided by TAs in both in-class and out-of-class situations, and our measurements did not distinguish between where support was provided. Measured variables included distractibility, confidence, motivation, disruptiveness, independence, and relationships with other students. Our results showed little evidence that the amount of TA support that students received over a school year improved their positive approaches to learning, except for those in Year 9 (13–14-year-olds), where there was a clear positive effect of TA support across all outcomes (Blatchford, Russell, & Webster, 2012). At that age, students with the most TA support had noticeably more positive approaches to learning. However, there was no trend for students in other year groups.

Summarising the Evidence on Impact

On the basis of the DISS project findings, and subsequent work focusing specifically on students with complex learning profiles who attend regular schools, it is difficult to avoid the conclusion that the students who receive high amounts of support from TAs receive a different and less effective pedagogical diet. TAs assume much of the responsibility for moment-by-moment pedagogical decision-making for these students and provide a high amount of verbal differentiation. They do this in part to make classroom teaching accessible, but also to compensate for the teachers' failure to make appropriate adjustments (Webster & Blatchford, 2015, 2019; Webster, 2022).

Importantly, as evidence from the DISS project showed, while TAs' interactions with students were well-intentioned, the nature and appropriateness of their interactions were qualitatively different to teacher-to-student talk. More detailed studies of adult–student interactions have found that TAs tend to close down talk, rather than open it up, as teachers do (Radford et al., 2011). Elsewhere, analyses by Rubie-Davies et al. (2010) found that, compared to teachers, TAs are more concerned with task completion and correction than learning. Other research points to concerns that TAs can encourage dependency, because they act in ways that do not encourage students to think for themselves (Moyles & Suschitzky, 1997). Evidence shows that over-reliance on one-to-one TA support leads to a wide range of detrimental effects on students, in terms of interference with ownership and responsibility for learning, and separation from classmates (Giangreco, 2010). Overall, the evidence of the impact of TAs on what we might call 'soft' outcomes is quite thin and largely based on impressionistic data. It is an area that warrants further research and greater attention from governments and education providers.

Making Better Use of TAs

We noted above that the DISS project findings were unable to be explained in terms of student factors. Importantly, these results were not attributable to TAs, either. The findings are best explained in terms of the situational and structural factors within which TAs work but, crucially, over which they have little or no influence. This is an important point, because the effects of TA support are consequences of decisions made *about* TAs, not decisions made *by* TAs. The wider pedagogical role (WPR) model (Webster et al., 2011) was developed to explain the DISS project results. It was built on the basis of an extensive data-collection effort, which combined results from classroom observations, staff surveys, interviews, and audio recordings of lessons (Blatchford, Russell, & Webster, 2012). The WPR model not only serves an explanatory purpose, but also a developmental purpose.

There are three main components of the WPR model: deployment, practice, and preparedness. The main explanation for the DISS project results on attainment appeared to be the way TA-supported students spent less time interacting with the teacher and became separated from the teacher and curriculum. In other words, there was a trade-off in terms of more TA support that meant pupils had less time with their teacher, and it is perhaps unsurprising that these students made less progress than their peers. The less-effective pedagogical diet we referred to earlier—where TA–student interactions are centred on task completion and correction—constitutes the second WPR component of practice. Writ large in the DISS project and other research on the effectiveness of TAs (Butt & Lance, 2005; Howes et al., 2003; Lee, 2002) is preparedness. Preparedness captures: (1) the time for joint planning, preparation, and feedback between teachers and TAs, before and after lessons (what we call the 'day-to-day' aspects); and (2) the training and professional development that teachers have received (or not) on how to manage and organise the work of TAs, and the extent and quality of training that TAs have had to help them perform their role optimally.

The debate about the deployment and effectiveness of TAs has been informed and sharpened in recent years by research and commentary on major reforms to policy and practice regarding the education of students with disability (Blatchford & Webster, 2018; Navarro, 2015; Peacey, 2015; Sharma & Salend, 2016; Skipp & Hopwood, 2016; Webster, 2022; Webster & Blatchford, 2013, 2015, 2019). It is difficult to avoid the conclusion that the model of 'inclusion' we have drifted towards over the last 30 years—which is more appropriately described as 'integration' by the *Convention on the Rights of Persons with Disabilities* (United Nations, 2016)—stands as a proxy for unresolved questions about how students with disability are taught in regular classrooms. Rather than improve the quality of teaching for students with disability (Hodkinson, 2009), the education system has looked to other forms of support and provision. In the case of the English system (and indeed others), this has meant a considerable increase in the number of TAs. A key conclusion from the DISS project aimed at policymakers and practitioners is that it is TA deployment that is the fundamental issue, not TA employment. In other words, the point of departure post-DISS is to ensure that schools make the best use of TAs, not get rid of them. In the remainder of this chapter, we use the structural components of the WPR model to put forward an alternative approach to TA deployment and practice, paying particular attention to how TAs can be prepared for these roles. We provide some practical strategies, many of which have been developed and validated by schools that have participated in the MITA program.

1 Deployment: Supplement, Not Replace

The essence of effective TA deployment is to ensure that TAs supplement, and do not replace, the teacher. This is essential in the case of students with disability, as a key conclusion arising from the evidence is that TAs are often used as an informal teaching resource for students with the most complex learning profiles. Guidance for school leaders, formulated on the basis of the evidence, makes it clear that decisions about TA deployment provide the starting point from which all other decisions about TAs flow (Webster et al., 2016, 2021). The critical first step is for schools to determine the broad types of role that TAs are required to perform. There may be a case for some TAs to have a full or partial role in non-pedagogical activities, such as easing teachers' administrative workload or helping students to develop 'soft' skills.

Ultimately, the requirements of the students must drive decisions around TA deployment. For example, teachers need to adopt the mindset of deploying TAs in ways that add value to their teaching. A practical suggestion is for teachers to first envisage the classroom as it would be with the teacher, but without the TA, and then make decisions about how the teacher would need to organise things to provide the best educational experience for all pupils in the class. Following this, the TA could then be introduced back into the classroom, so to speak, in such a way that they provide an additional resource. Furthermore, all staff and students need to be clear on the roles, boundaries, and expectations of teachers and TAs.

2 Practice: Scaffolding for Independence

The evidence is quite clear: students with disability who experience high amounts of TA support are at risk of developing learned helplessness. We can invert this by training TAs to foster student independence and ensure classroom talk focuses on the *processes* of learning, not products (e.g., task completion). One of the most promising ways to get TAs to foster student independence—and reduce dependence—happens to be one of the least expensive to implement. The work of Paula Bosanquet and Julie Radford (Bosanquet et al., 2021) has produced a straightforward and practical scaffolding framework that schools can use to improve TAs' interactions. It resembles an upside-down five-layered triangle, with each layer representing ever-decreasing amounts of student independence.[1] The framework recognises that you cannot really *teach* independence; you have to create the opportunities for students to experience and learn from it. In effect, the transformative potential of training and deploying TAs to scaffold for independence lies in another apparent contradiction: always give the least amount of help.

The TA's default position (layer one of the framework) is to observe student performance, allowing time and space for them to process, think and try the task independently. Bosanquet et al. (2021) refer to this as 'self-scaffolding' strategies. TAs need to get comfortable with students engaging in purposeful effort and recognise effort (as opposed to struggle) as an essential component of learning. Layer two of the framework is prompting or encouraging. Here, TAs might intervene with a nudge: "What do you need to do first?", "What's your plan?", "You can do this!" The third layer of the framework is clueing. Often students know the problem-solving strategies that the prompts are designed to elicit, but they find it difficult to call them to mind. Clues are a question or small piece of information to help students work out how to move forward. They should be drip-fed, always starting with a small clue. Prompts and clues are less effective when students encounter a task that requires a new skill or strategy. This calls for layer four of the framework: modelling. TAs, as confident and competent experts, can model while students actively watch and listen, then students can try the same step for

---

1 A summary of the framework is available online at: https://maximisingtas.co.uk/assets/content/scaffoldingframework.pdf.

themselves afterwards. Correcting (layer five) is where TAs provide answers. It requires no independent thinking and should be avoided in all but essential circumstances—for example, when there is a danger that doing anything else will frustrate the teaching and learning process.

What is significant about this alternative approach is how it shifts the purpose and prioritisation of the TA's support function. The starting point is to acknowledge the teacher as the pedagogical expert in the classroom, and to recognise that TAs' skills and pupil outcomes are maximised when TAs support problem-solving *alongside* the mainstream curriculum. Training TAs in this approach has been shown not only to improve TAs' talk behaviours, but also have a positive impact on pupil engagement (Dimova et al., 2021).

3 Preparedness: Teacher–TA Liaison for Planning and Feedback

Preparedness is a persistent problem, both in terms of pre-service and ongoing training, and especially in terms of the day-to-day aspects of readiness for lessons. The picture regarding day-to-day preparedness revealed through the DISS project is consistent with other studies (e.g., Butt & Lance, 2005; Howes et al., 2003; Lee, 2002). The majority of teachers had not had training to help them work with TAs in classrooms, nor did they have allocated time for planning and feedback, or other allocated time with TAs they worked with (Blatchford, Russell, & Webster, 2012). In their review of the literature, based on 28 peer-reviewed articles, Sharma and Salend (2016) cite international research published from 2005 onwards that identifies TAs "having effective communication and collaboration [and] planning time with supportive teachers" as "critical factors contributing to their efficacy" (p. 124). Conversely, where this is absent, TAs report that their performance was "hindered".

The comment below from a TA interviewed as part of our Effective Deployment of Teaching Assistants (EDTA) project (Blatchford, Webster, & Russell, 2012) typifies the reactive position that TAs are in when they do not have pre-lesson preparation: "You come into a classroom, you listen to the 20 minutes of teaching, and from that, you should know. And then you're to feed it to the children. It's scary" (p. 81). Unpacking this, we can see that in the absence of a pre-lesson briefing, this TA has to tune in to the teacher's whole-class input in order to understand the concepts being taught, the skills to be learned or applied, the tasks and instructions, and the intended learning outcomes. Then the TA is expected to apply her/his judgement and provide any differentiation (s)he deems necessary; this is what this TA meant by "feed it to the children". Add to this the very probable subject and instructional knowledge differential that exists between the teacher and the TA, plus the fact that the TA is working with the students who find it hardest to access the curriculum and teacher's pedagogical practices, and it is small wonder that this TA describes the situation as "scary".

The picture from the research evidence aligns fully with what we hear from school leaders, teachers and TAs in our work with schools. Over 1,000 schools have accessed the MITA program across the United Kingdom, and perhaps the most common refrain we hear from them is that the lack of opportunities for teachers and TAs to meet—to plan, prepare, provide feedback and talk about students' learning and progress—is the biggest barrier to fully unlocking the potential of classroom support. Few things exemplify the persistent problem of preparedness more vividly than the comment from the TA quoted earlier. Mitigating, if not avoiding altogether, the effects of TAs "going into lessons blind" (Blatchford, Russell, & Webster, 2012, p. 61) is an essential component of ensuring TA effectiveness. Finding extra time within schools is, of course, never easy, and it is probably why so many school leaders focus on this practical barrier in sessions on our MITA program. Nevertheless, without adequate out-of-class liaison, it is difficult for teachers and TAs to work complementarily and collaboratively.

In the EDTA project, schools found creative ways to ensure that teachers and TAs had time to meet, thereby improving the quality of lesson preparation and feedback (Webster et al., 2013). For example, head teachers standardised TAs' hours of work, so that they started and finished their day earlier, thereby creating essential joint-planning time between TAs and teachers before school. Other schools that have created dedicated liaison time report that teachers and TAs feel the benefits almost instantly, and TAs' sense of value and confidence soar. To ensure that teacher–TA preparation time is used productively, it may be necessary to set expectations of what it is (and is not) for. In the EDTA, one school had to introduce a loose planning framework to guide meetings, after TAs were found to be doing administrative tasks instead of discussing lessons and learning.

Although we emphasise *joint* preparation time, the responsibility for planning lessons and setting appropriate tasks for students rests with the teacher. It is essential that teachers plan lessons effectively, and explicitly plan the TA's role in them. Lessons should allow opportunities for TAs to be deployed in ways that supplement teaching. Teachers need to think about how to make use of the additional capacity in their classroom to achieve learning objectives and ensure that they—*the teachers*—spend time with students who require additional support. Effective and efficient lesson planning starts with a good understanding of what students can and cannot do at the end of the previous lesson. Teachers should encourage TAs to record their observations of students' performance during lessons, and be clear about what they want TAs to feed back at the end of the lesson.

Encouragingly, it is possible for schools to create time for teachers and TAs to meet, and the effects of achieving this are positive. In the EDTA project, the quality and clarity of teachers' lesson plans improved, and plans were shared with TAs and supplemented with daily discussions, which made explicit the role and tasks of the TA for each lesson (Webster et al., 2013). Indications from the MITA project suggest that primary schools can replicate and extend these practices and draw benefits. For example, school leaders report that TAs feel more valued, and some of the palpable problems of 'going into lessons blind' are being alleviated (Webster et al., 2021).

Acting on the Evidence

The evidence on effective TA deployment, practice and preparedness is relatively straightforward. Acting on it can be summarised in one clear principle: use TAs to supplement what teachers do, not replace them (Sharples et al., 2018; Evidence for Learning, 2019). At the same time, there are also clear benefits to schools in reframing the way TAs are used, in terms of student outcomes, school outcomes, and overall staff satisfaction and morale. Nevertheless, our experiences of working with schools to improve the way TAs are trained and deployed suggests that actually *making* those changes is not straightforward. It can be a complex process, requiring changes across the school (involving senior leadership, middle leadership, teachers, and TAs) that address the existing models of working, the provision of training at all levels and sometimes the implementation of structural alterations (in terms of timetabling and working arrangements). Encouragingly, we have seen that when schools overcome practical barriers to change, they do so by investing time, attention, and effort into making improvements—not by spending lots of money (Webster et al., 2021).

Our developmental work with schools (Webster et al., 2016, 2021) has revealed a number of key principles to successfully taking action on recommendations made in practical guidance (Sharples et al., 2018; Evidence for Learning, 2019). To conclude this chapter, we outline four steps that schools could consider. First, the school-leadership team, including the principal, should form and lead a small development team with responsibility for managing the changes. Involvement of the principal is essential, as staffing and contractual issues inevitably feature in decision-making, and change cannot be sanctioned without leadership understanding and approval. Second, the development team should schedule dedicated time over the course of two or three terms for discussion, planning, decision-making, and action. Time is ring-fenced for these discussions. As change is rolled out gradually, school leaders should encourage the testing of ideas and win support from staff across the school. The initial team is extended to include a small group of enthusiastic teachers and TAs who are interested in working with research evidence and willing to test new strategies and provide feedback on progress. Third, the senior leadership team should develop and communicate a clear vision for what the school needs from its TA workforce. The team should think about the TAs' role and contribution, and what students and staff will do differently as a result of improving TA deployment and preparation, as well as keep discussions open and positive. Finally, the school-leadership team should conduct a thorough audit of the current situation in their school. This audit can include:

- self-assessment of current practices,
- anonymous surveys of staff to gather their honest views and experiences,
- conducting observations and asking questions about teachers' decision-making regarding TA deployment,
- making an effort to observe and listen to TAs' interactions with students,
- a skills audit to collect details of TAs' qualifications, certifications, training, experience, specialisms, and talents, and
- obtaining and considering carefully the views of other school stakeholders, including students and parents and/or carers.

Conclusion

A constant refrain in both our research and development work is that, in order to bring about consistent and fundamental change, it is important that the whole school is involved, and that reform and improvement are driven by school leaders. That said, we know better utilisation of TAs is achievable at the classroom level when informed and motivated teachers become more aware of their responsibilities to both TAs and students with disability, and make changes in areas within their control, such as through more thorough lesson planning. This chapter has attempted to give a clear, evidence-based rationale for attending to TA deployment, practice, and preparedness, and provided field-tested strategies that teachers can use to ensure that TAs are used to supplement great teaching and add value to the classroom.

References

Alborz, A., Pearson, D., Farrell, P., & Howes, A. (2009). *The impact of adult support staff on pupils and mainstream schools*. EPPI-Centre, Social Science Research Unit, Institute of Education, University of London. https://eppi.ioe.ac.uk/cms/Portals/0/PDF%20reviews%20and%20summaries/Support%20staff%20Rpt.pdf?ver=2009-05-05-165528-197

Australian Government. (n.d.). *Education aides*. https://joboutlook.gov.au/occupation.aspx?search=alpha&tab=stats&cluster=&code=4221&graph=EL

Blatchford, P., Russell, A., Bassett, P., Brown, P., & Martin, C. (2007). The role and effects of teaching assistants in English primary schools (Years 4 to 6) 2000–2003. Results from the Class Size and Pupil-Adult Ratios (CSPAR) KS2 Project. *British Educational Research Journal, 33*(1), 5–26. https://doi.org/10.1080/01411920601104292

Blatchford, P., Russell, A., & Webster, R. (2012). *Reassessing the impact of teaching Assistants: How research challenges practice and policy*. Routledge.

Blatchford, P., & Webster, R. (2018). Classroom contexts for learning at primary and secondary school: Class size, groupings, interactions and special educational needs. *British Educational Research Journal, 44*(4), 681–703. https://doi.org/10.1002/berj.3454

Blatchford, P., Webster, R., & Russell, A. (2012). *Challenging the role and deployment of teaching assistants in mainstream schools: The impact on schools: Final report on the Effective Deployment of Teaching Assistants (EDTA) project*. UCL Institute of Education. https://discovery.ucl.ac.uk/id/eprint/10096860/

Bosanquet, P., Radford, J., & Webster, R. (2021). *The teaching assistant's guide to effective interaction: How to maximise your practice* (2nd ed.). Routledge.

Brown, J., & Harris, A. (2010). *Increased expenditure on associate staff in schools and changes in student attainment*. Training and Development Agency for Schools. https://dera.ioe.ac.uk/10981/1/increased_expenditure_associate_staff.pdf

Butt, G., & Lance, A. (2005). Modernizing the roles of support staff in primary schools: changing focus, changing function. *Educational Review (Birmingham), 57*(2), 139–149. https://doi.org/10.1080/0013191042000308323

Butt, R. (2016). Teacher assistant support and deployment in mainstream schools. *International Journal of Inclusive Education, 20*(9), 995–1007. https://doi.org/10.1080/13603116.2016.1145260

Clotfelter, C. T., Hemelt, S. W., & Ladd, H. F. (2016). *Teaching assistants and nonteaching staff: Do they improve student outcomes?* Working Paper 169. https://www.nber.org/system/files/working_papers/w22217/w22217.pdf

Cremin, H., Thomas, G., & Vincett, K. (2005). Working with teaching assistants: Three models evaluated. *Research Papers in Education*, *20*(4), 413–432. https://doi.org/10.1080/026715 20500335881

Department for Education. (2021). *School workforce in England: Reporting year 2020.* https://explore-education-statistics.service.gov.uk/find-statistics/school-workforce-in-england

Dimova, S., Culora, A., Brown, E. R., Ilie, S., Sutherland, A., & Curran, S. (2021). *Maximising the impact of teaching assistants: Evaluation report.* https://www.rand.org/pubs/external_publications/EP68731.html

Education Endowment Foundation. (2022). *Maximising the impact of teaching assistants.* https://educationendowmentfoundation.org.uk/projects-and-evaluation/projects/maximising-the-impact-of-teaching-assistants

Evidence for Learning. (2019). *Making best use of teaching assistants.* https://evidenceforlearning.org.au/education-evidence/guidance-reports/teaching-assistants

Finn, J. D., Gerber, S. B., Farber, S. L., & Achilles, C. M. (2000). Teacher aides: An alternative to small classes? In M. C. Wang, &, J. D. Finn (Eds.), *How small classes help teachers do their best* (pp. 131–174). Temple University Centre for Research in Human Development.

Geen, A. G. (1985). Team teaching in the secondary schools of England and Wales. *Educational Review (Birmingham)*, *37*(1), 29–38. https://doi.org/10.1080/0013191850370104

Giangreco, M. F. (2010). One-to-one paraprofessionals for students with disabilities in inclusive classrooms: Is conventional wisdom wrong? *Intellectual and Developmental Disabilities*, *48*(1), 1–13. https://doi.org/10.1352/1934-9556-48.1.1

Giangreco, M. F., & Doyle, M., & Suter, J. C. (2014). Teacher assistants in inclusive classrooms. In L. Florian (Ed.), *The SAGE handbook of special education* (pp. 691–702). SAGE.

Higgins, S., Katsipataki, M., Kokotsaki, D., Coleman, R., Major, L. E, & Coe, R. (2013). *The Sutton Trust–Education Endowment Foundation teaching and learning toolkit.* https://educationendowmentfoundation.org.uk/evidence-summaries/teaching-learning-toolkit/

Hodkinson, A. (2009). Pre-service teacher training and special educational needs in England 1970–2008: Is government learning the lessons of the past or is it experiencing a groundhog day? *European Journal of Special Needs Education*, *24*(3), 277–289. https://doi.org/10.1080/08856250903016847

Howes, A., Farrell, P., Kaplan, I., & Moss, S. (2003). *The impact of paid adult support on the participation and learning of pupils in mainstream schools.* EPPI-Centre. https://pure.manchester.ac.uk/ws/portalfiles/portal/32298068/FULL_TEXT.PDF

Lee, B. (2002). *Teaching assistants in schools: The current state of play.* National Foundation for Educational Research. https://www.nfer.ac.uk/media/1496/91172.pdf

Martell, T. (2018). *A lasting impact—6 lessons from the evaluation of ABRA.* EEF Blog. https://educationendowmentfoundation.org.uk/news/eef-blog-a-lasting-impact-6-lessons-from-the-evaluation-of-abra/

Moyles, J., & Suschitzky, W. (1997). The employment and deployment of classroom support staff: head teachers' perspectives. *Research in Education (Manchester)*, *58*(1), 21–34. https://doi.org/10.1177/003452379705800103

Navarro, F. M. (2015). Learning support staff: A literature review. *OECD education working papers*, *125*. OECD Publishing. https://doi.org/10.1787/5jrnzm39w45l-en

Nickow, A., Oreopoulos, P., & Quan, V. (2020). The impressive effects of tutoring on PreK–12 learning: A systematic review and meta-analysis of the experimental evidence. *NBER Working Paper Series*. https://doi.org/10.3386/w27476

Nicoletti, C., & Rabe, B. (2014). *Spending it wisely: How can schools use resources to help poorer pupils?* Nuffield Foundation.

Peacey, N. (2015). *A transformation or an opportunity lost? The education of children and young people with special educational needs and disability within the framework of the Children and Families Act 2014*. Research and Information on State Education. https://dera.ioe.ac.uk/38597/1/A%20 transformation%20or%20an%20opportunity%20lost.pdf

Radford, J., Blatchford, P., & Webster, R. (2011). Opening up and closing down: How teachers and TAs manage turn-taking, topic and repair in mathematics lessons. *Learning and Instruction, 21*(5), 625–635. https://doi.org/10.1016/j.learninstruc.2011.01.004

Rubie-Davies, C. M., Blatchford, P., Webster, R., Koutsoubou, M., & Bassett, P. (2010). Enhancing learning? A comparison of teacher and teaching assistant interactions with pupils. *School Effectiveness and School Improvement, 21*(4), 429–449. https://doi.org/10.1080/09243453.2010 .512800

Savage, R., & Carless, S. (2005). Learning support assistants can deliver effective reading interventions for "at-risk" children. *Educational Research (Windsor), 47*(1), 45–61. https://doi. org/10.1080/0013188042000337550

Savage, R., & Carless, S. (2008). The impact of early reading interventions delivered by classroom assistants on attainment at the end of Year 2. *British Educational Research Journal, 34*(3), 363–385. https://doi.org/10.1080/01411920701609315

Sharma, U., & Salend, S. J. (2016). Teaching assistants in inclusive classrooms: A systematic analysis of the international research. *The Australian Journal of Teacher Education, 41*(8), 118–134. https://doi.org/10.14221/ajte.2016v41n8.7

Sharples, J. (2016). *Six of the best: How our latest reports can help you support teaching assistants to get results* EEF Blog. https://educationendowmentfoundation.org.uk/news/ six-of-the-best-how-our-latest-reports-can-help-you-support-teaching-assist/

Sharples, J., Webster, R., & Blatchford, P. (2018). *Making best use of teaching assistants: Guidance report*. Education Endowment Foundation. http://maximisingtas.co.uk/assets/content/ ta-guideportrait.pdf

Skipp, A., & Hopwood, V. (2016). *Mapping user experiences of the education, health and care process: A qualitative study*. Department for Education & ASK Research. https://assets. publishing.service.gov.uk/government/uploads/system/uploads/attachment_data/file/518963/ Mapping_user_experiences_of_the_education__health_and_care_process_-_a_qualitative_ study.pdf

Slavin, R. E., Lake, C., Cheung, A., & Davis, S. (2009). *Beyond the basics: Effective reading programs for the upper elementary grades*. Institute of Education Sciences, United States Department of Education.

Slavin, R. E., Lake, C., Davis, S., & Madden, N. A. (2011). Effective programs for struggling readers: A best-evidence synthesis. *Educational Research Review, 6*(1), 1–26. https://doi. org/10.1016/j.edurev.2010.07.002

Thomas, G. (1992). *Effective classroom teamwork: Support or intrusion*. Routledge.

United Nations. (2016). *General Comment No. 4, Article 24: Right to Inclusive Education* (CRPD/C/ GC/4). https://digitallibrary.un.org/record/1313836?ln=en

Webster, R. (2022). *The inclusion illusion*. UCL Press.

Webster, R., & Blatchford, P. (2013). The educational experiences of pupils with a Statement for special educational needs in mainstream primary schools: Results from a systematic observation study. *European Journal of Special Needs Education, 28*(4), 463–479. https://doi.org/10.1080/08856257.2013.820459

Webster, R., & Blatchford, P. (2015). Worlds apart? The nature and quality of the educational experiences of pupils with a statement for special educational needs in mainstream primary schools. *British Educational Research Journal, 41*(2), 324–342. https://doi.org/10.1002/berj.3144

Webster, R., & Blatchford, P. (2019). Making sense of "teaching", "support" and "differentiation": The educational experiences of pupils with Education, Health and Care Plans and Statements in mainstream secondary schools. *European Journal of Special Needs Education, 34*(1), 98–113. https://doi.org/10.1080/08856257.2018.1458474

Webster, R., Blatchford, P., Bassett, P., Brown, P., Martin, C., & Russell, A. (2010). Double standards and first principles: framing teaching assistant support for pupils with special educational needs. *European Journal of Special Needs Education, 25*(4), 319–336. https://doi.org/10.1080/08856257.2010.513533

Webster, R., Blatchford, P., Bassett, P., Brown, P., Martin, C., & Russell, A. (2011). The wider pedagogical role of teaching assistants. *School Leadership & Management, 31*(1), 3–20. https://doi.org/10.1080/13632434.2010.540562

Webster, R., Blatchford, P., & Russell, A. (2013). Challenging and changing how schools use teaching assistants: Findings from the Effective Deployment of Teaching Assistants project. *School Leadership & Management, 33*(1), 78–96. https://doi.org/10.1080/13632434.2012.724672

Webster, R., Bosanquet, P., Franklin, S., & Parker, M. (2021). *Maximising the impact of teaching assistants in primary schools: Guidance for school leaders.* Routledge.

Webster, R., Russell, A., & Blatchford, P. (2016). *Maximising the impact of teaching assistants: Guidance for school leaders and teachers* (2nd ed.). Routledge.

Index

Entries in **bold** refer to tables; entries in *italics* refer to figures.

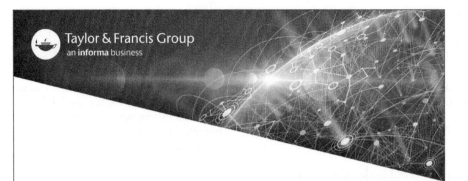

Printed and bound by CPI Group (UK) Ltd, Croydon, CR0 4YY

21/10/2024

01777040-0004